Second Nature

Book Two of the Coileáin Chronicles

M.J. FIFIELD

FAVORITE SPOON PUBLISHING

Printed in the United States of America
First Printing, 2018

ISBN: 978-0-9961074-3-3

Favorite Spoon Publishing, LLC
1720 Malabar Road #500509
Malabar, FL 32950

Book Design by Judy Maenle

Cover Design by Ravven; www.ravven.com

Also by M.J. Fifield

Effigy

For my mother.
Thank you for giving me the drive and determination
to do what I love.

Pronunciation Guide

Aelhaeran: Al-hare-an
Aodhan: Aid-in
Auryn: Awe-rin
Brollachan: Bro-lach-han
Bronagh: Bro-nah
Cathal: Cay-thal
Coileáin: Co-lee-ain
Darragh: Dar-rah
Einar: I-nar
Eluned: Elle-in-ed
Fáinne: Faw-in-nye
Faolan: Fay-lawn
Iollan Iuchar: Yoll-an Yuch-are

Laorans: Law-rans
Llian: Hlee-an
Luisiúil: Louis-shoo-elle
Mairéad: Ma-raid
Maoilriain: May-oh-ree-ain
Mireille: Me-ray
Revelin: Rev-lin
Rhoswen: Rose-when
Rhydwyn: Hrid-win
Rhys: Hress
Sighle: She-la
Ynyr: In-ir

Acknowledgements

To properly thank all those who helped this novel see the light of day, we first have to travel back to the dark ages of my high school career and Ben Greslick, who gave this book its name, and the teachers who kindly tolerated me creating stories in class when I should have been working on other things. Thank you for recognizing who I was destined to be, even back then.

Years later, when school had been exchanged for a day job, I had the pleasure of meeting Heather Hanscom, who agreed to read an early draft of this story. After reading one particular scene, she left a message on my answering machine so lovely and encouraging that I immediately took the micro-cassette out of service. (I still have that tape, by the way.) Thank you for making me feel as though I might be on to something.

I also want to give a shout-out to my amazing beta readers, Heidi and Michael Fox, who leapt at the opportunity to read this novel, even after slogging through multiple drafts of the first book. Thank you for sticking with me through all these years and all those drafts.

And then there is Jacob Jordan, who truly ascended the role of beta reader with this book. Thank you for always being willing to talk character and plot, for helping me craft some of my favorite lines in the book, and for providing me with such high quality literary analysis. Mrs. Guy would be proud.

Next are the two best critique partners for which a writer could ask, Tanis Thacker and Rita McCarthy. These wonderful women survived the trial by fire that is meeting me in a release year—and never once ran away screaming during my many crises of confidence. No easy feat. Though I still maintain that you give me entirely too much credit, thank you for always pushing me to do better.

I also want to thank Ravven, who once again turned my hazy thoughts into a gorgeous cover. If anyone gives this story a second glance, it's because of your talent.

And last but certainly not least, I want to thank my family. This can't be said enough: I couldn't do any of this without your love and support—especially Joe, who has always encouraged this journey, even though it means I keep extremely odd hours and a closet full of swords.

I love you all.

Prologue

Death had come to Quatara.

It came in the form of two twisted creatures silently slipping through the night-cloaked forest. Their names were unknown to the inhabitants here, as they were seldom seen in this land, and any unfortunate enough to lay eyes upon them never lived long enough to tell others of the horror they had witnessed. Death was their singular talent, and they had come to Quatara to once again practice their art. Someone would die before the dawn.

Unless he could stop them.

Faolan followed the two neruals as closely as he could. They left no trail detectable by mortal senses, but he was not mortal and their stench cut a wide swath as they moved nearer to Parthalan, Quatara's main settlement. It had been a city once, and would be so again, but now it was too newly ravaged by war and conquest. What business would neruals have in an already decaying land? Who here so threatened their masters that Yelsneh would unleash his fiercest weapons upon an unsuspecting population?

He was determined to find out.

It was why he had not yet engaged them, why they continued to slide through the woods stalking their prey. They had been dormant for so long, he needed to understand why they had been sent. Using an innocent as bait was not ideal, but if it would save the rest, he would lose one gladly.

A crash sounded behind him, and Faolan took his eyes off the neruals to make certain no threat lurked there. Only malevolence permeated the air. This hatred went beyond a nerual's limited emotional capabilities. Something else—someone else—was there.

Turning back to the neruals, Faolan found himself blocked by a wall—invisible, potent, and sophisticated. He couldn't get around it. Who had done this? Who could have? The neruals weren't responsible. They hadn't the skill.

"Yelsneh," Faolan said.

What had brought the god to this world? What could be so important that Yelsneh would come himself?

Faolan could handle the neruals. The dark god, however, would be beyond his reach. Far beyond his reach. Quietly, he summoned the goddess, holding out hope that the god would not realize what Faolan did behind his wall. Laorans would make her presence known to Yelsneh; Faolan didn't want to do it for her.

Upon her arrival, the wall vanished and Faolan moved forward, trying desperately to rediscover the neruals' now-obscured trail. He hadn't been held back for long, but the situation had been crucial enough when he thought the neruals to be the only dark creatures in the Quatari wilderness that night. Now that he knew the depth of the matter, every lost moment was the equivalent of a lost day.

As Parthalan grew closer, he was no nearer to finding his quarry—Yelsneh doing his part to keep his weapons protected. Faolan could feel Laorans's mounting concern as he navigated his way through the tangle of trees.

They must be found, the goddess said. *We must stop them.*

"I can't find..." Faolan stopped when the rank odor specific to the neru-als flooded his lungs. Looking toward Parthalan, he said, "They're coming."

They're not alone. They have something—someone.

"Alive?" he asked.

Alive.

Her tone made him nervous. Her actual response scared him. Neruals were dealers in death. They didn't know anything else. Their involvement, Yelsneh's presence, and the fact that his enemies' victim yet lived terrified him. Something happened here, something for which he was rather unprepared. He did not like to feel that way when Yelsneh was involved.

Faolan steeled himself and locked his gaze on the direction from which the neruals would come. All around him swirled the deities' power, determination and hatred like a strong wind heralding a destructive storm that would ravish everything in its path. Faolan prepared to do what he could for the human hostage. Laorans would contend with Yelsneh.

The gods collided, breaking like water upon rock, as the neruals came straight at Faolan. But where was their—oh. One nerual ran on three legs, holding a small bundle protectively against its body.

The hostage was a child. An infant.

What need would Yelsneh have for a human infant? What would he...No. Faolan forced the question aside. It didn't change what he had to do. There would be time enough for questions when the child was safe.

Faolan created a wall of his own, and the neruals slammed into it. As they were thrown back, he moved forward, hitting them again as they tried to right themselves. The infant fell from the nerual's grasp, and Faolan struck them a third time, harder than before, to force them back farther. Again and again he hit them, conjuring more power, draining his stores. Before he wholly exhausted his magic, he trapped them in the confines of a cage. It wouldn't hold for long, but it would contain them long enough to get the child somewhere safe.

Faolan glanced skyward to judge the status of the second battle. There was no reason to be truly concerned for the goddess's well-being. Had she been in any danger, he would have felt it before now, and he felt nothing save his own weariness. Yelsneh's outraged moan—deep, shuddering, and poisonous—was further evidence of Laorans's success. Satisfied, Faolan turned his attention to the red-faced, shrieking infant girl.

Her cries were interrupted by an explosion—the cage breaking. The child froze, eyes flying open and mouth gaping. Gasping for breath, she quivered and resumed her screaming. Faolan ignored it as he cast a spell to shield them both. The blue light stretched overhead but did not last. It shrank before disappearing completely, leaving Faolan bewildered. He should have had enough magic for a simple shield. What had happened?

A second attempt at the spell received the same result. He looked at the child. Was she the reason behind his failure?

"Who are you?" he asked, and she screeched in response.

He felt the neruals' fast approach and prepared to throw a barrier in their path when Laorans arrived, settling in between him and the neruals. The creatures yelped as they were hit with the might of the goddess's power. She only had to force them back once before they retreated through a portal of their own making and disappeared.

Both Faolan and the goddess waited a moment more, to see if their enemies had, in fact, been beaten back, but no more appeared, and the night air calmed once more.

It was done. The storm had passed, and they had won.

Faolan looked at the crying child. "She's immune to my magic."

Yes, that is most curious.

Faolan didn't think it was curious at all. It was unimaginable.

"What do they want with her?" he asked. "Who is she?"

I do not know, but we will find out.

"What should we do with her?" Faolan asked. "Did the neruals kill her family?"

No, Laorans said. *Her family comes for her.*

Faolan lifted his head to search the darkness. He could hear them, faintly in the distance, as they crashed through whatever obstacles were met in their quest to find their stolen child.

"I'll watch over her, then, until they arrive," he said.

Yelsneh will only send his assassins for her again, the goddess said. *We cannot give her back to her family. To do so would mean their death.*

"What do you want to do?"

Save them all.

There was more light then, bright and blinding. Out of its center emerged a tall, thin woman with long, dark hair and vibrant blue eyes. She wore gauzy robes in various shades of blue. Her feet were bare, but she walked over the rough terrain with a grace never found in humans. She knelt and touched the girl's face with her willowy fingers before gathering the blankets and lifting the child. Holding the girl close, the woman whispered in her ear, and the child stopped crying.

"Where shall we take her?" the goddess asked, gazing at the child with love and joy. "Where shall we hide our treasure so that she might be safe?"

"She won't be safe anywhere on this earth," he said.

"No," the goddess said, "I fear you are right."

"She may not be safe regardless of what earth she's on."

"It is true her protection will not be easy, but it is paramount that she be protected."

"I don't disagree. I just don't know who would be capable of—"

"I can think of one."

"I won't be its nursemaid."

"No," the goddess said, "not you."

"Who—?" He stopped when the answer came to him. Then he asked, "How?"

"There are ways," the goddess said.

Faolan knew exactly what that meant. He didn't like it, but there would be no changing the goddess's mind. He sighed. "Fine. What do you want me to do?"

"I require you to attend to another."

"Human?"

"Yes, human," Laorans said. "He is alone in this world, and I would have you look after him. Be *his* nursemaid."

"Why?"

"If tonight has shown us anything, it's that open war is rapidly approaching," the goddess said. "We shall need him."

"What would you have me do with him?"

"Protect him, guide him," the goddess answered. She was clearly enjoying this.

"Do you think Yelsneh and the rest would have such fun at my expense?"

This amused Laorans greatly. Faolan could hear it in her voice.

"That, and more," she said. "They would never take you, Faolan. You don't kill people."

Her levity trailed off toward the end. Eyes lifting, she studied the night. Faolan tensed and sniffed the air, expecting the scent of dark magic but sensing none.

"We must leave this place," the goddess said. "Her people approach, and it will do us no good to be discovered."

The goddess carried the child into the distant dark. As they disappeared, Faolan looked in the opposite direction. He could see the light of the torches the humans carried. They moved through the forest, searching for their lost child. One man cried out in agony, a name on his lips. Faolan could only assume he was the girl's father.

"Mireille!"

Part One: Schism

CHAPTER 1

When Faolan stopped talking, James remained silent as he waited to hear what might follow, but the pegasus didn't speak again.

James looked at the ground. "Mireille. That's her name? The queen's twin?"

"Yes."

"Where did you take her?"

"Another earth."

James looked up. "Earth?"

"Yes. Another earth," Faolan said. "Like this one, only different."

"No, you mean country. She's in another country."

"No, earth. She's on another earth."

"Separate from this one?"

"Yes."

"I don't understand."

"Neither will she. Keep that in mind when you find her."

"What? Me?"

"Who did you think we would send? Aaron?"

"No, but I can't go. I have to get back to camp. I told Ilya she'd not be abandoned."

"Don't dawdle."

"I can't go to another earth."

"Of course you can," Faolan said. "We'll go to the pond, and I will open a portal—a door of sorts—to take you to Mireille. When you find her, bring her back through the portal, and you'll be returned here."

"That's it?"

"Yes."

James shook his head. "You're not telling me everything."

"True."

"Don't you think you should?"

"No. It won't be helpful."

"It won't be helpful?"

"No," Faolan said, flying toward the forest. "Come on."

James chased after him. "Faolan!"

"She won't want to go with you," Faolan said. "You'll have to make her."

James was within arm's length of the pegasus and debated swatting him down. Perhaps Faolan sensed the impending danger because he stopped short and turned, hovering in the air.

"It won't be helpful," he repeated. "I could tell you everything, but that would take all day, possibly longer, and that wouldn't even include the hundreds of unanswerable questions you will have. But I suppose we could do that, if you want. I'll tell you everything while Haleine bleeds to death and Omur regroups."

"Faolan—"

"There's no time," the pegasus said. "You have to find Mireille, and you have to bring her here, kicking and screaming if that's what it takes. I don't care how you do it, just get it done."

"Do you believe she'll share the same powers as the queen?"

"Laorans does."

"All right. I'll go," James said. Did he even have a choice? "You'll need to get word to Ilya. Tell her what's happened, and tell her Dana will require help guarding the queen."

Faolan nodded. "I'll tell her. Anything else?"

James hesitated. "What about the boys—the princes? Are they safe?"

"You're worried about Haleine's sons?"

"I'm worried about Dana's sons. Are they safe?"

"Willem will protect them."

"Not what I asked," James said. "Are they safe? Should we be—I don't know—should we be—"

"Kidnapping them?"

"Aye."

"No, we should not kidnap the heirs to Lira's throne," Faolan said. "If Omur thought they were a threat, he would have done something about them by now. Willem will protect them."

"Omur isn't the only threat."

"They're safe. I promise you that Dana's sons are safe."

"Are your promises worth anything?"

"This one is."

James nodded. He supposed he would have to take the risk. "All right, then. Different how?"

"What?"

"You said it was different, this other earth. How is it different?"

"It would be quicker to tell you how it's not different."

"What does that mean?"

Faolan seemed to consider the question. Finally, he answered, "Let's just say that you're in for an interesting experience."

※

The fifteenth of June had been a perfect day, right up until the moment they told Cate her mother was dead.

Winter had lingered long past the point of appreciation, dumping a record amount of snow and ice on the city. May, keeping with a long-standing New England tradition, had been a month of wind and rain, saturating Boston and everyone in it until they were wet to the bone. June had been drier, but gray and unseasonably cool in its first two weeks. The city had been on the verge of rebelling until the fifteenth, when the sun finally appeared in all of its radiant glory. And with its arrival, the entire population was forced to decide between obligation and lounging in the warmth of a much-missed sun.

Cate had been no exception. It was the first day she cursed her decision to take a summer class at Harvard and had contemplated skipping her philosophy lecture altogether. Ultimately, she went—mostly because she didn't want to either lie to her mother about going, or suffer through a lecture about skipping.

So she sat in the windowless lecture hall with about fifty other students, few of which she judged as being enthusiastic about their attendance. She neglected to take notes and spent the time alternately drawing random patterns, staring off into space, and wondering why the first really nice day—the first really *warm* day—of the year wasn't automatically declared a city-wide holiday.

By the time class came to an end, Cate had filled two pages with Celtic-looking knots, pyramids, cityscape outlines, and a variety of stick figures in various death throes. She looked over her handiwork before shoving the notebook in her bag. Maybe she should declare a major in art or art history. It was something to consider later, though, because at the moment, she had friends with plans to waste time being marginally disreputable around Quincy Market. Her phone had been off during class—her professor insisted—and she turned it on to check in—at her mother's insistence—with Fiona, the housekeeper. Once the phone had come back to life, she saw she had a message waiting and accessed her voicemail to hear it.

"Catherine, love," Fiona's Irish lilt said, "you have to come home. Straight away."

The heavy melancholy in her housekeeper's voice brought Cate to a halt at the top of a flight of stairs. Lowering the phone, she held it against her

5

chest. She'd never heard Fiona sound mournful before. Angry, disappointed, appalled by Cate's sometimes questionable behavior, yes, but mournful? No. Not once.

Her friends called to her then, and she searched for them, but only found Daniel looking back at her. Daniel was her mother's man, Laura's jack of all trades, and he stood next to her friends at the bottom of the stairs. He was a man who made stoic people seem downright emotional, and the look on his face made her drop the phone and hold onto the stair railing for dear life.

"You have to come home," Daniel said.

"What happened?" she asked.

Daniel shook his head. "Come home, and we'll talk."

She had taken the train in that morning, but Daniel drove her back—a silent fifteen minutes that seemed to last fifteen years. Fiona met them at the door and enveloped Cate into a crushing embrace that answered every question she had. She knew what they would say before they gave it voice and begged for it not to be done.

But they said the words anyway.

Your mother's dead, they told her, Daniel and Fiona together, as they sat in the living room of Cate's Beacon Hill townhouse. *She's gone.*

Cate looked at them, dry-eyed, then turned her head to the left. The windows overlooked the street, and she watched the people walking past, wearing their shorts and short-sleeved shirts. Fiona settled beside her, taking her hand.

"I don't understand," Cate said.

And she hadn't. She hadn't understood it any better three days later when she was standing graveside, watching her mother's coffin being lowered into the ground. She still didn't understand it. It had been nearly a month, and still, she just didn't understand it.

Maybe if there had been a reason. People died suddenly all the time— some crazy tragic accident or something—but all Daniel and Fiona had said, or would say, was that her mother had a sort of cancer. And it killed her.

Cate knew they were lying. Laura Cole did not have a sort of cancer. The woman was healthy—the woman had *always* been healthy—never even a damn cold, forget cancer. If there had been, by some freak chance, a tumor, Cate would've known. Her mother never would have kept that from her.

Theirs had been the kind of sickly-sweet mother-daughter relationship that only existed in fairy tales or whatever, but not real life. Cate told her mother the truth—the *truth*—about things. Everything. Almost everything. Boys, fights with friends, the stupid stuff she did in school, the stupid stuff she did outside of school, and everything in between. And her mother recipro-cated. Of course, her mother never dated, didn't have many friends and never, ever did anything that could be counted as stupid. But still, she shared. She damn well would have shared that she was dying from a sort of cancer.

"Catherine?"

Cate came out of her reverie to find herself sitting in the waiting room of her doctor's office. The receptionist—Rosie?—stood in front of her, hand on her elbow.

"Hi," Rosie said, smiling her very best fake smile. "Sorry to interrupt your day dreaming."

Day dreaming. Right. "No problem," Cate said.

"Dr. Blaire's running a little late, but he'll be with you shortly."

The man chronically ran late, yet they expected her to show up for appointments on time. Whatever. It wasn't like it mattered. Cate nodded, and Rosie patted her elbow before retreating to her desk. Cate glanced at the clock on the wall and saw she'd been waiting almost thirty minutes.

Time sure did fly when one was obsessing over one's dead mother.

She leaned forward to select a magazine from the table in front of her. *People.* Swell. An outdated issue even. Bonus. Cate threw the magazine back. One would think, with the money she was paying this office, they could afford better magazines. Current magazines.

And better music. They seemed to be working their way through the elevator music genre's greatest hits. Only that was kind of an oxymoron, wasn't it? Cate cast a discerning look at the speaker in the ceiling before settling back in her chair.

She looked at the magazines again. As much as she didn't care about celebrity fashion or break ups, reading something—*anything*—would be better than letting her mind wander. It might be safer, too. She was reaching for the copy of *People* when Rosie called her name again.

"Catherine?" she said. "You can go on back. He's ready for you now."

Cate nodded and let the magazine stay where it was. For a moment, she considered continuing on with her time-killing plan and making the good doctor wait—just to see how he liked it—but pushed herself out of the chair, passed Rosie's desk, and walked down the hall to his office.

She opened the door without knocking. Dr. Richard Blaire sat behind his desk, looking at the contents of a manila folder. As she entered, he glanced up and smiled. She didn't smile back.

"Good afternoon, Cate," he said.

His voice was confident and warm, calm and comforting. Did they teach that in med school?

He gestured to the two chairs in front of his desk. "Have a seat."

Considering she'd made an appointment so he could later bill her for the privilege of his company, it was kind of him to invite her in. Still, she did as the man bade and sank into a chair.

"How are you?" he asked.

He posed the question as though they were friends or something. Like he'd known her all her life. While that was technically true, he wasn't her friend. If anything, he'd been her mother's friend. Laura had called him Richard. Cate generally called him nothing, but if asked, would have confessed to calling him Dick. She was nothing if not spectacularly immature when the opportunity presented itself.

"I didn't come for small talk," she said. "You can give it to me straight. I can take it."

The smile became less brilliant, and Dick put the folder on the desk.

"Well, Cate," he said, "there's absolutely nothing wrong with you."

She hadn't been expecting that. Cate gestured to the diplomas on the wall. "Are you sure those are authentic?"

"I swear you're in perfect health."

"But you ran all those tests."

"We ran all those tests because you were convinced you had a heart attack."

She loved his use of the past tense. Like she had somehow become less convinced in the two days since it happened. He'd known her all her life. He should've known that sort of thing didn't happen.

"I *did* have a heart attack," she said.

He smiled at her again. Kindly. Patronizingly.

"No." He held up the folder as if it meant anything to her. "You didn't."

If not a heart attack, then what? She'd been in the shower that morning, two days ago, when the pain started in her arms. A sharp, shooting, *burning* sensation so powerful, she could barely turn off the spray or open the shower door to get out. She was yelling to Fiona for help when her legs buckled, and her right knee erupted in pain. It was more agony than she had ever felt in her life, and Cate lay on the tile floor, shrieking until her heart seemed to explode. Then she lay in silence as other parts of her stopped working. Her lungs, her brain, everything. Life drained out of her until there had been nothing left.

She didn't know for how long she had stayed there, but all of a sudden, it had been like coming out of a trance, or waking up from a nightmare. Her knee had been throbbing, and her heart—her heart was beating where before it hadn't.

The doctors in the emergency room didn't believe her. They told her to rest her knee and sent her on her merry way because there had been no evidence in any of their tests that anything was wrong with her. 'Within normal limits' was officially her least favorite phrase because there had been absolutely nothing normal about that experience. Stupid emergency room doctors.

She looked at Dick. Stupid private practice doctors.

"What was it?" she asked. "What happened to me?"

"I don't know," Dick said. "Have you considered—?"

Cate sighed inwardly. This would be the part where he asked about her mental health because maybe she'd subconsciously invented some malady because her mother had dropped dead of some sort of cancer, and now she was scared it would make her drop dead, too.

It was an option she might have been willing to consider if it hadn't been for the sudden appearance of a scar on her chest, right over her heart.

She noticed it this morning when showering. It hadn't been there before. Not two days ago when she'd had her non-heart-attack experience, not last night when she'd changed for bed. But there was no denying its existence now. She was the proud owner of a shiny, ugly, purple gash that sat over her heart like she'd tried to cut the damn thing out of her chest with a grapefruit spoon. Since she most certainly had not done any such thing, she had come to Dick's office with the expectation of some sort of answer. Some reason why she'd felt her heart explode. Why there was physical proof something had happened.

Dick could prattle on all he wanted, but it wasn't in her head. Psychosomatic symptoms did not leave physical scars. It didn't work that way. At least she didn't think so.

While he talked, she looked out the row of windows behind him. Dick, for all his faults, had a gorgeous skyline view. It was a beautiful day, too. There had been a lot of them since June fifteenth.

"What sort of cancer was it?" she asked.

"Pardon me?"

His tone was high, tight. A stall tactic. Cate put her hand on her chest and felt the scar through her shirt. What would Dick have to say about it?

"The sort of cancer that killed my mother," she said. "What sort was it? Brain, breast, bone, lung, stomach? What?"

"You don't understand."

"Hence the questions. What sort was it? Pancreatic? Liver? Kidney? Skin?"

"She didn't want you to know," Dick said quietly.

"Cervical? Ovari—" She stared at him. Her hand fell to her side. "You're lying."

"I'm sorry, Cate, I really am sorry, but I am not lying."

"Fuck you," she said. "She would've wanted me to know. If there was some tumor eating her from the inside out, she would've told me that. The goddamn woman wouldn't let me leave the house in the morning until she'd given me a minute-by-minute itinerary for the day, and you want me to believe she wouldn't have prepared me for this? That she wouldn't have told me she was *dying*?"

"She didn't want you to know."

Cate nodded. "Fine. She didn't want me to know, but she's gone now. You can tell me now."

"She didn't want you to know."

There was some kind of pyramid-shaped paperweight on the desk, and she grabbed it and threw it at the windows. The paperweight bounced off them without doing any damage to either it or the glass. It only pissed her off more.

"She's dead," Cate hissed as she stood to lean across the desk. "She's fucking dead, and you *still* won't say anything."

Dick put his hands over hers, and she jerked away. He let her and sat back.

"Did Fiona tell you?" he asked. "Did Daniel?"

They hadn't. Cate shook her head.

"She didn't want you to know."

He said it slower this time, so he could emphasize the words. Her mother hadn't wanted her to know, and for whatever reason, instructed Fiona and Daniel and Dick to make sure it stayed that way. And because they were so loyal to her, so goddamn devoted, they would follow through, even if the woman in question was now rotting in the ground.

"You shouldn't be surprised, Cate," Dick said. "You knew your mother."

She was going to cry. If she spent one more moment in that room, she was going to cry. Crying in front of Dick—crying in front of *anyone*—was not something she was willing to do. Especially because she didn't know if she'd be able to stop.

"Guess not," Cate said and left.

James followed Faolan to the pond, apprehension growing in his chest with every step. It was one thing to say he would walk through a portal into another world. It was an entirely different thing to actually take the steps.

"I don't—I don't have a weapon," James said, his throat dry. "No sword, no dagger."

"You shouldn't need them."

"No?"

"No." Faolan looked at him. "Are you all right?"

James laughed. "I can't remember the last time I slept because I've been too busy killing and kidnapping, and now I'm waiting for you to open some kind of magical door to another world so I can kidnap yet another member of the nobility, and you're asking if I'm all right?"

"If it helps, she doesn't know she's a member of the nobility."

"I don't think it does help, no."

"Oh," Faolan said. "Well, she doesn't know. Be sure to take advantage of that."

Rustling in the brush caught James's attention. Faolan didn't react, but James tensed and reached for the weapon he didn't carry. When Luisiúil appeared, he breathed out in relief and lowered his hands.

"What is she doing here?" he asked.

"Helping," Faolan said.

"How?"

"Opening a magical door to another world isn't easy. She's here to help with that."

"What do I do?"

Faolan settled on the ground. "Stand there and be quiet."

James opened his mouth to apologize, but caught sight of Luisiúil's reproachful look and changed his mind. He nodded and stepped back to allow them to perform their magic.

They faced the pond, standing side by side with their heads bowed and eyes closed. A familiar stillness settled over the air, and once again, James held his breath as he waited.

A hole, no bigger than a man's fist, formed in the air over the water. It grew slowly, eating away at the surrounding daylight. Its perfection ebbed as it grew, becoming ragged with inky black tendrils stretching and reaching to claim more territory. Watching the thing move—seeing how *alive* it appeared to be—James realized what he was about to do. His earlier apprehension dissipated, replaced by fear.

"All right," Faolan said when the portal was large enough for James to walk through. "Go on."

James swallowed and pointed to the hole. "In there?"

"Yes, in there," Faolan said. "Do it now, do it fast. We can't hold this forever."

James inched his way forward. "How will I find her?"

"She's alone, secluded," Faolan said. "She should be the only person around the only house you'll find. Even if she isn't, she does bear a certain resemblance to the queen. I would think that would narrow it down for you."

James grumbled at Faolan's tone and approached the hole. Taking a deep breath, he stepped through.

—⁓—

The sidewalk was crowded, filled with people with a destination and a purpose. Cate leaned against the medical building, standing in its shadow, and watched them pass by.

Where to go? What to do? It was a riddle she'd been trying to solve for a month. What now? What next? There were minutes, hours, days, weeks, months, years, decades to fill, and she didn't have an answer for any of it.

She finally went to the nearest T station and got on the first train that pulled up to the platform. It was just as packed as the sidewalk had been, but she found an open seat in the back of the last car. As she swayed with the train's movements, she stared at an advertisement for a foreign language program offering classes in a variety of languages. They even taught Swahili.

Laura had probably known Swahili. Didn't seem like there was a damn tongue on the face of the earth in which her mother wasn't at least faintly proficient. Thanks to her fancy private school education, Cate could make herself understood in both French and Spanish, and knew more Latin than any one person not seeking a career in the clergy would ever need to know, but that was all. Her mother had never said so, but Cate had the distinct feeling that Laura had been disappointed by her daughter's lack of lingual talent.

Maybe that's what she could do—learn Swahili. She could do that. Learn to speak Swahili, and disappear wherever it was Swahili was spoken. Somewhere in Africa—Tanzania and Mozambique maybe. Because she'd blend in so well there.

No, if disappearing and blending were things she wanted to do, she'd be bound for the British Isles. She had the red hair and could fake a pretty decent accent. She'd be able to hide out there easily enough. Go hang out in London or Dublin for a while and—and what? Drink Guinness?

Well, it wasn't the worst plan ever.

By the time the train reached the end of the line, she had not thought of any better plans. She got off and crossed the platform to wait for the next train heading into the city. When it arrived, she sat in the last car and stared at an advertisement for Bunker Hill Community College, reading the same information over and over again until she had memorized it. She changed trains at Government Center and studied a poster detailing the symptoms of depression.

There was no need to memorize that one, so when the stop nearest her home was announced, she joined the line of people shuffling off.

The townhouse was mercifully empty when she arrived. Fiona must have been running errands, and she guessed Daniel was still out doing whatever it was he did all day. There'd been a time, shortly after Laura's funeral, when Cate was glad they weren't leaving her as well. They had started out as her mother's employees, but they had become family. Fiona was Cate's surrogate grandmother, and Daniel some kind of enigmatic uncle. But now, in light of horrible moods and a certain conversation with Dick, Cate was less pleased. They weren't staying for her. They were staying for her mother. She used to believe that essentially meant the same thing.

She didn't think that anymore.

Cate moved through the house, standing in each room for a moment or two, undecided again about what to do next. The light on the wall phone in the kitchen was blinking, indicating there were messages, and she stopped long enough to delete them. No need to listen to them anymore. The only people who called were her friends who had long since given up trying to reach her on her now-dead cell. They were always trying to entice her to come out and get away, forget all her troubles and move on with her life. They meant well, but it didn't change the fact that she wasn't interested in moving on. She was interested in wallowing and then wallowing some more.

She decided to wallow with a fifth of Jameson. Risky, maybe, because when Fiona came home, there would be hell to pay, but Cate didn't care about that. Let Fiona be mad. Cate was pretty mad herself.

Opening the liquor cabinet, Cate surveyed her options. Normally, there was a decent selection of hooch from which to choose—a courtesy for guests, as no one in the house was a big drinker. Cate, technically, was underage and therefore not allowed to be any sort of drinker, big or otherwise. She wasn't, either, but in her first year of Harvard, she had developed an appreciation for whiskey as well as the frat boys who also appreciated whiskey.

But Fiona hadn't purchased any Jameson nor anything else. It made sense. There hadn't been any guests to speak of since the wake. Cate closed the cabinet door and opened the refrigerator. Daniel had a six-pack of Sam Adams Summer Ale on the bottom shelf. Not ideal, but she'd make do. She was nothing if not flexible. When life gave her lemons and all that.

Locating the bottle opener, she stuck it in her pocket and went back for the beer. As she was sliding it off the shelf, the front door slammed open. Fiona burst into the kitchen next, her cell against her ear. She spotted Cate and looked both relieved and furious. Cate straightened.

"She's here, Daniel," Fiona said into the phone. "Yes, she's here in the kitchen. She's fine."

Another moment passed while Fiona listened to whatever Daniel said next. She agreed with him and ended the call. Cate nudged the six-pack back in place with her foot.

"Where have you been?" Fiona demanded.

Cate closed the refrigerator door. "Out."

"Doing what?"

"Drinking coffee with friends."

"You're lying," Fiona said, "and I don't like being lied to."

"Really? Because I find it to be delightful."

"What are you talking about?"

Cate shook her head. Telling Fiona what she was talking about would only lead to tear-inducing conversation, and she was still firmly against that. Fiona sighed and moved forward to give her a quick hug.

"Let's not fight, all right?" Fiona said. "I'll make us some tea, and we can talk."

Cate mimed committing hara-kiri. If there was one thing she wanted less than conversation, it was tea, but unfortunately, tea was Fiona's panacea.

"No thanks," Cate said. "I'm good."

Fiona wasn't discouraged. She opened a cupboard, extracted the kettle, and went to the sink to fill it. "Something happen at your appointment?"

She posed the question so casually, Cate wanted to laugh. She was sure Dr. Dick—doctor-patient confidentiality be damned—had wasted no time in phoning Fiona to tell her of how Cate had swore at him before trying to break the windows in his office with a paperweight. But if Fiona wasn't going to bring it up, neither was Cate.

"The appointment was fine," she said, sliding onto one of the stools. "Turns out I am a perfect picture of health."

Fiona set the kettle on the stove and turned on the burner. "I knew you would be."

That was because Fiona had been among the many disbelievers. She was the president of the Don't Be Silly, Of Course You Didn't Have A Heart Attack Society. Cate had spent a lot of time since her non-heart-attack calling her housekeeper Judas, Brutus, Benedict Arnold, and any other well-known traitors she could come up with. Yep, spectacularly immature. Every damn time.

"I had a heart attack, you know," Cate said.

Fiona set a delicate teacup in front of her. "No, love, you didn't."

So it would appear. Resting her elbows on the counter, Cate put her chin in one hand, while the other found its way back to her scar. Her fingers ran over it until Fiona brought the kettle over and poured hot water into the cup. Taking the teabag Fiona offered, Cate dunked it in and out of the cup, watching the water change color.

"I need to get out of here," she said. "I can't stay in Boston."

"Oh? Where do you want to go?"

"Maine, I guess. At least to start."

Her mother had owned a cabin up there, one right on a lake. It was a private place, with nothing for miles but quiet, solitude, and pine trees. Cate loved the city—she couldn't imagine ever living anywhere else—but an extended vacation in an isolated cabin deep in the woods currently held a certain appeal. She'd come back. Eventually.

"All right," Fiona said, "we'll go."

Cate shook her head. "No. Just me. I'm going alone."

"What do you mean you're going alone?"

"I mean I'm going to drive myself there and stay there by myself until I'm damn well ready to come home," Cate said. "You can stay here and drink tea."

As her eyes narrowed, Fiona folded her arms across her chest. Guess someone didn't appreciate her attitude. Cate couldn't blame her, but at the same time, Cate didn't care.

"You can't go by yourself," Fiona said.

"I think you'll find I can."

"Daniel won't like it," Fiona stated, as though it were the final word on the subject.

"Here's an interesting twist: Daniel works for me. He doesn't have to like it."

Fiona slammed her hand on the counter. "Catherine Mireille Cole! You stop this foolishness right now!"

Cate looked at Fiona in surprise. Her mouth hung open with the shock. Not only had Fiona assaulted the kitchen counter—which, in itself, would've been cause for astonishment—but she had also evoked the sacred power of her charge's middle name. No one used her middle name. No one but Laura.

"Your mother hired Daniel to look after you," Fiona said.

"I thought that's what you were for."

"Your mother brought him here to protect you."

"Protect me? Protect me from *what*, Fiona?" Cate asked. "A sort of cancer?"

"Your mother was involved in a dangerous business," Fiona said, angrier than Cate could ever remember seeing her.

Cate stood so quickly, she knocked over the stool. "Well, now my mother's not involved in any kind of business, is she?"

"There are still enemies, Catherine," Fiona said. "There are those who would like to see you hurt."

"Then I guess it's their lucky day," Cate snapped.

She was done talking. Brushing past Fiona, Cate returned to the refrigerator to liberate the beer. She went up to the roof and sat in the lawn chair she kept there. Fiona didn't follow, so Cate drank beer in silence as she looked at the sky. When it got dark, she looked at the stars. She was on her fourth bottle—and a little drunk—when Daniel arrived.

"Didn't know Harvard girls drank beer," he said.

"They do when the housekeeper fails to buy whiskey."

Daniel came alongside her, hands hidden in the pockets of his jeans. Cate looked him over and had another gulp of beer, daring him to stop her. He didn't.

"I hear you have some travel plans," he said.

"Damn straight. I'm going to Maine."

"I hear it's nice there this time of year."

Cate drank more beer. "Fiona tell you the part where I'm going alone?"

Daniel nodded but didn't say anything. He bent down and reached for a beer of his own. She handed him the opener, and he popped off the cap and took a drink.

"She thought you wouldn't like it," Cate said.

"I don't."

"That's it?" she asked. "No lecture, no yelling? No telling me I can't go?"

He shrugged. "You're nineteen. You can do what you want."

Cate toasted him with her beer. "Damn straight."

Daniel held up one of the empty bottles. "Do me a favor, though, and wait until morning before you go?"

Cate snorted. Hell, with the hangover she'd be nursing the next day, she'd be lucky if she hit the road before noon.

"Deal."

———ᴂᴂ———

James's next step led him into the pitch-black night. Blinded by the unexpected change from sun to dark, he stopped to allow his eyes to adjust. The air was still, the only sound water gently lapping against his boots. He looked at it as he stepped onto a stretch of sand. Faolan's portal was directly behind him, the black hole nearly invisible apart from the faint silver wisps outlining its edges. On either side, a lake glittered in the light of a full moon.

Turning back around, he saw the house of which Faolan had spoken. Even in the moonlight, it was unlike anything he'd ever seen before. This girl, this Mireille, may not have known she was nobility, but there was no doubt she lived as one.

He walked closer, marveling at the wall that appeared to be made entirely from glass. The palace didn't even have anything like that. Was it possible to be richer than a king?

The sand gave way to a wide wooden platform, and he walked across it, scanning for a way inside the house. How did people gain entrance? There had to be a door somewhere; he just had to find it.

Or make his own door. He put his hand on the glass wall as he glanced back at Faolan's portal. The pegasus hadn't told him for how long it would remain open. As reluctant as James was to do any damage, it was perhaps his best option. He couldn't risk becoming stranded there.

Stepping off the platform, he searched the ground for a sizeable rock, finally finding a row of them outlining a garden of some kind. He selected the largest and carried it back to the wall.

Passing the rock from one hand to the other, he sighed. "Well, here goes."

Cate's eyes flew open at the sound of breaking glass. She sucked in a deep breath and held it as she lifted her head to listen.

Someone was in her cabin.

If Fiona or Daniel had followed her, they would have used their key to gain entrance. They would have announced themselves, or turned on some lights. They would not be wandering around in the dark, broken glass crunching beneath their feet.

No, whoever was here did not belong.

She exhaled slowly. Okay, she had to think. Her cell didn't work here, and the landline was downstairs in the kitchen, so her first move was obviously the panic button on the nightstand. It was one of Daniel's gadgets, her direct link to the local law enforcement—or what passed for it in these parts—and probably the only reason why he let her come here alone without a fight. She'd never used it before, always thought Daniel was being wildly overprotective. The town couldn't have been more in the middle of nowhere. There was only one street light, and it only ever blinked yellow—at least until 10 p.m. when they shut it off for the night. It should have been safe, but as she pressed her palm down on the button, she was grateful for the man's paranoia.

Sliding out of bed, she crouched on the floor. Now what? She couldn't fit under the bed, and climbing out the window would get her nothing but a broken limb or two. That left the closet as a hiding place. A *dumb* hiding place. Could she say 'fish in a barrel'? No, she needed something else. What else was there?

Maybe she could make a break for her mother's room, or more specifically, the attached deck overlooking the lake. If she could get there, she could get out of the house, go hide in the woods, or find her way to the nearest neighbor. That was a workable plan—better anyway than hiding in the damn closet—but when she heard footsteps on the stairs, she abandoned all thought and went straight for it.

Better a dumb hiding place than no hiding place, right?

The logic was sound enough for her, but the footsteps reached her bedroom before she had arrived at her destination. Cate panicked and shrank back against the wall, knocking over her tennis racquet in the process.

"Hello?"

A strange male voice broke the silence—a strong baritone with a stronger accent that almost sounded English. Cate didn't recognize it, and found the racquet, gripping the handle tightly.

Why couldn't she have played baseball?

"Is someone there?" the man said.

Her digital alarm clock outlined him in a faint green-tinged light as he stepped inside the room. She didn't know if he could see her, but she didn't wait to find out. She lunged at him, swinging the racquet. As she made contact, he grunted and stumbled back. She swung again and again, forcing him back more each time.

"I am unarmed!" he exclaimed. "Would you *stop*?"

She didn't stop until she heard a thud, and the room exploded into light. Her advantage gone, Cate panicked once again and backed away to the other side of the room. The man didn't move.

He was young—probably not much older than her, but she'd always been a terrible judge of age, so she couldn't be sure. He was tall and well-built with brown hair in need of a trim and a face in need of—wait, was he wearing tights? Cate did a double take. Yep, he was wearing some sort of tights. Where the hell was this guy from? Was there a Ren faire in town she didn't know about?

"Who the hell are you?" she demanded.

The man didn't answer. He was too busy staring at the overhead light. The look on his face could only have been described as awe. He continued to stare, blinking furiously.

"What is that?" he asked.

"What *is* that?" she repeated. "You didn't seriously break into my home in the dead of night to discuss my lighting fixtures, did you?"

"No, I did not." He looked at her and pulled back. Unnerved. "God, you look just like her."

Cate didn't know to whom he referred, but she didn't like the way he looked at her. She adjusted her grip on her racquet. The intruder noticed the movement.

"What is that?" he asked.

"Your doom," she said. He looked doubtful so she added, "Tennis racquet."

"What do you plan to do with it?"

"Bash your head in on my way to a grand slam title?"

He tilted his head to the right. "I'm not sure that would be very effective for head bashing."

"Yeah, well, you haven't seen my backhand yet, have you?"

His forehead creased in confusion. "No, I have not."

"Great," Cate said. "Now that we have that settled, how about you get out of my bedroom? And my house."

He didn't move. She backed up until she bumped against the nightstand. Holding the racquet with her right hand, she felt around the surface for the panic button. Once found, she pounded the damn thing. Why wasn't it working?

"You're frightened. I've frightened you," he said.

"I am *not* frightened."

No, it was really more abject terror at this point. Not that she would ever admit it.

He held up his hands. "I am unarmed."

He did seem to be telling the truth about that. His shirt and vest were close fitting enough that she didn't know how he could conceal a weapon there. He definitely wasn't hiding *anything* in his tights. Fighting off a blush, she looked up.

"You better go," she said. "The police are on their way. They'll be here any second now."

He still didn't move. "Please, I don't want to hurt you."

She abandoned the panic button and again held the racquet with both hands. "But the voices in your head have other ideas?"

"What?"

"Get out," she said. "Get the hell out. Turn around, and go back to wherever the hell it is you came from."

For a moment, she thought there was remorse in his eyes. It didn't last and was quickly replaced by something with which she was even less comfortable.

"I can't," he said.

"You can't leave?"

"Not without you."

Resolve. That's what was in his face. That's what was in his voice. And it scared her.

"Well, you're sure as hell not leaving *with* me."

"You don't understand."

"You sure as hell got that right."

"I don't have a choice."

"So I'm just supposed to let you kidnap me?"

"It would be easier, but no," he said. "You could fight me. You would lose, but you could fight me."

"You don't know that. You don't know that I'd lose."

"With what do you mean to attack me? Your racquet there? Your backhand? Throw at me what you will, it won't be enough. I can't leave here without you, and I don't mean to."

"And I don't mean to let you kidnap me," she said. "I guess we're at an impasse."

He looked annoyed with her. That, in turn, annoyed her.

"I don't want to hurt you," he said again.

His tone suggested she was the unreasonable one in the room. How fucking ballsy was that? If he hadn't been attempting to kidnap her, she would have admired it greatly. He moved toward her, and she swung the racquet. He stepped back, hands in the air.

"You don't want to hurt me? Well, guess what," she said. "I don't have that problem. You come any closer to me, and I'll show you just how much I don't have that problem."

He dropped his hands. "You're making this bloody difficult."

"Am I? Good. I'm glad," she said. "I'm downright giddy."

"If you would only allow me to explain, Mireille, I could—"

"What did you call me?"

Without meaning to, she lowered the racquet. The man moved forward again and caught her wrist. He jerked her toward him, and with his other hand, tore the racquet out of hers. He spun it adeptly so he held the handle with the racquet's head tucked between his arm and his torso. She tried to pull away from him, but his grip was too tight.

"I'm sorry," he said.

CHAPTER 2

There was so much blood.

No matter how hard Bronagh scrubbed, the amount never lessened.

It was her penance. Michaela had charged her with Haleine's safety, and Bronagh had failed them both. She had tried, but did anyone know that? Did she care if anyone knew?

No.

Let them think what they wanted. Let them judge her, let them hate her. She had done what she had to do.

Haleine would have died had she stayed. Sending her off with the rebellion at least gave her a chance at survival. What other choice should Bronagh have made? The treason was easy—even though the price would be her life.

Should have been her life. She didn't know what had possessed him to do it, but Willem had saved her from that fate.

Her left eye was still swollen shut from his effort.

When you wake, he had said as she tumbled into darkness, *you tell them the rebels came for the queen.*

Climbing her way out of the shadows had been difficult. She wasn't certain how long it had taken, or how many times she had watched Haleine die as her husband laughed. When she finally succeeded at working through the layers of nightmare and confusion, Bronagh opened her sole functioning eye to see Rhys looking down at her.

"Ah, there you are. Good," the physician said. "Best not sit up just yet. You sustained quite the injury."

Aye, her head hurt. Why did it hurt?

"Do you remember what happened?" Rhys asked next.

She had started to shake her head when the memory returned. Willem, his fist, and his words. *When you wake, you tell them the rebels came for the queen.*

"The rebels," she said. "They came...they came for the queen."

A simple truth. Nothing the king and Omur wouldn't already know. What lie had Willem formed around it?

"Yes," Rhys said, obviously pleased with her. "Yes, that's right."

"Is the queen gone?" Bronagh asked. Please, let her be that. Let the rebels have gotten her away safely.

"Yes, but the soldiers are looking for her," Rhys said. "Don't you fret—the queen will be found before you know it."

Rhys didn't understand. If the soldiers found Haleine and brought her back, she wouldn't be safe. Far from it.

Bronagh shook her head and sat up. "I have to go."

"You have to rest," Rhys said, putting his hands on her shoulders. "Whoever hit you did so rather hard, and you will feel the effects for many days to come."

She laughed, pain rippling through her face. Aye, she would hurt for a good long while. Hiding wouldn't change that.

"I must go," she said. "I need to—"

"There's nothing, Bronagh," Rhys insisted. "Nothing you need to do. Nothing you can do."

Though she recognized the truth to his words, she had left his surgery and returned to the queen's chambers to look upon the proof of her failure—the proof of her treachery.

There was so much blood.

She would never be able to strip it away.

But she tried. Night and day, she scrubbed at the stains. No one bothered her. No one cared. It was easier to whisper about her when she wasn't around.

The queen's a traitor, they said. It was Bronagh's fault, they said.

And each day that passed without sight of their queen, the rumors only increased. Louder and more insistent. Her fault, they chanted. Her fault. Not one of them knew that it had to be done.

But there was just so much blood.

How could Haleine—how could *anyone*—survive such a loss?

"Bronagh," Omur said.

She ignored him. There had been a time when she would have risen and showed him the necessary courtesies, but that time was done. He could do nothing to her now.

He glided across the room, robes dragging along the floor. "You're quite put out, aren't you?" he said. "I should have come to you sooner."

For what purpose? What did she have left that he could want?

"I know you want the queen found as badly as I do," Omur said, stopping at her side.

If he thought that, he was a fool. She didn't want Haleine found at all.

"Surely you must know something that could help us find her."

"I have nothing to tell you," Bronagh said, pushing and pulling her brush across the stain. "I don't know where they took her."

"I think you know more than you claim."

"You're wrong," Bronagh said. "But even if I did know where she was, I wouldn't tell you."

"So hostile, Bronagh," Omur said. "That is my fault, I suppose, for having delayed this talk for so long."

"For having lied to me," she corrected.

"I never lied."

Bronagh's head snapped up. "You said she would not be harmed."

"I said I had no interest in harming her," Omur said, "but as I told you before, the king had—"

"You let him declare her a traitor," Bronagh said, throwing the brush back in the bucket with enough force that water sloshed out.

"She also happens to be a traitor, lest you forget."

Bronagh would never forget that. The rebel leader dragged that girl down, and Haleine never flinched.

I do not wish to be broken, Haleine had said time and time again.

But broken she had been. Broken, beaten, bleeding—*dying*.

Bronagh shook her head and used her apron to stop the water from spreading. "Why do you even want her back? All she ever did was fight you."

"Who said anything about wanting her back?" Omur asked. "I simply want to know how she fares. Is she dead or alive? You cannot tell me you don't have the same questions."

"No," Bronagh said, wringing out her apron over the bucket, "I cannot claim that."

"Then help me find her."

"I can't. I don't know where she is. The rebels neglected to tell me where they were taking her."

"Do they think you a traitor, too, Bronagh?" Omur asked, carefully stepping around her. "After all you did for them?"

"I didn't do anything for them but send their leader to his death," she said, watching his robes trail through the stain of blood. "That's all they care about. That's all any of them will ever care about."

"The queen as well?"

Bronagh hesitated. Aye, it was right to include Haleine in that. Even when Dana had devastated her so completely, she still sought to protect him from harm.

"Tell me," Omur said, "what sort of burial do you suppose the queen would receive in the forest?"

An image of a faceless corpse wrapped in a white shroud and dumped into a hole in the ground entered Bronagh's mind. Tears springing to her eyes, she retrieved the brush and attacked the floor.

"She's not dead," Bronagh said.

"How do you know?"

"I don't. I only hope."

"Is your hope not misplaced?" Omur asked. "Look at these stains. All that blood, Bronagh. How could anyone have survived the loss of so much?"

Was he in her mind? Could he see her thoughts? "I can't help you," Bronagh said. "I won't."

"I shall find her on my own, then."

"No, you won't."

Omur walked away. "We shall see."

———

After his interview with the maid, Omur returned to the king's library where Maddox sprawled across a sofa, staring at the ceiling. The king did not do much else of late. He slept, he drank, he fucked any girl within his reach, and he lay on that sofa, staring at that ceiling as he waited upon word of Haleine's whereabouts.

Maddox never had done well with infidelity. It was a curious quirk, to be sure.

"Did she know anything?" the king asked, his tone acerbic.

Omur glanced at the empty decanter on the floor. How many did that make for the day?

"No, my lord," he said.

"You are sure? She cannot lie to you?"

No, the maid could not lie to him. Whatever Dana had done with Haleine, the maid had not been involved. She had been scorned by the rebellion for turning to their enemies. Humans with good intentions always managed to hang themselves with them.

"Yes, my lord, I am sure," he said as he walked to the opposite end of the room.

Maddox sat up with one angry, fluid movement. "Someone somewhere must know *something*, Omur."

Omur sat in a chair facing the king. "I do not doubt it, my lord."

"Then find them!"

"We are looking, your majesty."

"You're not looking hard enough. I want my wife found," Maddox said. "I want her brought to justice. I want her to suffer for her crimes."

"She shall, my lord," Omur said. "She'll not go free. She'll not go unpunished."

"I will have her head," Maddox said.

"Yes, my lord."

The servant girl called Nonna entered then, carrying two fresh decanters, and the king's attention was lost. Maddox accosted her, backing her into a corner. What would he do if he knew the girl whose skirts his hand was under had worked with his wife against him? Omur imagined it would be more unpleasant than what he did to her now. Omur rose from his chair and turned his back to Maddox and the girl. He walked to the windows and looked at the city.

Varro and his men had already scoured it, searching every crack, every corner for the rebels and the queen. They had moved on to the forests, ever expanding their search when the last turned up nothing. Omur kept them at it, but Haleine would not likely be found by a random search. She was in the goddess's hands now, and Laorans would go to great lengths to keep her weapon safe. Omur could burn down the forests, every last twig and leaf, and still, he might not find the girl.

It was why he had given in to the king's demand.

When told of Haleine's disappearance, Maddox had wanted her named a traitor to the crown. He wanted the proclamation to reach every corner of his kingdom for all to hear. Their beloved queen was a faithless harlot who had renounced the throne and her husband for the rebel leader. Omur was inclined to allow the king his tantrum for, although there were a great many people devoted to Haleine and the rebellion, there were more loyal to the king, and perhaps word would come if Haleine were spotted amongst her people.

If she happened to be alive.

There remained the possibility that she was not.

Of what had happened in her chambers that night, Omur was unsure. He had loosed Maddox to dispatch the girl, to snap her neck, to choke the life out of her—whatever so moved the king—but Maddox had not killed her. He had walked away. Perhaps he thought he had done enough. Had his been the hand on the dagger? The maid thought it to be true, but there was something else.

Why would Maddox leave? The man who enjoyed the kill had walked away without seeing the life departed from the eyes of a most-hated, unfaithful wife? No, something had happened. Someone had interceded.

The queen herself perhaps? Her performance in the stables proved she had accessed potent magic. She had left Omur a wrecked heap upon his chamber floor. She easily could have turned her husband aside. But why not sooner? Why let her husband cause her so much bodily damage before stopping him?

No. Whatever had happened, he felt it had not been the queen. Something else.

It hadn't been the goddess, nor her vermin servant. He had not felt either of them since Haleine had stolen the unicorns from him. At the time, they had been wholly devoted to keeping their unicorns protected. Now, they were wholly devoted to keeping Haleine hidden. Or, if she had died, if she had indeed lost too much blood, they were scrambling to find another way to avoid extinction. No, they hadn't bothered with Maddox.

Who did that leave? How would he find out?

He had never before been so directionless. Would his lords offer him guidance?

The lass whimpered, and Omur checked on the king's progress. If Maddox held to his current pattern, he would be some time yet. Nonna whimpered again and looked at Omur, her eyes wide with a silent plea for help. How desperate the girl must have been if she thought him to be a viable source of aid. He smiled as he turned and placed his finger against his lips. She made another noise, a choked sob, and he shook his head, lowered his hand, and walked out.

Discovering Haleine, or uncovering what had become of her, was paramount. He would have to employ a new strategy. His men would search no more. No, they would *destroy*. The rebellion would be unable to ignore him for long if he once again burned the people and earth they fought to protect.

While that would draw out the human members of the rebellion, Omur suspected he may need to dig deeper still to find the queen. Forcing the pegasus to reveal himself would be best. The little beast had hardly left Haleine's side before the true extent of her value to the goddess had been discovered. Now that she was the key to their continued survival, the pegasus would assuredly tether himself to her.

Varro would have to be recalled immediately and kept close. There were hundreds of men Omur could order to raze any target he so desired, but Varro was the only one in whom Omur had enough confidence to be sent out after the pegasus and the queen. Omur would have to send messengers without delay. There would be no need to divulge much to them. Varro was a faithful pet, always coming when called.

After dispatching men to retrieve his captain, Omur returned to his chambers, where a lone guard stood outside the doors. The man pretended to pay him little mind, but Omur was well aware of his suspicion. The king's man he may have been, but it was in name only. Unless Omur was mistaken, his loyalty was given to Haleine's guard and, by extension, Haleine. Omur looked from the guard to his doors.

Sighle Coileáin had come to him. Why?

The guard did nothing as Omur passed and entered his quarters, carefully closing the door behind him. She sat by the fire, perched on the edge of a chair in which her father had sat once as he, too, waited for Omur's return.

"Lady Coileáin," he said. "How may I be of service?"

She looked at him. She was, without a doubt, Haleine's sister. Their relation was obvious in the way the girl carried herself, her shoulders back and her chin high. Her coloring had come from her father: pale skin, dark hair and eyes. She stared at him briefly before her pale cheeks flushed, and she sharply turned her gaze downward.

"My lord," she said as she rose. "I have come to beg a favor of you."

Omur crossed the room. "A favor?"

"Yes, my lord. Would you grant me a favor?"

"If it be in my power," he said.

Sighle lifted her head and offered him a smile he would have more expected to see upon the face of a gutter whore rather than Lord Darian Coileáin's youngest daughter.

"How kind of you," she said. "I can't begin to tell you how much that means to me."

Omur arched an eyebrow. "My lady?"

"Yes," she said. "Mine is right."

Omur frowned. "I beg your pardon?"

She stepped toward him. "Not yet. But you will."

"I am sorry, my lady," he said, "but I do not understand."

"Not to worry." She tilted her head to the left. "You don't have to."

He had made a mess of things. Oh aye, he had brought it all to ruin.

Dana sat in a corner of the cottage, his knees drawn to his chest. In his hands he held a dagger, *his* dagger, the one he had given to Haleine months before. He had found it sitting on the table, its blade stained with blood. How had it come to be there? Had James recognized it and brought it along? It didn't matter. Regardless of how the weapon had come to Enimode, Dana knew for what it had been used.

How had it come to this? How had he let it all get away from him?

On the other side of the room was the bed where Sarai, in times past, had taken her rest. Now, Haleine lay upon it, silent and still. Sarai sat upon a low stool at the bed's side as she administered to the woman she called queen.

Dana had moved to allow Sarai access to Haleine. It was the only time he moved from her side. Sarai worked efficiently—she always did—but no matter how quickly she resigned her position, it was too long a breach for Dana to bear.

Didn't he tell her—didn't he *swear* to her—that he would keep her safe? He had failed her once. He did not want to do it again.

He spent every moment he could at Haleine's side, the dagger in his belt, as he held her hand and stroked her hair. He called to her, his lips near her ear, cooing her name, trying to coax her back from wherever she had gone.

"Haleine, can you hear me, love?" he said over and over again. "You have to know how sorry I am. I'm so sorry, love. Haleine, please, can you hear me?"

He promised he would keep her safe, but he had left her vulnerable, and at the hands of a madman. Did that make him worse? Did it make him more terrible than the man who had cut her so deeply? Maddox never hid who he was; his cruelty was always obvious, always expected. Dana had buried his in false assurances and jealousy.

He thought of that scene, that dreadful confrontation, in her chambers. *I never turned from you*, she had spat at him. *Even when I should have.*

No, she had never turned from him. Did she regret that devotion now? For certes he did.

"Dana," Sarai said, standing in front of him.

He leaned to his left to see around her. "How does she fare?"

"When was the last time you slept?" Sarai asked.

So there was no change. Neither alive nor dead was his lover. And he was to blame.

The heavens know I've tried to stop it.

"When was the last time you ate?" Sarai asked.

Dana shook his head and shrugged. "I am neither tired nor hungry."

"You are, and I'll not have you lying to me," Sarai said. "Whatever else you are, you remain one of my boys. Go and rest. Tend to yourself."

"I don't want to—I can't." He finally looked at Sarai. "What if she wakes, and I am not here?"

"This house is not so large that you will not know it."

"I need her to know that—I need her to know how sorry I am. I didn't mean for this—I didn't want this."

The heavens know I've had every reason to, and yet I'm still here, my heart bleeding for love of you.

Her heart had bled with love for him, so her husband had tried to cut it out.

"She has to know," Dana said. "She has to know how sorry I am."

"When she wakes, you'll be here to tell her."

When. If. It had been days—*days* since they had brought her here. So many days, and still no change. Neither dead nor alive. For how long could a soul stay as such?

"This has gone on long enough," Sarai said. "There's work to be done, and if you're going to be on this farm, you're going to do your share. What with James gone, and my efforts spent here—"

She continued, but Dana stopped listening. James gone? Where? When?

"Dana," Sarai said.

Her tone made it clear that she was done asking. He nodded and dragged himself to his feet. Dagger in hand, he walked outside, not looking at Haleine. The sun was entirely too bright, so he walked to the shade of the forest and continued on to the pond. Once there, he stripped off his clothing and carefully placed the dagger on top of the pile. Wading into the water, he dove under once it was deep enough. He stayed there for as long as the air in his lungs would allow. When he returned to the surface, he floated on his back, looking at the sun through the filter of the trees.

After he left the water, he shook the excess liquid from his skin and raked the damp hair off his face. The summer air was hot, so it took him little time to dry. He put on his braies and trousers and sat beneath the shade of a tree, holding the dagger and staring at the water. He hadn't been doing so for very long when Faolan arrived. He flew into Dana's view and out again, coming to rest on a branch.

"I see Sarai finally got you to leave the house," the pegasus said. "That's good. We need to talk."

"Where is James?" Dana asked.

"Doing what you should be doing."

"That's no answer."

"That's all you'll get from me."

Dana nodded. "Why did you do it? I was a dead man. Why did you save me?"

"I didn't," the pegasus said. "Laorans decided you were worth saving."

"Why?"

"The goddess doesn't explain herself to me."

"You wouldn't have done it."

"No."

The word dropped between them like a stone.

"What do you want me to do?" Dana asked.

"It's not what I want that matters."

"What does your goddess want me to do?"

"What you were meant to do."

"I don't know that I can."

"Then leave," Faolan said. "Don't come back until you do know."

Leave. Another word. Another stone. Was there anything he hadn't poisoned?

"If I go," Dana said, "if I leave, she'll be unprotected."

He had failed her once. He didn't want to do so again.

"She won't be unprotected," Faolan said. "I have no intention of going anywhere."

"Because your goddess wants her."

"My goddess wants you, too. But not like this."

29

"This is what I am."

"It's not what you were meant to be."

"Mayhap it is," Dana said, "and your goddess is wrong."

"She's not wrong. Whatever you are—this pathetic, broken shell of a man—it's not what you were meant to be."

Dana nodded. He didn't know if there was truth to that. "Where would you have me go?"

"Go wherever you'd like," Faolan said. "I don't care."

Dana nodded again. If Faolan wanted him gone, he would go and follow the road wherever it took him. He'd lived that way once. He could do it again.

———

Haleine Coileáin wanted to die. She wanted to escape; she wanted to be free. She wanted to fly or sink or bleed. How it happened did not matter. She wanted only to be done with him, with them, with the world. To stay was too painful. To stay would be death anyway.

If you want to die, it won't be by my hand.

And she wanted to die.

But despite everything that had happened, everything she had done, she was not dead. What she was, Haleine could not say, but she was not dead.

She awoke on the shores of an expansive lake, her cheek pressed into fine, white sand. She sat up and brushed the grains from her skin.

There was nothing here, nothing but the crystalline waters and the sound of her heartbeat. She put her hand on her chest and felt the offensive movement beneath her fingers.

"Haleine?" he said. "Haleine, love, can you hear me?"

Her fingers curled, clutching at the white shift she wore and digging into her skin. She rose to her feet, eyes sweeping from side to side, but he was not to be found. She was alone in this place.

"Do you hear me?" his voice came again.

She could hear him. His voice was the only sound to be heard apart from her wretched heartbeat. They both echoed across the lake, surrounding her with her failure.

If you want to die, it won't be by my hand, the black-eyed beast in a monster's body had said.

So she had dragged her broken body across a cold stone floor as she sought to finish what her husband had started. The life would seep out of her of its own accord—he had done that much for her—but it would not come quickly enough. Her lover would come, her lover would save her, and Haleine did not want that.

No, she wanted to die.

She had taken up the blade, her lover's dagger. How fitting his would be the instrument to finish what his knife-shaped mouth had begun.

It had gone in harder than she had anticipated. She thought it would be like slicing through a tender cut of meat, but her skin provided more resistance than she had expected it might. A wall of bone followed, more easily defeated than seemed right, and then...Haleine felt it.

Relief.

No more than a pinprick with which to start, followed by a trickle, a thimbleful, and more until it poured out of her—her blood, her love, her life—onto a cold stone floor, onto a carpet, spilling everywhere and staining everything it touched.

It should have been enough. She didn't understand why it wasn't.

"Haleine," he said, "can you hear me, love?"

How dare he call her that? How dare he call her anything?

"I will not dream of you," she said.

She walked forward. The water was cold, icy daggers cutting her legs, then her arms, but she walked on. Her dress became so sodden that it tangled around her numbing limbs and slowed her pace, but she pushed onward. She walked until the soft sand beneath her feet gave way, and the dark current at the lake's center pulled her down.

It was quiet beneath the water's surface. Her heartbeat was muffled more and more until it was no more obtrusive than the steady pulse that beat at the base of her wrist. Her arms rose above her head as though they were reaching for the fading light. She looked at the dimming glow, her fingers curling in turn as they failed to grasp it.

She had been here before, seen this, done this. The pale-faced woman with the unicorn eyes had pulled her to the surface, her lungs burning with the effort of life, but that spark now lay dormant and hushed as she continued her silent sinking.

It would not be long. There would be peace soon.

Her arms fell from the ever-decreasing burn. They floated down—first one, then the other, independent of themselves, independent of her. She closed her eyes, head lulling back, then falling forward.

Soon.

But when there should have been peace, when she should have been free, she awoke once again on the white sand, this time her hands digging into it. Tears, fat and silent, rolled down her cheeks into the holes her fingers created. They disappeared, ineffectual and wasted.

"Haleine," he said. "Haleine, love, please, tell me you can hear me."

She rose to her feet and walked into the lake once again.

She would not dream of him.

Dead she may not have been, but beyond his reach she was. She would keep it that way. She would find her way free.

The rebellion could find another way to survive.

CHAPTER 3

The first thing, apart from the light of day, James saw when he carried Mireille through the portal into Enimode was Faolan hovering in the air.

The pegasus's head tilted to the side. "What did you—?"

"Seemed easier than kicking and screaming," James said.

"Oh."

"Can we go to the house? Is it safe?"

"Oh," the pegasus repeated before looking at James. "Yes, let's go to the house."

James left the forest and headed to the farm, Faolan flying at his side. Dana, Sarai, and Aaron were nowhere to be seen. Neither did he see anyone else. Perhaps they hadn't had enough time to arrive.

As they neared the cottage, Faolan flew on ahead, and the door opened without a single hand being laid upon it. James carried Mireille into the room where his parents had once slept. It didn't appear as though the room had been used for anything other than storage since their death. He wouldn't have used it now, except for his feeling that he would be better off containing Mireille as much as possible.

Laying the girl on the bed, he glanced at the wound on the side of her head. There was no blood, only swelling and bruising. She would hurt when she woke. He would have to ask Sarai to brew a tea to help with the pain.

But where was his grandmother? Where was everyone? Out in the common room, Faolan stood on the table, but a quick glance showed that the rest of the room was unexpectedly empty.

"Where's the queen?" James asked, looking at the wall where both the queen and the bed in which he had left her had been last.

"The root cellar."

"The root cellar?"

"I didn't think it would be wise to keep the queen of Lira on display where anyone could see her. They will have noticed that she's gone by now, which means they're looking for her."

"You put her in the root cellar?" James asked. "How did you manage that? It's not big enough to—"

"I made some modifications while you were away."

"Modifications? *You* made modifications?"

"Yes," Faolan said. "While you were away."

James's next question would have been how these modifications had been made, but if it had been Faolan's doing, magic had been involved. Sarai would not have been pleased by that. She was even more intolerant of magic than he was.

"While I was away," James said. "For how long was I away?"

"Four days."

"Four *days*?"

"I told you not to dawdle."

"But that's not right. It can't be," James said. "Four days? Faolan, that's impossible."

"You just walked between worlds, and you're telling me something is impossible?"

"I was not there for four days."

"Of course you weren't," Faolan said. "You walked between worlds, James. Time bends. Walking through dimensions like that…you lose time, and I can't explain it to you. Not because I don't want to, but because it involves a lot of concepts you're unfamiliar with, and a lot of concepts about those concepts with which you're equally unfamiliar. I know your travels appeared to be no more complicated than walking out the doorway to this cottage and back again, but the truth remains that it, the journey itself, takes longer than it seems. *You* lost days, and Mireille with you when you carried her through. Everything else stayed the same."

"That's not possible," James said. "It *shouldn't* be possible."

"You should work on loosening your understanding of that word," Faolan said. "It'll make things easier for you as we move on."

James ran his hand over his face. "The queen's in the root cellar?"

"Yes," Faolan said, sounding pleased that the subject had been changed. "Sarai is with her."

"Aaron? Where is he?"

"The barn, I think."

James nodded. "Find him and have him stand watch over her," he said, gesturing to Mireille.

"I'll stand watch."

"Your magic is ineffective on the queen, which means it'll likely be ineffective on her sister, which makes you a rather ineffective guard," James said. "Find Aaron. Have him stand watch."

Faolan flew off. James took another look at Mireille before crossing the common room to kick aside the deerskin concealing the root cellar's door. He opened it and peered inside, wary of what Faolan might have done. Where there was once a ladder were now steps made of earth. Lantern light filled the space, and he went below, finding his grandmother and the queen in a room near as large as the rest of the cottage above it.

"Gran," he said as he approached.

Sarai didn't look at him. "You made it back."

"Aye." He stood behind her and looked at the queen. She didn't look well. She'd grown worse since he'd brought her here. "How is she?"

"She's alive," Sarai said. "There's a fever, though, and I don't know that she's strong enough to fight it."

Especially if she didn't want to fight it. James stepped back and leaned against the wall.

"Has the physician seen her?" he asked.

"Faolan thought it best not to involve the man again," Sarai said. "There is nothing he can do for her that I cannot do myself."

James nodded. Was there anything any of them could do?

"What of the girl you've brought back with you," Sarai said then. "How does she fare?"

James looked at the back of his grandmother's head, surprised she knew anything about Mireille. "What did Faolan tell you about her?"

"He said nothing more than you had been sent to fetch her, that she was somehow needed. Is she all right?"

"Her head will hurt when she wakes. She'll need something to ease the pain."

Sarai turned toward him. "When she wakes?"

He shrugged. "She didn't want to come."

Sarai nodded curtly. "I see. I'll tend to it when I've finished here."

"I'm sorry. I'm sorry we've brought this on you, but with Dana and—" James looked around. Something was missing. Someone. "Where is Dana?"

"Gone. Faolan sent him off without a word to any of us."

"When? How long has he been gone?"

Sarai shook her head. "A couple of days? I'm not certain."

"Are there any others here?" he asked. If it had been four days, someone from the rebel camp should have been there.

"Just the lad and I," Sarai said.

No one else, and Dana gone. It was another thing to discuss with the pegasus.

"It wasn't supposed to be like this," James said.

Sarai nodded. "I know."

Cate was surrounded by trees—ancient, enormous, and covered by moss. Their branches and foliage shot out in every direction, weaving together to create a tapestry that blocked out the sun. She stood between two of them, a hand on each trunk.

She could feel something like a heartbeat beneath the moss, beneath the bark, something pulsating at the trees' core. It was unnatural, and it should have scared her or, at the very least, unnerved her, but in fact, it calmed her.

She looked up at the sound of growling. Standing in the distance was something she thought might have been a wolf. A big wolf. Werewolf? Or maybe a hellhound.

Whatever it was, it did not like her. She watched it, not removing her hands from the trees' soothing effect. The animal slowly wove its way toward her, never lowering its stare.

She didn't move. Not even when the wolf roared and charged her. Running away would have been wise, but she stood frozen, trapped in the glare of its yellow eyes. It pounced, knocking her flat on her back, and opened its mouth to snarl again.

When its jaws snapped shut, Cate opened her eyes and immediately wished she hadn't. She put her hand over her face, making the pain worse as her thumb made contact with a large lump on her forehead. Swearing softly, she carefully felt the wound, but stopped when she noticed the exposed beam running along the ceiling. It wasn't her ceiling. She swore again. Louder this time.

Someone laughed. "Never heard a lady use that word before."

She dropped her hand and pushed herself up, hands sinking into the feather-stuffed mattress. That was wrong. What happened to...It wasn't her bed.

She lifted her head. Standing in a doorway in front of her was a man she'd never seen before. Boy, rather. Not a man—though he was probably old enough to take offense at being called as much. There was something familiar about him, about the way he spoke, or maybe the way he leaned against the frame, but she didn't know what the something was. Her eyes slid down to take in his appearance. He was dressed almost identically to the other one.

"He kidnapped me," she said.

The boy shrugged. "Looks like."

"Who are you?"

"Your bloody guard, I guess."

He sounded bitter. Since she didn't care, she let that pass and checked out her surroundings. Plain, undecorated walls. Wooden shutters covering a small window to her right. No overhead lights. No lights at all. What was this place?

She looked at her guard. "Where am I?"

"The village of Enimode."

"Where the hell is that?"

"The country of Lira, which is on another earth," a new voice said. "Separate from the one you know."

The new voice came from her left. She turned toward it, but no one was there.

"Down here," the voice said next.

Her eyes dropped. Standing on an overturned basket was a—a pegasus? A very small pegasus? The sight of it made her forget about her head as she scrambled to the other side of the bed.

"Do you see that?" she asked the boy, pointing to the pegasus.

"He sees that," the pegasus answered.

"Did you *say* something?" she asked the pegasus before looking at the boy. "Did it just say something?"

The pegasus said, "Yes."

The boy shrugged again. "He does that."

"He does that?" she repeated. "And he sounds like that?"

"Like what?" the pegasus asked.

"Normal," Cate said, looking at it. "You sound normal."

"How should I sound?"

"I don't know. Like you represent the Lollipop Guild?" Cate groaned as nausea swept over her. She covered her face with her hands. "Oh, I think I'm gonna be sick."

"There's a pot under the bed if you need it."

That was a voice she recognized. She looked at the doorway again and saw the asshole who had kidnapped her standing behind the boy.

"You hit me in the head with my tennis racquet," she accused, nausea forgotten.

He shrugged. He and the boy were definitely related. Brothers.

"I told you I was unarmed."

"You told me you wouldn't hurt me."

"I told you I didn't *want* to hurt you."

"Oh, let me know when you're done splitting hairs."

"Mireille—"

"You called me Mireille," she said.

It wasn't the first time he'd done that. No, the first time was in her bedroom. *If you'd only allow me to explain, Mireille,* he'd said, and she had dropped her guard.

"Aye," her kidnapper said.

"Why?"

He seemed confused again as he glanced quickly at the pegasus. "It is your name, isn't it?"

It was her middle name, but not many people knew that. She didn't know why a freak in tights would have been one of them.

"My name is Cate," she said. "With a C."

"That's not what your mother called you, though," the pegasus said. "Is it?"

No. Her mother had called her Mireille. But how or why would a reject from a Disney animated feature know that?

She looked at him. "You familiar with my mother?"

"You could say that."

Cate gawked. How the hell was she supposed to respond to that? Her kidnapper, obviously uncomfortable, cleared his throat.

"Listen," he said, "my name is—"

"No need to tell me your name," she interrupted, still staring down the pegasus. "I've already given you one."

"You've given me a name?"

She nodded and turned her attention to him. He continued to look confused. She suspected he spent a lot of time looking like that.

"Asshole," she said.

There was a snort of laughter. The asshole's brother ducked his head, but not before she saw his glee. The asshole himself was less amused.

"Asshole?" he asked.

She shrugged. "Seemed fitting."

"My name is James ap Seoras," the asshole said. He gestured to the boy. "This is my brother, Aaron. The pegasus is called Faolan."

She folded her arms across her chest. "Ap Seoras? Is that your last name?"

"Last name?"

"Surname?"

"Aye."

"Was Seoras your father?"

"Aye."

"That's a Welsh thing, your surname," she said. "Or was. Are you Welsh, James?"

"Am I what?"

"Welsh, James, are you Welsh? Or did you steal from them?"

"I don't steal," he said. "Often anyway, and certainly not my name."

"Stole me."

"I told you I had no choice in that."

"Matter of life and death, was it?"

"Aye," James said. "If you would let me explain—"

"No," she said. "I'm not all that interested in your problems. A side effect, I would guess, of the goose egg here on my forehead. Or that whole kidnapping thing. Toss up, really."

"Cate," the pegasus tried.

"Tell me, James ap Seoras," she said, "is your father proud of all you've become?"

James stiffened. The brother also straightened, his pleasure from before disappeared. Apparently, the father was a sore point with them. She wondered why.

"I wouldn't think so," he said.

"Didn't raise you to be a kidnapper, huh?"

"No."

"Good to know there's some decency left in the world."

"Just not this one." James looked at the pegasus. "You wanted her, you deal with her."

He walked out. The brother seemed undecided, but stayed put. The pegasus snorted in what sounded to her like annoyance. She looked at him in surprise.

"That was rude," the pegasus said.

"Whoa, wait a minute," she said. "He kidnaps me, and *I'm* the one being rude? How's that work?"

"You should be mindful of how you speak," the pegasus said. "Aaron doesn't know what a minute is. No one here does."

"But you do?"

"A measure of time used where you come from. They don't use that here."

"What do they use?"

"Do you care about that?"

"Not so much, no," she said. "I'm more interested in not being here anymore."

"I'm afraid I can't help you with that."

"Can't?" she asked. "Or won't?"

"Perhaps both," the pegasus answered.

"What does that mean?"

"It means I need something from you. Until I get it, I won't be inclined to let you go."

Cate's hands went to her head. "How hard did that asshole hit me? This is fucking insane!"

Aaron made another noise. Never heard a lady talk like a sailor before. Well, he'd adjust, wouldn't he?

"Faolan," someone said in a schoolmarm tone, "that is enough."

Cate lowered her hands as she looked toward the door. An older woman stood at Aaron's side, holding a cup and wearing clothing that amounted to little more than rags. Cate could see the resemblance she bore to the boy. Nice to know her kidnapping was a family affair. The woman tapped Aaron on the shoulder, and he backed away and stepped out of sight.

"Cate," Faolan said, sounding unhappy, "meet Sarai."

Sarai stared. Her mouth was opened slightly, as if she couldn't believe what she was seeing. It reminded Cate of the way James had first looked at her, and she glared back.

Sarai didn't look away. "Leave the girl be."

"I'll return later, then," Faolan said. "You don't have to stay in this room, Cate, but you do need to stay in the house."

"Faolan," Sarai warned.

The pegasus took flight and left the room. When he was gone, Sarai came forward, moving like a drill instructor at a scary military academy. No wonder the boys had scattered on command.

Sarai sat on the edge of the bed. "I am sorry."

"What are you?" Cate asked. "The ringleader of the circus?"

"Am I what?"

"Are you the woman who makes decisions around here? I'm asking because they listened to you. Well, the string bean didn't, but he was already gone before you arrived."

"String bean?" Sarai echoed with a slight smile.

Cate shrugged. "You seem like a woman in front of whom one shouldn't swear. Why I should care about that, I don't know, but there it is."

This appeared to amuse Sarai more. Cate rolled her eyes.

"Glad to be so entertaining," she said. "I wouldn't want to be a boring hostage after all."

The gleam in Sarai's eyes dulled, and she drew away. "The lads are my daughter's sons."

"And the pegasus?"

"He belongs to another of my boys. Your ringleader, as you called it."

"Is he the one who sent your grandson to kidnap me?"

"I don't know about that," Sarai said. "But I am sorry he had to bring you here, and sorry for the manner in which he saw it done."

She held out a cup. Cate looked at it. "What's that?"

"Tea. It will help ease the pain of your head and make you feel less ill."

Tempting, but Cate didn't reach for it.

Sarai sighed. "There is a reason why—"

"Yeah, well, there's always a reason. Criminals always have reasons," Cate said. "Doesn't, however, mean they're just."

"Just. You'll notice that word has little meaning in this land." Sarai set the cup on the overturned basket. Standing, she bowed her head and gestured to the cup. "Drink it. You'll feel better."

"I'll feel better when I'm away from here."

"As will I," Sarai said. "I shall find you some clothing, and I'll come back."

Cate glanced at the Harvard tank and shorts she'd put on before bed. "Is that why everyone's staring?"

"I beg your pardon?"

"You, the string bean—you've been looking at me like you couldn't possibly be seeing what you're seeing," Cate said. "Is that because you can see my ankles, or because I look like someone I shouldn't?"

Sarai's eyes skimmed Cate's clothing.

"I can see more than your ankles," she said and left the room.

<hr/>

Faolan found James in the barn, staring at the ground as though he possessed the desire and ability to burn a hole through it. Speaking first would be unwise, so Faolan found a perch and waited.

"Where's Dana?" James said finally.

Faolan looked to the right where, resting against the wall, was Dana's sword. "Gone."

"Gone where?"

"Away."

James looked up. "What does that mean?"

"It means he's not here."

"Where did he go?"

"I don't know," Faolan said. "Neither do I care. He's not my concern."

"He should be," James said. "He should be here. He should be the one doing this."

Faolan had thought the same at first. He had said as much to Dana as he rousted the rebel leader from the homestead. But meeting Cate, being in that room with her—even for that short amount of time—had convinced him otherwise. Now, somehow, he thought there was no one better suited for this task than James.

"No," Faolan said. "He shouldn't be."

James's shoulders sagged. "We're putting all our hopes for survival on her?"

"We are for now."

"She's a nightmare. She's a bloody nightmare."

Faolan didn't argue. She was precisely that—a nightmare of the worst kind. James didn't know the half of it. He had no idea of the enormity of the risk they had taken in bringing her to their world. *Two from one, the first from moon, the next from dark.* Cate was the second. She was the dark. Faolan knew it as soon as he'd seen her lying unconscious in James's arms. The ability to turn the world to ash was inside her.

But he couldn't tell James that.

"You kidnapped her," he said instead. "What did you expect?"

James laughed. "You said you didn't care how it was done, so long as it was. Bring her back kicking and screaming, if that's what it takes, you said."

"I did say that. I meant it," Faolan said. "I don't care how it was done. But it would be ridiculous to expect her to be complacent and cooperative with us at this time."

James pushed off from the stall door and turned away. He paced the length of the barn and back again. Faolan didn't mind his irritation. He found it to be preferable. James was generally more useful when angry.

"What does that leave us with?" James asked.

"Convincing her to listen," Faolan said. "And later, convincing her to help us."

"You heard her in there. She's not interested in anything we have to say."

"We make her interested."

"How do we do that?" James asked. "Put her in a room with the sister she doesn't know she has?"

"No. We will not do that," Faolan said. "For the time being, I don't want her to know Haleine exists."

James stopped moving. "You mean to gain her trust by lying to her?"

"It's a lie of omission," Faolan said. "Cate doesn't know she has a sister. Cate doesn't suspect she has a sister. All you have to do is not mention it to her. We'll tell her about Haleine when the time is right."

"When will that be?"

"When it most benefits us."

James shook his head. "This will not gain her trust."

"It's not her trust we need," Faolan said. "But we will need her if we are to put an end to this war. Telling Cate about Haleine will only complicate things that are, as I'm sure you'll agree, already complicated enough."

James nodded, this time in defeat. He backed away and leaned against the opposite wall. His hands rested on his legs, and he looked at the ground.

"What do we do?" he asked. "How do we make her interested?"

Faolan couldn't tell James that, either. The tactics he thought would be necessary to sway Cate would be ones in which James would have no interest. As changed and hardened as the man had become, there remained a line he would not cross.

"*We* don't do anything," Faolan said. "*I* will do it."

"What do I do?"

"You catch her when she falls."

chapter 4

Once her kidnappers had left her alone, there was nothing to distract Cate from how badly her head hurt. It felt like James had taken something a lot heavier than a tennis racquet to it. Closing her eyes, she lay on her side and curled up tightly. Perhaps it was time to reconsider the head-curing tea Sarai had left behind.

Except...no. That's what they wanted—for her to accept their help. It didn't matter that they had caused the problem in the first place. If she drank that tea, she'd end up slightly more beholden to them than before, and who knew where that would lead?

No, thank you. She'd take her chances with the pain.

She could handle pain. Well, a headache, anyway. She could just treat it like a migraine—lay still in a quiet, darkened room until it went away. Besides, if she gave off the illusion of sleep, maybe they would leave her alone long enough for her to figure a way out of this place.

Wherever this place was.

It didn't take long for feigned sleep to morph into actual sleep. Too tired and sore to fight it, Cate gave in. She could come up with an escape plan later.

When she next opened her eyes, the room was darker, lit only by a dim flickering source. Sitting up, she surveyed the empty space, seeing nothing but a fire roaring in the next room. Where had everyone gone? Had they left her unguarded? Seemed a shame not to find out. Carefully, she slid off the bed.

"We did not poison the tea," James said.

Cate froze. Where the hell was he? Walking to the end of the bed, she found him sitting on the floor in the doorway, elbows resting on his knees. Not unguarded after all. Should have known that was too good to be true.

"Didn't think you did," she said.

He glanced at her. "Should I bother to offer you food? Or shall you only reject that kindness as well?"

She laughed. "You know, the kind thing to do would've been to not kidnap me in the first place."

He tipped his head back and looked at the ceiling. "I know."

"Well, so long as you know."

"I wish you would..." He shook his head. "You should get dressed."

She looked at herself. "I am dressed."

"You can't wear that. Not here."

"Oh, I didn't realize there was a dress code. You really should have mentioned that before you kidnapped me."

"My grandmother found you some clothing," he said. "It's there, on the bed. Put it on, please."

"Or what?"

He looked at her, seeming surprised that she was fighting the request. "Or what?"

"What will you do if I refuse," she said. "It's something to think about because I am refusing."

He stood. "Then I'll have to bloody well dress you myself, won't I?"

The statement lacked any true threat, but she moved back, hoping to appear intimidated. She looked at the clothes Sarai had left for her, then quickly at the shuttered window.

"You wouldn't dare," she said.

He stepped toward her. "Wouldn't I?"

She sighed. "Fine, I'll change. But not while you're standing there."

"I'll turn my back."

"You'll leave this room," she said. "And you'll close the door behind you because I will not, under any circumstances, be taking my clothes off in front of you."

He stared at her for a moment, then nodded. "Of course not. I wouldn't expect—I apologize. I'll go."

He backed away, pulling the door closed as he went. Cate tiptoed to the window. It wasn't very large, but neither was she. She could fit. Opening the shutters, she hauled herself through.

Her exit was graceless, and she landed in a heap on the ground. She didn't move right away, waiting to see if anyone had heard. No one said anything, and no doors opened, so she grinned and got to her feet.

Brushing dirt off her clothes, she looked around. All right, where was she? Her current guess was thirteenth-century Wales, which, in addition to being completely insane and highly improbable, meant the odds of running into someone with any sort of phone were likely slim. It was probably a bad idea to be out there in the first place, wandering around barefoot in an unfamiliar dark, but as her other option was to sit around an unfamiliar room trading barbs with an asshole and his personification pony, she went on.

As she moved away from the house, she glanced at the star-filled sky. The sight of it made her gasp. She was no stranger to stargazing. She and her mother would sit out on the beach in Maine and look at them. They'd sat on the roof in Boston and looked there, too. It had been nice to look at, but this sky above her now was awing. Open and clear and amazing. There were so many stars, it was like the black didn't exist. She searched for constellations she knew—the big dipper, the little dipper, Orion—without seeing any of them. That was discouraging, but it didn't necessarily mean anything. She wasn't an astronomer after all.

"Cate!" James shouted.

Time to go. She rushed onward, passing a paddock on her left and a building to the right. A barn maybe? It definitely smelled like a barnyard. A farm, then. She was on a farm. In thirteenth-century Wales. Because *that* made sense.

Behind her, a door opened, and James yelled her name again. Footsteps followed, and he quickly caught up with her at a smaller paddock filled with sheep. Keeping the sheep in between them, she looked him over. In one hand, he carried a lantern. The other held a sword.

"What are you doing?" he demanded. "You shouldn't be out here. It's dangerous."

She stared at the sword. "Why? Are the sheep evil?"

"You're being hunted, Cate," Faolan said, appearing at James's side.

"By the sheep?" she asked. "Those sneaky little ovine bastards. They never let on."

"Come back to the house," James said. "Please."

What she wanted to do was make a break for it in the woods behind her. But James would know them better than she did, and who the hell knew what else she might find in there? Lions and tigers and bears. Or—considering the presence of a pegasus—manticores, griffons, and dragons. Oh my.

Maybe she wouldn't make a break for it.

"Was I being hunted before you brought me here?" she asked.

James looked to Faolan. Faolan said, "No."

"Well," she said, "thanks for that."

Rounding the paddock, she pushed past James and returned to the house. Neither James nor Faolan followed. She could hear James's low murmuring but couldn't make out the words. Probably talking about her, though. Assholes. Once inside the cottage, she closed the door and leaned against it until noticing the bar resting next to it. She picked it up and set it in place.

"If you want to keep the pegasus out, you should bar the windows as well," Aaron said, his voice floating down to her. "To your left."

She glanced to her left and saw a window, the size of the one she'd climbed through. Closing the shutters, she hunted for the bar.

"Beside the fire," Aaron offered.

She put the bar in position and looked up. Aaron hovered near the edge of a loft, his face mostly shrouded in shadow.

"Thanks," she said, and he nodded before retreating into the darkness.

She went into the bedroom to close and bar that window as well. Returning to the main room, she bounced slightly as she looked around. There didn't seem to be anything left to do but find a seat and enjoy the show.

Just as she was pulling out a chair from the table, the latch lifted and someone pressed against the door. It didn't budge.

After a second failed attempt, James sighed. "Please unbar the door, Cate."

She didn't.

"Aaron!" he called then. "Aaron, let me in."

Cate's eyes flickered to the loft, but her accomplice stayed hidden. That made her smile.

"What is going on here?" Sarai demanded.

Cate whirled around to look at her. "Where the hell did you come from?"

Sarai ignored her as she crossed the room. Lifting the bar, she opened the door, but James stayed outside. His eyes swept the room, narrowing when they fell upon Cate. She stared back.

"Do that again," he warned, "and I will tie you to the damn bed."

"I'd love to see you try," she scoffed.

He came toward her, looking so goddamn menacing that she involuntarily retreated. What was she doing? She couldn't back down. If he wanted to get in her face, she had to get in his, too. Cate forced herself forward, but Sarai stepped in between them.

"Stop it, the both of you. That is quite enough," she snapped. "You've made enough noise this night to wake the dead."

"Did we?" Faolan asked. "Did we wake the dead?"

At this, James looked away. Cate followed his glance to an opened trap door in the floor. Was that where Sarai had come from? What was down there?

"No," Sarai said, sounding sorry. She looked at Cate. "Come, lass. I'll help you dress."

"Thanks," Cate said, "but I can manage on my own."

James snorted. "I'll be outside."

"I'll alert the media," Cate responded, going into her room and slamming the door.

No one followed.

———❦———

The magic was like a spark in the night. It stirred his senses, and Omur rolled onto his back as it pricked every nerve he possessed.

When he could no longer ignore it, he left the warmth of his bed and wrapped a robe around his body. He walked to the balcony and opened the doors wide. Stepping outside, he focused his attentions not on the city below him, but rather on what lay beyond the walls of Eluned.

Enimode.

Why hadn't he thought of it before? He should have—the village had long held some importance to Dana. The reason why the soldiers continued to find no trace of the rebellion in the forests was becoming clear.

They weren't there.

He breathed deep, inhaling the scent of magic, and opened his mouth to taste it. It was the opportunity for which he had been waiting. It was the muffled cry, the gasp for breath, the sliver of light in a blackened room. It was all he required to find his quarry. He wouldn't lose them again. He abandoned the balcony and opened the door to his chambers.

"Find Varro," he said to the guard in the hall. "Bring him here."

The man bowed, and Omur retreated to the fire to wait.

Varro arrived promptly, obviously having been roused straight from sleep, and bowed before Omur. "My lord, you have need of me?"

"The rebels are active once more," Omur said.

Varro did not ask how his lord knew this. The captain of the guard had learned long ago to never question anything his lord told him.

"I would have you run them to ground," Omur said. "Discover their secrets."

"The queen, my lord?" Varro asked. "Is she among their number?"

If only he knew. Omur couldn't be sure Haleine still walked this earth. He had seen the amount of blood the girl had lost. She very well could have died.

"It may be so, but I do not know," he said. "If she is with them, bring her here. Dana, too, should you come across him. The king has unfinished business with the pair of them, but kill the rest. He has no need for them. Nor do I."

"Gladly, my lord," Varro said. "Where will you have us start?"

"Enimode," Omur said. "Whether they are still there, I cannot say, but they have been there most recently. You will either find them, or their trail. The people may be of service to you."

"The people there gave us nothing the last time we sought information about the rebels."

"Yes," Omur said, "and you burnt their village to ash. Mayhap this time they will consider your questions more carefully."

"If they do not?"

Omur shrugged. "I'm sure they can be burned again."

Dana was drunk.

It made things easier. He didn't deserve that, but it wouldn't stop him from taking it. A lack of merit had never stopped him before, so why should it now?

Even his inebriated state was stolen, courtesy of the unguarded kitchens of a nobleman whose name Dana did not know. A day or two ago, Dana had pilfered from him a jug of ale and a loaf of bread. The bread was gone, but there was ale enough for one more night. He didn't know what he would do when the sun next set.

But that was a problem for later. His only goal since his expulsion from Enimode was to live through the night in front of him. He had chosen to spend this night in the burnt-out remains of what had once been a church in what had once been the village of Piangi. It was little more than a graveyard now. The king's men had seen to that. Why, how, when this had occurred was a mystery, and with each swallow of ale, Dana found he cared less and less.

It was all the more reason to keep drinking.

He took the village's destruction as evidence that Omur and the king were searching for him. The goddess may not have wanted him as he was, but Dana was still a wanted man. Neither Maddox nor Omur would care how broken and wretched he had become.

Nor, he suspected, would they care how drunk he was, except to lament that he wouldn't scream as much as the king would like when they cut into him. Dana had been in that dungeon once. He had never made it to the king's table, but he should have died there.

Yet, he hadn't.

Why had Laorans saved him?

He didn't know the answer, nor did he know where he might find it. Certainly it would not be here, in a house of worship devoted to a deity that was not the one he was meant to serve.

Again, another problem for another time.

Though meant for a nobleman's arse, Dana had selected a padded bench directly in front of the altar, or what remained of it. He didn't deserve that, either, that small measure of comfort, but the commoners' benches lacked a cushion upon which to sit.

He never did know his place.

He told that to Piala more than once. It was true of both of them, and they knew it. She had laughed at him, and he had laughed with her...until the night he had snapped her neck.

Raising the jug to his lips, he drank. It was uncommonly good ale to have been found in a nobleman's home. Unusual for it to be found there at all. Whiskey or wine was far more common among the nobility. He drank wine with Haleine once, served by her hand in a goblet worth more than anything he had ever owned.

He always did overreach. Mingling with those of a higher birth, treating them as though they might be equals. James never liked it. James had never met a nobleman whom he didn't distrust. But the drinking and carousing had been nothing compared to what Dana had done to Haleine. James would never forgive that. How could he?

Dana brought the noblemen to earth, but Haleine had raised him up. She had brought him too close to the sun, and he hadn't noticed until they were both scorched beyond recognition. The fall had been brutal. He wanted to think it was over, that he was finished falling—that he was in the ground, waiting for the dirt to cover him—but for some reason, nothing came.

Why had the goddess saved him?

Dana drank again. Whoever the man was, his taste in ale was to be admired. Dana had only ever known one other lord who was above such blatant snobbery, but that had been a lifetime ago.

Two lifetimes ago. Dana thought he was on his third now. Before. During. After. Before was tolerable. He didn't know what else was out there, did he? During—well, that hadn't gone well at all. His fault, he knew. His fault.

Which led him to After. He found he didn't care for After very much at all.

He took another belt from the jug, then set it on the floor to pull the dagger from his belt. The blade hadn't been cleaned. There had been no time to tend to it when the blood was fresh, and now he supposed it didn't matter. Running his fingers over the dark spots, he hissed as he sliced his thumb. As the bite registered in his ale-sodden brain, he dropped the dagger into his lap and looked at his injury. The blood, turned black by moonlight, rushed to meet the night. He pressed his thumb to his lips until the taste of metal had lessened. Once it had, he picked up the dagger once more, lightly dragging its tip along his arm.

It was a way out. But it was a coward's way out, and he wasn't a coward.

Wasn't he? Of course he was. Look at what he had done. Look at what he was doing.

And James—James was off doing what the goddess had meant for Dana himself to do.

I can't do this alone, Dana had said to Faolan the night he had been told of his destiny.

He never did know his place. Not before that night.

Dana ap Seoras, Lorcan had said. *I would speak with you.*

Dana ap Seoras. It was a name to which he had no formal claim. He had no formal claim to anything, and yet, Seoras's name was the one thing Dana was hesitant to take.

The world as you know it is going to change, the unicorn had continued. *And not for the better.*

That had been true. More true than Dana had realized at the time. His fault. Always his fault. He had always thought that everything was a damn game, some grand adventure to be had. A grand adventure, indeed.

Look what he had done with it.

Reaching for the jug, Dana allowed himself another mouthful of ale. If he wasn't careful, he would soon run out, and finding more wouldn't be easy. He couldn't afford to waste what he had. No, he'd already done quite enough of that. Whatever was left was precious.

He had to make it last as long as possible. It was the only way to keep from dreaming of Haleine.

"I can't do this alone," he said, just as he had the night his first lifetime had ended and the second had begun.

You don't have to, Faolan had responded then. *You and James both, you're destined to do this together.*

Now James would have to do it on his own, wouldn't he? Maybe it would be better that way.

Dana slid onto his back. Through the remains of the roof, he could see the moon.

"I never knew why you wanted him," he said. "I guess I do now."

Dropping his head, he looked at the altar, only to find Haleine, illuminated by moonlight. She wore the gown he had last seen her in, the front of it destroyed by the blood from her wound.

"You're not here," he told her. "Not really."

She said nothing.

"You're dying in Enimode. So go back there, and leave me to..." Lifting the dagger, Dana ran his thumb over the knot in the center of its narrow crossguard. "Just leave me. It is no worse than I deserve."

She did not respond. When he looked at the altar again, she was gone.

"No worse than I deserve," he repeated.

Draining the jug, he let it fall to the floor. The dagger he let lay on his chest, his fingers resting lightly atop it.

There had to be a place he could go, some place where her ghost wouldn't be able to follow. If he walked far enough, looked hard enough, he would find it.

He never had known his place, but it was time he changed that.

When the sun rose, if he was still there on that earth, wrapped in that skin, he would leave. He would walk until he found his place.

Back to the beginning he would go.
It was as good a place to start as any.

CHAPTER 5

Cate awoke the next morning, still lying on the scratchy and musty feather mattress on which she'd fallen asleep sometime after her foiled escape attempt. She stretched, pleased to find her headache had subsided almost completely, and looked to her left.

The pegasus was perched on the overturned basket. Grumbling, she flipped onto her stomach and pressed her face into the mattress. Maybe she could smother herself.

"I see you're dressed," the pegasus said.

She was dressed. The temperature overnight had dropped drastically, forcing her to relent and throw on the dress over her clothes. It hadn't helped much. She hadn't thought it would, but a second layer was better than nothing.

Cate sat up. "Don't think that means I'll be cooperating with anything else."

"I wouldn't dare," Faolan said. "What will you be doing? What's your plan?"

"Starve you out."

"Starve us out? This isn't a siege."

"That's exactly what this is, only in a castle scenario, you'd be the one trying to starve me out."

"But you're not in a castle," Faolan said. "None of us are."

"I guess metaphor isn't a part of your programming, huh?"

"What?"

"Look, you want something from me—you, your idiot lackey, and his happy little family. I don't know what that something is; I don't want to know; I don't *need* to know what that something is because—whatever it is—it means you can't hurt me. You want me to be whole and happy—well, maybe not happy, but whole and cooperative at any rate, which means you can be creepy and condescending all you want, and your lackeys can be scary and intimidating all they want, but you won't get what you want until you get through my defenses," she said. "Which you won't."

"That's a strategy?"

"The Boy Wonder will keep blustering; I'll keep deflecting," she said. "Since he doesn't strike me as one having been burdened by an overabundance of patience, I'll wear him down. Wear him out. Eventually, he'll throw me back."

"That decision doesn't rest with the Boy Wonder," Faolan said. "Otherwise, I'd say you had an excellent plan."

"With whom does the decision rest? You?"

"Not exactly."

She nodded. "It's great how damn specific you are."

"You want specifics?"

"No," she said. "Just making an observation."

Faolan tossed his head. "There's food and drink on the table out there if you want it, and a pot under the bed if you need that."

"You want me to piss in a pot?"

"I suppose you could hold it."

Cate laughed. "Well, shit."

"You'll have to do that in the pot, too."

She laughed harder. "This place keeps getting better and better."

"Wait until you ask for the specifics."

"I won't."

"We'll see." Faolan flew off the basket and headed toward the door. "Come out when you're done."

"We'll see," Cate said before sighing and sliding off the bed to look for the pot.

Afterward, she did go out to the cottage's main room. It wasn't like she had anything else to do, and besides, she was maybe a little hungry. Faolan stood on the table where a clay cup and two slices of a hearty wheat bread waited for her. Cate peered into the cup. Looked like water. Or very weak tea. Picking up the cup, she sniffed its contents. Tea. Swell.

"I suppose coffee is too much to ask for," she said.

"I don't know what that is."

"Of course you don't." Cate took a sip. She made a face and put the cup down. "Where's the Boy Wonder? Off kidnapping someone else?"

Faolan looked toward the door. "Milking a cow, I think."

"How very pastoral," she said. "What about the rest of the family? Where are they?"

"Aaron's also with the livestock, and Sarai's down below," Faolan said. "Why? Planning on running away again?"

"If I am," she said, "you'll be the first one I tell."

Cate broke off a piece of bread and looked at the animal hide—a deerskin maybe?—concealing the door in the floor. Why did Sarai spend so much time in that hole?

"What's down there?" she asked. "Meth lab?"

Faolan tilted his head. "I don't know what that is."

She dropped the bread and wandered over to the deerskin. "Whatever it is, it must be important."

"It's nothing. There's nothing down there."

"What about your waking-the-dead question last night?"

"Sarai's phrasing."

"Yeah, but she was sorry to be saying no," Cate said. "And the Boy Wonder, he was looking right over here when she said it."

"Why do you call James that?" Faolan asked. "Why don't you use his name?"

"Why are you changing the subject?" She used her foot to push aside the deerskin and crouched to lift the door.

"Cate," he said, "don't—don't go down there."

"Too late."

She ended up in a strangely modern-looking basement—although that might not have been what they called it. Root cellar, or something. Sarai sat on a stool at the opposite end, taking care of someone lying on a narrow bed. Cate crept closer. Why didn't Faolan want her to see this?

Sarai twisted around. "Oh dear."

"Cate," Faolan said. "Stop, please."

Cate moved to her right to see Sarai's patient. She saw the red hair first, then the woman's face. It was...Suddenly, her heart was pounding in her ears, and the floor rushed up to meet her. Tremors vibrated along her arms upon impact.

"You're all right," Sarai said, her hands on Cate's shoulders. "Let me help you."

"Who is that?" Cate pulled away. "Who the *hell* is that?"

Sarai looked at her, mouth open, but said nothing. Cate jerked to her feet and looked at Faolan.

The pegasus sighed. "Your sister."

———

James placed the milking stool next to the cow, stroking her hide and speaking softly to her. It had been a good length of time since he had last performed this chore. He actually smiled as he carefully positioned the bucket and lowered himself onto the seat. His hands moved efficiently, this work not forgotten in his absence from it. He settled into a rhythm and briefly forgot himself and his war.

It was almost normal.

"Your girl's on the run again," Aaron said.

The rhythm was broken, the normality lost. James lifted his head from the cow's flank and looked at his brother. Aaron leaned against the open barn door and gestured outside with a jerk of his chin.

"Your girl's on the run again," he repeated.

James sighed. "Which way is she running?"

"Toward the village, looks like."

Of course she was. James stood and stalked outside, collecting his sword from its resting place near the door. Faolan was flying toward him.

"What happened?" James demanded, buckling the sword belt around his waist. "What did you do?"

"Nothing," Faolan said. "She went—she went into the root cellar."

"Why did you let her do that? You were the one who said—"

"I told her not to go."

"Oh, I'm sure you did."

"Just go get her."

"Try not to lose the queen while I'm gone," James snapped, running for the village.

Finally catching up to Cate near the village center, he grabbed her from behind and pulled her close, but she elbowed him in the gut so hard, he was forced to let go. She kept walking. He stood briefly stunned, then sprang ahead to get in front of her.

"Stop," he said. "Wait."

Cate lunged forward to hit him. "Who is she? Who the hell is she?"

"Your sister." James held up his hands but did nothing else to stave off her attack. "She's your sister."

Cate hit him again. "I don't *have* a sister. Do you hear me? I don't have a sister, so who the hell is she, and who the hell are you, and why the hell did you bring me here?"

"I've been trying to tell you," he said. "I'm sorry, but I've been trying to explain—"

"Shut up! What makes you think I could possibly trust anything you have to say? You kidnapped me, you hit me on the head, and you brought me here. I don't even know where here is—except there's no electricity or indoor plumbing or coffee, but there is a tiny, surprisingly verbose pegasus with a master's degree in sarcasm, not to mention my long-lost identical twin stashed away, by the way, in the remarkably well-developed basement of your glorified mud hut, and I-I don't know what the hell is going on, who you people think you are, and—and *what* is up with all the genuflecting?"

"What?"

"Bowing," she said, looking past him. "People are bowing and kneeling in the street. Why? Why are people bowing and kneeling in the street?"

She pointed. He looked over his shoulder to see some of the townsfolk bowing and kneeling.

"Oh." He dropped his hands. "They think you are your sister."

Her eyes snapped back to him, looking as though she meant to hit him again, and he held up his hands once more.

"The woman you saw in the root cellar, the one who is not your sister," he said. "They think you are her."

"Oh," she said, sounding slightly mollified. "But why should that matter? Who is she to them?"

It seemed safe enough to lower his hands, and he slowly brought them to his sides. "Their queen."

"Queen?" Cate took another look at the people. "As in 'of all the land'?"

"Is there another kind?"

She shrugged. "Beauty, drama, dairy, homecoming, ice, prom, of hearts, dancing—"

"Dancing queen?"

"Young and sweet, only seventeen."

"What?"

"Nothing," Cate said. "So, she's the queen?"

"Aye."

"What is she doing in your root cellar?"

"Deciding whether to live or die, I think."

"In your root cellar? Interesting choice of venue."

"It wasn't her choice."

"Steal her, too, did you?"

He looked skyward and sighed heavily. "Aye."

"Starting a collection?"

"I didn't have a choice," he said. "Could we please discuss this back at the cottage? I'll answer every question you have, I swear."

She pretended to think. "No."

"Now you're just being difficult."

"I'd get used to that if I were you."

He blew out an exasperated breath and reached for her, but she jumped out of his grasp.

"Touch me, and I'll start screaming bloody murder," she said. "They think I'm queen. They'll come save me."

James was skeptical. His face must have shown it because Cate's smug expression quickly turned crestfallen.

"They won't come save me?" she asked.

"In another village, aye," he said, "they probably would."

"Well, damn," she said. "Why not this one? What's wrong with them?"

"Nothing's wrong with them. They understand something of what I do. They know there's reason behind it."

She wanted to ask what that reason was. He could see the question in her eyes—the wavering between curiosity and stubborn indifference. Deciding for her, he grabbed her shoulders and pointed her toward the village. She gasped but did not scream.

"Do you see that?" he asked. "Do you?"

"What? Colonial Williamsburg over there? Yeah, I see it. What about it?"

"Nearly a year ago, men came and destroyed all they could. They set fire to anything that held still long enough. They killed everyone they touched." James turned her to face the mill. "They ran down the miller's lad in the forest and shot him in the back." He made her look at the tavern. "The tavern girl, Rhiannon, she died, too. Do you want me to tell you what they did to her? Shall I tell you for how many days they tortured her before she died?"

Cate broke free and looked at him. "What happened to them has nothing to do with me. None of it."

"It has everything to do with you," he said. "It had nothing to do with them."

"If that's true, why did it happen? If it had nothing to do with them, why did it happen?"

"Because of you and me and this damn mess we're both in."

"I'm only in this damn mess because you brought me here."

"I only brought you here because of this damn mess," James said. "I'm not a monster, Cate, I'm not. I'm only trying to do what is right."

"Not by me."

"No, maybe not by you. But by them," he said, gesturing to the people. "My brother, my grandmother—"

"What about your father?" Cate asked. "Did you do right by him?"

Her words were another short jab straight to his gut. He wanted to respond in kind. His hands formed fists but remained at his side.

"If you want to know what happened to my father," he said, "I'll show you."

Seizing her arm, James dragged her back to the farm, holding firm even as she struggled against him. When they reached his parents' graves, he threw her on the ground in front of them. She tried to get up, so he shoved her down again and put his hand on the back of her neck to keep her there.

"There lies my father, and beside him my mother," he said. "Their throats were cut while my brother watched. He ran then, to hide, to save his own life, and has spent every day since hating himself for his cowardice."

Cate grabbed his wrist and dug her nails into his skin until he let her go.

"It's sad—heartbreaking, even," she said, getting to her feet. "I feel for your poor, emotionally crippled brother, but again, it's not my fault. Not my problem."

"Your sister felt otherwise."

She stepped toward him, chest heaving, but ready to fight again. He moved forward as well.

"You can believe what you want, Cate," he said. "It doesn't change what's true."

She pointed to the house. "*That's* not true."

"That *is* true," James said. "She's not the long-lost twin. You are."

Cate shook her head. "You're wrong."

"I'm not."

The urgent clangor of the church bell ended their conversation. James looked toward the village, his hand going to his sword.

"If you're late for something," Cate said, "don't let me keep you."

"Be quiet," he said, glancing at the barn.

Aaron had come running out, a sword in his hand. Faolan flew out of the cottage. Cate backed away as James turned to her. The color that had been in her face was gone. He was glad to see she at least had the good sense to be afraid of this.

"What's going on?" she asked.

James drew his sword. "They're here."

They were not all-around good guys. They were not the kind one invited to barbeques and barn raisings. They were the kind from which one apparently ran away and hid until they had gone. Or so Cate assumed because no one seemed to want to talk about them. Instead, Aaron dragged her through the woods to a cave where they were supposed to hide until James came and told them it was safe.

Seemed prudent, given how damn freaked out the Brothers Grimm were, so she let Aaron bring her to the cave and guide her through the oppressive darkness to the back where they sat facing each other. At least she thought they were facing each other. She couldn't see her hand in front of her face, forget anything else.

"Not friends of yours, I take it," Cate said.

"What?"

"They, whoever they are, they're not friends of yours."

"No."

She waited, but he didn't elaborate. "Who are they?" she prompted.

"The law of this land."

"And we ran from them," she mused. "Are you an outlaw?"

"My brother is," he said. "Do you want to die?"

She hadn't really thought about it. She'd thought about death a lot in the last month or so. A lot. And while she hadn't been exactly pro-life, it hadn't occurred to her to be anything else, either.

"I don't know," she said. "I don't think so."

"Then stop the bloody chatter," he snapped. "We're supposed to be hiding."

"Sorry. I've never done the whole running-and-hiding-for-my-life thing before," she said. "If there's something I should know, you should feel free to tell me."

"The first thing you should know is to shut the hell up."

Harsh. Cate made a face Aaron couldn't see. "The men...Are they the same ones as before? The ones who—"

"Are you an idiot?"

She shrugged. "Not according to the fine folks at Harvard."

"Then why can't you stop talking?" he asked. "Don't you understand what we're doing here? *Why* we're hiding?"

"No, that's why I'm asking," she said. "I can guess, I can assume why we're huddling here in the dark, but—"

"Shut up."

"Your brother—"

"What about my brother?"

The contempt was obvious and heavy in his voice. It wasn't just him being mad at her inability to keep her mouth shut, either. She had a lot of experience with that particular contempt. It sounded different.

"I know why I hate your brother," she said. "Why do you?"

"What do you care?"

He had her there. "Good point."

She was quiet for a moment and listened to Aaron breathe as she geared up for another round of questions. It wasn't that she couldn't see the sense in staying silent—she really wasn't stupid—but she needed answers and Aaron, unlike Faolan or James, lacked any other agenda.

"I'm sorry," she said, and Aaron groaned, "but are the ones we're hiding from the same ones as before? Are they the ones who killed your parents?"

"Them, or some like them."

"Why are they here?"

"Looking for you or the queen, I imagine."

"Why—why are they doing that?" she asked. "I get that they're looking for the queen because she's the queen, but why me?"

"This is the sort of thing James has been trying to tell you since you arrived."

"Arrived," she said. "That's an interesting word choice."

"Why do you talk to me but not him?"

"What do you care?"

"Good point."

They were quiet again. She looked around, thinking about how very *dark* dark could be, as she shifted against the cave to find a more comfortable spot for her back. After a few failed attempts, she gave up and hugged her knees to her chest. Finding a comfortable spot against a rock wall was probably just one of those things.

Fitting, though, wasn't it? Rock, hard place, and her stuck in between. Whoever they were, were doing whatever they did, all in the name of running her to ground. That was a new experience. Never been hunted before.

"What do you think is going on in the village?" she asked. Aaron didn't answer, which she didn't find encouraging. "Are people dying?"

Aaron still didn't answer.

"People are dying because I'm hiding in a cave," she said.

Aaron made a noise. "People are dying because there are men in the village killing them."

"Because they're looking for me, and I'm hiding in a cave."

"Keep talking, and you won't be hiding for long."

"Maybe I shouldn't be hiding."

"What should you be doing?"

"I don't know. I don't *know*, but I can't stay here, not doing anything. I have—I have to get out of here."

"Have fun with the soldiers," Aaron said. "They're bound to have fun with you."

"What?" she said. "*That's* why they're looking for me? What, do they have a thing for redheads?"

"No. They want you because the king wants you, and they'll bring you to him," Aaron said. "But do you think anyone will care if they rape you on their way to having you killed?"

"Oh," she said. "This is one of those places."

"Whatever that means."

"That means if they don't kill your brother, I just might."

"They haven't managed to kill him yet."

Cate held up her hands and crossed two fingers on each one. "Here's hoping."

Aaron laughed. "You're not very nice, are you?"

"And you're, like, what? The poster boy of good will?"

"I'm the poor, emotionally crippled brother."

"You heard that?"

"I hear a lot of things," he said. "I heard why my brother brought you here."

"*He's* into redheads?"

"He and the pegasus think you can help end all this."

"The killing?"

"Aye."

"How?" she asked. "With my grace and charm?"

"Oh, is that what that is?"

"Aren't you a funny, emotionally crippled boy," she said. "But seriously, what do I do? Carry a magic ring to the lava pit of Mount Doom and throw it in to eradicate evil from the face of the earth?"

"They didn't say. I suppose you could ask them."

"But that would go against my strict not-talking-to-nor-cooperating-with-my-abductors policy."

"You wouldn't have to do it for them," Aaron said. "I imagine the people dying in the village would appreciate it. They didn't have anything to do with you being here."

The way James told it, that statement wasn't entirely true. It was, however, enough to renew her guilt.

"Hey, we're supposed to be hiding here," she said. "Why don't you stop with the chatter?"

Aaron snorted but fell silent. They stayed quiet after that. Not speaking and barely moving until Faolan called to them from the cave's entrance. Cate heard the scrape of metal on stone and felt Aaron's hand underneath her elbow. He led her into the daylight, and she squinted while her eyes adjusted.

"Is it done?" Aaron asked.

"Yes," Faolan said.

He didn't offer any details. Cate thought about asking, but if Aaron didn't want to know, neither did she.

Faolan led the way through the woods. They didn't seem to be taking the same path, but she couldn't be sure. It was nothing but trees and more trees, and she wasn't one with nature. But again, Aaron didn't question the route, so she kept her mouth shut. She looked back at him once or twice, and each time he refused to meet her glance. He gripped his sword so tightly, his knuckles were white. As much as she didn't want to, she felt bad for him. He was only a kid. Sixteen going on forty, maybe, but he shouldn't have to do this.

"Where's James?" she asked Faolan and took note of Aaron's sharp intake of breath. "I thought he was coming for us."

"He's taking care of some things," Faolan said.

"But he's all right," Cate said. "Him, Sarai? All of them?"

Faolan turned and looked at Aaron. "They're all right."

Cate, too, looked at Aaron, who scowled at the pair of them. She glanced then at Faolan, which turned out to be a mistake because he landed on her shoulder. She tried looking at him, but couldn't turn her head in a comfortable enough way.

"What are you doing? Is something wrong with your wings?" she asked, shrugging him off. "Get the hell away—"

She forgot what she was saying as she stepped out of the woods and into the village. She stopped short and stared. This was the same place she had stood earlier that day with James, but now it was unrecognizable. Before it had been a tourist trap, some place camera-happy American tourists and British school kids might visit to see how life used to be and come to better appreciate technology and soap making.

Now, however, it was a picture in a magazine showing off the latest war-torn land. Everything was in ruins. Bodies had been hanged from trees, others beheaded, disemboweled, and burned. She choked on the smoke and gagged on the smell of charred flesh. Had there been anything in her stomach, she would have purged it. Her eyes watered, and she wiped away the tears only to have them instantly replaced with fresh ones. Covering her nose and mouth with her arm, she watched the villagers cope. They came out of the woods and moved through the wreckage, digging through the carnage as they looked for something, *anything*, to salvage.

"Come on," Aaron said.

He took her arm, but she didn't budge.

"People did this?" she asked. "*Men* did this? It wasn't something else?"

"Something else?" Faolan asked.

"I don't know," Cate said. "Fire-breathing dragon or something?"

"Dragons are myth," Faolan said.

Cate snorted. "Says the pegasus."

"I already told you who did this," Aaron said. "And why."

"I know, but..." She stopped again, not having anything to say. The concept of evil was hardly new. It wasn't as though she'd been raised in some violence-free utopia, but standing in the midst of such a scene that she had somehow been the cause of...What was she supposed to do with that? She lowered her arm. "How did they know to come here? How did they know I was here?"

"Remember when I told you not to leave the house?" Faolan asked.

She shrugged. "Vaguely."

"Remember when you *left* the house? Twice?"

They came here looking for her because she had somehow rolled out the welcome mat for them? It really had been her fault, hadn't it?

"They were watching the house?" she asked.

"Not the house."

"Tell me," Cate said. "Stop being so goddamn cryptic and *say* it."

"Do you know what an aura is?"

"Yes, I know what an aura is."

"I think the moment you set foot outside the house, the ones we're trying to hide you from could magically sense your aura and used it to find you."

"Why did the house matter?"

"I was shielding it," Faolan said. "Magically."

"You couldn't have told me that before?"

"Would you have listened before?"

No. No, she wouldn't have listened. She hadn't listened to most of what any of them had said to her. But there was a difference between saying 'you have to stay inside' and 'if you go outside, a lot of innocent people will die in a horrible, brutal sort of way.'

"I can't stay here," she said. "I cannot stay here. I won't. You can't expect me to—I have to go home."

"No," Faolan said.

"I'm not staying here. You can't make me stay here."

"What I can't do is let you leave."

"I'll run."

"I'll have James bring you back."

"He has to sleep sometime."

"I don't."

"What are you going to do?" she asked. "Watch me every minute? Dog my every step?"

"If I have to."

"Well, let me make it easy for you." Cate sat down. "I'm not doing anything. I'm not going anywhere. I will sit right here, and you can carry your own damn ring to Mount Doom."

"I can carry what where?" Faolan asked.

"That's right," she said. "The only thing I'll do for you is make your life miserable."

Aaron scoffed. "What have you been doing for the past two days if not making all of our lives miserable?"

"I'm sorry," Cate said. "Did anyone *ask* for your opinion?"

"No," Aaron said. "Fortunately, I didn't wait to be asked. Let's go."

"I'm not going anywhere," Cate said. "That's what I meant when I said 'I'm not going anywhere.' Sorry if I was at all unclear about that."

Aaron grabbed the neckline of her dress and hauled her to her feet. She was slapping his hand away when he came at her. Catching her by the waist, he tossed her over his shoulder and walked away. She thrashed around, but he held her as though she were nothing more than a sack of potatoes.

"Are you kidding me? What the hell are you doing?" Cate screamed. "Put me down!"

"Gladly," Aaron said. "Just as soon as we get back to the house."

"You'll put me down now, or I'll—"

"You'll what? Make my life miserable? You look around, and you tell me what *you* could do to make *my* life miserable."

"If you want me to look around, you'd better put me down because the only thing I'm seeing is your scrawny, farm-boy ass."

"Then you're not looking hard enough."

"You are in for a world of hurt, John Boy," she said. "The second you put me down—the very second my feet touch the ground—I'm gonna make you bleed."

That made Aaron laugh. She didn't appreciate it.

"You don't think I can take you?" she asked. "Because I can. And I will."

He laughed more. "Mostly, I think I don't fight girls."

"That makes two of us," Cate said, "but in your case, I'd be willing to make an exception."

"Are you calling me a girl?"

"It's an insult to girls everywhere, I know," she said. "I'll make it up to them after I've finished making you cry, you pain-in-the-ass emo freak."

"That's very cutting," Aaron said. "Or I'm sure it would be had I any idea what that meant. What else have you?"

"What else have I?" she echoed. "How about you take your stiff upper lip and shove it up your ass?"

That made him pause, but as soon as she started to struggle, he moved on.

"Oh please," she said. "That cannot have been the first time someone's told you to shove something up your ass."

"I can honestly say you're the first."

"What did you say the name of this town was?" Cate asked. "Mayberry?"

"This town's name is Enimode," Aaron said. "Since it's burning because of you, you'd do well to remember it."

"Because of me? You're changing your tune there, songbird. That's not what you were singing before."

"It's what I'm singing now," he said. "What of you?"

"What *of* me?"

"Your tune has changed as well, hasn't it?" he asked. "When we were in the cave, you said you couldn't stay there, doing nothing, when others were being killed."

"Yeah, well, I more meant me going home to work on my tan."

"That's not what you meant."

"Maybe not, but it's what I mean now."

"Liars, all of us, then."

"And to think, I actually felt sorry for you."

"Never asked you to."

"I won't make that mistake again," she said. "Don't worry."

"Aye," Aaron sneered. "*That's* what I worry about."

"Woe is you. Put me down."

"No."

"I will bite you."

"Go ahead," Aaron said. "Bite me."

Cate laughed. She couldn't help it.

"Something funny?" he asked.

"Trust me, absolutely *nothing* is funny," Cate said. "Seriously, though, you have to put me down. All the blood in my body is in my head, and it is not a good feeling."

"We're almost to the farm," Aaron said. "You can wait."

"For crying out loud," she moaned. "Just put me down and drag me by my hair the rest of the way. You're a caveman. That should appeal to you."

Aaron didn't speak to her again. He was telling the truth that they weren't far from the house, however, because before she knew it they had gone inside. Aaron didn't waste any time in dumping her on the floor. She sprung up and pushed him.

Aaron snorted. "Thought you were going to make me bleed."

"Give me a minute," she said, shaking out her arms. "I need to regain the blood circulation in my extremities."

"That is enough," Sarai said. "Stop it."

Cate looked at her. "Your grandson here—"

"Has mayhap saved your life," Sarai snapped.

Cate examined the woman in front of her, drawn and dirty and smeared with ashes. This was not a woman who had hidden in a cave. This was a woman who had probably gone after heavily armed men with a pitchfork. Cate should have backed down. But she didn't.

"A life," she said, "that wouldn't have needed saving had your other grandson not endangered it in the first place."

"Cate, please," James said from the door.

She took note of his exhausted tone before looking at him. His sword was out, hanging loosely at his side, its blade bloody. His other arm was across his stomach, suggesting he had sustained some sort of injury there, and his face was smeared with dirt, ash, and blood. Whatever had happened while she'd been hiding in the cave, James had done more—a lot more—than just protect the woman in the cellar.

Sarai hurried to James's side. Peppering him with questions, she tried to examine him, but he pulled away.

"Faolan, go outside and keep watch," he ordered. Then he looked at Cate. "You need to go into the cellar."

It was a request to which she should just agree, but Cate looked at the opened cellar door and shook her head. "I don't think so."

"It's only for your protection. Until I'm sure it's safe."

"Like you give a shit about my protection."

"I do."

"Right," she said. "You can't let anything happen to me. How, then, would I sacrifice myself for the greater good?"

"You do understand. I'm so glad," James said. "Please, will you do this?"

"No. If you want me to go down there, you'll have to make me, and I'm not sure you're up for the task."

"I am," Aaron said.

She had forgotten about him. He came up behind her and grabbed her arm, dragging her across the room and into the cellar before she even thought to struggle. As soon as she started, Aaron hit her back with his elbow, and she slid forward. Only his hold on her stopped her from falling all the way down.

"Stop it," he said.

"You stop it," she returned. "You can't just kidnap someone and throw them in a basement when they refuse to cooperate with you."

He let go of her, and she tumbled to the floor.

"Apparently I can," Aaron said as he walked back up the stairs.

"Hey!" she shouted, and he looked at her. "You wanna know what I'm doing right now? I'm wishing those genocidal soldier boys of yours had gotten their hands on you the first time around."

Aaron's eyes went cold. He nodded.

"You're not the only one," he said, and the door closed.

———※———

After James had sent Aaron and Cate into the forest, he left Faolan and Sarai to guard the queen and made his way into the village to do what he could for the people there. He went with the nagging feeling that he should have stayed behind to protect the queen, or that he should have been in the cave with Aaron and Cate, but he couldn't bring himself to abandon the village entirely. He never knew if he made the right decision, and each decision he did make was another weight upon his shoulders.

The village was already in flames and chaos when he arrived. The first attack had come after days of unsuccessful interrogation. Varro and his men had arrived, posing as lords seeking shelter on their way to somewhere else. They'd tortured the family that ran the tavern and inn, eventually killing all, save one. Varro had tried to wring information about Dana from them, but received not one single word, so he burned them, and the entire village along with them.

But if Varro had returned, intending to carry out days of interrogations, he would not receive his chance this time. The people of Enimode had learned—as so many of Lira's settlements had—to always be watching and waiting. James had heard it in the uncommon exigency of the church bell and had seen it in Aaron's eyes when his brother came charging outside. Something burned there, a light that had previously gone out the day of the first attack, a day that ended with their parents, throats cut, lying dead on the floor of their own home.

"I'm going," Aaron had said. "I'm going to kill them, and you can't stop me."

But James had done just that. He had disarmed his untested brother and stopped him long enough to convince him to take Cate to the safety of the cave. The house was vulnerable, and he couldn't move the queen, but he could move Cate. He could hide her somewhere else. In case the soldiers did get the house, in case they could get the queen, James had to be sure they couldn't get Cate as well. The cave was secluded and had already saved Aaron's life once. James had to chance that it would offer that same protection a second time.

Aaron agreed, snatching his sword from James's hand before pulling the stunned and scared girl into the forest. Once they had disappeared, James shouted for Faolan to guard the queen before running for the village proper to join the fight. He killed the men he had encountered while absorbing the occasional hit. The blade of a man's dagger had cut his cheek. He also had taken the flat of a sword across his ribs. The blow had knocked the wind out of him, and he had fallen to his knees, paralyzed until he could breathe again.

Nothing he wouldn't survive.

But whether he, or anyone else, would survive Cate, he honestly couldn't say.

James laid his sword on the table as he watched his brother, the latest victim of her fury, close the cellar's door. Aaron stood on top of it, eyes adverted and hands clenched.

"Aaron," he said.

His brother didn't look at him. "You'll have to lock that," he said as he walked past James and left the house.

"Don't," James said. "Aaron, don't—don't go far."

"You can't let him go out there," Sarai said. "It isn't safe."

"Faolan will look after him," James said and took in his grandmother's appearance. "Are you all right? Did they come close? Did you have to—?"

"Faolan kept us safe. Don't worry about that," Sarai said. "But there was fire. They got close enough for that."

She gestured to the damage in the corner of the house. He stepped up to scrutinize it, pleased to find it would be easily mended.

He shook his head. "I shouldn't have gone into the village. I'm sorry I left you alone."

"They needed you there more than I needed you here," Sarai said. "There was warning this time, but no one to fight for us but ourselves."

"We didn't know the first time," James said. "Not until it was too late."

"I don't place blame."

Maybe she should. The first attack had been because of Dana. Somehow, Omur had discovered Dana's ties to the village. It would stand to reason that the mage would seek to exploit that connection again.

"We'll go," James said. "In the morning. I'll take the girl, and we'll go."

"The girl," Sarai said. "James, you should—"

"Don't talk to me about her."

Sarai nodded and turned his head to give her a better look at the gash on his cheek. He didn't feel like submitting to her examination, but since she didn't press him further on the subject of Cate, he allowed it. He already knew what Sarai would say. He didn't care to hear it.

Cate was angry, frightened, and had every right to be both. He had decided to bring her here and put her life at risk without considering her. This wasn't her life. She hadn't been born into it; she had no investment in the land, and the only family she had here, the only blood tie, was a silent, dying stranger.

He should have stopped Aaron from handling Cate the way he did, but he had been too damn tired to intervene. But when she said those words—that she wished for Aaron's death—James found himself wishing he had thrown her down the stairs himself. He was suddenly so angry, too damn angry with her, and too upset by her apparent obtuse, self-absorbed state of mind to care what happened. How could she care nothing for those people she had seen in the village? Even if she knew nothing about them, how was she so unfeeling as to care nothing for their lives?

Sarai had gawked at him, as though surprised he had let it happen without a single word of protest, but at the same time, he had noticed her own silence. She remained quiet as she tended his wounds. Feeling her own shame over her inactivity? He should have told her to never mind that, that what they had done or hadn't done didn't matter, but his thoughts remained unspoken. He was too tired to give them voice. He was too tired to hear or respond to what might be said in return.

Too tired. That was a problem. He would have to find an opportunity to sleep that night.

When Sarai finished her fussing, James took his sword and went outside to clean it. Faolan stood atop a spilt stack of firewood that no one had yet taken the time to fix. He stared at the tree line and neither moved nor spoke as James approached.

What part had the pegasus played in the events of the day? James held a strong suspicion that Faolan had somehow orchestrated it all, but apart from the feeling deep within his gut, he had no proof, nor did he think he could bring himself to ask.

"Where's Aaron?" James said.

"The barn," Faolan answered.

James looked at the barn to assure himself that it was in no danger of an immediate collapse. Satisfied that it would remain standing for another night, he sat on a log at Faolan's side.

"Your plan didn't work," James said, dragging a cloth along the sword's blade.

"Plan?"

"There's always a plan. You always have a plan."

"And you think it didn't work."

"We have the queen and her sister trapped in the root cellar, one dying and the other a hostage," James said. "Please tell me that wasn't the plan."

"No, that wasn't the plan."

The pegasus still watched the trees intently. James scanned the line of the forest but could see nothing amiss.

"Is something out there?" he asked.

"Yes."

"Something I have to worry about?"

"No."

"Then why—?"

"Something to look at," Faolan said. "Are you badly hurt?"

James shook his head. "Bruises."

"The blood?"

"Messy, not deep. There's nothing wrong with me that time and rest won't cure."

"Good," Faolan said. "You should go inside and do that. Cate isn't going anywhere tonight, and the others will be here in the morning."

"They should have been here already. I told you to send for them days ago."

"You did."

"But you didn't, did you?"

"Part of the plan."

"The one that didn't work?"

"Yes."

"You burned Enimode for nothing, then."

Maybe he could bring himself to ask. James waited to see how the pegasus would respond. Faolan cocked his head but didn't say anything. He was silent for so long, James assumed his comment would go unaddressed.

"Maybe not for nothing," Faolan said finally. "She may come around yet. The plan almost worked."

"What happened?"

"She's not her sister."

There was truth to that. James had not had much interaction with the queen, but whenever they had spoken, she had been unfailingly polite to him. Even when he had been anything but that to her.

And Cate—well, Cate hated him. He didn't mind that—he didn't—because what she had said to Aaron was...

"You're so sure we have to have her?" James asked.

"Laorans is," Faolan said. "And until Haleine is conscious and upright, I have to agree."

"She doesn't believe that the queen is her sister."

"She will," Faolan said. "But that's the least of our problems."

That was also true. They had to convince her to help them. Even the thought of it, the idea of needing her, made him angry.

"I shouldn't have let Aaron treat her that way," James said. "She wouldn't have done what she did if I hadn't...It'll make it harder. She hates us, and—"

"That's not different."

"I hate her," James said.

Faolan looked at him. "I don't think that's true."

"What would you know about it?"

"Absolutely nothing. But whatever she said that riled you and your brother so very much is nothing compared to anything Maddox or Omur or Varro has done to this family."

Because words were only words, and a knife blade across one's throat was much more fatal.

"But be angry. Be as angry with her as you'd like," Faolan said. "You'll still do what needs to be done."

Would he? James wasn't so sure about that. "Why didn't you tell me what you planned to do here?" he asked.

"I didn't think you would support my decision to subject your town to this kind of destruction a second time," Faolan said. "Especially since, this time, it was my decision. Omur may have given the order, but he did so because I led him to it."

How many people had died that day? How many friends or neighbors had James lost? If their lives went to purchase a peace for the rest, was the loss worth it?

He looked toward the village where a plume of dark smoke rose into the sky. God help him, he'd do it again. What did that make him?

James nodded. "You tell me next time."

"If you'd like."

"As if that matters," James said. "We'll be leaving tomorrow, once the others have arrived. You and I will take Cate, and we'll go back to camp."

"This is the safest place to be now," Faolan said. "Varro's gone back to the palace to tell Omur that Haleine wasn't here."

"That's why we'll leave the queen behind. When she recovers, *if* she recovers, we'll bring her to join us, but you and I and Cate will go. She can't do what we brought her here to do from the root cellar."

"The roads will be dangerous."

"Maybe, but we've stayed here too long already," James said. Sarai called his name then, and he stood. "Take the first watch, aye? I'll relieve you later."

"No need. I can handle the watch on my own," Faolan said. "You should sleep, and nothing more will happen tonight. We'll be all right for a while."

"You shouldn't say that. That's a lie."

"Do you think so?"

James picked up his sword. "Things are bound to get worse. They always do."

CHAPTER 6

Revelin was exhausted. After confirming that he was alone in his father's study, he slumped in his chair and closed his eyes. He hadn't slept well since he gave the order for men to be sent to Lira. Most nights had been spent in front of the fire in his chambers or standing on his balcony overlooking the city.

His days were just as long, as the demands on his time only ever seemed to increase. They were spent sitting behind the desk that once had belonged to his father. He looked over report after report, waiting for news of Lira and her rebellion to reach him, yet no word came. The last message he had received from Darian was to inform him about the proposed taking of the rebel camp. What had happened since, Revelin did not know.

Despite his misgivings, sending men had been the appropriate choice. He had to send Darian. He had to send men to Lira to help end the fighting. His father had made the alliance, and Revelin was honoring that promise. He should have done it sooner.

Why, then, did he feel such dread? Had he chosen wrong?

"Regrets?"

His chest tightened as his heart registered to whom the voice belonged. It was the last one he would have expected to hear. He didn't correct his posture or open his eyes. There was no need. Haleine would always see him for what he truly was.

"What might you be doing here?" he murmured.

"Do you not wish for me to be here?" she asked. "I shall go, if you like."

He heard the rustle of her skirts. Eyes opening, he straightened and caught sight of her making her way to the door. "No. Stay."

Haleine turned. His eyes locked on hers.

"I do not wish for you to go," he said.

He held out his hand. She stood suddenly on the opposite side of his father's desk and studied his offering.

"Do you think you chose wrong?" she asked.

"Do you?" He withdrew his hand and shook his head. "No, do not answer that."

"Because you fear I will not say what you wish me to say?"

"I do not fear that."

"What do you fear?"

"That you shall leave," he said. "That you shall disappear through that door behind you."

"I'll not go," she said. "I'll not disappear through that door, nor anywhere else, until you wish it."

"I will never wish that."

"Won't you?"

"It was you who ordered me away, Haleine."

"It was you who called me a whore."

"I did that, yes."

"Tell me, then," she said, "why would I stay?"

"Because I want it."

"Why should I care what you want?"

"I do not know."

"Why am I here?"

He shook his head. "I do not know."

She backed away, fading more with each step. If he waited any longer, she would be forever lost to him.

"Your father has gone to kill your lover," he said.

That made her stop. That made her look at him.

"And therein lies your regret," she said. "You think you should not have sent him."

"I think I should have killed your lover myself," he said. "I had my chance, and I walked away. That is my regret."

"You still would have lost me."

"Mayhap," he said. "But at least I would have killed the one who stole you from me."

"He was dead long before that moment. You target the wrong man for the wrong reason."

"Why do you think so?"

"It is the Maoilriain way, is it not?"

"You are unfair."

"I am as I have been made," she said. "I am as the Maoilriains have made me."

"No one made you anything," he said. "And I honor an alliance made by our fathers."

"My father didn't make it."

"He would have."

Haleine nodded. "Because it was an honor to have been chosen. You men and your honor, your damned honor."

"Have you no use for honor any longer?" he asked.

"Can a whore have use for something like honor?" she responded. "Can a whore even understand what such a word means?"

"Will you punish me forever, Haleine?"

"You stood on that balcony, and you never looked back."

"You will not forgive me anything."

"Because you have forgiven what I have done?" she asked. "I gave to another—a vagabond, did you call him?—what should have been yours. You have forgiven me this?"

The words were his; he could not deny that, nor did he wish to do so. They were, however, words he had never spoken aloud.

"I did not tell you that," he said.

"You didn't have to."

"Tell me what you would have me do."

"I would have you open your eyes and see the evil that stands before you," she said. "I would have you listen and see—"

She stopped.

"See what, Haleine?" he asked, but she did not continue. "Haleine?"

"Careful," she said, her eyes turning to gaze at something he could not see. "We're not alone in this place anymore."

"I do not understand."

"My lord prince," Haleine said, squinting at him in concern.

"Haleine?"

"My lord prince?" she repeated. This time, the voice was no longer her own.

A hand on his arm brought Revelin back into awareness.

"Are you all right, my lord prince?" Darragh asked.

Revelin glanced at the corner where Haleine had first appeared. It was empty now. A dream, then. It had been naught but a dream. He sat up. "What do you need?"

"Our men have returned from Lira."

Revelin looked at Darragh. Their men returned? Without any word as to what had happened? It did not encourage him.

"Where is Darian?" Revelin asked. "What did he have to say?"

Darragh shook his head, eyes troubled. "I am told there was a battle, my lord, and—"

"Darian?" Revelin asked, dread washing over him. "Has he returned?"

"Not...not in the way we both had hoped, your highness," Darragh said.

Revelin sat back. Darian gone. Could it be? For so long the man had seemed indestructible. How could he be gone?

"It is certain?" Revelin asked.

Darragh nodded and motioned to a man standing near the door. "A messenger from Lira has come to speak with you."

The man stepped forth and bowed. His clothing implied he had come straight to Revelin's presence from the ship on which he had arrived. Most men did not. Revelin studied the man's face, trying to place him.

"Yes," he said, beckoning the man closer. "You are Maddox's man. Ceallach, is it?"

"It is, your highness," Ceallach said, bowing again. "But if it pleases you, I am the queen's man."

"Her majesty sent you?"

Ceallach nodded. "Yes, my prince," he said, and withdrew a letter from his cloak. "She bade me to give you this."

Revelin accepted the parchment and ran his hand over Haleine's seal before breaking it.

My father's coffin accompanies this letter, she'd written. *Please see him, as well as my family's obligation to the Maoilriains, interred alongside my mother.*

She had not signed her name. Revelin read the letter once more, then looked at the man who had carried it. "What happened?"

"The rebels took the battle," Ceallach said. "The rebel leader himself took the life of Lord Coileáin. It was...it was most gruesomely done, my prince."

"War is seldom known for its aesthetics," Revelin murmured.

He looked again at the letter, at her flawless script. At the absence of her name.

"Yes, my lord," Ceallach said.

Revelin allowed the letter to fall onto the desk's mahogany surface. "Thank you for delivering this news to me," he said. "I insist you take your ease with us a while. You will be quite comfortable, I assure you."

"I do not doubt the generosity of your hospitality, your highness, but I must return," Ceallach said.

"Of course you must," Revelin said. "But first, should you not attend Lord Coileáin's funeral? Would you have him interred with no one to bear witness on his daughters' behalf?"

"I would not dream of it, your highness," Ceallach said.

Revelin nodded. "Darragh will see to your needs."

Ceallach looked as though he wanted to say more, but his years in the Aelhaeran family's service held him in check. The man bowed and retreated from the room. Darragh followed until Revelin summoned him back.

"You will make the arrangements for Darian's interment?" Revelin asked.

"Yes, your highness."

"At Rhoswen's side."

"Yes, your highness."

Revelin waved Darragh away, then pushed back from the desk and walked to the window behind him. He stared at the cliffs that provided Mairéad such infallible protection, and the sea raging its never-ending war against the rock.

"Brother," a man's voice said.

Revelin closed his eyes. "Zoltano."

"You don't sound pleased to see me again."

Revelin turned. His brother leaned against the wall on the far side of the room. He was dressed simply, looking more the part of a hired sword than a crown prince.

"What are you doing here?" Revelin asked.

Zoltano smiled. "Is that any way to greet a beloved brother you have not seen—"

"In nearly a year?" Revelin asked, moving away from the window.

"I was grieving," Zoltano said.

"As was I."

"For our lost father or your little bitch?"

Revelin kept his eyes fixed on his brother, refusing to rise to the bait. Zoltano smiled again and encroached deeper into the room. He did not appear to be armed, but that did not make him less dangerous.

"Much has happened in my absence," Zoltano said, sitting in their father's chair.

Revelin crossed to the other side, keeping his back to the wall. "More than you realize."

Zoltano laughed. "I doubt that."

"How do you know what has happened here?"

"You didn't think I would go without, did you?"

"Have you ever?" Revelin asked. "Who told you?"

"It should have been you."

"I have been rather preoccupied."

"Busy stealing my throne?"

"It is not your throne."

"It is, and I've come to claim it."

Revelin shook his head. "You will lose, just as you did before."

"Yes," Zoltano said, "because the nobles are so devoted to our mother."

"She and Father treated them well, and she continues to do so," Revelin said. "There is no great mystery behind their loyalty to her."

"To you."

Revelin could not deny that. He did not try. "A lesson you should learn."

"I did not come to you for lessons," Zoltano said. "Only my crown."

"It is not yours to take."

"I think you'll find it is."

"I will stop you."

Zoltano smiled. "I invite you to try."

———

After the trap door had closed, Cate settled at the bottom of the steps, cramming herself into the corner as far as she possibly could, and kept her eyes focused on either her knees or the ceiling. She absolutely refused to look at the unconscious woman on the other side of the room.

She didn't know how long she sat there. There weren't any clocks of any kind, nor any windows she could use to judge the passing of time. If she'd known for how long the lanterns lighting the room would burn before needing to be refilled, she could've used those, but she didn't know, so she was left wanting and wondering.

The door opened again, and James and Sarai appeared, but only Sarai ventured down the steps. When she reached the bottom, she put a small plate of bread in front of Cate before continuing on to the queen. James stayed at the top and stared at her, his sword on his hip and his arms folded across his chest. The blood was missing from his cheek, but a bright red slash remained. He didn't look particularly pleased with her. Fortunately, Cate wasn't a person who cared about things like that.

"What are you going to do next?" he asked.

She didn't know. What would be an appropriate encore for the browbeating of an already traumatized teen? She shrugged. "Got any puppies I could kick? Cripples I could trip? Any nuns around? I could punch one."

He looked away. "We're leaving in the morning."

In the morning? Did that mean it was night? Had she honestly been sitting in this cellar that long? She examined the lack of bright light coming from behind James and decided she had.

"Have a safe trip," she said.

"You're coming along."

"Oh, you think so, do you?"

"I'll tie you to the saddle if I have to."

"You're big into bondage, aren't you," she said. "That's the second time in recent memory you've offered to tie me down."

"Offered?" he asked.

She narrowed her eyes. "Fuck you."

"Cate," Sarai scolded.

Cate looked at her. "You're not my mother."

"I am grateful for that," Sarai said.

Cate raised an eyebrow. "I'm not afraid of you."

Sarai stared. Cate stared back, then shrugged.

"I might be a little afraid of you," she allowed, and glanced at James again. "But even so, I don't think I'll be going anywhere come morning."

"We'll see about that, won't we?" James said.

"I guess we will."

Sarai swept past her on her way up the stairs. Cate watched her go, then engaged in another staring contest with James. He broke first, slamming the door closed. Cate traced his footsteps with her eyes. He paced, stopped, and then paced some more, followed by the sound of something being dragged across the floor. It stopped directly over the trap door.

She waited, but there was nothing to hear after that. Looked like she was in for the night.

Cate returned to sitting and staring at her knees. She didn't remember falling asleep—she didn't even remember *trying*—but it had to have happened because she was later jolted awake by blood-curdling screams. Instantly tense and afraid, she struggled to move. Her limbs were cramped and sluggish, and the more she thrashed about, the harder it was to untangle herself. Finally, she simply fell over and, in the lantern light, saw the woman on the bed writhing and shrieking.

Cate pushed herself up, eyes trained on the door above her head. Someone was bound to hear. The woman was howling like a banshee—probably everyone in a twenty-mile radius could hear. Sarai would come, and James would be at her heels, certain Cate was responsible for the disturbance.

But no one responded, and the screaming continued.

Cate backed against the wall. "I am not going over there!" she shouted at the ceiling. "Do you hear me? I am *not* doing it."

But they didn't hear her. Her goddamn doppelganger was making too much noise. Cate crawled up the stairs and pounded on the door, but whatever James had put there was deadening the sound. She didn't expect anyone to hear it anyway. If they couldn't hear the screaming, they wouldn't hear anything else, either.

The screaming ceased as suddenly as it started. Cate stopped pounding and crept down a couple of steps to investigate. The woman stood next to the bed, looking at her hands. Holding her breath, Cate stared at the bandages wrapped around the woman's chest, the bulk of which were centered over her heart. Over where Cate's own scar was located. It was too strange to be a coincidence, but it didn't make sense. Nothing here made sense. If she wasn't so damn freaked, she'd appreciate the consistency of it all.

Mindful of drawing attention to herself, Cate froze. What should she do? Not moving seemed like her best option, but her foot slipped off the edge of the step, and the woman's head turned as sharply as a hawk's.

When their eyes met, Cate felt something like a shock run through her. Now what?

"Who are you?" the woman asked. "What are you?"

Cate swallowed. "You mean besides mortified?"

"Mortified," the woman said, her eyes finally flickering onto something else. "The ghost of my soul I think you must be. Here I thought I would never see your like again."

"I'm not your soul," Cate said. "I'm not a ghost, either."

"Nor am I, I fear."

"You fear?"

"I was drowning," the woman said. "It was quite lovely, the drowning. You will know. You were there."

"I wasn't there."

"I thought perhaps I had finally done it—broken free of this flesh-and-bone, mortal misery—but it would seem that again I am a failure."

Cate thought about that. "*You* had done it?"

The woman nodded. "He said if I wanted to die, it wouldn't be by his hand. There was no option left to me but my own."

"So...you tried to drown yourself."

"Aye, I did that," the woman said. "He pulled me back before I could get away, then did not have the manners to make amends for his lack of etiquette."

"Lack of etiquette?" Cate echoed. "I'm not sure Emily Post would agree with you on that one."

The woman turned in a small circle, inspecting her surroundings. "I thought to let him beat the life from me, but even that he could not do. He walked away before he could finish. He always was so damned selfish."

"You *wanted* to die?"

"Want. My desire has not changed."

Great. A suicidal doppelganger. That was just what Cate needed. Maybe later she could get a hole in her head.

"What's your name?" she asked.

"A name is a human thing."

"Aren't you human?"

The woman smiled. "Something more, or so I'm told, but what that means, no one knows."

"They must call you something."

"Whore."

"Whore?"

"Liar," the woman said.

"Liar?"

"And those are the words of he who loved me."

"If that's true, I think you could probably do better," Cate said. "What about the people who maybe don't love you? What do they call you?"

"The one. The first."

"The one what? The first what?"

"Not one among us knows."

"Doesn't anyone know anything in this place?"

"Haleine," the woman said. "They called me Haleine."

That sounded like a name. "Haleine," Cate said. "Okay. Good."

"What are you?" Haleine asked.

"Word on the street is I'm your sister," Cate said. "I'll go out on a limb and say twin sister, and there you have it—the whole of my knowledge on this subject."

"A sister I have, but you are not her."

"Finally, someone who agrees with me."

"What are you?"

"Could you please stop asking me *what* I am," Cate said. "Besides being incredibly insulting to insinuate that I am a what and not a who, I also don't have any better of an answer for you than I did the first ten times you asked. If you want answers, you'll have to ask that asinine, little pegasus."

"Faolan," Haleine said.

"Yeah, Faolan."

"He is here?"

"Here in this cellar? No. Here in this general area? Yes."

"He has irritated you."

"That's one way of putting it," Cate said. "Hasn't he irritated you?"

"That, and more." Haleine released a soft sigh of laughter. "He can be rather endearing."

"Yeah, I thought so, too," Cate said. "Only I prefer the phrase 'compulsive-lying, manipulative, little malcontent.'"

"He has lied to us," Haleine said. "He has withheld from us."

"Thus the whole compulsive-lying thing."

"He lives to serve his cause. He should not be held at fault for that."

"Yeah, he should be."

"Where am I?"

"You're in a root cellar," Cate said, "in a village called Enimode in a country called...something."

"Lira," Haleine said.

"Yeah. Lira. Like the defunct Italian money. I remember."

"I do not know what that means."

"Neither do a lot of Americans."

"How did I get here?"

"I can't say anything about, like, mode of transportation," Cate said, "but a man named James—"

"James? He brought me here?"

"That's what I heard."

"James brought me here. If that is true, then what happened to him?" Haleine asked. "Where is he?"

"James?" Cate said. "He's busy being mad at me. I have this innate ability to piss him right the hell off. It's kind of great, actually."

"Not James, no," Haleine said, her tone becoming more agitated. "I've heard *him*; I've felt *him*. Asking if I hear him, calling me love as though he has a right to call me anything."

"Who?"

"Where is he?"

"Do you mean *Aaron*?" Cate asked. "Because I'm having a hard time picturing him—"

"No, not Aaron. I do not know this Aaron."

"Then I don't know who you're talking about," Cate said. "I haven't seen any other men around."

Haleine seemed to consider this. She touched the bandages over her heart and looked at Cate. "He is gone."

"Guess so."

Cate was losing patience. She had her own problems to deal with. She didn't need to be—nor want to be—saddled with those belonging to her suicidal, pronoun-reference-challenged doppelganger.

"Faolan claims we are sisters?" Haleine asked.

"That he does."

"I do not understand why he would tell such a lie, but how is it we knew naught of each other?"

"You didn't happen to grow up with only your father, did you?" Cate asked. "Because that would explain a lot. If we were in a Disney movie."

"A mother and father both I had," Haleine said, "for all the days of my childhood. As though I were somehow deserving."

Shit. Crazy sister aside, that meant if the pegasus was to be believed, Cate was adopted. Something else Laura had kept from her. Had anything ever been true?

"They are gone," Haleine said.

"What? Gone?" Cate asked. "Who?"

"Our mother," Haleine said. "Our poor mother, torn to shreds, or so they tell me, and I had done the ripping. Our father followed—oh, he was the worst of my sins, I think—and Revelin...To know I love the one who killed me—"

"You're not dead."

"You think because I have breath in my lungs, you think because my heart beats that I am not dead, but you know nothing," Haleine said. "The air is poison. Every breath I take burns me. And his words, his damn words, his words another dagger to my heart, and another and another and another—and still, here I sit."

"Stand, actually," Cate interjected.

Haleine cocked her head. "It doesn't matter, you know, this thing called blood. They tell you it does, but it matters not. They say your life, your blood, they are the same. Tied to each other, they are, and if you lose too much of one, the other is forfeit as well. But it's not true. You can spill a lake of it, an oceanful, and you do not die."

"It's good you're not being overly dramatic," Cate said. "I like that in a doppelganger."

"You mock me."

"Maybe a little."

"You mock me."

"Yes, but only because you sound like the rejected first draft of some sort of Shakespearean After School special."

"Proof. You require proof that what I have said is the truth," Haleine said, fingers tearing at the bandages covering her heart.

"Hey!" Cate stumbled down the remaining stairs. "Hey, don't do that."

"Why not?"

"Well, I'm kind of thinking that they're keeping your still-beating heart from falling on the floor."

"You think I care about that?"

"Ah, well, probably not, given that your life goal is to end it," Cate said. "But you shouldn't—"

She stopped when Haleine succeeded in removing the bandaging. She threw it to the ground and looked at Cate in defiance. The feeling behind the glare made Cate step back. She hadn't quite cleared the stairs and fell on her ass, staring at the blood filling the hole in Haleine's chest. Cate had never seen anything quite like it and couldn't bring herself to look away.

"You feel it, too," Haleine said.

"What?" Cate gasped. "I don't—what?"

Haleine nodded. "You feel it, too," she repeated, her voice soft. Her hand fluttered upward, her fingers gesturing briefly before falling back at her side.

Cate shook her head. She didn't feel anything except horror, but she looked around to see what, if anything, Haleine had been pointing to.

The front of her dress, over her heart, was stained dark. It was with a shaking hand that Cate touched it and discovered it wet with blood. She looked at her fingers, then yanked down the front of her dress to see an injury identical to Haleine's.

"What did you do to me?" she asked, pressing both hands against the wound. "What did you do?"

Haleine watched calmly, as though neither of them were bleeding to death. Cate stood—chest heaving, eyes watering, nose running—and searched the room for something to make it stop.

"It does not matter what I have done," Haleine said. "I have bled to death one thousand times and more, and still, I will not die."

"Shut up!"

Spotting a basket near the foot of the bed, Cate stumbled to it, knocking Haleine aside. She collapsed on her knees and dug through it, throwing away anything that could not be used as a bandage. Finding a wad of linen strips, she pressed it against her chest and closed her eyes.

"One thousand times and more," Haleine said, "I have died and been resurrected. One thousand times and more, I have bled and drowned. Why can't I die?"

Cate looked at Haleine. "My god, you're really just all kinds of crazy, aren't you? I can't—"

She broke off when she saw the silver object in Haleine's hand. It was some kind of cutting tool, a precursor to scissors or razors. It must have been in the basket. Cate held her breath as Haleine proceeded to drag the object across her wrist. Lengthwise, along the bright blue vein, just the way the experts claimed meant the person was serious about what she did. Blue became red and flooded everywhere. Slowly, Cate pulled one hand away from her chest and turned it over to see the inside of her wrist.

Her veins burst open, spraying blood far and wide.

She screamed.

—◦∿◦—

Unconvinced that Cate would be sufficiently contained in the cellar, James had bedded down in front of the door. He laid awake for a long time, but eventually succumbed to fatigue, only to be woken again by a relentless pounding. He bolted to his feet, tripping over his sword on his way to the window.

"There's nothing out there," Faolan said from the table.

More awake and aware, James looked at the chest he had used to cover the root cellar. Cate's voice was muffled and frantic, punctuated by her assault on the door.

"What happened?" he asked. "Do you know?"

"No."

"Are you lying?"

"Never mind that," Sarai said, climbing from the loft. "Just let the girl out."

Sliding the chest aside, James opened the door. Cate slammed into him, taking them both to the floor. She rolled away and curled into a ball, shaking badly. Her fingers were a bloody mess. Appalled, he stared at them. What had made her do such a thing? He looked at the open door and grabbed his sword.

"Help her," he said, disappearing below.

The cellar was silent and empty, except for the queen lying prone on her bed. James approached her and held his dagger beneath her nose to assure himself that she was breathing. Another look around showed nothing amiss, and he returned above stairs.

Cate was still on the floor. Sarai knelt beside her, rubbing her back and cooing gently as though Cate were a colicky infant.

"What happened?" Faolan asked. "Is Haleine—?"

"The queen's the same," James said. "I don't know what happened."

"That doesn't matter just now," Sarai said in the same soft voice. "Help me bring her into the other room."

Placing his sword on the table, James crouched to pick up Cate. She fought him the instant he lifted her, flailing so violently, he dropped her. He went to his knees, an apology on his lips, but the very moment he laid hands upon her, Cate screamed and lashed out. He fell back and looked at Faolan.

"I don't know," the pegasus said.

"James," Sarai said, "we can't leave her there."

He nodded. He understood he couldn't leave her there, nor did he want to, but he couldn't do anything for her when she was carrying on like she was.

Waiting until her spasms had lessened, he moved forward and scooped her off the floor as quickly as he could, holding her tight against his body. As expected, she resisted, but this time, he didn't drop her.

"Cate, stop it," he said softly. "Stop fighting me. I won't hurt you."

"No," she moaned, slumping against his chest. "Put me down, put me down, put me down. I don't want you to—put me down. Please, just put me down."

James carried her into the bedroom. "You're all right. I promise you're all right."

"Stop saying that like it means something," she spat. "You have no idea what I am."

As he laid her on the bed, Cate curled up again, this time smaller than before. Sarai followed, carrying a lantern and the basket in which she kept her medicinal supplies.

"Faolan, send Aaron to fetch me some water," Sarai said. "Go with him to make sure he comes back unharmed."

The pegasus flew out of the room. James listened to Aaron's angry footsteps and the cottage door slamming shut before turning back to Cate. Sarai sat on the edge of the bed, trying to coax Cate's hands away from the girl's chest.

"Leave me alone," Cate said, repeating the phrase over and over until she passed out.

Sarai released a sigh that betrayed her relief, and she opened Cate's clenched fists, sucking in a sharp breath upon seeing the damage. "Good God, lass. Did you try to claw your way out?"

James looked at the floor. It certainly appeared that way to him. What had driven her to do so?

As soon as Aaron and Faolan had arrived with the water, James returned to the root cellar, but there were still no answers to be found. He stared at the queen, then examined her hands. They were unblemished. Why he cared, why he even thought to check, he did not know.

When James climbed above stairs again, Faolan waited on the table.

"Is Haleine all right?" the pegasus asked.

"Aye, the unconscious, feverish woman with a bloody hole in her chest is quite well," James said. He gestured to the open door. "See for yourself, if you don't believe me."

"No need to be sarcastic."

"There's always a need when you're involved," James said. "Aren't you supposed to be keeping watch outside?"

"Call me if there's any more screaming," Faolan replied, flying away.

As if he would need to. James sat in a chair to wait, somehow even more bone-weary than before. Sarai finally reappeared, closing the door behind her.

"Don't," James said. Sarai nodded and pushed open the door. "Is she all right?"

Sarai shrugged. "I've bandaged her hands, and she's asleep. I do not know, however, if any of that makes her all right."

Neither did he. "Aye."

"Does Faolan know what happened?" his grandmother asked.

"He says no."

"Do you believe him?"

"This time."

Sarai placed her basket on the table and turned to the loft's ladder. "You have to stop this," she said as she started to climb.

He nodded. "Aye."

Once alone, James walked into Cate's room. He leaned against the wall and slid to the floor. There he stayed, watching his hostage sleep, while the sky exchanged its starry black for the purples and oranges of the dawn.

CHAPTER 7

When Cate opened her eyes, the first thing she saw was the early morning light seeping through the shutters. She looked at her hands next. They were completely wrapped in bandages, as though she were part mummy. It was proof that the night before had not been a nightmare, that it had been something else entirely—something unfathomably real. She sighed and, using her elbows for leverage, sat up. Faolan perched at the end of the bed. Swell.

"Do you know what the best part of waking up is?" she asked.

"Seeing me?"

Cate snorted. "It's that second when you can still think maybe it was all just a dream."

"It's not a dream."

"Thanks for clearing that up," she said, "because for a moment there, I had you confused with the tiny, talking, pain-in-the-ass pegasus from my universe."

"You saw him?"

She narrowed her eyes. Was he being serious, or just making some kind of incredibly unfunny joke?

"How are your hands?" he asked.

She looked at the bandages covering her hands like an odd pair of mittens. Itchy mittens. Next, she glanced at her clothing, finding them free of the blood that had stained them earlier. An examination of her wrists showed they were smooth and untouched. There was absolutely no sign that her veins had all but exploded the night before. Because *that* wasn't at all alarming.

"What happened?" Faolan asked.

She supposed it had been nothing more than a bad dream. The worst dream ever. But how could that be right? How could *that* have been a dream? It felt so goddamn real. The hole in her chest? And her veins...her veins had ruptured because Haleine had taken a blade to her own. Cate watched it all happen, understanding there was no way she could survive. So much blood, so little time.

But then she woke, crammed in the corner at the bottom of the stairs. Haleine was as motionless as the corpse she longed to be, and Cate wasn't bleeding anymore. At least not until she decided to dig her way out of the goddamn cellar.

"We can talk about it, Cate," Faolan said. "I may be able to help."

Nope. No way, no how. "Would you mind leaving me alone?" she asked. "You know, so I can piss in my pot without an audience?"

"Both Aaron and James are outside," Faolan warned as he flew away.

"Thanks for the update," she said.

Sliding off the bed, she crossed the room to bump the door closed with her hip, then dropped down to locate the pot. She looked at it in disgust. How much did she not want to do this? Maybe she could just stop eating and drinking altogether. A plan for the future, maybe, but here in the present, her options were rapidly thinning. It was either suck it up, or piss herself. With yet another sigh, Cate hauled up her skirt and assumed the position.

When she finished, she paced the length of the room—that stupid, tiny room with its one stupid, little window that she couldn't even climb out of— at least not without massive amounts of screaming and crying and dying following. There was a chance that the pegasus had been lying about that— that the village slaughter had been a terrible coincidence and not actually her fault—but it was too big a risk to take. As badly as she wanted—*needed*—to get the hell out of there, she'd have to find another way.

But what other way? There didn't seem to be any other goddamn options. Was she just supposed to live the rest of her life in that room? A new flare of anger drove her to kick the wall until she yelped from the pain.

Shit. She hated feeling like this.

But it made sense that she was on edge, right? If she had come out of the root cellar of horrors feeling nothing at all, she would've been accurately labeled a psychopath. Or a sociopath. She wasn't sure what the exact difference between the two was, but she didn't much want to be either. She stopped pacing and looked at her wrists. Still perfect.

God. Damn. It.

Her bandages were itching badly enough that she couldn't ignore it any longer, so she sat on the floor next to the door. She raised her left hand to her mouth to tear at the wrappings with her teeth, stopping only when the door flew open. Aaron stepped inside.

She lowered her arm. "I'm not running away. I'm sorry if that disappoints you. It definitely disappoints me."

Aaron didn't say anything. His face suggested he was considering kicking her in the ribs a few dozen times. Not that she could blame him for feeling that way.

"Now that you're here," she said, "could you please do me a favor and take these things off?"

She held up her hands. Aaron looked at them. He peered into the common room—checking for Sarai maybe—and nodded, then pulled her to her feet.

When he finished unwinding the bandages on her left hand, he held her wrist and examined her fingertips. She couldn't blame him for that, either. He had seen them last night, she was sure. She had seen them, too—skin and nails torn to shreds in her determination to get out of the cellar. But one wouldn't know that from looking at them now.

They were perfect. They were unblemished specimens. Not even a hangnail. She could have been a damn hand model.

"I guess your grandmother knows what she's doing," Cate said, twisting her wrist to free herself from Aaron's grip.

Aaron said nothing but kept his eyes on her fingers as he unwrapped her right hand. That one was perfect, too.

"Gran won't like that," he muttered.

Cate didn't care for it, either. She didn't know what Sarai's problem was, but hers was rooted in the idea that whatever was going on with her hands was both creepy and weird. It was shades of Haleine the Insane down in the cellar. *It doesn't matter, this thing called blood*, Haleine had said. *You can spill a lake of it, an oceanful, and you do not die.*

Apparently, you could also turn your hands to bloody ribbons without any discernable repercussions. Cate didn't like that, but what she disliked most was knowing she would have to ask Faolan for the explanation.

She followed Aaron into the deserted common room. "Where is everyone?" she asked.

"Not here."

It was nice of him to make this so easy for her. Cate gestured to the cellar's door. "Has anyone looked in on her?"

"Aye."

"Was she…okay?"

Aaron shrugged. He moved away and stood near the fire. Picking up an iron rod, he poked at the embers.

Cate sighed. "I'm sorry for what I said yesterday."

The words came out in a rush, much quicker than she had intended. Aaron stubbornly kept his head down.

"You can say what you want," he said. "I don't care."

"I do," she said. "And I'm sorry. It was mean. Even for me, it was mean, and I'm not like that."

Aaron glanced at her, eyebrow raised.

"Sometimes," she amended.

He nodded. "Which times? I wouldn't want to miss them."

"You do know I was kidnapped and brought here against my will, right?" she asked.

The door opened before Aaron could respond, and Cate looked over, expecting James or Sarai, but saw three strangers—two men and one woman—all armed with swords. Cate peeked at Aaron to see if she should be concerned. He seemed undecided but sidestepped closer to her.

The man in front laid eyes on her and bowed. The other man followed his lead. The woman curtsied.

"Your majesty," the man said.

"Or not," Cate said, and confusion crept over the man's face.

"She's not the queen," James said from the doorway.

He wasn't alone. In addition to Faolan standing on his shoulder, James was also flanked by two other men, each wearing a sword on his hip. The cavalry, it would appear, had arrived.

"Lucius," James said next, "it's good to see you well."

The man broke off his gaze and turned to James. Faolan flew off James's shoulder as the two men embraced. When James greeted the other arrivals, he didn't hug anyone else. Cate glanced again at Aaron. He shrugged.

The man James had called Lucius turned back to her and bowed again. It wasn't any less weird the second time.

"My apologizes," he said. "The resemblance is quite remarkable."

"Yeah," Cate said. "That's what I hear."

"This is the Lady—" James started.

Aaron snorted, and Cate flashed him a look.

"Sorry. Did you want to do that?" he asked quietly, and she grinned.

"Cate," James finished, glaring at them both. "The Lady Cate. She is the queen's sister."

Cate shook her head. "I'm not."

"Even if she denies it," James said.

"Which she does," Cate interjected.

James pressed on. "Cate, this is Lucius, Rhydwyn, Gair, Eion, and Brighid."

When his name came up, the man to whom it belonged bowed his head. The woman was last, and she curtsied again.

"Could you get them to stop doing that?" Cate muttered to Aaron, and he grinned. She looked at James. "Are these the merry men and woman?"

James didn't answer. He was staring at her hands, continuing to do so until she moved them behind her back. He then glanced at Faolan, resting on the table.

"The merry men and woman?" James asked, lifting his head to look at her.

"Is this the rest of your gang of ruffians?" she translated.

"Ruffians?"

"I heard you were outlaws," she said. "Plus, there's that whole kidnapping thing. It doesn't speak well to your character."

"This is not everyone," James said. "You'll see the rest once we arrive at camp. Rhydwyn and Gair will accompany us there. The others will remain here to help guard the queen."

Camp. Huh. Well, that didn't sound appealing in the least. As her idea of roughing it was using the public restrooms at Fenway, she couldn't imagine that she and medieval camping would be a good mix. Wherever this camp was, there probably wouldn't be anything as glamorous as a pot in which to piss. She preferred amenities. And a lot of them.

"Watch her," James said.

"Wait, what?" Cate asked. "Watch her?"

James ignored her as he and Lucius disappeared into the root cellar. After the door closed, Cate looked at her babysitters.

"I will give the entire contents of my trust fund to the one who gets me the hell out of here," she said.

They didn't react.

"I don't think they know what a trust fund is," Aaron said.

"Like you do."

"I'm still trying to work out what a pain-in-the-ass emo freak is."

"Look in a mirror," she said.

Aaron nodded. "Maybe I'll do that."

He walked out of the cottage. Cate watched him leave, insanely jealous of his ability to go outside, then took inventory of the remaining four.

Brighid stared, though she tried to make it look as though she wasn't. Gair stood in the doorway, his back to her. Rhydwyn was posted by the window, angled so she remained in his eyeline. Eion had moved so close to her, she was surprised she hadn't noticed before. She stepped back; he stepped forward.

"Hey," she snapped, "I don't know what your trauma is, but you need to back the hell off."

He didn't. He acted like she hadn't said anything at all. Running her tongue across her teeth, she considered her options. His eyes repeatedly darted over to his buddies. That made up her mind, and she moved toward him.

She kneed him in the groin, and he crumpled. Rhydwyn was on her almost immediately, his arm around her neck. He was pulling her back when she grabbed his arm and flipped him over her shoulder. He landed with a thud. The sword that had been in his hand came loose, and she picked it up. It was heavier than she thought it would be, so she didn't do much with it. It would probably destroy the ass-kicking illusion she had created if she tried to do anything more. She looked at Gair, who hadn't left the doorway. Jaw dropped, he stared at her.

"What do you say, tough guy," she said. "Wanna give me a go?"

Before he could answer—provided he would have—a hand clasped her shoulder and jerked her back. The sword was ripped from her fingers.

"What did you do?" James demanded, tossing her into a chair.

She shrugged. "I gave him fair warning."

Anger flashed in his eyes. "I told them to watch you."

"I told them to back off."

He shook his head. "You have to stop doing this."

"I don't have to stop doing anything."

James looked at Lucius. "Keep her in that bloody chair. Sit on her if you have to."

James stalked out of the house. As soon as he was out of sight, she looked at Lucius. "Gonna sit on me?"

"Will you make me?" he responded.

She grinned. "Haven't decided yet."

"Let me know when you have."

"Oh, you bet," she said as James returned with a length of rope. She laughed. "You are *not* serious."

"Aren't I?"

Jumping out of the chair, she moved away. "If you think I'll just sit there while you—"

James shoved her into the wall. She protested, but he turned her around and shoved her again. Pulling her arms behind her back, he wrapped the rope around her wrists. She screeched and tried to kick him, so he swept her legs out from under her, and she fell face first onto the floor. He put a knee on her back to hold her in place until he finished. When the rope was secure, he bent forward, his mouth close to her ear.

"You were saying?"

He jerked her to her feet and pushed her away. She stumbled a few steps before regaining her balance. Her face flamed with a mixture of rage and embarrassment while her eyes burned with the sting of tears. She blinked furiously, unwilling to give him the satisfaction of seeing her cry.

When he touched her again, her body shied away, curling inward. She hated it but couldn't seem to control the reaction. His grip lessened, and she hated that, too.

Leading her into the bedroom, he released her, this time not shoving her. She walked to the opposite corner, between the bed and the window, as she tried to put as much distance between them as possible. Turning around, she backed into the corner. She didn't look directly at him—she wouldn't—but she wanted to know where he was.

"I can't—I have to…When I come back," he said, "I'm going to talk, and you're going to listen."

Fat chance. But she didn't tell him that. She remained silent and stared at the wall until he left, closing the door behind him. He barked out orders, instructing someone to stand outside the window and someone else to watch the door. No one came inside the room, and she slid to the floor, drawing her knees to her chest.

The urge to cry, to outright sob, redoubled its efforts, but she wouldn't give in. She couldn't. She wouldn't let him—or anyone else, either—see her cry. It was much easier said than done, though, so she took deep breaths while pressing her face into her knees.

To distract herself, she tested the bonds on her wrists. The rough rope dug into her skin but held firm. She hadn't expected anything else. A farmer-warrior hybrid would surely be able to tie knots.

Okay—other means of escape. She lifted her head to scan the room for something she could use to cut the rope. The problem was, there wasn't anything in the room. No glass, no nails, nothing sharp. Nothing useful. Even the damn lantern was gone, so there was nothing for her to do but sit and wait.

New plan, then.

She could keep trying to wait them out. They wouldn't hurt her. Much, anyway. But they couldn't do worse because they still wanted her to do whatever it was they wanted done. Bring peace and harmony to all the land and joy to the little children. Whatever. The task itself didn't matter. The important thing was that they had need of her. She could bide her time. She could wait. If she was patient, opportunity would present itself. If she stopped fighting for a while, make them think they'd worn her down, they'd relax. They'd get lazy, they'd get sidetracked, something would happen, and she could maybe get away. She could maybe get back to where she belonged.

Just as soon as she figured out where she was.

The door opened again, and she quickly raised her head. She didn't look at James as he came in, keeping her eyes trained on the wall, but she saw him all the same.

"I'd like to talk to you," he said, closing the door. "If you'll let me."

Like she could stop him.

"It's not gone well," he said. "Your arrival here."

That was putting it mildly. She adjusted her shoulders and kept her eyes on the wall.

James shifted his weight. "I had to do it."

Did he mean kidnapping her, or throwing her into a wall so he could tie her up? Not that it mattered. He thought both actions were justified. Criminals always had reasons.

"You don't know," he said. "You can't understand."

That was true enough.

"Those people out there have been through hell. They have risked their lives for this land, their families, for me," James said. "I won't let you abuse them."

But she was supposed to be their Frodo Baggins or whoever, and it was open season on her. She shouldn't be surprised; she read the books. She knew how those things worked.

"They were acting on my orders. I told them to watch you. I told Eion to be your shadow," James said. "If you want to be angry with someone, be angry with me."

As a matter of fact, she did want to be angry with someone. And she was. But being angry at one person just wasn't enough. Hate and bile filled her, and even if she didn't know, even if she couldn't understand where James was coming from, she recognized that he felt the same way. The truth was in two grass-covered mounds. The truth was biting into her wrists.

"We're leaving soon," James said. "Brighid and my grandmother will come in when I leave to help prepare you. If you do anything to harm either of them, I swear I will—"

She looked at him, waiting to find out what threat he would make, what he would swear to do. He paused, then shook his head and walked out, leaving the thought unfinished.

———❧———

At the far end of her beach had been an outcropping of rock as white as the sand itself. When she could no longer bear to drown herself, Haleine had walked to it, thinking she might use it to aid in her pursuit. The rocks were as sharp as knives, and she spent days or weeks or months—she didn't know how long—using them to bleed herself dry. Every time, as the rush of pleasure—the relief of knowing it was almost done, that this time she had succeeded in freeing herself—pushed through her, she would awaken once again on that godforsaken beach, pure, untouched, and maddeningly alive.

The last time, she had climbed the rocks, cutting her palms and knees and the soles of her feet, leaving behind a trail of blood. When she reached the apex, she walked to the edge and looked at the water and the beach below. All was quiet and halcyon, devoid of everything but the peace that eluded her. She closed her eyes and spread her arms out to her sides. Raising her face to the sun, Haleine stepped off the edge.

But instead of hitting the water, she landed in a dark cell, broken and battered. She screamed at first, as she felt the hurt in her chest and limbs, but when the pain lessened, Haleine had gotten to her feet. She had seen the lanterns giving off their feeble light. And then she had seen the woman. A woman whose reflection was Haleine's own.

Not a ghost, not her soul but, the woman claimed, a sister, a twin. Faolan had told this woman of their relationship, but Faolan was a liar. It did not mean he lied this time, nor did it mean he spoke the truth. As she had told the woman, Faolan always served his cause. She did not fault him for it, but neither would she forget it.

How could she have a twin? How had she not known this? What had happened to this supposed sister of hers? Why had they not been raised together? Why had her parents never mentioned her name?

Haleine still didn't know her name. The woman hadn't said it, and Haleine, too concerned for other things, hadn't asked. What would Faolan tell her if she posed the question to him?

Regardless of what he said, regardless of the truth, there was no doubt there was some connection between the two of them. Magic at least bound them together, if not their lineage. Haleine watched the woman bleed when none had touched her. The hole over her heart first, then blood from her wrist, the injury identical to what Haleine had done to herself. More curious was the woman's reaction. While Haleine felt a flow of relief, the other woman had felt nothing but panic. She screamed—oh, how she had screamed—until she had disappeared, leaving Haleine to question if she had ever been there.

Haleine had not seen her since. How long had it been? She could not judge the passing of time anymore. Every time her eyes closed and reopened— no matter how briefly—she would wake up in another where, in another when, jerked back and forth and tossed to and fro. Forever anchored to Dana she thought she would be, for she saw him everywhere: in the ruins of a church, in a darkened forest, emerging glistening and wet from a sun-drenched pond.

She huddled in the corner, knees drawn to her chest and her arms wrapped tightly around them. Smaller. She had to make herself smaller. As small as possible—so small as to disappear entirely.

Light floated down from above, footsteps following, and Haleine raised her head to see two men appear. Unwashed, unshaven, shabby garments— they were commoners. The swords on their hips made them rebels. Did she know them? Had she seen them before?

Ignoring her, they spoke of things which held no meaning for her. Their voices were familiar, tripping an unclear inkling of a forgotten memory. She knew them, then. Had known them. Why couldn't she remember from where?

"What of Dana?" the taller man asked. "Where is he?"

Haleine flinched at the sound of her lover's name.

"Gone," replied the other.

She opened her mouth to demand what had become of him, but the first man asked the question before she could form the words.

"Where did he go?"

"I couldn't tell you."

"Does Faolan know?"

"If he does, he's not saying."

"Have you asked?"

"Once."

"But not since?"

The second man shook his head. "I've had other things on my mind, haven't I? He'll do what he'll do. I can't worry about him, too. I won't."

Haleine lowered her eyes to the floor. Where had Dana gone?

"Oh, your majesty," the first man murmured. "You poor girl."

She looked at him, surprised to have been addressed directly, and with such pity, and saw him lift a hand off a bed and cradle it in his own. She had not noticed the bed, nor anyone in it before. She stood to better see to whom the man spoke.

It was her in the bed.

As the realization hit her, a great crash came from above, and the second man raced up the steps. The other gently placed her hand back on the bed and followed.

Haleine stayed and stared at herself.

Rain was falling by the time they were ready to leave the homestead. James stood outside and looked at the sky. It would be wiser to stay another night to wait out the storm. It would be wiser to set out the next morning, but he didn't want to keep Cate there any longer. She had done enough damage, and he wouldn't give her the opportunity to do more. The rain couldn't hurt any of them.

His mind made up, James returned to the house.

"We're going," he said to Rhydwyn and Gair before continuing on to fetch Cate.

She sat on the floor in the bedroom, staring at the wall and wearing the cloak and shoes Sarai had provided. Cate hadn't spoken a word to him, nor anyone else, since he had bound her arms. Considering she hadn't kept her mouth shut about much of anything since he'd first encountered her, the change was both welcoming and concerning.

"We're leaving," he said as he approached.

She didn't look at him. If he made some other threat against her, would she stop staring at the damn wall and look at him again?

He held out his hand. She didn't react. He grasped her elbow to pull her up, but she was nothing but dead weight. He sighed inwardly, then yanked her to her feet. If he hurt her, she didn't complain. How hard would he have to push her to get her to break?

"Her hood," Faolan said when James led her out of the bedroom.

James tugged the hood of her cloak over her head. It wouldn't keep her dry—it was raining much too hard for that—but he supposed that Faolan's concern was keeping her identity hidden. James wanted that, too, but didn't know how effective a hood might be. Perhaps it could protect her from any human eyes, but the meager disguise would do nothing to shield her from Omur.

"Bearach is in the forest," Faolan said, settling on James's shoulder.

James nodded and looked for his grandmother. She smiled sadly as she held out a jar.

"A salve, for her wrists," she said. "If she needs it. When she needs it."

He accepted the jar. It felt heavier than its small size would suggest. He handed it to Gair, who carried a pack of provisions.

"Gran," James said, "I'm sorry that—"

"Go," she interrupted. "We'll be all right. Your people will see to that."

Lucius and Eion accompanied them to the forest. As soon as Bearach and Kynon came into view, Cate shrank back against James and whispered an expletive that went unheard by the others. Had she never seen a unicorn before?

As Rhydwyn and Gair mounted their horses, James passed Cate over to Lucius's keeping and climbed onto Bearach's back. Lucius lifted Cate and set her in front of James. The unicorn sidled, and Cate swayed, but both James and Lucius helped her to keep her seat.

"Ready?" James asked Rhydwyn and Gair. They nodded, and James lightly touched Bearach's neck to signal their departure.

The rain continued to fall as they rode. Faolan, flying at James's side, tried to speak to him more than once, but James brushed him off every time. He didn't want to hear about the damn tunnels. They weren't covering enough ground, however, and James was aware that a decision would have to be made when the light of day, already impeded by the clouds, started to fade. They would either have to find shelter or spend the night in the rain.

James looked at the back of Cate's head. She had remained silent the entire ride. She would have been motionless as well, were she not shivering madly. That made the decision for him. They weren't far from Eluned when James asked Bearach to stop. Rhydwyn and Gair pulled their horses alongside him.

"Gair," James said, "go on ahead and find out if Orla will begrudge us space in her stable for the night."

Gair didn't outwardly question the command, but neither did he move to follow it. James slid from Bearach's back and motioned for Gair to join him away from the others.

"They're canvassing the forests; they won't be looking for the queen in the city," James said quietly. "It'll be safe enough, and she needs a place to stay the night."

Gair took a furtive glance at Cate and nodded. Unbuckling his sword belt, he handed the weapon over before climbing back into the saddle and riding away. When Gair was gone, James returned to Cate and placed his hand on her leg, above her knee. As she jerked away and lost her balance, he grabbed her arm to steady her. Her head whipped in his direction, her jaw clenched and eyes dark with anger. Resisting the urge to shove her off Bearach's back, he pulled her toward him.

"I don't recommend kicking Bearach," he said, feeling the tension in her body. "He kicks back."

James set her on the ground. As soon as he let go, she kicked him in the shin. He swore. She didn't say anything, but he could guess her thoughts.

"Bearach, look to the perimeter," James ordered. "Rhydwyn, we can't take her through the main gates."

Both the unicorn and the man disappeared. Cate backed against a tree.

"Sit, if you want," James said. "They'll be a while in coming back."

Her response was to straighten and move away from both him and the tree. He let her go, satisfied with her staying within his sight. He adjusted his position to make sure she stayed that way.

Faolan landed on his shoulder. "If we'd taken the tunnels, we wouldn't be wet right now. We'd also be there already."

"I don't trust them."

"No one's watching the tunnels."

"I think I've heard that from you before."

Faolan sighed. "It was nice of you to let her kick you."

"I didn't let her kick me."

"You did, and it was nice of you. Good to know you didn't completely rob her of her will to fight."

"I didn't let her kick me," James repeated without much conviction. "Instead of talking nonsense, tell me what's wrong with Bearach. He's acting like a horse, and a damn skittish one at that."

"Bearach doesn't like to touch her."

"Who? Cate? He doesn't like to touch her?" James asked, pitching his voice low. "What does that mean?"

"Touching her is painful for him," Faolan said. "For all of us."

"Physically painful?"

"Not insurmountably so, but, yes."

"Is that unusual?"

"Yes."

James glanced at Cate. "Why did he agree to carry her if it hurts him?"

"You required it."

"It wasn't the only choice. She could have ridden one of the horses."

"It was the smartest choice."

"What does that make her?"

"I don't understand what you're asking."

"Don't you? You tell me it causes you and Bearach physical pain to come into contact with her, yet you can touch the queen, and I know Luisiúil can touch the queen. You tell me that it's unusual for a situation like Cate's to happen, but you don't understand what I'm asking? What is she? Who is she?"

"I'm not entirely sure who she is."

"She's the second, isn't she?" James asked. "The second named in your prophecy? Two from one, you said. You called the queen the first. The first for the goddess, and the second for the dark gods? Wasn't that what you said?"

"Yes. That is what I said."

"Could it mean twins? Two children from one birth? Two from one?"

"Maybe."

"Maybe? She could be the key to our ruin, and we brought her here," James said. "Why? Why would you do that? Why would your goddess want that?"

"Laorans believes Cate will help us," Faolan said. "Regardless of the prophecy."

"But if the goddess is wrong, we've unleashed someone—some *thing*—who could destroy everything."

"We have to make sure that doesn't happen."

"How do we do that?"

"We convince her to help us."

James nodded. That's what it all came back to, wasn't it? He looked at Cate, his eyes running down her back to the spot where her hands, concealed beneath her cloak, were bound. She hated him—she hated all of them—and for good reason. How would he ever convince her to help them?

There were more questions to be asked, but James, too wary of the answers, kept quiet. He required nothing else to worry about that night. Faolan abandoned the conversation as well, and flew from his shoulder in favor of a tree branch. They stayed separate and silent until Bearach and Gair returned.

Their perimeter was clear, and Orla's permission had been granted. Gair's horse was already stabled there. James lightly touched Cate's arm. She didn't pull away.

"We're taking shelter for the night," he said. "It's not far, but do you want to walk or ride?"

When she didn't respond, he picked her up and carried her to Bearach, depositing her on the unicorn's back. Both grimaced, but neither complained.

"Let's get out of the rain," James said, not bothering to hide his irritation.

When Rhydwyn saw them approach, he opened the hidden door in the city wall. Gair and Faolan went first. James pulled Cate from Bearach's back and went through the door, Rhydwyn following.

They had no trouble reaching the tavern. They used the stable entrance and took up residence in the back. Rhydwyn's horse joined Gair's, and James led Cate into the open stall next to them. He untied her cloak and removed it. He hung it over the side of the stall to allow it to dry. The stable was warm, but she was shivering, so he called for a blanket. Gair handed him one Orla used for her ponies. James shook it out and draped it around Cate's shoulders.

"It's always warm in here, so you shouldn't be cold for long," he said. "Sit, and get some rest, aye?"

She didn't say anything—not that he had expected her to—but neither did she move. He pushed down on her shoulders until she crumpled under the pressure and fell in the corner. Her eyes widened, but her mouth remained closed.

Aggravated anew and needing space, James stripped off his own cloak and left the others to guard Cate while he went to thank Orla for her hospitality. The tavern was quiet; only a few customers were scattered throughout the room, and none of them paid him any mind. Orla stood behind the bar, wiping the inside of a tankard.

"It's you," she said when she saw him. "Didn't expect that. Where's Dana?"

"Not here," James said. "I wanted to thank you—"

"Where is he?"

He understood her concern. The last time she had seen Dana, the rebel leader had been on the threshold of death. She would have no way of knowing what had happened since. But he didn't want to talk about it.

"I couldn't tell you," he said. "Thank you for the use of your stable. We won't be any trouble, and we'll be gone before the dawn."

"My favorite sort of guests," she said. "How many are you?"

"Four. But you don't need to—"

"I'll send supper in a bit," she said. "Go on back to the stable now. The castle guards get paid tonight, and those not on duty come here."

"Will it be safe?"

She shrugged. "As long as you don't come bursting in, waving your sword about and screaming your allegiance to Dana."

"No chance of that."

"Then there shouldn't be a problem," Orla said. "Go. I'll send the food."

True to her word, three of Orla's boys brought them bread, bowls of stew, and a jug of ale. James thanked them for the offering. He held out a serving in Cate's direction, to see if there was any interest, but she wouldn't lift her eyes from the wall.

"Starve yourself then," he muttered, turning away and setting her bowl aside.

He joined the others as they ate and talked. Faolan and Gair carried the majority of the conversation. Rhydwyn was silent, and James wasn't much better. He sat with his back to Cate, using every other sense he had to monitor her actions. But she did nothing.

After their meal, Gair and Faolan went outside to take the first watch. Rhydwyn, using his cloak as a blanket, stretched out to sleep. James covered himself with his own cloak and leaned against the stall's open door.

Later, he was startled awake by the horses and found himself looking at the stable roof. Had he fallen asleep? He hadn't intended to do that.

He propped himself up on his elbows. Rhydwyn slept soundly, which meant James couldn't have been asleep that long. He glanced to his right. The stall was empty, but he needed a moment to realize the significance of that. When he did, he scrambled to his feet and prodded Rhydwyn awake.

"Captain?" Rhydwyn asked.

"Get up," James said. "Cate's gone."

CHAPTER 8

When James dropped her into the corner, he inadvertently had provided her with the key to her release. A nail of some kind, either for wood, or maybe shoeing horses—she didn't know, she didn't care—was hidden in the straw. It jabbed into her palm, forcing her to bite her tongue to keep from yelping in surprise. Her fingers maneuvered it into position, slowly and carefully so she wouldn't be discovered.

James and the others made it easier, as they weren't paying much attention to her. They were distracted, busy discussing things that meant nothing to her. A trio of boys brought food—stew, from the looks and smells of it—and while her stomach growled its protest, Cate wouldn't even look at James when he offered her some.

It bothered him, her silent treatment, which was all the more reason to keep it up. He muttered something under his breath and turned his back to her. He sat at the end of the stall, talking to Gair and Rhydwyn and the pegasus while ignoring her.

She worked on cutting through the ropes, keeping her face blank as she continuously stabbed and sliced herself. What was a little blood when compared to not being a captive anymore?

By the time she succeeded, Gair had been sent outside for the first tour of guard duty. Much to her delight, Faolan went with him. Both James and Rhydwyn rolled themselves in their cloaks and went to sleep. She waited until they were both on their backs snoring, then quietly shed her blanket, stepped over them, and left the stable through the door the stew boys had used.

The door led to another room that, from the looks of things, was used as a storeroom. The only thing it was empty of was people. She went through to the door on the other side and entered what appeared to be a tavern. It was dark and quiet, probably close to last call, if such a thing existed here. A woman stood behind the bar, wiping mugs with a cloth, and they looked at each other. Unsure what the woman would be willing to do for James, Cate broke the stare and kept walking, quickening her pace as much as she could without breaking into a run. If some kind of alarm was about to be raised, she had to get away while she could.

The tavern led to a dark street. The rain had lightened to a drizzle, and the air was putrid, proof of a medieval city's sewer system. Gagging, she walked away from the tavern. She didn't care in which direction she went. Didn't know her way around anyway. Her goal was to simply get away from James and company. She would worry about getting out of the city—and this world—later.

She slipped into an alley and stood just inside of it, scanning for anyone lying in wait for an easy mark, as she was the very definition of an easy mark. The alley seemed empty enough, so she went forward, keeping one hand on the building to her right. She arrived at the other end safely and paused as she contemplated her next move. Left or right?

She went right, then decided to take a left into another alley. She was only a few steps into it when her luck ran out.

"Lost, lord?" a voice asked from behind her.

She gasped and whirled around. A hulking cloaked figure blocked the exit.

"Lady, I mean to say," he amended.

"Not lost," she said, mimicking his accent. "And I'm not much of a lady."

"Wouldn't think so." The man advanced upon her. "Being out and about all unescorted the way you are."

"Always been a maverick," she said.

For every step he took toward her, she took one away. She didn't get far before she came up against the wall.

"Maverick, eh?"

"That's not another word for whore," she said, slapping his hand away from her chest. "Just so you know."

"I've got coin, lass."

She heard the jingling of coin followed by the jingling of another kind. A belt.

"How nice for you," she said.

"Let's not be like that, love."

He was too close for her to effectively employ her signature knee-to-the-groin move. Her kingdom for a can of pepper spray.

"All right. How about I be like this," she said and drove the heel of her hand into his nose.

He yelped and backed off enough for her to knee his groin as hard as she could. Slipping past him, she ran into the alley. He wasn't thrown off for long and gave chase, launching himself at her and taking her down. She screamed as he flipped her onto her back and covered her mouth with a grubby hand. Something sharp pressed against her stomach.

"You bite me, bitch, and I'll cut you," he hissed.

Although it was nice to have been given a choice, it was hard to decide which option to take. Bite him and be stabbed, or don't bite him and be raped.

"Not if I cut you first," James said.

The man's head snapped back, and Cate was suddenly awash in a warm liquid. Blood. The man was hauled off her, and she scrambled away. Light flooded the alley, allowing Cate to see James standing over her, his dagger dripping red. Rhydwyn was behind him, holding a lantern.

Cate pushed herself up. "Could you be any more cliché?"

James looked momentarily surprised to hear her voice. When he recovered, he held out his hand. She shook her head. If he touched her, he'd figure out exactly how unsettled and nauseated she was. Turning her hands to fists so no one would see her fingers shaking, Cate stood on her own.

"Are you all right?" James asked.

Cate lied and nodded while looking at her assailant. Or what was left of him. Rhydwyn's lantern illuminated the man at her feet and the gaping hole James had left in place of his throat.

"You killed him," she said.

James crouched to clean the dagger on the dead man's cloak. "You are a clever one, aren't you?"

"No, I mean..."

James rifled through the dead man's clothing. "What do you mean?"

"I don't—I don't know. I just...You killed him for me."

"I killed him *because* of you," James said. He pulled out a pouch and tossed it to Rhydwyn.

"Okay," Cate said, "did you maybe not notice the part where he was about to—?"

James stood. "I know what he was about to do. I know what would have happened if I hadn't found you."

"Then why the—?"

"I had to find you. Because you ran away again," James said. "And because you ran away and because you were fool enough to run through the city streets in the dead of night and because I have to keep you safe, I had to track you down and I had to kill a man."

"Please don't tell me you're one of those assholes who thinks it's the woman's fault. That she was asking to be—"

"I'm one of those assholes who doesn't like to kill others."

"Well, aren't you in the wrong line of work."

"You don't have to tell me that."

"Apparently, I do because you're the one throwing a hissy fit over having rid the world of some lame-ass, wannabe rapist."

"If you hadn't run away—"

"He would've had some other girl underneath him."

"If he had found one."

"And you would've been all right with that."

"No, I wouldn't be all right with that." James looked at her in something resembling disgust. "You say that like it's that simple, that straightforward, and—"

"Isn't it?"

"No, it isn't. Of course it isn't," James said. "Bloody hell, Cate! It's not that I don't—I have to keep you safe. Do you understand that? Do you know what that means? I have to keep you safe. Whatever the cost, *I* have to protect *you*." He jabbed a finger at her, then turned and took a few steps away, only to come rushing back. "I don't care who that man is, or what he would have done tonight. He could have been Rhydwyn, and he would still be lying there with his throat cut because I don't care. I can't care. All that mattered was that *you* were in danger, and I have to keep you safe." He sighed and shook his head. "I don't like having to kill, Cate. Don't force that choice on me. Not when it can be avoided."

Well, then. There didn't seem to be anything to say to that. Cate wrapped her arms around herself. Rhydwyn, unperturbed by James's confession, set the lantern on the ground and walked to the end of the alley. James looked at the man he had killed.

After a moment, he frowned. "Did you break his nose?"

Cate shrugged. "Seemed the thing to do."

"How did you—?"

"Heel of hand, thrust up," she said and demonstrated.

He nodded. "Ilya will like you."

"I'm so glad." She sighed, momentarily curbed her annoyance, and added, "Thank you, you know, for the life-saving."

James looked as uncomfortable receiving her gratitude as she was in giving it. He offered her a curt nod. "I have to keep you safe."

"So you've said."

"It doesn't mean that I like you."

Cate fought off a laugh. "Never thought it did."

Rhydwyn returned then, moving at a pace that caused Cate's hackles to rise. Something had happened, or was about to happen. He scooped the lantern off the ground and gestured to James as though pointing out the emergency exits on an airplane. James nodded and slid his dagger into his boot.

"We have to go," he said to her. "The night patrol is coming, and you can't be found by them."

Unable to locate either her voice or the will to argue, Cate nodded and skirted the dead man. James placed his hand on the small of her back and guided her out of the alley. Rhydwyn doused the lantern and followed.

—◦◦◦—

Once more, a spell artfully wrought roused Omur from sleep. Its caster had tried to cover his tracks, but the job was hurried and sloppy, making the magic a veritable beacon. Omur left his bed and stepped onto the balcony, looking first at the moon before settling his gaze on the sleeping city below.

The pegasus was in Eluned. With him was something—someone?—worth hiding.

Omur laughed before he swept across the room and opened the door. The man standing guard turned to look at him.

"Find someone to locate Varro," Omur said. "Send him here."

The man bowed and Omur closed the door. He returned to his bed and pulled the covers to the floor, revealing the sleeping girl beneath.

"Out of here, you slut of a girl," he said, slapping her exposed thigh. "I've business to take care of, and I won't have you underfoot while I do it."

The girl stirred slowly as she pulled herself from sleep. Rolling onto her back, she stretched as though she were feline. She looked at him with her dark eyes.

"Is it my sister?" she asked with a slight quaver to her voice.

Sighle always wanted to know if his business involved her sister. He looked at her eyes, wide, brown, and hopeful. After a glance at the rest of her, he picked up one of the blankets from the floor and threw it at her.

"No, not your sister," he said. "Cover yourself and be gone."

Her face fell, and she slid from the bed in a manner that made Omur want to order her back to it, but it was better that she go. Varro never told a soul what he saw or heard, and it would not leave the man's lips if he did see Sighle in his lord's bed, but Omur felt the need for secrecy. He wanted to keep his pet for himself.

He watched impatiently as she leisurely slid her gown over her head. Why must she move so slowly? Why must she sway those narrow hips? He thought he might explode when she looked over her shoulder at him, brown eyes guileless.

"Tighten my laces?" she asked.

"Get out," he snapped.

"But my laces!"

"I am not your maid," he said. "Find your escort and go."

"Half-dressed?" she asked. "What will people say?"

"They'll say nothing. It is late enough that the only ones about are the two of us and the man you have waiting for you in the hall. Since all three of us already know what you have done here, there is none left over which to fret. Go."

She turned, eyes worried. "I've displeased you."

"I told you to go."

"Please say you aren't angry with me." Her voice quivered as she walked toward him with hesitant steps. "I couldn't bear it if you were."

"Annoyed," he said. "Not angry."

"That's not much better."

Stopping in front of him, she tangled her fingers in his robe. "Will you allow me to make amends?" she asked, her voice soft and repentant.

"Later perhaps," Omur said. "But only if you go now."

"As you wish, my lord."

She pressed a soft kiss to his throat and walked away. He watched her go, imagining the ways in which he would allow her to tame his frustration. She was quite the inventive piece. He was sometimes left wondering if Haleine had shared the same skill. If he ever found himself again in a room with the rebel leader, he would have to ask.

Varro arrived then, and Omur watched the captain of the guard enter the room, his head bent and eyes directed to the floor. Varro was nervous about this summons. There was good reason for the man to be concerned. Omur had been far from pleased when he had returned from Enimode with naught but fewer men.

They were waiting for us was the excuse Varro had offered him.

Thwarted once again by the people of Enimode, Omur had taken small comfort in knowing Varro had at least ordered the town burned before their retreat. He had thought that the destruction might drive the rebels elsewhere.

How interesting that they had come here.

Omur smiled and poured himself some wine before sitting in front of the fire. Varro came and stood before him.

"Your unfortunate blunder in Enimode may not have been so unfortunate after all," Omur said.

Varro's head came up. "My lord?"

"There are rebels in the city," Omur said. "As they cannot leave the city walls until morning, I don't imagine you'll lose them this time. I want you to find them and track them. They have something I want."

"The queen?"

Varro was near as bad as the girl. No, Omur did not think Haleine was with the pegasus. The longer he went without any sort of sense of her, the more he was convinced that she was already dead.

"No, I do not think so. There's something else. Someone else perhaps," Omur said. "I am not sure what that may be, but the pegasus is doing his level best to keep it hidden from me. I want you to find them and track them. I want you to discover who moves with them and, if you can, where they camp."

"Yes, my lord."

"You tell me what you find," Omur said, "and I'll tell you what to take."

Varro bowed. "Yes, my lord."

※

I've business to take care of, he had told her before dismissing her like a servant, like the child he thought her to be. A plaything to be tucked away out of sight until wanted again.

Oh, if only he knew.

Sighle Coileáin was well aware of his business. She had felt the magic, too, long before it had come close to touching her bedfellow's mind. The goddess's pegasus lurked nearby, and she knew what that meant. Still, Omur wanted her gone, so she allowed him to think that he had successfully sent her on her way, when in fact she stayed and sat in a chair where she could watch him give his orders. A puppet working the strings of another puppet.

He remained unaware of what secret the pegasus protected. But she was not.

Is it my sister? she had asked.

She had strived for a desperate, piteous tone. That particular combination worked well on him.

No, not your sister, he had responded, sounding so assured.

He thought she spoke of Haleine. He did not know any better. She found it curious that he did not. His dark lords had a purpose, she assumed, a reason for keeping their vessel ignorant of Mireille's existence, and Sighle was eager to discover what it was.

It would come to light soon enough. They were all headed for a collision. Not one of them, save her, saw it, but it was true all the same. They would crash, and when they did, all sorts of truths would be shaken free.

When that happened, she would have to be careful to keep her own secrets safely stowed. It would do her no service to be discovered now.

Omur would be particularly displeased with her. If he even suspected how much she had meddled with his grand plans, he would not hesitate to kill her. Nor would it be the first time he tried. When he had thought her to be nothing more than a means to weaken Haleine, he had tried twice to kill her. Twice he had tried, and twice she had thwarted him.

The first time, he had sent men to kill both her and her mother. He came away thinking the men he hired incompetent, but they weren't. They had intended to do the same unspeakable things to Sighle that she had watched them do to her mother. *Well, what do we have here?* the first of the two had said. *Hello, little girl,* the second man had added, a smile tripping over his lips. All too easily had she sent them away, their only souvenirs her mother's blood and her sister's letter.

The second time came after the death of her father. Omur arrived at her door under the guise of bearer of bad news. *I am so sorry to have to tell my lady this,* he would have said had she offered him the chance, but she already had known of his more sinister intentions long before he had set foot in her chambers. She remembered imagining how he would do it. Would he make it seem as though she had taken her own life? That the loss of first her mother, then her father would have driven her to such an act? She thought he might. That way would wrench her too-soft sister into further desolation, and Omur did love to see Haleine made wretched. It was what Sighle would have done if it had been hers to do.

But she never did find out. She never offered him the opportunity. He had entered the room boldly, relishing the idea of what he was about to do, and she had dismissed him without so much as a glance in his direction.

"Go away," she had commanded. "I'm grieving."

It was near to the truest statement she had ever uttered because, indeed, she did grieve for her father, the man who had given her so much. It was not playacting, as she had done before her liege prince. It was not pretend, as the tears she had squeezed out to mourn a weak, silly woman had been. Truly did she mourn her father.

If only he could see. If only Darian Coileáin could see how well she had learned all he had had to teach, but broken and mutilated her father had been, nailed in a box and left to rot in the ground, worms and maggots for pupils.

All living things must die, and she would one day include herself among their number, for if that dark horseman called Death had come for her father's pieces, he would come for hers as well. She did not fear it. There was no purpose in that. She could only hope that she would not be deprived in the same way her father had been.

A man who served his king so loyally, a man who never compromised, no matter the cost, a man who never wished he had been granted sons instead of daughters deserved better than the death he had gotten. The rebel leader had been the one to deal the blow, to strike off the head she loved, but she did not blame him for it. Love and war were two things that never played fair, and all living things must one day die. That acceptance, however, would not stop her from pulling the rebel leader up by his roots and rending him to pieces of broken earth because, while she did not blame him, she found she hated the man who had killed her unkillable father.

There was blame to be placed, nonetheless, and that mantle she would bestow upon the woman who had known full well what would happen, the woman who had seen it and had not stopped it.

Her sister, her lovely sister, with all her grace and charms, had sent their father to die because she was caught up in and ruined with love. Wrecked and poisoned she had been, she still was, and their father had paid the price.

You'll find love, Sighle had said to her sister, their parting words.

A warning no one heeded. A warning no one heard.

Her sister would find love. And it would kill her.

Indeed, Haleine had found her love and run straight into its arms. She welcomed the dagger thrust through her heart and begged for more.

Always begging was her sister. It was pathetic.

Mireille, Sighle suspected, would be different. Mireille would not beg. Mireille would not be broken.

The pegasus thought the same, only he did not delight in it as she did. He feared it, for an unbroken Mireille was of no use to him and his goddess, so he had used his magic to elicit Omur's attention. The pegasus was not hiding as Omur suspected. The pegasus wanted to be found. He wanted Mireille to be found.

But not taken. No, he did not want that. He could not lose control of her. But found, yes, that he much desired. Mireille did not want to help him nor his goddess, and the pegasus thought to use Omur to scare her into it.

Sighle thought, despite the pegasus's unfortunate associations, that she might like the little beast. His plan was not without merit. As hard-shelled and stubborn as Mireille appeared to be, there was no doubt that the girl stood on a knife's edge. A nudge here, a nudge there, and mayhap the girl would fall.

When that happened, Sighle would have to be sure her sister landed on the proper side.

Leaving the puppets to their planning, Sighle slipped out onto the balcony to look at the city containing her true sister. Haleine was a mistake, a failed experiment trying to crawl her way into the ground. Sighle would open it up and let it swallow Haleine whole if she could. Mireille would prove to be—

A sharp scream only Sighle could hear pierced the night. It was Mireille. In danger, in trouble.

Closing her eyes, Sighle located Mireille in an alley, being backed against a wall by a man thinking to do her harm. As her blood boiled, Sighle watched the man, a useless piece of filth, put his hands on her sister. How dare he defile her with his touch? How dare he think to do worse? Sighle would see him suffer for that. She could make him do all sorts of unimaginable things to himself.

And she would have. If not for the brown-eyed boy.

With one sure slice of a dagger, he saved Mireille and extended to her his hand. She didn't take it, hiding her fear in a cloak of anger. She didn't realize that her protector did the same.

There was trouble to be found there. The brown-eyed boy would have to be dealt with before the end.

With a sigh, Sighle opened her eyes and returned inside.

"I want you to find them and track them," Omur was saying to his servant. "I want you to discover who moves with them and, if you can, where they camp."

"Yes, my lord," the servant answered.

"You tell me what you find," Omur continued, "and I'll tell you what to take."

Varro bowed. "Yes, my lord."

"No," Sighle said.

She put herself in between the two men. They both looked at her without seeing her. She placed a hand on each man's cheek.

"This is what I want you to do."

As James and the others approached the tavern, Orla stood just outside the entrance, beckoning them inside. Did that mean her patrons had gone home for the night? He couldn't bring Cate into a room full of the king's soldiers.

Orla gestured more frantically. "Come on. It's safe," she hissed. "Get off the bloody street!"

James nodded and steered Cate into the barroom, breathing an inaudible sigh of relief to find it empty. As soon as Rhydwyn stepped inside, Orla closed and barred the door.

"All right?" she asked. "All of you?"

"Aye, we're fine," James said, his eyes on Cate. "Could we trouble you for a basin of water?"

Orla glanced at Cate and curtsied. Cate's wasn't the only confused expression.

"Did you just—?" James started, but the look on the barmaid's face convinced him not to finish.

"Come on, lass," Orla said.

As Cate followed Orla into the storeroom, James pulled out a chair at the nearest table and sank into it, Rhydwyn doing the same. They sat in silence, James fighting the urge to doze off. He couldn't very well fall asleep now. He shouldn't have even sat down. There was more for him to do that night. Every night. It never bloody ended, and wouldn't—he suspected—until Death caught him at last.

Orla emerged from the storeroom alone. One look at her face had Rhydwyn immediately on his feet.

James groaned inwardly. "What did she do?"

"What?" Orla said.

He stood. "Where is she?"

"In the storeroom having a good cry," Orla said. "Sit down and leave her be."

He stared at the storeroom door. Crying?

Orla sighed. "She's not going anywhere. The only ways out of that room are through here and the stable. You two are here, and Faolan and your other lad are there. So unless you're telling me that bit of a girl can best the lot of you, sit down and give her a moment's peace."

James glanced at Rhydwyn and saw the man's brief half-smile. Was he, too, remembering the scene at the farm that morning? Rhydwyn raised an eyebrow in question and gestured to the door. James shook his head and waved for him to stand down.

James lowered himself back into his chair. "She's crying?"

"Not in front of you lot," Orla said, joining them. "And don't you go mentioning it to her, either."

"Is she all right? Is she hurt?"

"Not physically." Orla shrugged. "Except for her hands and wrists."

James put his elbow on the table and his head in his hand. "She said she was all right."

Orla made a noise of agreement. "That makes you the fool who believed her."

He nodded. "I guess it does."

"Don't suppose it'll do me any good to ask you who she is," Orla said.

"No."

"She's not the queen."

"No."

"Are they both gone, then?" she asked.

"For now." James looked at Rhydwyn. "Stay here. Don't take your eyes off that bloody door. I'll send Gair to join you."

Rhydwyn nodded. "Aye, Captain."

After ensuring the street was clear of guards, James walked the short distance to the stable entrance. That door was locked as well, and James pounded on it until Gair opened it.

"We found her," James said, stepping inside.

Gair closed his eyes and sighed. "Thank the goddess," he muttered. "I'm sorry I didn't see her, Captain. I don't know how she passed by unnoticed."

James knew exactly how Cate had gotten past him. The answer stood on a barrel at the back of the stable. "She's safe; that's all that matters," he said and jerked his head outside. "Go into the tavern and help Rhydwyn keep watch."

"Aye, Captain."

Once Gair had gone, James barred the stable door and joined Faolan.

"Is Cate all right?" Faolan asked.

"She says yes. Orla says she's lying." James shrugged. "Orla's right."

He unbuckled his sword belt and sat on a stool. Placing the sword across his lap, he ran his hands over the worn leather sheath.

"Whatever you're doing," he said, "you have to stop it."

Faolan looked at him as though he were an object of mild curiosity. James ignored him and went on.

"I don't know what your plan is. I don't know what you're trying to do, but it stops now. It's done."

"What do you think I'm trying to do?"

"Manipulate her? Turn her? Kill her?"

"I'm not interested in killing her."

"Then what are you doing?"

"You wanted to know how hard you'd have to push her," Faolan said.

"I didn't say that to anyone."

"You didn't have to."

James knew what that meant. Dana had mentioned it to him before. "Stay out of my head," he said. "What's there isn't for you to know."

"You may not like it, but this has to be done, James. We have to break her."

Cate was already broken, and James suspected he was the reason why. He shook his head. "The way you're trying to go about it won't work," he said. "She won't cleave herself to us that way."

"There's an excellent chance she won't cleave herself to you in any way," Cate said.

Both James and Faolan looked to see her standing near the storeroom door, freshly scrubbed and wearing an ill-fitting dress that must have come from Orla's own wardrobe. She pushed up the sleeves to reveal white bandages wrapped around her wrists and palms.

"Hope I'm interrupting something," she said, coming toward them.

"Are you all right?" Faolan asked.

"Just dandy," Cate said.

James stood. "Orla says otherwise."

Cate nodded. "She would know, seeing as how she wasn't there and all."

"Cate—"

She put up her hand. "Save it, will you? I just want to sleep. You can go back to pretending you care about my well-being in the morning."

James nodded, and Cate walked past him into the stall where he had dropped her upon their arrival. Picking up her cloak, she shook it out and wrapped it around herself. She sat in the corner, leaned against the back wall, and closed her eyes.

"I'll fetch Gair and Rhydwyn," Faolan said.

James stepped in front of him. "It ends now," he whispered. "Do you understand?"

Faolan glanced at Cate. When his eyes once again rested on James, the pegasus nodded.

chapter 9

With the exception of an unmade bed, the room was immaculate. Polished stone floors were strategically covered with furs and carpets, while the walls were decorated with elaborate woven hangings. The furniture was rich, heavy, carved from a dark wood, and a fire roared in the large hearth. Cate hovered over it as though a ghost. What was this place? Why was she here?

The sound of tears caught her attention. She glided around the room, looking for the source, and spotted a redheaded girl sitting on the floor, leaning against the bed for support. Haleine?

Her mind changed when the girl raised her head, eyes fixed on something Cate couldn't yet see, and said, very clearly, "Oh shit."

The accent was hers. The vernacular was hers.

She was pulled toward herself the way magnets were drawn to metal. Just as she merged into her body, tall glass doors on her left shattered, and her now-corporeal hands shielded her face from the shards. When she looked up again, two of the hell hounds she had seen before in a dream were running toward her. There was no time to escape before they attacked.

They ripped through her clothing and into the vulnerable skin beneath. Their jaws found her arms, legs, and stomach, muscle and bone giving way beneath the force of their razor teeth.

Cate was still dreaming of yellow-eyed wolves mangling her body when James woke her. She was disoriented, lost in the dream and afraid, so she slapped his hand away and flattened herself against the wall at her back. James stayed crouched in front of her, not moving. When she realized where she was, she slumped into the straw.

"What's going on?" she said. "What are you—?"

"You were screaming," James said. "I couldn't risk someone hearing."

"Otherwise you would have let me scream," she said, running her hands over her arms to make sure they were in one piece.

James shrugged. "Maybe. I don't know."

"Swell." Cate checked her legs and torso.

"Are you cold?"

Her hands froze. She wasn't cold, but neither did she want to admit what she was doing. She rubbed her limbs harder for effect. "Maybe a little."

James stood and reached for his cloak, draped over the stall door. He held it out to her. "Put it on."

She shook her head. "No. I don't need it. I'm fine."

"Suit yourself," he said, and threw the cloak over his own shoulders.

When she was finally satisfied that she was in one piece, Cate pushed against the wall to help her stand. Her body was stiff and unresponsive at first, and she stumbled. James's hands shot out but withdrew just as quickly, as she regained her balance. An awkward minute passed between them that was made worse when James spoke again.

"Are your hands all right?" he asked. "Your wrists?"

Cate already knew that underneath the bandages Orla had applied the night before, her skin would be perfect. She didn't need to see it. She didn't need James to see it, either, and moved her hands behind her back, but James caught one wrist and stripped off the linen. He let it fall to the floor and stared at her completely healed hand. The instant his grip on her wrist relaxed, she jerked away.

"Have you always healed in such a manner?" he asked.

She shook her head. It was well past time to change the subject, so she searched for something she could use. Everyone who wasn't her appeared to be dressed and ready for traveling. Rhydwyn held a saddle in his arms. Gair carried a knapsack.

"What time is it?" she asked.

James raised an eyebrow. "Time to go."

"No, I meant..." She stopped. Right. Minutes weren't a thing here. She never did find out how they measured time. It hadn't been a burning issue for her then, or since. "Is it morning yet?"

"Almost," James said. "We'll be leaving as soon as Faolan confirms the way is clear. I'd like to be out of the city before the gates open."

"Stealthy," Cate said.

"Aye," James said. "Orla brought us some food. Eat something before we go."

Cate shook her head. "I'm not hungry."

"I didn't ask if you were," he said. "Eat something."

"Or you'll make me?"

"Aye. If I have to."

He would, too. She could envisioned him forcing food down her throat. It was not a pleasant image. Forcing herself to eat something was bound to be less traumatic.

"Whatever," she said.

Orla had brought them bread, some kind of hard white cheese, and a jug of cider. Cate had some of each, though she would have preferred not to. It had been a while since she'd last eaten, but she didn't have much appetite. Her stomach hurt. Hell, her entire body hurt. It was proof that her companion the past few days had been adrenaline, and now he was off doing something else. Maybe Orla had aspirin, or whatever its equivalent might be here. Or maybe she had some good, strong whiskey. Cate wasn't in a position to be choosey.

By the time she had eaten enough to satisfy James, Faolan returned, deeming the path clear. This also satisfied James, and he called for their departure. She and James led the way. He kept his hand on her arm just above her elbow. She didn't complain because her other option probably involved ropes. Rhydwyn and Gair walked behind them, leading their horses, while Faolan stuck to the shadows.

The rain had stopped, and the stars were beginning to fade as the sky lightened. Cate searched for the sun. Knowing how to find east was bound to be better than not knowing. Anything to help get her bearings.

Of course, there was the possibility that here—in Bizarre-o World—the sun didn't rise in the east. Everything else was wrong and backwards, so why not that, too, right? She would have to make some inquiries on the subject.

When they neared a structure that could only have been a palace, Cate stared at it, her mouth gaping. She'd been to England with Laura once, and while her mother had dealt with business, Cate had gone with Fiona and Daniel on a tour of old castles. They were impressive structures, even in their various states of ruin, and she had tried hard to imagine them in their full glory. Her imagination had not done it justice.

"Is that a castle?" she asked. "Palace?"

"What?" James said.

She pointed. "Palace?"

"Aye."

"What's it like on the inside?"

"Let's hope you never find out," James replied, pulling her into a well-concealed alley.

"Why? What does that mean?" she asked, and he shushed her. "Seriously, what does that mean?"

"It means he wants you to be quiet," Faolan said softly. "Ask your questions later."

James released her when they reached the end of the alley. It was nothing but a vine-covered wall. Where was the exit?

"Did you take a wrong turn?" she asked.

James shushed her again as he ran his hands over the vines. What was he looking for?

A moment later, a door in the wall opened. Cate gawked until James beckoned to her. He didn't mean anything by it, apart from wanting to make as little noise as possible, but she folded her arms in front of her.

"Ask me nicely," she said.

She couldn't see James's expression well, but the change in his stance was clear enough. Grabbing her cloak, he yanked her through the door and dragged her into the woods.

"Don't make me regret not tying you," he said, dropping her on the ground.

Lifting her head, Cate spat out the dirt in her mouth, preparing to call him every foul name currently coming to mind. She stopped when the unicorn appeared in front of her face. The animal probably wouldn't have cared what she called James, but the fact remained that he scared the shit out of her.

"Come on." James pulled her to her feet. "Rhydwyn will give you a boost."

Cate glanced at the boys. With their hoods shadowing their faces, she couldn't tell which was which, but neither stepped forward. She supposed the prospect of touching her didn't overly appeal to either of them. Deciding to give them a break, she turned to James, already astride the unicorn's back.

"I don't need a boost," she said. "Just your hand."

James obliged and, placing her hand in his, she used his boot as a stirrup. It was ungainly, but she made it onto the unicorn's back and settled in front of James.

"You can ride," he said.

She nodded. It was one of those things the woman she'd called her mother thought every well-bred young lady should know how to do, so Cate had taken years and years of lessons. Bet her mother had never imagined that her daughter would be one day riding unicorns.

"That's good to know," James said. "Bearach, put some distance between Omur and us, aye?"

The unicorn bolted. Cate yelped and buried her hands in the animal's mane. She didn't think he appreciated it, but until he slowed down, he would have to deal with it because she wasn't letting go.

They slowed once they were deep in the forest, and Cate relaxed her iron hold. They made their way down a well-traveled path, leaving it only to take cover whenever Faolan said people were approaching.

They stopped at what Cate judged as midday to rest the horses and eat some more of the bread and cheese Orla had packed for them. Cate was grateful for the reprieve, as her ass ached from all the riding. Yes, she could ride, but it normally involved a saddle and a far more leisurely pace. She glanced at the boys. How were they not screaming in pain?

After lunch, they hit the road again and proceeded in silence. They moved at a good rate, and the unicorn's canter was smooth enough that Cate found herself drifting to sleep. More than once, she started to settle into James, only to remember who he was and why she was riding a unicorn through a strange forest. Sure, the man had earned himself some points the previous night, but if he hadn't kidnapped her in the first place, she wouldn't have needed his help.

"It's all right to rest if you want to," James said. "Or need to."

"I don't want to," she said. "I don't need to."

She sat up as straight as she could, leaning toward the unicorn's neck as though she were a jockey.

"Cate," James sighed, "don't you think you're being—?"

"James!" Faolan's voice rang out.

The unicorn reared, dumping its passengers onto the ground. James was on top of her impossibly fast, hauling her away from the animal's hooves. She scrabbled to get on her feet, but James hissed and pushed her back down.

They stopped behind a large tree. She lay on her back, head and shoulders propped up against the tree's massive trunk. James faced the other direction, resting his hand on her shoulder.

"I thought you said no one was watching," James said under his breath.

Was he talking to her? He couldn't have been—she hadn't said a damn thing. Cate found the pegasus hovering above their heads. Where had the others gone?

"I was mistaken," Faolan said. "Omur must have…"

"What?" James pressed.

"Tracked me," Faolan said.

"You?" James asked. "You, and not her?"

"The magic," Faolan said. "I worked some magic in the city last night after she ran, and he must have felt it, sensed it. He knows I wouldn't be too far away from what he wants. Who he wants."

"Me?" Cate said. "This man, whoever he is, he wants me?"

Both James and Faolan looked at her. Neither acknowledged she was correct, but the expression on James's face was confirmation enough.

"How many are there?" he asked. "Do you know?"

"Not with any certainty," Faolan said. "Half a dozen is my guess."

"Why aren't they moving on us?"

"Bearach's taking care of them."

Cate had no idea what that meant, but James accepted it with a nod and glanced around the tree again.

"Rhydwyn? Gair?"

"They lost their mounts, but they're all right," Faolan said. "They've taken cover."

"Can they get to us?" James asked. "Can we get to them?"

"Bearach and I will get them here," Faolan said.

"Do it," James ordered. "Then we'll have to separate."

"Separate?" Faolan echoed.

"You and Bearach will lead the soldiers away. Omur will assume Cate is with you and will have the soldiers follow you, leaving the road clear for us. You'll know when we get to camp, so you'll know when it's safe to lose the men and make your own way back."

"Take the tunnels," Faolan said. "It'll be better to avoid the road entirely."

The pegasus flew away. Cate looked to James for explanation, but he held a finger to his lips. She nodded, seeing the sense in his request. A few minutes later, Rhydwyn and Gair silently arrived. She was impressed that she hadn't heard them approach.

The three men had another wordless conversation while Cate looked at the sky, straining to hear anything other than the singing of birds, until she felt James's breath on her neck.

"We're going to move now," he whispered. "The three of us will surround you. It should be clear, but we're not taking the chance. If something happens, look for cover and stay there, all right?"

It was not all right. Not by any stretch of her well-developed imagination was it all right. She stared at him as he pulled away. He didn't seem to notice how not all right she was, or maybe he didn't care. He lifted her under the elbow and maneuvered her into position. The other two took their places, and they moved out from behind the tree.

She thought they must look ridiculous—and an even bigger target than if they had walked on normally—but she didn't say so. That would require speaking, and her tongue felt thick and heavy and incapable of proper function, so she walked silently, following the pace set by her protection detail.

Rhydwyn and Gair were on her left, one slightly ahead of her and the other slightly behind. They carried swords on their hips, but they each had a bow, fitted with an arrow, in their hands. James was on her right, his head angled toward the road they had abandoned. His sword was out. He held it low in his right hand while his left stayed on her back. As scared as she was, she had to admire the man's strength. Those swords were damn heavy.

A twig snapping in the distance stopped them. All three men whirled around, weapons ready. Cate cringed, ducked, and covered her head as bravely as she could. No one moved.

"It's all right," James said finally. "Put your weapons down."

Cate straightened only after he lowered his sword. Gair and Rhydwyn lowered their weapons as well. James looked at the road and inclined his head as though acknowledging someone. Cate stepped around him to see.

A family stood on the road—father, mother, and two boys, all looking world-weary and half-starved. An ancient donkey attached to a small cart stood idly by. The two adults focused on her and dropped to their knees. The woman whispered something, and the boys dropped as well, the elder boy pulling down the younger.

The sight made Cate's eyes water. They thought she was Haleine. They were worn down and dejected. Their life was miserable, and *still*, they got on their knees for a woman they thought was their queen.

"James," she said, "you have to tell them I'm not—"

The sound of rapidly approaching riders interrupted her plea. The family lifted their heads as one and looked down the road.

"Run," the man said.

James was already moving, taking her with him.

"Wait," she gasped. "Wait, James, what about them?"

"Shut up," he hissed. "Do you want them to hear you?"

"No, but that family—"

"The soldiers aren't looking for them," James said. "They'll be all right."

They took cover in a copse of birch trees. She sat on the ground and leaned against the trunk of the largest tree. Rhydwyn and Gair were across from her, crouched and silent. James sat next to her, his head poised to listen as the horses came to a stop. Cate closed her eyes.

"You there," a man—a solider, she guessed—said. His voice carried clearly to their hiding spot. "We've reports of rebels in these parts. Have you come across anyone?"

"We've seen no one, lord," the man—the father—said.

Swords were drawn. Beside her, James tensed.

"You're sure of that?" the soldier asked.

"Aye, lord," the father answered.

Tell them, Cate thought. *Just tell them! Tell them we're in the goddamn trees. Tell them we went the other way. Tell them something.*

"Is that so?" the soldier said. "I saw you kneeling in the road when we came 'round that last bend. Seems odd."

"Giving thanks to our savior," the father said. "No time or place too odd for that."

Cate sank. What the hell had Haleine *done* for these people?

"Seen your savior in the trees, have you?" the soldier asked, his voice dripping with danger.

"We've come across no one on this road," the man said again, his voice firm and defiant.

"Please," James murmured.

Cate opened her eyes to look at him when the father screamed in pain. The woman and her sons wailed. Cate cried out, too, until James clapped his hand over her mouth.

"We're going to stop it," he breathed in her ear. "All right? We're going to stop it, but before we can, I need your word that you'll stay hidden and silent."

Leaves obscured the sky. By the looks of it, she could've been sitting in Boston Common. But things like this did not happen in Boston Common. Not for a long time, anyway.

"Cate!" James whispered harshly. "Do you promise?"

She nodded, and James dropped his hand. As the three men rushed out of the copse, she brought her knees to her chest and buried her face in her borrowed clothing. This would be the perfect opportunity to run away, but she couldn't make herself move, so she listened to them rush through the trees and brush to get to the road. The sounds of swords clashing and men dying followed.

She couldn't stay here. Wouldn't stay here. She'd get away. She'd find a way to get home. She'd do whatever she had to in order to get free of this. And she would, too. Just as soon as she persuaded her legs to start working again.

She was still hiding her head and plotting an escape when James returned. He touched her shoulder, and she nearly jumped out of her skin. As he apologized for scaring her, she stared at him and the layer of blood he wore like a second skin. She couldn't keep the horror off her face. He seemed to understand why and swiped at his face with the sleeve of his shirt. It didn't help.

"The blood's not mine," he said.

That did *not* make it okay. She looked away.

"Thank you for not running," he said.

Thank her legs for not moving because if she'd had any say at all in the matter, she'd already be three towns away.

He crouched beside her. "Cate, we have to leave. We can't linger."

She nodded. It made sense. She just couldn't convince her legs of that fact.

"Are you hurt?" he asked.

The blood wasn't hers, either. She shook her head.

"I'm going to pick you up," he said.

She shook her head again. She didn't want him to *touch* her. Picking her up was completely out of the question.

"Then get up on your own," James said, his voice sharper than before. "And do it now, or I will carry you because I can't leave you here, nor can we stay any longer."

She put her head in her hands. "Is he dead? The father?"

"Aye," James said.

"He died thinking he was protecting the queen."

"Aye."

She looked at James. "What did she do for these people?"

He paused. "Gave them hope," he said finally. "Come on."

She followed him out of the copse and back to the road. Though she had been perfectly aware of what James and the other two had been doing, it didn't prepare her for the sight of their handiwork. Her stomach lurched, and she stumbled, falling against a tree for support.

"Don't look," James said quietly.

There was no way not to look. It was everywhere. The bodies of six men littered the road. Their horses stood by, tethered to trees. Gair knelt, searching a corpse. It wasn't the first time she'd seen that done, but she still found it hard to watch. Looking away, she witnessed Rhydwyn dragging a body to the side of the road. That was worse, so she turned to see the body of the man who'd died to protect her lying in his family's cart, his legs hanging over the edge. Her eyes burned with tears, and she jerked away, only to find his family looking bloodied and shell-shocked. When they noticed her presence, the mother started to sink.

"No." James swiftly crossed the road and caught the woman's elbow. "She doesn't require it of you."

The bread and cider Cate had eaten what seemed like eons ago came up then, and she fell to her knees to purge in the undergrowth off the road. When she finished, she wiped her mouth on her cloak and sat in a miserable heap until James pulled her to her feet.

"Can you ride?" he asked.

She glanced at the road and saw it cleared of corpses. Blood had pooled there, and she watched Rhydwyn kick at the dirt to try and obscure it. Her stomach heaved again, and Cate turned her head.

"Cate?" James shook her. "Can you ride?"

"What?" she said.

"Come on." He led her to one of the dead men's horses. "Just don't fall off, aye?"

Don't fall off. She could do that. Ignoring James's offer of help, she stuck her foot in the stirrup and scrambled into the saddle. The dress made it awkward and uncomfortable, more so than sitting the unicorn's back had been, but she wasn't about to complain.

"Are we ready?" James asked, holding her horse's bridle.

They seemed to be. Rhydwyn had taken control of the donkey and the cart. One of the horses was tethered to the end. Gair sat in the saddle of another horse and held the reins to a third. The mother and her youngest son were mounted on one of the two remaining horses, while her eldest son, who couldn't have been more than ten, rode the last.

Cate felt another stab of guilt and shame. They were the ones who had lost someone—someone whose name they actually knew, someone they had loved. They were the ones who had seen it happen, knowing they would be next. She was the one who had cowered under the cover of a bunch of trees before puking in the bushes.

Big bad Cate. Shown up by a ten-year-old.

She leaned forward to claim the reins. James felt the motion and looked at her.

"I'm fine," she said. "I can ride."

James didn't let go of the bridle. Was he worried she would make a break for it and ride off into the sunset? If he thought about it long enough, would he realize why she couldn't—or wouldn't—do that? When his eyes flickered over to the boy on horseback, she knew he had.

He still didn't trust her, though. He called for Gair to bring the last horse to him and didn't release her horse's bridle until Gair had taken hold of it. James swung into the saddle. His horse protested, but James easily brought the animal under control.

"Let's get to camp," he said. To Cate, he added, "Ride in front of me, please."

Cate nodded and urged her horse forward.

⟞⟝⟞

They had burnt so much of the day that when nightfall came, they were nowhere near the rebel camp. The addition of the woman and her two children had slowed their pace drastically. There was nothing to be done but to bear it, for they were in no condition to be on their own. James had pushed them as hard as he could, thinking only to put as much distance as possible between them and the road on which the king's soldiers had died.

Though it could not be avoided, he did not favor the idea of spending the night in the forest without Faolan and Bearach to add to their protection, especially when Varro had not been among the six dead men. That meant there was at least one other group of soldiers prowling the forest paths. How would James properly defend everyone?

He should have made use of the damn tunnels, but as reluctant as he was to trust their safety, he was even more hesitant to show their existence to outsiders.

He called for them to stop and make a camp with the meager supplies given to them by Orla and those gleaned from the dead men. There was little comfort and less food, but at the very least they had water enough for the horses.

The woman sat with her sons, each of them wrapped in grief thicker than any blanket they possessed. She rocked them gently, hushing any errant sobs. Cate watched, her back against a tree. She didn't make a single sound. For the first time since her arrival, James was not concerned that she would run off. That family's sacrifice had anchored her to him—to them—for the time being. It would not last, but he would take advantage of it while he could.

He and Rhydwyn and Gair guarded the camp's small borders. Two would keep his back to the camp at all times, watching the black for any sign of danger, while the third was responsible for the souls within the perimeter. None of them slept, and the night passed without sight nor sound of another human.

The following morning, they silently shook off their exhaustion and prepared for another day's travel. They moved slower than the previous day, fatigue weighing them down, and when they had stopped for a midday's rest, James worried that another night would have to be spent outside of the camp.

A consultation with Gair left him reasonably assured that reaching camp before dark, or shortly thereafter, could be done, so as the sun sank in the sky, James let Gair lead them deeper into the thick and imposing Donasien Woods.

James rode at the back, focusing on Cate. She stared straight ahead, allowing her horse to plod along, following the horses in front of him. The brutality of what had happened on the road had shaken her deeply. Whatever the world in which she had been raised was like, it was not like this.

"You left the other men," a voice said, interrupting his thoughts.

James shook his head to clear it and saw the elder boy on his right. This was the first time he had spoken to James, or any of them, apart from his mother or brother. Considering the boy's age and what he had experienced, he rode exceedingly well.

"You dragged them off the road to the trees," the boy said.

"Aye," James said, "I did that."

"But not my father. You brought him with us. Why?"

James looked at the cart where they had put the man's body. "Your father deserves a proper burial, or at least as proper a burial as we can give him."

"But not the other men?"

"They murdered your father. Would you see them properly buried?"

"I think so."

"You're a better lad than most," James said. "You don't have to worry. They'll get their burial, but we won't be the ones to do it. They'll be seen to, I'm sure."

Someone would find their bodies eventually. Anyone with a working set of eyes would see a fight had happened on that road and that lives had been lost there. They had hidden the evidence as well as they could in the time James had been willing to give to the task, but it was only a matter of time before Varro knew where to start looking for the rebels.

"What's your name, lad?" James asked.

"Iestyn ab Ynyr. My mother is Llian, and my brother is Aodhan."

"I am sorry about your father, Iestyn," James said. "Soldiers killed my father, too, so I know it is no condolence to hear those words, but I am sorry I did not save him."

"Did you kill the men who killed your father?" Iestyn asked.

"Not yet," James said.

A whistle came through the trees—a signal that they had reached the outskirts of the camp. He waved to make sure the guards saw him, if they hadn't already.

"Join your mother, Iestyn," he said.

"What is it?" the boy asked.

James smiled and spurred his horse forward. "We're here."

As guards appeared on the path, he reigned in his mount alongside Cate's. "Put your hood up, please," he said to her. "You'll cause a commotion in camp that I'd rather avoid."

Cate complied without argument. She was retreating into herself. James could see it in the curve of her shoulders and the emptiness in her eyes. What would he have to do to bring her back out?

Gair had already gone through the barrier that hid the camp from human eyes. James dismounted and handed off the reins to one of the guards. He motioned to Llian and Iestyn to do the same.

"Follow Rhydwyn," he said. "I'm placing you in Hanah's care. She's our healer, and she will see you tended to. All of you."

Llian nodded. "Thank you," she said, her voice barely audible.

After they disappeared through the barrier, he turned to Cate, holding her mount's bridle. One of the other guards took the horse, and Cate looked at James.

"Go ahead," he said. "I'll be right behind you."

He wasn't sure if that would reassure her or only offer her an opportunity to mock him, but she merely nodded and followed the guard into the camp. James lingered a moment longer, scanning the forest before fading through the barrier himself.

When he appeared on the other side of the enchantment, both Ilya and Hanah waited to greet him. He nodded to them both but searched for Cate, finding her standing with Rhydwyn and Gair.

"What happened?" Ilya asked.

"We had some trouble." James gestured to the refugees from the road. "Hanah, I need you to care for these people."

"And you?" Hanah asked. "Do I need to care for you?"

James shook his head. "The blood's not mine."

"Whose blood is it?" Ilya asked, but James ignored her as he approached Rhydwyn and Gair.

"See that the horses are cared for, and the gear is safely stowed," he said. "Then get cleaned up, eat something, and rest. God knows you've earned it."

"Captain," Gair said, "you'll need—"

"I don't want to see you until morning, at least. *Late* morning," James said. "I mean it."

"Aye, Captain," Gair said, and walked away with his brother.

"Now will you tell me what happened?" Ilya asked.

"I told you." James placed his hand on Cate's back and steered her toward the tents. "We had some trouble."

Ilya fell into step with him. "Some trouble? You're covered in blood. You're all covered in blood."

"Not all of us."

"James."

"It's their blood," he said. "Not ours."

"Whose?" Ilya stepped in front of him. "Tell me what happened."

"Soldiers. There were soldiers in the forest," he said. "Faolan thinks Omur tracked him and sent men to run us to ground. Bearach and the two horses took arrows. Bearach should be fine. The horses are lost, but we found new ones."

"Where are Faolan and Bearach now?" Ilya asked. "Why aren't they with you?"

"They were running interference," James said. "They were trying to draw the soldiers away from us so we could get safely here. It worked for a time, but the soldiers came back, or another group found us—I don't know which—and I don't know where Faolan and Bearach are, but they'll turn up. Tell the sentries to keep alert. Varro's out there somewhere. He'll find those bodies sooner or later, and he'll know where to start looking."

"You left bodies on the road?"

"I left bodies on the side of the road," James said. "I couldn't take the time to do anything more."

"Are you all right?" Ilya asked. "Does Hanah need to see you?"

"I'm fine," he said. "What I need is a tent—a place for her. I need her out of sight."

Ilya glanced at Cate, who was staring at the ground, arms wrapped around herself as though she were cold.

"This way," Ilya said.

She led them through the camp, stopping at a tent in the center of activity. He ushered Cate inside and dropped his hand. Ilya lit a lantern, setting it on a table. James looked from the maps on its surface, to the single chair, to the row of baskets lining the back wall. This was Dana's tent, then.

Cate rotated unhurriedly, pushing back her hood and running her fingers through her hair. Upon seeing her face, Ilya inhaled sharply and looked at him in astonishment.

"It's not—she's not the queen," James said.

Cate acted as though she hadn't heard him. Ilya looked between him and Cate. It wasn't nearly enough explanation for Ilya—as James knew it wouldn't be—but he didn't want to talk about it in front of Cate. When her back was turned, he shook his head at Ilya. *Later*, he mouthed.

She nodded. "There are some things to which you should attend."

"Me? Isn't Dana—?"

Ilya shook her head. "We've not seen him."

James had to swallow his shock. Dana was really gone, then. Just disappeared into nothing. Why? How could he walk away from this—from them? Taking a deep breath, James exhaled slowly, then repeated the exercise. He had told Lucius that he didn't care where Dana had gone. He hadn't realized that he had been lying.

"Who sleeps in here?" he asked.

"No one sleeps here," Ilya said.

He didn't want to, either. The only things missing from the tent were Dana's personal belongings. Where might those have gone? Lost, as their owner had been?

"In the morning, Ilya," he said. "I'll tend to whatever you want in the morning. If it's waited this long, it'll keep until then. Please. Just give me the night."

She nodded. "Until morning."

She left, and James turned his back to Cate to prevent her from seeing his mounting frustration.

Where the hell had Dana gone?

chapter 10

There was no hill to be found in the hamlet known as Tamzin Hill, only a small settlement found deep in the forests north of Mahile. Dana didn't know how the village had received its name and doubted any of its residents did. They wouldn't be the sort to ask, either. The people of Tamzin Hill kept to themselves.

It had taken Dana the better part of three days to make his way here. He left the church in Piangi at the first sign of light and walked the road that would lead to Mahile. He saw no one and passed through one skeleton of a village after another. He thought Tamzin Hill, because of its seclusion, might have been spared, but when he came upon it, he found he had been wrong.

It had been, to the best of his recollection, a full day since his last swallow of ale, so it was with a sobering eye and aching head that he walked through the ruins. Maddox's soldiers had been particularly cruel to Tamzin Hill, leaving nothing behind but remnants of what had once been a thriving community. They hadn't even spared the holy house that had once stood at the village's edge. He stopped in front of the structure's charred remains.

It was here that Dana had been born and his mother had died. The women who lived there had taken in his mother, sick, dying, and in travail. As he had breathed his first, they later told him, she had breathed her last.

He stayed in the holy house after that. Had he been orphaned in a village like Enimode, finding a home for him would have been all too easy, but Tamzin Hill was an isolated place inhabited by private, untrusting folk. A pregnant woman, alone and unknown, sick and dying, was something none there wanted anything to do with. Neither was her infant son, so the sisters had cared for him. At least they had until the day he disappeared into the forest behind the holy house. He'd gotten lost, so turned around in the labyrinth of trees that he couldn't find his way back. He'd found Faolan instead.

What would he find now?

Dana walked through the embers of his first home to reach the small cemetery where the sisters had buried their own.

Buried his mother.

He had stopped asking the sisters about her years ago. They had no answers for him. She had told them she was called Alais but had offered nothing else. He had her coloring, from her hair to her skin. His eyes, the sisters had told him, likely came from his father, whoever that man might be.

The identity of the man who had given him life was something in which Dana had never put much consideration. Seoras was his father in every way that mattered. As he stood in front of his mother's grave, Dana spared a thought for both men. At least one of them would be disappointed to see what he had become.

He touched his mother's grave marker and moved away to stand amongst the other fire-singed mounds. There were new graves, too, so new as to not have a stone to mark whose remains lay beneath the earth. So many new graves. Too many. As the other villages he had passed through had only mass burials to offer their dead, Dana suspected Tamzin Hill was not as deserted as it appeared.

"You've come back to us," a woman's voice said.

It was one of the sisters who spoke. He recognized the voice but no longer recalled her name. He looked at her, thinking she reminded him of Sarai. Short, plump, and steel in her veins. She was not dressed as the women of her order traditionally did, wearing instead the clothing of a townswoman. In an earlier lifetime, she had tried to teach him to read and write. He managed the basics, but he never did grasp the finer points of the skill.

Enough for my purposes, he had told Haleine once.

He turned away at the thought of Haleine. The woman moved up beside him and stood so close their arms touched. She did not know, then. She did not know he had been named pariah.

"How long?" he asked. "How long has it been like this?"

She shook her head. "It's been just short of a week."

He didn't know why either Maddox or Omur would have an interest in so thoroughly destroying Tamzin Hill. Were they that restless and bloodthirsty? Or had they somehow learned of his ties to this village as well? Piala had betrayed his connection to Enimode, but how would Omur have learned about Tamzin Hill? No one but the sisters and Faolan knew of it. Not even James knew. Dana had never brought him here.

"Are you all that's left?" he asked.

"No," she said. "But there are a scant few of us here."

"Did the soldiers come because of me?"

"Does it matter why they came? Would it make the destruction any less senseless?"

"Enimode burned because of me."

"Enimode burned because of our king," she said. "As has the rest of this country."

"I tried to stop it," he murmured so softly he wasn't sure she would be able to hear him. He wasn't sure if he wanted her to hear him. "I tried to stop him."

"Have you given up?" she asked.

He supposed he had. Why else had he come?

"Are you here alone?" she asked, and he nodded. "But what of...There's no one?"

No, he had failed every last one of them. James, Aaron, Sarai, everyone in camp, everyone who had died fighting for him. They all had come to the rebellion because he had made them believe that something good could come from it. What a liar he turned out to be.

And then there were his sons—his *sons*—in the palace, guarded by one man after another who—for one reason or another—hated him, and would— for one reason or another—kill him on sight.

You'll never get near them, the maid had told him. *Not without the queen.*

And now Haleine was lost to him, too.

"Not anymore," he said.

His eyes started to water, but he made no move to hide the tears nor wipe them away. The sister nodded and reached for his hand.

"Come with me."

"Where?"

"Follow me, please."

She released him and left the cemetery without waiting to see if he followed. He stayed amongst the graves another moment, then turned to catch up to her.

"It's been quite some time since we saw you last, but I suppose you've been busy. Do you remember me?" she asked as they walked.

"You taught me my letters," Dana said. "Or you tried at least. I wasn't a very good student, I know."

"I also taught you your prayers."

Dana shrugged. "I remember the letters."

She smiled. "My name is Navlyn."

"Your garb has changed," Dana said.

Navlyn nodded. "It is sometimes best to keep one's true self hidden when strangers appear. The king's men are not the most devout souls you will find."

"Not a loss of faith, then?"

"No," she said. "Faith has been difficult to hold on to—I can't lie about that—but we maintain it. This land, and its people, will be saved in the end."

Had that not been his responsibility? Had he not been the one who was supposed to save the land, free the people? That hero's mantle was meant to be his, but he couldn't bring himself to throw it around his shoulders again.

It was better left where he had dropped it. Someone else could claim it. Someone who wouldn't bring it to ruin.

James, he thought. It would be James's to take now.

"I hope you're right," he said.

He followed Navlyn to a barn. The door opened before they reached it, and Navlyn stepped through. Dana hesitated, looking at the black and not liking it. Navlyn's face reappeared in the doorway, eyebrows raised in question.

"I shouldn't," he said.

"Why did you come here?"

"Just passing through."

"On your way to where?"

Navlyn knew him to be a liar. He could hear it in her voice. He looked at the road on which he now stood. He had come from the south, but if he continued on that road, he would turn west. West would bring him to Feond.

"Have you anywhere else to go?" she pressed when he did not answer.

He looked at the ground. "Not just now."

"Then you'll stay," she said. "For now."

Dana nodded and stepped toward the barn. "For now."

<hr />

The next letter from Lira arrived mere days following Zoltano's return. Revelin had left his chambers after another night of bad dreaming and insufficient sleep and made his way to the library to discover what Darragh had waiting for him, only to find Zoltano behind their father's desk.

"Letter for you, brother," Zoltano said.

Revelin looked at the opened parchment in Zoltano's hand. "Who has sent this letter?"

Part of him wished to hear Haleine's name on his brother's lips. Part of him wanted desperately to read a letter written in her hand asking him to forgive and forget what she had previously written. Part of him wanted this, even though he could not believe Haleine would willingly put quill to parchment for his benefit. Had she not made that clear in her last letter? The Coileáin obligation to his family was to be buried the same day as her father. No, the letter would not be from Haleine.

"Maddox's advisor," Zoltano said. "Apparently, your girl's gone missing."

Haleine? Missing? Revelin's step faltered. "My girl?"

"Don't play the idiot, Revelin. It's never suited you."

"What happened?"

Zoltano shrugged and held out the parchment. "Taken by the rebels."

Taken by her lover. Revelin took the parchment and scanned it. Omur had offered few details. The circumstances behind her disappearance were unclear, but what was certain was that she had sustained some sort of injury. The blood, Omur had written. There was so much blood that they presumed her dead.

Good God. Revelin sat.

"I heard she was fucking the rebel leader," Zoltano said. "Do you suppose that's what she's doing now?"

"He says she was hurt," Revelin snapped. "Presumed dead."

"He says he thinks she was hurt," Zoltano said. "But as she's gone and disappeared, how are we to know? Maybe they stuck a pig or a servant to make it appear as though she were so grievously injured. They'd want to be alone, I'd think. Wouldn't want anyone coming to look for them, would they?"

Revelin set the letter aside. "What are you doing here?"

"Reading your letters primarily," Zoltano said. "You know, I believe some of the noblemen actually do think the sun rises out of your ass."

"What are you doing here?"

"I told you I came for my crown. I came for my kingdom," Zoltano said. "I can't very well regain what you've stolen from me by lazing around my bedchamber."

"I have stolen nothing."

"You may call it what you like. I do not care. It does not change what you have done."

"And what is that?"

"You gave away something that did not belong to you, and now I want it back."

Quatara? He meant to go after Quatara? Revelin recalled a conversation with Darian on the subject. *We will prepare for his coming*, Darian had told him. But they never had.

"You will not use the crown's men for this," Revelin said.

"My crown, my men."

"It is not your crown. Nor are they your men."

"This is rather tiresome, Revelin," Zoltano said. "It is my crown, and they are my men. If you like, you can throw a tantrum and hold your breath until you're blue in the face, but simply saying I am not your king does not make it so."

"What need have you for such a conquest?" Revelin asked. "Quatara was always more trouble to hold on to than it was worth. We are stronger without it."

"I disagree. And I want it." Zoltano shrugged. "For my bride."

"You are not married."

"But I intend to be. Now that I am king—"

"You are not king."

"If only wishing made it so," Zoltano said. "She is a queen now, Revelin. You can't expect me to enter into our union a beggar."

"You are far from that, and I doubt the queen of Feond would be much impressed by the gift of a war-scarred country."

Zoltano smiled. "Fine. I don't want it for my bride. I want it for myself. Quatara should have been mine years ago, but our father refused to take it away from his damned lap dog. Or do you forget?"

Revelin thought about how Darian would have reacted to being called a lap dog. It almost made him smile. "No. I do not forget."

"I could have taken it from him. From them."

"You would have lost."

Zoltano nodded. "So I recall you telling me. Did you come on your own to protect me? Or had Father sent you to bring me to heel?"

"You know which."

"I suppose I do," Zoltano said. "I watched you afterward in that garden with your whore. Did you know that?"

No, he had not known that. Revelin could well remember the day he had stood in the snow with Haleine. It was a stolen moment. All they ever had were stolen moments.

"She is not a whore," he said.

"I think Maddox might have a thing or two to say about that." Zoltano leaned back in the chair and put his hands behind his head. "Tell me, Revelin, do you think she pushes away her lover the way she did you that day?"

Revelin stood, wanting nothing more in that moment than to hurt his brother. He took a single step toward the desk but no more. Restraint. He needed to demonstrate restraint.

"Did I upset you? I didn't mean to," Zoltano said, his smile supporting his disingenuous tone. "Why are you doing this, Revelin? You won't last. You're holding on by the skin of your teeth as it is. You don't sleep, you don't eat—"

"How would you know?"

Zoltano sighed. "They're called spies, Revelin. Did Darian teach you nothing?"

"He taught me how to handle you," Revelin said.

Did you stop him? Haleine had asked him all those years ago.

Do I ever? he had responded, wanting so very much to lose himself in her.

Every time.

There will be a day when I cannot, he had confessed.

Revelin looked at Zoltano. Had that day arrived at last?

"Did he?" Zoltano said. "When do you intend to use what you have learned?"

Revelin didn't answer. He sank back into his chair and picked up the letter from Maddox's advisor. He crushed it into a ball and dropped it on the floor.

"I will stop you," Revelin said.

Zoltano smiled and straightened. "I think we've discussed this before."

"And we shall surely discuss this again," Revelin said. "I will stop you if you cannot stop yourself."

"But think of Mother," Zoltano said. "She will be heartbroken should her sons fight."

"I would not count on that," Revelin said. "She knows this country would have been better served if you had been drowned at birth."

Zoltano shot to his feet and, with a mighty heave and anger-fueled groan, flipped the massive desk on its side. "You do not say such things to the king!" he shouted.

Revelin smiled, every bit as calm as Zoltano was not. "You are not the king."

Zoltano laughed, the dangerous sound far removed from amusement. "Look who thinks he knows how to play."

Revelin shook his head. "I do not play."

"Neither do I," Zoltano sneered.

His brother stalked forward, fists at his side. Revelin rose, preparing to defend himself, but before Zoltano could land a single blow, Darragh burst through the library doors and rushed toward them. Zoltano backed away as Darragh dropped to his knees before Revelin and bowed his head.

"My lords," Darragh gasped.

"What is it?" Revelin asked.

Darragh lifted his head. "Your mother."

Despite their exhaustion, James doubted either he or Cate had slept well during the night. After Ilya had left, Cate spurned his attempts to see to her comfort and ended up huddling in a corner of the tent as far away from him as she could get. Leaving her be, James had stripped himself of weapons and stretched out across the tent's entrance, too tired to tend to anything else.

Cate must have fallen asleep at some point because she started screaming, just as she had in Orla's stable. He located the lantern and lit it before calmly shaking her from the dream. She had the same reaction to him as before—

fear, followed by recognition and withdrawal—and moved to a different corner of the tent. He sat in the opposite corner, and together they watched the dark give way to light.

Ilya appeared shortly after the sun, bringing with her two bowls of Hanah's porridge. His stomach rumbled at the thought of proper food; his last meal had been the bread and cheese provided by Orla. Cate had later purged that meal in some roadside brush, but if she was at all aware of, or interested in, what Ilya had brought, she didn't show it.

Placing the bowls on the table, Ilya looked him over and sighed. She went to the back of the tent, waving Cate out of her path, and retrieved a basin and jug of water. She put those on the table as well before returning to dig through the baskets. Shirts and trousers in a variety of sizes and colors appeared and disappeared until she found what she desired.

"I could have done this on my own," he said, taking the bundle she shoved against his chest.

"Yet, you didn't," she said. "Wash your face, change your shirt. Your breeches, too. There are things for you to do, and it'll go better if you don't look as though you've recently bathed in blood."

"It's not that bad," he said, dumping the clothing onto the chair.

"It's bad enough," Ilya countered. "Really, James, you should have—"

"There was barely enough water for the horses," he interrupted. "I wasn't about to waste any of it so that I could have a bath."

"Do it now, then," she said. "But quickly, aye?"

James nodded. "Aye. Give me a moment."

After Ilya departed, he cleared the table and poured some water into the basin before turning to Cate. She sat on the ground, watching him impassively and rubbing her wrists. Did they still have Sarai's salve? If not, perhaps Hanah had something that could help. He would have to ask.

"I'm going to do this here," he said in way of apology, gesturing to the basin.

Cate looked disinterested. "Well, if I see something new, I'll be sure to throw a dollar at it."

"A dollar?"

"Fine. Two dollars," she said. "But if you're expecting any more than that, you'd better start shaking your money maker."

"What?"

Cate sighed. "Take your bath, Boy Wonder. I'll try to contain my excitement."

Her tone was irritating and her words maddening nonsense, but at least she had spoken to him. That had to be progress.

James stripped to his braies and washed in the small basin. Dressing quickly, he buckled his sword belt around his waist and looked at Cate.

"I have to go—" he said.

"Be the leader?"

"I'm not the leader."

"Maybe you don't know what that word means."

"I know what it means," he said. "I won't be long. You can stay here."

"Oh, can I? Can I really?"

He gave her a warning look she didn't notice. "I'll have someone bring you—"

"I don't need anything."

"Fine," he said and left.

Rhydwyn and Gair waited with Ilya outside the tent. Their presence was hardly a surprise, but James still shook his head. At least they had washed and changed.

"Make sure Cate stays where she is," he instructed. "If she asks for something that isn't a means of escape, see that she gets it, but don't abandon your posts."

"Aye, Captain," Gair said, and Rhydwyn nodded.

James looked at Ilya. "Well?"

Ilya smiled and gestured to her right. As he passed, he gave her a warning look as well, but she only laughed as she fell into step with him.

"So, Cate," she said. "Care to tell me who she is, or where she came from, or why exactly she's the spitting image of the queen?"

He didn't. "Has there been any sign of Faolan or Bearach?"

"None that's been reported to me," Ilya said. "Are you going to ignore my question?"

For as long as he could. "When was the last time you saw Dana?"

Ilya shrugged. "When you went to fetch the queen. How long has it been since you last saw him?"

"Six days? A week now? Longer? I don't know," James said. "Faolan sent me to find Cate. I was gone four days, and when I came back, Dana was gone. Faolan didn't say where. I'm not sure he even knows."

"Shall I send people to look?"

"Look where? If he's not here and he's not at the queen's side, I don't know where he would be. We'll have to make do without him."

"All right," Ilya said. "Now tell me about Cate. Who is she, and why did Faolan send you to find her?"

James sighed. "Ilya, I—"

"I'll only keep asking," she said. "Best get it over with."

Bloody hell. He sighed again. "She's the queen's sister, but I don't recommend saying that to her unless you want something heavy thrown at your head."

"Where did she come from?"

"You wouldn't believe me if I told you."

"Four days' journey," Ilya mused. "You could have covered quite a distance."

"You have no idea."

"Going out from Enimode, you could have—"

"Ilya," he said. "Where I went? You won't find it on any map."

"What does that mean?"

"I don't know," he admitted. To distract her, he added, "Lucius looked good."

Ilya nodded. "He looks better. He still has some recovering to do, Hanah says, but he insisted upon going to Enimode. He's fond of the queen. He'll look after her well."

"No one better," James said. "What of the other wounded?"

"We found families in villages to care for those who couldn't travel. When they're well, they'll rejoin us."

"Defenses?"

"Lorcan and Luisiúil saw to that," she said. "Our supplies are holding reasonably well, all things considered. The arrow stores were rather depleted, but I've got people making more."

"Then what—?"

"Hostages."

Hostages. James honestly had forgotten about them. The battle in which they had been acquired felt as though it had happened years ago.

"They're still here," he said.

"Aye."

"Where are they?"

Ilya pointed. "This way."

"What have you been doing with them?" James asked.

"We've treated their wounds, kept them alive. We've tried to get information from them, but I don't think there's anything to get."

They were foot soldiers, likely. They were men who went where they were told to go and killed who they were told to kill. He wasn't surprised they knew nothing, but neither did he know what he was supposed to do with them.

"Have they a leader amongst them?" he asked.

"The one in the center seems to have taken charge."

James nodded. "Good. Let's go."

The prisoners sat in a line on the ground, each partaking in a portion of porridge. James was annoyed to see them eating an entire meal when he had been forced to leave his behind.

"Are they worth anything?" he asked.

The man Ilya had indicated as their leader cocked his head and appraised James carefully. The others snuck looks at him before turning their attention to their bowls.

"Don't let Hanah hear you say that," Ilya warned.

"Right. All life's bloody sacred. Well, are you?" James nudged the leader with his boot. "Are you worth anything?"

"I was," the man answered calmly. He set his bowl on the ground beside him. "Then your leader cut off my leader's head."

"What of Haraszty, your queen?"

"If my queen knows any of us are here, I would be surprised."

"Didn't she send you here?"

"I came at the behest of my lord, who came at the behest of the queen's second son."

James thought he had done well to remember the queen of Tanuba's name, but of her second son, he had no knowledge. He glanced at Ilya.

"Revelin," she said.

The name meant nothing to him, but James nodded. "Will Revelin not be interested in your safe return?"

"I doubt it. Men like us are expendable to men like him."

"The answer is no, then," James said. "No, you're not worth anything."

"I suppose that would be your decision, but I hear life is sacred. All life."

"Shall I say those words over the graves of the men and women you killed?"

"Because you've never killed a man?"

"Day's young yet," James said, turning to leave.

"You're undecided what to do with us, yet you're collecting more prisoners," the man called.

James stopped.

"I saw you leading my lord's daughter," the man said. "Your queen."

An unexpected protective surge rushed through James, and he turned to better contemplate the man at his feet. He had noticed Cate, hooded and huddled, in the failing light of day. James didn't care for that. He looked down the line of men. Their leader was the only one to meet his gaze.

"She's not the queen," James said and walked away.

"But she's a prisoner?" Ilya asked when she caught up to him. "Our prisoner?"

"For now," James said. "Get rid of them."

"Get rid of them?"

"If there was anything to be had from them, you would've gotten it by now, so get rid of them. We don't need to keep feeding or guarding them, so blindfold them or drug them, and lose them in the woods a long way from here. Let them fend for themselves."

Ilya nodded. "If that's what you want."

"Except their leader," James added. "Does he have a name?"

"Idwal Kai."

"Keep him," James said. "We'll have to put a guard on him for now, but I'll speak to Faolan when he returns. If his wall can keep people out, it can keep someone in."

"Why are we—?"

"I don't know," James said. "I think there may be a use for him yet."

And the man had recognized Cate. He thought he had seen the queen, but James didn't want to release him with that knowledge. Mayhap it wouldn't matter, as Omur was already on their trail. How was he to know?

Damn Dana. Damn Faolan. Damn them all.

"All right," Ilya said. "Is the lass really our prisoner?"

James shrugged. "I don't know. What I do know is that she's tried to run a good many times already, and I'm certain she'll try again. Make it known throughout camp that should anyone—*anyone*—see her walking about unescorted, they become her shadow, and they find someone to tell either you or me because we can't afford to lose her."

"I'll take care of it."

"I'd also warn them not to touch her if they don't have to, nor get close enough to be touched."

"Why?" Ilya asked.

James thought of Rhydwyn and Eion on the floor of the cottage, and the man in the alley with his broken nose. He smiled in spite of himself and shook his head.

"Let's just say you'll like her," he said.

———※———

The dream had been of James and Rhydwyn and Gair. The dream had been of their battle against six agents of an unknown enemy, six men whose bodies and blood Cate had seen on a forest path a day earlier. Before she had only witnessed the aftermath, but now she stood in the middle of it.

James and the other two used the element of surprise to take out two of the riders with the bows Rhydwyn and Gair carried. Swords came next, and Cate found herself ducking as steel sliced through the air. Stumbling, she fell onto a blade. Her mouth dropped open, expecting to scream in pain, but there was no sound, nor any feeling at all, as the sword passed through her as though she were a hologram.

She looked in horror at her undamaged torso and surveyed the skirmish. She fell to her knees, curling inward to make herself smaller. Turning her head, she saw the mother, clutching the donkey's tether, while her two children crouched in the shelter of the cart. The youngest wailed. The elder boy looked directly at Cate.

"Emotion is what hangs you in the end," he said.

Then, he transformed from a child to the yellow-eyed hellhound of her earlier nightmares. It threw itself at her, as it had in her other dreams. Its jaws were closing around her throat when James shook her awake.

She hoped it wasn't the start of an alarming trend. She could tell from the look on his face that James shared a similar desire. He wanted to know what was wrong with her. She kind of wanted to know that, too.

But they didn't talk about it. They didn't talk about anything. They'd spent the rest of the night sitting and staring, not talking and not sleeping. He wouldn't sleep if she didn't, and she sure as hell wasn't going to sleep.

But not because she wasn't tired. She was beyond exhausted, but too afraid to sleep. The nightmares were too vivid, too realistic, just too goddamn scary. She didn't want to experience them anymore.

But, *damn*, she was worn out. Her nerves were frayed—hell, her nerves were raw. She was on edge. Or over the edge, hanging on by her once nicely manicured nails. Sarcasm was part of her sparkling personality the way water was a part of the human body, but when combined with all the rest, the resulting side effect made her mean. Especially mean. *Exceptionally* mean. That part didn't worry her so much. She didn't care how badly James's feelings were hurt. James would deal with it. He had to.

What did concern her was the anxiety-induced claustrophobia she seemed to be experiencing. She didn't know why she should start panicking now—she was no worse off than she'd been at any other point since her kidnapping—but whatever the reason, the calm was crashing down.

The tent wasn't big enough. It was better now that she was alone, but the canvas felt like it was shrinking, and she couldn't breathe. She needed to get out and get away.

Pushing through the flap, she barreled head-on into Rhydwyn. He caught her, holding her arms to either steady her or to keep her from running away. Although no words left his lips, his eyes questioned her welfare. She hated the way he never said a damn word and broke free to retreat to the tent.

She still couldn't breathe, so she sat in the chair, lowered her head, and concentrated on changing that. In and out, in and out. One breath at a time. That's all she had to worry about. The trick was to keep breathing.

It took a while for her breathing to return to normal, but she currently seemed to have nothing but time. Time and anxiety. When the worst of her panic had passed, she sat up and looked around the tent, not focusing on the walls. Plenty of other things to check out. She didn't have to worry about the walls at all.

Looking at the table, she wrinkled her nose at the basin containing the remnants of James's bathwater. How nice of him to leave it behind. She couldn't hold it against him, though. He had only been in a hurry to get as far away from her as he possibly could. Nothing wrong with that.

On the opposite edge were the two bowls the warrior princess had brought in. At the time, Cate thought she could smell food, actual hot food, but had been determined not to look at either Xena or James. But now that she was all alone, she could be as interested as she wanted in the prospect of food.

It reminded her of Cream of Wheat. She held a bowl to her nose. It didn't have much aroma to it, but as it was medieval refugee camp cooking, she was probably fortunate it wasn't a selection of edible roots and leaves. It wasn't hot, more lukewarm, but her stomach wouldn't mind. Combining the contents of both bowls, she drank. It was tasteless, but filled her just the same. It didn't do much for her mood, but she suspected nothing—with the exception of a one-way ticket back to Boston—would do anything for that.

The reality of that thought made her sigh. This was supposed to be when she plotted an escape, but she didn't have it in her. She'd made plans and formed strategies that had flown right out the window the very second they were needed or challenged. James may not have understood her reaction to things, but neither did she. She was supposed to be stronger than this. More capable. She was supposed to kick ass and take names, but all she felt like doing was huddling in the corner of her small canvas prison and having a good long cry.

But crying was still not an option.

She would have to do something. Anything. Who cared if she didn't have a plan? She could make it up as she went along because it didn't matter what she did. If she was doing something, she wouldn't be huddling in a corner crying her eyes out—and anything would be better than that. Almost anything.

Perhaps it was time to revisit her earlier strategy—the one where she would wait them out—but with one minor addition.

Make them rue the day they decided to kidnap her.

She could be difficult. There were people who would claim that being so was her default setting. James was likely one of them by now. What would he do if she turned up the volume on that? Forget eleven, she'd go all the way to twelve.

Having a plan—as wanting as it was—fueled her, and it was with determination that she stood, grabbed the basin, and stuck her head out of the tent. Rhydwyn was still there.

"Hey, Rosencrantz. Where's Guildenstern?" she said. Rhydwyn looked at her blankly. She smiled and offered him the bowl. "Find a place to dump this, would you? Maybe rinse it out before you bring it back?"

Rhydwyn took the bowl, and she slipped back inside. She stood in the center of the tent and counted to sixty before looking out again. Rhydwyn hadn't moved. The bowl, however, had gone missing. She looked at his empty hands, then his expectant face.

"Well played," she said, and withdrew once more.

Maybe she could crawl out the back. She went to the opposite end of the tent and moved the baskets out of the way. When a suitable space was clear, she dropped on her stomach and lifted the bottom of the canvas to crawl out. She'd freed her head and shoulders when a voice stopped her.

"Looking for something?"

Gair. Of course. She looked at him. "Did James tell you to keep me in here?"

Gair nodded.

"Do you always do what he tells you?" she asked next, even though she was already too well aware of the answer.

Gair nodded then, too, and Cate crawled back inside the tent, thinking of several new and unflattering names for James.

A few minutes later, Rhydwyn came inside long enough to hand her a clean basin. Setting it on the table, she looked at the jug James had left on the ground. Guess she could wash, too.

She poured water into the basin, undressed, and washed. There were no towels, so she air-dried while poking around in the baskets. Finding clothing, she replaced her dress with woolen leggings, a linen shirt, and a leather vest. She found a belt, too, and cinched it around her waist. The ensemble was slightly too large, but she preferred it to the dress.

Afterward, she wandered around the tent, examining everything she could find. Sadly, there were no weapons. There wasn't much of anything, apart from basic supplies with which she could do nothing useful, so she went back to the table and started leafing through the layers of parchment.

One sheet looked like a list of names. Names of what, she had no idea, but she was pleased to see she could more or less read the words. She exchanged the list for a map. In the corner was written the word 'Eluned.' It might have been a city name because the map itself reminded her of an old map of London. She put it down and reached for the next one. It seemed to be a map of the entire country. What had Faolan and Haleine called it? Lira? Eluned was on it, as well as Enimode. There were four named forested areas: Aerona, Piangi, Donasien, and Brandubh. Not that she had any idea in which one she was currently being held hostage. Details.

In one corner of the parchment was a symbol. She would have called it a Celtic knot if she thought Celtic was a thing around here. Tracing the pattern with her index finger, she stopped when she remembered two pages in a notebook on which she had drawn the day her mother died. She had sketched this knot. The drawing on the map was more precise, but she was certain it was the same damn design. Her stomach clenched.

Coincidence? She thought not.

Someone outside shouted. Startled, she jerked and dropped the map on the ground. People shouted back, but the noise died down and no one came near the tent. She bent to retrieve the map, but froze as soon as she laid eyes on it. After a minute, she picked up the parchment but didn't stop staring.

She was still staring, still trying to figure out how she was seeing what she was seeing, when James returned.

"You changed your clothing," he said.

He sounded surprised. Since his surprise couldn't possibly be greater than hers, she ignored him.

"What are you looking at?" he asked.

She turned it to let him see.

"Trying to find somewhere else to run?" he asked. When she didn't respond, he added, "You're holding it wrong, you know."

She did know. The lettering was all sideways now, as were the little drawings meant to be trees and mountains and cities.

"This is a map of England," she said. "Kind of."

"Lira," James corrected. "With Feond, there, on the other side of the mountains."

She turned the map so that the lettering was right-side up. "*This* is a map of Lira and whatever you said after that."

"Feond."

"Whatever." She turned the map again. "But this? This is a map of England. And Wales and Scotland."

"I don't—what?" James looked at her. "I don't understand what you're saying."

Cate laughed. "*I* don't understand what I'm saying. I don't understand how it is that I'm seeing this map, this map that I've seen before—or at least something like it—except where I come from, the orientation is different, and the country names are different, but—"

"What are you saying?"

"James ap Seoras," she said. "You remember?"

"My name? Aye, I remember that."

"No, no, I asked you—I asked if you were Welsh because your surname is, or was, anyway, and look!" She pointed to Enimode. "Here's your village located where Wales is, or at least would be, if we were somewhere where things made sense."

"That place certainly isn't this tent." James took the map and scrutinized it. He held it both ways and shrugged. "I don't see it."

She snatched the parchment from his hand. "Of course you don't see it. Why would you see it? You don't know what England is, or Wales, or any of it. You're only aware of the meaningless ravings of the lunatic woman standing in front of you."

"I can't argue with that."

"Where's the winged monkey?"

"The winged monkey?" James considered this. "Do you mean Faolan?"

"Yes, Faolan. Do you have another winged monkey? Wait...do you? Do you have another winged monkey? Like, an actual monkey with wings? I guess I can't put it past you to have something like that floating around somewhere, can I? You've got unicorns and a pegasus, so a winged monkey isn't all that crazy. Kind of pedestrian, I'd say."

"I don't—I don't know where Faolan is," James said, "or even if he's returned yet, but if you want to speak with him, I'll send someone to try to find him."

"He knows," she said. "He can explain this."

"I wouldn't count on that."

"You think he doesn't know?"

"Oh, I'm sure he does," James said. "I don't think there's much he doesn't know."

"Then why—?"

"He guards information more closely than anything. He won't say a word unless he stands to gain from it."

"He's still trying to gain me, isn't he?"

James was suddenly very still, looking as though he didn't dare hope she had just said what he had heard her say. Or maybe he was boggling over the fact that she had said it because of a map. She could have told him about the knot, too, but that felt like too personal a thing to share, so she kept quiet and waited him out. Finally, he nodded and stuck his head outside the tent.

"Rhydwyn," he said, "send someone to find out if Faolan's returned. I'd like to talk to him."

"Aye, Captain."

Cate laughed. James looked at her, his eyebrow raised.

"Those are the first words I think I've heard him speak. Also, he called you 'captain.' It tickles me somewhat," she said. "I know you're the leader and all, but you don't seem the type to put a lot of store in titles or ranks or anything like that."

James shrugged. "Rhydwyn has always called me that. I asked him not to once, and do you know what he said?"

"Aye, Captain?"

James nodded. "Aye."

"Well, I promise never to call you that," Cate said. "Unless I'm following it with hook, crunch, kangaroo, or tightpants."

"Captain Tightpants?"

She shrugged. "Just making an observation."

James looked down at himself. "What about 'asshole'?"

"Captain Asshole? No." She shook her head. "Admiral Asshole, maybe. I do like alliteration an awful lot."

"Well...good, then." James let out a huff of laughter, as though he couldn't decide whether to be amused or annoyed by her. "Even if he is in camp, Faolan will likely be a while in coming. Now that he knows—"

"I get it," she said. "He's kind of a bastard, that one."

"You have no idea."

"But I'm getting one."

"I suppose you are," James said. "While we wait, would you like to eat, or maybe like the chance to bathe more properly?"

"Bathe? You mean, like, a bath?" she asked, and James shrugged again. "Surely you jest."

"Why would I jest about that?"

"Because you are both cruel and sadistic."

"Cruel and sadistic?" he echoed. "If you think that I am cruel and sadistic—"

"Which I do."

"—then it is a sheltered life you have led indeed," he finished.

"You know, you're right," she said. "I *did* lead a sheltered life. Right up until the moment you kidnapped me and dragged me back here to the dark ages."

"I carried you," he said. "Never dragged."

"Oh, we are so not arguing semantics right now."

"I don't know what that means."

"That means as the indignant kidnapping victim, if I want to say dragged, I say dragged."

"Brilliant. Say whatever you want. Now, do you want the bloody bath or not?"

"Is there soap?"

"Soap? Where do you think you are? The bloody palace?"

"Okay, you have a tiny, talking pegasus who pulls more faces than Jim Carrey, and you're acting like me asking for soap is outlandish?"

"We're in the middle of a forest."

"Yet you're offering me a bath."

"A bath, aye," he said, "in a pond."

"A pond? Well, I guess that answers the hot water question."

"Bloody nobility," James seethed.

"Bloody peasants."

"Bloody peasants?"

"Bloody nobility?"

"You are a member of the nobility," James said.

"And you are a member of the peasantry," Cate returned. "Not a very popular one, either. At least not outside these woods. Whichever woods these are. Hey, which woods are these?"

James looked at the map she'd left on the table. "I think I preferred it when you weren't speaking to me."

"No, you didn't."

He moved away. "Because you know me so well."

She shrugged. "I don't really know anything about you. But I do know that."

"What do you want to know?"

"How I get out of here," she said. "How I get home."

James nodded. "Something we have in common, that."

Cate was quiet. She didn't like it when he said things like that. There was no trace of a lie. No wisp of deceit. Just the inkling of shame she felt because she didn't want to get involved.

"How do I know you're the white hats?" she asked.

"The what?"

"How do I know you're not the villains? How do I know you haven't done worse than—"

"Than what? Than what was done to Enimode? Than what was done to that family on the road?"

"I'm not saying you don't have a strong case. I'm just asking how I know. How do I trust you?"

"I don't know."

"You kidnapped me, and you've kept me here against my will, thrown me around, tied me up," she said. "You've done all these things that would suggest you are, in fact, not the good guys, but you killed a man for me—"

"Because of you."

"You saved those kids—"

"Kids?"

"Children," she said. "The tiny versions of adults you killed six hulking monsters to protect? You saved those boys, and I don't understand. I don't get it. You kill yourself to protect your men, and you kill yourself to protect those kids, and you bring me here so I can stop the killing or whatever, and you kick me around like some unwanted pest of a puppy, and it doesn't seem like how you should treat your chosen one."

"My what?"

"The chosen one," Cate said. "I'm, like, your freaking chosen one."

"My freaking chosen one? What does that mean?"

"Your brother told me you and your My Little Pony kidnapped me so I could—I don't even know what—stop the absolute insanity that is this universe. Is that true?"

"Possibly."

"What led you to me?" she asked. "Some sort of cryptic, ancient prophecy?"

"There's a prophecy, aye."

"Okay," she said. "That makes me your chosen one."

James snorted. "Hardly."

"What does that make me, then? The one you'll settle for in a pinch?"

This time he shrugged. "That sounds more accurate."

"Well, that's terrific. I'm incredibly flattered," she said. "Tell me, Boy Wonder, how am I supposed to go about saving the world? I know I have an impressive command of sarcasm, but it's more of a passive power than anything else."

"I've noticed."

"You're not too bad yourself, cowboy."

"Cowboy?"

Cate shrugged. "Did you bring me here to help stop your—I don't know—what do you call it? Your war?"

"Aye."

"What made you think I would ever give a damn about your war?"

James shook his head. "Thought there might be some humanity somewhere inside you," he said, "if we could only just find it."

"Kind of stupid of you."

"I see that now."

"Then let me go! Let me leave! You can keep me here as long as you want, but you won't be able to Patty Hearst me," she said. "I'm sorry, but that won't happen."

"How could I be trying to Patty Hearst you? I don't even know what that means."

"It means you're on your own for the big heist, cowboy, because as enticing as your proposal is, I think I'll pass."

"Pass?"

"Yes, as in me not being interested in helping you," she said. "But don't lose hope yet. Last I heard, Frodo was in the Grey Havens and therefore unreachable, but you could try Harry Potter. And if he's not around or interested, you should look up the Pevensie children. I hear those kids come with good Christian values."

"What?"

"Prim and proper young ladies with a healthy fear of lipstick are probably right up your alley," Cate said.

James stared at her, his mouth gaping. "How is it we speak the same language, yet I never understand a bloody word you're saying?"

Cate shrugged. "Just one of those things, I guess."

"Are you two finished?" Faolan asked. "Or should I come back later?"

They both looked at the pegasus hovering inside the tent.

"I heard you were looking for me," Faolan said.

"Did Bearach make it back with you?" James asked.

"Yes, he's fine," Faolan said. "Ilya told me you had some trouble."

"Yeah, trouble," Cate said. "With a capital T that rhymes with 'me,' and that stands for 'answer my damn questions.'"

"What?" Faolan said.

She snatched the map off the table and held it out to the pegasus. "Explain this."

"It's a map." Faolan's head tilted. "By the way, you're holding it wrong."

"I know it's a map."

"Then why did you ask?"

"I recognize this map," she said. "Why?"

"Have you seen it before?"

"I will shove this thing down your little throat," Cate said. "Don't you think I won't."

James stepped in between them. "Cate, that's not helping."

"*He's* not helping," she said. "Are you seriously defending him after we spent all this time talking about what a manipulative little bastard he is?"

James glanced at the pegasus.

"Do you think you're the first to have that conversation?" Faolan said.

"Okay, look." Cate spread the parchment on the table. "This map is wrong. It's just—it's wrong. If I'm in another place, another...*whatever*, I shouldn't be looking at this map. It doesn't make sense."

"The map itself doesn't make sense?" Faolan asked. "I assure you, it's quite accurate."

"I know. I know, right?" Cate said. "It's crazy accurate. Only it isn't."

Faolan looked at James.

James shrugged. "I didn't understand, either."

"This map?" Cate said. "It exists in my world, too. But that's not right, right? I mean—I don't know what I mean."

"At least we all agree on that," James muttered.

She ran her hand over the Celtic-esque design in the corner. "And this knot," she said softly.

"Have you seen that before?" Faolan asked.

His tone was irritatingly polite. She touched the drawing again and shook her head. "I just—I just wondered what, if anything, it meant. If it stood for something."

"Oh," Faolan said, "I wouldn't know about that."

The hell he wouldn't. "I will use this map as a fly swatter and take you down," she said.

"I'm not sure what that means, but it doesn't sound good," Faolan said. "Maybe I should go."

Faolan shook out his wings and flew toward the exit. Shocked, Cate looked at the map, then back at him. What the hell?

"Specifics," she blurted before he could leave. "I am asking you for the specifics."

Faolan returned to the table. "Why didn't you say so in the first place? Let's talk."

chapter 11

"Your name is Mireille Coileáin," the pegasus started.

Her name was Catherine Cole. Her name was Cate, but she bit her tongue to keep from speaking. She'd never get to the truth if she interrupted. There was the distinct possibility that she'd never get to the truth anyway, but it would be better if she let Faolan go on unimpeded. But her name was Cate. Mireille was just a middle name—a middle name no one but her mother had ever used.

"Your mother's name was Rhoswen," Faolan said next.

Was. Past tense. She knew what that meant, but she didn't want to ask about it. *Our mother*, Haleine had said, *torn to shreds, or so they tell me, and I had done the ripping.*

"My mother's name was Laura. Laura Cole," she said.

She didn't mean to say it. Not out loud, anyway. She'd already had the adoption revelation back in a root cellar in Enimode. Faolan's announcement shouldn't have shaken her that much.

"The woman who gave birth to you," Faolan said. "Her name was Rhoswen. She—"

"Skip it," Cate said. "I know she's dead. I don't want to know anything else."

"How do you know she's dead?" James asked.

She glanced at him, standing in the corner. He didn't know she'd spoken to Haleine. Maybe he suspected it, but he didn't have any proof. She wanted to keep it that way.

"I'm a goddamn English major at an Ivy League school. I know what the past tense is and what the use of it signifies," she said, taking note of his confusion. "Which is more than I can say for you."

"Yes," Faolan said. "Your mother is dead."

"Both of them," she said. "When we first met, you claimed you were familiar with my mother."

"Yes. Both of them."

"How?" she asked. "How would you ever be familiar with Laura Cole?"

"We couldn't leave you with just anyone," the pegasus said.

"You mean like my real mother?" Cate asked.

She hated the sentence as soon as she said it. Laura Cole was her real mother. To call her anything else was a betrayal, and Cate wasn't willing to do that.

But hadn't Laura betrayed her?

"Yes," Faolan said. "Like that."

"Why?" Cate asked. "Why couldn't you?"

"Neruals," was the answer.

James's body jerked. It had been a small movement, possibly involuntary, but Cate looked at him as she asked her next question.

"Neruals?"

"Lycanthropes. Entirely evil lycanthropes, who can kill a mortal man with naught but a scratch," Faolan said. "I think perhaps you've dreamt about them."

Her hands went instinctively to her torso as she remembered the sound and feel of teeth tearing at her skin. Shuddering, she said, "I called them hellhounds."

Faolan nodded. "That would also be an apt description. When you were an infant, they came for you."

"They came for me?" she asked.

She'd barely gotten the sentence out before an unseen force shoved her out of her chair and into darkness. It came upon her without warning, engulfing her whole. For a short while, she fell, and when she landed, she lay on her back and cried.

She was a red-faced, bawling infant, lying in a cradle, helpless but aware. The neural hovered over her, not on four legs as she had seen it before, but on hind legs, like a man.

And like a man, it swaddled her tiny, flailing body in the blankets upon which she laid. It turned its massive paws to the task, being surprisingly gentle. She heard a growl rise in its throat and saw the flash of its claws pass overhead as its foreleg somehow swung out in a wide arc.

A man screamed, and Cate's vision was tainted red. When it cleared, she was on the move, looking up at a starry night sky. Cradled in the creature's paw and pressed against its furnace-like body, she wasn't afraid. She was protected, and she was precious.

She didn't know what happened to change that. Jarred from the creature's warmth, she fell. This time, when she landed, it was on the ground, cold and hard. She cried again, her infant shrieks hurting her ears. Faolan appeared, hovering over her. Another flash of light—brighter than before—followed and washed over her senses, causing the pegasus and everything else to disappear.

"Mireille!" a man shouted.

It stopped then. She was back in her own body, but could see only black. Something held her up, which was good because she lacked feeling in her extremities. Taking several shallow breaths in quick succession, she waited for the world to right itself.

"What the hell was that?" she gasped when she could again move and see.

She'd fallen out of the chair and was leaning against James, who apparently had the presence of mind to catch her before she did a complete face plant on the ground. He appeared as freaked out as she felt. She pushed away and stalked to the other side of the tent. When Faolan didn't respond, she looked at him.

"What the hell was that?" she repeated.

"You had a vision," Faolan answered.

"What?" Cate said. "I had a what?"

"A vision," Faolan said. "It's a—"

"Yeah, I understand the concept of a vision," she said. "What I don't understand is how the hell I had one, or what the hell you were doing in it."

"What did you see?"

She had seen those same monsters that had ripped her apart in other dreams, only this time, they had been so careful that she had felt safe in their possession. How did they get from one to the other?

"I assume I saw what happened when the devil dogs came for me," she said. "But you know what they say happens when you assume."

"What?"

"That you make an—never mind. It's not important," Cate said. "Were you there? When those things came for me?"

"Neruals," Faolan said. "Yes, I was there."

"Why? Why were you there? Why were they there? Why was any part of some mystical menagerie remotely interested in me?"

Faolan said nothing. She looked from him to James, who now stood along the tent wall, his arms folded across his chest. He wasn't looking at either of them.

"James?" she asked.

He lifted his head, but didn't say anything. Because he didn't know, or because he didn't want to tell her?

"You won't want to believe me," Faolan said finally.

Cate looked at him. "I already don't believe you."

"You won't want to trust me," Faolan said.

"How will that be any different than now?"

Faolan sighed. "There's a prophecy—"

"You can save the prophecy talk," she interrupted. "I don't believe in prophecy."

"I don't see how that matters."

"I think it matters quite a lot."

"Did you believe in unicorns before you saw one?" Faolan asked. "Did you believe in the existence of a talking pegasus before you had a conversation with one? Did you believe in parallel universes before you ended up in one?"

No. Of course she hadn't. But she'd be damned if she would admit that to him.

"Is that what this is?" she asked. "A parallel universe?"

Faolan nodded.

She'd read the occasional fantasy novel. She'd read her share of sci-fi. The concept wasn't completely foreign to her. Or, at least the concept conceived by the writers in the world in which she had been raised wasn't completely foreign to her. She supposed she didn't have any real way to know how accurate their ideas were. The pegasus probably wasn't as well-versed in modern fiction as she was.

"I still don't believe in prophecy," she said.

"Again, I don't see how that matters," Faolan said. "You may not believe in it, but the beings who sent the neruals after you in your infancy believe in it quite a lot, and this prophecy is the reason the neruals were sent for you at all. You may not believe in it, but you should at least understand it."

She thought about that. It wasn't the craziest idea ever. "Fine. Tell me about your prophecy."

"It's not my prophecy."

"Well, whoever's prophecy it is," she said, "tell me about it."

"It foretells the existence of a woman who has the power to stop the forces of darkness from encroaching upon the goddess's earth," Faolan said.

James's head rose. The movement wasn't much, but she caught it. The pegasus was lying.

"I'm that woman?" Cate asked.

"Your sister is that woman," Faolan said. "But as she is—"

"Suicidal and insane?" Cate supplied, promptly earning James's full attention. She smiled at him. "That's right. You thought she was willing to die for your cause, but it turns out she only wants to die because of it."

That was a stupid thing to say. Now he would want to know how she knew that, and she didn't have any smart-ass comebacks. But she wasn't interested in reliving her night in the root cellar with Haleine. James didn't say anything, though, so they only stared at each other until Faolan interrupted the contest.

"Your sister has certain skills," he said. "Magical abilities that mark her as our chosen one."

"Magical abilities?" Cate echoed. "Like, slight of hand? Smoke and mirrors? Pick a card?"

"I'm talking about real magic," Faolan said. "Not tricks."

"Okay, let's speculate that such a thing as real magic does exist," she said, skating over the fact that she was stranded in a parallel universe surrounded by unicorns and having a conversation with a talking pegasus. "What does all that have to do with me?"

"We believe you and your sister share similar powers," Faolan said.

Cate shook her head. "Well, you're wrong. I don't have any powers. Not magical ones, anyway."

"Your vision is proof otherwise."

"I never had a vision before. Not before I was kidnapped."

"I'm certain you have," Faolan said. "You might have thought it was only a dream. I doubt it would have taken much of a toll on you."

"Why would that be?" she asked. "Why the change?"

"The visions are advancing," Faolan said. "You're closer to it, you're submerged in it, whereas before you were sheltered—even more sheltered than your sister. Her powers, I believe, started to grow upon her arrival in Lira, and I suspect yours are doing the same."

"It? What is *it*?" Cate asked. "What is it that I'm closer to? What is it that I'm submerged in?"

"I don't know that I have a good answer for you."

"I would have been surprised if you had."

"This fight, this war, that we're asking you to help us with has been going on since long before you were even born," Faolan said. "Centuries passed without any mortal knowing of the conflict raging around them. We—the mystical menagerie, as you called us—have always been able to keep the struggle from spilling over into the human realm, but that's changed. It's flooding this world now, and humanity, as you've seen, is drowning in it. Lira has become the epicenter. I don't know why. I only know that your sister's arrival on Liran soil was a catalyst that has brought us to where we are now."

"What does that make my arrival?" Cate asked, her voice taut.

"A lifeline," Faolan said. "Our last lifeline."

"I'm your last hope?"

"Yes."

"Huh," she said. "That doesn't bode well for the world."

James made a quiet sound that indicated he agreed with her. Faolan didn't say anything, but Cate could tell he shared a similar view.

"There was a man in my vision. He called out my...He called out for me," she said. "Who is he?"

"That man was your father," Faolan said. "Darian Coileáin."

Was. More past tense. But Haleine had hinted at that, too. *Our father followed*, she had said after describing their mother being torn to shreds. *Oh, he was the worst of my sins, I think.*

"Is he dead?" Cate asked.

James glanced at the pegasus. Curious, maybe, to find out how Faolan would field this question?

"Yes," Faolan said. "He was a soldier, and he died in battle."

"A battle involving your rebel forces?"

"Yes."

"Oh," she said. "But he wasn't one of your rebel forces?"

"No."

"Oh." She'd have to file that away to be sorted through later. "Tell me again why you brought me here."

"I believe you share a connection," Faolan said. "You and your sister."

She thought about that, and the night in the root cellar—specifically Haleine's injuries and what she had done with the small silver blade. Yeah, they had a connection.

"Is that why I have this?" she asked.

She opened her vest and pulled down her shirt low enough to reveal the scar over her heart. Both James and Faolan gawked. It was especially disturbing coming from a tiny talking pony who shouldn't have been able to gawk at all.

"The scar, you idiots," she said. "I'm talking about the scar."

"I was looking at the scar," Faolan said, but James declined to comment.

Cate rearranged her shirt so that everything was once again covered. "Explain, please."

"I don't know that I can," Faolan said. "There's so much that we don't know about your magical abilities. All I can offer you are theories."

"Theorize away, little Einstein."

"I—who?" Faolan said.

"Never mind. What are your theories?"

"The goddess Laorans took a special interest in your protection," Faolan said. "She went to great lengths to keep you hidden from the dark gods, and in doing so, it is my belief that a connection, a bond, was formed between the two of you."

"A bond? Between me and a goddess?"

"Yes. That is my belief."

That thought was funny. The idea that she could, in any way, have a bond with a higher power was damn near hysterical. Cate had never been one for religion. Her mother never pushed her in any one direction. Fiona lacked any strong religious convictions, and Daniel definitely wasn't the sort to be worshipping anyone. That wasn't to say Cate was an atheist or anything because she wasn't. It was more that she didn't care one way or another. She didn't know what that made her.

"Interesting theory," she said. "But what does that have to do with the scar?"

"There's also a connection between your twin and the goddess. It was forged not long ago, when your sister accessed her powers to pull the goddess back from the brink of defeat."

"You think we're connected through the goddess?" Cate said. "And that means we somehow feel each other's pain?"

"I don't know how else to explain your scar," Faolan said. "Unless you also tried to take your own life in a fashion mirroring your sister's attempt."

"I'm not suicidal."

"I'm glad to hear it."

"As I'm your great white hope, I'll just bet," Cate said. "How do I access it?"

"The magic?"

"No, your offshore bank account," she said. "Yes, the magic."

"The magic is a part of you. All you have to do is use the force—"

Cate laughed. A lot. When she started to have difficulties breathing, James and Faolan exchanged glances.

"Are you all right?" James asked.

"Yeah, sorry, I'm having a moment," Cate said once she'd gotten the hysterics under control. "Here I am, sitting in the woods on some alien planet with a Muppet telling me to use the force. It's—yeah, it's funny. No other word for it."

Faolan pushed on in absolute seriousness. "But do you understand—?"

"Yes, use the force I must," she interrupted. "Understand this I do."

"Good?" Faolan said.

Their talk continued after that. Faolan spoke so much about things Cate didn't understand that eventually his words stopped sounding like words and just became noise.

"Stop," she said finally. "I need a break from this, from the specifics. It's—it's a lot, and I don't know what to think about it. Any of it."

Especially when she took into account how selective with the truth the pegasus had been. How would she get around that? She glanced at James, thinking he would be her best bet. It didn't encourage her.

"All right," Faolan said.

"Could I have a minute—a moment to myself?" she asked. "Alone? To think?"

James nodded. "I'll be outside."

"Lucky me."

James regarded her a moment, but she didn't return the look. He shook his head and walked away. Faolan followed.

"There endth the lesson," Cate said when she was alone. "Shit."

—⫘⫘—

Faolan followed James out of the tent and landed on the man's shoulder once they were in the open air. As James turned to keep an eye on the entrance, Rhydwyn went around to the back.

"What do you think?" James asked.

Faolan couldn't tell James what he thought. As much as he didn't want to involve Cate in any of this, they were desperate and short on options. They had to take the risk.

But he didn't want to.

Laorans believed Cate would come around, come through for them—for *her*—so he would continue to work toward that goal, but it didn't prevent him from feeling doubt.

There was something wrong. With Cate, with everything.

"She'll come around," he said. "She's nearly there."

James nodded. "She said we wouldn't be able to Patty Hearst her. Do you know what that means?"

"No."

"I think it means she won't help us."

"She'll come around," Faolan repeated. "She's nearly there."

"Nearly there, but not there yet," James said. "There's quite a difference between the two, Faolan. How long will we wait? How long can we afford to wait?"

"We don't have Haleine, so we have to have Cate," Faolan said. "We turn her, or we die."

James looked at the camp. "You think you know what needs to be done, but what if you're wrong?"

Faolan tensed.

You think you know what needs to be done.

He had heard that exact phrase two months earlier—from the lips of the same being who had first spoken the prophecy.

Not long after the birth of Haleine's sons, Faolan's spies discovered the crone. She lived in a hovel in the wilds of Quatara on the very edges of the land abutting the sea. For weeks, they pressed her to give up those words the dark gods and their followers considered sacred, but she remained silent. Finally, one night when Haleine would be as safe as she could ever hope to be, Faolan left her in the care of her lover and her guard to travel to Quatara. He meant to see this woman for himself. He had to discover what the prophecy foretold, and he could not leave it to the others any longer.

The crone's shelter was easily determined, for it was the only available locale in which a human might take refuge. The door opened as he approached, and he flew through it without hesitation, curious as to whom he would find inside.

She wasn't human. Faolan could smell it in the air along with the scent of burning herbs. She sat in front of a small fire pit at the back of her hut. Her hands worked the air as though carding wool. She had magic within her—he could sense it without effort—but it lay dormant. Across from her lay an overturned bucket. He landed there and looked at her. She may not have been human, but so well done was her visage that no mortal would have realized the truth. Her silver hair was thin and unkempt. Her skin was the color and texture of tanned leather. She looked ancient, yet Faolan was certain she was much older than that.

"I know why you've come," the woman said. She glanced at him briefly, revealing violet eyes. "I've been waiting for you."

"Tell me what I want to know."

"Kept me waiting for so long, you have, I don't know if you're welcomed here."

"You opened the door for me yourself," Faolan said. "But if you want me gone, tell me what I want to know. I won't leave before."

She laughed, the cackle sounding as old as the rest of her. "Oh, I know you won't. You think my words will save your mistress."

"I won't know that until I hear them."

"You think you know."

"I don't know," Faolan said. "It's why I am here. Tell me your vision."

The crone's hands worked harder, her fingers impossibly nimble. She closed her eyes and began to rock back and forth gently.

"Two from one, they'll come, they'll come," she said, her voice now lower and heavier than before. "The first from moon, the next from dark."

Two from one. Haleine and Mireille. The dark gods had to have thought Mireille was the second. It would explain why they had sent the neruals to take her. But why had they left Haleine alive?

"The fate of the world in their hands they'll hold," the crone said.

"What else?" Faolan asked.

"They'll live, they'll fight, they'll love, they'll die."

They'll die. "What else?"

"Blood against blood, light against flame," she said. "Two from your blood will start it all. One from your blood will see it done."

"Whose blood?" Faolan asked.

"Not for you to know," the woman answered, her voice returned to its ancient creak. She stopped rocking and opened her eyes. Her hands continued their manic movement.

"I must know."

"Must means nothing," she said. "Only over the dead man's body will you ever know, for he'll not speak of it before."

"What is for me to know?"

She seemed to consider his question. Her hands stopped and grabbed her thighs as she leaned toward him.

"Know this," she said. "The throne of the dark lords will be reclaimed when the rivers run red with the blood of the moon."

As he stared into the crone's violet eyes, he saw it: the end. He forced himself to look away, surprised by the effort it took.

"Go ahead," the woman said. "Try and thwart it."

"I will," he said. "You'll see."

"You think you know what needs to be done," she had called as he flew away, "but I tell you now, you've never been more wrong."

He had never forgotten the crone's parting words, but it wasn't until he saw an unconscious Cate in James's arms that he believed the wise woman might have been right.

"Faolan?" James said then. "Did you hear me?"

"No," the pegasus said, returning to the present. "No, I didn't. What did you say?"

"I said she knows you lied to her."

"She knows you think I lied to her."

"I only think that because you did lie to her."

Faolan looked at the tent. Yes, he had lied to her. He couldn't tell her the truth about the prophecy. Not now. Maybe not ever.

"And now she knows it," Faolan said. "Try to do better the next time, won't you?"

He left James before a response could be made and flew straight to the depths of the forest where Luisiúil and Lorcan waited.

Landing on a tree branch, Faolan shook out his wings and folded them against his body. Meeting Luisiúil's patient gaze, he said, "We need to talk."

—❧—

Needless to say, Cate did not sleep well after her talk with the pegasus. She was beginning to think she would never sleep well again unless serious narcotics were involved. There were too many questions spinning around her brain, questions that refused to be silenced, even for the span of a night, so when James left her alone in the tent to complete a security check of the camp's perimeters, she decided to take a walk of her own.

This was made possible by the fact that Rhydwyn and Gair were spending the night elsewhere, and her new guards weren't nearly as vigilant as James's matching pair of automatons. The new guys had received specific instructions on keeping her where she was, but she supposed they thought the danger was external. They didn't seem to realize the trouble she was capable of causing, so it was easy to put on her cloak, pull up the hood, and slip out into the darkness unnoticed.

The camp was fascinating. At least the atmosphere was. The camp itself was poor and kind of depressing, but the atmosphere was electric. How much of that could be attributed to James?

Based on the people's response to his appearance, at least part of it could. It had started with the guards outside the camp borders and had only intensified once they were inside. They hadn't fallen to their knees at the sight of him or anything, but she thought some of them had considered it.

He was obviously their leader. It was interesting he didn't think he was. It was interesting how he recoiled, almost physically, from the mere suggestion. *I know what it means*, he'd snapped. Right before he had gone to do whatever it was that had needed doing.

She suspected he spent a lot of time doing that. She'd gotten a pretty good look at him—well, most of him—that morning. One did not come by the sort of bruises and scars he was sporting when one did not care. *I'm only trying to do what is right*, he'd told her.

But not by her.

He didn't like her. She hadn't given him much reason to like her, but he had put up with her. Anyone else would have thrown her back by now. Or killed her and left her in a ditch. One or the other.

Which was also intriguing. In a completely infuriating sort of way. She'd never met anybody before, with the exception of Daniel and Fiona, whom she couldn't intimidate into leaving her the hell alone.

She walked past a group of—of what? Campers? Refugees? Cannon fodder? Whatever they called themselves, they sat around a bonfire, eating, talking, warming their hands. She glanced at them as she passed but stopped when she saw the woman whose husband had died to protect her.

To protect Haleine, rather.

The woman sat, her youngest son in her lap, and her older boy at her side. The older boy's head shifted, his eyes falling on Cate. He stared at her the way he had in her dream. She held her breath. Did he know it was her? Was she dreaming again? His mouth moved, but she couldn't hear what he said. The boy's mother lifted her head to look at Cate as well. Okay—

probably not a dream. Caught, Cate lowered her hood and moved toward them.

"Your majesty," the woman mumbled, catching the attention of those within earshot.

They stole glances at her before ducking their heads and speaking in whispers. Cate wanted to tell the woman not to address her as royalty because she was far from royal, but her husband had died thinking he was protecting the queen. What would she think if she knew her husband died to protect some stranger who wanted nothing to do with their troubles? Would it be kinder to lie?

"I am very sorry for your loss," Cate said, adopting Haleine's accent.

As the woman nodded, Cate sat and smiled at the boy in her lap. He hid his face in his mother's clothing.

"What was his name?" Cate asked. "Your husband."

"Ynyr," the woman said. "Ynyr ab Ivor."

"I know what he did for me," Cate said. "I will never forget it."

"I know," the woman said. "Your majesty, I know."

"Your name?" Cate said. "And your sons?"

"I am called Llian," the woman said. "My sons are Aodhan and Iestyn."

She touched each boy on the head when she spoke his name. The eldest, Iestyn, didn't shrink away from Cate's focus. Cate nodded, then spotted James standing on the other side of the fire, his eyebrows raised in concern.

"I beg your pardon," Cate said, rising.

Llian only nodded, and Cate walked around the fire to join James.

"What are you doing?" he asked.

"Offering my condolences," she said. "It's the least I could do considering they're all in mourning because of me."

"You didn't kill that man."

"I may as well have."

James leaned in. "You can't think like that. You didn't kill that man, and he didn't have to do what he did. He could have told them where we were. He could have—"

"He didn't think he had the choice."

"No one here does."

She glared at him. People were openly watching her now. James noticed it, too, and he didn't seem to like it any more than she did.

"Are you finished here?" he asked.

He didn't wait for an answer before he took her elbow and led her away.

"However did I manage to walk before I met you?" she said.

"What are you going on about?"

Cate pulled free. "You! I'm going on about you, Mr. Grabby-Hands, with your hands always on my arm, or my back, leading me around like I'm incapable of walking on my own."

"I'm not—"

"I'll have you know that I was walking all on my own for years before you kidnapped me, and I certainly don't require your help to do so now."

"I didn't..." James put his hands in the air as though she were holding him at gunpoint. "My apologizes. It won't happen again."

"It better not."

They had attracted an even larger audience now, and Cate slowly lifted her hood over her head. It probably didn't matter anymore, though. Everyone seemed to think the queen was in their midst.

"Are they how you found me?" she asked.

"They?"

Cate gestured to their spectators. "I didn't leave a note saying, 'Hey, here's where I went, be back soon,'" she said. "Did word get back to you that the queen was out and about, mingling with her subjects?"

"Subjects?" James echoed, his tone insinuating he didn't care for the word.

"Or whatever."

"Aye," he said. "Word got back to me."

"Because you're the leader."

"I'm not," he said. "Are you finished?"

"Oh. Yeah, sure. I just..." How much did she not want to admit this? "I don't exactly know my way around, so you'll have to, you know"—she sighed—"lead the way."

James folded his arms across his chest. "Now you want me to lead the way?"

She rolled her eyes. "It can be done without manhandling me."

"I didn't manhandle you," he said, walking away.

She stayed on his heels. "No, you just knocked me unconscious, threw me over your shoulder—"

"I did not throw you over my shoulder."

"Indignant kidnapping victim," she sang.

James threw his hands in the air again, and they walked the rest of the way in silence. He knew the camp impossibly well for someone who'd only arrived that day. She couldn't have gotten around without a bread trail of some kind. She only knew they had reached her tent when she saw Rhydwyn and Gair standing at the entrance.

"Do you ever give your backup dancers a night off?" she asked.

Looking exhausted—and maybe a little frightened—James said, "Do I what?"

"Frick and Frack over there." Cate indicated the two men. "Do you ever let them sleep?"

"I tried to," James said. "But you ran off again."

"You couldn't just kick the asses of the incompetent people who were here earlier?"

"Rhydwyn and Gair are—"

"Loyal?" she asked. James shrugged. "And you say you're not the leader."

"I'm not. That is—was—someone else."

"Where is the someone else now?"

"Gone. He's gone."

"Dead?"

"Might as well be."

James's tone made her uncomfortable. There was clearly some back story there. But for now, it was time to change the subject.

"Well, don't Rhydwyn and Gair have girlfriends or wives, or kids or dogs who miss them?" she asked.

"They did once."

Once. That probably meant their story would end with soldiers killing massive amounts of innocent people. She didn't need to hear it. She'd already gotten the visual.

"Doesn't mean you shouldn't let them sleep," she said.

"Apparently, they won't sleep until I sleep, and I won't sleep until you stop trying to run off," James said. "Maybe you should let them sleep."

"What makes you think I care about that?" she asked. "The more tired you all are, the less vigilant I suspect you'll be."

He held open the tent flap. "You care."

"Hey," she said, stepping inside, "just because you caught me caring once does not mean it'll happen again."

He stayed outside and studied her, his lips eventually curling into a smile. "You care."

She nodded. "Just for that, I'm going to run away twice."

CHAPTER 12

After taking a last walk through the camp and checking in with the night's sentries, James returned to the tent. Rhydwyn and Gair were standing outside of it, so Cate hadn't yet run away. Or, if she had, they'd already brought her back.

"Has she run off?" he asked.

Gair shook his head. "She's asleep."

That was a bloody miracle. "Good," James said. "Find a couple of replacements, put the fear of Ilya and Hanah in them, and get some sleep. You'll not do me any good if you don't."

"Aye, Captain," Gair said.

James entered the tent and was pleased to find Cate asleep on a bedroll. She appeared to be shivering, so he found a blanket to cover her. Turning the lantern light low, he waited to see if she would start thrashing and screaming, but she stayed quiet. He spent the remainder of the night sleeping lightly, waking at every noise, however slight, but Cate never moved.

When morning came, she continued to sleep, and James moved around the tent quietly to avoid disturbing her. People came in and out with various questions. Hanah sent one of her apprentices with food and water for washing. Stripping to his waist, James washed and was contemplating shaving when Cate spoke.

"People are going to think you're doing the queen."

He jumped. How long had she been awake? He looked at her, still lying on the bedroll.

"Thank you for the blanket." She sat up, keeping it wrapped around her shoulders.

"What did you say?" he asked.

"Thank you. It's a phrase used to express gratitude."

"Not that. The other part."

"I said people are going to think you're doing the queen."

"Doing what to the queen?"

Cate stretched, the blanket falling away. "Having sex with her."

James pulled a shirt over his head. "What?"

"You do know what sex is, right?"

"I'm familiar with it, aye," he said, "but they won't think that."

She stood. "Why? Because the queen's all chaste and pure?"

"No."

"Because you're all chaste and pure?"

He laughed. "No."

"Why then?"

"They know better than to think I would..." He sighed. "They know better."

"Oh. Because she was having sex with someone else?"

James indulged in a moment to marvel at the inanity of the conversation. "Her husband, I suppose."

"Besides her husband."

"What makes you think I'd know about that?"

"You seem so sure your huddled masses out there won't think any impropriety is going on in this tent," she said. "You know something. They know something. Everyone who isn't Cate knows something. So, with whom was she having sex?"

"Does it matter?"

"It might. I won't know until you tell me."

"That night in the cellar," James said. "What did she say?"

"Your grandmother? She said she was glad I wasn't—"

"Not her."

"Does it matter?"

"It might. I won't know until you tell me," James said. "What did she say?"

"Nobody said anything."

"I don't believe you."

She shrugged. "Your prerogative."

She turned away and stubbornly kept her back to him. He watched her, amused and perplexed, until Gair called to him from outside, and another of Hanah's students came in. He nodded at her, and she curtsied, which James took to mean she had noticed Cate.

"Hanah sent me to tell you Ynyr ab Ivor would be buried this morning," the girl said. "She thought you'd want to be there."

"Aye," James said. "I'll be along."

The girl nodded, curtsied again, and backed away, her head bowed.

"I'd like to go as well," Cate said. "The man died because of me."

"For you," James corrected.

"For Haleine," Cate said. "I should be there."

It was the first time he'd heard her call the queen by name. Who had told her? He hadn't, and as far as he knew, neither had Faolan, and Faolan was currently the only being in the entire camp in the habit of using the queen's name. Until now.

"Please?" Cate asked. "I promise not to run away again for at least a full day."

"Rhydwyn and Gair will be pleased to hear that," James replied. "If I bring you, you have to stand in the back with your hood up and your mouth shut."

"Not a problem." Cate bent down for her cloak.

"Who told you the queen's name?" he asked. "It wasn't me, nor do I recall Faolan saying it."

She straightened slowly. "Aaron. He mentioned it. When we were in the cave."

James suppressed a snort of laughter. "You are an accomplished liar."

"I like to think so."

He nodded. "Come on."

Ynyr ab Ivor was buried in a glen outside of the camp's protection. Someone had dug a grave between a pair of trees, and the body had been wrapped in a white shroud. The man's family stood at the grave's side. Llian held Aodhan's hand tightly in her own. Dry-eyed, Iestyn stood apart from his mother and brother, looking into the hole that would contain his father's body.

James and Cate watched from a distance. She had made good on her promise thus far. She hadn't opened her mouth once since their arrival, and was currently focused on the ground, her hand frequently disappearing beneath her hood to clear her face of tears. Why did she hide it? Did she find it shameful to cry? He would have shed tears of his own were he capable of such a thing, but he had dug too many graves and borne witness to too many burials for that to still be true.

"What will happen to them?" Cate asked afterward, as they walked through the camp.

"Who?"

"Llian and Iestyn and Aodhan. What happens to them now?"

"That depends on what they want," James said. "They'll be welcomed here for as long as they like, but if they want to go elsewhere, we'll help them get there safely."

"I don't think she knows what she wants."

"Well, we'll keep them safe until she does know."

"That might take a while."

James shrugged. "Then it takes a while."

She nodded. "Spoken like a white hat."

He stopped. "I am."

Cate stopped, too. She studied him for a moment, her eyes roaming his face before glancing back toward the glen where Ynyr ab Ivor had been laid to rest. Sighing, she nodded and walked away. What conclusion had she reached? Curious, he followed her to their tent, intending to ask, but his question fell away when he found Ilya and Faolan waiting inside.

"What are you doing here?" he asked, watching Cate remove her cloak and retreat to the back of the tent.

"We need to talk," Faolan said. "Decide upon a course of action."

James nodded. "Hanah will want to be here for that."

"Well, she's coming to look at you properly," Ilya said. "We can talk when she gets here."

"Coming to look at me properly?" James asked. "What does that—?"

"You're one of her charges," Ilya said. "She wants to see for herself that you're all right."

Bloody hell. Knowing there would be no easy way around it, he sighed. "Fine. We'll wait."

Hanah arrived promptly, nodding to Faolan and Ilya before turning toward him. She found Cate first, sitting on a basket in the corner, and she stopped, her jaw dropping slightly. Cate stiffened as the stare lingered, and she looked to him, eyebrows raised in question.

"Hanah," James said, "this is—"

"The queen has a twin?" Hanah said, looking at him.

"Aye," he said. "How did you know it wasn't her?"

Hanah shook her head. "I wasn't sure at first, but I've met the queen and spoken to her. I do not believe she would be so panicked were she to see me again."

Cate rolled her eyes. "I was not panicked."

"This is Lady Coileáin—Cate." James smiled as Hanah curtsied. "Cate, this is Hanah, our healer."

"My lady," Hanah said.

Cate gave James a withering look and faced the wall. Confused, Hanah looked at him, but he shook his head to discourage her from asking about it. He didn't want to explain it. He wasn't sure he could.

"You're all right?" Hanah asked then. "Truly?"

"I told you I was."

She stood in front of him and turned his face from side to side. Her genuine concern surprised him. The last time he had seen her, she hadn't been at all pleased with him.

"You've been fighting," she said, dropping her hand.

He laughed. "We've *all* been fighting, Hanah. It's one of the disadvantages of being at war."

"Which is why I think it's something we can turn to our advantage," Ilya said.

"How?" James asked.

"You know we've taken a significant loss," Ilya said. "People and supplies. If we don't find some aid soon, I don't know how much longer we can hold out."

"Why didn't you tell me?" James said. "I asked, and you didn't tell me. You claimed they were holding."

"They are. For now," Ilya said. "But I don't know that we could survive another winter on our own. And if Omur were to attack again, as he did before, or if Varro arrives on our borders with even a portion of the king's army, we wouldn't even last until winter."

"What advantage is to be found in all this?" he asked. "You did mention one, didn't you?"

"The nobles are hurting, too. They have also lost, and they are also tiring of this war," Ilya said. "The king is draining their coffers faster than they can fill them. I think it may be possible to sway them, or at least some of them, to our side. Glean some aid from them, if nothing else."

"You would trust them to help us?" James asked.

"What else can we do?" Ilya said. "The country's so bloody poor now, there's no one else with the means. If we were to approach them—"

"Approach them?" James said. "There's no one here who could convince nobles of anything. Dana is the only commoner I've ever known who could talk sense to a noble."

"Don't use a commoner," Cate said. "Use a noble."

Everyone looked at her as she unhurriedly examined her hands. Running her fingers over her wrists, she raised her head to look at him.

"We happen to be running a bit low on nobles," he said, "but thank you for your suggestion."

"How many do you need?"

"How many do you think we have?"

"I think you have at least one."

"Do you mean yourself?"

Cate shrugged. "You said I was a member of the nobility, didn't you?"

"Aye, your blood makes you nobility," he said. "But your mouth marks you as a sailor's whore."

Out of the corner of his eye, he could see the offense taken by both Ilya and Hanah. Cate didn't seem bothered. She appeared almost amused. Her mouth quirked with something that could have been considered a smile.

She nodded. "Those who want to swear like a pro learn from the pros."

"I couldn't send you to talk to anyone anyway," James said. "No one would understand half of what came out of your mouth."

"Nothing but the profanity," she agreed.

James turned away. "No, what we need is—"

"Do they like Haleine?" Cate interrupted. "Do they revere their queen?"

He froze. "Everyone does."

"Everyone?" she said. "Your tone suggests that's a bit of an untruth."

James looked at her. "Why do you ask?"

Cate sighed and licked her lips. "I ask because perhaps the best person to sway these nobles to your cause would be a noble whom they hold in the highest esteem."

Her voice was a perfect mimicry of the queen's. He stared. "How did you...How did you do that?"

Cate shrugged, breaking the illusion. "I don't know," she said, her voice returned to normal. "I've always been good at picking up accents. It made me popular at parties. Incredibly boring parties."

"But to do what you just did," James said, "you would have had to talk to the queen. When did you—?"

"Look, I'm offering my help here," Cate said. "Do you want it or not?"

"We want it," Faolan responded quickly.

"Then it's settled," she said.

Encouraged, Ilya spent the remainder of the meeting working with Faolan on a strategy for their new plan. Neither James nor Cate contributed anything else. He crouched in one corner, his hand covering his mouth, and watched Cate. She sat nearly motionless, staring off at nothing. He couldn't even be sure she was listening.

When the meeting came to an end, Hanah, Ilya, and Faolan departed, leaving James alone with Cate.

"Do you truly want to do this?" he asked.

Cate shook her head. Her eyes were bright with tears. "No. I really don't."

"Why offer?"

"What wouldn't you do," she said, "to get back home?"

———

Revelin sat at his mother's bedside as he watched her sleep. He leaned forward to study the rise and fall of the bed covers. The physician, upon his last visit, had expressed some concern over the queen's breathing, and now Revelin found himself quite unable to stop wondering which shuddering breath would be his mother's last.

The physician had been unable to discover a reason for the queen's illness. The wear of age and grief had been proposed, but Revelin had dismissed it as soon as the idea had left the man's mouth. His mother was made of hardier stock than that, and his father had been gone for some time now. No, there was something else afoot here.

Revelin suspected Zoltano.

He did not know what his brother had done or how he had done it, but Revelin was certain Zoltano was to blame. Haraszty had fallen ill after his brother had returned from exile, determined to claim the crown. There was too much coincidence to be ignored. But coincidence was not proof, and he would require that, and more, if he were to bring his brother down on a charge of treason.

He would have to consult someone. One of the noblemen, to be sure, for their support would be vital, but whom could he trust? They had supported him thus far, fearing what Zoltano's rule would mean for their own wealth, but would that continue to hold true were Revelin to accuse his brother of treason? Would they rally to that, thinking it a way to keep themselves safe? Or would they view it as a desperate attempt by a second son to secure for himself a throne?

If only Darian were there.

Revelin had insisted on being present when Darian's coffin was opened, needing to see for himself that the man was dead. He had regretted it immediately. The murder had been most gruesomely done. Revelin didn't know why it had surprised him so. War was known for its unflinching brutality, and never before had he seen such a well-illustrated example.

Darian Coileáin had deserved better.

But since Revelin could not change what had happened, he had done what he could to see Darian properly honored in death.

It was tradition, when a commander of Nathan Maoilriain's army died in battle, to spend the night before the fallen's interment holding vigil. Darian's vigil had been held in the room where Revelin had watched his father die. He arrived at sundown and stayed the entire night. He had not been the only one to do so. Many had stood alongside him, wanting to pay homage to the man who had served the crown so well.

The funeral had been a crowded affair, a testament to Darian's importance in the Maoilriain reign. Haraszty and Eamonn were both in attendance, as were as many of the noblemen who had been able to reach Mairéad in time. Revelin, sitting between his mother and brother, spent the service with his head bowed, as he turned over in his brain the image of what a Liran bastard-born commoner had done to Tanuba.

The rebel leader would pay for what he had done. For this, for everything. Revelin would make sure of it. He would not let another chance pass him by.

"My lord?" Darragh asked.

Revelin lifted his head. He had not heard the man come in. "What is it?"

"The physician is here, my lord, to tend to your mother."

Revelin nodded and rose from his chair. "Show him in."

The physician and two of Haraszty's maids entered. Revelin waved them to their work and retreated to stand against the wall.

Darragh joined him. "Your highness, I do not wish to disturb you here, but—"

"Lira or the crown prince?" Revelin asked, not taking his eyes from his mother's bed.

"The crown prince is asking for reports on the armies. He wants—"

"He wants Quatara. Give him nothing."

"My lord, he is—"

"I know who he is," Revelin said. All too well did he know that. "Give him nothing."

Darragh bowed. "Yes, my lord."

As his advisor left the room, Revelin folded his arms across his chest and leaned against the wall. He had hoped that Zoltano would have given up on this quest by now—that being back at court would provide enough of a distraction to prevent his brother's mind from turning east. But if Zoltano was requesting information on the army, he was only more determined than ever.

The matter of Quatara had been settled long ago in Gweneria. It was true he and Darian had both worried over Zoltano's reaction when Revelin gave control of the country back to Einar, but as his brother had stayed inactive and hidden behind the walls of his fortress, Revelin had let himself believe that perhaps Zoltano no longer desired the land.

But the obsession with regaining what had been lost was wrong. The reasons his brother claimed he wanted it were shallow. Even for Zoltano, they were shallow. There was nothing to be gained from reclaiming Quatara. It would be a never-ending fight against Einar and the other rebels, just as it had been when his father and Darian had tried. Zoltano knew that. His brother was selfish and cruel, but not ignorant. He knew what a deathtrap Quatara would be.

Why did he want it?

As greatly as Revelin wanted an answer to that question, the more pressing concern would be stopping Zoltano before this country's men died to steal back another. Too many men had been lost already, and Revelin no longer cared to sacrifice them. Not for Quatara. Not for Einar. So long as the man stayed behind his own borders, Revelin was content to let Einar do as he pleased. Einar could—

Einar. Could it be that simple?

Revelin looked at his mother's attendants. "Stay with her until I return."

Revelin found Darragh alone in the library, reading a letter. The resemblance to Darian was so strong. How many times had Revelin thought how alike the two were? How many times had he witnessed Darragh's absolute devotion to Darian? At the vigil, Darragh had refused to leave his lord. Even when Revelin had ordered him to rest, Darragh had not.

Darragh had served Darian long before he served the Maoilriains. If anyone would know what Darian Coileáin would do, it would be him.

"Not more news from Lira, I hope," Revelin said.

Darragh's head whipped up. He dropped the parchment and bowed. "Oh, my lord, I am sorry. I had thought you would be occupied with your mother a while longer. Have you need of me?"

"The letter?" Revelin asked.

"Not from Lira, my lord," Darragh said. "Truly, it is nothing with which to concern yourself."

Revelin nodded. "I need you to find me a messenger. I shall soon have a letter to deliver."

"Yes, my lord. To where will the man be traveling?"

Revelin moved to the window behind his father's desk and watched the waves punish the cliffs.

"Quatara," he said. "My brother is not to know of this. Do you understand?"

"Of course, my lord. Will there be anything else?"

"One thing more," Revelin said. "Bring to me, in secret, a nobleman. I want no one to know that we meet."

"Which one, your highness?"

Revelin rested his head against the glass. "The one Darian would trust."

———※———

Their next meeting came the following day. It was held in the cover of the trees outside the camp because Faolan reported the unicorns held an interest in the plans but did not want to come to the center of camp. James obliged them, leaving Cate behind with a pair of guards on each side of the tent. Since none of them were Rhydwyn or Gair, he had no true illusions that Cate would be there when he returned. Regardless of the warnings he issued, she always managed to slip past them. Perhaps it didn't matter anymore.

What wouldn't you do to get back home? she had asked him. She was resigned to helping them now.

It was exactly what he had wanted.

Why did it make him so bloody miserable?

With a sigh, James leaned against a tree. Rhydwyn and Gair waited on either side of him, keeping a careful watch on their surroundings. They were outside of the camp's protection, but James wasn't worried. Omur wasn't hunting for them.

Ilya arrived first, with Hanah at her heels. Soon after, a tall, redheaded man James knew as Semias joined the group. Semias, he supposed, had taken Lucius's place. If Ilya trusted him enough to bring him into this inner circle, James could be assured of his capabilities. Ilya wouldn't have let just anyone in.

Faolan, flanked by Lorcan and Luisiúil, arrived last. The unicorn mare kept her focus on James, but he refused to meet her gaze.

"Let's start this," he growled.

Ilya watched him the way she used to look at Dana when she hadn't approved of the rebel leader's moods. James hadn't liked it then. He hated it now.

Glaring at her, he challenged, "What have you got?"

"We need a nobleman to approach," she said. "I've been considering some names, and I thought perhaps—"

"Emrys," James said. "We go to Emrys."

Emrys was the lord of Labhras, a town located on the edge of the Donasien Woods. He was a rotund man who liked to drink and eat his wealth. James had first met him through Dana, as the lord of Labhras's keep was one of Dana's favorite feasting halls.

"Emrys?" Ilya asked. "You mean Emrys of Labhras?"

"Aye. He's close, and he should do us the courtesy of at least listening to our proposal. He's a decent sort, for a lord."

"A decent sort," Ilya echoed. "You know him?"

James nodded and, feeling the unicorn's stare intensify, looked at the ground. "I've been in his hall."

"Does he know you?" Ilya asked.

Would he? Probably. Dana had made the introduction with enough frequency that even a careless lord might remember it.

"I suspect he wouldn't know me from one of his grooms," James lied. "He had a rapport with Dana, though, and they seemed to like each other well enough. We can use that."

Awkward silence followed the mention of Dana's name. James continued to look at the ground until he felt something like fingers stroking his mind.

He scowled at Luisiúil. *Get out of there*, he thought. *You're not welcome.*

The unicorn blinked, and the feeling within his mind subsided. She didn't, however, look away.

"Let's talk about defenses," Faolan said, looking between James and Luisiúil. "The unicorns and I—"

"Will stay in camp," James interrupted.

"In camp?" Faolan asked. "I don't think that's a good idea."

Ilya, Hanah, and Semias agreed with Faolan. James couldn't tell what the unicorns were thinking, but he didn't have to bother looking at Rhydwyn or Gair. They would follow him. Even if they shouldn't.

"We've got to keep the lass protected," Hanah said. "Who better to do that than the unicorns?"

"I'll keep Cate protected," James said.

He couldn't let anything happen to her. How, then, would she sacrifice herself for the greater good?

"By yourself?" Ilya asked.

"I'll take a small group with me," he said. "Humans only. It'll be better."

"We can help," Faolan said.

"Omur tracked you before. He'll track you again," James said. "I want us to pass by unnoticed. I want us to be invisible, and with you, we won't be."

"That may be true, but as best as we can tell, Varro's still out there," Faolan said. "He'll concentrate his search in this area after the message you left him, so if it's invisible you want to be, you'd best plan to use the tunnels."

James shook his head. "No. They're not to be trusted."

"No one's watching, James," Faolan said.

"You keep saying no one is watching, yet it seems someone always is," he said. "We're not using the tunnels. I won't bring her down there. Everything—*everything*—hinges upon her, and I won't—"

Put her at risk. The words nearly left his mouth, but he bit them back.

"Just get this done," he said. "Put people in the village and on the road. I want to know who or what is out there."

Ilya looked at Semias, who nodded and backed away. "We'll send Cate to Emrys on the morrow," she said.

"No, I want to be certain the roads are safe first," James said. "Besides, she'll need a day, maybe two, to prepare. For us to prepare her. Sounding like the queen is one thing. Acting like the queen, however, may take some doing."

Behind him, he heard Rhydwyn's quiet snort of laughter. Damn him, he was *amused*. James glanced over his shoulder, and the sound died instantly.

"A day or two will be enough?" Ilya asked. She hadn't missed Rhydwyn's reaction. She never missed anything.

"It'll be enough. Make the arrangements, aye?" James said. "I'll find Cate."

Cate took off again when James had taken both Penn and Teller to attend to some secret task, the details of which he didn't want her to know. She didn't want to know, either, all things considered, so she was fine with being left behind. The problem was, sitting in the tent still made her claustrophobic, even more so since her offer of help had been made. She wasn't interested in running away—*probably* not interested in running away, anyway—but she was as equally disinterested in waiting. The guards he left her with this time were more vigilant than the previous set, but she eluded them easily enough and set off in search of something to see or do.

Wandering aimlessly until the sound of clashing swords caught her attention, Cate ended up on the edge of a clearing. A cluster of trees offered her privacy as she watched a woman she didn't know lead the troops in swordplay exercises. Others shot arrows at straw targets. A third group worked with quarterstaffs. That could be interesting. How did one gain an invitation to the party?

"I'm sorry, your majesty," a small voice said.

Cate swiveled to see one of the boys from the road standing there. The older one. What was his name? Iestyn?

Assuming Haleine's accent, she said, "Why are you sorry, Iestyn?"

She wasn't eager to impersonate Haleine more than she absolutely had to, but it was how he knew her, and she wasn't sure how to tell him the truth. Or even if she should. It was something to consider, though, because the kid looked petrified.

"I didn't mean to disturb you," he squeaked.

She plastered a smile on her face, hoping to reassure him, and some of the tension left his shoulders. "You're not disturbing me."

Iestyn looked at the ground. "Yes, your majesty."

"Have you come to watch the sparring?" she asked, and the boy nodded. "You should come closer. You can't see properly from back there."

He hesitated, but moved alongside her. Together, they watched the training session, Iestyn's shoulders twitching in sync with the students' movements.

"Do you know how to do that?" she asked. "Fight?"

Sinking into himself, Iestyn shook his head.

"Do you want to learn?" she asked, and he nodded. "Well, if you go find a pair of suitable sticks, I'll teach you."

Iestyn scrutinized her closely. "You're the queen. And you're a girl."

"You're half right," Cate said.

"Did your father teach you?" he asked.

She shook her head. "I never knew my father."

"Who taught you, then?"

The fencing instructors at her overpriced private schools had taught her. Thrust, block, and parry. Sure, a foil or an epee wasn't the same as the swords carried by James and friends, but like the horseback riding, the basic skill set would be transferable. Especially as her weapon would be a stick.

"A woman called Clara," Cate said. "Clara Parker."

"A woman?" Iestyn asked, unconvinced.

Ever since Cate had come to the conclusion that she was somehow stuck in a clone of the middle ages, she had been prepared to face some degree of misogyny. However, she hadn't expected it to come from a scrawny, pre-pubescent half-pint.

Cate gestured to the leader in the clearing. "She's a woman."

"She's not a queen."

What did that have to do with anything? Cate shrugged. "Fine, I won't teach you. Your loss."

"You'll really teach me?" Iestyn asked after a moment. When she looked at him, he added, "Your majesty?"

"Enough to get you started," she said. "Go find those sticks, and we'll begin."

He ran away quickly, making little noise. His return was nearly as speedy, and he presented her with two relatively straight sticks of a workable thickness. She nodded and selected one.

"Good," she said. "This should work just fine."

She took a couple of practice swings. It felt silly to be doing so, but the earnest look on Iestyn's face hastily curbed those feelings. She positioned him in front of her and demonstrated the proper grip. He copied her.

"First, you bow to your opponent," she said. "Or salute, I guess."

"No one bowed to my father before running him through," Iestyn said.

No, but he had bowed before her.

"Good point," Cate said. "Don't bow."

Where should she begin? Teach him to block first? Thrust? Clara had started her students with stance and footwork. Cate had performed endless lunges with her sword arm outstretched and empty while her free arm was held behind her at shoulder height, her elbow sticking out like a bird's wing. She moved forward, keeping her front foot pointed straight out and her back foot angled sideways. She moved backward the same way, doing it over and over again until it was no longer awkward but the most natural thing in the world for her body to do. Boring, maybe, but it had been the proper way to learn the sport.

She looked at Iestyn. He didn't have the time nor the patience for the right way. This wasn't a sport for him.

"You never come into your opponent straight on," she said. "Never. You present too large a target that way. You're still small, so you wouldn't be much of a target anyway, but you never come in straight on. Understand?"

He nodded once, a stony look overtaking his face. She moved beside him and demonstrated a forward lunge, then had him practice strikes on a tree. After a while, she put herself in front of him. He balked for the first time.

"If the queen commanded something of you," she said, "would you do it?"

"Aye, my lady," he said, eyes on the ground.

"Then I command you to attack me as though I were that tree, as though I were one of the soldiers who killed your father."

Ordering him was the wrong thing to do—she felt it immediately—but Iestyn obeyed. Flushed and not thinking, he came at her head-on. She took advantage of his mistake and used her makeshift sword to jab him, not too forcefully, in the chest, directly over his heart. He stopped in his tracks, looked at the stick, and then at her.

"What did I tell you about attacking straight on?" she asked.

"Don't."

"That's right. I said don't, and it was the very first thing you did when pressed," she said. "If this stick had been a sword, and if I had been a soldier, what would you be right now?"

"Dead."

"Yeah," she said, though she was pretty sure it was something Haleine would never say. Her accent was wavering. Had Iestyn noticed? "Don't do it again. Got it?"

He nodded and readjusted his hold on the stick. "Again."

They repeated the exercise six more times. The first three, Cate won easily. The following two were more of a contest, but she maneuvered her way around him. The last time he surprised her, striking her sword arm hard enough to make her yelp. Iestyn pulled back, horrified.

Cate laughed. "Don't look so terrified. That's what you were meant to do."

Iestyn didn't appear convinced.

"You know, you might do better with a dagger," she said. "At least until you grow a bit more. It'll be easier for you, I think. You're small, you're quick. With a dagger you could get in, do the—"

She paused, stunned to be saying these things to *anyone*, much less a kid.

"Your majesty?" Iestyn pressed.

"You get in, do the damage, and get out," she finished. "Before they even realize you were there."

He nodded and thrust his weapon forward, this time attacking an imaginary opponent. The determination on his face made her queasy. She wanted to tell him to go away, that she'd taught him enough for one day, for a *lifetime*, but her mouth refused to form the words. Fortunately, James arrived to do it for her.

"Iestyn," he said, "go back to your mother now, aye?"

"Aye, Captain." Iestyn dropped his stick and bowed to Cate. "Your majesty."

"You can call me Cate," she said.

Iestyn looked unsure about that, but nodded and ran off.

James picked up the stick. "He can call you Cate?"

"They'll all find out sometime that I'm not the queen," she said, trying to infuse more conviction in her voice than she had in her head. "I don't see how *when* matters."

James nodded and sliced the stick through the air. "Where did you learn?"

She shrugged. How long had he been watching? "I had an uncommonly good education."

"You're not bad. You lack passion, though."

"You think I lack passion because I chose not to go medieval on some little kid's ass?"

James was quiet while he attempted to puzzle out what she had said. Then he shrugged and tossed the stick aside. "The boy has a reason to pick up a sword," he said. "It puts a passion in you—one that can't be taught. No matter how good your education may have been."

"Vengeance isn't the same as passion."

"It is when it's all you have to live for."

"He's just a kid," she said. "A baby."

"He stopped being that on the road, and you know it," James said. "Otherwise, you would have shown him nothing."

"You're speaking from experience, aren't you?" Cate asked. "You, Aaron, both of you?"

"There was a lad," James said, "a bit older than Iestyn. His name was Owain, and he was from Enimode."

"And he lived happily ever after with his trusty golden retriever?" she asked, already knowing that whoever Owain was, he did not live happily ever after.

"He lost his mother, his father, his sister—all his family—in the first attack on the village," James said. "He came to us, a green lad, sick with grief, much like Iestyn."

Did James ever tell stories with happy endings? Or, at the very least, stories that didn't involve the massacre of innocents?

"The last battle we fought..." James stared off into the trees. "That last battle, we were outnumbered, so badly outnumbered, none of us thought we'd see another day. We emptied camp of everyone and anyone who could not fight. We tried to get the lads to go, too—Owain and the others. The ones with families went, but—"

"But not Owain," she interjected.

"No," James said, "not Owain."

She steeled herself. "What happened to him?"

"Your father killed him."

What was she supposed to make of that? What did he want from her? She hadn't known Owain. The story made her squeamish, but all of James's stories had that effect on her. But she didn't personally know the kid, so her horror was limited. Neither had she known her father. He was a completely unknown entity in her existence. She didn't even know what the man had looked like. She had never called him 'Dad' or gone to any father-daughter events with him. What did James suppose she would feel? What response was he trying to elicit from her?

Her expression must have mirrored her new inner turmoil because James shook his head.

"I didn't mean to…" He sighed. "I don't know why I said it like that."

She didn't, either. She tossed away her stick and looked at the ground.

"You can't keep them from it," James said. "The horror, the death. They're drawn to it. If we hadn't taken Owain, he would have fought them another way, and maybe he only would have died sooner. All you can do is prepare them the best you can."

"And hope," Cate said.

James looked at her sideways. "Some do, aye."

But not him. The message was clear. She nodded. "You're keeping Aaron from it."

"I need Aaron to stay on the homestead."

"Yeah. To keep it in your name for you," she said. "For when you come back from this."

James shook his head. "I'm not coming back from this."

"Because you think you're going to die?" she asked. "Or because you died when your father did?"

"Aye," he said.

It hadn't been a yes-no question, but the response was still appropriate.

His openness on this subject was curious. She doubted that he talked to everyone like this—or *anyone* like this. She didn't think it was an act, either. If it was, the man deserved a damn academy award.

"You forgot to leave a note," James said.

She nodded. Share time was over. Thank goodness.

"I knew word that the queen was watching weapons training would get back to you," she said. "Figured I shouldn't waste the parchment."

"Aye," James said.

They both watched the training then. Some people had left, but Ilya had arrived and had moved those who remained on to target practice. They mostly used traditional bows, but there was a pair of crossbows as well. Cate had never fired one, but the idea didn't bore her.

"Xena down there seems to be a good instructor," she said.

"Ilya, you mean," James corrected. "Her name is Ilya."

"Ilya. Sure. My mistake."

"She could teach you, too, if you'd like."

"I'm sure that'll thrill her to no end."

"I could teach you," he offered, sounding less certain about that.

She smiled. "Now say that as though you don't think it'll come back to bite you in the ass."

He shrugged. "Can you draw a bow?"

She could draw a bow. Her high school physical education class had also contained an archery unit in which she had excelled. But could she draw a bow from this time—whatever time it was?

"In theory," she said.

"Part of your uncommonly good education?"

No kidding. Her education was starting to feel tailor-made for this experience. That was one hell of a coincidence. Part of her adoption agreement, maybe? You can have the kid so long as you provide her with arcane weapons training?

"Were you honestly worried that I had disappeared?" Cate asked. "Or did you maybe want something?"

"They're ready to move forth."

Move forth. With the plan. The plan she hated. The plan she proposed.

"Oh," she said. "That didn't take long."

"No," James said, "it did not."

She looked at him. Forget the fact that he had somehow managed to Patty Hearst her—even after she had vehemently told him he would not—he appeared and sounded downright irritated with his success. It was unexpectedly interesting.

"So...you need me to go—"

"Back to the tent," he said. "Aye."

But he didn't move. Huh. He really lacked enthusiasm for this plan, didn't he?

Cate wasn't all that excited by it, either, but it was potentially her ticket home. Pointing in the direction in which she thought the tent might be located, she started off.

James tagged along. "We need to spend some time preparing you."

"Preparing me?" she asked.

"You need to do more than sound like the queen."

"How will you do that? Create charts and flash cards, or—"

"Flash cards?"

"Okay, maybe not flash cards," she said. "What are you going to do?"

James sighed. "Teach you to be a lady, I suppose."

That was funny. "*You're* going to teach me to be a lady?"

"Well, your uncommonly good education seems to have some holes after all."

Cate nodded. "Never did get around to finishing school."

"I don't know what that means."

"It doesn't mean anything."

"Then why did you say it?"

"It's what I do," she said. "But I wouldn't worry too much about the prep work. I could probably tap into my inner princess or something. I'm sure that would get the job done."

"I don't know what that means, either."

"It means that somewhere in this soft and cuddly exterior of mine lies an ice queen waiting for her opportunity to put the smackdown on the Y chromosome."

"I'm sorry—what?"

"You worry about getting us to wherever we're going without being seen by whoever's looking. I'll do the rest."

"Is your plan to confuse the nobles with your gibberish until they're so helplessly confused, they don't know to what they're agreeing?"

"Do you think that would work?" she asked. "Because I could do that."

James laughed. She started to look at him but was distracted by a pair of unicorns standing at the edge of camp. The smaller of the two seemed to glow. A trick of the light? Or was it something else? Cate stopped to stare.

James stopped as well, following her gaze. "Is something wrong?"

She shrugged. How the hell would she know? "Your unicorns don't like me."

"They don't like anybody."

James was not an accomplished liar. But she didn't say so.

CHAPTER 13

The one thing, apart from suspicion, that the people of Tamzin Hill had in abundance was ale. Stored in a hidden cellar of the barn in which they had taken refuge was a cache of brew. Dark and strong, it would grant a man a night of dreamless sleep. It was as good a reason as any for Dana to stay on past that first night. Indeed, he had stayed three nights now, spending each one sitting before a fire and sharing a bottle with a pair of men old enough to know how deep his ties to this village ran.

The men were called Cado and Hagan. Dana had only the vaguest memories of them, but their recollections of him had been much stronger. Along with Navlyn, they were the only ones who knew the draw Tamzin Hill held for him. The other residents were all too young to know his history. They knew his name, though. Navlyn had not told them, but it had not mattered. They knew him anyway. There wasn't a corner of the country where his face wasn't known. He'd have to escape to Feond to find anonymity. The idea held some appeal for him. Somewhere in the wilds of that country was a place where he would be a stranger—a nobody—and not the face of an uprising of which he was no longer a part.

But they didn't know that in Tamzin Hill, none of them, and though they were wary of why he hid in their small hamlet, they asked no questions. They scrutinized every gesture and step as Dana helped them reconstruct a life from what had been crushed. They were curious why he helped tend their little garden, or hunted game for their supper instead of hunting those who had done the crushing, but they did not lend voices to their queries.

He suspected Navlyn was responsible for their silence, and for this, Dana was grateful. Theirs would be questions to which he did not have answers, questions to which he did not want the answers. A look, a glance—those could be politely ignored. He could go on drawing their water and repairing their walls while pretending he hadn't seen their stares.

This latest day had been spent thatching the roofs of two cottages nearest to the barn. The work was good—hard, exhausting, and more importantly, distracting. There had been a time when Dana had almost forgotten why he was thatching roofs at all. Almost.

But now there was no such distraction. Cado and Hagan offered no conversation, only a nudge from time to time to either offer or reclaim their shared bottle. Their silence hadn't mattered the first two nights, and Dana didn't know what had changed.

What he did know, what he could feel, was that the demons that had tracked him from Enimode were creeping up on him again. The ale no longer seemed to be enough to keep them at bay. He looked at the bottle, currently in Hagan's hands. His own hands started to shake, so he turned them to fists and pressed them into his gut to steady himself.

Was he really so far gone?

Hagan handed the ale to Cado and left without a word. Dana slid closer, staring at the bottle the way a man might stare at a woman, maybe the way he used to look at Haleine. Cado noticed—how could he not?—and frowned. Dana knew he should look away, but the demons were closing in, and his desperation rising fast.

"Here, lad," the man said, holding out the ale.

Dana accepted it, trying and failing to hide his eagerness, and Cado rose to his feet, using Dana's shoulder to help steady himself. Once his balance was restored, Cado shuffled away. Dana sat alone, humiliation churning inside him. How had he become this...thing?

Holding the bottle before the firelight, he judged how much ale remained. Now that it was his alone, there was perhaps enough to get him through another night. What would he do the next time when he needed more? What would he do once the supply ran out? He couldn't go on like this. He flexed his ankle, lifting his heel off the ground. The dagger inside his boot shifted with the movement.

Maybe he did know what he would do.

Dana put the bottle on the ground between his feet and looked at the fire. Holding his fingers just out of the flames' reach, he watched them try to taste his skin, leaping and missing but rising up to try again. Slowly, he lowered his hand. The flames caressed his skin and tore into his palm.

How long before he turned to ash?

Dropping his hand deeper into the flames, he set out to find the answer. The pain made him close his eyes and grit his teeth. A scream likely would have followed had someone not grabbed his arm and shoved it up.

"What are you doing?" Navlyn demanded, her eyes wild.

Dana looked at his hand and smiled. It hurt.

Lowering his arm, Navlyn knelt and turned his hand over. His palm throbbed and his skin cracked as the heat continued to work its will. It hurt enough to bring tears to his eyes. Mayhap he was still human after all.

"Why would you do this?" Navlyn said.

She didn't wait for a response before ordering a woman he didn't know to fetch her supplies. Bandages, salves, water. He should have told her not to bother, not to waste what limited resources they had.

"It hurt," he said.

"You put your hand in a fire. Of course it hurt," Navlyn said. "Tell me what made you do such a thing."

She looked at him this time, wanting an answer. Silence would no longer be acceptable, so he decided to tell her the truth.

"I didn't think it would matter. I wanted to find out."

"You didn't think it would matter if you put your hand in a fire?"

"No."

"Why would you ever think that?"

The woman returned then with everything Navlyn had requested and laid it out carefully. Navlyn stared at him, waiting for him to continue, but he was unwilling to consider it in a stranger's presence. After a moment, she seemed to realize this and sent the woman away.

"Answer me," Navlyn said, using a tone that would give even Sarai pause.

"You don't know," Dana said. "You don't know the things I've done."

"Don't I?"

As Navlyn washed his wound with cold water, Dana closed his eyes. "You know what they want you to hear. You know what tales they decide to tell. You don't know the truth."

"Tell me the truth, then. Tell me why you are here."

He was tempted. He wanted to admit his sins and tell her of the girl he killed, the girl he let die for him. He wanted to beg for forgiveness—from her, from her god. He didn't know, he didn't care, but surely Navlyn would have answers. She was a woman of a holy order who had presided over his very entrance into this world. She would know why he could not seem to leave it, why the goddess had saved him only to dismiss him. She could tell him why he hadn't opened his veins in Piangi when he had no true reason not to. She could tell him why he hadn't done it since.

"Dana?" she prompted. "Why did you come here?"

"I had nowhere else to go," he confessed.

"I don't understand," she said, applying a salve to his hand. "What about the war? *Your* war?"

The salve brought relief to the injury. For the span of a shallow breath, his hand ceased to burn.

"They didn't want me anymore," he said. "They told me to go."

Navlyn laughed as she wrapped linen around his hand. "Since when have you ever done as you were told? The lad I knew—"

Anger rushing through him, Dana stood. "Don't tell me how it used to be. How *I* used to be," he snapped. "It's meaningless now; don't you see that? The lad you knew is gone. He disappeared into that bloody forest and never came out again."

"What happened to him?"

Navlyn's voice was calm. That made it worse; it made everything worse. Suddenly, the barn was too small and growing smaller still. The walls, covered with his tormenting demons, were closing in on him, so he stumbled to the door and pushed his way through.

The moon and stars were hidden behind a barrier of clouds, making the night as dark as any Dana had known. He relied on instinct to find his way to the forest and did not stop until he was a good distance away from the village.

He leaned against a tree for a moment before righting himself and screaming until his lungs burned as badly as his hand. Turning to the tree, he attacked it, hitting and kicking it over and over again until the rage finally drained out of his body and seeped into the ground. Then, he rested his forehead against the trunk and squeezed his eyes shut. Tears escaped anyway, running down his cheeks, dripping off his nose and chin, and disappeared into the void alongside his anger.

He had done this before—screaming, yelling, crying. He had assailed a wall in Orla's alehouse, pushing against a force that refused to push back while a hole in his gut threatened his life. It should have killed him. Why couldn't he break free?

The pond. It was nearby. He could go there and slip under the surface. He could stay there until his lungs begged for air, then find a way to stay under until they could beg no more. He should have done that in Enimode. The sisters should have done that the day he'd been born. Tossed him in and never looked back.

"Dana?"

Navlyn had followed him. Of course she had. Her faith had instilled in her the belief that everyone could be saved, that no one was without hope. Obviously, her god had never known the likes of him. His uninjured hand formed a fist, and he drove it into the tree a final time, grinding his knuckles into the bark before letting it fall to his side. He turned around.

"What happened to him?" she asked.

He slid against the tree until he sat on the ground. Navlyn stood in front of him, so he looked away and stared into the woods. Somewhere in there was the answer to her question, the place where everything had begun, where his four-year-old self happened upon a tiny pegasus perched atop a boulder. That was the day Dana left the holy house.

That was the day they killed him.

"Dead," he said.

"I don't believe that's true."

He looked at his burned hand. The injury was alive, pulsating and refusing to be contained. It was one thousand daggers attacking at once. It hurt, but it didn't hurt enough.

"You don't *want* to believe that's true," he corrected. "But it is. They took that boy, the goddess and her minions, and they hollowed him out. They made him what they wanted, what they could use. They made him their pet—they made *me* their pet, and I let them because I didn't know that I shouldn't."

Navlyn's posture changed at the mention of the goddess. She knelt on his left, put her lantern on the ground, and opened a small satchel she wore on her hip. Pulling out a roll of linen, she continued what she had started in the barn. She didn't speak, and Dana wasn't surprised. Few were comfortable talking about a deity that wasn't their own. But he appreciated her silence. Now that he had started, he found he didn't want to stop.

"They did it to me, and then, because they wanted it, I did it to her," he said, resting his head against the tree.

"Her?"

"The girl I killed."

This made Navlyn more uncomfortable. She stopped touching him and drew her entire body away. "Is that not the nature of war?"

Despite his confession, she wanted to forgive him. He smiled at her with genuine affection, but she did not see it. She had returned to what she'd been doing, but her movements were now hesitant. It spoke volumes about her disapproval and disappointment. He hated to see it, but it was good she understand what he was.

"There's nothing natural about war," Dana said.

He couldn't help but remember a similar conversation with Haleine. Sacrifice and war. Then, she had been the one telling him what he had to do and how he had to do it. He had to divorce himself from the cost of winning. *War is about sacrifice*, she had said. *Even the victors suffer loss.*

Which of them had been the victor?

"There's even less natural about what I did to her," he said, brushing the memories away. "She loved me, and I destroyed her."

Navlyn finished fussing with the bandage. "Your other hand now. Let me see it."

Her concern made him laugh, but he did as she asked, stretching his arm across his chest. She took his hand and examined his knuckles closely.

"You can't make me whole," he said.

"Nor am I trying to. All I hope to do here is to keep you from falling apart further."

"All I want is the opposite."

"I don't believe that's true," she said, wrapping a bandage around his hand.

Dana pulled free. "What *do* you believe?"

"That no matter the number of roofs you thatch, you'll not find what you're looking for here."

There was truth in her words, and he hated it. He looked away and saw Haleine, somehow glowing faintly in the darkness as she stood amongst the trees. An odd whimper left his throat.

What manner of witchcraft was this?

Navlyn glanced over her shoulder. She did not appear to see Haleine. Taking advantage of his distraction, she grabbed his hand once more. He was too caught up in Haleine to care.

"I brought everything to ruin," he said.

It was not what he should have said. It was a paltry apology, another insult, and Haleine deserved more, much more, than that.

"Ruins can be rebuilt," Navlyn said, tying off the bandage. She did not know he hadn't been talking to her.

"But not the girl."

Navlyn took his face in her hands and forced him to look at her. "Are you so certain she is lost?"

He lifted his eyes to the trees. Haleine's apparition had disappeared. "I'm certain."

Navlyn nodded. "Then you find another way."

She dropped her hands to restore order to her satchel. Dana watched her, noting how efficiently she worked. If she hadn't been so entrenched with Tamzin Hill and its people, he'd send her to the rebellion. She would see the war ended in spectacular fashion.

"What if I can't?" he asked.

A valid question. All he could see was the bottom of a bottle of ale and the ghost of the girl he loved. He couldn't do this; he couldn't be what she thought he was.

"You owe it to the girl to try."

Was it that simple? Dana looked again to the spot where Haleine had been. He flexed his fingers, testing their limits.

"Aye," he said. "I owe her that."

———✦———

Instead of lessons on how to be a proper lady, James sat Cate down to talk about where they were headed and what they would do there without actually giving her any details. He was starting to make Faolan look forthcoming. She told him so, and he responded with an eye roll.

"The man you're going to meet is Lord Emrys," James said, "and if you talk to him the way you talk to me, this plan will never work."

"I'll try to keep a civil tongue in my head," Cate said.

"Please do."

"Emrys? Is that what you said? Is that his given name or surname?"

"Surname."

"What's his given name?"

"I don't know."

"Would Haleine?"

"I doubt it."

"Okay," Cate said. "Why Emrys?"

"Pardon?"

"I'm sure there are scores of noble families in your realm here. Why did you choose Emrys?"

"He's the closest."

Cate blinked. Wow. James was truly a terrible liar. She'd offer to help him improve in that area if she didn't think she could use it to her advantage.

"Let me see if I understand this," she said. "You based this entire decision—a decision which very possibly will make the difference between the life and death of your cause—on proximity?"

"No," James admitted.

"I didn't think so," she said. "That means you, or someone you trust, are familiar with him."

"Not someone I trust."

The intonation he used belonged to what she had decided to call his backstory voice. She'd wager all the money in her not-insignificant trust fund that the someone he didn't trust was the same as the might-as-well-be-dead leader.

"Have you met Emrys before?" she asked.

"I've been under his roof."

"Kind of cryptic, but okay. Has Haleine ever met this man before?"

"I wouldn't think so. Lord Emrys was never one for palace life, and the queen seldom left the palace."

"What's his idea of the good life? What does he like?"

"Drinking, whoring, and gambling. Sometimes in that order."

"We should have a deep discussion someday about your class prejudices," Cate said.

"Why would we do that?"

She shrugged. "It seems as though you harbor a lot of hatred for the nobility. That kind of thing can be unhealthy, you know."

"What have they ever done for me?"

"And that's why I'll be doing the talking. I'll have a better chance of hiding my seething dislike for the man."

"You've never met him," James said. "Why would you have any dislike at all for him?"

"You're sort of missing the point," Cate said. "My fault. I've been told my sense of humor is a little dry. And lacking."

"Humor?" James echoed. "Something you said was supposed to be humorous?"

"Supposed to be, yes," she said. "And, in my head, it was both clever and amusing."

"Best keep your humor in check when we're in Lord Emrys's presence."

"I'll do my best."

Now James looked as though he wanted to tell her that he needed more than that. She didn't know what stopped him. Maybe he was afraid she'd keep on talking. There was precedent.

When Gair entered the tent, James looked away. "Something wrong?"

"They're calling for you, Captain," Gair said.

James sighed. "I'll be right back," he said to her. "I'll leave Rhydwyn and Gair here, if you need anything."

She nodded, and James disappeared outside. His change of phrasing was interesting. Starsky and Hutch were no longer her captors and guards. Nope, if she needed anything, they would be at her service. How unexpected.

Cate reached for the parchment on top of the table. It was the map of the entire country. Finding Enimode, she walked her fingers across the surface, trying to work out where she had gone after leaving there. The biggest location on the map was Eluned, and even included a drawing of a castle. That had to be the city. Everything else, though, was a mystery. It probably didn't matter anyway. Her navigational skills were the product of a post-GPS world.

"Who are you?"

She didn't recognize the man's voice. The accent seemed more refined than those of James and his band of misfits. Not to say that they were a group of Eliza Doolittles or anything, but the man speaking to her now had the same sort of clip to his words that Haleine had. He was Henry Higgins. He was upper crust. Nevertheless, she kept her eyes on the map. She didn't care about crusts, upper or otherwise.

"My name is Inigo Montoya," she said with a slight Spanish accent. "You killed my father. Prepare to die."

"I did not kill your father," Henry Higgins said.

She put down the map. The man standing before her was all-around average. He was older, at least middle-aged. He was shorter than James, but taller than her, with brown hair and eyes and weathered skin. His build could be described as neither fat nor slim, but suggested he had a certain amount of strength. A soldier, maybe?

"You knew my father?" she asked, dropping the accent.

Her mystery guest nodded. "Who are you?"

Not enjoying the way he looked at her, Cate glanced at the tent's entrance. James had left Rhydwyn and Gair on guard duty. There wasn't any way they would abandon their post, but neither could she imagine them letting just anyone in—and this man reeked of being just anyone.

"How'd you get in here?" she asked.

"Your rebels aren't the only ones capable of stealth."

"*My* rebels?"

Henry Higgins wasn't listening. "He said you weren't the queen. I see now that is true."

She didn't know about whom he was talking, but the fact that he referred to the rebels as hers was a red flag. That meant they weren't his, which couldn't possibly mean anything good for his presence in the rebel camp. She looked to the tent's entrance again. Should she bother to call for her big, strong, and oblivious bodyguards?

"I mean you no harm," Henry Higgins said. "Nor did I do anything to harm the two men outside."

"That's good to know," she said. "If you're not one of the rebels, who are you?"

"My name is Idwal Kai," he said. "I served with Darian Coileáin, and later for him. I was with him when he died."

He didn't mean it to be shocking. He was merely stating a fact. He had been there when her father had died. That was interesting, too. No one had said anything to her about how that had happened. *Our father followed* had been all Haleine had offered, and Faolan had stopped after admitting Darian had died in a battle against the rebels. Cate watched Idwal move around the tent. What would he tell her if she asked?

"They told me he died in battle," she said.

"Yes, he did at that."

"Is there something more to it?"

"You should perhaps ask your rebel leader about that."

"He's not my rebel leader," she said, looking at the entrance again. Was it too late to call for the boys?

"You do not have to call for your guards," Idwal said. "I sincerely mean you no harm."

"What do you want?"

"Please, who are you?" Idwal asked. "You are not the queen, but who that does make you, I think I cannot believe."

"Who do you think I am?" she countered. "You come in here, claiming to know my father, but you don't know who I am?"

"Mireille," Idwal said softly, and she flinched. "They thought—we all thought—you were dead. What happened to you, my lady? How did you come to be here?"

That was a question she wasn't ready to answer. Or could answer. "How did you come to be here?" she said instead.

"I was taken prisoner during the same battle that killed your father," Idwal said. "Are you a prisoner, too, my lady?"

She didn't want to answer that, either. When James's low, angry tone broke the resulting silence, she was grateful.

"What are you doing here?" he demanded.

She looked at James. His eyes were riveted on Idwal.

"You told me to stay here," she said. "Remember?"

"Not you," James said, not breaking his stare. "How did you get past the guards?"

"Stealth," Cate said. "He used stealth."

James looked at her in bewilderment. She didn't quite understand why she wanted so badly to diffuse the situation, either, but suspected it had something to do with the fact that Idwal had known her father.

"What of the men set to watch you?" James asked, turning again to Idwal. "Did you use stealth to lose them, too?"

"Subterfuge," Idwal said. "Don't be too hard on them."

"Get out of here," James growled.

Idwal turned to her and bowed. "Ever your servant, my lady."

Cate watched him go, perplexed by the entire exchange.

"Are you all right?" James asked.

"What?" She looked at him. "No, I'm fine. I just—I'm fine."

"What did he want?"

She shrugged. "He wanted to know who I was."

"Did you tell him?"

Cate shook her head. "I didn't have to."

—⟨∿∿⟩—

There was a time when the utterance of Mireille's name was a sacred thing, whispered by only the most worthy. Sighle remembered it well—she remembered everything well—but now that time was gone. Now that Mireille walked amongst them once more, her name had all but disappeared. It was a river bed in the summer heat, cracked and parched and crushed beneath an oblivious heel of a boot belonging to her once-lost sister, for Mireille called herself Catherine Cole.

A false name for a false girl who belonged neither here nor there.

She called herself Cate and demanded everyone surrounding her do the same. They had given in to her request—even the pegasus, who knew what Mireille did not, had lowered himself to use that untrue name—but Sighle would not. She would only think of her sister by the name destiny had assigned to her.

Mireille Coileáin.

I want to meet her. I want to stand before her and see her with my own eyes. I want to smell her and touch her with my own hands. This child of reverence, of sky-exploding color, shielded by a goddess and coveted by the dark. A child lost, a woman found.

I will be what she needs, too.

No longer was Sighle's path uncertain. The fireflies had been replaced by the sun, beating down and illuminating all. Everything was clear now—what she was meant to do, what Haleine's role was to be. Mireille, too—Sighle saw her purpose as well. Oh, how she wanted that.

The desire for Mireille grew more potent with every breath. It made her skin itch. She scratched at herself until her skin turned red and her maid had to bandage it. She ached inside, so badly did she want this. A hole, a pulse, sat in her stomach like a stone. No, not a stone. A stone was nothing; a stone was not alive, and what was in her, what pined for this stranger, was very much alive. She wanted to cut it out. She wanted to take a knife to her belly and slice and score her skin and let it ooze out of her before it could rip its way free. Claws it had, scratching at her, making holes as it went, filling her with its venom, filling her with its need.

Poison. Mireille was poison within her. She possessed Sighle as Sighle had worn others, and the only cure was to capture the ghost and force it into flesh.

I will make her mine.

Mine.

Every day, every moment, spent watching her sister, Sighle wanted her more. Every breath formed the phrase. Her heart began to beat the word.

Mine.

I will make her mine.

Mine.

Mireille would be what Haleine was not. Mireille would be the stuff of legend and bring the world to its knees. She would step on its neck and hold it there. Destroyer her name would be.

And it would be done because Sighle so desired it.

But there was also the matter of the brown-eyed boy.

At times, she studied him more closely than Mireille. Trouble. There was such trouble there. She could not ignore him. Watching the pair of them in Enimode and Eluned had been simple, but once they were within the protective walls of the rebel camp, her pastime became a chore.

At first, she spied upon them through the gray eyes of the boy from the road. Iestyn, her sister had called him. Sighle had a kinship with the lad, although he did not know it and never would become aware of it. They both had watched their fathers hacked to pieces, grabbing their necks when the killing blow came. From the seclusion of her bed chamber had Sighle watched her father die, her eyes closed and her head bent to her chest. Her body jerked as she felt each blow her father took. Iestyn witnessed his sire's death the length of a man away. He felt his father's blood hit his face. Never again would he find his face clean.

He had not cried at the burial, but he wept into his sleeve when hidden by the night. He thought it made him weak, to cry, but Sighle did not care about that. She had seen Darian Coileáin cry openly and without shame. Tears did not make a man weak.

Neither did a lack of tears make a man strong. The more she watched the brown-eyed boy, the more concerned she became. He scowled and paced and questioned every command he issued, cursing those who had made him lead. And for those who would make him send her sister to her death, he harbored a deeper hatred still.

If Haleine were the sacrifice, he would not be so opposed. If Haleine were the one he had to burn, he would happily build and light her pyre. The brown-eyed boy's heart echoed Sighle's own.

But his determination would not stop her. He could not keep Mireille. He would not keep her.

I will make her mine.

Mine.

Sighle also made use of her father's man. He'd been left behind in Mairéad after Nathan's death, part of her father's effort to safeguard the queen. She had been aware that Idwal Kai had come to Lira, but had lost track of him when she had lost her father. As she eased in and out of his skin, she found she was pleased to have him back. Idwal Kai had served her father well. Now he would serve her.

She made him whisper her sister's name and watched Mireille respond as though it were something dangerous.

Then she witnessed the brown-eyed boy act the lion as he drove her father's man away. *Get out of here*, he snarled. She could have made Idwal Kai stay just as easily as she had made him do everything else, but her father's man acquiesced and walked away. Let the brown-eyed boy think himself strong.

There would still come a day when he would find she would not be so easily turned aside.

Sighle worked her way out of the camp's defenses and lay wasted and trembling on her bed. A small rivulet of blood trickled from her nose. Running her thumb across it, she examined the smear before dragging her hand across the coverlets. Each time, the amount of blood lessened, but it remained a sign of the exertion the magic required. She was not accustomed to being so weak after working her will. It had come so easily for so long that to meet any sort of resistance was frustrating and exhausting. She took solace in knowing that no matter the toll her body took, she could do what the pegasus thought no one could.

Nor would it drain her forever. She would get stronger, and defeating their barricades would get easier. She looked at the ceiling as she waited to settle once again in her own body, then turned her head to find her maid.

The girl's name was Nonna, and she had been Haleine's favorite, sent to spy upon Sighle after Darian's death. Nonna, though none knew it, had belonged to Sighle ever since.

"Fetch me food," she said to the girl tending the fire.

Nonna dropped what she held in her hands and left to fulfill her mistress's request. When the door closed, Sighle sat up, moving slowly, as she was usually lightheaded after an extended visit to the rebel camp. This time was no exception, and she drew her knees to her chest.

There was peace in her head for only a moment before, unbidden and unwelcome, the whispers flooded in. Whenever her guard was down, she would hear them all, every soul within the palace walls and even some beyond those barriers. She heard their every thought, and felt every impulse, every desire, every joy, every sadness. Rising to the top of the clamor was one distinct voice, one of the two whom Sighle had long shadowed.

It belonged to Haleine's maid. Bronagh was thought to be a traitor by those who loved the queen, and her guilt was slowly rising water in her lungs. Sighle had spent days at Haleine's side, watching her sister drown herself over and over again as she tried to abscond from that which could not be escaped. While Haleine had tried to give her body over to death, Sighle had discovered only serenity.

Would she find the same release were she to enter the maid's body? Would the guilt Bronagh felt be enough to take her down and settle her, as Haleine's rage had been? Sighle thought to try it, to drown along with the maid, until the voice of her puppet lover intruded and brought her abruptly back to her purpose.

Omur meant to flood the forest with his men. The brown-eyed boy had left a gift of death rotting in the brush. The captain of the guard had been shocked by this discovery, as though finding his soldiers slain by their enemy in a time of war was a thing over which one should be surprised. He shouted for the rebel leader's head, not knowing Dana had naught to do with this. Omur's man could scream all he liked, and the rebel leader could kill as many of the king's army as he liked. She wouldn't let anyone touch Dana.

Dana was hers.

Nor was it the way to find Mireille.

Why did Omur not see it? The pegasus, the unicorns, and all their human followers could hide for years in the Liran forests, and he would not find them again. The first time had been a fluke, a perfect storm of circumstance that Omur would never be able to replicate. Flooding the forest with his minions would only drive the rebellion deeper into hiding, taking him farther away from Mireille.

Taking her farther away from Mireille.

She despised having to depend upon him to do this. How often did she listen to him complain about the ignorance of others, when his own incompetence was a more grievous slight? He would ruin everything. Why had the dark gods placed such power and faith inside such an idiot?

She would have to guide him.

When she arrived, his chambers were crawling with milling men making their plans. She walked through the room until she stood in front of him.

"Look at me," she demanded, her voice soft in volume but firm in tone.

His eyes immediately found hers.

"Send your men to Labhras. Tell them to lie in wait in the forest outside the village," she said. "They'll find her there. They'll be able to bring her back to you."

Back to her.

She wound her way, unnoticed, through the men to stand by the balcony doors. When she heard Omur give his man the command she had given him, she smiled.

Now for the maid.

———⟿⟿———

There was still just so much blood.

Bronagh had scrubbed at the stains until her own hands bled, but she could not erase what had been done. She never would, yet she had continued on until her body had given out and she could worry about it no more.

Since then, she lay on the floor in the queen's chambers, her palm pressed against the stain of her lady's blood, as though she might derive something from it. She stayed there day into night and back again, feeling the life leave her body a little at a time. It seeped out her fingers, absorbed by the tarnished floor.

For how long would she lay there? Was this how she would die? Would she be nothing but dust and bone before any sought her out?

"They found her," a voice whispered into her ear. "The queen. They've found her in the forests near Labhras. They're going to bring her back."

Though Bronagh did not move and could not see who had spoken, a spark was relit. The queen found. The queen *alive*, and in the forest near Labhras. It wouldn't be long before they brought her back.

How could Dana have allowed this to happen?

Bronagh rose as the trumpets sounded, and from the queen's balcony, she watched the soldiers march through the city. When the last of them had left her sight, she made for the nursery, rumors and whispers chasing her every step. Willem stood sentry inside.

"They think they found the queen," she said. "Did you hear?"

Willem didn't say anything. He didn't acknowledge her presence.

"They sent men to bring her back," she said. "I just watched them go."

He offered her nothing. There had been a time when things had been so different for them both. They had never loved each other, only the woman they served, but there had been companionship and comfort. She wanted to move in close and wrap her arms around him. She longed to feel his hands on her skin, anywhere on her skin, but she doubted he would ever touch her again. They weren't those people anymore.

"All right, then," she said and walked away.

Before she reached the door, he said, "I've seen to it."

What did that mean? Bronagh turned around. "You've seen to it?"

"If they do find her, if it is her," he said, "I've seen to it."

He didn't elaborate further. Grateful he had told her even that much, she nodded. Willem would do what he could. They would both have to hope that it would be enough.

"If it is her, if they do find her," Bronagh said. "Willem, they think she's a traitor."

He nodded. "She is."

How could he say it so plainly? "They'll treat her as a traitor," Bronagh said.

"Aye."

Did he not understand what that meant? Sabine had been named traitor, too, and Bronagh's body still shuddered to think what had been done to her. She could hear the girl's screams and the sound of the whip cracking skin. It would be much worse for Haleine. Bronagh's stomach rolled as she looked at Willem in disbelief. How could he stand there so calmly while they discussed the fate of the traitor queen they both loved?

"What will we do for her then?" she asked.

Willem shook his head slowly. "I don't know."

CHAPTER 14

The last thing for Cate to do before embarking upon their fucked-up mission was to look the part—starting with an honest-to-goodness gown that would have made Cinderella jealous. Hanah held it up for inspection, and Cate looked it over with a serious amount of skepticism. Made from a dark blue material that might have been silk, it seemed to be nothing but laces and plunging necklines.

"I'm supposed to wear that?" she said.

"Is it not to your liking?" Hanah asked. "I do apologize, but we have nothing else."

"Yeah, no, I wouldn't expect you to be flush with women's formal wear or anything," Cate said. "It's just…Why can't I wear what I already have on?"

Hanah looked at Cate's shirt and pants. "That's hardly appropriate."

"It's clean. Clean-ish."

"That doesn't make it appropriate for the queen," Hanah said. She shook the gown. "Come on, now. We haven't time to waste."

Cate sighed and pulled her shirt over her head. "Let's get this over with."

The gown was heavier than it looked, and the weight of it held her in place as Hanah worked on the laces running down her back. Each pull was more uncomfortable than the last. If they were tightened any further, Cate's kidneys would be looking for a new place to live.

"I will be able to breathe in this thing, right?" she asked.

"Of course," Hanah answered.

"Just checking."

Hanah gave the laces one last tug. "You may sit now."

"How magnanimous of you," Cate said, but gratefully sank into the chair. It helped, but not much, as the gown prevented her from slouching. So this was what it was like to have good posture. If only her mother or Fiona could see her. Sitting up straight *and* wearing a dress. They'd be so pleased.

Hanah set to work on Cate's hair, first running a comb through it, before braiding multiple sections. Apparently, ponytails weren't appropriate for the queen, either. Eventually, Cate's head was forced down, giving her an up-close-and-personal view of her brand new cleavage.

The neckline was worse than she'd thought. She had worn less revealing bikinis. Cate attempted to yank it up, but it was determined to stay put.

"Please tell me there's a shawl or something to complete this ensemble," she said.

"No. No shawl. Nothing else," Hanah said, and tapped beneath Cate's chin. "Head up, please."

Cate obliged. "I'm just supposed to go out there like this?"

"How else would you go?"

"Not on display for all to see, maybe?" Cate asked. "How is this okay, but my tank top was indecent?"

Hanah knelt in front of her. "Tank top?"

"Never mind," Cate said. "What are you doing?"

Hanah held up a pair of shoes that looked to be an early version of Mary Janes. "You cannot go barefoot."

"Well, I can put them on myself."

Hanah sat back and looked at her. "Can you?"

Given that she couldn't even slouch, Cate knew the answer was no. She sighed again. "Fine. Whatever."

"All right, then," Hanah said, and reached beneath Cate's skirts to locate her feet.

"Where did this dress come from anyway?" Cate asked. "It's a tad extravagant for a group of people squatting in the middle of a forest, isn't it?"

Hanah laughed. "Indeed. It belonged to the queen."

"How did it end up here?"

James walked in before Hanah could respond. He looked Cate over, his expression one of complete derision. A moment later, he shook his head and the look disappeared.

"How much longer?" he asked Hanah.

She stood. "We're finished."

He nodded. "Give us a moment, then?"

Hanah squeezed Cate's hand. "Be careful out there, aye? I would prefer it if all of you returned in one piece for once."

Cate didn't know Hanah well, but she hadn't come across as one prone to hyperbole. Did that mean ending up in multiple pieces was a possibility? Cate looked at James. At no point in time was that mentioned as a risk. Who the hell were they going to see? Sweeney Todd?

"It'll be fine, Hanah," James said.

She patted his cheek on her way out. "See that it is."

"Everything all right?" Cate asked once they were alone.

"Not for a long time," he answered.

Drama queen. Cate made a face he didn't notice. "You don't like Haleine much, do you?" she said.

"Does it matter?"

"It might."

How many times would they have variations of the same conversation? There was no give-and-take between them. What happened in a game of chicken when neither player was willing to flinch?

James shook his head. "It doesn't."

"If you say so." She stood, using the table for support until she was sure she could stand on her own. "What did you want to talk about? Did something happen?"

"No, I just wanted to..." James touched the map on the table. "Here. We're here. In the Donasien Woods."

Cate turned to get a better look as he traced a line she thought was meant to be a road.

"We'll travel along this path to the village of Labhras," he said, his finger tapping the word. "Lord Emrys's keep is found there."

Had he decided to trust her? Or did he think they were walking into a death trap, so it wouldn't matter if she knew where she was?

"We'll be on horseback," he continued. "You, me, and three others. An advance guard has already been sent, and there will be a rear guard as well. We'll keep you safe."

Maybe he didn't think they would die. He wouldn't put all those people at risk for nothing, would he?

Whatever the cost, I have to protect you.

Maybe he would.

"Horseback," she said. "Not unicorns?"

James shook his head. "They're staying behind. Faolan, too. Any other questions?"

"Does the sun rise in the east?"

His face creased in fleeting confusion. "Aye."

She nodded and glanced at the map. "Does this mean you trust me, or you think we're going to die?"

"I'm not sure."

She sighed. "This is a horrible plan, isn't it?"

"Can't think of one worse."

Cate smiled at the immediacy of his response. "Well, we should go. Burning daylight, advance team advancing, and all that."

"Aye," James said. "I just..."

"What?"

He didn't finish his thought. He stayed silent for so long that she carefully patted her hair. Did she not look all right? James shook his head, actually smiling as he took her hand and lowered it to her side.

"Thank you, Cate," he said. "For doing this."

"You don't have to thank me."

"Aye, I do."

This time, it wasn't the gown's laces making her uncomfortable. She shrugged and left the tent before anything else could be said.

A small group, armed with swords and bows, had gathered outside. The rear guard, presumably. Some acknowledged her with a simple nod, while others treated her to a full-fledged bow. Cate nodded back. How many of them knew she wasn't their queen?

Her protection detail—Rhydwyn, Gair, and a redheaded man—waited to the group's left, five horses between them. Cate followed James over to them.

"Cate, this is Semias," he said, and the redheaded man bowed. "He'll be accompanying us."

"Hi," she said.

Semias smiled warmly. "My lady."

"Let's get you in the saddle," James said. "The mare is yours."

Gair led a tall, bay horse forward. James crouched at the mare's side, fingers laced together. As there was no way the gown would allow her to get up there on her own, she raised the hem of her skirt and lifted her foot, but stopped when she saw the saddle. There was something wrong with it. Why did it look like that?

When she figured it out, she put her foot down and looked at James. "Sidesaddle? Seriously?"

James straightened. "It's a woman's saddle."

"It's a joke, that's what it is," she said. "I can't use that. What do you expect me to do?"

"Not fall off. Do you need a hand up, or can you manage on your own?"

"What I need is a different saddle. A *real* saddle, like what everyone else has."

"You can't have one," James said. "It's what she would use, so it's what you will use."

Cate placed her hands on her hips and glared, but it did nothing to weaken his resolve. Finally, she sighed with as much annoyance as she could muster and allowed him to give her a boost.

"When we arrive at the keep," James said, "you're to stay in the saddle until I help you down."

"But I won't need help getting down. Especially because it's a sidesaddle, and most likely, I'll already be on my face in the dirt."

"It's not a matter of needing help. It's a matter of propriety."

"Propriety. Right," Cate said. "I forgot my vagina makes me—"

"Stop talking," James pleaded. "I know you're some kind of man-eating demon woman—"

"Man-eating demon woman?" she echoed, too amused to try and hide it.

"—but the queen is not," he finished. "Whatever else she may be, the queen is—"

"Proper?" Cate offered.

"Aye, and you're about as far away from that as one can get."

"Thank you."

"That's not a compliment," he said. "Sounding like her won't be enough. You have to *be* her."

"I highly doubt you want me to *be* a raving, suicidal lunatic."

"I don't want you to be any sort of lunatic," he said. "I want you to—"

"You want me to convince Emrys to throw his support to you and your ragtag group of followers," she said, dropping the humor. "I know the plan. I was there when it was made, remember?"

"I remember."

"I'm pretty motivated to make this happen," she said. "You need to have some faith that I'll be able to pull this off."

"Faith." James smiled. "You really don't know me at all."

"Be a drama queen on your own damn time," she said. "Just get on your horse, and let's go."

With the hint of another smile, James called for everyone to move out.

As they left the camp, her protection detail fell into formation. James took point, Rhydwyn and Gair were on either side of her, while Semias brought up the rear. They rode for the better part of the morning. No one said much. They were too focused on the woods and the road, worrying about what might be lurking around the next bend, to be bothered with conversation. The silence only increased the tension, and Cate found herself sincerely glad of the idiotic sidesaddle, as it gave her something else on which to concentrate besides the ever-increasing doubt and fear.

The forest gave way to an open dirt road, bordered by fields of crops and livestock, and the occasional cottage and barn. Dwellings became more frequent as they progressed, until they were surrounded by multi-story buildings on either side. The stone-paved streets were crowded with villagers, who paid them little mind as they went about their day.

The keep was not nearly as impressive as the palace in Eluned had been, obviously built for protection and endurance rather than aesthetics. But it was solid and formidable, and Cate's heart beat faster as they grew closer. This had 'death trap' written all over it.

But they pressed on.

Four sentries blocked the entrance, and James brought his horse to a halt. Cate stopped at his side, while the other three formed a line behind them.

"The queen of Lira has come to see the lord of Labhras," James said. "Let us pass."

The sentries stared at her. It was some time before one of the men stepped forward.

"She can come in," he said. "The rest of you can wait out here."

"No," Cate said in her borrowed accent. "You will not deprive me of my escorts. Move aside, and allow us to pass."

"Not armed," the sentry said.

"Yes, armed," Cate countered. "Are your lord's soldiers so lacking that these four men alone are a threat?"

As the sentries looked at one another, unsure how to answer, Cate urged her mare forward, forcing the men to part. Behind her, James swore, and the sentries shouted a protest. The clattering of hooves and boots chased her into a muddy, crowded courtyard.

James caught her first, leaning over to grab the mare's bridle. The expression on his face indicated that if Lord Emrys didn't kill her, he would. The sentries were still shouting, catching the attention of every last soul within earshot. They stopped what they were doing and gawked at her.

The only people not shouting or staring were a group of men engaged in swordplay at the far end of the yard. Watching them was a stout, older man who appeared to be wearing the well-tailored remnants of a circus tent. When the guards' cries reached his ears, he looked over his shoulder, straightening as his eyes landed on her. He barked out something she couldn't hear over the ruckus, but the men ceased their practice and went down on one knee, their heads bowed.

As the roly-poly man crossed the yard, other people dropped to their knees, or bent low at the waist. Even the irate sentries stopped their shouting and bowed deeply. Did that make him the lord of Labhras?

Sliding from the saddle, James waved the other three back. He didn't look happy as he lifted her from the horse, but she no longer seemed to be the reason why.

"Coming toward us," he whispered, setting her on the ground.

He stayed at her side, and together they watched Emrys approach. The lord of Labhras's eyes skimmed over James and settled on her. Cate stared back until he not only had looked away, but also knelt in the mud before her.

"Your majesty," he said. "You are alive."

"Obviously," Cate said. "Please, rise."

Lord Emrys stood. "There are a great many men searching for you."

"Are you one of them?" she asked.

She thought she could feel James's anxiety grow. He didn't want to be there—neither did she, really—but was his fear justified?

Emrys smiled. "Not anymore."

"But you were."

"Looking for you? Yes," Emrys said. "I am as the king commands me, your majesty. He is desperate for your recovery and return."

"I'm sure that he is," she said. "Is there a place where we might speak privately?"

"Your majesty," Emrys said, "I am..."

"Yes?"

Emrys glanced at James, then at the other three members of the rebellion. They had fanned out, monitoring Emrys's men. No weapons had been drawn, but hands on both sides were poised in a prime position to do so.

"The circumstances of your arrival are—well, they are quite unexpected, to say the least," Emrys said.

"You do not realize how deep that truth runs," she said.

"They told us you were—"

"Kidnapped? Likely murdered?"

"Yes, your majesty. Among other things. There are many rumors surrounding your disappearance from the palace."

Just the kind of murky waters she wanted to have to wade through. Yipee. "Let my presence amongst these men prove otherwise. I clearly am not dead, neither was I snatched from the palace by anyone," she said. "I left of my own volition to join with these people, and now I have come here to speak with you. Privately, if you please."

"Of course, my queen," Emrys said, bowing quickly. "Come this way. Your men can stay here."

"They are not my men. They are quite their own," she said, and then gestured to James. "But he will accompany me."

Emrys looked at James again. "As your majesty wishes."

He turned toward the keep. Cate hesitated, glancing at James. This was what he wanted, right? When he met her eyes and nodded, she followed Emrys inside.

———✺———

Upon taking his first step inside Emrys's keep, James had to stop himself from grabbing Cate and running straight back to the forest.

Coming here, bringing *her* here, had been a mistake. He knew it so clearly now that he hated himself for not seeing it sooner. Why had he agreed to such a foolhardy plan? She was the key to everything, and he had brought her here to chase a ghost of a possibility, that a nobleman might feel remorse for what had been done to a people lesser than himself.

She would sacrifice herself for nothing, and James would have to watch it happen because he would never be able to protect her.

As Emrys led them above stairs, a small detachment of soldiers trailed behind. James glanced at them, counting seven. That was to be expected. The queen's appearance would not go without suspicion, and Emrys knew exactly whom James served.

Emrys opened a pair of doors and moved aside to allow Cate to enter first. Looking at someone behind James, he gave a miniscule nod. Four men attacked James then, wrestling him to the floor and pinning him there, leaving only his head free.

"What are you doing?" Cate exclaimed, rushing out of the room. Her accent nearly failed in her panic. "What is this?"

"Your majesty," James said, speaking as firmly and clearly as he could. "It's all right."

A punch to his ribs followed. "Shut it," a man ordered.

James swallowed a groan and lifted his head. Cate had placed herself in between him and Emrys.

She pointed to James. "I demand you release him at once. Tell your men to let him go."

"This man is an outlaw," Emrys said.

"As named by a murderer," Cate said. "Let him go."

"Your majesty, I cannot. He is an outlaw. A rebel. My duty demands that—"

"I care nothing for your duty. Release him."

Emrys hesitated. "I must ask, your majesty…is it your desire to be parted from these people?"

Cate didn't answer. James didn't want to look at her, but his eyes drifted to the back of her head.

There is a chance that this won't work, Ilya had said to him before their departure. *There's a chance she'll turn on you. If you go in there, you may not walk out again.*

I've thought of that, he had said in response. *But I don't think she will.*

Why?

Ynyr ab Ivor, had been his answer.

Now, here he was, held by men loyal to the king. All she had to do to rid herself of him was speak a word. Aye, she did wish to be parted from these people, and James would find himself missing a head.

What choice would she make?

Cate drew the dagger from Emrys's belt, grabbed the surprised man's neckline, and pulled him to her. Judging by the awkward angle at which

Emrys held his head, she had to be holding the dagger beneath the man's chin. The three remaining men drew swords, but she continued on as though they weren't there.

"If it were my wish to be parted from these people," she said, backing Emrys against a wall, "do you think I truly would have ridden in here and extolled their virtue as I have done?"

"Forgive me, your majesty," Emrys said, "but mayhap you would if you were under duress, or in fear for your life. Do they have some hold on you?"

"They have no hold on me, nor am I in fear for my life," she said. "Now, you will release this man, and I shall release you, and then we will talk in a civilized manner."

"Yes. Your terms are acceptable," Emrys said. "Release me, and I will release your man."

"Him first," Cate said.

There was a moment's hesitation before the men released him. As James stood, Cate looked at him, a hint of concern in her eyes. He offered her a slight nod. Lowering the dagger, she walked into the room. A bewildered Emrys followed. James was last, closing the doors behind him.

"May I offer you wine, your majesty?" Emrys asked.

"No, you may not," Cate said brusquely, sitting in a chair that provided a view of the entrance. She laid the dagger across her lap and rested her hands lightly atop it.

Emrys bowed, then poured himself some wine. He took a long pull from the goblet and refilled it before sitting across from Cate.

"Will you not offer my companion some wine?" she asked. "I had heard you were a hospitable man, Lord Emrys. I would hate to think those tales untrue."

Emrys looked at him, and James bit back a smile. He shook his head and took up position to Cate's left.

It was unnerving to watch Cate transform into the queen as seamlessly as she had. How did she do it? Nobility was her blood, but it was difficult to accept that this was the same girl who had fought him every step of the way, who had sworn at him and about him, who had run off every chance she could either find or manufacture. The same girl who had landed two of his own on their backsides, broken a man's nose in an alley, and pulled a lord's dagger on himself was now the embodiment of royalty, sitting in a nobleman's chamber, looking at the man coolly, as if this were as natural as breathing for her.

"Your husband has named you a traitor to the crown," Emrys said. "Was your majesty aware of this?"

No, she wouldn't have been aware of that. James hadn't known to tell her.

"Is that why your household knelt before me upon my arrival?" Cate asked. "Are they in the habit of showing obeisance to traitors?"

"I should think not."

"Yet, all of them did. As did you, if I recall correctly," she said. "Do I recall correctly, Lord Emrys?"

Emrys grunted and reached for his cup. "You do, your majesty."

"Well, then, what shall you do?" Cate asked. "Arrest me? Return me in chains to your king?"

James looked at the doors. How many men stood out there, waiting for such a command? Were there still just the seven, or had more joined them? The number hardly mattered. Even if there were only seven men, he would never be able to get Cate out alive.

Why had he done this?

He was pondering the possibility of using the lord of Labhras as a shield when Emrys answered Cate's question.

"Not before I at least hear what has brought you and your...your companions"—Emrys glanced at James—"to my keep this day."

"Generous of you," Cate said.

Emrys bowed his head. "Your majesty."

"I have come, as I am sure you now suspect," she said, "to ask for your assistance in ending this bloody war."

"You ask me to side with these rebels," Emrys said. "These outlaws."

"Yes. Now I shall ask you to cease speaking of them as though they were less than you. They may not hold a title nor your riches, but they also do not dream of such things, my lord," Cate said. "They care nothing of your coffers and even less for what is inside. What they do dream of is living their lives free of the horror that their king has inflicted upon them. Have you seen a village once my husband's men have finished with it? Have you seen the travesties to which these people have been subjected?"

If Emrys had been uncomfortable before, he was more so now. He shifted in his chair and rubbed at the stain of mud on his knee. "These rebels, my lady, have—"

"Your majesty," Cate interrupted.

"I beg your pardon?" Emrys asked.

"These rebels, your majesty," she said, emphasizing each syllable. "Surely that is what you meant to say. I am, after all, your queen."

Emrys drained the contents of his cup and set it on the floor. "These rebels, your majesty," he said with a dip of his head, "have earned the wrath of the king. They killed the old king—"

"We did not kill the old king," James stated flatly. "You know that full well."

Emrys sat back and looked at him. "You truly have aligned yourself with these—these people, your majesty?"

"These people," Cate said, mimicking the disdain in Emrys's voice, "have been through hell. These people have risked their lives for this land, their families, for me."

James stiffened as he recognized the words he had spoken to her. It was strange to realize she had been listening.

"Have you ever had a man sacrifice himself to keep you alive, my lord?" she asked. "I assume you have sent men to battle, sent men to die in your name, but have you ever had one place himself in between you and your own death?"

Emrys shook his head. "I cannot say that I have."

"You are fortunate," Cate said. "I cannot. It is not the sort of thing one dismisses easily."

"I would not think so," Emrys said.

"Then how could I do anything less than align myself with their cause? How could I offer them anything less than my life for their pursuit of justice?" she asked. "Because justice is all they want. Will you not help them achieve this? Are you not a just man, Lord Emrys?"

"It is not a matter of justice," Emrys said.

"I don't know how it is not," Cate said. "But if I cannot appeal to your humanity, perhaps I can appeal to your common sense."

"Your majesty?"

"You want this war to end. It's ugly, it's expensive, and the reasons for it are not your own," she said. "You've backed the king thus far because he is your king, and you have always been a loyal subject of the man who has worn the crown, whoever he might be. You thought you were backing the stronger side, but you were wrong, and now you stand thigh-deep, stuck in a quagmire not of your making.

"The rebellion is throwing you a lifeline, Lord Emrys. They cannot be stopped. They cannot be crushed. Their wounds go too deep for that. As long as my husband wears the crown, the fighting will not end. Continue to side with your king, and you will lose everything," Cate said. "However, should you help us remove the king from his throne, the war will cease. The fighting will end, peace will be restored, and you will be free to go back to your drinking and whoring and gambling, and whatever else it was you did before the woes of this country so rudely interrupted."

"You make it sound so petty," Emrys said.

Cate shrugged. "It is. But that is human nature, is it not? No matter how lofty we think our ideals to be."

Emrys fell silent. Was he beaten? Had Cate convinced him? James watched the man's jaw work.

"You bring Dana here," Emrys said finally. "You bring him to me so that I might speak with him, and I shall think upon your offer."

"The words of your queen are not enough for you?" Cate asked, her voice cold enough to freeze water.

"I do apologize, your majesty, but no," Emrys said. "You are not of this land. You—"

"Do not tell me I am not of this land. I may not have been born here, but my name has since been written here in blood."

"You bring Dana here," Emrys repeated, "and I shall think upon your offer."

"You truly require him?"

"Dana, your majesty, is the face of your rebellion. People rally to him."

"The rebellion, my lord, has a new face now," Cate said. "One to which the people will respond, I assure you."

"I want Dana," Emrys said. "You bring him here, and I shall think upon your offer."

"Then I shall be sure to send him along," she said, her tone still icy. She looked at James. "I believe we are finished here."

She swept out of the room without another glance at Emrys. James followed, quickening his pace to keep up with her. It seemed every soldier Emrys retained had moved inside, but in the absence of an order from their lord, none moved to pursue.

Before she could escape outside, James caught Cate's arm and pulled her back. She looked at him—furious, not afraid—but he held firm.

"Easy," he said softly. "Any peace out there is fragile. Go out angry, and it will break."

She stared for another moment, then nodded. Dropping his hand, he waited for her to regain her composure. A glance over his shoulder showed the soldiers were monitoring them. They maintained their distance, but were watching, waiting for any reason to pounce.

"Your majesty," James murmured.

Cate looked at him, then her eyes landed on something behind him. Her shoulders squared, and she continued on.

Together, they emerged from the keep. Rhydwyn was already in the saddle while Gair and Semias had possession of the remaining horses. As Cate marched determinedly to her mare, James stepped to Rhydwyn.

"We're not being chased—not yet, anyway," he said, "but get the others moving. Get them in place. I don't want to linger longer than we have to."

Rhydwyn nodded and rode through the gates. Gair handed James the reins to his horse. Cate was already aboard the mare, straddling the saddle as though it were a man's, with her skirts hitched indecently high. Gair and Semias hid smiles while James merely shook his head.

"Is there a problem?" Cate asked.

James pulled himself into the saddle. "None at all, your majesty."

He led the way out of the keep and the village. Emrys's men did not give chase.

Upon reaching the forest, they settled between the advance and rear guards. James sent Semias to the front, Rhydwyn and Gair to the back, and rode at Cate's side himself. He glanced at her, concerned, and his gaze lingered upon the jeweled dagger tucked inside her bodice. How long had that been there?

Cate looked at him. "Take a picture, it'll last longer," she said, her accent gone.

"Do what?"

"What are you looking at?"

"You didn't steal that dagger's sheath."

"Wasn't interested in the sheath."

"Aye, I know, but—"

"What?" she asked. "Do you have a problem with petty larceny?"

If only he knew what that was. James gestured to the dagger. "Isn't that a dangerous place to keep your prize, lacking a sheath the way you are?"

"Are you planning to stick your hand down there?"

"No! God, no!"

"Then it should be just fine."

She was truly irritated, wasn't she? She hadn't been playacting for Emrys. His refusal to help had bothered her greatly. James almost smiled. Would she ever stop surprising him?

"You're staring again," she said.

"Sorry," he said. "I just...I didn't realize you could be so eloquent."

"Yes, ladies and gentlemen—the sailor's whore can be taught!"

A sudden sting of shame left him without breath, and James found himself unable to answer until it had abated.

"I did not intend to offend you."

"Yes, you did," Cate said. "But it's all right. It takes a lot more than that to offend me."

"A kidnapping, perhaps?"

She laughed, a short, staccato sound. "Yeah, that was pretty offensive."

He opened his mouth to apologize again, but said, "You could have rid yourself of me—of all of us—today."

"True."

"Yet, you chose to hold a dagger to a nobleman's throat and demand my release."

"Oh, so you were paying attention."

"Why?" he asked.

She shrugged. "Better the devil you know, right?"

"Aye." James hesitated, then added, "Thank you for your help. Thank you for being willing, even after I—"

"I didn't do it for you."

"Thank you anyhow. I believe you have done us a great service today."

"Getting him to think about it was a great service?"

"In truth, it was more than I expected. Though, I thought he might…"

Cate nodded. "Me too. Maybe your class prejudices are justified. Where I come from, the rich would have been abashed enough to at least have a telethon to get the middle class to pay for it."

"I don't know what that means."

"Doesn't matter," she said. "Is Dana your leader? The one who's gone?"

"Aye."

"If you want Emrys, or at least Emrys's resources, you'll have to find Dana."

"Aye."

"You said he was as good as dead, or might as well be dead, or something like that, didn't you?"

"I did."

"Won't that make it kind of difficult to track him down? Can a man come back from the dead?"

James shrugged. "He's done it before."

"Oh," she said. "I assume you don't mean a literal resurrection, although I suppose it wouldn't come as that much of a shock if you did. Not after everything else."

He smiled. "No. Not a literal resurrection."

She asked him something else, but he had stopped listening, focusing on the woods to her right. She didn't hear it, but he did.

It had happened before, when he was escorting the queen to Eluned. They had come out of nowhere, and his only sign that something was about to happen had been the smallest sound, the snap of a twig.

"James?" Cate said.

He heard the distinct whistling of an arrow cutting through the air and threw himself at her, knocking her from the horse's back. She landed on her stomach, and he on top of her. Shielding her body with his own, he pushed himself up to appraise the situation.

Chaos had erupted. Men dressed in the browns and greens of the forest had emerged from their hiding spots to surround his small band of warriors. Swords clashed, arrows flew. Rhydwyn and Gair battled on either side of him—protecting him, protecting Cate. He had to get up, had to move her, but where could he go?

"James?" she whispered, and he hissed at her to be quiet as he eased his sword from its sheath.

His first priority had to be her safety, but he couldn't abandon the others. He wouldn't. A place to leave her, then. That's what he needed. Where could she go? Where could he send her? Where would be safe? Not the woods—the ambushers had made them dangerous. Too many enemies, too many un-knowns. Where, then? Looking over his shoulder, he saw the bodies of two fallen horses.

"Come on, come on." He got to his feet and hauled her up. Pulling her in front of him, he directed her toward the horses. "There, between the horses. Stay there, stay flat, and keep your head down."

He heard a sword being drawn and didn't have time to see if she listened before whirling around to block a killing blow. He barely had dispatched the man dealing it before another man was on him. A third and fourth man fol-lowed, then more. As soon as one fell, another took his place. James kept pushing, fighting, killing. They were surrounded, overwhelmed. More of his people were down than up.

Too many. There were too many. They would never...He had to get to Cate. Get her out, and take their chances in the woods. It was the only way. It was—

"James!" Cate shrieked.

Driving his sword into the man he faced, James turned to scan the melee. He saw the flash of her gown—a stark contrast to the browns and greens of the warriors—and the two men dragging her off.

"Rhydwyn! Gair! Semias!" he shouted, not knowing if they were up or down, alive or dead. "Someone! Anyone!"

But they were gone. All of them gone, or swarmed by their enemy. He would have to reach her himself.

As he fought his way toward her, Cate struggled against her captors, flailing wildly. After freeing one arm, she reached inside her bodice to remove the dagger. She stabbed one man in the thigh, and prepared to do the same to the other when he caught her arm and jerked it back. Cate screamed and slumped in pain, the dagger slipping from her hand. The man she had stabbed punched her in the face, and she fell to the ground. She didn't move again. The man kicked her stomach before picking her up and throwing her over his shoulder.

James continued his pursuit, taking the most direct line he could, step-ping on the fallen, and battling past the rest, and did it all without thinking or looking away from the man carrying off an unconscious Cate.

Maybe if he had, he would have seen the crossbow.

The first bolt took him in the shoulder with enough force to spin him around. The second hit his chest on his left side, just below his heart, and he dropped to his knees. He gasped for breath before falling onto his back in the dirt.

A man peered down at him. Varro. The captain's gaze switched from him to the sword resting uselessly in his hand. Varro's head tilted, and a smile crossed his face. He kicked the sword away and knelt beside him.

"Your leader once warned me of you," Varro said. He pulled a dagger from his belt and ran his hand along its blade. "Told me I'd best pray you'd not find me. Somehow, I thought you'd be tougher."

James fought to breathe. He couldn't do this. There was no time for this. For Varro. He had to get up. Get to Cate. She was getting farther away, and he had to stop her. Save her. His dagger—there was a dagger in his left boot. Could he reach it? No. His hands shook too much for that. What, then? His eyes flickered to Varro's weapon. Could he grab that?

Varro didn't miss the glance. He smiled again. "Well, you don't quit. I'll give you that."

That wouldn't be true much longer. It was harder to breathe now, as a hand James strongly suspected belonged to Death pressed on his chest. He wouldn't be able to fight that. Not for long.

"Seems a shame to slit your throat, so I'll tell you what I'll do," Varro said, "I won't."

The dagger slipped back into its sheath.

"I'll leave you here. Perhaps you'll survive, perhaps you won't. I'm certain you won't, but I must admit I hope you do," Varro said. "I'll be taking the queen and my sword now. If you don't die, I invite you to try to take them back."

Varro stood and shouted for his men's departure. They had gotten what they wanted; there was no need to linger. James listened to their retreat, then to the sounds of the forest. Birds chirping, his people dying.

The hand pushed harder; he couldn't breathe. He collapsed beneath it, plunging into darkness.

Part Two:
Lineage

chapter 15

Haleine stood in the corner of her prison and watched them watch her. They did not see her there.

Three people took it in turn to sit with her body—tending its wounds, holding its hand, and muttering words of comfort for its hearing. The first two were women of which Haleine knew nothing. The third was a man she had seen before, a man she knew from stolen secret moments. He was the man from the rebel camp, the one Dana had used as their go-between. He had told her his name once.

She didn't remember it now.

She didn't care to remember. She remained in her corner and watched them, judged them. Their careful attention would keep her anchored to this world of which she wanted no part. Did they think they were serving their queen? Saving their land? Ignorance abounded, and she was helpless to say otherwise.

Someone was always with her. She had not been alone since her reflection had left screaming. She had gone, bursting through the door and taking with her Haleine's only hope of peace, replacing it with a root cellar in a town that had burned. She could smell the ash and death in the air. She didn't know how the others could stand it.

Nor did she know to where the woman, her twin, had gone. She had disappeared, and no one had said anything about her since. Mayhap she had never been there. Haleine would not be surprised to find the woman had been nothing more than some invention of her fragmenting mind, for further and further from herself did she fall.

She looked at her body and the man who sat with it. He cradled her fingers between his two palms. He spoke to her, urging her to return to them, return to life, breaking off only when the door in the ceiling opened, and Faolan appeared. The man rose to greet him, but Faolan flew past without a word as he came to the corner where she stood.

"Haleine," he said, looking her in the eye, "you need to come back to us."

She stared at him, then glanced at the man standing behind him. The man was as shocked as she.

"Faolan," he said, "what are you—?"

"Go above," Faolan ordered.

The man looked at her body and nodded. He backed away to the stairs and climbed them slowly, not turning until the last possible moment. She wanted to call out for him to stay. She had never been afraid of the pegasus before, but now she was wary of being alone with him.

"Haleine, look at me," Faolan said. When she did, he went on. "Your wandering needs to end. You need to come back to us now."

Why? So they could use her further? She had no interest in that. She'd not be their weapon. She'd not be their slave.

"You're afraid, I know," Faolan said, "but you can't hide any longer."

Afraid? He thought she was afraid? Whatever she might be, she most certainly was not *afraid*.

If she spoke, would he hear her? Or would her voice be lost as long as she stayed where she was? Turning her head, she glanced at her shell, that broken and useless husk.

"She told us what you did," Faolan said. "That your hand was on that dagger. No one else's. Yours."

Who had told? Her false twin? Haleine had spoken those words to her. What of the goddess? Would Laorans have known of her attempt to free herself from a life of servitude? The goddess had known of everything else, hadn't she?

But it did not matter who had done it; it had not been theirs to tell.

She glared at Faolan. Would he scold her for her actions and take her to task for her selfishness? The world would collapse without her to hold it up. Did she not care?

She didn't. Not anymore.

"I don't think that's true," Faolan said.

She felt herself shrink. He could not do this. He could not touch her. He could not compel her to do anything she did not wish to do.

"That is true," Faolan said. "But you claiming not to care? That is a lie."

How would he presume to know that?

"Because I know you."

He only thought he knew her, but he didn't. He couldn't. No one did. She didn't even know herself. A stranger both in and out of her own skin whose only conviction was an unwillingness to be used.

"We did that, yes," Faolan said. "I never wanted to, but—"

But the world demanded it. She turned away. There had to be an escape—a way to be free.

"Haleine—"

She put her hands over her ears, thinking to block his voice from her mind.

"You'll still hear me," he said. "You can't shut me out. Not that way."

Then which way? Her hands slid down and encircled her neck. She stole another glance at her body, abandoned on its poor little pyre. Could she destroy it? Use the lantern to set it ablaze? Would that at last set her free?

"Even if you could do that," Faolan said, "I wouldn't let you."

He couldn't stop her. Why did he continue to claim the opposite?

"Would you leave your sons alone in this world?"

She hadn't left them alone. She had left them in Willem's care, and he would see them safe. He would protect them better than she ever could.

"What about Sighle?"

Her sister—oh, her poor sister. But no, there was nothing to be done there. Sighle was her father's daughter. She would find her way.

"Are you not your father's daughter?"

No, she was not. Darian Coileáin's daughter would not wish so desperately to die. Darian Coileáin's daughter would not try to claw her way into the ground. And if there was ever a time when Darian Coileáin's daughter needed to do so, she would not fail at it as completely as Haleine had. Days, weeks, months, years—how long had it been? She didn't know. Each moment spent bleeding, drowning, and sobbing over an earth that would not have her.

"Weeks, Haleine," Faolan said. "Two weeks. That's how long it's been."

She lowered her hands. Two weeks? She did not know how it was he saw her, how it was he heard her, but he did not know where she had been or what she had done there. It had not been two weeks. He was wrong again. Was he never right?

Locking eyes with him, she flooded her mind with her days on the beach and let him watch her failures one after the other. She let him watch her die and be resurrected again and again. She did not stop. Even when he winced and looked away, she did not stop.

"Haleine," he said gently, sadly, "you need to come back. She'll die if you don't."

She was surprised Sighle still lived. Why had Omur not yet taken her? Once he had said he would see to Sighle personally. What had stopped him?

"Not Sighle," Faolan said. "Mireille."

The name meant nothing to her. Haleine shook her head and walked to her body, careful to keep her mind blank as she looked at it.

"Did she tell you her name when you spoke?" Faolan asked. "Perhaps she called herself Cate."

When they spoke? She hadn't spoken to anyone since…Did he mean that woman? Her self-righteous reflection? Her false twin? She had called herself nothing.

"She's not false," Faolan said. "She is your flesh and blood, Haleine. She is your twin. Your parents called her Mireille, and the dark gods took her from your cradle when you were infants. Your parents thought her to be dead."

Why did he think she might care who the woman was? She was nothing to Haleine. Not her soul, not her ghost. Nothing.

"Your people believe she's you," Faolan said. "One of them has already given his life to protect her. Others will follow."

Was she supposed to care about that? Haleine extended her hand and held it above the one lying on the bed. What would happen if she lowered her hand? Would she pass through herself, or would she be trapped and dragged down once more? Better not to risk it. She withdrew and was about to step away when she was forced forward. A boot on her back, shoving her down.

"Haleine?"

Faolan called for her, his tone making obvious his innocence in this. She tried to rise, only to be thrown down again and crushed by a heavy body, pushing her to the floor, and through it, until she fell.

Hands groped and grabbed her body, tearing and pulling. There were flashes of faces—brutal and determined—belonging to men she had seen before, men who served her husband.

He had found her. He had come for her.

Horror was engulfed by pain as the attack continued. She screamed for help with a voice that was not her own. Help did not come, so she fought them herself, striking out any way she could, but her efforts were not enough. Her left arm felt as though it had been torn from her body. A fist in her face and a kick to her stomach followed before the assault ended, leaving Haleine gasping for breath and searching her body for injuries that were no longer there.

When the pain stopped, she was in her body once more, lying on her back, and looking at the worried faces of her caregivers. Terror gripped her, and she tried to scream, tried to push away, but she was unable to do either. They touched her, checking old injuries, searching for new ones. The older of the two women ran a hand over Haleine's hair and down her cheeks, shushing her little grunts of protest.

It was too soon after the assault; she couldn't abide it. Haleine wanted to order them to stop, to leave her alone, but her tongue fell uselessly against her teeth, making no sound any but her could hear.

"Stop," she begged, her voice cracked and weak. "Please stop."

But they did not hear her.

"Haleine, what did you see?" Faolan asked.

She groaned. The elder woman heard the noise and soothed her.

"Tell me what you saw, Haleine," Faolan pressed.

He repeated his question again and again. The elder woman hissed at him to stop, but he wouldn't. Haleine twisted from the woman's touch and turned her head, hands searching for an escape. How could she return to the beach?

"Haleine, stay with me," Faolan said. "Stay with me, and tell me what you saw."

An ambush. Her husband's men attacking her, capturing her. She had cried out for help and—

No. She hadn't cried out at all. The voice hadn't belonged to her. Her husband's men hadn't attacked her. It was...Haleine didn't know her name. What had Faolan called her? Mireille? Her sister. Her *twin*.

Her head rolled in the other direction, and the pegasus appeared in her line of sight.

"Tell me," he said.

"Her," Haleine gasped. "I saw her."

"Your sister? Mireille? You saw Mireille?" Faolan asked, and Haleine nodded. "What did you see? What happened?"

"They've taken her."

———

When Cate started to come to, the first thing of which she was aware was how goddamn badly her head—her *face*—hurt. Pain radiated everywhere, pulsating and pounding, keeping beat like a sadistic drum line ready to march her off the mortal coil. She'd go, too—what the hell, right?—if only she could find her legs. They didn't seem to be attached to the rest of her anymore. Or maybe they were. She didn't know. There didn't seem to be anything else. Just the pain, the dark, and her. Maybe she was just a head. A head in a box with no one to accept delivery.

No. No, she still had legs. They had to be those logs below the pit of nausea located where her stomach used to be. She'd open her eyes to check, but they didn't seem to be working, either. Maybe they weren't there anymore. Maybe they were melted, liquefied, and evaporated like rain. Dust in the wind was she. A kind of heavy dust that wouldn't even move in an F5 tornado.

Except she was moving, wasn't she? Rocking gently side to side, as though she were on a boat. Why would she be on a boat? She hated boats.

Damn, her brain was scrambled. Could she get a side of bacon with that? Maybe some wheat toast? Pancakes? Pancakes would be good.

She tried opening her eyes. The effort turned out to be a mistake. A white-hot flash filled her field of vision. The pounding in her head increased to the point where she honestly thought it might explode, and the pain was so bad she wasn't sure if she would care.

What would that be like? How would it sound? A quick *pop* like a pin-stuck balloon? Or would it be louder and messier like a car bomb—all alarms and sirens, smoke and fire, and splattered gray matter sizzling on a flame-licked windshield?

She closed her eyes again. Her stomach lurched, bile was rising, so she flipped on her side to avoid choking.

Also a mistake.

More white-hot pain. More white-hot flashes. Only a sense of self-preservation she didn't know she had kept her from screaming both loud and long. Indulging in a cautious, quiet whimper, she eased onto her back and lay there, blind and hurt, panting and crying. What the hell had happened?

The vision swallowed her whole before she knew it was happening, but once inside, she recognized it for what it was. The herky-jerky nature made her stomach protest violently, but she was helpless to do anything but watch.

She rode next to James, talking with him almost as if they were friends. Without warning, he threw himself at her, and they both fell to the ground. The dagger whose sheath she had not stolen sliced into her skin, but the fall had robbed her of the breath needed to cry out. There wasn't time to linger on it because James shielded her again, dragging her somewhere safe.

But not safe for long. She'd done as he asked. She'd stayed as still and flat as she could, but they found her anyway.

She fought, using her stolen dagger to stab one of them. She would have stabbed the other, too, if he hadn't been faster. The second man jerked her arm back, twisting her wrist and disarming her. The first man, the one she had stabbed, came at her and put his fist in her face.

The vision ended then, leaving her feeling as though she had been dropped from the top of the Empire State Building, even though she hadn't moved at all. She swallowed another scream, choking with the effort. Her body somehow hurt more now that she remembered what had happened.

Her arm. She thought that was the worst of it. Well, that and her head, she supposed, but the goddamn bastard just about tore off her arm. She ran her hand up the injured limb. Regardless of how it felt, it was still attached.

Maybe it was dislocated. She'd dislocated her shoulder once before when she had fallen off a horse after trying to tackle too ambitious a jump. The horse was fine. Cate, not so much. She had been trussed up on one of those backboards and rushed to the hospital where Fiona paced while Daniel and her mother sat in the waiting room. Cate had been subjected to a battery of tests both she and her mother had said were unnecessary. Cate came out of it with nothing more than the shoulder injury. The damn thing hurt like hell for a while, though—and that was *with* the quality pain meds that had come along with her sling.

This hurt more. This hurt *a lot* more.

She felt her face next. It was tender to the touch, but it didn't feel like anything was broken. That was something for which to be grateful. A broken nose would be no good in a place like this. A broken *anything*, really. A dislocation was proving to be bad enough.

Then there was the concussion. If it was a concussion. She didn't think she'd ever had one before, so how the hell was she supposed to know what it was? It didn't matter what she called it. It hurt, and it was bad. She attempted to open her eyes a second time only to experience the same results as before: white, blinding light, followed by nausea and dry heaving.

Closing her eyes yet again, she lay in the dark. Waves of unconsciousness came back like a tide returning to shore. She was the soft sand crumbling beneath it. Defeated, she slipped into the welcoming arms of sleep.

The next time she woke, the rocking had stopped. Her body still hurt from head to toe, but the pounding in her head had been reduced from a full-fledged drum line to a well-struck quartet of tympani. She thought she might vomit but took the risk and opened her eyes, considering it a victory when she wasn't instantly struck blind by pain.

There was little light, but some was better than none. Moving cautiously, she felt around. Wood. Both beneath and surrounding her. There was a wall to her right. A low wall, like she was...A box. Was she in a box? A *coffin*?

Panicking, she struggled to prop herself up on her right side. Okay, not a coffin. A wagon. She was in the back of a wagon. At the end of it were two men, facing the other direction. Beyond them were a number of small fires, and the silhouettes of men sitting around them. Camp, then. Whose camp, though?

Her elbow gave out then, and she fell, strangling a cry as she hit. Her guards turned around, and she froze.

They weren't Rhydwyn or Gair.

She wasn't in the rebel camp anymore, was she?

"Oi," one of them said. "Awake, are you? Cap'n will be pleased."

The man walked away, but Cate stared at the one who remained. He licked his lips and grinned.

She didn't grin back.

———※※※———

Night had fallen by the time Faolan reached the rebel camp. He searched for James as he wove his way through a crush of people. An unpracticed eye would see nothing but chaos, but Faolan saw only recovery. They had done it before, and they would do it again.

Haleine had offered no details, except to tell him of Cate's abduction. *They've taken her.* They'd taken her in such a manner that the impact had been enough to force Haleine back into her body. It was all the evidence Faolan required to know that whatever had happened in Labhras, it couldn't have gone much worse.

"Faolan!" Ilya called, coming toward him. "Do you know what's happened?"

"I know Cate's been taken," he said. "Other than that, I know nothing."

"They went to Labhras and spoke to Lord Emrys. What was said no one knows, as James and the queen's sister were the only two privy to the conversation, but he allowed them to leave unchallenged."

"Where were they challenged?"

"In the forest. An ambush the advance guard didn't see," Ilya said. "It was the king's men, Varro at their head. They killed who they could and took the queen's sister captive."

"Where's James now?" Faolan asked. "Has he gone after Cate?"

"No, he can't," Ilya said. "He's dying."

"Where?"

"His tent," she said. "Come on."

He followed her, watching the people clear a path as she walked. When they arrived at the tent, Ilya held the flap for him, and he flew inside.

James lay unconscious on a bedroll spread on the ground, bleeding from multiple wounds. Hanah knelt at his side, working frantically to save his life, but the smell of death permeated the air. She would fail.

"Get Luisiúil," he said, and Ilya left.

Hanah twisted around. Her face bore the stain of both blood and tears. "I'm trying, Faolan. I'm trying to save him."

"You can't," he replied. "He's beyond your skills."

"I won't let him die!"

"Neither will I," Faolan said. "Just keep his heart beating."

"What are you going to do?"

"I'm going to save his life. Or, rather, Luisiúil will do it."

"Magic?"

"It's the only way, Hanah. Keep him alive until she gets here. That's all you need to do," he said. Hanah nodded and turned back to James. "What kind of wounds are they?"

"Bolts. Crossbow bolts. Two of them."

"You removed them?"

"Not me, no. Someone else."

"All right," Faolan said. "It's fine. It's better, actually. You'll see. Luisiúil will fix this."

"She won't." Ilya stepped inside. "She'll not come. Lorcan told me that she refuses."

Faolan nodded. He should have expected as much. "We'll have to take James to her."

"He's barely holding on as it is," Hanah said. "You can't think to move him!"

"We either move him to Luisiúil, or we move him to a grave," Faolan said. "Make your choice."

Hanah looked to Ilya. "We need others."

Ilya dashed out, quickly returning with Gair, Semias, and a third man. Ilya positioned herself at James's right side, near his head. Semias stood beside her, and the other two men moved to James's feet. On Ilya's count, they lifted the bedroll. Hanah stayed at her patient's side, her hands pressed down on his chest.

Faolan followed the slow procession as it winded its way to Luisiúil. Lorcan waited with her. He hadn't been far from her side since her capture. Dana's absence made it easier for him to stay there.

The humans laid James on the ground and backed away. Hanah knelt to keep pressure on the wounds, but Ilya pulled her up and forced her to leave his side. Luisiúil ignored them and fixed her eyes upon Faolan.

Do you know what has happened?

Him first, Faolan responded, nodding toward James. *Then we'll talk.*

Faolan, this is grander than one human.

He's needed. Heal him, and we'll talk.

"Faolan?" Ilya asked.

"A moment," he said.

"James doesn't *have* a moment."

"I know," Faolan said. "Luisiúil will make sure it doesn't stay that way."

The unicorn mare pawed at the ground. Tossing her head, she ran straight at James, acting as though she intended to trample him. Hanah gasped while both Gair and Ilya leapt forward.

"Don't!" Faolan shouted.

Gair and Ilya dropped to their knees. Luisiúil stopped short and threw an angry glance at Faolan before dipping her head gracefully and performing her healing magic. None of the humans had seen it before, and this time, Hanah was not alone in her cries. Faolan spoke again, sharply, telling them to stop, to be quiet, and they fell into immediate silence.

When Luisiúil had finished, she looked at Faolan. *Send them away.*

"You can take him back to camp now," Faolan said.

Ilya stepped toward James. "Is he—?"

"He's fine," Faolan said. "Take him back, and have someone sit with him until he wakes."

"When will that be?" Hanah asked.

"Soon," Faolan answered. "Take him and go."

Ilya called for their departure. Hanah's concern for James overrode any suspicion she may have held for Faolan's claim, and she ran to keep pace with the others. Faolan waited until they were gone before turning to the unicorns.

"What's happened?" he asked.

We'll not get near her.

"Mireille?"

She is being protected by magic. Dark magic, the likes of which this world has not seen.

"It is true," Lorcan said. "We heard the human's report and went to see for ourselves if she could be reclaimed. The magic stopped us, and there is no way around it."

"Omur?" Faolan asked.

This is deeper, darker than him. Whatever drives these men wants Mireille. And more than that, it doesn't want us to have her.

"Yelsneh," Faolan said.

Mayhap, but it feels different.

Something else. Someone else. Haleine? Cate? Who else could do something like this?

"Is it Mireille?" he asked. "Is she doing it?"

Neither Luisiúil nor Lorcan answered. They knew the prophecy as well as he. They knew what role Mireille was fated to play, and like Faolan, they could feel the darkness inside her.

"Keep searching for another possibility," he said.

When he returned to James's tent, Ilya sat in the chair, monitoring a still-unconscious James. She glanced at Faolan as he settled on the table.

"How does it work?" she asked. "The magic."

"You're the first one to ask."

"What's the answer?"

"Our powers—the unicorns' and mine—are drawn from the earth and its elements. If you looked at the spot where James was healed, you would find everything around it has died. To give life, one must take life. It's the reason why Luisiúil doesn't often use that particular skill."

Ilya nodded. "How long will he be like this?"

"Hard to tell. He could wake at any moment, or it could take days. It'll depend on James, but he will wake," Faolan said. "Did anyone tell you what happened on the road during the ambush?"

Ilya shrugged. "Some. What do you want to know?"

"What did Cate do?"

"She was their target," Ilya said. "She would have been the first to die had James not knocked her from the horse. Gair claims she fought them, the men who took her, but they won in the end and carried her away."

"Do we know where Varro is now?" Faolan asked.

"We know where they are, and we know where they're going," Ilya said. "But that's not the problem, is it?"

"It will be once they get there."

"We can't touch them, Faolan. We can't get near them."

"I heard that, yes."

"Can you explain why that is?"

"Magic," he said. "But I can't offer you any more explanation than that. At least not yet."

"Omur?"

"No. Someone else. *Something* else."

"Something else," Ilya echoed. "We didn't need there to be anything else."

"I know."

"What now, then? What do we do?"

"We wait."

"For what?"

Faolan honestly didn't know anymore. "A miracle, I suppose."

—◦◦◦—

The injury to his hand forced Dana to spend his days watching the others work while he sat in the shadows of the barn with nothing but a bottle of whiskey to keep him company.

Three days now, he had sat and watched and waited. He needed to leave. He didn't want to keep taking from people who had nothing, especially when he had nothing to give in return. He wanted to leave. He couldn't stay here any longer when Navlyn knew so much, and he knew so little, and Haleine's damned ghost was there to witness it all.

Would she find him in Feond?

He looked at the road. Taking it west would lead him there, to Feond, and perhaps a life where no one knew his name. He would only need a day or two to reach the border. A day or two's walk, and he could disappear.

Why didn't he go?

The answer was obvious and terrible, and the next swallow of whiskey had nothing to do with how badly his hand hurt.

You owe it to the girl to try, Navlyn had said. Try to find a way to repair what he'd broken. He had a way, though. James. James would do it. James would see it done.

Dana gulped another mouthful of whiskey and stared at the western road until a young girl, no more than ten, came running from the opposite direction into the village. Searching for Navlyn, he supposed. Owain had come to find him that way once. *There's an army,* the boy had said to him.

"Someone comes," the girl said to Navlyn.

Running to the barn, Navlyn rang the bell hanging outside the door. Everyone stopped their work and hid any evidence of their existence before retreating to the barn. Was this what they had done when he had turned upon their path?

"Come on," Navlyn said to him when the others were inside. "You too."

Dana accepted her help to stand, and he entered the barn first. Although he had watched everyone go inside, there was no sign of life to be found. Navlyn closed the door, enshrouding them in near darkness, and climbed the ladder to the loft. He didn't follow her—his hand wouldn't allow it easily—so he moved to the left of the door and looked out a crack in the wall to see who approached.

It took some time, but eventually a lone traveler came into view. Wearing a ragged cloak and carrying a worn sack, the man walked slowly, practically dragging his right leg. He stopped to lean against the shell of the church. His pack slipped to the ground, and the man eased himself down to sit alongside it. The man's aged face and obvious exhaustion signified to Dana that he was no threat to any who lived there. When he heard Navlyn climb down from the loft, he knew she agreed.

"I'll go," he said.

"You're drunk."

"Not so much." He held out the bottle. "Let me go. Please."

Navlyn nodded and took the whiskey. He thanked her and stepped outside.

"Don't mean no harm, milord," the man said as Dana approached. "Just looking for a place to rest some before I continue on."

"I'm not a lord," Dana said.

"My 'pologies, young master."

That title wasn't much better than the first, but Dana let it go. "Have you a name?"

"That's the one thing we all have, ain't it?" the man asked. He was pleased with himself until he noticed Dana did not share in his amusement. Then he shrugged and added, "You can call me Rab, milord."

"Where are you headed, Rab?"

"Away. Don't know more than that. Somewhere there ain't fighting, if there be such a place anymore. My bones can't take no more, aye?"

"There's been fighting?" Dana asked. "Recently?"

"Oh, aye. Ain't there been here? Looks like the king's men have been 'round," Rab said. "And you look as though you've seen your fair share of trouble, that's for sure."

It hadn't been a fight so much as a slaughter, but Dana didn't say that. Neither did he comment on his troubles. "Where do you come from?"

"Here and there. I follow the wind mostly. Ever do that?"

"A long time ago, aye," Dana said. "Where have you seen them fighting?"

Rab studied Dana, his jaw working as though chewing on something. He spat. "Someone who 'spects an old man to answer questions might offer him a drink first."

Dana nodded. "I don't have anything to offer but water."

Rab grinned. "So you claim."

"Aye, so I claim. If you wait here, I'll bring you some."

"Bit o' food wouldn't go amiss, neither, milord."

"I'll see what I can find," Dana said.

He returned to the barn where Navlyn waited eagerly. He pulled her away from the opening to keep her unseen, and she looked at him with concern. He ignored it as he moved to the food stores.

"Do you think he's a danger?" she asked.

Dana shook his head and picked up the remains of the bread they had eaten for breakfast that morning. He worked it underneath his arm to pick up a jug of water.

"No," he said. "Still, I'd like to find out what he knows. What happened to him and when. Why it happened, and if they'd have reason to follow him."

Navlyn nodded. "What do you need?"

"Water, bread, and for you to stay here. You can administer to all his needs when I'm through."

"What do you think he'll tell you?"

"Maybe nothing. I won't know until I ask him."

Dana walked back to Rab and held out the jug. The old man bowed his head in thanks as he reached for it and took a long drink.

"I don't mean no harm," he said. "Not to you, nor them hiding in yonder barn."

"There's no one there," Dana said. "What happened to you?"

"Set upon by thieves, if you believe it. I try to outrun the war and land straight in the hands of brigands. Took everything they thought they could use. Starting," Rab said, "with my horse. Wasn't a sorrier creature to be found this side of the Endellion Sea, and yet—"

"It was more than what they had," Dana finished.

"Aye." Rab drank more of the water. "The bread, lad?"

Dana gave it to him, watching the man gnaw at the bread's heel before sitting at his side.

"They let you live," Dana said. "The thieves."

Rab choked on the bread and laughed. "Aye. Not everyone takes their cues from our esteemed king."

"No, not everyone," Dana agreed.

"I've seen you before." Rab swallowed the last of the bread. "I know who you are."

"No, you don't."

It was true. This stranger might have recognized his face, but he didn't know the man behind it. No one did anymore.

"What are you doin' here," Rab asked, "when your people are dyin' in the south?"

"You don't know me," Dana stated. "And my people are already lost."

He stood and walked away. Navlyn could have Rab. She could take care of him, and Dana could move on. If he pushed himself, he could be halfway to Feond by the time night fell.

"Always thought you to be stupid, challengin' the king the way you did," Rab called out. "Didn't figure you to be a coward as well."

Dana stopped. "I'm not who you think I am."

"No, I 'spect not. Not if you're here and not there."

"Where?" Dana asked before he could stop himself.

Rab chuckled. "Labhras, lad. They be in Labhras. I was in the lord's keep when they arrived, the queen at their head."

Dana's heart pounded worse than his hand. "The queen?"

"Aye, a lovely lass, that one," Rab said. "Just rode in, she did, surrounded by rebels, and actin' like she owned the place—like she hadn't been named traitor, like she hadn't been missing or thought dead—and demanded an audience with his lordship."

Rab had to be wrong. It hadn't been Haleine. It couldn't have been Haleine. She was dying in Enimode. She was already dead. She was a ghost haunting him everywhere he went. How could she possibly have been in Labhras?

"You've seen the queen before?" Dana asked.

"I get what you're asking, lad. I'm telling you it was her."

Dana turned. "What did she want with Emrys? You said she was named a traitor. Why would she ever go to a nobleman loyal to the king?"

"Don't know. She didn't take the time to tell the likes of me, did she? Spoke to his lordship and rode out again, them rebels trailing behind her. Emrys ain't been seen since word of the attack came."

The attack.

"How would you know?" Dana asked. "Labhras is days from here."

"Labhras is days away when you're walking, lad. I told you I had a horse until recently, didn't I?"

Horse or not, Labhras was too far away. Even with a unicorn, it would have been too far. Unless he had somehow gained access to one of Faolan's tunnels, Rab had made impossible time. Someone had used him to deliver this message. Did he not realize it?

"So you claim," Dana said.

"Ain't no reason to lie to you. Your people died in Labhras. A real massacre, aye?"

A massacre in Labhras. What had James done?

Despite attempts to sway him, Emrys had stayed loyal to Maddox. Dana had never faulted Emrys for that. The man had only done what he thought was necessary to protect his people.

And while Emrys had never been an outright threat—always doing just enough to keep his king satisfied—he wasn't a friend to the rebellion. James knew that—he had told it to Dana a time or two—so why would he ever go to Labhras? What had changed?

Dana looked around. What *hadn't* changed?

"Is the queen dead?" he asked.

"Not yet," Rab said. "But as I hear it, traitors never last long in the king's dungeon."

What had James done? He bore Haleine no love, but he knew how vital she was to the rebellion, how necessary she was to Laorans's survival. Why had he brought her to Labhras?

Why was she still fighting? How?

"Strange you don't know," Rab commented, "seeing as how they're your people."

"They're not my people," Dana said. They were hers now, and if not hers, they belonged to James.

Rab nodded. "Aye, I forgot. You ain't who I think you are."

"No one ever is," Dana said.

He went back to Rab's side to help the man to his feet. They walked to the barn, Navlyn coming out to meet them. She spoke to Rab, words of concern, but her eyes were fixed on Dana.

He left the village and relieved a pair of men on guard duty. When they left, he sat in their hidden spot, holding his dagger in his good hand. He watched the moon because the road would be clear and waited for Haleine to show herself, but she did not appear. She had found her purpose, and it no longer involved haunting him.

"What did you do, Haleine?" he said. He posed the question to the night, as she had not been considerate enough to show herself. "How did you do it?"

The night offered no answers. There would only be one place where he thought they might be found. Wherever she was—that's where he needed to be.

Could he make himself go?

Would she allow him to stay?

He sat in the watch post the remainder of the night, contemplating the road beneath him. When two men arrived after dawn to replace him, Dana emerged onto the road and saw Navlyn waiting for him.

"You're leaving us, aren't you," she said.

"I have to."

"Where will you go?"

Dana looked at the road. He did not look west.

CHAPTER 16

The night in the wagon was the longest of Cate's life.

Sleep would have helped, but as there was no way—barring another bout of sudden unconsciousness—that was likely to happen, she moved as far back into the wagon as she could and curled up as tightly as her injuries would allow. The one small sliver of good news was that no one approached her. Her two guards hardly paid attention to her. They looked over their shoulders from time to time, but they had to know she was in no condition to be running off.

Perhaps that was why their captain had yet to put in an appearance. She couldn't go anywhere anyway, so why rush? For a while, she had waited for him, anxious to know whom she was up against, but when movement in the camp died down, and her guards had been swapped out for different men, Cate assumed she'd not encounter the man until morning.

That left her free to worry about other things, so she looked at the forest. Were any of the rebels out there? Squeezing her eyes shut, she attempted to summon a vision of what had happened to the rest of them. When nothing came to her, she glared at the moon.

"Come on," she muttered. "Show me *something*."

But she continued to see nothing more than the moon. How did the damn magic work? How did she make it work? Or…Oh. What if it *was* working? What if the reason she saw nothing was that there was nothing to see. Had any of them survived?

That thought carried her into the next morning when she uncurled and propped herself against the wagon's side to watch the men break down their camp. She counted fifty of them. Which one was in charge?

One of the fifty broke off and came toward her. With the exception of the major black eye he sported, his features were rather nondescript. Brown hair, brown eyes, average build. He was young, young enough that he probably didn't shave yet on a regular basis. He wore a sword on his hip, but that told her nothing. Everyone in the camp who wasn't her wore a sword on his hip. His clothing, however, was much more informative, especially the sleeveless tunic of blue and silver he wore over his long-sleeved shirt. That screamed quality—something her guards lacked entirely. Who was he? Probably not the captain—her guards lacked any interest in his approach. A knight, maybe? Did they have those here?

"Go on," the man said to her guards, a significant length of rope in his hands. "I'll take her to the captain."

Cate looked at the rope. They thought she was the queen. They thought she was a traitor. Of course restraints would be involved.

"I need you to come forth, your majesty," the man said when they were alone.

He spoke quietly, as though afraid of being overheard. Why? The other men were making enough noise that she thought she could break into song and dance and not be noticed.

"Please, your majesty." The man put the rope on the wagon's edge and held out his hand. "I need you to stand. If you don't, this will go harder for you."

She still didn't move. The man nodded and took a quick look around before leaning in closer.

"My name is Fionnbar," he whispered. "Willem sent me to look after you."

Obviously, that was supposed to mean something. Whoever Willem was, though, there was an excellent chance he hadn't sent Fionnbar to look after her. It didn't seem like a good idea to tell him that, so she nodded and slid forward. Fionnbar was a potential gift horse, and she had no intention of looking him in the mouth. At least not yet.

He helped her stand, and as she felt the ground beneath her feet, she realized for the first time that her shoes were missing. She looked down. Her dress was torn to hell, too, but since she was a woman in a camp filled with men who considered her an enemy to their king, she counted herself fortunate to be wearing a dress. Or *anything*, for that matter.

Fionnbar held her gingerly. "Can you stand on your own, your majesty?"

Standing was one thing, but if he expected her to do anything else, he would likely be disappointed. The way she was feeling, she wasn't convinced she could walk. Sure, there was a marked improvement from the previous night, but it would be a while before she'd be able to turn cartwheels or do anything that didn't involve holding her arm while grimacing in pain.

Cate never thought she would say this, but she missed Sarai.

The whole thing begged a question. If she was supposed to be some kind of magical whosewhatsit, shouldn't she have been harder to hurt? It was seriously demoralizing.

"Have you a need to relieve yourself?" Fionnbar asked, looking uncomfortable with the question.

She stared at him. No way, no how was that going to happen. His uneasiness increased until he broke eye contact and nodded.

He removed a bag from his belt. "Water? You must be thirsty."

She was thirsty. She was beyond thirsty. But she was also stubborn and mad as hell. She didn't give a shit who had sent him or why.

"Please, your majesty?"

She stared some more. Fionnbar looked worried but returned the water bag to his belt.

"Your hands," he said. "If you please."

It didn't please her to hold out her hands, no matter how politely he had asked. He was going to tie her up, and it was going to hurt like hell. She looked away to see a well-dressed man watching her from atop a great roan stallion. Was this perhaps the elusive captain?

She didn't know why, but after seeing the man in charge, Cate held out her hands as best as she could.

Fionnbar took them and carefully drew out her left arm. Reaching behind his sleeveless tunic, he withdrew a wide linen strip and secured it around her wrists. The rope followed. There were two lengths: one to bind her wrists, and a second to act as a leash.

When Fionnbar finished, he looked at her, his eyes apologetic. "I am sorry."

Not as sorry as she was.

As Fionnbar led her to the man on horseback, she stumbled, working through the pain residing in every limb, muscle, and appendage she had. The ruins of her gown didn't help much, either. Fionnbar looked sharply at her but didn't move to help. He couldn't now. Too many others were watching.

"Oh, your majesty," the man on horseback said when she was close enough. "You've been a very naughty lass."

She opened her mouth to respond with the rudest comeback she could think of but bit her tongue instead. There was no way rising to the bait would work out in her favor.

"It was quite a merry chase you led us on," the man continued, "but here you are at last. My lord will be pleased to see what we've brought him."

Fionnbar presented the rope. "Captain."

The captain dismounted to accept the offering. He gave the rope a vicious tug, and she was jerked toward him. Legs tangling in her gown, she fell, landing hard on her injured arm. As men laughed, Cate commanded herself not to cry.

The captain knelt and pulled her up by her hair. His eyes were so dark, they looked demonic.

"I know who you are," he sneered softly in her ear. "And who you aren't."

Her blood ran cold. She kept quiet, as her only defense was to keep her damn mouth shut. He hauled her to her feet and tied her leash to his saddle.

"Shall we go, lads?" the captain said.

They went. She walked behind the captain and his stallion. It slowed their progress back to their lord, but she understood why they did it. They—or most of them anyway—thought she was the queen, a traitor. This was meant to be her perp walk.

The perp walk took them out of the forest and onto a wide, dirt road. Any other travelers they came across would move to the side to allow the soldiers to pass, keeping their heads bowed but for the occasional stolen glance at her. No one made a move to intervene. Neither did the rebels attempt a rescue. Maybe under the cover of night. Maybe they would come then.

They walked through one village and then another, each filled with people who stopped to gape openly at the procession. What were they called? Where was she on that map she had studied?

She supposed it didn't matter where she was. Didn't she already know where they were taking her? *The king wants you,* Aaron had told her. *They'll bring you to him.*

She tried hard not to think about what Aaron had said following that. The part about whether anyone would care if the soldiers raped her on their way to having her killed.

She cared. She cared a lot.

When the captain gave the order to stop for the night, Cate was both relieved and terrified. If they had made her walk much farther, she would've collapsed from exhaustion. But while they were slouching toward Eluned, the soldiers hadn't been able to do anything more than leer at her, but now that they were making camp—now that they would be stationary until the next morning—Cate didn't know what they might do or how she would stop it.

On his command, two men—neither of them Fionnbar—escorted her to a tree and looped her leash around an overhead branch. They pulled her arms over her head and secured the rope. She cried. The pain was so bad, she couldn't help it.

The men talked, but she couldn't focus on them—not when staying conscious was proving to be so much work. She shut them out until a hand landed on her leg, fingers sliding up the inside of her thigh and caressing her skin. Anger surging, she looked at the man to whom the hand belonged, and twisted to keep him from feeling anything else.

"So you're a crier," the man said. "You a screamer, too, yer majesty?"

"S'pose we'll find out," the other said. "Long night, lots of willing lads."

She stared at them. If she ever got out of this mess and found her way back to James and Faolan, she would kill them both. Then she would find a way to resurrect them so she could kill them a second time.

As his companion crept closer, the first man tried to feel her up again. She twisted, trying to kick them back. The first caught her ankle and forced her leg down.

"S'pose we find out now," he growled in a low voice.

"Suppose you go fuck yourself," Cate said in a similar tone.

He grinned. "Oh, I'd much rather fuck you, yer majesty."

As the second man helped hold her still, the first man's knee forced her legs apart, and his hand ran up her waist until his fingers were cupping and squeezing her breast. She spat in his face. He swore and slapped her. After he wiped the spittle from his cheek, he put his hands on the neckline of her gown and tugged at it while the second lifted the remains of her skirts.

No, no, *no*—they couldn't do this. She wouldn't let them do it, and if they thought it would be easy because she was tired, or tied, or hurt, they had another thing coming.

She sure as hell wouldn't go down without a fight.

She thrashed violently, her injured limbs screaming with the effort. She screamed, too, kicking, twisting, spitting—anything to get them off her body. One kick landed in the second man's face, forcing him back with a sharp yelp of pain. Cate was delighted to hear it and snarled at the other one.

"You there!"

Cate caught sight of Fionnbar stalking toward them. The second man scrambled away, holding his nose, but the first man stayed until Fionnbar pulled him off and shoved him aside.

"The captain wants you back," he said. "I'm to watch the queen."

The first man didn't flinch. "Ain't finished here, lad. The queen and I, we have a score to settle."

Score? What score? Cate's eyes slid down his figure to the bandages wrapped around his right thigh. Oh. That. If only her aim had been better.

Placing himself in front of her, Fionnbar drew his sword. "The captain says you are. Best go before he decides to have you whipped."

The man glanced at her. "Later, then."

As her tormentor walked away, Fionnbar looked at her. She turned her head, trying to control her tears.

"He won't bother you again. He won't touch you again," Fionnbar said. "None of them will. I'll make sure of it."

How would he do that? One man versus all the rest? One man standing against all the willing lads wanting to see if she was a screamer? She didn't want to come off as fatalistic, but it seemed more than a little hopeless to her.

"Your majesty," he said.

From the corner of her eye, she saw him reach for her. He wouldn't hurt her—his actions throughout the day had convinced her of that—but unless he intended to let her go, he could keep his hands to himself. She turned her head away as far as she could until he got the message and dropped his hand.

"I will keep you safe," he said. "I swear it."

She'd find out, wouldn't she?

Night fell, and she lost sight of Fionnbar in the darkness. She struggled against her bonds, hoping either to find a way free or make herself pass out. Unsuccessful on either front, she spent the night crying big, fat, silent tears of abject misery. She was hurt, she was scared, and never more in her life did she want to be at home with her mommy.

The rebels didn't appear that night, either. What the hell were they waiting for?

The morning couldn't come fast enough. Fionnbar looked like hell as he released her from the tree. She wanted to thank him for his efforts, but her tongue refused to form the words. He held up the water bag and looked at her, his eyebrows raised in question. She shook her head. The whole damn idea was humiliating, and she didn't want it. She didn't want to give in.

"Your majesty, please," Fionnbar whispered. "You must."

As stubborn as she wanted to remain, he was right. She nodded, and he held the spout to her lips and tipped it. Cool, crisp water ran down her throat. She choked and ended up spilling more than she swallowed, but took in enough to take the edge off her thirst. She wanted more, so much more, but thought it best to go slow. Having Fionnbar help her relieve herself was an experience best delayed as long as possible.

Next came food. Fionnbar explained they weren't planning on feeding her. As she already had watched everyone else in camp enjoy four meals, she wasn't shocked. Fionnbar didn't have much to offer, just a bit of bread, but it was better than the nothing she had before. He ripped the bread into bite-sized pieces and fed her. When it was gone, he offered her more water. She spilled less the second time around.

After that, it was back to walking. The scenery was an endless loop of trees and road, so she mostly stared at the stallion's hindquarters. When the soldiers stopped for lunch, she stared at the ground and ignored their jibes.

Later in the day, when their pace had slowed even more to accommodate her dwindling energy, she glanced at the mounted soldiers behind her. Fionnbar was asleep in the saddle. Insane jealousy followed, but begrudging him the opportunity to rest was unfair. He had spared her from being gang raped after all, and he would likely have to do the same every night until they reached the king. He should sleep while he could.

Turning to face front, she stepped into a small hole in the road. It wasn't anything more than a slight dip, but it was enough to send her to the ground.

The men laughed, no one trying to hide it, but neither the captain nor his horse noticed as they dragged her along.

As her face burned with anger, she twisted her wrists into a position to grab the rope. Bringing her legs in to her chest, she used the rope and the horse's weight to propel herself to her feet. The first attempt only landed her back on her stomach. The men laughed harder, making enough noise that the captain turned to look at her. His face was impassive, except for eyes that betrayed his amusement.

Her second attempt, though awkward, was successful. The captain's dark eyes changed, looking at her in approval. Cate didn't care for it. She didn't want him looking at her in any way, but he most definitely would not look at her like that.

Grabbing the leash again, she yanked it as hard as she could. Her impact was minimal. Less than minimal. The captain laughed and turned around. She gave the rope another useless tug while imagining the bastard falling from the horse's back and landing on his face in the road. She would kick him as she passed, just before he was trampled by his men and their horses.

It was a satisfying daydream, one that sustained her through the rest of the day.

The next night was spent in another nameless village. The captain and the mounted men received rooms in an inn. The foot soldiers were given space in the stable. Cate was gagged and tied to an outside post with only Fionnbar for company.

Just let me go, she wanted to say to him. *Untie me and let me run.*

There was nothing—literally nothing—she didn't hate at that moment.

She spent the night alternating between crying, more crying, passing out, and waking up, only to cry some more. She was awake when the sun started to rise. As she had a front row seat for the event, she knew she was facing east. Not that it changed one goddamn thing.

"We will reach the palace today," Fionnbar said when he removed the gag.

Oh, so there would be an end to the scenic walk of shame after all. How nice. Of course, as it would be exchanged for the king and any other untold horrors the palace held, it kind of sounded like a lateral move.

But what the hell would she do about it?

"He sent you to look after me," she whispered. "Willem?"

Fionnbar nodded vigorously. "Yes, your majesty."

"He wants you to keep me safe?"

"Yes."

"Then let me go."

"Your majesty—"

"You know what they'll do to me. If you don't let me go—if you don't help me escape here and now—they'll kill me, and you know it. Is that what Willem wants?"

"No, your majesty, but—"

"Let me go."

"They're not out there," Fionnbar said.

His words came out in a rush and hit her in the face. She stared at him as he continued.

"They didn't come for you, and they're not going to."

It wasn't true. It couldn't have been true. There had to be a reason why they hadn't come for her yet. But they would. They had to. They needed her, for crying out loud, to save their sorry world. They wouldn't let her hang.

Would they?

No. They wouldn't. James needed her. All right, so he needed her to sacrifice herself for the greater good, but that greater good wouldn't be served by letting her stay in the hands of his enemy, would it? There was a plan. He had a plan, and he would get her out.

Wouldn't he?

Left with disturbing thoughts, Cate refused the water and food Fionnbar offered, then followed him to the captain's stallion without an ounce of resistance. When the other men had assembled, they left the village and resumed their slow march to Eluned.

When they entered the city, they didn't crawl through some hole in the wall under the cover of dusk or dawn. No, they came through the city's main gates with the afternoon sun blazing down, when everyone and their mother stood outside, watching the man on a horse drag her along.

The captain was all about making a statement, and as no one threw rotten vegetables, or booed or hissed, she understood he was sending a message to the masses as much as her. James had told her once that Haleine had brought the people hope. If that were true, then they were now watching that hope be taken away.

The captain led her through the palace gates and brought his mount to a halt. She gawked at the palace. It was much more imposing than when she had seen it last. Two soldiers came up behind her to take her arms, and a fresh surge of pain coursed through her. She squeezed her eyes shut, willing herself to stay conscious.

"What do we have here?" a new voice, male and smooth, asked. "What have you brought me, Varro?"

"The queen, my lord," the captain—Varro?—said. "We have brought you the queen."

Was she about to meet the king? Cate forced her eyes open.

The new guy wore deep-red robes that trailed in the dirt. A braided belt of gold wrapped around his waist. He was well-groomed and bathed—which was more than she could say about a lot of people she had encountered in Lira—and his face was a step or two below handsome. A series of scars on his cheek marred it, as though he had survived a run-in with Freddy Kruger, or maybe someone else. Someone else was probably more likely.

But as normal as he looked, there was something about him. Something wrong. It wasn't anything physical because she couldn't see it, but she could sense it. Somehow, that was scarier.

"Have you," Scarface said, coming slowly closer. "The king will be so pleased."

Okay, so not the king, then. Who did that make him?

Scarface stopped just short of an arm's length away. He stared, examining every inch of her as though she were a painting he suspected of being a forgery. He smiled in a manner that turned Cate's veins to ice.

He knew she wasn't Haleine.

Scarface stepped back. "Bring her below."

Below? No part of that sounded like a good thing.

As Scarface withdrew to the palace, Varro motioned to the men holding her. They moved forward, dragging Cate between them. The fact that she was nothing but dead weight didn't faze them in the least.

Below was a dungeon. A dark, dank, and dreary dungeon complete with moaning and groaning, and the scurrying of unseen rodents. She couldn't see any other prisoners, but the sounds of their misery were crystal clear.

She should fight—needed to fight. What had happened to all of her goddamn fight? Had she left it in the woods? Tied to a post in a village whose name she didn't know? Where had it gone? Why was she doing this, just...doing *nothing* while they dragged her through a dungeon—a goddamn *dungeon.*

A man—the jailor, she assumed from his possession of a large ring of keys—rose upon their arrival. He looked her over but said nothing as he led them down a hall, unlocked a door, and pushed it open.

The soldiers didn't untie her before they threw her inside. Unable to stop her momentum, she hit the wall, slid to the floor, and landed on her left side. She couldn't breathe for the pain, and it was with gratitude that she passed out.

—⚬⚬⚬—

James was yanked out of the drowning dark and pulled into the light. He lay on his back, floundering and sputtering, until his eyes adjusted.

"James," Faolan said.

He groaned. "Even in death I have to listen to you."

"You're not dead."

How was that possible? Recalling the bolts tearing through his skin, James put his hand on his bare chest. He felt the area where the first bolt had gone in. The bolt was gone, but neither was there a bandage. At the very least, there should have been a bandage, but there was only a scar he didn't have before. He dropped his hand below his heart where the second bolt had struck. It, too, was scarred and tender to the touch, but appeared otherwise free from injury.

"Luisiúil?" he asked.

"Yes."

James sat up. He was back in his tent. How had he gotten there? He looked at Faolan, standing on the table. "I appreciate the effort."

"We couldn't lose you, too."

The pegasus spoke the truth. They'd already lost too much—Dana, the queen, Cate. He wasn't nearly as valuable as the rest, but it went to show how desperate their situation had become.

"Down to your last hope," James said.

"Cate is the last hope."

"Then we'd best get her back. Tell me what happened."

"Do you remember the attack?"

"Hard to forget that," James said. "Tell me what happened afterward. How did I get here?"

"Not everyone took multiple bolts to the chest," Faolan said. "The ones who didn't fetched help for the rest."

"How many did we lose?" James asked.

Twenty-five had departed from the camp. How many had returned? Faolan didn't respond. He didn't care for this part, talking about death, loss, and sacrifice. The numbers didn't matter to him. They were all justified, all worthy losses, in pursuit of his grand plans. James would have to ask Ilya. The numbers—and more—mattered to her.

"Do we know if Cate is alive?" James asked then.

"Omur won't kill her," Faolan said. "At least not yet."

"He knows who she is?"

"I imagine he knew it when he saw her."

"Why did you allow it to get that far?" he demanded, getting to his feet. "Bloody hell, Faolan, what—?"

"We had no choice," Faolan said. "Something, someone other than Omur, protected those men—protected Cate—from us. We couldn't get near them. All we could do is watch."

Something else. Someone else. It was too much. When would it end?

"She's in the palace now?" James asked.

"Yes."

"Is anyone in the palace with her? Any of ours?"

"Rhydwyn. He's there, but he can't do anything on his own."

No, he couldn't. James would have to find men to go to the palace with him. Gaining entry would be easy enough—the maid had showed them a hidden passage—but would it matter? Would it be enough? If Omur wanted Cate, would it matter how many men James had?

"She's alive, James," Faolan said, misinterpreting the silence. "Whoever—whatever—is doing this wants her alive."

For now. But that would change. It always did.

"What do we do?" James asked. "How do we get her back?"

"We go to Eluned," Faolan said. "We watch, we wait, and we learn. An opportunity will present itself, and when it does, we'll take her back."

"It's not a very good plan, as plans go."

"Doesn't matter," Faolan said. "That's all there is right now."

James sighed. This was his fault. Cate's loss was his fault. His people's death was his fault. Had Luisiúil bothered to save any of the rest? God help him, he should have listened to Faolan. If only he had done that.

"Is Gair dead?" he asked.

"No. He's here in camp."

James nodded. "Find him. Ilya, too, and bring them here. There are plans to be made."

The pegasus didn't move. "I know what you're thinking."

"How can you know when I don't?"

"I know what you're thinking," Faolan repeated. "You're wrong."

"I've told you before to stay out of my head."

"I didn't need access to your head to know this," Faolan said. "You're thinking you should have listened to me. You're thinking I should have come along, that maybe Bearach or Lorcan should have come along. You're thinking that would have made a difference."

"Wouldn't it have?"

"Not this time," Faolan said. "The magic that's keeping us from Cate would have kept us from doing anything other than dying in that ambush. Your stubbornness saved us."

"That was luck," James said. "Nothing for which I should be praised."

"And that's why you're the leader," Faolan said.

After Faolan left, James moved around the tent slowly, feeling as though he were a stranger in his own skin. Running his hand up his left arm, he breathed a small sigh of relief when he came to the scar he had received in his first battle. He checked his right arm then, and found the scar running from his wrist to his elbow, received in a fight that had nearly cost the queen her life.

Had he ever made a proper decision? Why did every choice he make lead to someone else's suffering? Someone else's loss?

"Is she truly gone?"

James startled and turned, finding Idwal Kai standing inside the tent.

"Make some noise next time, will you?" James said.

"Is she truly gone?" Idwal Kai repeated.

James nodded. "Taken on the road."

Idwal Kai considered this. "I'll help you get her back."

"You'll *help* us?"

"She is my lord's daughter," Idwal Kai said. "I have concluded that you mean her no harm, but if the king believes her to be a traitor…"

There was no need to finish the sentence. They both knew how it would end.

"Take me to Eluned with you," Idwal Kai said. "I will help you."

James had thought the man might have a use. He never imagined this would be it.

"How could you help me?" he asked. "You don't know the city or the palace as well as I."

"I don't know the city or palace at all, but I know noblemen. I know royalty," Idwal Kai said. "And I know how to fight."

"You'll fight for us?"

"She's my lord's daughter."

"You're loyal to Tanuba."

"To my lord."

"Who was loyal to Tanuba."

Idwal Kai conceded this point. "At this moment, I care about the girl. Nothing else," he said. "Which, I believe, makes us allies, at least for a while."

"Maybe, maybe not," James said. "You'll stay here. If I find a use for you, I'll let you know."

"I tell you, all I want is the girl."

James nodded. "You're not the only one."

—◈—

The girl was not the queen. However much she looked the part, the girl was not Haleine. But who she was or from where she had come, Omur could not say. She had value to the goddess, though, which meant she would be of value to his own lords.

When he returned to the privacy of his chambers, he proceeded to the fire to summon his lord.

"Yelsneh," he cried, "god of the north and commander of my will, I beseech you to appear before me now!"

Why is it you have summoned me? Yelsneh asked.

"My men have brought me a girl," Omur said, his head bowed.

A girl, you say? What of her? Surely she must have some significance for you to have summoned me here.

"The extent of her worth I do not know, but she is the very image of the queen. She is her twin."

Yelsneh said nothing, but a pulse in the thickened air indicated the dark god was most intrigued by the announcement.

"Who is she?" Omur asked. "Please, my lord, I must know."

She is here? She is on this earth? The goddess has brought her back?

Brought her back?

"Please, my lord, my god," Omur said, "tell me who she is. Tell me what value she has to you."

She is ours. The goddess took her from us nineteen years ago. But you say she has been returned?

"She is in the king's dungeon as we speak, my lord."

The dungeon? You placed our chosen vessel in the dungeon?

"I did not know who she was; I did not know what she was," Omur said. "The men who captured her think her to be the queen. She has neither said nor done anything to make them doubt."

Then raise her to this position. Remove her from the dungeon.

"The queen is disgraced—a traitor," Omur said. "The king will have her killed."

Convince him otherwise. The queen of Lira can wield great power for our cause, if the right woman should be on her throne.

"Yes, my lord," Omur said. "That is easily done, but...I have concerns about the girl's loyalties. She has been living amongst the goddess and her followers, and it is my belief that she has aligned herself with them."

Convince her otherwise.

"Yes, my lord."

You will turn her to our cause, Yelsneh said. *You will make her ours. You will make her what she was meant to be.*

"As you have commanded," Omur said, "so shall it be."

When Cate woke up, she was still in the dungeon. She lay on her back and looked at the stone walls surrounding her. They were covered in mold, mildew, and a variety of other science projects. A pair of iron rings protruded from the wall above her head, the kind from which she imagined both chains and people were hung. One such ring was digging into her leg, so she knew they also ran along the floor. The only window was the small barred one in the door, and the only light was the flickering of a torch.

Which meant it would be awfully difficult for someone to bust her out of there.

Why hadn't they done anything already? Why hadn't they tried for her back in the forest where there were infinitely fewer obstacles to overcome? Could it be possible that none of the rebels had survived? She had to consider the prospect. The captain and his boys had held the element of surprise. They'd had greater numbers, more weapons—better weapons. It wouldn't be completely out of the ever-expanding realm of possibility to think that maybe the only survivor of the attack was the person currently rotting in the damn dungeon.

Not only was it possible, but Cate found it was also debilitatingly depressing. It didn't matter that she was so parched swallowing hurt. It didn't matter that her stomach was this growing pit of aching emptiness. It didn't matter that she didn't have any damn energy. It didn't matter that she couldn't so much as take a deep breath without wanting to pass out in pain.

Nothing mattered. Because she was going to die here. Some people would say she was being pessimistic, but she preferred to think of it as realistic. They thought she was the queen. They thought she was a traitor, and the only people who knew the truth were missing in action. So unless a traitor's death in these parts was death by chocolate, she really didn't have much to look forward to.

When the door opened and two men came in, she didn't move except to look at them.

"Pick her up."

That was Scarface. Cate looked for him until the two men hauled her up. The sudden movement hurt, and she swooned, but a hand across her face brought her out of it. She let out a noise she couldn't identify and looked at the captain—Varro, Scarface had called him—standing in front of her.

"My lord wishes to speak with you," the captain said.

"Thank you, Varro," Scarface said, stepping inside the cell.

He wore the same red robes as before. Did that mean it was the same day, or was Scarface's sense of fashion that limited? It didn't *feel* like the same day, so it was probably the latter.

"Here we are." Scarface approached with deliberate, over-careful steps. "Long have my lords waited for this. Waited for you."

His lords?

"Do you know what fate awaits the queen?" he asked. "I am sure you do. Or, if failing that, I am sure you can guess."

So he didn't want to talk to her so much as he wanted to talk *at* her. That was fine by her. She didn't have the energy for bantering.

"Why have you not told them your true name?" he said.

"Would that have made a difference?" Cate asked. She didn't bother with the accent. "Would they have believed me if I had? Because I don't think so."

Scarface smiled. "And here you would sit anyway."

"I was more lying prone on the floor," she said, "but sure, we can say sit."

Maybe she had a little energy for bantering.

"Your injuries, yes," Scarface said. "They are regrettable, but they shall be attended to."

"Oh yeah? Bound by the Geneva Convention, are we?" she asked. "You should've reminded your captain of that. I do believe some of your boys had less than honorable intentions."

Scarface smiled at the floor. "You will have to forgive him—"

"Unlikely."

"—but he does not know who you are."

"Who is it you think I am?"

"I know exactly who you are," Scarface said. "I know better than you."

"Everyone says so. What makes you any different?"

"Shall I show you?"

"I think I'd rather you not show me your anything."

Scarface smiled yet again. "Very well," he said. "Now, you will have to forgive me, but I am curious."

Before she could ask what had piqued his curiosity, Scarface put his hands on the neckline of her gown and cleanly ripped it from neck to navel. She yelped and brought up her hands to cover herself, but he forced them back down. She yelped again, this time for other reasons.

He studied her chest. "Interesting."

"What's the matter?" she asked. "Haven't seen a pair of breasts before?"

Scarface revealed his biggest smile yet. She was so damn glad she could be so damn amusing.

"I've seen a fair few," he replied. "But that is not what interests me."

"What does?"

"Your scar." He nodded to the mark over her heart. "How ever did you come by it?"

"Don't you know you should never ask a lady about her scars?" she asked. "It's impolite."

"I've never been one for the rules of polite society."

"Well, color me surprised."

"You will tell me from where you received that scar."

"The hell I will."

His hand lashed out and pressed against her stomach. "You will tell me."

She looked at his hand. As much as she didn't care for him touching her, as far as torture went, it was pretty mild.

"No," she said, "I won't."

A growl sounded low and deep in Scarface's throat. He took his hand from her stomach and put it around her throat. She gasped for breath, choking and crying, and tried to hit him, but couldn't muster anything more than an ineffective rapping of his chest.

She thought she was on the verge of passing out—maybe death—when something flickered in his eyes, and he backed off. Coughing and sputtering, Cate slumped against the men holding her.

"Are you trying to make me cry?" she asked when she was able.

"I can't say I would be opposed."

"Like to make girls cry, huh?"

"I like to do more than that."

"I'll bet you do," Cate said. "You know, my mother warned me about men like you."

"I have no doubt your mother warned you about me," he said. "After all, I have been trying to kill her for quite some time now."

Cate locked eyes with him and struggled against her guards until their hold on her tightened. Using them as an anchor, she pushed off the floor and kicked Scarface squarely in the chest, sending him sprawling back. The captain hit her across the face, and she cried out before she could stop herself.

"Varro, no," Scarface said, once his balance had been regained. "There's no need for that."

The captain backed away, his head bowed. Scarface came forward and lifted her chin.

"It's quite all right," he said. "I don't mind her resistance. She doesn't understand."

Cate couldn't think of a truer statement.

"She will soon enough, however," Scarface said.

Now Cate couldn't think of a scarier statement. The combination of Scarface's soft inflection and dark, ominous eyes was somehow worse than anything she could have imagined.

"Bring her above," he ordered.

"What's above?" she asked.

Scarface smiled. "You'll find out."

CHAPTER 17

Dana went to Labhras first. His choices were either that or Enimode, and Emrys would see him, even if he didn't want to. Dana truly wanted to find the camp, but he didn't know where it might be now, nor if he would be able to find it. The walls were made to keep out enemies, and though he had been able to access the tunnels, there was no telling what they might consider him. Starting with Emrys made the most sense.

When he arrived, he slipped past the guards on watch and entered the keep through the kitchens. Emrys wasn't in his own hall, so Dana went above stairs to the solarium. There he found the nobleman sitting in front of the fire, a goblet in one hand, and a dagger in the other. A plate of untouched food waited on a tray at his side.

As Dana stepped inside, Emrys looked up and laughed. "She sent you along, by God, just as she said she would."

Dana did not laugh.

"Sit, won't you?" Emrys said, chuckling. "Pour yourself some wine, if you'd like. Don't want my hospitality to be in question, eh?"

Dana did nothing.

"Don't be like that," Emrys said.

The nobleman continued to squirm under Dana's scrutiny. He placed the dagger on the tray and leaned forward, resting his elbows on his knees. He held the goblet loosely between his hands.

"What were you thinking?" Emrys said, his humor disappeared. "Why weren't you with her? You send her on that fool's errand without you?"

He hadn't sent her nor had she sent him, but Dana didn't say that. He only waited to hear what Emrys would say next.

"I sent men out as soon as we heard. One of the village women came in screaming about it. Murder done on the road. A massacre, she said, and I sent men to see." Emrys tilted the goblet and studied its contents. "When they arrived, there was nothing left but the dead. Some of theirs. A lot of yours. More than the four I saw in my bailey. We buried them. I'll show you the graves if you want to see them, but the queen was not among the dead. Neither was that lad who accompanied her inside. Your lad."

Did that mean James had survived? What had he been thinking?

"He's got her again, that damned king of ours," Emrys said. "He'll have her locked up in his bloody dungeon by now. Do you know what he'll do to her?"

Finish what he started the last time he had her. Dana looked at the floor.

"I didn't think I would like her so," Emrys said.

Dana nodded. He hadn't thought so, either, the first time he met her.

"She took this from me," Emrys said, swapping his goblet for the dagger. He turned it over in his hands. "Ripped it from my side and held it to my throat until I agreed to let her man go. Did she tell you that? Did she have the chance?"

No. There hadn't been the chance to say a lot of things. Dana looked at the dagger and approached the nobleman. Her man, Emrys had said. Why had James done this?

"They found it on the road, my men," Emrys continued. "The blade was covered in blood. Hers, theirs—I don't know, but I like to think she put up a fight."

She always did.

"Here." Emrys slid the dagger into its jeweled sheath. "You take this, and you give it to her when you find her. Tell her I'll give her what she wants."

Emrys held out the dagger, but Dana didn't take it. He stared at the weapon. What had she done? What had she asked of him?

"You will get her back, won't you?" Emrys asked.

Dana met Emrys's eyes briefly before taking the dagger and walking out.

Bronagh sat on a bench in the corner of the kitchens, plucking chickens, when Omur entered. Servants everywhere bowed their heads at his presence. Bronagh did not, but when he stopped in front of her, she lifted her head.

"Do you want something?" she asked.

"Come with me," he said.

"What for? I don't serve you."

"Perhaps not," Omur said. "But you do serve the queen."

She stopped working, staring at the half-plucked chicken in her hands, as the meaning of Omur's words settled in her brain.

"You found her," she whispered.

"I found her."

There was malice in his voice. She heard it clearly, and suddenly, she couldn't see. She couldn't breathe. Dropping the chicken, she clutched the edge of the bench.

They found her. God, they found her.

"Come, Bronagh," Omur said. "You must be pleased by the queen's recovery."

The shock faded, and her senses returned. She looked at Omur. "What do you want from me?"

"I want you to do your duty," he said. "I want you to tend to your mistress."

"Where is she?"

"Her chambers."

"Her chambers?"

"The king has pardoned her. He has forgiven her sins."

"Why? Why would he do this? Why would you want this?"

"I am as the king commands me, Bronagh."

"That is not true."

Omur smiled. "I am as my lord commands me."

That was true. She did not know who his lord was—she didn't want to know—but Omur spoke the truth. She had heard enough of his lies to know the difference.

"The rebels will come for her, Bronagh. They'll not be content with her loss, and they will come," Omur said. "You should decide now whose side you are on because this time, should they try to take her away, I won't be so lenient. She won't make it out of these walls alive."

That was truth as well. Bronagh's eyes turned to the floor. That wasn't a choice at all. If Haleine wouldn't make it out of the palace alive, Bronagh would keep her within. She wouldn't seek to harm the rebels when they came, but neither would she help them.

"Do make haste, Bronagh," Omur said. "You don't want to keep the queen waiting."

He swept out of the room, his robes swirling around him. She looked at the floor, taking deep breaths until her fingers were able to relax their hold on the bench. When they had, she stood and walked out of the kitchens, ignoring the eyes focused upon her.

———

Varro and two of his guards brought Cate through narrow, torch-lit hallways. The captain took the lead while the other two half-led, half-carried her to wherever this mysterious above was located. So far there had been three flights of stairs followed by a labyrinth of corridors. Cate didn't know where above was, but for the sake of her legs, she hoped they reached it soon. Otherwise, her escorts would be carrying her outright.

Finally, they stopped in front of a door, and Varro gave the command for her hands to be untied. Cate held her breath while the guard on her right worked the knots. It had been days since she'd had the use of her hands, and almost as long since there had been feeling below her elbows. As grateful as she was to have the ropes removed, she understood that it was going to hurt.

The ropes fell away, and all three men were left looking at the linen strip Fionnbar had used to protect her skin. Varro pulled it off and let it fall. When the strip had settled on the floor, he smiled.

"The things you inspire my men to do," he said.

Cate declined to comment. He opened the door and motioned for her to go through. The guards dropped her arms, and Cate took a few uneven steps forward. The door closed behind her, leaving her alone, so she rubbed her wrists and took in her new location.

Above was better than the dungeon. Above was *way* better than the dungeon. Above came with windows and natural light, area rugs, and a bed—an honest-to-goodness *bed* with blankets and pillows, and a mattress probably stuffed with something soft. Above screamed luxury, and Cate tried to keep from drooling as she collapsed in the nearest chair.

She thought she could learn to like above.

Only there had to be a catch, right? Scarface had ordered her to be brought here, and he hadn't filled her with warm, fuzzy feelings. There had to be a catch. If she waited long enough, the catch would find her, but the passivity inherent in that plan irked her, so she gathered her strength and pushed out of the chair because above was begging to be explored.

It wasn't the room from her dream, but it was close. Similar in its richness and furnishings, but different enough that the dream could still safely be considered a dream, and not be upgraded to a vision. That was likely wishful thinking on her part, but she had other things, more immediate things, about which to be concerned.

Like escape.

Her first stop was a set of glass doors that led onto a balcony. She looked at the city and the forests before glancing over the wall to confirm that she'd need a radioactive spider bite or some serious repelling gear to turn that into a viable getaway. Back inside, she tried another set of double doors—solid, wooden, and locked.

She sank to the floor to better examine the lock. She'd broken into her fair share of high school classrooms for various lame pranks, but those doors never required anything more than a library card. These doors required more, but she had that skill, too. Daniel, of all people, had taught her. It had been a joke between them because why would she ever need to know how to pick a lock? They had laughed about it.

She wasn't laughing now. If she could get her arm working again, and find some pins, she maybe had a way out. The thought made her want to smile, but that felt too much like tempting fate so she got up and walked away.

Spotting a third door, she crossed the room, bypassing a vanity on her way and avoiding the mirror at all costs. There was absolutely no need to experience the horror that would be her reflection. When she passed the bed, she dared only to lay her hand on it. Holy crap, that was soft. She gave the bed a loving glance before moving on to Door Number Three.

It was a bathroom. An actual bathroom. Okay, so maybe there wasn't a flush toilet, but there wasn't a bush to squat behind, either, and there was a tub—a beautiful, white marble vision of perfection—sitting in the middle. Her eyes watered at the sight.

Perhaps it wouldn't matter what the catch was. It would be worth it for the opportunity to have a bath in this room. Just to have a *bath*. She stepped closer to the tub and reached out to touch it, afraid it would disappear.

"They have brought you back, my lady?" a timid voice asked from behind her.

Cate quickly pulled her hand away and turned to see a gaunt, black-haired woman standing in the doorway. Judging by her utilitarian, apron-covered dress, she was a servant of some kind. And a haunted one at that.

The woman frowned. "You are not the queen. Who are you?"

Cate said nothing.

"Who are you?" the woman repeated, but Cate stayed silent. "You have no reason to fear me. I will not harm you."

It wasn't the first time someone had told her that. Yet here she was, in the worst physical condition she'd ever been in. *Ever.*

"Please," the woman said, "tell me who you are."

"Who are you?" Cate said.

"My name is Bronagh. I serve the queen."

"Did someone tell you I was the queen?" Cate asked, and Bronagh nodded. "Scarface?"

"I beg your pardon, my lady," Bronagh said, "but to whom are you referring?"

Cate had forgotten that Scarface was unlikely to be his given name. "Tall, dark, scars on his face? Wears red robes, and likes to make girls cry."

Bronagh nodded. "That man is Lord Omur. He is the king's advisor, and aye, he told me you were her."

Omur. Cate had heard that name before. He had sent the soldiers to look for her because, according to James and Faolan, Omur wanted her for some reason. Did that mean he was perhaps more than just the king's advisor?

"Who are you?" Bronagh asked, sounding as though she was on the verge of tears.

"Cate. I'm Cate. They tell me I'm Haleine's sister."

"They?"

Cate studied the wall. Was it safe to tell her the truth? Was it safe to tell her anything? Hell, she may have already told this woman too much. If only she knew what the goddamn catch was.

Cate tried to shrug, but only her right shoulder worked. "The voices in my head, I guess."

"The rebels," Bronagh said. "Dana?"

Cate shook her head. "I don't know who that is."

A lie in the strictest sense, but claiming any knowledge of him was probably unwise when the people holding her prisoner were the same people trying to exterminate the rebellion.

Bronagh nodded. "I don't know from where you came, but I know the rebels were involved. Dana and that damned pegasus, they brought you here, sent you here."

"I told you I don't—"

"I don't care about that," Bronagh interrupted. "I don't care about them, or why they may have sent you here. Just tell me, please, if you have seen the queen. Is she alive?"

Cate didn't look at the wall this time. She thought what she was about to say would kill the maid, but if letting her think Haleine was gone for good could possibly lead to an end to the village attacks, Cate wouldn't hesitate. It wouldn't be much of a lie anyway.

"Haleine's gone," she said. "Dead."

Bronagh released a sad, little whimper and closed her eyes, her hands clenched and pressed against her chest. A lone tear slowly rolled down her pale cheek. Whatever else this woman was, at one point she must have been Haleine's friend.

Bronagh opened her eyes and studied Cate. "You're hurt."

"You get used to it."

"I'll summon the physician to look at you."

A doctor. Well, considering her arm was incapable of doing anything but dangling like a strand of limp spaghetti, a visit from a person of medicine might not be completely unwelcome.

"Is there a possibility of me putting on something less revealing before the good doctor arrives?" Cate asked.

Bronagh seemed to notice for the first time what Cate was wearing. Or, what was left of it, at any rate. It was hard to tell if she was startled, or maybe embarrassed by Cate's disheveled state, but it soon turned to curiosity. Bronagh had to be looking at that damn scar. Everyone was so intrigued by it, and other than the theories of a pint-sized pony, she had no idea why she even had it.

"Hey." Cate snapped her fingers. "Eyes up here."

Bronagh shook her head. "I do apologize, my lady. It's just...your scar. It's—"

"Yeah, I know. It's been real popular with everyone."

"What about..." Bronagh indicated the cuts between her breasts.

"I didn't steal the damn sheath. Live and learn, right?"

Bronagh nodded as though she had understood. "I'll fetch a robe. It'll be best. Rhys will need to see—"

"Rhys?"

"The physician. He will need to examine you. He knows the queen..."

Bronagh stopped. Cate waited.

"Your scar," the maid said. "How do you have—?"

"Beats me."

"I do not understand."

"You're not alone. How about that robe now, huh?"

"Aye. I apologize, my lady."

"Yeah, it's okay if you don't call me that," Cate said, but Bronagh looked as though Cate had suggested she eat a plateful of broken glass. "Or whatever you're comfortable with. You know, if you point out the general direction of the robe, I could get it myself."

That proposal went over about as well as the first, and the maid left the bathroom. Had she insulted Bronagh past the point of tolerance? Did that mean the doctor wouldn't be summoned? Crap. How could she get Bronagh back?

Cate was in pursuit when Bronagh returned, a lush, blue robe with white fur trim draped over her arm. Setting it down, she motioned for Cate to turn. Even in its ruined state, the gown took a while to remove, and Cate was openly crying when it finally pooled at her feet.

"Here." Bronagh shook out the robe. "Rhys first, then food and a bath."

Cate put her right arm through the sleeve. "With hot water?"

"Of course," Bronagh said, helping with the useless left arm. Cate's tears were renewed, and Bronagh let out a distressed gasp. "I hurt you! I'm so sorry, my lady."

"No, you didn't hurt me," Cate said. "Well, you did, but that's not why I'm crying. Not the only reason, anyway."

"Then why?"

"Oh, it's dumb. It's materialistic and shallow and means I'm a bad, bad person, but damn, I really want a hot bath."

Bronagh came around to face her. "You are quite curious."

Cate smiled. "Since I know you don't mean 'inquisitive,' I should thank you for finding such a polite way of putting it."

Bronagh smiled as well, the action sitting oddly on her face. "I'll find Rhys for you now," she said. "You can rest in the other room until I come back."

Cate followed the maid into the bedroom and sat on a sofa near the fire. "You said Omur told you I was the queen?"

"Aye, my lady."

"Why does he want people to think I'm her?"

"Does he perhaps not know the truth? The resemblance is—"

"He knows," Cate said.

He knew, and he had sent an attendant who would be sure to know the difference, too. Maybe it meant nothing, and she was just reading something into it that wasn't there. Maybe Omur had only sent Bronagh because Bronagh was Haleine's maid, and it was her job to attend to the queen. Maybe Bronagh was working with Omur to find out what Cate knew. If that was the case, they would be disappointed because the only thing Cate had let slip was her name and how badly she wanted a bath. There wasn't much they could do with that information, except withhold the bath. It would be an evil thing to do, sure, but like Omur's hand on her stomach, it was something she could survive.

"I'm sorry, my lady, but I do not know," Bronagh said.

"Never mind. It doesn't matter." Cate watched the maid head toward the door through which the guards had brought her. "Do you know where those corridors go? You must, right? You work here, so you must know your way around."

Bronagh turned. Her countenance had shifted from concerned caregiver to psychotic prison warden. "Escape will be useless."

"You promised me a hot bath. Why would I want to escape?"

"You will. And when you find you can't, you will pray for death."

Well, that had taken an unexpected turn, hadn't it? Cate wasn't quite sure how to respond.

Finally, she shook her head. "I don't pray."

—✺—

After Bronagh found an idle boy to fetch Rhys, she went to the kitchens. The space was crowded with other servants, whispering to each other and staring at her. She kept her head down and her mind focused on her task. Bread. A bowl of broth. Wine, and a goblet in which to put it. She set everything upon a tray and was preparing to leave when she spotted him.

One of the rebels. She'd seen him before, that night they took the queen. She couldn't recall his name, but whoever he was, he was in need of a bath and a shave. And a change of clothing. He currently wore a kitchen smock over trousers and boots that had seen far better days. Why bother with that? How far did he think the smock might carry him when his filth betrayed him so badly? None of the palace servants would ever look as unwashed as that, not even the stable lads.

He looked at her then, and she glared back. Omur had told her they would come. She hadn't thought they'd be here so soon, but it didn't change what she had to do. Carefully placing the tray on a table, she motioned for him to follow.

"What do you want?" she asked when they were outside.

"The lass. Where is she?"

"You won't be able to get to her," Bronagh said. "There are too many guards."

There weren't any guards, not yet, but Omur would send them soon enough. But even if he didn't, she couldn't allow the rebels access to the girl.

"Where is she? The dungeon?" he asked.

Bronagh shook her head. "The queen's chambers."

"How many?"

"Guards? Too many," she said. "How many are you?"

He didn't answer. What did that mean?

"Why isn't Dana here? Is he..." She remembered the condition in which she had last seen the rebel leader. He hadn't been much better off than the queen herself. "Is he gone?"

The man didn't answer that, either. Had the rebel leader died? Could it be that both him and the queen were lost?

"Who leads you now?" she asked. "Who sent you here?"

"Will you help me get to the lass or not?"

"I can bring you to her, but it won't do you any good," Bronagh said. "There are too many guards both in the room and surrounding it. They're Omur's men, and they'll know you don't belong. It's not safe to try and take her."

"It's not safe to leave her there."

"Which is why you were supposed to take her and keep her safe," Bronagh spat.

"We did."

A flair of anger bloomed within her. Dead was safe? Well, mayhap it was. Haleine would be beyond any of their reach now.

"You know the truth about the lass, don't you?" the man asked. "You know she isn't—?"

"I know." Bronagh sighed. "You can't loiter around the kitchens looking the way you do. They'll notice."

"I'm not leaving the palace. Not without the lass."

He would have to be hidden, but where could she conceal him? She couldn't place him with the servants. Too many spies and wagging tongues. The same reasoning eliminated the soldiers' barracks.

"Come on," she said. "Follow me."

The man didn't move. "Where?"

"A place you can stay."

"Where?"

"I have a house along the palace wall. You can stay there. You, or whoever else needs to hide. I assume you're not here alone."

"You have a house?"

"There was a time when I was believed to be a loyal servant to the queen."

"Michaela."

She nodded. "Will you come?"

"Aye."

It had been so long since she had set foot inside her little house that she was unsurprised to find a family had taken up residence there. She unceremoniously threw them out and, once they had gone, busied herself with checking to see what belongings remained and what had been pilfered.

"You shouldn't have done that," the man said, hovering near the door.

"They'll find somewhere else to go. It's not my problem, nor is it yours," Bronagh said. "Now, I must return before I'm missed. Stay here, stay close. I will do what I can to help you."

The man bowed his head and stepped inside. "Thank you."

She nodded, not bothering to tell him that he should save his gratitude. "I'll bring you what I can, when I can. Food, as well as information. Water for washing. Maybe some clothing if I can find it."

"I need the lass," he said. "Everything else is secondary."

She knew what he meant. "Omur doesn't want to let her go."

The man shrugged. "Doesn't matter."

James took Gair with him to Eluned. Idwal Kai campaigned hard to be permitted to come, but James didn't trust him and finally asked Lorcan to keep the man in place. Bearach and Fáinne carried both him and Gair to the city, leaving them and Faolan outside the walls. They used the hidden passage to gain entrance and parted ways with Faolan before moving into the general public.

"Meet us at Orla's," James said to the pegasus. "Mind you stay out of sight."

"Same to you," Faolan replied and flew away.

James tugged the hood of his cloak over his head and stepped onto the street. Turning left would lead to Orla's. Right would take him by the palace.

He went right, Gair following close behind.

Upon reaching the palace, James stood outside its walls and looked at the castle. He should go inside. Just to see if he could find Rhydwyn, or Cate, or discover where they were holding her. It would be safe enough, just the two of them. If the guards were looking for anyone, it was Dana. Not him.

Would she be in the dungeon? James had freed Dana from there once before. Could he do it again?

James walked along the outer wall to the hidden door. After checking for witnesses, he went straight at it, only to be shoved back before he could reach it. Rubbing away the sting in his chest, he glanced at Gair. On his second try, he moved faster and was forced back harder and farther, the ensuing sting worse. Gair made his own attempt with no better results. James advanced a third time, walking slowly with his hand outstretched until he met resistance. It looked as though he touched nothing, but he could feel it. Cold, smooth, solid. Alive. A sharp pain worked its way up his arm.

"Bloody magic," he muttered.

Forming a fist, he hit the wall and was thrown to the ground. He stood, clenching and unclenching his now-burning, throbbing hand, and stared at the palace walls he couldn't reach. His sword. Perhaps that could get him through.

Gair touched his elbow. James glanced at the pair of guards heading in their direction. They didn't seem to be focused on anyone in particular, but James nodded and walked away.

They took a roundabout path to Orla's and entered through the main door. The barroom was crowded with patrons. Orla was delivering a pair of tankards to a corner table. James and Gair pushed their way to the bar to wait for her return.

"What'll you have, lads?" she asked when she got to them, her attention on something beneath the bar.

"Ale," James said. "Two."

Orla looked up. She was even less pleased to see him than usual. Faolan must have already arrived. She filled a single tankard and set it in front of Gair.

"Come with me," she said to James. "Your bloody bird is in my storeroom."

James pushed off the bar and followed Orla into the next room. He closed the door behind them and leaned against it. Faolan stood on a nearby barrel.

"This came for you today," Orla said, pulling a small, folded square of parchment from her apron. She thrust it at James. "Are you having your letters delivered here now?"

A letter? Who would be sending him a letter? James took the parchment and unfolded it to find a short missive from Rhydwyn. Cate had been moved from the dungeon to the queen's chambers. Too many guards to risk retrieval at this time.

"I've a business to run, lest you've forgotten," Orla said. "Tell me what it is you want. A stall for the night?"

James shook his head as he refolded the parchment and fed it to the nearest lantern. "I need a room."

"I ain't got that many."

"I only need one. You know which."

"Occupied," Orla said.

"Not anymore," James said.

"You don't run my tavern."

"Move them elsewhere, or I'll do it."

"All grown up now, aren't you?" Orla asked. "Making threats like a man."

"Please, Orla," Faolan said. "We need your help."

"Have you got coin?"

"You wouldn't ask Dana that," James said.

Orla shrugged. "You're not Dana."

"No, I'm not," James said.

They stared at one another until Orla said, "They took your girl from you."

"I'm aware," he replied.

"They marched her through those streets, like she was"—Orla shook her head—"like she was you."

"I'm going to get her back," James said.

Orla seemed to consider this.

"How did she look?" Faolan asked.

"How did she look?" Orla gaped at the pegasus. "She looked like a bloody prisoner, that's how she looked. What sort of question is that?"

"Was she able to walk?" Faolan asked. "Was she—?"

"She's alive," Orla sighed. "She's alive, and she walked, head held high, right into that bloody palace. But she won't be alive for long, I'll tell you that. Not with what they'll do to her."

"I'm going to get her back," James repeated. "You'll either help me, or you won't. Which is it?"

"Where's Dana?" Orla asked. "What's happened to him? Is he…"

"Not dead," James said. "Not so far as I know."

"Where is he?"

"Gone."

"Gone where?"

"Disappeared off the face of the earth," James said. "I don't know where he's gone, nor do I care. I don't need his help to get the girl back. I need yours."

"Aye, all right," Orla said. "The room's yours."

"Thank you."

"They think she's the queen, James," Orla said, surprising him with the use of his name. He couldn't remember her ever having used it before. "They're going to kill her."

James shook his head. "They won't have the chance."

CHAPTER 18

The physicians had yet to discover a cause for his mother's illness. Revelin sat at his father's desk, his hands pressed against his mouth, as he listened to their discussion. Theories followed by arguments, then more theories and more arguments, but no consensus and no answers.

Poison was the word on Revelin's mind, but he was reluctant to give it voice in this room in front of these men. It had not been proposed in any of their discussions, and he viewed its omission with suspicion. He saw everyone in the same way now, not knowing whom among them belonged to his brother. Enemies everywhere, and Revelin was helpless to stop them.

The one man Revelin did trust entered the library then, and the physicians' conversation died away as Darragh made his bow.

"Your carriage is ready, your highness," he said.

Carriage? Had he asked for a carriage? Revelin lowered his hands to ask, but Darragh gave him the smallest of nods, and Revelin understood. His nobleman had been found. He stood, and the physicians bowed.

"We will continue this at a later time," he said, and they murmured his title in agreement.

Darragh said nothing as they walked to the courtyard. As Revelin climbed inside the waiting carriage, his advisor offered him nothing more than another small nod before calling for the driver to depart.

Revelin rode alone as the carriage left the palace grounds and made its way through Mairéad's streets. It did not take him long to realize his destination.

The Coileáin estate had once belonged to the Maoilriains but had been given to Darian upon his marriage to Lady Rhoswen. Nathan's noblemen were left jealous and some furious by the gift, as few believed that an upstart soldier from a family of no name was worthy of such a wealthy property. Whether Darian had ever been aware of these opinions, Revelin never knew, but it would not have mattered. Darian would not have cared anyhow.

Upon Revelin's arrival at the estate, a servant escorted him to the library where Adomnan Cathal lounged on a sofa. He stood when Revelin appeared and bowed.

"Your highness. How may I be of service?"

"What did Darragh tell you?"

"Only that you wished to speak with me. I presume from our locale that secrecy is paramount."

Revelin glanced at the servant standing against the wall. "Secrecy, yes."

Cathal also looked at the servant. "Fetch wine, please."

The servant bowed and exited the room. Cathal gestured to the sofa. Revelin stepped toward it but stopped when he saw a portrait of Haleine and Sighle hanging on the wall.

"It is safe to speak here, my lord," Cathal said.

Revelin continued to stare at the portrait. "Is it?"

"Darian Coileáin was unfailingly loyal, and he inspired that same quality in those who served him. The palace walls have ears, your highness, but this is not the palace. It is safe here."

Revelin nodded and sat on the sofa. On the opposite wall hung another portrait, this one of Darian and Rhoswen. Ghosts everywhere he turned.

"I have not seen you at court since Darian's vigil," he said.

Cathal sat in a chair. "Nor would you when you buried my reason for being there."

"The queen has need of you."

"*You* have need of me, your highness," Cathal said. "How fares your mother?"

Revelin looked away. "You are a nobleman's son."

"I am, my lord."

"As was your father and his father and his father before him."

"Yes."

"The sons of noblemen do not often associate with the sons of farmers."

"Not often, no."

"Even less frequently do they spy on the other's behalf," Revelin said, and Cathal smiled but did not comment. "Why did you?"

The servant returned with a decanter and two goblets. Neither Revelin nor Cathal spoke until everything had been laid out. Cathal dismissed the servant and poured the wine himself. When he offered Revelin a goblet, Revelin shook his head. Cathal placed the goblet on the table and returned to his seat.

"I trust your highness will forgive me this," Cathal said, "but I forget how young you are."

The thought almost made Revelin laugh. He did not feel young, only the opposite. "What does my youth have to do with anything?"

"It is the reason you don't already know the answer to your question." Cathal sighed. "You're very much like him, you know."

That thought was more absurd than the last. Revelin worked to squash his rising irritation. "You do not know why we meet, yet you seek to flatter me?"

"Not flattery, your highness. Just remembering." Cathal had some wine and looked toward the windows. "Darian was an infantry man—a foot soldier. Such men are usually commoners, bastards, criminals. They're nameless men—boys, really—most of which have no training and have never held a sword, and their purpose is to enter the fray first while the noblemen and their sons stay back to issue their orders and play their war games.

"Most of them don't live long, you'll understand, and there's no reason why they should. It's why they're sent in the first place. They're expendable; they're no one. They're our shields, and they die so we don't have to."

Revelin reached for the goblet. "I am afraid I do not understand."

"Darian was different. He shouldn't have been—a farmer's son with a farmer's education? He should have died young with a spear in his belly, but do you know what he did instead?"

"He lived."

"Too right he did. And because he lived, I lived."

"He saved you."

"More than once." Cathal looked at Darian's portrait. "I was my father's second son. He called me his spare and had more regard for his hounds than he did for me, so I set out to make a name for myself by serving the king, your father. I was a reckless fool, even for a lad at war, but I wanted so badly to prove myself to your father, to my father. I should have been dead many times over.

"It didn't take long for me to learn about Darian. Everyone talked about him. He had this...this ability." Cathal paused to drink more wine. "He knew. He always knew where there would be danger, when things would go badly. Mine was not the only life he saved."

Revelin's goblet was empty, and he reached for the decanter, knocking it over. The sound startled Cathal back to the present, and he stood to tend to the spill himself.

"How does any of this make me like Darian?" Revelin asked.

Cathal refilled Revelin's goblet, then his own. "Darian Coileáin never should have been born a commoner," he said. "And you, my lord, never should have been born a second son."

Revelin put the goblet on the table and left it there. He looked at Cathal. Cathal stared back.

"Darian thought the same, your highness. He thought you shared the same instincts and told me once that I should trust you as I did him," Cathal said.

"Yet, you departed court as soon as Darian was interred."

"I did. He was more a brother to me than any of my blood. I sought to mourn his loss in private. But I am here now." Cathal slid to the edge of his chair. "Your highness, I am, of course, happy to answer any questions you wish to ask until all your suspicions have been quelled, but would your lady mother not be better served were we to discuss the reason you had your man bring me here today?"

"He was Darian's man first."

"Now he is yours," Cathal said. "As am I."

Revelin nodded and gestured to the chair nearest him. Cathal sat.

"My mother is ill, and her physicians have not yet been able to determine the cause."

"But you believe you have."

"Yes."

"Poison?" Cathal asked, and Revelin offered a curt nod in response. "You suspect the crown prince?"

"I do."

"Evidence?"

"I have none. I have only..."

"Instinct."

"Yes."

Now Cathal nodded. He laced his fingers together and leaned back into the chair. "None of the physicians have posed such a theory?"

"They have not." Revelin waited a moment before adding, "I do not seek the throne for myself."

Cathal laughed. "I can't imagine anyone—with the possible exception of the crown prince—would think that, your highness. Though most of those same people would be most relieved if that were your intention."

"I am a second son, not an anointed king."

"Neither is your brother."

"But he should be."

"Mayhap that is his birthright," Cathal said, "but your highness knows too well what has happened to Lira since Maddox Aelhaeran came to power. If your mother were to succumb to her illness and your brother were to ascend the throne, it is my belief—and yours as well, I think—that Tanuba would share a similar fate."

"You do speak plainly, Lord Cathal."

"Is that not why you summoned me here?" Cathal asked. "Tell me what you would have me do."

Revelin sat back and looked at Adomnan Cathal. "My brother intends to take the crown. I want you to help me stop him."

Cathal bowed his head. "As you wish."

———✺———

The physician Bronagh called Rhys was a squat man with a thinning head of dark hair, but he seemed clean and well-meaning enough that Cate submitted to his examination. He instructed Bronagh to give her a cup filled with a bitter tea that seemed to have no purpose other than testing her gag reflex. Shortly after Cate had choked it down, her pain subsided and the examination began.

Rhys asked her the occasional question, and she declined to answer any of them. She didn't utter a single sound until he set her shoulder. Then she screamed. A lot.

Rhys apologized profusely as he wrestled her arm into a sling. Having already accepted that the experience would be painful as hell, Cate found the apology unnecessary. Bronagh was not as forgiving and hurried Rhys through the rest of his assessment. He pronounced her in need of rest and nourishment and poppy-laced wine. It was a diagnosis Cate could get behind.

The wine made her sleep, and when she woke again, the sun had been replaced by candlelight. She lay on her back and admired the cherubim and seraphim on the ceiling until a man's voice interrupted her quiet interlude.

"Your majesty?"

Right. That was her, wasn't it? Cautiously, she stretched and looked for the speaker.

He was tall and muscular with dark hair cropped close to his head, and a sword strapped to his side. His clothing marked him as a palace guard, and though he was much older than her, he wasn't old. Daniel's age, maybe. How did he fit into Haleine's world?

She pushed herself up onto her uninjured elbow. "May I help you?" she asked in the queen's accent.

The man's head tilted, but he didn't speak. Struggling to sit up, Cate searched the room for Bronagh, calling her name.

The maid emerged from the bathroom, stopping dead in her tracks when she saw the man. "What are you doing here?" she asked, and the man finally took his eyes off Cate in order to look at her. "Oh, you heard, didn't you? Someone told you the queen was returned."

The man looked at Cate.

"I'm sorry," Bronagh continued. "It isn't true."

The man nodded, and Bronagh moved in front of him. She placed her hand on his arm, and he let it sit there briefly before pulling away. He had turned toward the servants' entrance when Cate decided to speak.

"Who's this?" she asked, voicing her question in a louder-than-necessary tone. When Bronagh and her mystery guest looked in her direction, Cate smiled and waved. "Hi."

"His name is Willem, my lady," Bronagh said. "He's—"

"I know who he is," Cate said, losing the accent. "He's the one who sent Fionnbar the Beardless to look after me."

Willem looked so sharply at her she was surprised he hadn't given himself whiplash.

"Well," Bronagh said, "to look after the queen."

"Right," Cate said. "To look after the queen. The one who anyone with an opinion that carries any weight around here thinks is a traitor."

Willem squared his stance and stared at her.

"That man did not sleep for three days because of you and your orders," she said. "If you wanted it done, why not do it yourself?"

"He couldn't," Bronagh said. "The queen charged him with the protection of her sons."

"Sons?" Cate asked, suddenly distracted from her train of thought. "Sons she...gave birth to?"

Cate pantomimed a pregnancy belly and a delivery as best she could. Both Bronagh and Willem looked at her strangely, but only Bronagh answered, "Aye."

Cate snorted. "I did *not* feel that."

"I do beg your pardon, my lady," Bronagh said, "but I don't—"

"Nothing," Cate said. "What about Lurch here? Does he have the ability to speak for himself, or do you do all his talking for him?"

"Lurch?" Bronagh asked.

"I can speak for myself," Willem said. "But to you, I don't know why I should bother."

"Sassy," Cate said. "I like that in a bodyguard—not that I've actually had a bodyguard before. I had a panic button once. It didn't work."

"You have no bodyguard now," Willem said, walking away.

"Are you the one she was fucking?" Cate called.

Willem turned and stared. Bronagh made a strange little noise in her throat.

"Yeah, I swear a lot," Cate said. "I've been told that my mouth marks me as a sailor's whore, but enough about me. Let's talk about Haleine. Was she a soldier's whore? Are those your sons you're so intent on guarding?"

Willem came toward her, walking with purpose. He had gone to great lengths to see to Haleine's security, but what would he be willing to do to an identical, button-pushing stranger?

Bronagh stepped in his path, forcing him to stop. "Willem."

He glared at Cate, then spun on his heel and left the room.

"That's interesting," Cate said.

"You insult his honor," Bronagh scolded.

Cate shrugged. "It's what I do."

"You'll need him, if you wish to survive."

"What if I don't? Wish to survive, that is. Will I need him then?"

"You don't mean that."

"I might."

"Why did you ask him those things?"

"For the same reason most people ask questions: I wanted the answers," Cate said. "I get nothing but lies and half-truths from everyone around here, and I'm tired of it. It pisses me off, and if I can't get straight answers, I'll settle for pissing off everyone I come into contact with. What do I care? We can all be pissed off together."

"Pissed off?"

"Are you kidding?" Cate asked. The look on Bronagh's face assured her that the maid was, in no way, kidding. She sighed. "To be angry. Or, as a verb, to anger profusely."

"No," Bronagh said. "No, you can't do that. You can't set out to anger everyone who comes into this chamber."

"Why not?"

"If you anger the wrong person, my lady, it will mean your death."

"Everything on this earth means my death."

"You do not know whom you fight."

"Lurch? You mean him?"

"Willem will not harm you. He would never cause you harm, no matter how many slurs you cast against him. I am speaking of the king. He is cruel—more than cruel. He enjoys pain and enjoys causing others pain."

"Even his wife?"

"Especially his wife."

"What did he do to her?"

"What you might expect," Bronagh answered. "And worse."

Cate sat back. Had Omur put her there so the king could torture her? Did he plan on beating her into submission? Would she be able to withstand something like that?

She looked at Bronagh. "What would the king do if he knew I wasn't Haleine?"

"He would kill you. If you were lucky."

The answer came without hesitation.

"Let's assume I'm not lucky," Cate said. "What happens then?"

"I told you before—you will pray for death. You claim you do not pray, but should the king not deign to kill you, you will. You will pray for death with every breath; you will seek it out, but you will never find it because he will never let you go. Not until he is satisfied, and he is never that. You will pray for death."

"Oh," Cate said. "Okay."

That would be a problem. Her Haleine impression went only so deep and failed outright when faced with anyone who apparently had ever had a conversation with her. There was also the fact that Cate lacked an entire lifetime of knowledge. She'd never be able to pull it off for long, but maybe she could keep it up long enough to figure a way out.

"You'll have to help me," she said. "Teach me."

"Teach you?"

"To be Haleine."

"To be..." Bronagh shook her head. "Are you mad?"

"Pretty much exclusively. Doesn't change the request, though."

"Have you not heard me?"

"Oh, I've heard you. I know how miserable a place this is, and just how shitty my chances for survival are," Cate said. "But I'm not giving up. If they want to take me down, they're going to lose a few vital body parts in the process."

Bronagh was quiet. She opened her mouth more than once but closed it again without uttering a syllable. Finally, she said, "You should be careful what you say and how you say it. The queen would not say such things."

"Maybe she should start." Cate sighed again when she saw the depths of Bronagh's frown. "If it will make you happy, I won't say such things, but it's not only my mouth getting me in trouble. I didn't even *say* anything to you, and you knew I wasn't her. How'd you do that?"

Bronagh turned her gaze to the floor. "You didn't look at me in hatred."

"Haleine would have?"

"Aye."

"Oh. Did she have a reason?"

Bronagh walked away, never lifting her eyes. "You should rest. You'll need your strength."

Guess she could consider that confirmation. Cate nodded. "Sure thing."

— ✦ —

Cate's education began early the next morning as a steady parade of people flowed in and out of the room. They came for different reasons, but all of them stopped to gawk at her. The worst offender was a young, dark-haired, pale girl who stood in the corner, looking like she'd wandered off a horror movie set somewhere. Cate didn't know who she was because, despite the girl's fancy dress, Bronagh ignored her, and Cate quickly had learned that if the maid ignored someone, she should ignore them, too.

But Cate discreetly watched the girl out of the corner of her eye until a thin, white-haired man entered the room.

Bronagh curtsied. "Lord Ceallach."

He nodded to Bronagh before bowing to Cate. "I am so pleased to see you returned to us safely, your majesty."

Safely. Sure. Cate didn't know how or if she should respond, so she kept her mouth shut. Lord Ceallach continued to talk. He acted genuinely pleased to see her—even if he thought he was welcoming back Haleine—posing several questions that she didn't care to answer. Her silence did not discourage him from asking other questions, or from settling in for an extended stay.

She looked at Bronagh. Who the hell was the guy?

"My apologies, my lord," the maid said then, "but her majesty was just preparing for a bath."

"Very well," Lord Ceallach said. "I shall return later."

When he was gone, Cate checked the rest of the room. No servants remained, and the medieval Wednesday Addams also had disappeared. She turned to Bronagh.

"Who was that?"

"Lord Ceallach. He calls himself the queen's advisor."

"What is he really?"

Bronagh shrugged. "The queen didn't trust him."

"Good to know," Cate said. "Were you serious about the bath?"

"If you're sure you're well enough."

"I'm sure."

It wasn't a lie. Her arm was tender and sore but could function again. Her head didn't hurt at all. Apparently, her unexplained accelerated healing abilities weren't only because of Sarai's skills. Still freakish and worrisome, but she had to admit they were handy.

"All right," Bronagh said. "I'll order a bath."

Ordering a bath required the maid to leave the room. Realizing she was unchaperoned, Cate traded the bed for the vanity to rifle through its drawers. There had to be hairpins—or something like them—in there somewhere. When she found them in the back of the second drawer, she cackled with glee. They were perfect for the task.

"Haleine?"

Cate's head came up, and she shoved the drawer closed before turning around. She hadn't been aware that anyone had come in, but there he was—a bedraggled blond man hovering near the bathroom door. He was unwashed, unshaven, and—judging by his stealthy arrival—unsanctioned.

And he had called her Haleine.

"What do you want?" she asked. Her accent sounded a bit rough, but Homeless Ken didn't seem to notice.

"This is what you say to me?"

"You expected something different?"

"We were in love once."

Terrific. He was a guy with whom Haleine had history. Cate looked at the servants' entrance. Where the hell was Bronagh?

"Once, perhaps," she said. "But not now."

"Not now," Ken echoed softly. "Haleine, what are you doing here?"

"Preparing for a bath."

"A bath?"

"It's a socially acceptable means of cleansing oneself," she said. "You should try it sometime."

Ken shook his head and started forward. "Stop it. Just stop it and tell me—"

"You stop." Cate backed toward the balcony. "I'll not have you coming any closer to me. We may have been in love once, but that time has passed."

Ken stopped. "We've come to this."

"Looks that way," she said. "Tell me what you're doing here. What do you want?"

"You went to see Emrys."

"Heard about that, did you?"

"Word is bound to travel when the traitor queen appears from out of nowhere to visit with her nobles."

Cate wanted to roll her eyes, but it didn't seem like something a queen should do. "You make it sound as though I was there for a spot of tea. Did word happen to mention the purpose behind my visit?"

"Emrys told me you rode with the rebels, and that the king's men took you on the road."

"I did, and they did."

"Now you are here?" His tone was angry, accusing. "You let them kill those people, and you let them bring you here?"

She was starting to understand why he and Haleine were former lovers. This time she did roll her eyes.

"Yes, I wanted so badly to come here that the soldiers dragged me for three days behind a horse's ass and the stallion he rode," she said. "You can save your accusations. I have done no wrong."

"Then why are you here?" Ken demanded. "I thought he would finish what he started. I thought he would cast you in his dungeon."

"He did. Now I'm here."

"Why? How?"

"Stairs were involved." Cate sighed. "Don't ask me what I'm doing here when I hardly know myself."

Ken was quiet now, studying her carefully. She suspected the reason and glanced again at the servants' door. How long did it take to order a damn bath?

"You're not Haleine," Ken said. "Who are you?"

"You know full well who I am."

He charged, moving quicker than she would have thought him capable, and grabbed her by the shoulders to pin her against the wall. She winced when her left side hit the stone.

"Don't lie to me," he said. "Tell me who you are, or I'll—"

"You'll what? Breathe on me?" Cate said in her normal voice. "Although now that I bring it up, don't. Did you take a bath in a barrel of whiskey?"

"Please, for the love of the goddess, tell me who you are."

She stared at him. Despite the unfinished threat and the aggressive way he held her, she wasn't afraid. This was the man Haleine had loved, and she pitied him.

"Tell me where she is," Ken begged. "Please, just tell me."

"She's dead," Bronagh offered.

Ken released Cate and spun to look at the maid. "You're wrong."

"I'm not," Bronagh said. "She's dead, and you being here won't change that, Dana."

Dana? Cate looked at the back of Ken's head. *This* was Dana? The might-as-well-be-dead leader of the rebellion? No wonder they were losing.

"You can't be here, Dana," Bronagh said. "You need to leave, and you need to do it now. I'll call the guards if you don't. You have no idea how many men wait on the other side of those doors, and they'll skin you alive if you're caught. You won't stand a chance."

Dana made a noise that might have been a laugh. "How many times will you send a man to his death, Bronagh?"

"If you stay here, you'll find out."

Some time passed where no one did anything. It was so quiet Cate found herself holding her breath as Bronagh and Dana stared at each other. Who would be the first to break?

Dana looked at Cate. "I will find out the truth."

She slumped against the wall. "Before or after you meet up with Scooby and the rest of the gang?"

Dana walked out onto the balcony without responding. Cate slid to the floor.

Bronagh was at her side almost immediately. "Are you all right? Did he hurt you?"

Cate shook her head and jerked her thumb toward the balcony. "Where does he think he's going?"

Bronagh shrugged. "Off the side."

"Off the side?" Cate twisted to see the balcony. Dana had disappeared. "What, did he...kill himself?"

"I'd never be that lucky," Bronagh said. "No, he climbs over the side and down the wall."

"And no one notices the Amazing Spiderman's gravity-defying escape?"

"They haven't yet. Or, if they have, they don't care."

"Which do you think it is?"

Bronagh's shoulders fell, and she whispered, "He knows everything."

He was probably Omur, and though Cate could offer no substantive supporting evidence, she said, "No one knows everything."

"He does."

"Where does that leave us?" Cate asked.

"Damned," was Bronagh's answer.

———ᘉᘉᗷ———

After Faolan's departure, Haleine was made to rejoin the living.

She would have preferred not to. She would have preferred to stay in the dark, but the woman Faolan had called Sarai insisted, and it would seem she was not a woman to be gainsaid. The man she knew from her past carefully lifted Haleine from her little bed and carried her into the light. He placed her in a chair set before a small table. The room in which she sat was plain. A cottage in Enimode, her twin had said. Plain, but bathed in sunlight. Haleine ducked her head as the brightness burned her eyes.

"I will make you some tea and something to eat," Sarai said. "You need to regain your strength, and this will help you do that."

Haleine was at a loss. She had no appetite of which to speak, but to argue would be a waste of energy she did not possess, so she said nothing and did nothing as Sarai moved around, gathering what she required.

"Here, I want you to drink this. All of it, mind you." Sarai placed a cup on the table. "I need to go to the barn, but I won't be gone long. Don't move from that spot, aye?"

Sarai needn't worry. Haleine doubted she'd be able to move. Her legs felt useless, as though they weren't attached to her at all. Sensing, though, that her nurse waited for a response, Haleine nodded and Sarai departed, closing the door behind her.

Haleine stared at the roughly crafted cup. A peasant's cup.

She hated the thought as soon as it appeared in her mind. She didn't know why it should be there at all.

When the door opened again, she picked up the cup before Sarai could say anything about it and raised it to her lips. The warm liquid was bitter, but soothing, as it slid down her throat. She swallowed and looked over at Sarai who, from the sound of it, had yet to come through the door.

But it wasn't Sarai standing there. It was Dana. He had come back.

Haleine dropped the cup. It was difficult to breathe as she stared at him. What did he want?

"What business have you here?" she demanded once she had found a voice.

Dana stepped into the house. "They told me you were dead. I came—"

"You came to what? To mourn me?"

"I mourned you already," he said, coming closer. "I came to see if they had spoken true. I came to see if you were, in fact, dead."

"I do not know what I am."

He took another step toward her. "But you are not dead."

"If you say."

Another step. "Haleine—"

"Don't."

He stopped. "Don't?"

"Don't say my name like that," she said. "Like you—like you love me."

"But I do."

She shook her head. "You are incapable of that."

"I've given you no reason to think otherwise, I know."

"Then we are in agreement," she said, "and now you can be on your way."

"Haleine, you have to give me—"

"There is nothing I have to give you," she said. "Nor is there anything I will give you. You think I don't know what it is that brings you here? You think I don't know what it is you want?"

"Forgiveness," Dana said.

She lacked the strength to stand. She lacked the strength to do anything more than sit. Oh, how she longed to attack him, to throw herself at him and beat her fists against him until he crumbled beneath her fury. She wanted to make him bleed for having the audacity to utter such a request in her hearing. Placing her palms on the table, Haleine pushed herself up. She slid her hands across the rough surface and gripped the edge.

"You are not here for forgiveness," she said, turning toward him. "Do not tell me that you are."

"Why do you suppose I am here, Haleine?" he asked. "If not for you?"

"Yes, you are here for me. But it is not my forgiveness that you seek."

She shoved off the table but couldn't manage a single step before she fell. He caught her, his arms wrapping around her, pulling her close, and she hit him. Her hands turned to fists that beat against his chest, his face, any part they could reach. He didn't stop her. He didn't protest. He held her until her arms went slack. Then he moved her back to the chair and helped her sit. Kneeling in front of her, he placed his hand on her cheek. She tried to shove him away but lacked the fortitude to move him.

She snared a fistful of his shirt. "You listen to what I have to say: you can't have me. Not for your damned war, nor for anything else. To you, to your goddess, I am dead, and no amount of begging on your part will change that."

Dana's hand dropped. "Laorans did not bring me here today. I serve her interests no longer."

She released him. "Of course you do. You have never done anything else. You do not know how to be anything else."

"For you, I will learn."

"I do not want that. I do not want you."

"I am not anyone without you," he said. "Not the man I must be. Not a man at all. I am a ghost, a shadow. Without you, I am nothing."

"Mayhap you should have thought of that sooner," she spat.

Dana bowed his head. "Haleine, please, I am as you command me."

"No, *I* was as you commanded me. I was as you made me. I made myself a liar, a whore. For you I did this, and still, you dared to call me traitor."

"Tell me what to do. Tell me what you want," he begged. "I'll do it. Whatever it is, I'll do it."

"Go away from here, Dana, and do not return," she said. "I have no desire to ever lay eyes upon you again, and we have no more to say to each other."

A moan left his lips, but he stood and backed away. Opening the door, he hesitated and looked at her.

"Your words today have killed me, Haleine."

She did not hesitate. "Good."

———

Dana staggered out of the cottage. The sun was suddenly too bright and the air too thin. Two steps, three, and he collapsed on the ground, his lungs

277

burning with the effort of keeping him alive. Behind him, Haleine screamed, cried, sobbed, and his fingers grasped at the dirt, searching for an escape, as the sound burrowed its way into him, through him. His body responded in kind, developing a howl of its own, and he pushed himself up. He wouldn't—couldn't—let it go. Too many demons were already in the world; he'd not allow another to run free.

Haleine wailed again, and Dana stood. Whoever guarded her would hear, they would come running, and he couldn't be there when they arrived. He had to be somewhere else, anywhere else.

The first few steps were unsteady and threatened to take him down again, but he pushed forward. The forest was close, dark and empty. He could lose himself there, and no one would ever find him.

"Dana?" Sarai called. "Dana!"

He kept his eyes on the ground and continued walking. She caught him anyway, first her hand on his arm, holding him back, then pulling him into a suffocating embrace.

"Oh, you're here," she said. "Oh, my boy, where have you been? I'm so happy to see you. James and the others—they've been talking as though you were dead."

"As well they should," he said. "It is what I am. What I should be."

Sarai shook her head firmly and released him. "No, Dana. Come inside and—"

"I can't. She doesn't—she doesn't want it. Me. She doesn't want to see me."

Sarai looked past him to the cottage. Haleine was quieter now, but he continued to feel her sobs.

"We do have a barn," Sarai said. "You need food. Rest. Care. Please, Dana."

"No. I have to go. She doesn't want me here; I shouldn't have come."

"Why did you come?"

"I needed to know," he said. "They told me she was dead, and I—I needed to know. Now I do."

"Where will you go?"

He didn't know. He'd come here for answers, desperate to discover how Haleine had found her way back, but it hadn't been her. Some stranger was in her place, and the true queen of Lira could barely stand. So consumed in hatred was Haleine—hatred for him and what he'd done—that she was perhaps every bit as lost as he was. Mayhap she didn't want to find her way back, but where did that leave him?

"I don't know," he confessed. "I don't know where to go. I don't know what to do."

"James was in Eluned, last I heard. You go there, and you do what's right."

"I don't know what that is anymore."

"Of course you do," Sarai said. "You always have."

Dana looked at the cottage. There was no sound coming from it now. "Tell that to her."

He walked away. Sarai called his name but did not follow, and he entered the forest alone. The trees surrounded him when he collapsed again, pressing his forehead into the soft dirt.

Do what's right. That was how he had lived before—*tried* to live before—and why he had ever followed Faolan down a path of war. But now the war was within himself, and he was trapped in a hole from which he thought he might never escape.

He had never intended to lose his way, to end up in this place, and couldn't remember when that had happened. Haleine had been the reason why, just as she had been the reason he had left Tamzin Hill, why he'd gone to Emrys and the palace.

But he hadn't been chasing Haleine. It hadn't been Haleine taken on the road, nor Haleine he encountered in her chambers. No, that had been someone else. A stranger to this land. From where had she come, and what was her purpose?

Whatever it was, he envied it. To have a purpose was a marvelous thing. He had one once, something beyond a desire for ale and a need for dreamless sleep. Once he had been something apart from Haleine. How could he reclaim that?

The obvious answer was to return. To James, to Faolan, to the rebellion. Would they have him back, or would Faolan merely send him away again? Could he convince them that he could finish what had been started? Could he convince himself?

There was only one way to find out.

CHAPTER 19

Mireille did not use her power. She ignored her birthright, as she did not know it was there inside her, secured in a locked box she had never sought to open. How she, and Haleine before her, had remained ignorant to its existence, Sighle did not know, for she herself had been aware from the moment of her birth.

Sighle left her room, allowing her guard to follow her to Haleine's chambers. Omur had placed Mireille there, thinking she could take the position of the lost queen, convinced she would serve him where Haleine had only fought him, but he was wrong. His lords were wrong as well. The plan was good, sound, but it would not work. Not yet. It couldn't when Mireille was so infested with the brown-eyed boy and his cause.

But Mireille did not know that was within her, either.

When Sighle reached her destination, she abandoned her guard to wait with the four Omur had stationed outside the doors to keep Mireille where she was. They weren't inclined to allow Sighle to pass, but that was easily altered, and she went inside.

Omur's imposter, Sighle's blood, slept in the great bed. Even in the low light, Sighle could see the marks and bruises the soldiers had left on Mireille, and though it was no longer there, Sighle could see the blood.

She walked through a field of wrath rooted by the thought of lowborn trash touching sacred flesh. It soon gave way to the cloud of grief and anger surrounding her sister, but beyond that was the darkness clinging to Mireille like a second skin.

How did she not know it was there?

Mireille had yet to awaken, so Sighle climbed onto the bed and crawled to her sister's side. She rested on her knees and kept her hands clasped in her lap as she examined the woman before her, absorbing all that Mireille was. She hadn't gotten this close on her previous visit, choosing to stay in a corner to observe in secret. But she was tired of studying and watching and skulking. Mireille was capable of greatness, and Sighle was eager to bear witness to the waste.

She lay on her side, facing Mireille, and breathed in when her sister breathed out. So long had she waited for this—a chance to see, smell, touch, taste an enigma. She'd gone to great lengths to keep Mireille protected from her brown-eyed boy and his beasts so that she might have this chance. Reaching out, her hand hovered—fingers trembling, stretching, flexing, curling—but did not touch the body before it.

Her hand fell when the servants' door opened, and the maid entered. Sighle rolled onto her stomach to lay as flat as she could. In her haste, she brushed against Mireille, elbow skimming elbow, and a jolt raced through her. Mireille must have experienced a similar shock, for she came awake and bolted upright.

The maid took notice immediately, and Sighle collapsed in on herself. As she rose from the feather mattress, her eyes were wide and glistening.

"What the—?" Mireille looked at the stranger beside her, and her true voice quickly gave way to Haleine's. "Back again, are you?"

Back again? Her sister's words made no sense. She wouldn't have, couldn't have, seen Sighle before, but there was no time to consider the question, nor the implications, as Bronagh rushed over, desperate to stop a mistake before it was made.

"Lady Sighle! Oh, I did not see you there," she said. "You'll have to forgive your sister, my lady. She has been in much pain and..."

The maid continued, but neither Sighle nor Mireille listened. They stared at one another, Mireille forgetting who she was supposed to be as she marveled at what she was. Her heart pounded as she remembered Haleine's words. Sighle could see them forming in Mireille's eyes. *A sister I have, but you are not her.*

But she was.

"I was so frightened, so scared," Sighle said.

There was the hint of tears in her voice, a small tremor from the little girl trying to be brave that caused all who heard it to stumble. The maid stopped splashing in her stream of nervous chatter to swim in a river of pity and guilt. Mireille did not falter, building a wall of stone to shield herself from caring. Could Sighle break it down?

She threw herself at Mireille, wrapping her arms around her sister's neck. There was no jolt this time, Mireille's wall protecting them both. Sighle sobbed into Mireille's shoulder and felt the wall strengthen. Her sister's determination made Sighle cry genuine tears until the maid intervened and gently pulled her away.

"I'm sorry. I'm so sorry," Sighle said. "But they—they killed our mother, they killed our father, and they took you away. They stole you from me, and I thought—"

"It's all right, my lady," Bronagh soothed. "She's here now, and she's safe. You both are."

Sighle looked at Mireille. "They thought you were dead."

Mireille shook her head, but the motion was stiff and reluctant. "I'm not that easy to kill."

No, she wasn't, and she didn't know how true her words would prove to be. Sighle could see that, too, and the vision overwhelmed her.

The edge of the world was an ugly place, a stark brown land where nothing grew, nor ever would, with a lump of coal acting as the sun. Mireille appeared before her, wielding a great sword, and drove it into the ground in front of Sighle. The land cracked and crumbled, giving way to a river of molten rock that swept Sighle away, pulling her under. Flesh burned and melted, bones following their lead, while the last to disintegrate was her heart.

As the vision ended, Sighle sat on the bed, gasping for breath from newly formed lungs, while Mireille watched with icy detachment. Did she know? Did she know what Sighle was?

"My lady?" the maid said. Her tone proved that all of Sighle's defenses had fallen. "Are you all right? My lady, your nose. You're bleeding!"

Sighle brought her hand to her nose and wiped away the blood she had not expected to be there. The amount of it surprised her, and she stared at it before Bronagh grabbed her hand and washed away the stain with a damp cloth.

"Oh, you poor girl." Bronagh held Sighle's face between her hands. "What happened to you? What did you do? I'll fetch the physician for you, and he'll—"

"Bronagh, she's fine," Mireille interrupted.

"She's not! She's—"

"She's fine. Let her go."

Sighle wriggled free as the need to retreat swallowed her. "I am. I-I'm sorry. I-I shouldn't b-be here. I j-just thought—I should go. I'll go."

Mireille didn't utter one word of protest, and Sighle quickly slid backward. She hit the edge of the bed and fell, but the maid was there to catch her. Bronagh attempted to help Sighle regain her balance, but Sighle pulled away and stumbled from the room.

She was forced to rely upon her guard to find her way back to her own chamber, and as soon as she was behind her closed door, she sank to the floor, clutching her stomach. She rocked forward, pressing her forehead to the stone, and stayed like that—laughing, crying, shivering—until she was herself once again.

Though she had acted it a myriad of times, she had never truly been afraid before, but knew instinctively that's what it was. Fear, terror, dread—building a nest inside of her like an unwelcome colony of rats. How did a soul survive such a thing day after day?

How did Mireille—who did not know what lurked within her—do *that* to Sighle? In and out of visions and thoughts and dreams and bodies for years now Sighle had been. As natural as breathing it was—until this moment—because always and never were two words with no meaning when applied to her. But now her body ached, and when she closed her eyes, she saw that river of fire covering her face and making her blind as it ate away every other part of her.

The only thing left behind was a terrible truth: Mireille would destroy her. And Sighle was afraid.

How did one conquer fear?

Omur's voice interrupted her musings. He hadn't paid Mireille any attention since having her moved from the dungeon, but he would end that now, as he marched the king to see his false wife. Did Omur think to use the king to intimidate Mireille into helping him? What an odd little man he was. Did he not realize Mireille was made of sterner stuff than that?

Sighle sat up. "Nonna."

The girl appeared before her. "Aye, my lady?"

"Go and tell Bronagh that Omur and the king are coming," Sighle said. "Be sure to run."

After Sighle left, Bronagh followed to track down Rhys and tell him what had happened. Cate watched them go, then left the bed, removed her sling, and retrieved the hairpins she had found in the vanity. She sat in front of the doors Sighle had used and set to work on the lock. It wasn't as easy as she had thought it would be, so she was still attacking it when Bronagh returned.

"What are you doing?" the maid asked.

"What does it look like I'm doing?" Cate said. "I'm getting the hell out of here."

"You can't do that."

"Oh, I think you're witnessing some pretty compelling evidence to the contrary."

"You don't know what's beyond those doors."

"Give me another minute, and I will."

"I'll not give you anything," Bronagh said. "You can't do this."

A pin slipped from her hand, falling to the floor. Cate left it there and looked at Bronagh.

"No, what I can't do is stay here any longer. You tried to warn me. You told me I didn't want to do this—I didn't want to be Haleine, and you were right. You were so right, and I should have listened to you. I'm sorry that I didn't. I let myself get suckered in with that whole bath thing, but I'm over it now, and I have to leave. I can't be what that girl wants, what that girl needs.

I can't do it! That kid is seriously screwed up. Do you know that? She makes me look incredibly well-adjusted, and that's just wrong." Cate dropped the second pin and stood, pulling at her robe. "Look at this! It's soaked through with her tears! She threw herself at me, and she sobbed about how they killed our mother, they killed our father, and how she thought they killed me, but that wasn't me. That was Haleine. It was never me, and it never will be me. She wants me to...I don't know what she wants, but I can't do it. I won't. Thanks for the bath and the first aid, but I'm leaving now."

Cate dropped to the floor to search for the hairpins. She had them both in hand and was returning to her task when Bronagh spoke again.

"Even if you could get the doors open, the men outside won't allow you to leave."

"Fine!" Cate abandoned the lock entirely. "I'll go off the balcony. It worked for Homeless Ken, and if he can do it, I sure as hell can."

She marched with determination toward the balcony, but Bronagh latched on to her arm and held her back.

"It won't work for you," she said. "Lord Omur doesn't want you to leave, and he'll do everything in his power to make you stay."

"I don't care what he wants. I don't care about his power. He can't make me stay here. He can't make me do anything I don't want to do—not one goddamn thing—and that includes being anything at all to Sighle. I don't care what game he's running, or she's running, but I won't—"

"There's no game. Not for her," Bronagh said. "I don't believe that lass has done anything but mourn since she came here. She only wants her family, and if you are the queen's sister, then you are her sister, and you are her family. The only family she has left."

Cate's shoulders sagged. "Why did you ignore her?"

"I did no such thing."

"You did."

"When?"

"Yesterday, or the day before, maybe. I don't know when, but she was standing in this room, and you ignored her so I thought I should, too, and she—"

"She wasn't here, my lady."

"She was! She was standing right over there"—Cate waved her free arm in the direction of the other side of the room—"for...I don't know for how long, but she was there, and you ignored her."

"I promise you I did not see her."

"How didn't you see her? You saw every single other person who came into this room, so how did you miss the noblewoman to whom I am supposedly related?"

The servants' door flew open, and another girl, another stranger, rushed in and ran toward them. Cate closed her mouth and dropped her arm. This didn't look like a portent of good things.

Bronagh released Cate. "Nonna?"

"The king is coming," the new girl panted.

"When?" Bronagh demanded.

"Now. Maddox comes now, and Lord Omur comes with him."

Bronagh's face paled. She ordered Nonna to leave, grabbed Cate's arm, and dragged her away from the balcony.

"Bed, get in the bed now, and your sling—where's your sling? Why did you take it off?"

"It's in the—"

"Find it and put it on, and get into bed and—no," Bronagh said. "Not the bed. The chair. Sit in the chair by the fire. Over there. Go and—"

"Take a breath?" Cate suggested.

She retrieved the sling and worked her arm into it as Bronagh pushed her toward the chair.

"Don't make jests. Don't speak unless spoken to. Don't speak at all unless asked a direct question. Be meek—"

"Meek?" Cate snorted. "Yeah, right. Meek is not in my repertoire."

"Be penitent and gracious. He'll say awful things, horrible things, and you have to let him," Bronagh said. "Don't provoke him. Whatever you do, don't provoke him. You don't know the sort of man he is, and if you offer him even the smallest slight, it will be the last thing you do. He thinks you are his wife. He thinks you betrayed him and made him a fool, and he'll not forgive that."

"Maybe I should've stayed in the damn dungeon," Cate hissed as the doors opened and Bronagh scurried away.

A handsome young man, impeccably dressed and groomed, came in first. Scarface was right behind him, wearing his red robes and that same shit-eating grin. Bronagh murmured greetings. Your majesty. My lord. She curtsied, too. She hadn't mentioned if Cate should, so Cate opted to stay seated and silent.

The king came forward, walking carefully, almost stalking her like a two-legged jungle cat. Omur skulked along for a few steps before stopping in the middle of the room, allowing the king to approach Cate on his own.

She wasn't sure where to look. Making direct eye contact could be seen as provocation, but looking at her lap seemed pathetic and not particularly useful, as she needed to figure out what she was up against. Undecided, she alternated between looking at him and her lap, but Maddox ended her dilemma when he took her chin, lifted her head, and turned it side to side.

"They hit you," he said.

Yeah, they had hit her. They also punched her, kicked her, and starved her. They'd tied her up, dangled her from a tree, and dragged her behind a damn horse, too. If it hadn't been for Fionnbar, they would've done a lot worse, but Cate didn't offer any of those details.

Maddox indicated her sling. "My men caused this injury as well?"

"Yes," Cate said.

Something changed in his face then, an unseen frown becoming deeper. There was a pulse in the air that hit her like another fist in her gut. Her stomach contracted and absorbed the blow. No one else moved or gave any indication that they had experienced something similar.

"Omur," Maddox said, "I will want to speak with Varro about this."

"Yes, your majesty," Omur replied.

Maddox knelt and slid his hand to the back of Cate's neck. "You are my wife. You are their queen, and it is unacceptable that they have laid their hands upon you and treated you so roughly. I'll find the ones who did this and strike off their hands for it, if not their heads, and you'll stand beside me and watch it be done."

Well, wouldn't that be festive. Cate stared at him, forgetting how to do anything else. Staring was the only thing that made sense in that moment. It wasn't like she could verbalize a response. What did one say to that?

"You would like that, wouldn't you?" Maddox prompted softly.

The correct answer—the answer he expected—was obviously yes. It wouldn't cost her anything to offer that single syllable. It wouldn't mean anything, just another day, another lie, all in her quest to survive.

"Yes," she whispered.

Maddox's resulting smile would've made her blood run cold had it not already frozen long before this point. He rose and kissed her forehead, leaving a cold impression on her skin. As he pulled away, she imagined a sinkhole in the shape of his lips had been created, and little by little her skull crumbled into it.

"The physician is caring for her?" Maddox asked Bronagh.

"Y-yes, your majesty."

"Properly?"

"Yes, your majesty. He has been most concerned and most attentive."

Maddox nodded. "You will inform me should that change."

"Yes, your majesty."

Cate glanced first at Bronagh's terrified face, then at Omur. The king's advisor grinned. As he was the only person in a good mood, Cate was suspicious. What was his game? What did he want from her?

"Omur," Maddox said, "I wish to speak with Varro now."

Omur bowed. "Yes, your majesty."

Maddox took Cate's right hand and lifted it to his lips. Another kiss, another sinkhole. When he released her, Cate looked carefully at her skin, expecting to see it decomposing and surprised to find otherwise.

"Your majesty," Omur said. He bowed to her before following Maddox out of the room.

When the doors closed, Cate looked at Bronagh. The maid appeared as though she were about to faint.

"That's the Big Bad Wolf, huh? That's the man everyone's afraid of?" Cate said. "Somehow I'd thought he'd be scarier."

Bronagh stared at the closed doors. "So did I."

—⟿—

From the moment Omur had first appeared in the kitchens with claims of Haleine's return and pardon, Bronagh had been wary. When she had found Haleine's unknown twin standing in the queen's place, she had become doubly suspicious. The lass appeared innocent, if difficult, and if Omur had a purpose for wanting that girl, no good could come of it.

Something needed to be done. Cate required protection, and Bronagh needed help to do it.

The rebellion would seem an obvious choice. They wanted Cate back, and at least one of their number was living in her house. She had checked on the man every day, bringing him food and assuring him of Cate's continued recovery. He would ask about the defenses Omur had in place, and she would lie to him.

Because Omur wanted Cate. Bronagh understood that so completely now, and he would rather see her dead than in the rebellion's hands. Telling the rebels meant they would try to take her back, so she went to Willem.

When charged with another's protection, Willem never failed, never faltered. He walked a fine line where his own well-being was concerned but, to Bronagh's knowledge, never crossed it. Compromising his health would not best serve his cause. But ever since Haleine had charged him with the guarding of her sons, Willem had become a demon possessed.

She started her search in the nursery, but Willem was not to be found. He'd changed the routine yet again. There were five men, two at each entrance and one in the room itself. They all looked at her as though she were diseased, but they made no move against her, nor spoke a single word, not even when asked where Willem might be.

She went to the barracks next. The off-duty men watched her as she made her way to Willem's bunk. If they were Maddox's men, they thought her a traitor who should be dead, or worse, in the dungeon. If their loyalty was to

Willem, they didn't know what to do with her. Condemn her or respect her, they couldn't decide, so they would settle on hating her. She didn't care what they thought, any of them. The staring didn't affect her anymore. Everywhere she went, eyes followed.

The only set of eyes that didn't take notice of her belonged to the man she had come to find. He stood next to his bunk, frowning. He was shirtless, his exposed skin glistening and his hair damp.

"Were you training?" she asked.

He picked up his shirt and pulled it on. "What are you doing here?"

"You have to protect her."

Glancing around quickly, Willem nodded to a pair of men who stood and acted as a shield between them and the others.

"I don't have to do anything for her," he said.

"Haleine wanted her sister to have protection," Bronagh countered. "Isn't that what you told me? That she wanted her sister to have guards?"

"She wanted Lady Sighle to have guards, and that I have seen done."

"Willem!" Bronagh said. "Stop fighting me. You have to do this. The girl in that chamber will die without your help."

"There is nothing I can do. The queen commanded me to guard her sons."

"Do you do this because she questioned your honor?" Bronagh asked. "Do you leave her unprotected because she accused you of loving the queen?"

"She did not accuse me of loving the queen."

"No, but she did call your honor into question, and I wonder why that bothers you because I know you have done the same. You have doubted your actions ever since Haleine was taken. You have—"

"You gave her to them."

"To save her life."

"To save your own."

She shook her head. "That's not true. Willem, please, you didn't see her. She does not fear the king."

"That is not my concern, nor should it be yours."

"He was good to her. He cared for her. He was *kind*," Bronagh said. "She does not know the danger she is in."

"What do you hope to gain from this? From her? Do you think you will redeem yourself if you save this stranger?"

"Do you think you will redeem yourself if you save Haleine's sons?" Bronagh asked. "Find Fionnbar, and tell him to guard that girl."

Willem shook his head. "There are rebels within the palace walls. Give her to them. Let her be their concern."

"I cannot allow them to take her," Bronagh said. "Lord Omur told me he will kill her before he lets her leave the palace. He does not lie. Not about this."

"Does he know she is not the queen?"

"Lady Cate says he does."

"Does she also say what Omur's interest in her is?"

"No, she doesn't know what he wants with her."

"Why does he want us to believe she is the queen?"

"She doesn't know that, either."

"What does your Lady Cate know?"

"She knows what happened to Haleine."

Willem pulled away and looked around. It didn't seem to her that anyone was paying any kind of attention to them, but he thought differently. He took her arm and led her out of the barracks. The two men he had set as watch followed until he barked at them to go back inside. He dragged her around the corner of the structure and pushed her against the wall. He covered her with his body. One hand held her at the waist while the other was braced against the wall near her head. To any passers-by, it would appear as though they were two lovers engaged in a private moment, but Bronagh knew better than to think Willem might actually hold her that way again.

"What does she say happened?" he asked, his mouth close to her ear.

Bronagh couldn't stop herself as she placed her hand on his chest. "She says the queen is dead."

For a moment, Willem did nothing. Then the hand near her head became a fist that he drove into the wall. She flinched.

"You did this," he accused.

"They were going to kill her, Willem," she said. "Omur and the king, they were going to kill her. They *tried* to kill her. I told you this before. The blood—you didn't see the blood. She was alive when I gave her to the rebels. I thought maybe they could save her."

"You were wrong."

"Aye, but she would have died for sure had I not done it." Bronagh sighed. "I'm not asking you to forgive me, Willem. I don't care if you ever again spare a kind thought for me. Just don't leave the girl unprotected. Find Fionnbar, and set him to watch her like you did when you thought she was the queen."

"Fionnbar."

"She knows him, and what he'll do for her," Bronagh said. "You trust him. You wouldn't have sent him to look after Haleine if you didn't."

"That girl is death waiting to happen," Willem said. "I'll not put any of mine on that path."

"Willem, please—"

"There is a man living in your house," he said. "Did you know that?"

"Aye, I put him there. He's one of them, one of the rebels. I told him I would help him."

"Take the lass."

She nodded. "Aye."

"Do they not yet know they can't trust you?"

She supposed she should have been insulted, but she was far too tired and numb to care about so slight a transgression. Besides, there was too much truth there.

"I guess not," she said.

"Did you tell him Omur will not let her go?"

"Aye. He says it doesn't matter."

"Who is that girl?" Willem asked.

Bronagh shook her head. She didn't know.

———

Standing in between James and Cate were the outer walls protecting the palace. Men walked up and down them all through the day and night, and the number had only increased since Cate's capture.

But he could get past them. A door in the wall, unguarded and secret, would gain him entrance. Beyond that were the palace walls themselves, even more easily defeated than the others, as another hidden passage would get him inside the kitchens.

Then there were the guards. According to Rhydwyn, the regular patrols had been doubled. In addition, ten men guarded the entrance to the chamber in which Cate had been placed, and another ten stood watch in the servants' passage. More were in the room itself, and together they kept any unauthorized persons from entering.

But the problem with Cate's recovery wasn't the walls, nor the guards on the walls, or in the halls, or those who stood in the room with her. The problem was the wall James couldn't see.

Invisible to the human eye and potent, the damn thing encircled the entire palace grounds, and had stopped him from getting inside more effectively than all of the king's men ever could.

Magic was to blame. But to whom the magic belonged, Faolan didn't know. James had immediately suspected Omur, and just as quickly, Faolan had told him no. All magic, the pegasus claimed, left a signature that could be traced back to the one responsible, and he was very familiar with Omur's work. Whoever had created this barrier was frighteningly powerful and completely unknown.

After time spent watching others walk in and out of the palace without trouble, Faolan had formed the theory that the shield was designed to prevent any with knowledge of Cate's existence from passing through. James was inclined to agree with him, but the idea did not provide them with a way to free Cate, so James was left watching and waiting.

Orla provided distraction in the form of chores, and while James welcomed the work, he made sure to spend part of each day lingering in the shadows outside the palace walls. There was nothing to do but count how many more guards had been added, but he went anyway.

Currently, he kept his futile watch from the window in his borrowed tavern room. Faolan lurked somewhere behind him. Gair had gone below stairs to see if Rhydwyn had sent any more messages.

That was all any of them did anymore—stared, lurked, waited. They were wasting time, so much time, but James had no solution for that, either.

"We have to do something," he said, looking at Faolan. "Why haven't you found a way around that bloody wall? It's magic, you're magic—shouldn't you have worked something out by now?"

"Magic isn't always easy."

James turned from the window to lean against the wall. "And never useful, either."

"I wouldn't say that. You're alive, aren't you?"

"For all the good that's done."

"I understand you're aggravated, and—"

"I don't need you to do that. I don't need you to understand what I am," James said. "I need you to find me a way through that damned wall."

"I don't know that I can."

"We can't keep sitting here," James said. "We have to do something, and if we can't get to her...we'll have to make them bring her to us."

"All right. How do we do that?"

James sighed. "I have no idea."

The door opened, and Gair stepped inside, wearing an expression that inspired suspicion. Either Rhydwyn's letter contained very bad news, or something else was wrong.

"What is it?" James asked.

"You should come and see."

James nodded and reached for his dagger. He slid it into his boot and followed Gair below stairs. The reason why he had been summoned stood in the center of Orla's barroom, dressed in commoner's clothing and scanning every patron. The queen's guard. Willem.

James examined the room. Nothing appeared out of place, but he turned to Gair anyway. "Keep watch outside. He may not be alone."

"Aye, Captain."

As Gair moved to the entrance, Willem finally laid eyes upon James. Would Willem recognize him? They'd only had the one encounter, and James hadn't been the man's focus at the time. He hadn't been anything other than a swiftly tossed-aside barrier, but all doubt disappeared when the guard approached him. Willem appeared to be unarmed, but he probably didn't need weapons. Just liked them.

"I want to talk to Dana," Willem said when they were face to face.

"Yet, you can't. You can talk to me, or you can leave."

"I could beat you bloody."

"You could, aye," James acknowledged. "But it won't get you any closer to what you want."

They fell into a stare, and unless Gair came bursting through the door announcing the imminent arrival of the king's guard, James wouldn't break. Willem seemed to hold a similar determination, and they held their stance until Orla interrupted.

"Whatever the two of you are doing, do it somewhere else," she said. "You're making my customers nervous, and I like them a lot more than I like either of you."

James didn't blink. "That's unfair. You don't even know him."

"I don't have to," she said. "Go measure your swords in the stable. But if you spook my horses, I'll kill you both."

Willem looked at Orla as though he didn't quite know what to make of her. Finally, he nodded. "As you wish, madam."

James gestured to the storeroom door. "King's men first."

"I am the queen's man."

"I wasn't aware there was a difference."

"There is a great deal of difference," Willem said. "You'd have a blade in your gut otherwise."

"You seem to be lacking a blade at the moment."

"You're not."

Willem walked away and had disappeared into the storeroom before James moved. He took the dagger from his boot and placed it in his belt, all the while not knowing if he was making it easier to protect himself, or just easier for Willem to stab him.

"Tell Faolan the queen's guard is here," he said to Orla. "If you would."

"Is there going to be trouble?"

"The horses will be fine."

"What about you?"

He looked at her. "Are you worried?"

"About you? No. I don't fancy cleaning up a mess is all."

"You won't be inconvenienced. I promise."

"See that I'm not," Orla said. "I'll find Faolan. You deal with your mysterious man."

James nodded and went to the stable. Willem stood halfway down, hands at his sides and eyes fixed on the wall. Did he ever stop being a soldier?

"I did not think I would find you here," Willem said.

James sat on top of a barrel of grain and laid his dagger in his lap. "I'm not the one out of place. Aren't you supposed to be protecting a pair of bastard boys?"

"The queen's sons are none of your concern."

"Dana's sons are."

Willem looked at him. "Where is he?"

"Not here," James said. "Did the maid tell you where to find us?"

"I've always known where to find you."

Why had James never considered it before? If Willem knew, it stood to reason that others did as well. Not only was James at risk, but the danger to Orla was even greater. The king would not suffer traitors to the crown, and harboring members of the rebellion would see the alewife hang.

"And the rest of the king's guard?" James asked. "Do they know where to find us? Should I be expecting them?"

Willem shook his head and came toward him. "That's not why I'm here."

"That's right. You came for Dana."

"I came for answers."

"I haven't any answers for you."

"Which is why I want to talk to Dana," Willem said. "Where is he?"

"His whereabouts are none of your concern."

"The queen's are."

"Not anymore."

Willem stopped and leaned into the nearest stall door. He closed his eyes. "It's true, then."

James didn't know what might have been true and didn't care to either ask or guess, so he stayed quiet and waited.

Moments passed before Willem pushed off the door, his eyes focused on the floor. "Who is she? Why is she here, and why does Omur want people to believe she's the...the queen?"

James was slow to respond. "That also is none of your concern."

Willem lifted his head. "I seek only to help you."

"Your help is not needed."

"Isn't it? She is surrounded by guards, and none of them are mine."

"If that's true, it doesn't sound like you'd be much help at all."

"How many men have you?"

James didn't answer. He had three men and a pegasus, but numbers didn't matter. Even if he had an army that rivaled the king's, it wouldn't matter. There would be no getting to Cate inside the palace. Willem repeated his question, and James laughed.

"I'm not going to tell you anything, and I don't know why you ever thought I would," he said. "I don't trust you; I *can't* trust you, and neither would Dana. You're wasting your time. And mine."

"You're wasting time. She's been in the palace for days now, and you've done nothing."

James didn't require that reminder. He was already well aware of what he hadn't done, but he wouldn't admit that to Willem, either. "Why do you care?"

"That girl—whoever she is—she's not the queen. She doesn't belong there, and I want her out. I want her gone."

James smiled at the frustration in the guard's voice. "Spoken with her, have you?"

Willem turned and walked away. "Just get her out."

"That is the plan," James said once the man was gone.

"You know," Faolan said, "there may come a day when you'll have to trust someone."

Even though Faolan had misspoken, James didn't respond. He had trusted someone once, and he'd followed Dana into this bloody mess because of it. Look at where it had brought him.

He folded his arms across his chest. "Willem says Omur wants people to believe Cate's the queen. Why would he want that?"

"Because she's not the queen."

James looked at Faolan. "He wanted to kill the queen."

"He wanted to kill Haleine. The queen of Lira is a position of power, or could be, and if he has someone in that position he thinks he can control, or use to his advantage—"

"The second. He believes Cate's the second."

"Yes."

"Omur thinks Cate will serve the dark gods, and the goddess believes Cate will serve her."

"Yes."

"They can't both be right."

"No."

"Who's wrong?"

"Time will tell."

"You think you already know, don't you? You think your goddess is wrong."

"It doesn't matter what I think."

James stood. "Well, would you like to hear what I think? To hell with time. To hell with your prophecy."

"It doesn't work like that."

"To hell with that, too. Prophecy can be thwarted. It can be changed. Isn't that what you told Dana? Was it the truth, or was it only a lie to get him to do what you wanted?"

"James, I—"

"Is that why we haven't defeated that bloody invisible wall yet? Is it yours? Did you put it there to keep me from her because you think Omur's right? You think she's...She helped us, Faolan. Cate helped us after we—after I—she helped us when she had no reason to, so I don't care what you think or what your damned prophecy says. She's not our enemy and she never will be."

"Let's hope you're right."

"I am."

Returning the dagger to his belt, James stalked out of the stable and headed toward the palace. Gair fell in step with him as he passed.

"Did he go this way?" James asked.

"Captain?"

"The guard—the queen's guard. Did he come this way?"

"Aye."

James lengthened his stride. Gair stayed on his heels as they maneuvered their way through crowded streets. As soon as Willem was in sight, James motioned for Gair to drop back and approached the guard alone.

He put his hand on Willem's shoulder, intending to turn the man around, but ended up on his back with his own dagger under his chin. Willem hovered over him.

"Bloody hell," James said. "Do you have to keep doing that?"

Willem's expression changed from anger to annoyance, and he moved the dagger. "God damn it, boy, do you want to die?"

"Not important." James got to his feet. "Tell her we're coming for her. Tell her we're going to take her back. You can tell Omur and the king, too, if you'd like."

"I do not serve Omur, nor the king."

"Tell them anyway," James said. "And when they ask how many will come for her, you tell them I have every single soul in this land that they have wronged, both living and dead. Every man, woman, and child who has suffered at their hand will be at their gates, and no amount of force will be enough to keep us from what we seek."

Willem stepped back. The corner of his mouth curled into a smile, and he nodded. "There will be a man with her. A guard," he said. "He is not there to keep you from her. He is there for her protection, and I would appreciate it if no harm were to befall him at your hands."

"You set a guard on her?" James asked, and Willem nodded again. "Why would you want to protect her?"

"Whoever she may be, she does not deserve what they will do to her," Willem said. "Whatever you think to do, do it soon."

He dropped the dagger and walked away. James watched him go and was not surprised when Willem passed through the palace gates without trouble. The guard was long gone when Gair stepped alongside James, stooping to recover the abandoned blade.

"There are three of us," Gair said. "Four, if you include the pegasus."

"I know."

"How will we—?"

"That's Faolan's problem," James said. "I need you to return to camp, find Idwal Kai, and bring him to me."

"Idwal Kai?"

"Aye," James said. "Tell him I found a use for him after all."

chapter 20

The next time Bronagh disappeared through the servants' passage, Cate decided to follow. She waited a suitable amount of time to allow Bronagh to get wherever she was going before opening the door.

The narrow hall was blocked by six guards standing in pairs of two. They stared at her, and she stared back as she contemplated her options. When she stepped forward, every guard moved in her direction. One of the two closest men put out his hand to prevent her from taking a second step.

"We cannot allow you to pass, your majesty," he said.

"On whose orders?"

"The king's, your majesty."

She nodded. Six men. Six men watching every move she made. They were supposed to keep her in and others out, but the man had called her 'your majesty' and maybe that was something she could use. Maybe they wouldn't dare stop her.

She stepped forward again, but the man who had spoken to her grabbed her arm and forced her back into the room.

"Do not open this door again," he warned as he released her.

Cate watched him close the door. How the hell was she supposed to get out of this place? How was it that climbing off the balcony was her only viable option?

Returning to the balcony, she peered over the side. It hadn't changed since the first time she'd looked. Unbelievably high and lacking a ladder. How had Dana pulled it off? He looked barely able to hold on to his sanity, let alone free climb down a stone wall. Yet he had done it, and here she was, still trapped.

If only she had some rope. The closest she came were bed sheets. How far down would they get her? Or was that a bad idea?

It was, but she went inside to do it anyway because—bad idea or not—it was the only one she had. She stripped the bed down to the mattress and sorted the bedding into two piles—things that could be turned into some kind of rope, and things that could not. She was on her knees, trying to rip the largest sheet into strips, when Bronagh returned.

"What are you doing now?" the maid asked warily.

"Same thing as before," Cate answered. "Getting the hell out of here."

"How?"

"Any way I can."

"What purpose will destroying the linen serve?"

The sheet gave way. Cate put the first strip aside and started on the next. "Ah, well, probably none," she admitted. "We are rather high up, after all, and there aren't a ton of sheets here. Still, it's better than sitting around waiting to find out what fun new relative will pop through the door next."

As she tore the second strip free, the door opened.

"You've got to be kidding me," Cate moaned, swiveling around to see who had entered. Recognizing the new arrival, she smiled and slipped back into her borrowed accent. "If it isn't Fionnbar the Beardless. What are you doing here? Come to tie me up again?"

"Willem sent him to protect you," Bronagh said.

She sounded happy. Thrilled. A glance at Fionnbar proved Cate wasn't the only one who found that strange.

"How do you know that?" Cate asked.

"I know Willem," Bronagh said. "You insulted his honor, but he wouldn't leave you unprotected."

"Aren't I special." Cate looked at the guard. "Is that true, Fionn?"

"It is, my lady."

"Willem told you who I was?"

"He did."

"He told you who I wasn't?"

"Aye."

Cate nodded and dropped the accent. "For how long will you protect me?"

"Until Willem tells me otherwise."

She hated all the no-questions-asked loyalty running amuck around this universe. She didn't want anyone to take a bullet for her. Ynyr ab Ivor had been enough. He'd been more than enough. She wasn't interested in carrying around a second millstone of guilt.

"Thanks, but I don't need protection," she said. "I don't want it."

"Willem won't care," Bronagh said.

Cate raised an eyebrow. Who the hell did Willem think he was? "Then I'll make him care. Just as soon as I see him again."

Bronagh put her hands on her hips. Cate couldn't blame her for being irritated. The maid was only doing things the way they had always been done. It wasn't her fault that Cate was who she was.

But because Cate was who she was, she ignored the maid and turned her attention to Fionnbar. "You were there."

"Where, my lady?"

"The ambush in the forest," she said. "You were there. You were a part of it."

"Aye."

"Tell me what happened."

She would have added a 'please' to the end of her request—her mother had taught her manners after all—but thought the guard would respond better to something sounding like a command.

Fionnbar was paralyzed anyway. His nervousness overpowered everything, showing in his stance and the beaded sweat on his forehead.

"I need you to tell me what happened," she said. "I know all the awesome things that happened to me. What I don't know is how the others—the rebels—fared, and I need you to tell me that."

"The man you stabbed is called Rhydoch," Fionnbar said. "He is one of the captain's most trusted men. He does not like you."

"And here I was thinking his fist in my face meant we'd be best friends," Cate said.

"He was one of the men who tried to…"

When Fionnbar stopped speaking, Cate nodded and looked at the floor. Rhydoch was one of the men who had tried to rape her. She remembered. It would be difficult to forget the night she'd spent dangling from a tree in the darkness, and the two men who had managed to put their hands on her.

Shaking her head, she looked at Fionnbar. No one had ever laid so much as one finger on her after the initial skirmish. That can't have been easy to accomplish. What might he have to do for her in the future?

What the hell was Willem thinking?

"What happened to the others? The rebels," she asked, wanting to stop thinking about Rhydoch and those nights on the road. Again, Fionnbar hesitated. "I know you killed some of them. You would have had to, and while I don't mean to suggest that I don't care about that, I don't care about that. I know people died, but I need to hear about it. Everything you remember."

"Captain Varro knew the rebels were in Labhras."

"How?"

Fionnbar shook his head. "I don't know, my lady. He told us where to go, and we went. No one asked why or how."

Cate nodded. Of course they wouldn't.

"He led us to a section of the forest, near the road," Fionnbar continued, "and bade us to hide on either side of it. We were to wait for you and the others. We thought we were after the queen. We all thought you were the queen."

Varro didn't. He never thought she was the queen. Cate nodded. "What next?"

"You came."

Fionnbar described how they had watched the rebels move along the road. Rhydoch, armed with a crossbow, had taken aim at Cate's head. When Fionnbar realized the man's target, he deliberately broke a fallen branch and bumped Rhydoch's elbow as the man took his shot.

"I'm betting he didn't like that," Cate said.

"No, my lady, he did not."

"Is that where you got the..." She gestured to her own eye, indicating her guard's still-healing shiner.

"Aye, my lady."

Cate felt ill, physically sick, thinking about what Fionnbar had done because Willem had told him to protect the queen. "What happened next?"

He told her, chronicling everything he saw. From the number of times he hesitated, she was reasonably assured he wasn't hiding much.

But he hadn't mentioned James.

"What about their leader?" she asked finally. "The man who rode beside me? The one who knocked me down when Rhydoch took his shot? What happened to him?"

Fionnbar looked at the floor.

Cate's stomach lurched. "What?"

"He took two bolts. I don't know who shot them, but your man was hit first in the shoulder, then the heart."

The heart. Cate's hand moved to cover her own heart. She could feel her scar.

"The captain knelt at the man's side," Fionnbar said. "He drew his dagger. I didn't see what happened, but..."

"Right," she said.

With a bolt in his heart, what would Varro's dagger matter?

"So," she breathed, "that's that."

———※———

When James returned to the tavern, Orla stood behind the bar talking with one of her customers. He thought he might pass by unnoticed, but she abruptly abandoned her conversation and caught up with him at the bottom of the stairs.

"Not dead, I see," she said.

"Sorry to disappoint. Is Faolan here?"

"Above stairs, last I knew. Your friend coming back?"

"Not tonight," James said. "Thank you for your help, Orla. We've put you at a terrible risk, I know. You don't have to do it, and I don't know how to thank you."

"Maybe you could do some more chores later."

James nodded. "Later, then."

He climbed the stairs and entered his room. Faolan waited in the opened window.

"The wall isn't mine," the pegasus said.

James closed the door. "Why should I believe you?"

"The goddess wants Cate. That means I want Cate."

"But you don't trust her. You think she's a danger to us."

"Laorans doesn't, and her will is what matters most to me."

That was probably true. Faolan had made questionable choices before, all in the name of serving his goddess. James crossed the room to sit in a chair.

"Why are you so convinced Cate is a danger? Your prophecy?"

"Yes, but there's something more. There's something about her. Her aura is...James, she could destroy us all."

"She might not."

"Also true. Where's Gair?"

"Gone back to camp. I needed him to fetch something."

"Something?"

James shrugged. "Someone."

"Who?"

"Idwal Kai."

"Doesn't he serve the Maoilriains?"

"Aye."

"What do you plan to do with him?"

"Use him to get Cate back."

"You have a plan."

"Starting to," James said. "We can't get in, but if Idwal Kai could get inside and convince Maddox—*Omur*—that he's escaped and that he over-heard our plans—if he tells them we're coming for her—"

"They'll put every able-bodied man they have in between us and her."

"Aye, but if he tells them we're coming at them with every weapon we have, it could give them pause."

"It could." Faolan didn't sound convinced. "What do you need me to do?"

"Persuade whoever is responsible for that wall that what Idwal Kai says is true. Make them believe we're coming through it. You claim Laorans wants Cate back, so make them feel it," James said. "We don't actually have to de-feat the wall, but if you, Luisiúil, Lorcan—I don't know who, but if enough of you gather together, surely you can do something that resembles a threat, something that will frighten them."

Faolan nodded.

"It's not a particularly good plan, and there are a great many things that could not work or could go wrong," James said, "but this is what we have to do. She's untouchable in the palace, but if we can force them to move her, there's a chance at least, isn't there?"

"We couldn't touch her before she was in the palace, either," Faolan said.

"I know, but we have to change the circumstances however we can."

"We do," Faolan said. "All right. I'll talk to Luisiúil and see what she..."

Faolan looked at the door, and James reached for his sword. Had Willem decided to send soldiers for them after all?

"Is something wrong?" he asked.

"No, nothing's wrong," Faolan said. "I...I'll be back later."

As the pegasus disappeared through the window, James leaned his sword against the wall and considered Faolan's abrupt departure. What possibly could have scared off the little beast?

The answer arrived when the door opened, and a filthy, emaciated man smelling strongly of ale and whiskey walked unsteadily inside—one of Orla's customers lost and confused over where the ale was found.

James stood to usher the man back below stairs. "Sorry, friend. Private room."

"James," the man rasped.

Stepping back, James peered at the figure before him. "Dana?"

"Who is she?" Dana asked.

"What the hell are you doing here?"

"I heard Haleine—"

"Of course," James said. "Why else would you come?"

"The girl in the palace. Who is she?"

James fought to extract himself from the wave of resentment washing over him and clenched his hands into fists. "The girl in the palace?" he asked, his tone soft and careful. "What girl would that be?"

"Haleine's bloody twin. Who is she?"

"You saw her? When? Where? How?"

"Who is she?"

"The queen's bloody twin," James said, caution forgotten. "Tell me where you saw her."

"She was in Haleine's place, in her chambers. Bronagh waited upon her."

"You got in and out of the room? How? How many guards were there?"

"There weren't any. Not in her rooms," Dana said. "Willem wasn't even there."

The maid had lied. The bloody maid had lied. James reached for his sword. "I'll kill her."

"Who is she? Where did she come from?" Dana asked. "She's not Haleine. I saw Haleine in Enimode, so who is the girl pretending to be her?"

No, a sword was too good for Bronagh. Too quick. A dagger to her kidney would be better. Slower.

"James?"

"I told you who she was. She's the queen's twin."

"Haleine doesn't have a twin."

"Obviously she does," James said, "because not even your witch of a whore can be in two places at once."

"Why did Bronagh tell me Haleine was dead?"

James laughed. "All that woman has ever done is lie to us. You can't possibly be surprised that she's done it yet again."

He moved toward the door. He didn't know where he would go—he couldn't get into the palace, and he wouldn't leave the city—but he didn't want to stay in that room any longer. He'd get a message to Rhydwyn. Tell him that the maid had lied. Tell him to kill Bronagh in the slowest, most painful way possible. Dana, however, blocked his way, stumbling with the effort.

James looked at him in disgust. "Are you drunk?"

"Not currently. What's happening here?"

"Nothing that concerns you. Just go back to the rock from under which you came. You're not needed."

"Was it Haleine's twin you presented to Emrys?"

James stepped back. "How did you know about that?"

"I heard it from a stranger on the road. Then I heard it from Emrys himself."

"You spoke to Emrys?"

"Aye," Dana said. "He's besotted with her, whoever she is. He thinks she's the queen, but you didn't send Haleine there, did you?"

"You spoke to Emrys?" James repeated. "What did he say?"

Dana sighed. "That she held a dagger to his throat."

"She did that, aye," James said. "What else? Did he say anything else?"

"He wanted me to give her this."

Dana tossed something onto the floor between them. It was Emrys's dagger, the one Cate had taken from him. James crouched down but didn't touch it.

"He said he'd give her what she wanted," Dana continued. "Who is she, James? What does she want from Emrys?"

"Why do you want to know? What are you doing here?" James asked. "Your bloody lover's in Enimode. Isn't that all you care about?"

"No."

"No, that's right. You left her, too. You left all of us and walked away to go God-knows-where," James said. "But now you're back. Why? Run out of ale?"

"I want to make things better. I want to make them right. For her, for you. I want—"

Dana wobbled again, this time giving James the opportunity to reach the door. He opened it and gestured to the hall.

"Orla keeps the ale below stairs," he said. "I'm certain she'll be more than happy to serve you."

Dana leaned against the wall. "I don't want—James, I didn't want to go. Faolan told me to leave."

"And you do everything he tells you." James shook his head when Dana protested. "Stop. I don't care. I can't care. I can't stand here listening to you make excuses. There's nothing you can say that would change anything, and all you're doing is keeping me from what needs to be done."

"What needs to be done?" Dana asked. "Why are you here and not in camp? Is that girl a prisoner? She didn't look to be. She looked quite comfortable to me."

James picked up the dagger and tucked it in his belt. "Don't be here when I return."

—◦◦◦—

The morning following Fionnbar's revelation was Cate's third day in Haleine's chambers, and she decided to spend it in bed. Why confirmation of what she'd already suspected felt like such a sucker punch, she didn't know, but it did. So she lay beneath layers of linen and fur and took stock of her situation. It didn't take long.

James was dead, and she was screwed.

Bronagh didn't argue with Cate's inactivity. Early on she had inquired about her charge's health—did the physician need to be summoned?—but Cate claimed that she was just tired, and Bronagh had gone on with her day. Cate supposed the maid was so thrilled that the escape attempts had stopped that she'd allow Cate to stay in bed for the rest of her life. While that wasn't a great plan, it would work for now because as the only unguarded way out was the damn balcony—an option that would almost certainly lead to her broken and mangled body on the ground—Cate had decided to save it for when she was truly bottom-of-the-barrel desperate.

She wasn't there yet. At least she didn't think so.

That meant a new plan was in order. However, devising a successful one would be a damn miracle, considering her entourage's sole purpose in life was to prevent her from leaving. Bronagh, Fionnbar, six nameless guards with sharp, pointy weapons standing out in the servants' passage, plus the promise of more outside the main doors.

And Ceallach. Cate heard his voice as he entered the room. Great. Haleine's untrusted advisor was back, and Bronagh wasn't getting rid of him. Maybe she was bottom-of-the-barrel desperate.

"Your majesty," Bronagh said softly.

"No," Cate said *sans* accent. "Whatever it is, no."

"We're not alone," Bronagh whispered.

"Don't care."

"The king has summoned you."

Cate lifted her head. "Summoned me? Like, he wants me to go to him?"

"Aye."

"He wants me to leave this room and go to him?"

"Aye, your majesty," Bronagh said, "but if you are too ill—"

"No, I'm fine." Cate sat up and switched to Haleine mode. "I'll be more than happy to answer the king's summons."

Bronagh didn't care for that announcement, and she glared as Cate slid from the bed. Cate smiled back and looked at Ceallach.

"I'll need a moment to make myself presentable," she said.

Ceallach bowed. "I'll be in the hall when you're ready."

She smiled brightly until he left. As soon as the door closed, the smile disappeared.

"What do you think you're doing?" the maid demanded.

"Getting out of here any way I can," Cate said. "Now, where would I find some clothes?"

When Cate left the room fifteen minutes later, she was a study in silk, wearing an emerald-green gown that did nothing to leave her cleavage to the imagination. Her hair was coiffed in some complicated knot, and her remaining bruises had been hidden beneath powders.

"Did you do that for Haleine a lot?" she had asked a still-angry Bronagh, but the maid hadn't answered.

Fionnbar accompanied her as she followed Ceallach through one elaborate hallway to another. The palace may not have been Versailles, but was still very impressive. The only thing it lacked was an unguarded exit. The throne room was doubly extravagant and stuffed to the gills with people. Men and women, young and old, stared at her before dropping into bows and curtsies.

Ceallach and Fionnbar escorted her to the other end of the room where Maddox sat upon a throne. Omur stood on the king's left. She ignored him as she bowed her head slightly to Maddox. The king gestured to the empty chair on his right, and Ceallach guided her up the few steps. As Ceallach joined Fionnbar along the wall, she perched nervously on the edge of the seat.

"Bring them in," Maddox said.

The doors opened, and Varro appeared. Behind him, two men were forced forward by pike-wielding guards. They were the men who had tried to force themselves upon her after the ambush—Rhydoch and the other whose name Fionnbar hadn't mentioned. She glanced at Maddox. Were heads and hands about to roll?

Varro bowed when he reached the dais. Rhydoch and his buddy did not. Omur stepped forward.

"You have been brought before the king this day for crimes committed against the queen," he said. "For laying hands upon her majesty and causing her grievous injury, his majesty, the king, has decreed that you shall lose those hands."

A murmur traveled through the audience. They backed up as a massive wooden block was rolled in and placed on the floor at the foot of the dais. Was Maddox seriously planning to do this here and now?

"Have you anything to say before your punishment is carried out?" Omur asked.

Rhydoch looked at Cate and spat. "Never did find out if you were a screamer."

A rush of anger flowed through her and drowned everything else. She stood and walked down the steps to stand in front of him. The action made everyone who wasn't Maddox or Omur nervous. From the corner of her eye, she saw Fionnbar rush in her direction, only to be stopped by Ceallach.

"Now you never will," she said to Rhydoch.

"Take that one's tongue as well," Maddox ordered lazily. "Do you wish to give the command, my dear?"

Cate felt his hand on her back and realized that not only was he standing beside her, but also that he had been talking to her. She looked at the two men about to be mutilated. The correct answer would be yes, just as it had been when he had asked if she'd enjoy watching this scene. Maddox did not appear to be a man one refused, but Cate didn't want to give the command to remove Rhydoch's hands.

She wanted to do it herself.

The more she looked at him, the more she wanted to do it. Hack off his hands, cut out his tongue, and remove whatever she found between his legs. Then she'd fire a crossbow bolt into his heart because no matter what Fionnbar claimed, she knew this man was the one responsible for James. Even if he wasn't, he'd make a perfectly acceptable scapegoat.

But she couldn't do any of those things—could she?—so she swallowed and said, "Do it."

The two men were forced to their knees, and Rhydoch was dragged to the block first. Two guards stood behind him, and a third held down the man's outstretched right arm. Another guard offered Maddox a short sword shaped like a machete. He took it, running the flat of the blade across his own hand, as he moved to the side of the block.

Rhydoch, Cate learned, was a screamer. At least until they removed his tongue.

She didn't move until after the two bodies had been dragged away. She wasn't sure she could; she felt she'd been turned inside out and tied into a pretzel. Blood and gore coated the floor, shouting at her until Maddox took her elbow and ushered her to her seat. Omur came forward, but Maddox stopped him and turned to the crowd once again.

"These two men were not the only ones at fault for the mistreatment of my wife. There is one more I would see punished this day," Maddox said. "Captain Varro."

Varro blanched. "Your majesty?"

"These men were under your command, were they not?"

"They were."

"Your men follow your command, do they not?"

"They do."

"You allowed them to do these things? You advocated treating your queen in such a foul manner?"

Varro looked between Maddox and Omur. Cate could imagine what he was thinking. He'd only been carrying out orders, she was sure, and now Omur was letting him take the fall for it.

"Your majesty," Varro pleaded, "my lord, I—"

"Kneel, and present to me your sword."

Kneeling in the blood, Varro drew his sword. He held it in both hands above his head.

Maddox walked down the steps and took the blade. "Now crawl to the block and lay your head upon it."

Cate opened her mouth to say something—to protest maybe—but caught sight of both Ceallach and Fionnbar shaking their heads. Fionnbar actually mouthed *No*, so Cate bit her lip and cowered in her seat as Varro crawled the short distance to the bloodied block. She didn't want to watch—seeing the hand and tongue removal demonstration was quite enough horror for one lifetime—but she didn't think she could close her eyes or look away.

When Maddox brought the sword down upon the captain's neck, she clapped both hands over her mouth to keep from screaming, or possibly vomiting, as her insides were suddenly in a full-scale revolt.

The rest of the onlookers were silent, though a thud from the back of the cavernous room suggested that someone had fainted. Cate hadn't ruled out that possibility for herself. Being unconscious was much more appealing than sitting in an uncomfortable chair while watching people lose body parts.

Maddox dropped the sword in the expanding pool of blood and approached her. She lowered her hands and gripped the skirts of her dress as she watched this blood-spattered, happy man coming for her. When he was close enough, he leaned in and touched his forehead to hers.

"For you, my love," he said and shifted to kiss her.

He didn't seem to notice that she wasn't kissing him back. Even if she was interested in kissing a blood-spattered psychopath—which she wasn't—all of her energy was currently being channeled into controlling her stomach to keep from vomiting all over everything and everyone. The part of her that had wanted to do the maiming was gone, and Cate was mortified that it ever had been there at all.

Maddox pulled back and studied her. "You're unwell."

All hail the king of the understatement. Cate pressed her fingers to her lips. Before, when he had kissed her, her skin had been cold and decaying, but now her lips were overly warm. It felt as though they were on fire, but not in a good way.

"No," she said, "I'm—"

"You're unwell," Maddox repeated. "The fault is mine. I was too eager, and I should have waited until you were more recovered. Will you forgive me?"

He wanted forgiveness for his *timing*? Cate looked past him to where a pair of men were lifting the headless captain's body onto a small cart. Behind them, a boy placed the severed head into a basket.

Skipping breakfast had possibly been the best decision she had ever made in her entire life.

Cate looked at Maddox. "Yes, my lord."

He nodded. "Good. We will get you to your chambers and summon the physician to tend to you."

"No, I'm—"

Why was she arguing? Did she want to hang around and watch them squeegee blood off the floor? No, she'd go back to her very lovely cage, crawl into bed, and stay there until she woke up somewhere else, preferably somewhere with electricity and vodka. Lots of vodka.

"Yes, my lord," she said.

Maddox helped her stand, and the king's stunned and silent court watched Ceallach and Fionnbar lead her out of the room. She waved off her escorts when they were far enough away from Maddox and walked on her own power back to her cell where an anxious Bronagh waited. Ceallach told her what had happened as Cate searched the room for the darkest available spot.

Once located, Cate crammed herself into it. Her knees came up to her chest, and she covered her head with her arms. It wasn't dark enough, so she squeezed her eyes shut as well. It was still too bright, but she suspected that not even the bottom of the Mariana Trench would be dark enough.

"You can't stay in the corner," Bronagh said at some point.

The hell she couldn't. Everything in this stupid world was about what she couldn't do. She couldn't stay in the corner; she couldn't go home. She couldn't use a normal saddle; she couldn't make people angry. It sucked, and she was done with it. She'd stay in that corner until she was good and ready to come out of it.

Omur arrived first, and though Cate was far from willing to concede her position, she did lift her head to watch him sweep into the room. The air dissipated as he moved, and the scent of malice made her choke. But no one else seemed to notice that, either.

Ceallach offered Omur a shallow bow. "My lord."

Omur ignored the gesture. "Leave," he said. "All of you."

Cate assumed that order didn't include her and slowly got to her feet as Ceallach walked out. Bronagh practically crawled toward the servants' entrance, but as she was moving, both Cate and Omur looked at Fionnbar. Her guard was determined to hold his ground, standing rigidly with his hand on his sword.

"He'll stay," Cate said, approaching the man in red.

Omur bowed his head. "As you wish, your majesty."

Fionnbar didn't relax. Cate couldn't blame him. For all she knew, she had just signed that kid's death warrant.

"What do you want?" she asked in her normal voice. Omur seemed surprised to hear it and glanced at Fionnbar again. Cate shrugged. "He knows."

"Very well," Omur said. "I thought we might have a chat."

Cate sat in one of the chairs by the fire. "Super. What were you hoping to discuss?"

"Your reason for being here."

"Your headless henchman ambushed me in the forest and quite literally dragged me here," she said. "*That's* the reason I'm here."

Omur shook his head. "That's how you came to be here. Not the reason why."

"Oh. You mean that prophecy."

"They told you about it?"

"Everything there is to know."

Omur chuckled and sat across from her. "I doubt that."

Fionnbar moved to stand on her left, his hand gripping his sword. Did he know it likely wouldn't matter how prepared he was?

"Your mistake," Cate said.

"Yours is thinking that you can and should lie to me."

"Hey, it's my kidnapping, and I'll lie if I want to," Cate said. "What are you going to do about it?"

"You should be tied to a block, having your back whipped bloody. You should be stripped naked and lashed to the rack, begging for death. You should have a noose around your neck, and the crows should be pecking the eyes from your skull," Omur said. "The king should be inflicting a host of horrors upon you right now, and do you know why he isn't?"

"Because I'm not Haleine."

"Because I will it."

"Because I'm not Haleine."

"Well," Omur said, "at least you know that."

"I know far more than you think I do."

"Go on, then. Impress me."

"Sure. Because impressing you is what I care about," Cate said. "Just tell me what you want already, so I can tell you how that's never going to happen."

"How certain you sound. Did you tell that to the rebellion as well?"

Loudly. And frequently. "Jealous?" she asked.

"Curious."

"Don't be."

Omur smiled. "I do like you."

"Terrific. I can die happy."

"The idea is for you not to die at all."

"You think I need your help for that?"

"I know it."

"How certain you sound," Cate said. "But I haven't heard what it is you want."

"You," Omur said. "I want you."

"I should hope so. Otherwise, this whole incarceration deal is a real waste of taxpayers' money," she said. "*What* do you want with me? *What* did you bring me here to do?"

"Fulfill your destiny."

"I don't believe in destiny," she said. "How does that fit into your plan?"

"It doesn't matter. You'll come around."

"How do you figure?"

"Control," Omur said. "You lack it, but you want it. I can give that to you."

"Wouldn't that just be you controlling me?"

"I'm doing that now."

"Well, you're trying real hard, and that's what counts," Cate said. "Don't let your evil overlords tell you different."

"Are you so sure I am the evil?"

"I've caught your act a couple of times now. I'm sure."

"I saw you in the great hall. I saw the pleasure in your eyes."

"You're wrong about that."

"No," Omur said. "I'm not."

"Then you and I have two very different interpretations of what that word means because there was no pleasure in my eyes or any other part of me."

"There's no need to be ashamed."

"Do you know the definitions of any words?" Cate asked. "I'm not ashamed. I'm horrified and disgusted and will never sleep again, but I'm not ashamed."

"You gave the order. You wanted to do the violence yourself."

Both true. While she could explain away the former, it was the latter that was the real sticking point. She looked away. "Wanting and doing are two different things."

"They don't have to be," Omur said. "I can give you that, among other powers."

"Do any of these other powers come with tights and a cape?" Cate asked. When Omur failed to react, she added, "That joke is, of course, funnier in a world where tights and capes aren't everyday wear."

Omur leaned back against the chair and laced his fingers together. "Tell me—do you resist everything?"

"Yes," she said. "Any other questions?"

"It will go easier on you should you not resist this," he said. "It is your own true nature that you fight."

"What would you know about that?"

Omur smirked. "I know far more than you think I do."

"Go on, then," Cate said. "Impress me."

"When the pegasus told you of the prophecy, he would have said how you were needed to save this land and those souls within it. He would have told you how the loss of your sister necessitated your return to this world, and he would have claimed that you and that wretched creature shared not only blood, but also the same magic," Omur said. "You don't."

"Which is what I told him."

"What I suspect he did not tell you is that there were two named in this prophecy. Your sister, the woman in whose place you now sit, is the first. You, my dear girl, are the second."

"What does the runner-up in the Miss Save The World Pageant get? A lifetime supply of Rice-a-Roni? Teeth whitener and Vaseline?"

"I believe you misunderstand me," Omur said. "The prophecy does not foretell of you saving this world, but rather of how you will destroy the goddess, and her earth along with her."

Faolan definitely had left out that part. Of course, she had suspected he'd been lying. James's reaction—the way his head had come up—had been a giant red flag.

"Yeah, that doesn't sound like me," she said.

"You have no idea what's inside you."

"That's not true. I did very well in anatomy."

"I shall prove it to you." Omur looked at Fionnbar. "Kill her."

"What are you doing?" Cate asked. "He's not going to—"

But the sound of a sword being drawn made her look at Fionnbar. His eyes were gone, replaced by solid black pools. She scrambled out of the chair, tripping on that ridiculous gown, and fell to the floor. Fionnbar's sword swung over her head and stuck in the chair.

"What the hell!" she screeched. She looked at Omur. "What are you doing?"

He wasn't doing anything but watching the scene in front of him as though it were C-SPAN. It pissed her off, but she didn't have time to do anything about it as Fionnbar freed the blade and came for her. As the sword went over her head again, she ducked and crawled away. Omur stayed in his seat, looking toward the balcony.

On the other side of the chair, she stood. Fionnbar was close behind and moving at her with maniacal focus, so she continued to back away, one hand out in front of her, the other behind, on the lookout for any obstacles.

"What the hell are you doing, Fionnbar?" Cate cried. "I don't think this is what Willem had in mind!"

Her heel caught on the hem of her gown and she went down again, so she scuttled along the floor until she came up against a wall. Fionnbar was almost on top of her, and Omur still showed no sign of intervening.

"Goddammit, Fionn!" she exclaimed, throwing her hands up as he readied the sword to strike. "Stop!"

Squeezing her eyes shut, she braced for the bite of steel, but nothing came. After a moment, she opened her eyes and peeked through her fingers.

Fionnbar was frozen, stopped as though someone had hit the pause button. The sword was in mid-thrust. He would have killed her for sure.

She lowered her hands. "What did you do?"

"I did nothing," Omur said.

She edged her way around Fionnbar's unmoving form. "You started the rampage."

"You ended it."

Cate looked at Fionnbar again. "I didn't do that. I didn't do anything."

"You stopped him."

Was that true? Could it possibly be true? He had to be lying. There was no way she could've done that—paused someone, *frozen* someone—and not known it.

Was there?

"You have no idea what's inside you, and neither does anyone else," Omur continued. "Truly, we speculate, we claim we know, but it may be that your power is limitless. I will help you, show you. I will teach you. Unlike the goddess and those who follow her, I never have and never shall lie to you."

Cate folded her arms across her chest and pressed her fists against her body. "There you go again, using words you don't understand."

"You are the one who doesn't understand." Omur stood and walked toward the doors. "Don't resist this. Allow me to help you discover who you are. You won't regret it."

"I already do," Cate said, but if he heard, he didn't respond. The door closed behind him, and she looked at the still-frozen Fionnbar. "Shit."

What the hell was she going to do? If she had done this to Fionnbar, how had she managed it? How did she undo it, and what would happen if she did? Would Omur's mind control still be in play, or would the Kill Cate part of Fionnbar's agenda be over? Would he know what had happened? Would he remember?

Dropping her arms to her sides, she slowly uncurled her fists. She moved behind Fionnbar and touched his shoulder with the flat of her hand. He was instantly released, and the blade clashed against the wall with enough force that Fionnbar was jolted back. The sword clattered to the floor as Fionnbar fell to his knees, his body expanding and collapsing with deep breaths. A minute passed before his head turned from side to side. His shoulders straightened and tensed. When he whirled around, Cate moved.

"My lady?" he said, getting to his feet.

She held out her hand. "You stay there, but kick the sword away from you. Far away from you."

He searched for the sword. The expression on his face confirmed he didn't understand why or how it had gotten onto the floor behind him, but he did as she asked. The weapon skidded and spun away. Cate kept her hand raised as she went after it. She picked it up with her other hand.

"My lady, what—?"

"What's the last thing you remember?"

"I..." Fionnbar hesitated. "We were by the fire, you sitting, and I—where is Lord Omur?"

Cate laughed. "Lord Omur is gone—off to do whatever the hell it is the evil do after they've successfully messed with your head."

"My lady, what happened?"

Fionnbar stepped toward her, but she jumped back, sword in tow.

"Stop," she said. "Stop now."

No magic intervened this time, but Fionnbar halted and held up his hands. "What happened? Why are you afraid?"

"Lord Omur ordered you to kill me," Cate said. "And you tried."

"No, I would never—"

"You did. He told you to kill me, and you went for it. You attacked with gusto, and if I hadn't"—if she hadn't *what*, exactly?—"if I hadn't stopped you, your sword would've gone through my head instead of losing a game of chicken with the wall."

Fionnbar's hands fell, and his eyes darted nervously around the room. "No, I would never—"

"I know, but he compelled you to do it. He had some sort of control over you, and you did just what he wanted—what you would never do."

Fionnbar said nothing.

"You can't be here anymore," she said. "I can't let him use you against me."

"He won't."

"He just did, and neither you nor I have any idea how he did it, or how to stop it if he decides to do it again. It was luck, just blind luck, that I'm not a shish kabob right now," Cate said. "You have to leave."

"I can't leave you unprotected."

She shook her head. "I don't need protection. Omur doesn't want to kill me. Not in any traditional sense, anyway."

"My lady, Willem—"

"Get out," she said. "Get out now, and don't come back. I don't care what Willem wants, or what Willem says, you get the hell out of here. If he has a problem with that, tell him to take it up with me."

She tossed the sword at Fionnbar's feet. He looked at it and then at her. "My lady, please."

"Just go. I'll be all right."

"Are you certain, my lady?"

"Yeah," she lied, "I'm sure."

———◦◦◦———

Sighle screamed.

As soon as the oxygen had left her lungs and the sound died, another rose in its place. Again and again she did this, as the pain of Mireille's magic seared her mind.

When the pain abated at last, and Sighle was once again in control of her faculties, she curled up on the floor, shivering as tiny tremors worked their way through her.

That small bit of unintentional magic had burned her. If Mireille ever managed to unlock her true potential, Sighle would be nothing but ash.

But those Omur called his lords wanted it this way. They wanted Mireille's powers, needed her heart black, and Sighle intended to see that done.

But she did not want to die in the process. The woman who sat upon Feond's throne thought it would be a beautiful, noble honor to die in the service of her lords, and mayhap it was—certainly Darian Coileáin would agree—but Sighle was not eager to find out. She liked being alive. She liked what she could do and wanted to keep doing it for as long as she could.

A vision had showed that she would die a fiery death, killed by molten rock and melted into nothing, but it didn't have to happen like that. A vision was one possibility for the future, determined by one's current path. If that path could be altered, the vision could become naught but a dream.

If Mireille were molded properly, Sighle need not die at her hands at all. If Mireille were made ally and not enemy, that death could belong to someone else.

It was what Omur aimed to do, but she could not leave the task to him. He and Mireille were too ill-matched. He would continue to push and provoke her, and she would push back—that was her nature—and no true ground would be gained. Not when Mireille remained tied to the rebellion and the brown-eyed boy who led it. Mireille would never be what they needed until she was free of that.

Distance, and a new mentor—that's what Mireille needed.

Sighle carefully washed and dressed for Omur. Such effort was normally wasted—the lecher would bed her if she were dirty and infected with a pox—but Mireille had damaged Sighle's equilibrium, and having as much control as possible over Omur would be paramount. She would do anything she had to in order to make his mind easier to manipulate.

As soon as she was properly prepared, she went to Omur's chambers and entered unannounced. Omur sat cheerfully in a chair, a goblet in his hand, reliving over and over his encounter with Mireille. Sighle crossed the room and knelt in front of him.

"My lady," Omur said, surprised. "What brings you here?"

"Take her away. Take her home." Sighle placed her hands on his thighs and spread them. "You'll find the one you need there."

chapter 21

They had moved Haleine into a small room on the main floor. A shuttered window, a bed barely wide enough for two. This was her cell now, and she lay upon the thin mattress, curled on her side, and stared at the windowless wall. She listened to the one keeping watch outside as he paced and fidgeted with a sword that would do nothing to save either him or her. Which of them was it? The task to guard the cottage and the queen inside alternated between three—the boy, the man, and her messenger from another life.

The day Dana had come and gone, the messenger had reached her first. Haleine had been on her knees, hands shredding the linen covering her heart. She had wanted to rip it from her chest, throw it on the floor, and tear it to pieces. She would succeed where a blade had failed. She no longer wanted it there, nor did she need it. It only sickened her further, poison running so deep there was no chance of recovery. Removal was the only choice. A quick death, a clean death, not this hanging on, a body not knowing when to let go.

But the messenger pulled her hands away and pinned them to her sides. He let her scream until her lungs burned and the emotion became ash and drifted away. Then, as she sobbed, he pressed her against him and allowed her to cry until her body was nothing more than an empty shell.

She hadn't spoken nor slept since, so she was awake when Mireille had...Well, Haleine didn't know what it was that Mireille had done, only that it rippled through her like fire on a dry field of hay, and that Mireille was responsible. How or why Haleine should know this, she did not understand, but recognized the truth behind it. She didn't know why she should be aware of the presence of two unicorns in the forest, but she was. Each time their hooves struck the earth, she could feel it as though that were what powered her heart.

Mayhap that was the way of it. She was tied to this land in a way she did not comprehend and could not escape, no matter what she did.

Haleine lifted her head and scanned the floor to see if either of the two women—one young, one old—slept there. They had done so every night since

Dana's return and departure. Some nights they slept on either side of her, other nights only one slept at the foot of her tiny bed. Ready to wait on her should she want anything, ready to hold her down should she scream again, ready to save her should she try to die.

How could she make them stop? How could she convince them to let her go?

Her companion that night was the young woman, sleeping on the floor beneath the window. Haleine carefully and quietly slid from the bed, grateful the chamber was small, that the wall was close, because she required its help to both stand and walk. When she reached the door, Haleine leaned against it and watched the old woman sew by the weak light of her lantern.

"Sarai," she said when the name came to her.

Haleine hadn't meant to say it out loud, but it was too late to recall the words. The woman to whom the name belonged turned her head and gasped.

Sarai stood. "I'm so sorry, your majesty. I did not mean to wake you."

Haleine shook her head. "You did not wake me."

"May I get you something, your majesty?"

"You should not call me that," Haleine said. "That is not who I am anymore."

"Of course it is," Sarai said. "You'll never be anyone else."

"I cannot be that anymore."

"But if you cannot be who you are and cannot be anyone else, where does that leave you?"

"I wish I knew."

"Here." Sarai patted the chair. "You sit, and I shall make us some tea."

"That is not necessary."

"Many things are not necessary," Sarai responded. "But we do them anyway."

She helped Haleine to the table and saw her settled before moving to the fire. Stoking the embers, Sarai added a fresh log, then fetched a small kettle and filled it with water from a bucket on the floor.

"This is your home," Haleine said, glancing at Sarai's work. Tunics, leggings, and stockings. A dress as well.

"Aye."

"Is he yours?"

Sarai looked at her, a puzzled crease forming across her brow. "Dana, you mean?"

"Yes."

"As much mine as anyone else's, I suppose," she said. "I don't know from where he came, but he first appeared here when he was just a wee lad. My daughter's husband found him asleep in the barn one morning and brought him in. He stayed for a bit, then disappeared to somewhere else, but he came back after a time. He always came back."

"Always?"

"It was true in the past. I don't know if it's so now." Sarai laughed. "Oh, how my daughter used to worry about him when he was gone. I did, too, at first, but the winds always blew him back this way eventually."

"Your daughter and her husband," Haleine said, "where are they?"

Sarai set the kettle over the flames and joined Haleine at the table. "They were killed in the first attack on the village."

"How many have there been?"

"Two." Sarai offered Haleine a strained smile. "You were here for the second."

Haleine looked away. "I was the cause of the second, you mean."

"I believe it was the other lass. Your sister, my grandson has told me."

"I never knew her," Haleine said. "I never knew I had a twin. I still don't believe it, really. My mind is..."

Broken. Like the rest of her, a fragmented, disjointed mess.

"So often now I don't know where I am, or who I am," she continued. "I see people who can't be here and places that don't exist, and I never know what is real anymore. I may soon awake to find that sitting here with you now was naught but a dream."

"You will heal," Sarai said. "You will grow stronger, and you will heal."

Yes, she probably would. Haleine could feel that, too, like she felt each step the unicorns took. Her body would heal itself. Her body would grow stronger. It did that now, though she had only strived for the opposite.

"The world will right itself once again for you," Sarai said.

"You should not believe that."

An unexpected thud interrupted Sarai's response, and they both looked to the fire. The lid had fallen from the kettle, landing on the stone floor of the hearth. As Sarai rose to tend to it, the cottage door opened, and Haleine's messenger—why couldn't she recall his name?—stepped inside.

Sarai waved him off. "We're fine, Lucius, but I thank you for your diligence."

He bowed to Haleine. "Your majesty."

"Lucius," she said. Would she remember his name now? "Thank you."

Lucius bowed again and returned to his post. When the door closed, Haleine glanced up to see both the man and the boy peering at her from above, and the young woman standing in the doorway. One by one, they slowly retreated to their beds—the boy first and the woman last—but Haleine was embarrassed to have woken them at all and stared at her lap until Sarai returned, a cup in each hand.

"You will be all right in time. I do believe that," Sarai said, placing a cup in front of Haleine. "Just as I believe this war will end, and that the side of good will stand victorious when it does."

Haleine looked from the tea to the woman who had made it. "How do you do that? Your daughter, her husband—after everything, how can you believe? How do you have faith?"

Sarai stared intently at her own cup. "Aye, there has been loss, and there surely shall be more to come before this war finds its finish, but does that mean I should resign myself to some bleak future? That I should give up hope?"

"I did. I gave up hope. I have none now," Haleine said. "The only reason I remain on this earth is that you and some malevolent force hold me here, refusing to let me go."

Sarai lifted her cup to her lips and took a sip before placing it back on the table. She looked at Haleine for a long time, then nodded and walked away. She was near the other end of the cottage when she stopped and stared at the floor.

"The king's soldiers slit my daughter's throat here and killed her husband over there. I wasn't here when it happened; I found their bodies when I returned home. I don't know if you've ever seen a body that has had its throat cut like that. I don't know if you understand the amount of blood that comes from such an act, and all of it was on this floor. I know I didn't understand it, though I saw it, stood in it, knelt in it; and every time I see a blade, all I think of is what was done to my family in this room," Sarai said. "I don't like weapons in my home. I make the lads keep them outside. They understand, I think, and mostly"—she reached into a bucket in the corner and pulled out a dagger—"they respect it. But they worry about you and their ability to protect you. As have I."

Sarai carried the dagger to the table and laid it in front of Haleine.

"But it would seem we should not have bothered," Sarai said. "Would you care to slit your wrists, or shall I cut your throat for you, your majesty?"

Haleine looked from the dagger to Sarai. "Why not both? Find another blade, and I'll cut my wrists as you cut my throat," she said. "It doesn't matter what I do, or what is done to me. I awake alive and whole."

"You're not whole."

"No, you're quite right; I'm not, and I can't change that," Haleine said. "You don't know all that I've done, how many times I've felt myself die, only to find it wasn't true. It does not matter what happens; I cannot leave this place, this world."

"Then you must stay."

"To what end?"

"There is still a war to be fought, a war to be won," Sarai said. "Once you did great things for this land and its people. For my boys. You can do so again."

"It wasn't enough."

"Try again."

"If it still isn't enough?"

"Try until it is."

"You make it sound simple."

Sarai sat. "If you think that, you are a fool."

Haleine laughed, then quickly covered her mouth with her hands. How long had it been since she had felt even the smallest amount of honest mirth? She hadn't realized that her body remembered how to make such a sound.

"Of course it isn't simple," Sarai said, "but perhaps it could be less difficult than you believe when you realize that you now only sit at this table and yet, you undermine them."

Haleine's hands dropped to the table, and she stared at them. Sitting was such a passive act—it did nothing to weaken anyone. How could it?

Sarai took Haleine's hands in her own and squeezed. "They wanted to kill you. They wanted you dead, and every day that you live, every day that you survive, is a day that you win. That *you* hurt *them*." Releasing Haleine, she gathered up the dress and squinted at her needle before setting to work again. "Imagine what you could do if you stopped just sitting."

Haleine stared at Sarai and resisted an urge to laugh again. It was still too simple an idea—a ridiculous thought to believe that she could hurt anyone in any way—but her host only sought to be kind, to trust in something, and Haleine did not wish to dash that faith. She had none, but surely she should not ruin it in others. She reached for the tea and had some of the lukewarm liquid before replacing the cup and looking at the dagger lying next to it.

It was not the one she had used before. Where that weapon had gone, she did not know, but this was not it. Almost involuntarily, her hand moved toward it and rested atop the blade. Sarai inhaled sharply—she was not as unconcerned as she would have Haleine believe—but her watchfulness didn't matter. The dagger would lead Haleine nowhere new. She didn't understand it, but she could try to accept it. The only way to survive life would be to live it.

"I can sew," she said finally, as she drew away from the dagger.

Sarai looked at her. "What, dear?"

"I can—I can sew," Haleine repeated, her voice struggling for strength. She swallowed. "I can help you."

"Queens do not darn stockings."

"This queen does."

Sarai smiled and handed her needle to Haleine. "As you will, your majesty."

A storm moved in that night. It was a heavy, soaking rain that would have clogged drains and flooded low-lying streets back home. Had she been there, Cate wouldn't have given the weather a second thought, tucked away all warm and dry and ensconced on the couch watching something stupid on television while Fiona knitted next to her. Daniel would've been restless, pacing and acting as though being inside hurt, and Laura—

That didn't matter. Laura was long gone, and Cate wasn't in Boston anymore. Her fortress of solitude had been exchanged for a much larger and better guarded version, and instead of being oblivious to the weather, she stood between the opened balcony doors and watched the rain pound against the stone.

Somewhere out there, a group of people hid in the forest, seeking shelter in tents that had more holes in them than Swiss cheese. There was no reprieve to be had for them, nothing to do but wait it out. Of course, the same could be said for them even when it wasn't raining.

And she was supposed to help them. Unless Omur was to be believed. Then she was slated to destroy them. Kill them all, and anyone else who got in her way. She didn't think an evil entity bent on global destruction was overly discerning where body count was concerned.

Not that she wanted to be an evil entity bent on global destruction. She didn't want to be anything but Catherine Cole, college sophomore and girl about town—whatever that was. She didn't want to be evil—and she wasn't. Maybe she occasionally *thought* evil things, but who didn't?

But maybe she didn't get a choice. Free will didn't seem to be a hugely popular concept in these parts, and maybe that was because it didn't exist here. Laws of nature were crazy and backward, and your fate was laid out for you whether you liked it or not.

If that were the case, Cate chose not. She did not like it. Not one bit. She didn't want to be anyone's damn puppet, a mindless marionette doing some cosmic soft-shoe dance until the curtains came down on this messed-up universe.

But how could she get out of it?

Cate took a step forward. The rain splashed up from the balcony and quickly soaked the hem of the nightgown Bronagh had given her for bed. Maybe she could throw herself off the balcony and take her chances. She was apparently supernatural—maybe she'd bounce. Or maybe she'd splatter like a dropped egg. Her feet didn't seem willing to take the risk, though, and stayed right where they were, allowing the cold water to soak them, too. She may have been supernatural and potentially evil, but she wasn't suicidal. She'd leave that to Haleine.

Behind her, doors opened and closed, and someone walked toward her. Who would be paying a visit at this time of night? Hadn't she banished every-one from the room—Bronagh and Ceallach included? Who did that leave?

She had her answer when Maddox's arms wrapped around her waist and pulled her against his body. He kissed the back of her neck, slowly moving his lips toward her ear, and this time she didn't feel anything but revulsion.

He ran his tongue along her ear. "I've been thinking."

"About not licking me ever again, I hope." Cate twisted out of his grasp and faced him.

"About you," Maddox said. "About how you've changed."

A little robot was suddenly in her head, warning her of impending dan-ger. She stepped back, but his fingers hooked into the neckline of her nightgown and kept her close.

"I don't know what you're talking about," she said.

"Don't you?"

She pried his hand from her clothing, but he wasn't discouraged. Quite the opposite, she thought, as they fought briefly, a vertical arm wrestle, each struggling for control. Maddox won, forcing her arm down and squeezing her fingers in his. His other hand came up and rested on her side, below her breast. She tensed as she waited to see what would follow. She wasn't wearing the full gown anymore, so she could knee the hell out of his groin if he tried to do much else—though assaulting the Head Psycho In Charge in any manner—provided that she could—might lead to something worse than letting him cop a feel. Then again, letting him do *anything* was probably a bad idea. He didn't strike her as the sort of man to believe that no meant no.

"I've wanted you dead, you know. Oh, how I've wanted that," Maddox said. His hand slid to her hip. "For so long, I've wanted you dead, and I almost didn't care how it happened so long as I could look upon your corpse."

"Is that why you're here now?" Cate asked, trying and failing to free her hand. "To kill me?"

"No. I don't want to kill you anymore. I'm not sure why that is." His hand continued to stroke her side. "It's wrong, these feelings. After all that you've done, after taking that bastard-born traitor into your bed—"

"Would you have preferred a noble-born traitor?"

Maddox grinned, but his eyes showed his amusement didn't run deep. His hand glided up, over her breast, and stopped under her chin. "You're different."

"I'm really not."

"You are," Maddox said. "I'd very much like to know who you are because I dare say you are not the woman I married."

"What would you know about her?"

"My wife is weak. Pathetic. An incorrigible whore."

"Sounds like a lovely girl."

"She cried and sobbed and wailed, always mewling over one death or another."

"Imagine that."

"But you," Maddox said, "you enjoyed watching those men suffer today. You reveled in it."

"Would you look at that—another man in need of a dictionary," Cate said. "You don't know what you're talking about."

Maddox released her. "You're angry now."

"Not just now."

She darted right and he blocked her, so she went left. This time he let her pass but stayed close behind.

"Tell me why you're angry," he said.

"I'm here? You're here? Take your pick."

"You don't like me."

Cate stopped by the servants' entrance and put her back against the wall. "Does anyone?"

"Of course not. I am the king." Maddox sat in a chair by the fire and looked at her. "And you, whoever you are, are my queen."

Cate swallowed and lost the accent. "Wrong again."

Maddox didn't react to the change in her voice. "You're here, aren't you? In the queen's rooms, wearing the queen's clothes, being attended by the queen's servants—"

"Being harassed by the queen's husband?" Cate finished. "Yes, I am currently doing all of these things, but I wouldn't get too attached, if I were you. I'm just passing through."

"On your way to where?"

"Somewhere else."

"My man wants me to believe you are her. He wants you to play the part."

"Your man? Do you mean Omur?" Cate asked, and Maddox nodded. "Generous use of the word 'man' there, don't you think? I find him to be more parasite-like."

"Don't be so harsh," Maddox said. "The man will grow on you."

"Like a malignant tumor, I'm sure."

"You really don't care for him, do you?"

"Feeling less special now?"

Maddox smiled again. "He should have known it would never work. He should have realized I would know you were not my wife."

"What gave it away? The accent? The speech patterns?"

"You are sparring with me. You are fighting me, and my wife stopped doing that the day I first broke her."

Cate looked away. Broken. That was an apt description of the woman she had encountered in a cellar in Enimode. Between Maddox's abuses—and there had to be more than anyone had let on—and whatever had happened with Dana the Unwashed, Haleine's state of mind didn't come as much of a surprise anymore. Had Cate been subjected to that, she imagined she would have fared a lot worse.

"Physical breaking, or mental breaking?" she asked as though it made a difference. It didn't. He would still be a despicable, horrible human being that she hated.

Maddox shrugged. "Take your pick. She resisted longer than I thought she might. I would beat her, I would break her bones and bruise her body, yet she would only defy me again and again. But I bested her in the end. I always do," he said. "You, all of you women, you break so easily. A twig, a pane of glass, a piece of parchment—that's what you are. Sometimes I ponder how you can survive at all when you are so very fragile."

"I don't break easily."

"I should very much like to test that."

Cate lifted her head. "You try it, and I'll kill you."

"How would you ever manage that?"

"I'm very resourceful."

"Oh, I'm sure you are." Maddox rose from the chair and took slow steps toward her. "Brave, too, I think. For you to stand there and so boldly threaten me harm—"

"It was more a promise than a threat."

Maddox smiled again, the delight reaching his eyes and beyond. "I can't begin to tell you how much I shall love breaking you."

"Not as much as I'll love kicking your ass."

"Would you like to hear how I finally crushed your twin? How I brought her to her knees and made her call me master?" he asked. "I killed a boy, not even an important one. He was a flea-infested street whelp so thin you could practically see through him. I found him, tore him from his mother's arms, and brought him into the palace, into the great hall where she sat upon the same throne upon which you sat this very day, and I put a dagger through his tiny, little heart while he stared at her with his big, sad pauper eyes.

"She begged me not to do it; she pleaded with me to spare him, for he had done no wrong, but I killed that wretch anyway. And as that boy died, I watched her collapse. It was a beautiful thing, really, and all for a brat whose name she didn't know."

Maddox stopped in front of her. One arm rested against the wall near her head; the other landed at her waist.

"Now, who do you suppose I could kill to get you on your knees?" he whispered. "A young sister? A pair of bastard boys your twin called sons perhaps?"

Provoking him to hurt her was one thing—a stupid thing, some would say—but dragging either Sighle or innocent infants into this mess was something else entirely, and that was something she wasn't willing to do. Defeated, Cate slumped against the wall. Maddox grinned and leaned in to nuzzle her neck.

"I think you shall be my most amusing conquest yet," he said.

Oh, screw this. Cate sharply introduced her knee to his groin, and then his face when he went down to his knees. He slumped onto his side, and she stomped on his exposed nose for good measure.

"What do you think of me now?" she asked.

Looking between both entrances, Cate screamed. Guards rushed into the room, and she greeted them with high-pitched, nonsensical babble as she pointed to Maddox. As the guards surrounded their king, Cate walked out the main entrance, only to find Fionnbar standing in the hallway. They looked at each other without saying anything. Her escape window was growing smaller, so she spoke first.

"Do you know where to find Omur?"

"Aye, my lady."

"Great. Let's go," she said, but Fionnbar didn't move. She sighed. "I'll track down that jackass with or without you. You know you won't stop me, so either help me or forget you saw me. What's it going to be, Fionn? Make a decision because I won't wait much longer."

Fionnbar gestured down the hall. "This way."

"Thank you," she said.

When they reached the room Fionnbar claimed belonged to Omur, a single guard stood outside the doors. He bowed when he saw her and uttered the title that didn't belong to her. Cate took that for an encouraging sign.

"Move aside and let me pass," she said.

"My lord Omur is—"

"I don't care. Move," Cate said, and the guard bowed again before complying with her request. She looked at Fionnbar. "Wait here. Make sure we're not interrupted."

Fionnbar bowed. "Aye, your majesty."

Inside the darkened room, the only source of light came from the fire. Her eyes required a moment to adjust, but when they had, she could see Omur in the bed at the other end of the room. He hadn't appeared to notice her arrival, so she went to him.

"Hey!" she exclaimed, advancing to the bed. Every available source of light burst into flame. She hesitated, unsure how that had happened, but decided to press on. "I thought you should know that your puppet just became a real boy. A very real boy, and—oh my god!"

Omur was, indeed, in bed. Naked. With a girl. Doing...Cate registered the sight and whirled around, surprised she hadn't instantly been struck blind.

"What the hell are you doing?" she asked.

"I would have thought you'd recognize it," Omur said.

"Okay, I know what you're doing, but who in their right mind would ever be depraved enough to—"

"What are you doing here?" Sighle said.

Cate's insides collapsed at the sound of the girl's voice, heart and lungs and everything else dropping into her stomach like someone doing a belly flop. Her head screamed with white noise as she slowly turned to stare at her naked sister sitting in Omur's bed.

"What are you—what are you doing? Just...*what* are you doing?" Cate looked at Omur. "And you! What the hell do you think *you're* doing? What kind of disgusting game are you playing here? She's a child!"

"I'm not!" Sighle insisted. "I'm not a child!"

Cate swiveled back to Sighle. "You know what, Lolita? When you're caught naked and in bed with...with *that*"—she pointed to Omur—"you don't get to argue. Now get your damn clothes on, and let's get out of here."

"You can't tell me what to do."

Cate's eyes narrowed. "Get. Dressed. Now," she said. "Or I'll dress you myself."

Something in her voice made Sighle relent, slide from the bed, and start the search for her clothing. Cate didn't want to think about the activities that had led to her sister's dress and undergarments being strewed around in such an impressive radius, so she looked to see what Omur was doing.

Tall, Dark, and Creepy had found a robe to throw on and was now watching Sighle dress, causing Cate to question whether she had the ability to liquefy his eyeballs. Focusing on his face, she imagined his eyes melting into rivers of slime that would run down his stupid, evil cheeks, but nothing happened. What the hell good were these goddamn powers?

"I'm ready," Sighle said in a small voice.

She sounded on the verge of tears. Cate didn't want to make the kid cry—didn't want to see or feel it—but what was she supposed to do? Leave her there to do things Cate didn't want to think about?

Misery weighing her down, Sighle dragged her feet, but Cate had no patience for it. Stalking across the room, she put her hand on the girl's back and ushered her to the hallway at a more brisk pace. Both Fionnbar and the other guard snapped to attention.

Cate looked at Fionnbar. "Bring her back where she belongs and make sure she stays there."

Fionnbar bowed. "Yes, your majesty."

He took Sighle's elbow and led the girl away. The other guard started to follow, but Cate put her hand on his chest and held him in place.

"You're her guard?" she asked. "You're responsible for keeping her safe?"

"Yes, your majesty."

Cate nodded. She grabbed the collar of the man's tunic and pulled him closer. "Then you listen to me carefully," she said. "If you ever bring her to this room again, or anywhere near the man who lives here, I will personally do to you what was done to your friends earlier today. Only I won't be so nice about it. Do we have an understanding?"

"Y-yes, your majesty."

"Good lad." She released his tunic and patted his cheek. "Now get out of my sight."

The guard bowed quickly and hurried down the hall after his charge.

"No one will question your ability to deliver a threat," Omur said.

"Not a threat." Cate turned around. "As for you—"

"Not interested," Omur said. "I am, however, curious what brought you to my door in the dead of night."

"Oh, your puppet king—and my new best friend—stopped by my door in the dead of night looking for conversation and, I'm guessing, a nice rape. And though he didn't know it before, he somehow knows I'm not his wife. Then there's the super fun part where he's looking forward to breaking me the same way he did her."

"But you stopped him."

"You bet your ass I did."

"Did you kill him?"

"Not yet. But if you don't keep a tighter grip on him, I will."

"However much I would like to see that," Omur said, "there is no need to kill him."

"Oh, there really is."

"He never should have breached your doors this night—I do owe you an apology for that—but the lapse was inadvertent. I was distracted, you'll understand, and my hold on the king momentarily slipped."

Cate frowned as she remembered his distraction. "I could kill you, too, you know."

"No, you couldn't."

"You touch that girl again, and we'll find out which one of us is wrong."

Omur laughed with genuine delight. "I must say you are marvelously entertaining."

"You are both evil and annoying," Cate said. "Are you going to stay away from my sister, or am I going to castrate you while you sleep?"

"Cooperate with me, and I shall stop bedding your sister," Omur said. "I will also better control the king, I assure you."

Another crappy choice. How unusual. "I will find a way out of this," she informed him. "One way or another, you won't be able to manipulate me forever. And when that blessed day arrives, you'd better start watching your back."

"There may come a time when you won't want to find your way out of this."

"I wouldn't hold my breath if I were you," Cate said. "Unless that will kill you. Then you should feel free to go right on ahead."

Omur smiled. "You needn't worry about me touching Lady Sighle. We will be leaving before the next night is out."

"Leaving? Who's leaving? You and me?"

"And the king."

"But not Sighle?" she asked, and Omur nodded. "Leaving for where?"

"Home," Omur said. "I shall be taking you home."

"Somehow, I don't think you mean my home."

"I do. Wherever the goddess stashed you these many years is not your home."

"I have documentation that proves you're wrong. I don't have it with me, or anything, but it does exist."

"Lies. All of it. This world is the one in which you were born. This world is the one in which you were meant to be."

"Yeah, well, unless this world has chocolate lava cake and you all have been holding out on me, you're wrong about that, too."

"I am not wrong," Omur said. "The goddess and those who serve her have done nothing but lie to you."

"They've stretched the truth from time to time, but—"

"They have ignored the truth."

"—I know what I've seen," Cate finished. "I'm not interested in aligning myself with someone so careless about human life."

"Have they not been careless with your life? Were they not reckless with the life of your twin?" Omur asked. "I offer you the truth. I offer you the opportunity to discover who you truly are and from where you truly come. The decision should be easy for you."

He told the truth—it should have been obvious. One did not cooperate with the forces of evil. One did not agree to play some twisted version of *This*

Is Your Life with the forces of evil. But if there was some truth to be had out there, some answers to be found, shouldn't she at least try?

She folded her arms across her chest. "How did I stop the guard?"

"Your abilities are tied to you, to your emotions. The stronger the emotion, the stronger the response," Omur said. "You were angry and afraid, and so channeled that power accordingly through your hands."

"How? I've never done anything like that before, and it sure as hell wasn't the first time I've ever been angry. What was different about this time?"

"Another lesson for another day," Omur said. "Provided you accept my offer."

Cate let out a breath and lowered her arms. "Okay," she said and delivered a short jab to Omur's groin. As he doubled over, she walked away. "I'm in."

—◦∾◦—

Cate may have demanded that they all leave her chambers, but Bronagh suspected the command would not hold up to a challenge and decided to return. Though she believed Omur to be at fault, she didn't know what had caused Cate to issue the order to begin with. Fionnbar had said very little about what had transpired, but he appeared absolutely miserable about it, and Bronagh wanted to know why.

When she arrived at the queen's chambers, the hall was empty of guards, and the door was open. She rushed inside to see six guards carefully lift the unconscious king from the floor and place him on a stretcher. Rhys was there as well, bidding the men to be careful. The stretcher was lifted, and four guards carried the king from the chamber, Rhys trailing behind them. The remaining guards milled around, talking so quietly that Bronagh could not hear what they discussed. One by one, they returned to their posts, leaving her alone in an empty room, kneeling near the blood on the floor.

What had Cate done?

Cate returned some time later, appearing to be unharmed, but Bronagh's eyes were soon drawn to the stain of blood on her shift.

"Where have you been? There's blood on the floor. There's blood on your clothes!" Bronagh exclaimed. "What happened here?"

Cate looked at the blood on the floor. "That's not mine."

"No, it's the king's! I watched them carry him out of here on a stretcher! What happened? How did his blood get on both you and the floor?"

"He hit his head."

"On what?"

"My knee," Cate said. "Then the bottom of my foot."

"The bottom of your...What did you do?"

"I tried to crush his head like a grape. Do you know what that is? Do you have grapes here? You must, right? This place is lousy with wine," Cate said. "Anyway, it doesn't matter. It didn't work. I may have broken his nose, though."

Bronagh felt faint. "You may have broken his..."

"I also kneed his groin pretty hard. That felt good," Cate said. "Well, not to him, but to me and every other woman he's ever even glanced at, it felt great."

Bronagh sank to the floor. "You didn't."

"I did. Trust me—he had it coming."

"No." Bronagh shook her head. "No, he didn't. He didn't have it coming. He's the king, and you can't—"

"Can. Did. Would definitely do it again."

"Do you not understand what you've done?"

"Oh, I understand. It makes me feel all warm and fuzzy inside to know that somewhere in this labyrinth you call a palace is an unconscious asshole whose little buddy won't be functioning properly for a while."

Bronagh sighed. "My lady—"

"Hey, how long has my little sister been banging the Crypt Keeper?"

"Who? What?"

Cate flopped onto the sofa. "Sighle—you remember Sighle, right? Dark hair, pale skin, soon to enter puberty?"

"What?"

"I caught Sighle—the child you claim is my sister—naked, and in bed doing unspeakable things with and to Omur."

Bronagh paled. "No, that's not right."

"I agree."

"No, you must be mistaken."

"I'm not mistaken. She was getting freaky with the freak."

"I—I don't understand."

"That makes two of us," Cate said. "So, here's what's happening now: Omur, the asshole, and I are going...You know what? I have no idea where we're going. He claims he's taking me home, but I don't know where he thinks that is."

"The queen was from Tanuba," Bronagh offered. "It's a country across the ocean."

"Across the ocean," Cate echoed. "How would one get across this ocean?"

"By ship."

"Ship?" Cate grimaced. "Are you sure there's no land bridge or anything like that available?"

"Yes, I'm certain."

Cate sighed. "Well, before I board the *S.S. Minnow* with Tweedle Dee and Tweedle Dum, I want to make sure that you and Fionnbar will look out for Sighle to make sure that no one else is doing anything to that girl that they shouldn't."

"Should she not go home with you?" Bronagh asked.

"Not with the cradle robber on board. She stays here, and you watch her like overprotective hawks."

"Aye, if that's what you want."

"It's what I want," Cate said. "Sighle may not like it, but you're in charge. Don't let her order you around."

"Aye, my lady, we will see her protected," Bronagh said. "Did Lord Omur say when you would depart?"

Cate shrugged. "Before the next night is out."

"Did he say for how long you would be gone?"

"No."

Bronagh sighed. "Oh, my lady, why did you agree to this?"

"The other choice wasn't acceptable," Cate said, a hint of worry finally creeping into her face. "There's other stuff, too, but it's nothing you'd know anything about."

Bronagh nodded and stood. "Then I will make sure you are properly packed and prepared."

"I'll need more than dresses and petticoats for that."

"Aye, you will," Bronagh said. "I'll be back shortly. Please don't cause bodily harm to any other members of the monarchy while I'm gone."

"No promises."

Bronagh hurried away. Continuing to leave Cate unattended would be dangerous, but to whom could the task be trusted? Fionnbar would refuse— he wouldn't get any closer than the hall—and Willem would never leave the nursery. There wasn't another soul who knew the truth behind their imposter queen's identity, and as Cate was unable to hide it, there was nothing for Bronagh to do but to complete her task as quickly as she could.

Rumors were circulating rapidly amongst the servants, centering around the king, the queen who had injured him, and what the pair would do next. Bronagh gathered each whisper she heard, not knowing what was truth and what was wrong. It would not be for her to determine. She would tell them what she had heard, and the rebellion could decide on its own what was to be believed.

When she arrived at her little house, the rebellion's man lay on the cot, one arm behind his head as he stared at the roof.

"Where are the rest of you?" she asked.

He looked at her. "Around."

"Where? I've only ever seen you here."

"I'm all you ever will see. Safer that way."

She nodded. "You'll have to make them come out of hiding now, or take me to whoever is leading you."

"Why? What's happened?"

"They're taking her."

The man sat up, swinging his legs over the side. "Let's go."

———⟡———

James didn't return to Orla's until morning, choosing to walk the palace perimeter again and again, searching an invisible wall for a weakness he already knew didn't exist. As a result, he was soaked through, exhausted, and angrier than ever.

The tavern was warm and mostly empty. A pair of men talked in a corner, a plate of bread between them, and a lone man sat at the far end of the bar. Two serving boys hovered nearby, whispering to each other. Orla busied herself behind the bar. Though she had glanced up at his arrival, she now seemed to be working hard to avoid looking at him. James suspected Dana was the reason why and approached the bar to wait.

"Where is he?" James asked when she had made her way to him.

"What did you do?" she said. "Stand in the rain all bloody night? Are you trying to catch your death?"

"Where is he?"

"I'll heat some water for you and have the lads bring the tub to your room. You can—"

"Where is he?"

Orla sighed. "The stable. He said you didn't want him here."

James nodded and pushed off the bar. "I don't."

"I won't make him go."

James shrugged. "Your tavern. Do what you want."

"I will," she said. There was a slight pause before she added, "He looks awful."

"That's not my concern."

Out in the stable, Dana sat on the floor, resting against the wall with a jug of ale in his hands. He appeared both unsurprised and unconcerned to see James.

"You told me to leave the room," he said, putting the jug on the floor. "I did that."

James nudged the jug with his boot. "You're pathetic."

"I know. Oh, I know." Dana laughed, the sound turning into a hacking cough. When he had it controlled, he dragged his arm across his mouth. "But say the word and I'll go."

"Go where?"

"A place that will have me."

"Is there such a place?"

"Maybe one."

"Where is that?"

"A long way from here," Dana said. "Well? Do I stay, or do you mean to lay claim to the stable as well?"

"Orla wishes for you to stay."

"But not you."

"No. Not me," James said. "Why does she care so much for you?"

Dana shrugged and took up the jug again. "I've never promised her anything. I'm sure that helps."

James had never promised anything to Cate, either. Not that it mattered. He still had let her down. He stripped off his sodden cloak and laid it over a stall door. The mare occupying it pushed her head against his chest until he absently stroked her neck.

"James?" Dana said.

James turned, unfocused, as his eyes searched for a target. They found the ale first, then Dana. "Stay if you want. We won't be here much longer anyway."

"Where will you go?"

Wherever Cate went. Wherever they took her, he would follow. He would do whatever he had to do in order to get her back. He'd swear that to her now, even though she couldn't hear it.

"Doesn't matter," he answered. "You're not coming."

"I'm not a threat, James. You don't have to hide your plans from me."

"Why would I bother? I could tell you everything, and you'd only run in the opposite direction."

"Try me." Dana swallowed a mouthful of ale. "Tell me about the girl."

James slumped against a barrel and took Emrys's dagger from his belt. "I already told you she's the queen's sister."

"Aye, but where did she come from? Where has she been?"

"Another bloody world," James said. "I should have left her there."

"Why didn't you?"

James shook his head. "Trying to save this bloody world."

"Faolan means for her to take Haleine's place?"

"Aye."

"I can help you get her back."

James ripped the ale from Dana's hands and tossed it aside. "Stay away from her."

"I'm not your enemy."

"You're not anything else, either."

"No, not now," Dana agreed as he struggled to stand. "But I could be."

"I don't care. I can't be bothered with you."

"Why did you come in here, then? If you can't be bothered with me, why seek me out? Why stay?"

James looked at the floor. He didn't know. "It doesn't matter. I'm leaving now, and I won't be back again."

"Isn't that what you said last time?"

James didn't think as he punched Dana in the face. Dana reeled back until he hit a stall door. The horse startled and reared, striking the door with his hooves. Shoving Dana out of the way, James opened the stall and went inside to calm the horse. Afterward, he backed out carefully and closed the door. Retrieving the dagger from the floor, he glanced at Dana, wiping blood from his nose, and shook out his swollen knuckles.

The stable door opened before either of them could speak, and James turned, expecting to see Orla coming to check on her ponies, but found himself looking at Rhydwyn.

"What are you doing here? You aren't supposed to—" James stopped when he saw Bronagh standing behind Rhydwyn. "What is this?" He used the dagger to point at the maid. "What is she doing here?"

"I've come to help you," Bronagh said.

"Help us?" James asked. "I don't know that I could think of anyone whose help I would want less."

"Mine?" Dana offered.

"Will you never trust me?" Bronagh asked.

"Not likely," James said. "You do have a habit of lying to us."

Bronagh shrugged as though her past were irrelevant and looked at Dana. "Found your way here, did you? Discover your truth yet?"

"Still searching," Dana answered. "You came to help?"

Bronagh nodded. "Omur plans to take your girl from the palace. I think he wants to get away from you, or he wants you away from her."

"You think?" James asked.

"He didn't sit me down to explain his intentions. I'm just telling you what I heard," the maid said. "What you do next is your choice, but he's planning to take her from the palace."

James looked at the floor. What had changed? They hadn't put their plan into motion yet—Faolan hadn't even reappeared. No, the rebellion had been sitting outside of the palace doing nothing, unable to do more, for days. They couldn't possibly have been a threat. Why would Omur risk moving her?

"Just Omur?" Dana said.

Bronagh shook her head. "The king, too."

"Where are they taking her?" Dana asked.

"Mairéad. They don't think you'll be able to follow her there."

"Mairéad? Is that—where is that?" James was forced to ask.

"Tanuba," Dana said. "They're taking her to Revelin."

"When?" James asked.

Bronagh shrugged. "Tonight? Sooner? Omur wants it done. I'm surprised they haven't already gone."

James nodded and looked at Rhydwyn. "See her out."

"Don't bother. I can find my own way," Bronagh said.

"Then do so," James said. "But if I find you've lied to us again—"

"You'll what? Hurl more insults at me?" Bronagh shrugged and backed toward the door. "Do your worst. You're not clever enough to hurt me."

She slipped out of the stable, and James stared at the door.

"Captain?" Rhydwyn said. "I don't believe she's lying. Not this time."

James nodded. God help him, he agreed. "You have to go to camp, as fast as you can," he said and held out Emrys's dagger. "Give this to Ilya. She can use it to get what we need from Emrys. Tell her also what we mean to do, and that she'll be on her own again for some time."

"What do you mean to do?" Dana asked.

"You'll also have to track down your brother," James continued. "He went to fetch Idwal Kai, but you'll have to find them and tell them—perhaps Idwal Kai can use his lord's name to secure passage for the three of you, but however it's done, get yourselves to Mairéad and find me there. Bring Faolan along, if you find him."

"You can't go to Mairéad," Dana said. "Not alone."

"You trust Idwal Kai?" Rhydwyn asked.

It was as close to questioning him as Rhydwyn had ever come. James almost smiled. "No," he answered. "But I need him."

"How will we find you?" Rhydwyn asked. "Where will you be?"

"Wherever she is," James said. "Get going now, and don't tell Idwal Kai about Dana, aye?"

"Aye, Captain." Rhydwyn took the dagger and left.

"Who is Idwal Kai?" Dana asked.

James looked at him. "Are you still here?"

"Let me help you."

James left the stable to return above stairs. Tanuba. Mairéad. How would he get there? Could he find a ship? If he left now, he could arrive when she did, perhaps even before. Before would be better. If there was to be another wall, he needed to be on the inside before it was created. Finding the palace wouldn't be difficult—getting inside would be a challenge, but he would find a way. He had to find a way.

Orla's boys had brought the tub into the room, but James had no time for that now. On one of the beds was a clean tunic and breeches, carefully folded. Had Orla washed his clothes?

"James, wait, please," Dana said, slipping into the room. "What are you doing?"

James kicked off his boots and stripped naked to change. "I'm going to Mairéad."

"You can't do that."

"If she's going there, I'm going there."

Dana eased onto the chair. "You can't go by yourself."

"We can't travel in a group. It will take too much time, and there's too much risk, so I'll go now on my own. Rhydwyn and Gair will follow with Idwal Kai. They'll find me; it'll work. It *has* to work."

"I can go with you."

"Haven't you a pressing need to get drunk? A keg of ale requiring your attention? A noblewoman to seduce?" Turning his back on Dana, James threw his belongings into a rucksack. "You're not coming."

"I can help. I want to help."

"I don't need your help."

"You need someone's help. Especially if you can't trust this Idwal Kai."

James whirled around. "Dammit, Dana! Why are you still here?"

Dana stood. "You want me to leave?"

"I can't say it any plainer."

"All right. Tell me who Idwal Kai is, and why he may not be trustworthy. Then I'll go."

"He served your whore's father," James said. "Right up until the moment you cut off your whore's father's head."

"James—"

"He was taken prisoner in that battle, along with some others. Did you know we had prisoners?" James asked. "Doesn't matter; we don't have them anymore. We cut them loose. I don't know what happened to them, but Idwal Kai? Him we kept."

"Why?"

Because he had recognized Cate.

"Because I thought he might have a use," James said. "Turns out I was right."

"He serves the Maoilriains, and you're going to trust him to hand you Cate?"

"No. No one will hand me Cate. I'll get her back on my own. I trust Idwal Kai will help me keep her alive."

"I will help you keep her alive."

James looked at his hand and traced his swollen knuckles with his thumb. "If only I could trust you," he said. "Be sure to close the door on your way out."

Dana sighed but walked away, closing the door as he left.

James continued to look at his hand long after Dana had gone. Only when certain he would not encounter Dana did he slide on his boots. Making sure he had packed all he owned, he departed.

Orla sat at a table in the now-empty barroom, looking tired and forlorn. Dana hadn't returned to the stable, then.

She stood as James approached. "You're leaving."

"I have to," he replied. "I'm sorry to ask more of you, but if the other two or Faolan should come looking for me, will you tell them, please, that I've gone to Mairéad, and that they should find me there? I don't think they will come here, but if they do…"

She nodded. "I'll tell them," she said before quickly adding, "Dana's gone."

James shrugged. "That's what he does. It's what he's always done. You know that, and I should have remembered it." He made his way to the door, but before he left, he looked back at the alewife. "Thank you, Orla."

She nodded again. "Try not to get yourself killed."

"Same to you."

Once on the street, James turned toward the palace. This time he thought he could feel the wall long before he stood in front of it. It seemed to hum. Could anyone else hear it? But why would they? That barrier was nothing to them; it was everything only to him.

He touched it, just as he had that first day, and every day since. A shock of pain ran through his body, but that had happened every day, too. He glanced at the palace. Was she still in there, or had they already gone?

How would he ever find her in a country to which he had never been?

However it was to be done, he wouldn't be able to do it by standing still, so he backed away and headed to the harbor. He walked amongst the people, examining both the sailors and the ships for Tanubian colors. A number of vessels appeared to be unguarded but were too small to offer him a place to hide. He stood at the end of one pier and stared at the boats too large to dock in the harbor. They would suit his needs, but how could he get out there unseen?

"Thinking about swimming?"

Dana. James put a hand on the dagger in his belt before turning around. Dana stood a few feet away, the hood of a cloak he hadn't had before pulled up to shade his face. James released his weapon as he looked at the sword strapped to Dana's side. That was new, too.

"What are you doing here?" James asked.

"I've found us passage to Tanuba."

"You found *us* passage?"

"Aye," Dana said. "They're sailing soon, so we should be going."

James didn't move. "How did you find passage?"

"I'm not completely without friends," Dana said. "I know the harbor-master. He found me a ship that will take us to Odhran."

"What is that?"

"It's the Tanubian harbor closest to Mairéad, where they're taking her."

"There's a place for us to hide on this ship?"

"There's no need to hide," Dana said. "Tanubian sailors have no idea who you and I are. They think we're looking to escape the war, and they're willing to have us aboard so long as we're willing to earn our keep."

"Are you capable of that?"

"I'll manage," Dana said. "Come on, James. You want to get your girl back, don't you?"

"She's not my girl."

"But you want her back, aye?"

"You know I do."

"Then trust me."

Trust. That was about the last thing James wanted to give to Dana. He didn't deserve it; he hadn't earned it, but James did need help. As stubborn and alone as he wanted to be, he needed help to get to Tanuba, and if Dana could provide that, James thought he could at least try. For Cate's sake, he would try.

James nodded. "Let's go."

Chapter 22

It was a dangerous game they played with Darian Coileáin's second-born. Faolan and his goddess weren't alone in this; Omur and his dark lords faced the same risks, the same rewards.

Volatile and unpredictable, Cate remained an enigma, and it was impossible to know which girl—Laorans's daughter or Yelsneh's servant— would prove to be her true self, but Faolan became more and more convinced with each day that it would be the latter.

The very moment James had carried her through the portal, her magic, though dormant, had screamed to Faolan so much more than it ever had during his initial days with Haleine. There were not many things that frightened him; however, the uncertainty surrounding Cate was chief among them, so though she'd been brought to this world to work magic, he hadn't pushed her to unlock that which lurked inside her.

But he hadn't lied to James about wanting to recover her. As much as Faolan didn't want Cate in the rebel camp, he recognized that he couldn't very well leave her in Omur's hands. If he could have broken through that damned barrier, he would have.

Then came the night when Faolan had felt the first burst of active magic from her veins. How or why she had done it—what Omur might have done to get her there—he didn't know, but that almost didn't matter when the magic itself—Cate's magic—had struck Faolan at his core and left him frozen with fear and the confirmation that he had been right not to encourage her.

He remained frozen, which was why he had not joined James's quest to bring Cate back to these shores. In deference to the goddess's wishes, he hadn't stopped James and Dana from their fool's errand, nor had he said anything against Rhydwyn and Gair's subsequent departure with Idwal Kai. But he would not go himself. He would not waste days being weakened by an extended exposure to salt for a girl who would, more like than not, become his enemy.

Instead, he joined Ilya in an expedition to safeguard a flagging rebellion and went along to visit the lord of Labhras. Cate had somehow convinced a stubborn nobleman to turn ally, and Ilya carried the symbol of his agree-ment—a jeweled dagger—that would ensure Jaspaer Emrys's aid and the rebellion's continued survival.

After leaving the safety of the tunnels for the open air, Ilya rode in front, flanked by Semias and another man, Dawe. Bearach and Fáinne traveled in the woods on either side of the road while Faolan acted as rear guard. They were taking such careful precautions on this road that had so recently seen the deaths of too many of their own, but whatever evil had permeated the forest that day was gone. Faolan supposed there was no reason for it to linger—not when Cate now sailed the Endellion Sea.

The unicorns stopped at the edge of the trees, but Faolan followed the humans as they rode into Labhras and neared the keep's opened gate. When they stopped, Faolan landed on Ilya's shoulder and watched a guard ap-proach. Two others stayed in front of the gate.

"I hope you're right about this," Ilya murmured.

Faolan held a similar hope. He had not been to Labhras in some time, only ever putting in the occasional appearance whenever Dana paid a visit to its lord. Whereas Dana had been fond of Jaspaer Emrys, Faolan had never fully trusted the man. If the instructions they followed had come from anyone other than James—who had trusted Emrys even less—Faolan couldn't say he would have taken the risk.

"State your business," the guard said.

Ilya removed the jeweled dagger from a saddlebag and held it for the guard to see. "My business is with your lord. Tell him we're here, won't you?"

The guard looked at the dagger and then at Faolan. His eyes flickered to Semias and Dawe before he called the other two sentries forward.

"You'll surrender all weapons here," he said, "and wait in the bailey until my lord deigns to see you."

Ilya laid the dagger in her lap as she unbuckled her sword belt and handed it to the guard. Behind her, Semias and Dawe did the same. Soon Emrys's men had an impressive array of blades in their possession, but Ilya had not yielded the jeweled dagger.

The first guard looked at it. "That, too."

"No," Ilya said. "Now fetch your lord and let us pass."

The air thickened with her refusal. Faolan looked from the gate guards to the pair of men watching from the wall walk. The trio attempting to gain entrance had caught their attention as well—even if they didn't know who Ilya or her companions were. Faolan willed all involved to keep their tempers in check. Eight people he could manage—maybe as many as fifteen or twenty—but if trouble started, more than that would be drawn to the fight, and with the exception of a single dagger, the rebels were unarmed. Avoiding a brawl would be vital.

Emrys arrived before the standoff could escalate further, and Faolan was thankful to see him. The lord of Labhras came through the gate and stared hard at Faolan.

"Let them pass," he said to the first guard. To Ilya he added, "Keep the dagger if you wish. The rest of your weapons you may reclaim upon your departure."

"Fair enough," Ilya said.

Emrys went back inside. The three gate guards stepped aside, glaring at Ilya as she nudged her horse forward. Semias and Dawe followed, Faolan hovering behind them. Inside the bailey, more guards watched the rebels hand over their mounts to waiting grooms. Too many people now, too many souls. Faolan would never be able to control the situation.

"We'll talk in the stable," Emrys announced.

The rebels followed him into the structure where their only witnesses were the nobleman's horses. It was ideal for Faolan, and he found a perch on the edge of an empty stall's door. Semias and Dawe remained at the entrance, Dawe watching Ilya while Semias focused on the bailey. Ilya and Emrys moved deeper into the stable.

"I suppose Dana's gone off to Tanuba after the king and our newly pardoned queen," Emrys said, taking a seat on a stool. "Sent you here in his place?"

"Is that a problem?" Ilya asked. "Does that change what you've agreed to do?"

Emrys shook his head. "I gave the queen my word, and I intend to keep it," he said. "What is it you want?"

"Supplies and information, to start."

"What sort of information?"

"What sort do you think?"

"What makes you believe I would know anything that would be of value to you?"

"You know the queen's on her way to Tanuba," Ilya said. "It's not common knowledge."

"You know it."

Ilya smiled. "You're one of the king's trusted noblemen."

Emrys barked a laugh. "Only until the king finds out about this. When that happens, I think you'll find my favor gone."

"Then the king best not find out," Ilya said. "You needn't fear us; we haven't any interest in jeopardizing your standing at court."

"Of course you don't. You want to make sure I remain of use to you."

"Aye, we do," Ilya said. "Please don't be difficult, my lord. I'm sure neither of us wishes to waste time playing these games."

Emrys nodded. "Very well. What would you like to know?"

"Do Varro and his men have orders to march? If so, where will they go?"

"The king isn't in the country."

"The last time the king wasn't in the country, much of the west burned," Ilya said. "Does the army have any orders?"

"I haven't heard of any such orders," Emrys said, "but I can assure you that Varro is no longer a threat to your people."

"Why is that?"

Emrys shrugged. "He's dead. The king took his head for what was done to the queen when he dragged her back to Eluned."

Faolan hadn't expected that. Neither had Ilya, and she looked at him in surprise. It didn't last long, as she quickly realized she should not have acknowledged him that way in that place, but Emrys noticed anyhow.

"Dana used to do that, too," Emrys said, gesturing to Faolan. "He'd look at that little beast that way, as though he were capable of responding, or of having an opinion at all."

"Dana has always been capable of having an opinion," Ilya said. "I'm sure you've heard him offer them from time to time."

Emrys sighed. "Fine. Keep your secrets."

"I intend to," Ilya said. "Has a replacement been named? Who will take Varro's command?"

"No one has been named that I have heard, and I would have heard," Emrys said. His pride was bruised now, and his tone showed it. "Have you considered that they might not care about your rebellion anymore? They've already reclaimed the queen, your leader's a ghost, and your people won't survive without my aid. Why should they bother with how you spend your days?"

Ilya smiled. "Find out if that's the case, won't you?"

Emrys was not amused. "I've become fond of the queen, and I have always liked Dana," he said, standing, "but you, I merely tolerate, and barely so, for their sake. You should keep that in mind as we proceed."

Ilya dipped her head. "I did not mean to offer you offense, my lord."

Emrys's laugh suggested he didn't believe Ilya's apology to be sincere. "How about you offer me some truth to make amends," he said. "What changed the king's mind?"

"My lord?"

"You found his pardon of the queen to be as unexpected as I did, but I suspect you may understand why it was done. I wish to understand it as well."

Maddox hadn't changed his mind; he'd had it changed for him. Ilya glanced at Faolan again, and the pegasus shook his head slightly. He wasn't yet willing to reveal that the true queen of Lira was hidden in a northern village while an imposter—the woman of whom Emrys was fond—sailed to Tanuba in her place.

"I can't answer your question," Ilya said. "At least not yet."

"More secrets." Emrys shook his head. "Dana would not withhold from me were he here."

"If Dana were here, we'd not be talking in the stable," Ilya said. "There is trust to be gained on both sides, my lord. We should allow it to come naturally, for all our sakes."

"As we should," Emrys said. "Let us discuss, then, what other aid I may provide your cause."

When the talk turned to medicine and food rations, Faolan left the stable. Things were quiet in the bailey; with the exception of a few soldiers, the population had gone back to their normal routines. The soldiers watched as Faolan flew into the village. From there, he waited in the forest with Bearach and Fáinne until Ilya, Semias, and Dawe joined them.

"Lord Emrys was suspicious of your departure," Ilya told him.

"He was suspicious anyway," Faolan said. "Did you get what you needed?"

Ilya shrugged. "Enough to be going on with for now. I just hope we can trust him not to poison anything."

"If he does, we'll detect it."

"It might have been easier if you would have only spoken to the man."

"That'll come."

"Like telling him about Cate and the queen?"

"Let's see if he poisons anything first," Faolan said. "I have to leave you here, but Fáinne and Bearach will accompany you back to camp."

"Where are you going?" Ilya asked.

"Enimode," was Faolan's answer.

———※———

Once Haleine stopped fighting against life, her body began recovering quickly. Too quickly, she realized, for Sarai's comfort. Too quickly for her own comfort as well, truth be told, but Haleine understood she could not change it.

What she could do was hide the exact extent of her recovery from Sarai and the others with whom she came into contact. Though she did not feel it, Haleine frequently feigned weakness and exhaustion. She favored her left arm, holding it tightly against her body, and refused help when the time came to change bandages covering wounds that no longer existed. Haleine couldn't be sure her efforts had their desired outcome, but kept at it if for no other reason than it kept her own mind occupied.

Sarai had given in to Haleine's ceaseless requests to help with whatever work needed to be done, but neither she nor any of the rest would allow Haleine to leave the shelter of the house. Faolan had forbidden it during a previous visit, and either her caretakers didn't know or wouldn't admit as to why the edict had been issued. Hence, Haleine could go no farther than the door. One of their small number was always left behind to make sure she complied.

Haleine found it terribly amusing to think of Sarai's earlier posturing, trying to be so subtle in her attempt to turn Haleine toward returning to the fight, only to bar her charge from stepping foot outdoors. So carefully they guarded her, and though Haleine understood why, she suspected it was an effort wasted, for who would possibly care where she was or what she did there?

"Haleine," Faolan said.

She lifted her head to see him hovering in the opened doorway. Brighid stood behind him, looking uncertain for some unknown reason.

"Will you leave us, Brighid?" Haleine said. "Faolan will ensure that I do not endanger myself in any way."

Brighid curtsied. "Aye, your majesty."

She turned and walked away as Faolan came inside and landed on the table. Some time was spent studying one another, Haleine waiting for him to speak first.

"You look better than the last time I saw you," he said.

That was laughable. The last time they had occupied the same room, Haleine had been a ghost unable to sever the tether to her body, and Faolan had been the only one to notice.

"Should I be concerned about you endangering yourself?" he said.

She didn't respond to that, either. He didn't think her serious. The last time they were face to face, she had forced her memories into his mind, so he had seen all that she had done—drowning and bleeding and dying—but he did not understand it. Mayhap he lacked the ability.

"What are you doing here?" she asked. "What do you want of me now?"

"Only your continued recovery."

That made her smile. "I have no choice in that."

"That's not entirely true."

"What would you know of it?" Haleine shook her head. "Don't answer that."

She moved to the doorway but did not set a single toe beyond it. In the center of an empty paddock, Lucius gave the boy a swordplay lesson. Brighid sat on a stool in front of the cottage, and though Haleine could not see them, she felt the two unicorns standing guard in the forest.

"What of Mireille, Cate—whatever it is you call her," Haleine said, watching the lesson. "Did you take her back from my husband's soldiers?"

"Not yet."

"Why not?"

"There were complications."

Wasn't that always the way of it? Was there anything in the world that wasn't complicated?

"Where is she?" Haleine asked.

"On a ship bound for Mairéad. Omur is taking her there to keep her away from us."

"Will it work?" Haleine asked. "Will you be able to follow?"

"Dana and James are doing that now."

Haleine studied the sparring. Dana had gone to Tanuba? Why had he done such a thing? To prove something to her? To himself?

"Will they be able to recover her?" she asked.

"I don't know."

"Should you not be there with them?"

"No."

"Will they not require aid?"

"They're not alone. They have help."

"Whose?"

"A man named Idwal Kai," Faolan said. "He—"

"He served my father." Haleine looked at the pegasus. "How do you know him?"

"He was taken prisoner in the battle that...that killed your father."

"You take prisoners?"

"We did that time. We have since let them go."

Haleine nodded. "Why would my father's man agree to help you?"

"He wanted to keep his lord's daughters safe."

Daughters. Haleine shivered and wrapped her arms around her body. "Does he know who it is he chases?"

"Yes."

"How? Did you tell him?"

"We didn't have to. He already knew."

"How? How did he know? How did you know?" she asked. "How did everyone know I had a sister—a twin—but me?"

"Your parents thought she died when you were just an infant. Perhaps they never told you because it was too painful an admission," Faolan said. "If Idwal Kai has been in your father's household since your birth, he would have known about Mireille."

"You never spent a day in my father's household. How did you know?"

"Because I'm the one who took her."

Haleine was forced to look away again. Lucius was showing the boy how to block and attack, and she watched as she contemplated Faolan's confession. When they moved from instruction to practice, she went back to the table and sat.

"Explain."

"The dark gods sent their fiercest servants to steal Mireille from her cradle, but Laorans and I stopped them and hid her away to keep her safe from any future attempts," Faolan said. "You were the twin about whom I didn't know—not until Dana sent me to your side."

"How disappointing to discover you don't know everything after all," Haleine said. "With all your claims about my great and mysterious destiny, how did you not know about me?"

"I never spent a day in your father's household."

"But you took Mireille and allowed her to be raised by a stranger in some strange place in order to keep her from your enemy, to keep her safe."

"She wasn't a stranger, but yes," Faolan said. "Our aim was to protect Mireille."

"Why did you bring her back?" Haleine asked. "Was it because of me? Because I—you wanted her to take my place."

"Needed," Faolan corrected. "Not wanted."

Swords continued to clash outside, Lucius periodically shouting instruction. Haleine looked at her hands, one folded over the other.

"Before," she said, "before you told me that people thought she was me, and that they—*someone*—had given his life to protect her. Was that true?"

"Yes."

"What was Mireille doing when my husband's soldiers captured her?"

"Helping us," Faolan said. "We needed the aid of a nobleman, and she convinced him to provide it."

Who was this woman, and why did she help them? Why would she? It wasn't her land nor her people. This country, this strife, was nothing to Mireille, so why would she care? *How* could she care?

Why couldn't Haleine do the same? Was it perhaps like life? The only way to get past it was to do it? Could she pretend to care and find her way clear?

"I can't hide anymore," she said.

"Haleine?"

"I have been selfish, so selfish, and I didn't care. I still don't, not truly," she said, "but this stranger you call my sister has done what I was meant to do, what I once *wanted* to do. You brought her here for that purpose; you put her at risk because of me."

"Haleine, you—"

"I have to find a way to do this. I will find a way to do this. Somehow. I won't hide in this house any longer. I won't hide anywhere."

"I can protect you in this house," Faolan said. "Here, I can shield you. If you leave, and they're looking—"

"They're not," she said. "There's no one left to look."

"That may not be true."

She shrugged and moved to the door. "Let them come."

"Haleine, please—"

She ignored him as she walked outside and crossed the yard. Lucius and the boy stopped their play when she reached them. Lucius bowed, but the boy did not.

"Your majesty," Lucius said.

"I would have you teach me to fight," she said. "If you would."

Lucius smiled. "With pleasure, your majesty."

If Haleine believed there was no one left to look, she was mistaken. But Sighle had come to expect nothing else from her fiercely flawed sister.

It bothered her. Though their paths were not the same, and though Haleine's failure would only be Sighle's gain, Sighle remained irritated and angry at her sister's inability to thrive. How could she consider herself a Coileáin? Not once had Haleine called herself by her husband's name. Never Haleine Aelhaeran, always Haleine Coileáin. It should have been as such. Coileáin women did not need another's name, but Haleine could not be worthy of such a distinction now. She would crawl into the ground, into her lover's arms, and let the weight of it crush her. Mireille—who had never called herself Coileáin—was far more deserving of the name.

Would that change with Mireille's exposure to the Coileáin life? Some shift in demeanor would be expected, but when she saw all that her name could command, how far would she slide? Which way would she go? Would destiny be embraced at last, or would she, too, become something Sighle despised? Curiosity filled Sighle the way a rising sun infused darkness with light, bringing her to the point where she almost regretted not sailing to Mairéad herself.

But keeping her distance was better.

Now that Mireille was steadily moving farther away, Sighle could once again breathe—full, deep breaths that slowly expelled the poison in her blood with each push of her lungs and beat of her heart. Magic flowed freely in its place, unhampered, unchecked by Mireille's accidental interference, allowing Sighle to wander as she so desired.

As there was no one within the rebel camp who held Sighle's interest, she had entered the mind of the young common woman attending Haleine and listened to every word of her sister's discussion with the pegasus. Haleine claimed a desire to fight, but Sighle did not feel it. Haleine only acted as she thought she should, trying to remember how it was to want to be alive. Would she ever find her way?

Or would Sighle have to do it for her?

"My lady, are you all right?"

Bronagh. Yes, gone were the toxins, but Mireille had left behind two shadows in their place—Haleine's maid and the boy guard—and Sighle had not yet been able to touch their minds. She had been trying since their first appearance in her chamber, meaning to turn them away, but found that her commands merely rolled off them like water on an oiled cloth. They would not leave her alone; they would not be ignored. What Mireille had said or done to make this feasible, Sighle could not guess nor counter. Until she could, she was resigned to having two unshakable chaperones.

The maid spoke again, and Sighle extricated herself from her host. When she had settled back into her own body on her own bed, she opened her eyes to look at the maid hovering over her.

"Are you ill, my lady?" Bronagh asked. "You've not moved in quite some time."

Yes, she would know that. Never before had Sighle been watched so closely as she was now. Bronagh had hardly left the room, sending Nonna to fetch what was wanted or needed. She slept on the floor, waking at every small sound. When she was awake, she stared, stared, stared, marking each move Sighle made, and apparently noting any she didn't make. If Bronagh had given Haleine this sort of attention, the princes might never have been born.

"I'm not ill," Sighle said.

She curled onto her side and looked at the guard, Fionnbar, standing by the door. Before Mireille, he would have fallen upon his sword if Sighle had requested it. Now if such a demand were made, he would simply ignore it, dismissing her as a child making empty threats during the midst of a tantrum.

That's what they thought she was—no longer the child in mourning, to be coddled and pitied, but rather a foolish girl who knew not what she did.

"You don't need to stay here," Sighle said. "I can care for myself."

"No one suggested otherwise, my lady, but your sister—the queen—commanded it," the maid replied. "She wants you taken care of. Protected."

Mireille had told Bronagh about Omur, and Sighle's dalliance with him. The maid's horror at what Sighle had done—and who she had done it with—almost made Sighle laugh, but she turned it into petulance.

"She wants me locked away and hidden."

"She wants you to be safe."

Safe for now, perhaps, but that would come to an end. Sighle had seen it, felt it. Fire and ash, and she would burn because Mireille desired it.

"Until she kills me," Sighle murmured.

Bronagh looked up. "Did you say something, my lady?"

Sighle closed her eyes and felt her body disintegrate. "No."

ChApTER 23

There was truly no hell greater than sailing. James had spent days thinking that if he managed to survive the voyage and set foot on Tanubian soil, he might never leave. He would never doubt again that he was meant to be a farmer and that his feet were meant to stand on the ground.

When he wasn't vomiting over the ship's side, he worked, trying to complete the job of two men so that Dana—who could not manage after all—would not be tossed overboard. Scrubbing, hauling, dumping, fetching, raising and lowering the sails, and even taking his turn on the oars when the wind disappeared. It was miserable work, all of it, and kept him on his feet from first light to last, and occasionally through the night as well, but it was a better way to pass the time than sitting, waiting, and worrying.

When the opportunity to rest did arise, and the weather wasn't too wretched, he chose to stay on deck. The crew's quarters were cramped, dark, and putrid. Sitting on the deck, wrapped in his cloak and counting stars was a vastly preferred option.

But that night, James stood on deck and looked at Odhran. He'd never seen a village from this side before. Should he dare hope that a voyage home would be the last time he would ever have to endure that sight?

With no answer available to him, James went below deck. The weather was fair and the cabin mostly empty, but Dana slept in one of the lower hammocks near the entrance. Any others in the room were at the opposite end, Dana's continued sickness guaranteeing their privacy. James grabbed the hammock's side and pulled it down until Dana tumbled onto the floor. Dana groaned loudly and slowly pushed himself up.

"Come on," James said. "We're leaving."

"Are we there?" Dana asked.

"No, I just thought we might swim the rest of the way."

"What?"

"Aye, we're there." James picked up Dana's pack and sword. "Come on. I want to get off the ship before anyone notices we're gone."

Dana nodded and started to get to his feet. He needed the help of both the hammock and the wall to accomplish it. Why hadn't he left Dana behind? Why hadn't he let the sailors throw him overboard? Surely Dana would be no help at all in getting Cate back. He'd do nothing but slow down James's own efforts. But it also remained true that, at present, Dana was the only source of aid that James had, so he walked out of the crew's quarters without further comment.

"James," Dana said when they were both on deck. He was pale in the moonlight, but it was more color than he had had in days. "Wait."

"If you're going to vomit again, please aim for the ocean," James said. "I just swabbed the deck."

Dana smiled. "I don't think I have anything left in me to vomit."

"Wait a bit. I'm sure you'll find something."

"There's no need to sneak away," Dana said. "It could be more suspicious if we do."

"Then it's a good thing they don't know anything about us, isn't it?" James said. "Where does their participation end? We ask them to help us find our way to Mairéad? We tell them we're going to the palace to kidnap the queen of Lira? No, I don't care if you don't think there's a need or not; I don't want to involve them anymore."

"All right."

"I've half a mind to leave you here."

"Only half?" Dana asked. "That's better than I was expecting."

James shoved Dana against the rail. "Shut up," he said. "I don't want to hear anything out of you. We will do this my way, and if you again question anything I say—any decision I make—I will leave you behind. I will throw you to the bloody wolves and let you die."

Dana eased free of James's hold and gestured to Odhran. "Lead the way."

James got them off the ship without being seen, and they took their first steps on Tanubian soil. He followed the stone-paved street, lingering on the edge of shadow, as he moved deeper into the town. He had no more bearings here than he did on the sea. That was the first thing to be done. Work out where they were, and how they would get to Mairéad.

He paused at a corner to examine the three possible paths open to him. There was nothing but cobblestones and darkness on his left and in front of him, but to the right was a wooden sign moving slightly in the ocean breeze. The lanterns hanging on either side of the door allowed him to read the words *The Thirsty Whale*.

A tavern. There were worse places to start, he supposed.

"Here," he said, pulling Dana along. "In here."

James chose a table in the corner, and they sat with their backs to the wall. Dana put his head on the table and promptly fell asleep while one of the serving girls came toward them. She was a young, full-figured lass with dark hair tied back with a red scarf. She stopped in front of them and put her hands on her hips.

"Best cover up those swords," she said. "People are nervous, and seeing strangers with weapons only makes it worse."

James adjusted his cloak to cover his sword and did the same with Dana's. "Thank you."

"You're new here. From Lira?"

"What makes you say that?"

"You have this…war-weary look about you that I've seen on some other Lirans that have stumbled through here," she said. "So? That you? Just off the boat? Looking for a new beginning?"

James nodded. "Something like that."

"I wager you're fighters," the girl said. "With swords like those, I don't figure you for farmers."

James smiled. "I was once."

"What changed?"

"Everything."

"Are you any good?" she asked. "Fighting, I mean. Not farming."

"Haven't died yet."

"I suppose that's something." She pointed over her shoulder. "Do you see that man over there?"

James looked around her to see a lone man at the bar, a pint of ale in front of him.

"Name's Rowan," she said, "and he's the captain of the queen's guard. They're always looking for experienced men, and if you're as good at not dying as you claim to be, he might take you on."

James looked at Rowan again. "The queen's guard?"

"Aye. At the palace in Mairéad. Maybe you don't know, but it's not far from here and—"

"No, that would be—that would be very good luck indeed," James said. "It's been so long since…Thank you. I—I'm sorry, I don't know your name."

"Cailean," she said. "Now, what will you have?"

He needed a moment to realize what she was asking. "Oh, we haven't any money. We had to work for our passage just to get here."

"I know."

"Then why—?"

"If you're going to see Rowan about work, you'll want to have eaten first. There's also a water barrel out back. You should use it to wash so you don't smell like you've been on a ship for more than a week, and if possible, you should shave. Especially your friend. Is he all right?"

James looked at Dana. "He's been ill. The journey's been hard."

Cailean nodded. "I'll bring him something that'll help."

"I will repay your kindness," James said. "Somehow, I will do that."

"Don't worry about it," she said. "New beginnings are expensive, and I'm all right. Besides, I'm going to tell Rowan about you, and if he takes you on, he'll pay me more than I'll be out tonight."

"You don't know us. Why take the risk?"

Cailean shrugged. "You have an honest face. Whoever you are."

"James," he said. "My name is James."

"It's a pleasure to meet you, James the Farmer," she said. "I'll be back in a moment, aye?"

He nodded and watched her go. When she was far enough away that she wouldn't hear him, he laughed. Surely this small change of fortune should be questioned.

"Palace guards?" Dana said. He had turned his head, but his voice was muffled by his arm.

James continued to watch Cailean and Rowan. "You're awake."

"I was never asleep," Dana said. "You mean for us to become palace guards?"

"I intend for me to do that. You'd have to be able to hold your head up first," James said. "But it would be a bloody good plan. Access, weapons. No one in the palace will know who we are; it should—"

"Revelin," Dana muttered.

"What about the prince?"

"Revelin's seen me."

"When? How?"

"Two months ago? Maybe three? I don't...It was after the children were born, and I went to—to see her. He was there, and we...He saw me."

"Are you sure?"

Dana coughed. "He had his sword at my throat. I'm sure."

"Bloody hell, Dana."

"But your plan is good; it's still good," Dana said. "Revelin wouldn't be involved in the acquiring of palace guards. We'll get in; we'll avoid him. It'll work."

"Or I get in, avoid him—though I won't have to because he's never held a bloody sword to my throat—and you stay here. Or, better yet, go back to Lira."

"You could do that, too," Dana said. "For how long will you hate me, James?"

James sat back and shook his head. "I don't know."

Dana straightened. "You told her you were a farmer."

"Was I wrong? That's what my family's always done. It's what they do now—what's left of them."

"You never wanted that life."

"Maybe not," James said, "but after everything that's happened, after what I've seen and done, after seeing you like this, after Cate...I'll gladly take farming." James sighed. "Why don't you go wash and shave—if you can manage to do it without drowning or slitting your throat."

"I'll do my best," Dana said after a moment.

He left the table and worked his way to the back. Cailean reappeared, caught his elbow, and led Dana through a door. When Cailean returned to the barroom, she came toward James bearing two trenchers piled with food. She set one serving in front of him.

"Your friend is in terrible shape," she said. "Or is he your brother?"

James glanced at the door again. "Neither."

———❧———

Revelin stood against the wall in his mother's bedchamber, watching the physician tend to his charge. Though nearly three weeks had passed since the queen of Tanuba had fallen ill, no reason for it had been discovered. Physicians from all over the country had been summoned to make their own examinations and offer their own thoughts on this puzzle. Revelin had lost track of the number of theories posed to him, but not one suggested the possibility of poison. Neither had Cathal uncovered any such evidence, leaving Revelin to speculate whether his instincts were to be trusted at all.

As Revelin pondered this, Eamonn slipped into the room. Haraszty's youngest son was seventeen now and had lost the look of a child he had held just the year before. Tall and lean with the Maoilriain features all three brothers shared, he always had been even-tempered and jovial. The cheerfulness had started to fade after their father's assassination; what remained evaporated more each day his mother's illness lingered.

Eamonn glanced at Haraszty before joining Revelin. "How long can she stay like this?"

Revelin shook his head. "I do not know."

"It can't be much longer, can it? Look at her. She's..."

"Strong," Revelin said. "Our mother is strong and stubborn. She will survive this."

She had to. Revelin could not allow Zoltano to claim the throne. That would only end in disaster for the entire country, but if Haraszty died, Revelin did not know what he would do.

"We don't even know what ails her," Eamonn said.

"We will."

The door opened again. Darragh stepped inside and nodded to Revelin, a signal that Cathal waited at the Coileáin estate. Would he have anything new to report this time?

"I need to go," Revelin said to his brother. "Will you stay here and—?"

"Yes," Eamonn said. "I'll stay with her."

Revelin followed Darragh out of the queen's chambers. They didn't speak as they passed through the palace to the courtyard where a lone carriage waited. Two men sat on the drivers' bench, and two guards stood on the platform at the rear. None of them acknowledged Revelin as he climbed inside. Darragh closed the door, and the carriage started its journey, trading the protective palace walls for the exposure of the city.

"Your highness."

Revelin's head snapped to the left, and he saw a hooded man sitting in the opposite corner. The man pushed back his hood, allowing Revelin to see his face. Reamann Einar.

"Stop the carriage!" Revelin shouted, but they rambled on. "I said, stop!"

"They heard you," Einar said. "But they're not your men, you see, so they've ignored you."

Revelin forced himself to take a calming breath, then another when the first proved to be insufficient. "What is your purpose here? Do you mean to take me hostage?"

Einar laughed. "Why bother? Who do you suppose would ransom you?"

A harsh truth, to be sure. Revelin swallowed his irritation and glanced out the window again. They did not appear to have changed course.

"Why are you here?" he asked, looking back at the Quatari.

Einar reached inside his cloak and removed a folded piece of parchment bearing Revelin's seal. "You sent me an invitation."

"I sent you a warning."

"Now I seek to return the favor."

"Of what could you possibly need to warn me?"

"The Black Wolf has crossed into your lands. Into this very city."

"The Black Wolf?" Revelin said. "The mercenary?"

"Do you know of another Black Wolf?"

No, Revelin did not. Cold broke in his head and trickled down his spine, spreading through his veins. "Even if I could believe anything you have to say, why should I care where he is or what he does there?"

"Given the man's penchant for sowing discord and political unrest everywhere he goes, I thought you might be interested." Einar shrugged. "But I'm sure he's only in Mairéad for the view."

"Is he here because you sent him?"

"I haven't any interest in your country, so long as you continue to refrain from spilling onto my side of the border," Einar said. "But I can think of someone who has great interest in who wears Tanuba's crown."

Zoltano. Always Zoltano.

"My brother wants Quatara."

"Not as much as he desires his birthright," Einar said. "He hasn't so much as looked at our borders since your dear mother fell ill."

According to Adomnan Cathal, Zoltano hadn't done much else, either. Revelin couldn't determine his brother's game. The goal was to rule—what else would it be?—but the methods used thus far were nothing but disjointed madness.

Revelin sighed. "So you rush here to bring this news to me."

"Would you have trusted one of my messengers?"

"No. But neither do I trust you."

"Don't," Einar said. "I'm certain the rabid dog you now travel to meet will tell you the same. Eventually."

Apart from Darragh and the servants at the Coileáin estate, no one was supposed to know about Revelin's meetings with Cathal. Even the men who accompanied Revelin to and from Darian's home thought their prince did nothing more than oversee the estate's management in Haleine's absence.

"You know far more than you should," Revelin commented.

Einar smiled. "I do, don't I?"

Nothing to be done there. At least not yet. He would have Darragh, or perhaps Cathal, make some sort of investigation into that as well. From where and whom was a Quatari rebel's information coming?

"Rabid dog?" Revelin said.

Einar's relaxed posture changed. "I've not forgotten what your father and his army did to my people and my lands."

"Then why warn me of anything?"

"I like your mother on the throne. She makes life…simpler. I wish her a long and prosperous reign."

"Is that so?"

"It is," Einar said. "Though I suppose I could tolerate you wearing the crown. A man so honorable he won't lay claim to the throne, even to the detriment of his country? That is a man I want on the other side of my border."

"It is not mine to claim."

"Neither did Quatara belong to your father," Einar said. "That did not stop him."

"You have it back now."

"Yes, I do, and I wish for it to remain that way." The carriage slowed, and Einar glanced out the window. "We appear to have reached your destination, your highness. I trust you can make other arrangements for your return to the palace."

"Are you stealing my carriage?"

"I know I have done you a great service, but do try to remember that I am an outlaw here," Einar said. "I wouldn't be able to live with myself if I didn't steal your carriage."

Revelin smiled. "We would not want that."

"I'm happy we agree."

Revelin laughed. "There is nothing upon which we agree."

"Neither of us wants your brother on Tanuba's throne," Einar said. The carriage door opened, and he gestured to it. "Your highness."

Revelin slid from the carriage and stood outside the manor, watching the Quatari men depart with their prize. After they had disappeared from view, Revelin remained still as he contemplated what had been said and the possible implications. He stayed so long that some servant must have told Cathal, for the nobleman joined him outside.

"Your highness?" Cathal said. "What are you doing?"

Revelin shook his head. "I do not know."

—◈◈◈—

Cate hated boats. Canoes, kayaks, row boats, motor boats, sail boats, paddle boats, lobster boats, pontoon boats, yachts, ocean liners, those big cargo barges—she hated them all. Even the little swan boats in Boston's Public Garden. It didn't matter that she'd never set foot on the vast majority of them; she hated them just the same. There was something about being at the mercy of a thin barrier that could give way and send her plunging without warning into a dark, watery abyss filled with things that might want to eat her that simply did not appeal to her. Okay—so maybe that didn't apply as much to the swan boats, but still, she hated them.

Which made her current circumstances all the more shitty because she was on a boat in the middle of the deep blue sea. Or maybe it was a ship. She wasn't sure what the difference was between the two. Maybe there was no difference. She could swear like a sailor, but that's where the similarities ended.

The vessel on which she had been a passenger for days now was large and wooden with three thick masts, each boasting a set of white sails. A blue flag with a silver unicorn in its center flew from their pinnacles. She'd seen the same thing in the palace and figured it was the Liran crest.

Tapestries with the same design also hung in the cabin to which she had been assigned. Despite the three windows, the room was dark and cramped, but was probably real luxury as far as medieval-esque sailing accommodations were concerned. There was a bed large enough for two against the wall, as well as a table and two chairs nailed to the floor. She hated to see furniture nailed to the floor. It only acted as a portend of what could come once they were out on the open water.

Fortunately, it hadn't been too much of an issue thus far. There had been one night of rough seas, which had seen an unprepared Cate tossed around the room like a rag doll until she crammed herself in a corner, braced between the walls and the bed. She had stayed there until the storm passed and hadn't strayed too far from that spot since. She sat either there or on the bed, clutching the pot in which she was meant to piss and puke.

Cate was starting to miss the dungeon. But not terribly so.

And though she had been ill more days than not, it wasn't like being on a wooden deathtrap surrounded by miles and miles of shark-infested salt water was completely without benefits. The food was surprisingly decent, the women sent to wait on her were discreet and not interested in conversation of any kind, and there was a refreshing lack of guards. Not only that, but she hadn't seen Maddox since they boarded the ship back in Lira. She didn't know where Omur had stashed him but supposed a box lacking air holes would be asking too much.

Omur himself dropped by at least once a day to make sure she hadn't jumped ship and to say something rude or sarcastic before storming out again. He hadn't forgotten nor forgiven her assault on his person, but neither had she forgotten nor forgiven the reason she had done it.

The seventh morning of a journey she feared would never end, Cate sat upon her bed, waiting for a giant tidal wave to come and flip the boat over, when Omur entered. Neither of them said anything at first, she looking at him with suspicion, him looking at her as though she were the most pitiful thing he had ever seen. Which, at the moment, she likely was.

"Your maids tell me you've not been eating much," he said.

Cate shrugged. "You throw up less that way. Of course, as it turns out, you dry heave more, but there's always a trade-off, right?"

He surveyed the cabin with one long look. "Come."

She raised an eyebrow. "I'm good, thanks."

"You mistake this as a choice."

"Thought you were all about giving me choice. Giving me control," she said. "That was you, wasn't it? Or is there some other megalomaniac running around trying to recruit me for his evil plan to take over the world?"

"Come."

"Is the boat sinking?"

"No."

"Then I'm staying here," she said. "Unless you come up with an equally good reason why I shouldn't."

Omur raised his eyebrow. "You agreed to this."

"I agreed to this trip," she said. "Not to sunrise walks on the lido deck."

"I thought we might talk," he said. "But I'll not do it in this dank room."

Cate felt suddenly defensive. "Hey, you're the one who stuck me in here."

"You're the one who turned it into a prison," Omur said. "Come."

She smiled and slid off the bed. "Well, since you asked so nicely."

She followed Omur out of the cabin and above deck. The sun was much brighter without filthy windows to filter it. Cate used her hand to shade her eyes and trailed behind Omur as he walked across the deck to the bow of the ship. When he stopped at the rail, she stood beside him and took in the view. For days, her windows had offered her nothing but water. Now there was the promise of land—a thin, dark strip breaking up that endless blue. Seeing it nearly made her laugh in relief.

"Is that where we're headed?" she asked.

"Yes."

"When will we reach it? Will it be soon?"

Omur glanced at her. "Your twin wasn't afraid of sailing."

Her twin was also obsessed with killing herself, so Cate didn't consider Haleine to be the best role model ever.

"But," Omur continued, "I don't suppose it does her much good wherever she is now."

"If you dragged me out here to talk about Haleine, I'm going back inside."

"What is it that frightens you?"

Shit, what *didn't* frighten her? She gripped the rail and cautiously peered over the edge.

"Is it drowning? Do you fear that?"

"No, I hear drowning's a lovely way to go. Why would I fear that?"

"Is it the waves? Are they making you ill?" Omur said. "If they bother you, command them to stop."

"I can't stop the waves from doing anything."

"You stopped the boy from killing you."

"Allegedly and accidentally stopped the boy from killing me," Cate corrected. "I still have no idea how it was done, or even if I did it at all. But if I did somehow work that hocus pocus, it's a far cry from commanding the damn ocean to calm its ass down. *That's* a force of nature, and—"

"*You* are a force of nature," Omur said. "Bending the ocean to your will shall only be the beginning of what you can do. It is my belief that your powers

will be near limitless. You were born with this magic; it runs in your blood—
it *is* your blood—and so long as you have a single drop remaining in your
veins, you will possess that power."

"How are you so sure? Were you born with it?"

"No. My skill was a gift from the lords I serve."

"A gift, huh? What was *that* party like?"

Omur's face darkened. "That is something I shall not divulge to you."

"Shy?"

"No."

"Okay, then, tell me about this supposed magic. Dazzle me."

"Tell you about it," Omur said faintly. "In what sort of world did the
goddess place you that you would make such a request? You ask me for something I cannot give. You desire a history of magic, as though it were something
that could be accounted for by days and years, as though it has not been here
longer than the world itself."

"Is that possible?"

"From what, do you suppose, was this world and the one from which
you came created?"

"Layers of rock. Lots of carbon and whatever-based life form you
happen to be," Cate said. "Is there some kind of asshole element on this side
of the portal? I ask because you and your pet monkey seem to have it in
spades."

Omur looked at her blankly.

"I don't require a history of magic. I don't give a shit about days or years
or whatever reverence you think pulling a rabbit out of a hat deserves," she
said. "What I *do* care about is understanding how I stopped in his tracks a
man intent on murdering me. So stop with your goddamn rhapsodizing already, and give me an answer to my question."

Omur looked over the rail. He was silent for so long, Cate assumed he
wasn't going to say anything else. She had turned to leave when he spoke
again.

"You have seen my scars, I trust."

"You mean with my two working eyes? Yeah, I've seen them."

"They were a gift from your sister, though I do not know if she was ever
aware of what she had done," Omur said. "She was so blind with fury and
fear that it would not surprise me if she saw nothing else."

"What had you done to her?"

"I held her by the throat against a wall, intending to choke the life from
her, and threatened the lives of her bastard lover and their bastard boys,"
Omur said. "Her blood boiled, she struck me—a slap across the face—and
my flesh burned as your sister walked away. I had never been hurt like that
before; I hadn't realized that I could be."

"So, in the dungeon, when you touched my stomach…"

"An experiment. A failed one."

"You thought you would burn me."

"I thought I might, yes."

"And you couldn't because you weren't afraid or angry enough?"

"Perhaps."

"But you don't think so."

"No."

Cate nodded. "What about the stunt with Fionnbar? What was that? Another experiment?"

"A much more successful one."

"Did you think I would burn him?"

"I didn't know what you would do. Burn him, kill him—I didn't care what happened to the boy; I didn't care what you did. I only wished to learn what it would be."

"I stopped him."

"I saw."

"I told him to stop, and he did."

"Yes, with my two working eyes, I saw this."

Cate folded her arms across her chest. "You're a real bastard, you know that?"

"That has never been proven."

"Whatever," she said. "Are you disappointed that I didn't do anything more violent?"

Omur smiled. "That will come, I think, in time."

"Why do you think that?"

He laughed. "Because that is who you are, my lady. It does not matter who or what opposes you, you fight. You always fight. Your body craves it; your soul demands it, and so you battle every single living soul you encounter."

That was a lie. It might have been true if one only considered her time in Lira and on this damn boat—and given those circumstances, why shouldn't it have been true?—but it hadn't been true in Boston. She hadn't fought with Laura. She hadn't fought with Fiona or Daniel, either. At least not until Laura lost her fight to stay.

If she had fought to stay.

"I also include yourself in that number," Omur said. "You fight against yourself most of all."

"Maybe not *most*," she offered.

"When those men died in the throne room, you delighted in it. You denied it then, and you'll do so now, but I know what I saw—what I *felt*. I do not lie when I claim you are a force of nature. You do yourself a disservice ignoring that which is so obviously plain," Omur said. "You may not have been raised to believe such a thing, but there is a darkness inside you, and when you do stop fighting yourself—when you do accept this truth—you will be unstoppable. I believe that now more than ever. You can master the waves and make the ocean as smooth as glass. You can move the tallest of mountains with your mind. If you so desired, you could pull the moon down from the night sky and turn it to dust with your bare hands."

Damn. That was one hell of a sales pitch.

"You want me to do all those things? Like, literally, control the ocean, move mountains—destroy the moon?" she asked, feeling idiotic to be saying it out loud. Could he be more of a cartoon villain?

"Some more than others."

"Why?"

"It's what my lords want. It's what they want you to give them."

"What will they give me in return?"

"What won't they give you?"

What would be left? Screwing with nature—with the *world*—in the manner in which Omur had described would be more than detrimental. The endgame would have to be nothing but destruction. What would his lords do with the ashes?

Did she honestly care?

"Will they let me go home?" she asked.

Omur gestured to the strip of land. "There is your home. You will find all you seek there—the truth of your past and your destiny."

"I don't believe in destiny," she said.

It was her Pavlovian response to the suggestion that her future was predetermined by something or someone other than herself. But the longer she remained in this world, being attacked on all sides by beings who claimed her destiny was to help and serve their particular cause, the more she had to wonder if it wouldn't be easier to have that be true. There might be less fighting that way.

She sighed. "Is this a ship or a boat?"

Omur appeared surprised by her change of topic. "Both, I suppose. Does it matter?"

Cate looked from the devil to the deep blue sea and the unknown looming ahead. She shook her head. "Nothing ever does."

Chapter 24

The palace in Mairéad was a thing of beauty. Polished, gleaming white stone walls and towers, golden gates made to look like walls of ivy—it was pure art. At first glance, it appeared to serve a decorative purpose only, while offering nothing in the way of protection to those who lived there.

However, the yard in which Dana, James, and the six others vying for a position in the queen's guard stood claimed the opposite. The rock walls here were a dull gray, and a line of iron pikes bearing heads in various stages of decay ran along the top. Dana scratched at his beard as he imagined who they had been and what crimes they might have committed.

He didn't like the beard. Dana had tried to keep his hair short and his face clean-shaven. Better in a fight, that way—nothing for an opponent to grab hold of. He'd done it to others and had no desire to have the same done to him, but as there were those in Mairéad who wanted him dead as much as Maddox or Omur, the beard—despite the possibility that it would make no difference—became an easy precaution to take.

The tavern girl James had befriended had taken pity upon Dana and helped when his shaky hands had proved too incapable to complete the task on their own. When he wouldn't allow her to cut his hair short, nor shave him, she settled for making him appear neat and deliberate, rather than an unmitigated mess. James had only shrugged upon seeing the transformation, but Dana maintained hope it would effectively conceal his identity to any who might recognize him.

Rowan, the captain of the queen's guard, did not. He walked the line of eight men seeking to secure a post and examined each of them closely. One man was forced out immediately. James had received an approving nod—a result of their conversation the night before, Dana supposed—but Rowan stopped and frowned at Dana.

"Tell me," the captain said, "out of which gutter in our fair city did you drag yourself?"

"None," Dana answered. "I am not from the city."

"From where do you hail? We don't trust the welfare and protection of the royal family to just anyone."

Dana was well aware of that already, having encountered Darian Coileáin once. But he couldn't very well tell that to the man standing in front of him.

"I should hope not," he said. "Should you allow me the opportunity, I will prove myself."

"A bold gutter rat. The very worst kind." Rowan stepped back and folded his large arms across his chest. He took a harder look at Dana—which Dana returned—and pointed to a wooden platform at the other end of the yard. "That's where we hang or behead thieves and rogues and men who over-reach. Fail this test, and I'll see the same done to you."

"Will you hang or behead me?"

"Both."

Dana nodded. "What's life without stakes?"

"Let's see if you feel that way when the noose is around your neck." Rowan turned his head and shouted, "Otto!"

A mountain of a man stepped into the yard and lumbered toward them. His head was bald, and his arms were bare apart from leather cuffs on each wrist. His mammoth chest was covered by a leather jerkin, and a broadsword hung at his side. If he had a weakness, it would have been his limited mobility and lack of speed. Dana was quick—or he had been in another lifetime when his head didn't endlessly pound and his hands didn't shake while his stomach continuously flipped end over end. In that lifetime, he could have dispatched Otto with little trouble.

But now—whoever, whatever he was—he wasn't sure. Beside him, James swore under his breath. He didn't think Dana could do this. What was unclear was whether James would later thank Otto for his efforts.

"Best Otto, and I'll give you a post," Rowan said. "Lose, and I'll see your corpse returned to the sewer."

"What of my head? Another trophy for your wall?"

Rowan smiled. "Scraps for the pigs."

"Fair enough," Dana said. "When do we be—?"

Otto's fist landed squarely in the center of Dana's face, sending him sprawling to the ground. He closed his eyes and gritted his teeth as his aching head flooded with fresh pain. James swore again, louder this time, but in a tone which suggested that Dana was on his own in this. Rowan wasn't the only one who wanted proof of his abilities.

"Don't kill him," Rowan called as Otto picked up Dana and slammed him against the nearest wall.

"I'll try not to," Dana gasped.

Rowan laughed. "I wasn't talking to you."

Otto relaxed his hold only to slam Dana against the wall again. This time, one meaty arm came across his throat, cutting off Dana's ability to breathe. The giant grinned, revealing a mouth of broken or missing teeth. Dana flailed, slid into blackness once, twice, before he fought his way out of it. His head swam worse than ever, unconsciousness threatening to take him, but he pushed against it and forced it back. He had to stay here; he had to best Otto. James expected failure, and Dana couldn't give it to him.

The first step was staying conscious. The second step would be freeing himself. Dana gripped Otto's arms to steady himself, then drove his thumbs into the man's eyes. Howling, Otto dropped Dana on the ground.

Next step: end this quickly. He could never manage an extended bout. Dana stood, drawing his sword before throwing himself at his opponent. After an elbow to the gut and a hilt to the face, the big man staggered back a few steps, and Dana kicked his stomach to bring him down. Dana advanced, placing the tip of the sword at Otto's throat.

The yard was dead silent until Rowan spoke.

"Don't kill him."

Dana waited a moment more before lowering the sword. He offered Otto his free hand and struggled to help him stand. When both men were again on their feet, they looked at the captain of the queen's guard.

"That'll do," Rowan said, a begrudging smile on his face.

Dana looked at James next. There was no smile.

—◊◊◊—

The sun was setting when the ship—boat?—finally arrived at its destination. Cate had spent the day on the bow, watching their progress, but once the vessel had docked, her handmaidens brought her to her cabin. They helped her wash as best one could in a tiny basin, and then dress to impress whoever lived on this side of the ocean.

When she was deemed ready, Cate was escorted from the ship to a carriage where both Omur and Maddox—still looking a little worse for wear—were waiting. The three of them rode in silence through the port town and the winding incline of a road that led to a walled city untouched by the fighting and poverty that accompanied war. Impoverished, they were not.

When the carriage arrived at the palace, Maddox departed first. Omur motioned that Cate should follow, and she slid out cautiously. Coming toward them was a young man who would have been handsome if not for the air of arrogance and the scent of crazy coming off him in waves.

"Zoltano!" Maddox cried. "I didn't know you'd be here!"

"I had to come back," the young man said. "This place hasn't seen a decent party since I left."

Maddox and Zoltano embraced briefly and slapped each other on the back. Cate took their evident fondness for each other to mean that she would find Zoltano about as appealing as a rabid opossum.

The rabid opossum politely greeted her as Haleine and ignored Omur completely. That made Cate smile, and with a spring in her step, she followed Beavis and Butthead into the palace. As the two men carried on a lovely conversation about great breasts they had known, Cate took note of guards and possible exits. There were all too many of the former and a severe lack of the latter.

The small procession ended in a large and lavish room filled with people in the midst of a serious party. At the far end of the room were two elaborate golden chairs upon which sat two bare-breasted women. Zoltano and Maddox headed in their direction. Other girls gone wild populated the room, dancing, flirting, and fucking their partners. Alcohol appeared to flow freely while music played. Cate wasn't a stranger to Boston's nightlife, but she had never been anywhere like this.

"Was Caligula the party planner?" she asked Omur.

"Who?"

"No one," she said. "What the hell am I supposed to do here?"

"Enjoy yourself?" Omur stopped a passing servant and took two goblets from the tray he carried.

"You want me to participate in...that?"

Omur handed her a goblet. "You may find it instructive."

"More like repulsive."

He shrugged. "Either way."

He walked away, immersing himself into the celebration and giving off no indication that he was an evil bastard hell-bent upon destroying the world. Cate sniffed the contents of her cup. Wine. She considered dumping it, but after another look at the bedlam surrounding her, she not only kept the goblet but took a tentative sip of the dark liquid inside.

"Your majesty."

Cate choked, and the goblet was removed from her hand. Inquiries as to her well-being followed, and she made a half-hearted effort to wave them off. As soon as she could breathe again, she looked at the brown-haired man who had spoken to her.

He was the average sort, someone who wouldn't stand out in a crowd, someone whose face one would forget almost as soon as it was seen. His clothing was nice, but not fancy, so while he wasn't a complete nothing, neither was he someone at the top of the food chain.

"I apologize, your majesty," he said. "I never intended to startle you in such a manner."

"Oh?" she responded, automatically employing Haleine's accent. "How did you intend to startle me?"

The man laughed, and Cate's stomach twisted. Before falling into Wonderland, Cate had never put much store in the concept of a sixth sense. Sometimes, though, she would encounter another person who made her hackles stand on edge. That sixth sense she didn't believe in would go off like an air raid siren, and Cate would put as much distance as she could between them.

But now that she had fallen through the rabbit hole to a world where magic was somehow a very real factor in her life, she found she needed to revise her thoughts on the sixth sense.

Because whether it was magic or just her gut, the alarms were going off now. More so than when she had met Omur or his pet boy. It led her to a singular conclusion: this man—whoever he may have been—was not a good guy. Other people might not remember his face, but Cate wasn't likely to forget it.

He bowed, being careful not to spill the contents of the cup he held. "Forgive me, your majesty. I wanted only to welcome you to court and tell you how glad it makes my heart to see you again."

Creepy. Cate managed a smile and took the goblet back. "How nice."

She spotted an empty bench in a relatively empty corner and abandoned the glad-hearted man to claim it. Poor manners, perhaps, but she was an acting queen, and he was not, which meant he would have to deal with it and later thank her for her graciousness.

She sat rigidly on the bench, sipping wine while watching Maddox and Zoltano fondle their admirers. Maybe it would be worth tapping into the so-called malicious darkness Omur claimed was inside her if it meant she could eviscerate those two using nothing but the powers of her mind.

A black-haired woman wearing more jewels than Cate had ever seen in her entire life sat next to her and said, "They're disgusting, aren't they?"

Cate smiled politely, but neither agreed nor disagreed with her statement. The spectacle before her was disgusting and degrading and all kinds of other things, but as she didn't know the identity of the woman beside her, it was best not to offer any potentially harmful opinions on anything.

"Zaide Romanza," the woman said next.

"What?"

"That is my name. Zaide Romanza Brollachan. I am the queen of Feond, the country which borders Lira."

Feond. Had James mentioned that before? Cate scanned her memory banks for any previous mention of Zaide Romanza but couldn't come up with one. "I know who you are," she replied anyway.

Zaide Romanza smiled. "You don't, but that's all right, Mireille. I'll never tell."

Cate glanced down. Was she wearing a nametag? "I think you may have me confused with someone else."

"I don't. I know well who you are, and I have waited for so very long for this chance to speak with you," Zaide Romanza said. "For this chance to merely sit in your presence."

Cate stared at her new stalker. "I'm definitely not who you think I am."

Zaide Romanza nodded. "He said you've been resisting."

"Who?"

"Our mutual friend."

"I doubt we have any friends in common."

"Acquaintance, then."

Omur, maybe? Cate looked over the crowd until she found him staring back at her. He raised his goblet in acknowledgement. Cate was tempted to flip him off in return but restrained herself.

"That's still too friendly a term for him," she said, losing the accent.

"I feared he might be making a mess of your recruitment," Zaide Romanza said. "I should have intervened sooner."

"Or not bothered at all. Leaving me alone would have been a perfectly valid option."

"Not for us. One day you will understand that, and when you do, you shall thank us for our persistence."

"I wouldn't count on that."

"He clings to his grand plans and his vision for the future. He's so focused on what our lords want that it does not occur to him to start somewhere smaller." Zaide Romanza held her palm over the flickering flame of a nearby candle before twisting her wrist and scooping the flame into her hand. She held it in front of Cate, who stared at it in a mixture of fear and fascination. "After all, it takes a single spark to start a fire of any size, does it not?"

"Neat trick," Cate said.

"It's not a trick." Zaide Romanza closed her hand and extinguished the flame. When she opened her hand again, the flesh was undamaged. "Neither is our proposal. There are grand plans; they do involve you, and we will be relentless in our pursuit of you. But what we will give you in return will far outweigh any annoyance you have endured thus far. I promise you that."

Doubtful. Cate looked away and caught sight of her brown-haired friend from before standing at Zoltano's side, bent at the waist in order to hear what Zoltano was saying.

"Who's that?" Cate asked, nudging Zaide Romanza. "The man standing next to the gigantic asshole over there—who is he?"

Zaide Romanza laughed. "The gigantic asshole?"

"Zoltano."

"Prince Zoltano?"

"He's a prince?"

"The crown prince."

"That sucks for the kingdom."

"It...what?"

"Never mind," Cate said. "Do you know who the other man is?"

"That is Darragh. He serves the Maoilriains. Why do you ask?"

Cate shrugged. "He came off as overly happy to see me. It was weird."

"He did serve your father before the rebels killed him. I suppose Darragh knew Haleine well. Perhaps he cared for her."

Swell. It was too much, and Cate looked at her goblet. There wasn't enough wine in the universe.

"Well, as riveting as this has been," she said, "I need some sleep in a bed in a room that isn't swaying from side to side. I assume that exists somewhere around here."

"Of course. I'll have one of the servants show you the way." Zaide Romanza signaled to a young girl, who approached and curtsied when she stood in front of them. "Take the queen of Lira to her rooms. Make sure she has everything she requires."

"Yes, your majesty."

Zaide Romanza leaned in and kissed Cate once on each cheek. "I'll call upon you in the morning. We can continue our chat then."

Cate stood and placed the goblet on the bench. "Oh good. Something to look forward to."

Zaide Romanza smiled. "You wait. You'll see."

———

Revelin was reading in the silent solitude of his chambers when Darragh appeared. He didn't speak right away, wringing his hands in front of him, and Revelin waited, expecting to hear that his mother's health had worsened, or that Zoltano's ridiculous gathering in the throne room had set the palace on fire, but Darragh only said, "The king and queen of Lira have arrived."

Revelin lowered his book. "What? Here?"

"Yes, your highness. They are in the throne room with the crown prince and his...court."

"They are here," Revelin said. "*Haleine* is here?"

"Yes, your highness."

Revelin stood, the book falling to the floor. His entire body felt heavy, the worst of it centered in his chest. "Did we—did anyone know they were to arrive?"

"Judging by his greeting, I'd say the crown prince was aware, but the queen's reappearance surprised me as well, your highness," Darragh said. "The last word we had from Lira was…"

"'Presumed dead' I believe was the employed phrase."

"Yes, well, they were mistaken."

"Yes." The pressure in Revelin's chest did not lessen. "Why have they come?"

"I have heard nothing official, but the rumor is that the rebels have been relentless. They want to reclaim the queen, it would seem. Their leader doesn't want to let her go."

It was strange to have something in common with a lowborn traitor. Revelin nodded. "Have you seen her?"

"She looked well."

"Have you spoken with her?"

"Only briefly, your highness."

Haleine, here, alive and well. He had to see her. He had to make things right between them again.

"Did you say she was in the throne room?" he asked.

"Yes, your highness."

Revelin nodded. "Thank you."

Darragh bowed out of the room as Revelin bent to retrieve his fallen book. He set it carefully on the table beside the chair but didn't remove his hand from it.

The last time he had seen her, spoken to her, he had said such horrible, ugly things, sick with jealousy that she could love another—a man such as Dana. Her responses had been equally terrible, especially her parting blow.

May you fall in love so desperately, you are blind to all else, she had said to him. *And may that love forever be unrequited.*

His blood had run cold then, he remembered, and had not thawed since. He would require her forgiveness to change that—they each would have to pardon the other—and he could not find that by hiding here in his chambers.

The throne room was nothing short of a circus. Revelin stood against the wall near the entrance and searched the crowd for Haleine. Zoltano and Maddox occupied the thrones, oblivious to everything apart from their wine and women. Eamonn sat at a table surrounded by the sons of Tanubian nobles, appearing intoxicated, yet solemn. Maddox's advisor also stood amongst the crowd, but Revelin did not see Haleine.

"If you've come looking for Haleine, she isn't here. She's retired to her chambers for the night."

Zaide Romanza. Revelin would recognize her voice anywhere. No one else ever caused that shiver to run down his spine with so few innocuous words. He gathered himself before turning to his left.

"Your majesty," he said, bowing. "I must apologize; I did not realize you were at court. No one told me."

"Titles are tiresome, Revelin. I would have you call me by my name."

"As you wish," he said. "Have you been here long?"

"Long enough, I suppose."

"Why have you come?"

"It's time to renegotiate my engagement to your brother."

"To end it?"

Zaide Romanza shrugged and slid closer to him. "That will depend upon the terms. I am a queen now, as you know, and your brother is not a king."

"He will be someday."

"Yes, and your mother is so ill. I have seen her."

"Was she awake when you visited?"

"No. The nurse told me she does not wake often," Zaide Romanza said. "Such a terrible illness to have befallen her."

It was not an illness. Revelin was more convinced of that than ever. The Black Wolf would think nothing of poisoning a queen if the price were appealing enough. Revelin searched the crowd again. Was the mercenary here as well?

"You look so serious," Zaide Romanza said. "I am certain she will recover fully."

He nodded. "That is my hope."

Zaide Romanza smiled and put her hand on his arm. "It's kind of you to humor me, but you didn't come here to make small talk with me. You came to see Haleine."

"Am I so transparent?"

"Only where she's involved. But I wouldn't fret too much about it. I'm certain there are women who would find your penchant for ceaseless devotion charming."

"You are not one of them?"

"Oh, I'm far too jealous a creature for that."

"What reason would you have to be jealous?" he asked. "I am but a second son. For you, Zoltano is the appropriate match. The superior match."

"Yes, and if I were solely interested in one day calling myself the queen of Tanuba, there wouldn't be this conflict," Zaide Romanza said. "But I have never been one to be solely interested in anything. I prefer to have everything."

"Yes, your majesty."

"Say my name, Revelin."

"Zaide Romanza."

"Now say it like you would say Haleine's name." Zaide Romanza's hand moved to his chest. "I wish the rebels had killed her, don't you? I would think you must because then you wouldn't be feeling this way now." Her hand stopped over his heart. "If she were dead, you wouldn't have to suffer the daily torture of knowing that her heart belongs not only to another, but to the one who killed her mother, her father, *your* father. You wouldn't have to live with the knowledge that she loves that monster and not you, the righteous, selfless soul pining for her."

It did not matter if Haleine were above or below the ground, he would suffer anyway. He would always remember their last encounter and the words he had thrown at her.

Revelin lifted his head and looked at Zaide Romanza. "Why are you doing this?"

"I've already told you—I'm ravaged by jealously. I wish there were a loftier answer to give you, but there isn't. I've always wanted you to look upon me as you would her," Zaide Romanza said, her fingers grazing his mouth. "Now give your future sister-in-law a kiss, and we'll speak no more of this."

Revelin hesitated briefly before taking her face in his hands and kissing her hard upon the mouth. When he released her, she stumbled back and leaned against the wall, a grin crossing her now-flushed face.

"That is not a kiss one gives to his sister-in-law," Zaide Romanza said, patting his cheek. "Don't make this too easy, Revelin. I'll feel cheated."

He said nothing as he walked away.

—⟊⟊—

The room to which the servant had brought Cate looked as though the court of the Sun King had exploded. Her digs in Eluned had been nice, but this room took her breath away. This room was straight out of Versailles.

The walls were covered with gold carvings of angels and intricately woven lion tapestries that ran from the ceiling to the floor. Candelabras were everywhere, some tall and freestanding, while others rested on painted tables throughout the room. The ceiling itself was worthy of the Louvre. Two chandeliers hung at either end, loaded with candles. In its center was painted a complicated gold-and-white knot. At one end of the room was a large four-poster bed with drapes for privacy. In front of the fireplace were two beautiful sofas and a single chair carved from dark wood. There was no balcony, just a wall of tall windows—none of which opened—hidden behind emerald-green drapes.

With a precursory search of the room complete, Cate began a more thorough one. Escape wasn't the necessity it had been in Lira, but that would come around again, like a boomerang, and when it did, she'd have a fire exit in mind.

She touched everything that could be reached, and moved everything that could be moved. In addition to the main entrance, there were two other doors. One led to a bathroom, and the other to the servants' passage where two guards stood. Cate took note of their weapons—swords and daggers—before closing the door and checking behind the tapestries for potential secret passages. When none were found and her search came to an end, she stood undecided in the center of the room.

Bed was the obvious choice. It looked clean and comfortable, and she hadn't been lying to Zaide Romanza when she'd claimed to be exhausted. Sleep wouldn't be the craziest idea ever. She could even crash in her gown to avoid having to call upon anyone to help her undress.

But she didn't go to bed.

Stalking over to the nearest candle, she stared at the flame. Zaide Romanza had held fire in her hand. In her *hand*, and if it had hurt the woman at all, she hadn't shown it. Her skin hadn't shown it, either. There had been absolutely no sign of injury, not even simple irritation. How was that possible? Cate was prone to sunburns, and the earth was a good ninety-two million miles away from the damn sun. Imagine what her skin would do if she were dumb enough to stick it directly in a fire.

But…if Zaide Romanza had done it, Cate could do the same. In theory, she could do *better*. They wouldn't be harassing her otherwise.

Cate held her hand, palm down, over the flame and slowly lowered it until the lick of fire tickled her skin. It didn't hurt; it didn't burn. Odd, she thought, as she twisted her wrist the way Zaide Romanza had. Her hand passed through the flame, this time feeling the heat and pain. Cate hissed and pulled her hand back. Son of a bitch.

Blowing on her palm, Cate glared at the candle. Then, with a decent amount of irrational anger egging her on, she attempted the trick a second time. She held the flame in her palm for a few seconds before the burning began in earnest, causing her to swear and drop the fire on the floor. She stomped it out.

"Your majesty?"

Shaking out her throbbing hand, Cate whirled around to see a new face standing at the main entrance. It was a handsome face—possibly the most handsome she had ever seen—attached to a well-dressed man. It was official. She had fallen into a parallel universe filled with nothing but beautiful people. Maybe it was all the wine.

"Haleine, I…" the man said.

This was a social call, then. Now the question became how Mr. Darcy knew her sister.

"I apologize for the lateness of my visit, but I dared not delay in coming," Mr. Darcy continued. "I thought you were gone. They told us you were…lost, dead, and I—Haleine, when I remember how we last parted, the words we spoke to one another, I cannot breathe."

Oh. Theirs was a stormy history. But that shouldn't have come as a surprise. Was there anyone in the entire damn universe with whom Haleine didn't have a stormy history?

Her silence seemed to agitate Mr. Darcy. He stepped forward, and she moved back.

"Please tell me you are not still angry with me," he said. "Haleine, please, I know we said hateful, hateful things, and I never should have—"

"Yeah, I'm going to jump in and stop you right there," Cate said, skipping the accent altogether. "It's late, I'm tired, my hand hurts for some reason, and I'm also not Haleine, so maybe you would like to save this startling confession of…whatever for another time. And place. And person."

Mr. Darcy stared. His striking face was on the verge of cracking an emotion. Judging by the shiny sheen his dark eyes had taken on, she guessed it wouldn't be a happy one.

"I know I look a lot like her—identical, some would say—and though I don't at this particular moment, I can sound a lot like her, too," Cate continued. "But I'm not her, and as you seem like a…Well, I don't know what you seem like—intense, for sure, but other than that, I don't…I just thought you should know I'm not who you think I am."

Mr. Darcy continued to stare. Cate bounced as she waited. Finally, she said, "Are we finished here, or—?"

"Mireille?"

She stopped bouncing. "Come again?"

"Mireille. You are Mireille." Mr. Darcy laughed softly. "I do not know how that is possible, but you are her. You have to be. How else would you…"

He covered his mouth with his hand and shook his head. His eyes remained bright.

"I prefer Cate, actually. Or Catherine, if you're feeling formal," she said, "which I'm guessing you usually are."

Mr. Darcy lowered his hand. "Catherine?"

"Or Cate. Who might you be?"

He looked surprised by the question. "I am Prince Revelin Maoilriain, the second son of the queen of Tanuba."

"Well, that's a mouthful."

"I was told Haleine was here." Prince Revelin Maoilriain was becoming increasingly irritated. "I was told you were her."

"That's understandable. I have been pretending to be her."

The prince came forward again, his pace angry. "Why do you pretend to be her?"

Cate held out her hand. "I think that's close enough. You should stay there. Or maybe back up a few steps."

Revelin stopped short, looking confused, then appalled. "I would not hurt you. I would never harm you; I swear it."

"Even so. Keep your distance."

"If that is what you want."

"It is."

Revelin nodded and took a deep breath. "I apologize, my lady. I came here to beg your sister for forgiveness, and find I now need to ask the same of you. It was never my intention to make you feel unsafe," he said. "This has been a shock—to find you here in her place, wearing her name—and I seek only to understand it. Why do you pretend to be Haleine?"

It was a nice apology; she didn't know if she had ever received one nicer. She should have told him the truth but answered, "What can I say? I just get so bored sometimes."

Revelin wasn't amused. "The true answer?"

"Too long a story. You wouldn't be interested."

"You could not be more wrong about that," he said. "I would hear this story; I would have you tell it to me. I shall summon the physician, and have the servants provide sustenance, and you will tell me this tale."

He returned to the main entrance before she could tell him how that wasn't going to happen. While he ordered the guards in the hall to do his bidding, Cate drifted in the opposite direction. The prince of Tanuba had sounded sincere in his promise not to hurt her, but keeping a good amount of space between them still seemed the way to go.

"My lady?" he asked.

She turned to him. "Why did you summon the physician?"

"You said you injured your hand, did you not?"

Cate glanced at her burnt palm. "Yeah, I did that."

Revelin sat at an empty table. "He shall treat it."

She nodded. "What about the sustenance?"

"If this tale is as long as you claim, we will both require food and drink to sustain us, will we not?"

Cate laughed and settled on the sofa facing him. "You think of everything, don't you?"

Revelin looked away. "Not everything."

They sat in an uncomfortable silence, each scrutinizing the other with suspicion, until the physician arrived. The older, white-haired gentleman greeted Revelin first, then turned to her and bowed. "Your majesty."

She nodded, waiting to see if Revelin would give her up, but the prince said nothing as he escorted the physician across the room, all the while being careful to maintain his own distance. The physician knelt in front of her, placing his bag at his side. She offered him her hand, and he gingerly examined the affected area.

"How did your majesty do this?" he asked.

"It was a silly accident. Retelling it shall only embarrass me further."

She had answered with her Haleine accent, and Revelin's face grew more serious upon hearing it. She caught his eye and shrugged. She had warned him.

"Is there much pain?" the physician asked.

Truth was, it didn't hurt much anymore, but as that wasn't what a normal person would have answered, Cate said, "Some, I'm afraid."

The physician nodded and reached into his bag. He pulled out a small silver jar, removed the lid, and liberally applied a strong, foul-smelling salve to her skin. She attempted not to gag as he wrapped a bandage around her hand.

"It's not a terrible injury, your majesty. I have seen far worse," he said. "This should heal nicely. The salve will help dull the pain and mend the skin. It has a strong scent, I know, but it works well on burns. Though I've done what I can for now, I shall return in the morning to see how you fare. Send for me immediately, however, should you experience any discomfort during the night."

"I will," she said, knowing she would be washing away all traces of his salve the first chance she got. "Thank you for your services."

He placed the jar back in the bag and stood. Offering her another bow, he took his leave. Revelin walked him to the doors and said something to the guards she couldn't hear. Afterward, he returned to his seat at the table.

"How did you burn your hand?" he asked.

"An unfortunate run-in with fire," she responded, still employing her accent.

"Do not do that," Revelin ordered. "I will not tolerate you doing that."

"Is there something wrong, your highness?" she asked, mock innocence in her borrowed voice.

Revelin bolted to his feet, fists clenched at his sides, but a stream of men and women emerging from the servants' entrance prevented him from doing anything else. What would he have done if they hadn't been interrupted?

The servants brought enough food and wine to feed an army and arranged it with such care on her painted table that Martha Stewart would have been impressed—and perhaps a little jealous. Cate looked over the selection—fruits, cheeses, breads, and meats—from the safety of her sofa. When the servants had finished, Revelin dismissed them, then poured the wine. He filled two goblets with burgundy liquid and held one out to her. She didn't move.

Revelin sat and drank deeply from his cup before gesturing to the chair across from him. "I promise I will not hurt you."

Cate dropped the accent. "That's what they all say."

"When I make a promise, I keep it."

"Admirable."

"Are you always this obstinate?"

"You think I'm obstinate because I'm declining to drink alcohol with a man I don't know, a man who's already threatened me once?"

"Threat?" Revelin lowered the cup. "What threat?"

"I will not tolerate you doing that," she said gruffly, mimicking his tone and accent.

"That was not a threat."

"Sounded like a threat."

"I did not mean that I would hurt you."

"Oh? What did you mean? You'd have someone do it for you?"

"No, of course not."

"You are a prince. For all I know, you have an entire staff devoted to hurting obstinate women who won't—"

Revelin slammed the cup on the table. "I will not hurt you! I do not hurt women."

Cate smiled. "Oh, you hero. You true humanitarian. Does Betty Friedan know about you?"

Pouring more wine into his goblet, the prince shook his head. "Do what you want."

"Thanks for the permission."

Revelin raised the cup but set it down again without taking a drink. "If I have made you feel unsafe, if I have made you feel as though I would hurt you—as though anyone would hurt you—I apologize most sincerely. It was unconsciously done."

He sounded sincere, but she still didn't move.

"You'll have to forgive me if I don't trust you," she said. "It's nothing personal, I just don't trust you. You came here looking for Haleine, and I don't know what that means for her, or for me."

"I do not know, either."

"Reassuring," she said. "If Haleine were here instead of me, what would you be doing right now?"

Revelin picked up his goblet but did not drink from it. "I would beg for her forgiveness."

More sincerity. If he was a liar, the second son of the queen of Tanuba was a good one. Cate pushed off the sofa and joined him, positioning her chair to keep the table between them. Revelin slid the second goblet toward her.

"What do you want to know?" she asked.

"Tell me what has become of Haleine," he said. "Yes, please, start with that."

Drinking would be a bad idea. A terrible idea. The worst idea in the history of ideas—but Cate took the goblet anyway. She studied the liquid inside as she contemplated the request and her response.

"She's dead," Cate said, lifting the cup to her lips.

Revelin's expression did not change. In fact, only the single twitch of a muscle in his cheek was proof that he was more than a fine wax statue. Cate had more wine and leaned back in her chair.

"Not that I care or anything, but you don't seem particularly upset," she said. "After hearing about how you couldn't bear the way you last parted, the complete lack of emotion comes as a bit of a surprise."

Revelin drained his cup, Cate following his lead. When she put her goblet on the table, he leaned over to refill it.

"I have been mourning her loss longer than you know," he said.

Cate nodded as Revelin polished off another serving. Was that his fourth?

"Yeah, I'm getting that," she said. "You know there's a difference between social drinking and drowning one's sorrows, right?"

Revelin refilled his goblet a fifth time and raised it as though giving a toast. She returned the gesture.

"How did it happen?" he asked. "How did she die?"

"Stabbed. She was stabbed through the heart."

"Who did this? Was it Dana?"

"No."

"That man is a murderer."

"Maybe so, but he didn't stab Haleine."

"Then who?"

"Who did he stab?"

"Who stabbed Haleine?"

Cate shrugged and had another sip of wine. "How many other people did she have in her life?"

Avoiding direct answers whenever possible was a good thing—partially because she was lying, but mostly because she didn't know anything about the prince except for his mild anger management issue, obsession with Haleine, and high tolerance for wine. Maybe there wasn't anything else to know.

"The king, then," Revelin said.

There wasn't any harm in letting him think that, so Cate shrugged in response. Revelin nodded as though she had shown him irrefutable proof and drank more wine.

"Good God," he said softly. "When?"

"I don't know. It happened before I arrived."

"From where did you arrive? Where have you been all this time?"

"Somewhere else. Somewhere a long way from here," Cate said. "You haven't heard of it."

"I am well-educated, I assure you."

"No doubt, Prince Revelin Maoilriain," she said. "But trust me, you haven't heard of it."

Revelin nodded. "Then tell me why you are masquerading as your sister."

"No."

He looked at her, eyes hard. "No?"

"Oh, come on. You're a charming devil, but surely someone somewhere must have told you 'no' before me."

"Why will you not tell me?"

"I don't see how it's your business."

"You made it my business when you told me who you were."

That was a valid argument. Cate shrugged again. "Then I guess I'm just stubborn. Don't bother trying to order me or intimidate me into telling you, either. It would take someone a lot scarier than you to be successful at that."

Now Revelin looked as though he didn't know what to do with her. His solution involved more wine. "If it concerns Haleine, it concerns me."

"I don't think so. See, when I embarked upon this incredibly moronic mission to pretend to be Haleine, I received a fast lesson in all of the important things and people in her life. Your name never came up—not even in passing. No one thought I should know your name. No one," she said. "So as much as you hoped to be a knight in shining armor, the only soul who might have cared is gone, or—considering all those hateful, hateful words that were spoken—was never there at all."

Cate finished the wine in her cup and reached for the bottle to pour more. She looked at Revelin. "Was that too mean? Are you going to cry now?"

Revelin surprised her by laughing. It wasn't a jolly sound, but a laugh all the same. "You are not at all like Haleine."

"Yeah, funny how that works, what with me being a different person and all."

"How does Maddox not realize the difference?"

He had once, but Cate wasn't interested in discussing that. "Haleine and I do happen to share a certain resemblance. Also, I don't think he knows there is a Mireille. That helps."

"For how long shall you do this?" Revelin asked. "Live as your sister, keep this secret."

"For as long as I need to. For as long as I can," Cate answered. "What about you? For how long will you keep this secret?"

"You need not worry about me, my lady. I shall keep this secret for as long as you require."

Cate raised her goblet. "I'll drink to that."

Revelin drank to that, too, then said, "I could help you further, if you would allow me."

"What makes you think I need help?"

"You, who has been presumed dead nearly all your life, are pretending to be your dead twin sister," he said, his words clipped. "I cannot imagine you do this for the food."

Cate grinned and gestured to the spread they had yet to touch. "You have to admit, it's damn impressive. People have done a lot more for a lot less," she said. "Seriously, though, thanks for the offer, but I'm not in the market for a knight in shining armor."

"I am a prince, not a knight."

"I need one of those even less," she said. She laughed and had another swallow of wine. "Now that I've insulted you yet again, may I pose a question?"

Revelin shrugged. She didn't know him that well, but it felt like a strange thing for him to do. Too informal or something. Maybe the wine was finally starting to get to him. It was definitely going straight to her head. Why wouldn't it? The last real meal she had eaten had been back in Lira. Maybe she should have some bread. A lot of bread.

"How did you know about Mireille?" she said. "Not a lot of people do."

"Your father told me some, my mother the rest."

She reached for the bread, but it was too far away. "You knew my father?"

"Yes. Did you mourn his loss?"

"Would you pass some—" She looked at him. "What?"

"Your rebel leader murdered him. Did you know that?"

"Heard a rumor to that effect," she said. "Still, he's not my rebel leader. Could you pass some—?"

"You defended him."

"I said he didn't stab Haleine, which he didn't. If you want to call that defending him, then sure, I suppose I did. Bread, please."

"Why?"

She figured he wasn't talking about the bread. "Because he didn't do it?" she said. "Look, I'm guessing that you don't like Dana because he had this hot and heavy thing with a girl you thought was yours, but—"

"He killed your father," Revelin said. "Does that not bother you?"

"No, you know what? It doesn't bother me, and do you know why?" she said. "Because I never knew my father. I never knew a damn thing about him until they brought me here and dumped this dysfunctional branch of my family tree on me. Why should I be bothered by the death of someone I didn't know that happened before I even came here?"

"He was your father."

"According to you."

"You presume I would lie?"

"You might. How am I supposed to know?"

"I am not a liar."

"You know what's funny? I hear liars say that all the time."

Cate stood to get the damn bread herself. She carefully worked her way around the table, keeping her hand on the edge as a guide. She took two thick slices of a crusty white bread and headed back.

"What will it take to prove myself to you?" Revelin asked.

"A miracle, probably," she said. "I've been told that I have trust issues. Many have tried to overcome them; most have failed."

"Most, but not all?"

As Cate slumped back in her chair, James popped into her mind, unbidden, unwanted. She put down the bread, picked up her goblet, and drank until the cup was empty again.

"No," she said. "Not all."

"How was such an impressive feat managed?"

He was mocking her. It was mildly annoying, but she wouldn't take the bait. She wasn't interested in talking about James. Not to Revelin. Not to anyone.

"Oh hell." Cate ignored the bread and reached for the wine. "Let's just get drunk."

———✺———

In the palace in Eluned, James had been comfortable, if not welcome. He had known where the guards were posted, how many could be found in any given area, what weapons they were likely to carry. He had known many of their names, when their watches ended, and where they went afterward. James had known how to get out of that palace—with or without the aid of a goddess or one of her damn pets.

Now, in Mairéad, he knew none of that. He had been given Maoilriain colors to wear—emerald and gold with that brazen lion in the center of his chest—two hearty meals each day, and a bed in the soldiers' barracks. It was truly the finest bed he had ever had, with its mattress not stuffed with straw, or made on the unforgiving ground.

But despite the luxuries, life as a member of the Maoilriain queen's guard was proving to be deathly dull. Perhaps that was only true in a city where there was no rebellion with which to contend, but most of James's day had been spent standing on a wall walk at the front of the palace, lending secondary support to the guards at the gate as merchants and knights, lords and ladies, and others made their way to and from the castle itself. No one of note had passed by, no one interesting.

No Cate.

What if she wasn't here—what if she wasn't coming at all? Bronagh had a history of lying to the rebellion; what if she had done so again, just to drive him away? It had been a risk to come, to leave Cate behind, but at the time, it had felt like the right decision—the *only* decision—that could get him what he wanted.

As night had fallen, his fears had been temporarily alleviated when another carriage arrived. It passed unstopped through the gates, and James moved to the other side of the walk to see who would step out.

The king of Lira had been first, James's heart pounding at the sight. Cate followed, and James had swallowed hard. She was all right—healthy, whole, and alive.

She was *alive*.

His relief had disappeared when Omur emerged from the carriage, and Tanuba's crown prince appeared to greet the trio. It had been a reminder that his task was far from finished, and that the danger was still very real.

The rest of his watch had passed with no further sight of her, and as he had no plausible reason to be wherever she had gone, he returned to the barracks when his replacement arrived. There, he stripped off his Maoilriain colors, ate a small meal of bread and cheese, and lay on his bed to wait for Dana.

When Dana returned from his post, James allowed him time to change out of his uniform before standing and gesturing to the door. Dana nodded, and they exited the barracks and went out to the empty yard.

"She's here," Dana said. "Did you see her?"

"Aye, but I don't know where they're keeping her."

"I do. There are four guards, two outside each door. I don't know if any are in the room itself, but there is…"

"What?"

"Revelin."

The goddamn prince. James looked at Dana. "Did he see you?"

"I'm still alive, aren't I?"

James hadn't made a final decision on that. He checked to ensure they were alone before saying, "We could kill them. We could kill two men. If we did it right, the other two wouldn't know until it was done, and we were gone."

"What about the prince?"

James shrugged. "We kill him, too."

"Tanuba already hates us."

"Tanuba doesn't know we're here."

"If we kill their prince, they may start to suspect."

"Does it matter?"

"It might to Haleine."

"What makes you think I care at all about what may or may not matter to your whore?" James asked. "I came here to get Cate back, and I'll do whatever I have to—*kill* whoever I have to—to make that happen."

"I know, James. I know you want to get her back," Dana said. "But I want you to survive the attempt."

"You don't have to concern yourself with me."

"Someone does."

"Not you."

"Aye, me," Dana said. "I'm all you've got, and until that changes—"

"All right, stop." James sighed. "Tell me about the prince. What's his interest in the queen?"

"They were to be married once," Dana said. "A love match."

A love match? James gave Dana a sideways look. "Did the prince know that you—?"

"Aye."

James smiled. "No wonder he hates you."

"Something you have in common, that."

James's smile faded, and he nodded. "Can we use him?"

"Use him?"

"Aye, use him. Would he help us?"

"I can't imagine so."

"Would he help her?"

Dana was silent.

"Dana," James said, unable to mask his irritation, "would he help her? Do you think he might help Cate?"

"Cate."

"Aye, Cate. Surely he knows who she is by now. He may have gone there expecting the queen, but he must know now that she—"

"He doesn't."

The answer was immediate, certain. Dana slid against the castle wall until he sat on the ground. Bending his knees, he rested his elbows on top of them.

"How could he not know?" James asked.

"You don't know her."

"I know her better than you."

"Not Cate."

"You mean the queen."

"I do. I don't know what went on behind those doors this night. She may well have told him everything; he may have realized it on his own, as I did," Dana said. "But he'll forget. He won't remember. He'll look at her and think of Haleine. He'll talk to her and believe, if only for a moment, that he's talking to Haleine. And that will be just long enough to convince him that Haleine never left."

"How are you so sure?"

"Because I'm doing the same thing," Dana said. "I left Haleine in Enimode. I know it, and yet seeing Cate this night made me forget it all. I thought I was looking at Haleine; I *keep* thinking that, and until you say Cate's name, I am, each and every time—"

"Lost," James said.

Dana shook his head. "Found."

CHAPTER 25

As far as Omur's servants went, the former captain of the king's soldiers had been a good, if oblivious, man. Sighle had ridden in his skin on more than one occasion. The first had been the day her father died, the last coming the day Varro had captured Mireille to drag her back to Eluned.

I know who you are. And who you aren't, she had forced him to say.

The day he had died, she had watched it happen through the eyes of a borrowed courtier's body, as no one had thought to invite her to the event itself.

His replacement had been named before Omur boarded the ship alongside his puppet and his prisoner. The king had said the name—Garbhan—likely without knowing who the man was, and left him the command of the army. Sighle had not been aware of Garbhan before hearing the king utter his name but had quickly come to approve Omur's decision.

Garbhan was not a good man.

His physical appearance would be considered pleasing by anyone who cared about such things. If not for his age—which Sighle judged to be nigh on forty—he might have been mistaken for a bastard son from Amatheon's loins, so closely did he resemble Lira's current king. One difference between them—and the one about which Sighle most cared—was the brand of Maddox's army Garbhan wore upon his left arm. The mark reminded Sighle of her father, his devotion to his king, and his ruthlessness in battle.

Garbhan was ruthless. Sighle could feel his temper burning bright, a well-stoked but contained fire. He should have been Omur's selection from the start, but Omur had chosen Varro, thinking a desire for vengeance enough of an impetus to do successfully what needed to be done. In another man's hands, it might have been; in Garbhan's hands, it likely would be. The prospect delighted Sighle, and she dreamt of riding his skin in more ways than one.

But the persistence of her shadows prevented her from doing anything more. Bronagh and the boy guard remained irritatingly vigilant, only leaving when there was no other option open to them. The boy had to sleep and could not make his bed in a lady's chamber, so he departed each night, leaving another man to stand outside Sighle's door alongside the man Haleine had placed there so long ago. Bronagh had continued to sleep on the floor by the fire. It wasn't until she required time to tend to her own needs that she would go. Nonna was set as chaperone in her place, and Sighle was free to roam as she would until Bronagh's inevitable return.

But that never lasted long enough. Brief bursts of exploration that merely tantalized Sighle further. Never satisfied was she, making her more and more restless and frustrated, which only increased Bronagh's paranoia about what Sighle did and with whom the act took place. The maid had to be dealt with, Sighle finally decided, and the physician was summoned to her chamber when Bronagh was absent.

"I have need of a poison," Sighle had said to him. "Not much, just enough to make one ill and confined to bed for a length of time. Have you access to such a potion?"

"Yes, my lady," had been his response.

"Bring it to me," she had commanded.

From the physician's hands, Sighle had taken the tiny vial and placed it in Nonna's. She repeated the instructions the physician had offered.

"Ill, not dead," Sighle had said then. "Make sure of it."

Bronagh was Mireille's servant now, and therefore she was Mireille's to kill.

Nonna proved to be competent with poison, and two days later, Bronagh was abed, writhing with fever and twisting in pain, stopping only long enough to gasp out a request to an attentive Nonna to carefully guard their charge. Sighle had looked at her through Nonna's eyes and swore to see it done before gleefully hopping from one soul to the next until she came to rest within Garbhan's skin.

The new captain had protested her intrusion at first; the strong ones always did. She didn't begrudge their objection. It was a queer sensation, she imagined, to have another pass through your skin as though you were a cheesecloth separating whey and curds. A man wanted to believe he was solid, unbreachable; to feel otherwise would be difficult to accept.

But as every soul Sighle borrowed had done, Garbhan came to accept her presence. It helped that she had whispered to him his place and purpose. Every soul craved that as well, and Sighle satisfied that yearning. To some she had told grandiose lies—not all souls were destined for greatness—but to others the truth had sufficed. Just the promise of serving a superior power could make them yield.

Garbhan had required more. He may have served in the king's army, but he could have been well-suited as a mercenary. Garbhan desired wealth and flesh and a name people remembered. He did not care if that name were soaked through in notoriety or raised to the sky in a hero's chant. He wanted only to make a mark; Sighle could help him do that.

But first, he would help her.

Haleine was in Enimode, and Sighle could have easily sent Garbhan to fetch her, but she had chosen another target: Loreton. It had no value, no purpose—which was why Omur had never bothered with it. For that reason, Sighle thought its selection would hurt Haleine greatly. Perhaps any village would; Haleine cared that way.

Garbhan and his men left the palace in the early morning. Sighle lay on her bed and rode with them. Loreton was not far from Eluned; it did not take long to reach it. It took less time to destroy it. Blades, flame, and blood—so much blood. It saturated the earth until the earth would take no more, then pooled on top of it.

At her insistence, the soldiers had kept one alive. The man sat on the ground outside of the charred church, dirty and bloodied and breathing heavily.

Garbhan knelt in front of the last living man. "Have you a name?"

The man—a boy, really—nodded. "Aye, my lord. I'm called Caleb."

"Know this, Caleb," Garbhan said, "I don't care about the rebellion or your support for it. I don't care if you don't support it. Whatever side you fancy yourself to belong to, it poses no threat to either me or the one I serve. You—all of you—are nothing to us but gnats to be brushed away."

"Then why—?"

"The rebellion has the queen. They have Haleine Coileáin," Garbhan said. "I want her; you will help me take her from them."

"How can I—?"

"I would have you deliver a message to the rebellion. They'll come much too late—as they always do—but they will come, and you will be here when they do."

"What do I tell them?"

"Tell them to bring me the queen. Alive or dead does not matter, but I will have her. I will have Haleine," Garbhan said at Sighle's request. "Do you understand?"

"A-aye," the boy gasped.

"Will you remember?"

"A-aye."

"Are you certain? It is an important message."

The boy nodded earnestly.

"I wish I could believe you, Caleb, I do, but—"

"I'll not fail you. I'll tell them, I will. I swear it."

Garbhan nodded. "Yes, well, men often swear. They seldom make good, however."

"I will," Caleb muttered, the fight and determination draining from his face as well as his voice.

Did he see his end? Did he know what Garbhan meant to do? What she meant to do? She whispered the words, and Garbhan took his dagger—an ugly, nasty, jagged blade—and drove it into Caleb's gut. Caleb screamed as Garbhan dragged the blade through his body, destroying flesh and organs and leaving no chance for survival. When the boy fell to the side, arms trying and failing to prevent his life from leaking out, Garbhan flicked blood from the blade as though it were water.

"This way is better," he said to the dying boy. "You understand."

He returned his knife to his belt and lay the boy's body on its back. Some life lingered there, prolonging Caleb's existence past the point of his appreciation. Garbhan reached into the wound he had created and withdrew his hand, red with blood. He stood, located a span of wall that hadn't burned, and began to write.

———

It required time, but the lord of Labhras allowed the rebels inside his home. They met in a small chamber on the lower floor. As Ilya and Emrys sat across from one another at a table discussing the rebellion's current needs, Dawe stood guard in the doorway. Semias waited at the opposite end, behind Emrys, while Faolan had chosen a perch on the arm of an unoccupied chair.

Ilya had requested that he accompany her to the keep once again, meaning for him to monitor the nobleman's moods and mindset, but Emrys appeared to have settled well into his role as spy and supporter. The rebellion now enjoyed regular deliveries of food and medicine, as well as a steady stream of information.

Perhaps the information flowed so freely because there was so little to report. With Omur, Maddox, and Cate out of the country, and with Dana and James following, the happenings in Eluned had died down. Omur's focus was Cate; the war he had started now held little of his interest.

Emrys stopped talking when Dawe allowed a messenger to enter the room, and the boy handed a letter to his lord. Ilya looked at it with open interest; Faolan was more circumspect. Emrys opened it and read its contents. When he finished, he sighed heavily and looked at Ilya.

"Can you read?" he asked.

She glowered at him as she snatched the letter from his hands. After reading it, she started to look at Faolan, but corrected herself and said, "The king's men have attacked Loreton? Who sent you this?"

"A contact at court."

"Why didn't your contact tell you before the attack had occurred?"

"Haven't you a contact at court? Why are you only learning of this now?" Emrys countered.

They were only finding out now because their best palace spy was hiding in Enimode. Faolan closed his eyes to send a message to Luisiúil. Loreton would be in need of aid and relief, and it would be up to the rebellion to provide it.

"It must not have been *all* of the king's men who marched. A small group could slip out at night without notice. It's happened before," Emrys said.

Ilya stood and nodded to Semias. "We'll have to end our discussion early, my lord. My people and I have somewhere else we need to be."

Emrys rose as well. "I'll—I'll rally my men, and we will—"

"No," Ilya interrupted. "You have never gone to the aid of an attacked village before. If you do now, your allegiance could be suspect. Better for you to remain here. We will take what you have given us and help them."

"I could go there. I could pass through on my way to Eluned. There is nothing suspicious about that."

"Do you have business in the city?"

"I could have business there. You don't know; neither does anyone else."

Ilya smiled, and Faolan flew from the chair to her shoulder. "Stay here, my lord," she said. "We shall talk again."

She offered him a slight bow of her head and left the room, Semias and Dawe on her heels.

"Get word back to camp," she murmured to Faolan as they left the keep. "Tell them to meet us in Loreton, and make sure Hanah comes with them."

"It's already done," he replied just as softly.

He hovered in the air while they regained their mounts and flew at Ilya's side as they rode through the forest. The tunnels carried them to their destination swiftly, and the sun was still in the sky when they arrived in Loreton, offering an unhindered view of what had been done.

His first thought was how merciful Varro had been. It was a ridiculous notion; Varro had been only the opposite, and Faolan had often considered him to be unflinchingly cruel, but whoever had taken his place was much, much worse.

Enimode had been rebuilt. Loreton was nothing but ash.

Faolan was consumed with questions of who that man might be, and who had sent him. Though his deeds were done in the king's name, Maddox had not given the order. Neither had Omur. Who else would have sent the soldiers? Who else *could* have?

Faolan left Ilya to contend with the ruins and survivors to scour the village and its perimeter for any hint as to the one responsible. Discovering such a thing would be unlikely, and surely he wasted time, but he kept at it. He needed to know who had done this.

He stopped his fruitless search when Ilya called his name. Her voice, normally loud, clear, and commanding, was now tainted by fear. Its presence was unexpected; Ilya was so seldom afraid.

Faolan returned to the village where Ilya stood staring at a half-burnt wall that had been part of a church. He settled on her shoulder and looked at the wall, understanding at once why she had called for him.

A message. Written in blood.

Bring me Lira's queen, it read. *Bring me Haleine.*

He continued to stare at the words until Ilya moved suddenly, dropping to her knees at a boy's side. Faolan hovered while she checked the body for the life she had to have known was long lost.

When she accepted the horrible truth, she settled on her heels and looked at the wall. "We need to know who did this," she said. "This is different than before. The intent behind it...This is different. We need to know why it was done in this manner."

Faolan didn't disagree. "It is, and we do."

"We need to know," she repeated. "Perhaps Lord Emrys could make inquiries."

Emrys could make inquiries, and might have been doing that already, but it would likely be for naught. There was only one person who could bring them the answers they sought. He loathed to put her in danger, to test her when she was so fragile, but perhaps it could not be put off any longer.

"I think we may need the queen," Ilya said, her voice quiet and reluctant.

"Perhaps we do," Faolan responded. "I'll fetch her."

—⟋∿∿⟍—

Though Haleine was exhausted, she did not sleep. Her mind was too busy and her body too sore to allow it. Sarai had offered her teas and salves to soothe her aching, but Haleine had declined. This was a pain onto which she would gladly hold. It was nothing for which she had not asked.

The first step, Lucius decreed, in teaching Haleine to fight was to build up her strength. A farm offered no shortage of hard work, and it was his thought to have her take advantage of that fact. Despite Sarai's protests that the queen of Lira should not perform such manual labor, Haleine toiled from dawn until dusk, doing everything Lucius asked of her: tending to the animals, working in the wheat field, and kneading dough for Sarai. She carried pails of milk from the barn to the cottage and hauled water from the pond in the forest.

Each foray into the woods brought her a sighting of the two unicorns. Both stallions—one as black as the darkest night, the other a smoky gray—watched her and whoever her escort was that day dip their buckets into the water and carry their load back the way they had come.

When she did not do chores, Haleine learned how to handle weapons. Lucius started with daggers, teaching her the proper way to hold one and how best to strike. She had spent time in her childhood watching her father's men train in Parthalan, but watching and doing were vastly different things. Brighid sparred with her and against her, murmuring apologies whenever a hit was made.

As Haleine grew more competent, Lucius gave her a short sword, and she practiced for a time alongside Sarai's grandson. He did not care who she was, always attacking as though she were one of the soldiers who had raided his home and killed his parents. Fearing for her safety, Lucius sent the boy away. After that, either Brighid or Lucius was her partner.

Haleine worked until her hands formed blisters, and those blisters bled. Each evening, Sarai would apply a salve and wrap Haleine's hands in linen. Each morning, her hands were healed, and Haleine would begin again.

The unicorns witnessed this as well, though she never saw them on the farm itself. Perhaps they followed her movements the same as she could follow theirs. She was constantly aware of their presence. It was always there, that knowledge, in the back of her mind, hovering behind her the way Willem used to. Fitting, she supposed, for were they not her guard now?

A question for Faolan—another on an endless tally that could very well go unanswered for all time, as the pegasus was avoiding her. She felt his reluctance to be near her, to answer her questions, but could not understand it. Why seek to avoid her? Didn't he—his goddess—want her to fight? Hadn't he been pushing for it? He should have been thrilled, beside himself with glee over his good fortune. Haleine had been shamed, continued to be shamed, and now sought to atone for her selfishness. She would do anything he asked; he must have realized that. Why did he stay away?

The same questions had plagued her each night, and this night was proving to be no exception until she heard voices in the other room. Sarai first, then Lucius, and—

Haleine smiled. Faolan had returned.

The voices were hushed and unclear, but she was aware of the urgency behind their words. Something must have happened. Was it Mireille? Sighle, perhaps? Her sons? Dana?

Haleine glanced at Brighid, sleeping soundly on the floor. Quietly, Haleine slipped from the bed and opened the door to see into the common room. Sarai sat near the fire, her head bent over her sewing. Lucius sat at the table, his back to the bedroom. Faolan stood in front of him.

Sarai noticed her first and rose. "Your majesty."

Lucius broke off from his conversation and twisted around. Upon seeing her, he stood and bowed. "Your majesty."

"Haleine," Faolan said.

She said nothing as she moved into the room, carefully closing the door behind her.

"May I get you something, your majesty? Tea, perhaps?" Sarai asked, stepping forward.

Haleine shook her head and looked at Faolan and Lucius. "Has something happened?"

Lucius looked at Faolan. Faolan said nothing.

"I'll rephrase," Haleine said. "I know something has happened. Tell me what."

"There was an attack," Faolan said.

"On the rebellion?"

"Not directly."

"On a village?"

"Yes."

"Where? Which one?"

"Loreton," Faolan said. "It's—"

"I know where it is," she interrupted.

Though she had never set foot within its borders, she could find it on a map. In the early days of the rebellion she had studied whatever maps she could find, thinking it would help her better serve the rebellion and protect Lira's people. Loreton was south of Eluned and north of Trutina. The soldiers would have passed it both times they had marched on Trutina, and again when they went to raid the southern coast. They hadn't touched it before. Why had they done so now?

"Did any survive?" she asked.

"We're still unsure," Lucius answered. "There is much chaos in the wake of such a thing, and those who can run often do. It takes time to account for them all."

Haleine nodded. "But you will account for them?"

"Yes, your majesty. As best as we are able."

"Why was Loreton chosen?" she asked as she approached the table. She didn't look directly at either of them but saw the glance Lucius gave the pegasus.

"We never know that," Faolan said.

"You know this time."

"Why do you think so?"

"I have eyes, Faolan. I have ears. I have seen you looking at each other; I have heard your whispers. Tell me what it is that you do not wish me to know."

"We don't know why Loreton was chosen, but there was...The new captain of the king's army left behind a message," Faolan said.

Haleine sat in the empty chair. "New captain?"

"Varro was put to death by the king," Faolan said.

"For what reason?"

"Mistreating the queen."

"Mireille, you mean."

"Yes."

"Omur wants them to believe she is me?"

"Yes."

Haleine looked away. "What did this message say?"

"'Bring me Lira's queen. Bring me Haleine.'"

"How was this message delivered?"

"It was written on the ruins of the village church," Faolan said, "with the blood of one of the villagers."

She closed her eyes. "Who did this? Who sent the soldiers to Loreton?"

"They were the king's men," Lucius said.

"Aye, but Maddox believes Mireille is me; Omur wants him to believe it," Haleine said, opening her eyes to look at him. "Who, then, was responsible for this message? Who else knows the truth?"

"I don't know," Faolan said in a way that informed Haleine he did not lie.

"How am I to know, then, to whom I should turn myself in?"

"Haleine." Faolan's voice was suddenly tight. "You can't—"

"No? What should I do? Let them slaughter more innocents and leave more messages in blood?"

"No, but—"

"What?" she demanded.

"They'll kill you."

"Let them. Let them try. I couldn't do it; why should they succeed?" Haleine stood and stalked to the other end of the cottage, cursing its small size. She stopped before the fire and stared hard at it. "You don't even know who they are or what they want."

"They want you."

Now Faolan was annoyed, almost angry. Haleine could hear it and, somehow, feel it. She nearly smiled as she said, "They can have me."

Sarai placed her hand on Haleine's arm. "Your majesty."

"I can't let that happen," Faolan said. "I won't."

Haleine whirled around. "I am not your hostage. I'm nothing—I'm not even the queen anymore," she snapped. "No, another girl with my face wears the crown I never wanted. I cannot do a thing to help her, but I can do something for these people, and I should. You should! Isn't that what we are all here to do? Do we all not want to save as many souls as we can and not just one useless shadow of a soul?"

"You are far from useless, your majesty," Sarai insisted.

"No, I am not," Haleine said. "I could fetch every pail of water or milk from here to Feond and back again, yet nothing will be gained."

"Your health," Lucius offered. "Your strength."

Haleine shook her head. "Both have been long recovered. I continue to do as you instruct because I wish to learn how to fight, but a blade or bow is not the only way I might wage war."

"Your majesty?" Lucius said.

Sarai didn't move, but Haleine could feel the woman retreating from her. She understood the turn the discussion was taking and did not care for it. As she looked at Faolan, Haleine wished she could do the same.

"I tore down a wall that could not be touched by you, nor any of the goddess's servants," she said. "I tore down Omur; I *hurt* him, and I can do it again."

"Omur is in Tanuba," the pegasus said.

"Then I will hurt the one who has taken his place. I will hurt the one who has staked a claim on me using the blood of my people. I will tear them down instead."

"We don't know who is—"

"We will if I surrender," Haleine said. "If I give myself over, we will see who is behind this."

"You don't know that. You can't know that," Faolan argued. "If you do this, we will lose you. Then where will we be? What will we do?"

Haleine shrugged. "You have another, do you not?"

"Cate isn't you."

"That is for the better, I imagine." Haleine returned to the table but did not sit as she looked down upon the pegasus.

"Losing you will never be for the better," Faolan said, almost muttering.

"Still fond of me?" she asked. "After all that I've done and all that I've failed to do?"

"You haven't failed anything or anyone."

"You've told many lies this night, Faolan, but none as grievous as that. Now tell the truth," Haleine said. "You need to know with whom you are dealing. Putting myself in their path will grant you that opportunity."

"That's not necessarily the truth," Faolan protested. "You have no way of knowing what will happen."

"I have one way."

"Did you dream it?"

Faolan was fully angry now. The heat of his fury pushed against her. She pushed back.

"No," she admitted.

"Well, when you have, you let me know." Faolan's ire continued to grow. "Haleine, you don't know the sort of magic you'll encounter. *I* don't know the sort of magic you'll—"

"I know nothing of magic at all," Haleine said. "Only that you claim it is a force within me that you once promised to help me tame. What happened to that promise?"

"Cate," Faolan said. "She changed everything."

"Because now you are afraid."

"No, I—"

"You are. I can feel it; I can see it coming off you," Haleine said. "For some reason, Mireille frightens you and—"

"Mireille doesn't frighten me. She *terrifies* me. What she can do, what she *could* do—but this isn't about Mireille," Faolan said. "This is about who-ever tried to keep me and James and all the rest from getting your twin out of Eluned. *That* we know nothing about."

"Then it is time we change that," Haleine said. "Is it not?"

Faolan sighed. "As you will, your majesty."

His easy acceptance irritated her further. "You say that as though you did not just gain precisely what you wanted."

"Your majesty," Lucius said, "this is not what Faolan intended. He didn't want us to tell you that—"

"Don't let him fool you, Lucius. Faolan has argued admirably this night, but he wanted me to know of this," Haleine said. "And this is the decision he wanted me to make."

Faolan shook out his wings. "That's not true."

"Isn't it? If you hadn't, you would have had this conversation in the barn, or the forest, or any of the other numerous places not within my hearing. But you had it here, where you knew I would take notice," Haleine said. "I will act upon this, Faolan. With or without you, I will do this."

"We'll not let you do this alone, your majesty," Lucius said.

"You will not *let* me do anything," Haleine said. "But I will happily ac-cept your aid."

Lucius worked to conceal a smile. "Very well, your majesty. How would you care to begin?"

"Take me to Loreton."

"In the morning," Faolan said.

"Now."

"The very first light of day," Lucius countered. "Really, your majesty, it will be better. There is nothing to be gained by departing now."

She looked at him. "Only distance."

"We will make excellent time come morning, your majesty, I assure you."

"We could make excellent time this night," Haleine said. "Please, Lucius. Take me there now, or I shall take myself."

Lucius glanced at Faolan, and Haleine made a noise of disbelief. She stalked back to the bedchamber, Sarai and a lantern following close behind.

"I'll need a horse," Haleine said, "and clothing—something suitable for riding, and—"

"You cannot think to go alone, your majesty," Sarai said, closing the door.

Haleine watched a bewildered Brighid rise from the floor. "They'll follow. I've left them with little choice."

Sarai put down the lantern and started to shake out Haleine's clothing. "Is it wise, your plan? Is it not too great a risk?"

Haleine pulled the shift over her head. "Life is risk, and I've been hiding—*sitting*—for far too long. This is my chance to change that. If I am to end this war, I have to do something, and this is where I shall start."

"I do not argue that something needs to be done, or that you should act," Sarai said, handing off rejected garments to Brighid. "You know that."

"What is your argument, then?" Haleine shook her head when Sarai offered her a pair of breeches. "Not those, no."

Haleine had never worn trousers before, only relenting when Lucius insisted it would improve her mobility when she fought. Though he had been correct about that, she found them odd and indecent. They certainly were not the proper attire for this occasion.

Sarai continued to hold them out. "They're better for riding long distances. You'll be more comfortable."

"What does my comfort matter, Sarai, when people are dying?"

"My argument is this, your majesty"—Sarai's voice was crisp and cool—"there is a fine line between risk-taking and stubborn stupidity. Do be certain not to cross it."

Haleine looked from Sarai to Brighid and back again. She smiled and accepted Sarai's offering, slipping into the breeches.

"I should move you into the palace when this is over," Haleine said. "I shall require a good advisor."

Sarai sniffed and held out a shirt. "I would not come, but you will always be welcome here."

"A very fine offer, that," Haleine said. "I shall endeavor to be worthy of it."

Sarai kissed Haleine's cheek. "I know you will, your majesty."

Haleine put on the blouse and allowed Brighid to fit her with a leather vest that Haleine could only assume belonged to Brighid herself. As the girl worked on the side laces, Sarai braided Haleine's hair down her back. She was tying off the braid when someone knocked on the door. When Brighid opened it, Lucius stepped inside and bowed.

"Your horse is ready, your majesty," he said, then looked at Brighid. "Yours as well. Gather your weapons."

Brighid nodded and slipped past Lucius. He looked to Sarai next. "I will require both Eion and Brighid to accompany me. Will you—?"

"My grandson and I will be quite fine on our own," Sarai said. "You do your best to protect our girl."

"Always," Lucius said. "Your majesty?"

Haleine pulled on the boots Sarai had set out for her. Did these belong to Brighid as well? "I'm ready."

Faolan refused to travel to Loreton, so when Haleine rode out on her borrowed mare, she was accompanied by the three human members of the rebellion. Brighid rode in front, reins in one hand, a lantern in the other. Lucius, armed to the teeth, was on Haleine's left, while Eion, carrying a lantern of his own, acted as rear guard.

They left the village and abandoned the road in favor of the forest where the two unicorns joined them. The brightness of the moon increased, penetrating the overhang of trees to the point where lanterns were no longer necessary, but both Brighid and Eion kept them lit.

"Should we not be moving quicker?" Haleine asked. "At this pace, we'll never reach Loreton."

"We will get there, your majesty," Lucius said, bringing his horse to a stop.

Haleine stopped alongside him. "In time to do any good?"

"Yes, your majesty. We will make excellent time, just as I already promised," Lucius said. "Brighid?"

Brighid slid from her horse's back and advanced to the nearest tree. She pressed her hand against it, and an opening in the trunk appeared. Haleine looked from it to Lucius in astonishment.

"A tunnel, your majesty," he said as he dismounted. "It will take us safely to Loreton."

Faolan had told her of this once; she remembered that. She hadn't thought about it since but now watched Brighid take her lantern and her mare inside. When she had faded from view, Haleine looked at Lucius again.

"We go on foot from here," he said.

"On foot?" She glanced at Eion to see he, too, had dismounted. "But you said—"

"I said we would make excellent time, and we will. I assure you we will reach Loreton by dawn," Lucius said. "Please, your majesty. Trust me."

Reach Loreton by dawn on foot? Could such a feat truly be possible? Haleine looked at the two unicorns. Of course it was possible. She had spent enough time in Faolan's presence to know that nearly anything was.

She nodded and slid from the saddle. "I trust you."

Brighid and her lantern led the way through the tunnel. Haleine followed closely, soon realizing that while she moved no faster than Brighid, she covered more ground than one could with a normal step. It was as though she glided across the ground, the way one might skate on ice. She studied the ground, then the wall to her left. Now that she concentrated upon it, she could feel something there.

"There is magic here," she said. "Isn't there?"

"You feel it, your majesty?" Lucius asked.

"I sense something," she responded. "It must be magic, though I am unable to give it a more specific name. Would you know?"

Lucius laughed. "No, your majesty, I wouldn't. None of us would. We haven't your abilities."

Her abilities. She grew tired of hearing about them, of knowing they existed, but being unable to use them. If Faolan continued to refuse to teach her, she would have to find someone who would.

As Lucius had promised, they arrived in Loreton as the sun was breaking over the horizon. Haleine had never seen firsthand the destruction her husband's men could cause. She had seen the refugees in the rebel camp, but until now had not witnessed what had driven them there.

Smoke and ash spoiled the air, as did the scent of death—blood and excrement and vomit mingled together, turning her stomach. Just as she could feel Faolan's fear, she could sense the grief and anger coming from those who had survived. The sensation burrowed into her, making its home beneath her skin. Emotion overwhelmed her, tears soon filling her eyes.

They moved slowly down Loreton's main road. She urged her mare closer to Lucius.

"Is it always like this?" she asked.

"Aye."

She nodded and forced the tears back down. The writing on the wall came into view, and she abandoned both the mare and her escort. She approached slowly, first looking at the dead boy, his eyes open and vacant, and then at the gaping wound in his gut. Tears threatened again, but she blinked them away and raised her eyes to read the message that had been written in his blood.

Bring me Lira's queen. Bring me Haleine.

It was exactly as Faolan had told her, but the way the words had been written—the strokes with which the letters had been formed—was familiar. She moved as close to the wall as she could without disturbing the corpse at her feet and reached out to touch her name.

Her fingers had barely grazed the blood when the words, the wall, the body, and all of Loreton fell away, replaced by a single face.

Sighle.

Opening her eyes, Haleine stared at the writing. "Did any see the one who wrote this?"

"Their leader," someone answered.

"A man, then," she said.

"Aye."

A man had not written that message. A man had not written her name like that. It was too feminine, too juvenile, and the leader of her husband's soldiers would be quite the opposite.

Haleine looked at the boy. "He did this as well?"

"Aye."

She nodded and knelt at his side. "I am sorry you were so ill-used," she said, leaning forward to close his eyes.

Touching him pulled her into another vision, this one of Sighle wielding a jagged blade, driving it into the boy's stomach. Haleine jerked away, mind whirling and stomach twisting. A scream was growing louder, and she put her hands over her ears to muffle the sound.

Strong hands clamped onto her shoulders and yanked her back to the village. She opened her eyes and looked again at the bloody message written by her sister. Not her sister—a man. The witness had said it had been a man, but...

Sighle.

"Your majesty, are you all right?" Lucius asked. "What is it?"

Sighle, it was Sighle. Good God—how could it be possible that a man had written a message in her sister's hand? How was it possible that Sighle could have wielded the dagger that had done this? How were they one and the same?

Haleine lowered her hands and lurched to her feet. She turned from the boy and the wall, unable to look at them anymore.

"Your majesty, are you all right?" Lucius repeated.

Haleine shivered and wrapped her arms around herself. Lucius touched her shoulder again, his concern radiating from his core, but she could not answer his question, nor could he answer hers. There would be only one soul who could. She circled slowly until she had ascertained the location of her unicorn shadows, then stalked out of the village and into the forest, not stopping until she stood before them.

"Tell Faolan that I require to speak to him," she said. "Tell him to stop hiding and to face me, or I shall track his cowardly self down, and he will be sorry for having made me do so."

The gray unicorn departed, while the black stayed and stared. She stared back until Lucius spoke. She had not realized that he had followed her.

"Your majesty?" he asked cautiously. "Do you—do you know who is responsible here?"

Haleine saw again her sister's face. Sweet, innocent—a child.

Oh Sighle, what have you done?

"No," she answered.

CHAPTER 26

Cate's head pounded so badly when she woke that she was at first suspicious that she had been knocked unconscious yet again. But it wasn't just her head. Her throat was uncomfortably dry and scratchy, her mouth felt full of cotton, and her stomach was in a complete state of rebellion. What the hell had she...The wine. She hadn't been knocked out at all. Just stupid.

She and Prince Sex-On-A-Stick had put a serious dent in the fermented grape supply the night before. She'd kept up with him for a while—a mistake to even try, she realized now—but that hadn't lasted long. The last thing she recalled was the good prince announcing that she needed to be put to bed and—

Shit. Cate patted her body. She appeared to be fully clothed in the gown she'd been wearing the night before. Good. She didn't need to add a drunken, awkward hook-up to her list of problems.

"Your majesty?" a woman said. "Mireille?"

Swell. It was that crazy woman from the party last night. What did she call herself? Queen something-or-other. Cate groaned and disappeared beneath the covers where light couldn't reach her and any further sounds would be muffled.

The woman threw back the covers. "Are you ill?"

"No. Yes." Cate opened her eyes and squinted at the queen of a country whose name she couldn't recall. "I might have a slight hangover."

"A hangover?"

"Do you call it something else? I drank a copious amount of wine and then decided to drink even more," she said. "What's your name again? I know you told me last night, but I seem to have forgotten it."

"Zaide Romanza." The woman frowned. "You barely touched the wine in the throne room. Why overindulge here?"

Cate shrugged. "I didn't want to do it, but it was the only way to get him to stop talking."

"Him?"

"Prince Revelin May-something."

"Maoilriain."

Cate closed her eyes. "That sounds like it could be right."

"It is. Revelin was here?"

"Yeah."

"What did you talk about?"

"Mostly about how I'm Mireille and not Haleine. He sure was stuck on that subject," Cate said. "Hey, what might I have to do to get *you* to stop talking? Or, at least, stop talking so loudly."

"You told him?"

"I told him I wasn't Haleine. He filled in the rest on his own. Guess he already knew about Mireille. Me. Whatever. Whoever? However that works, he already knew."

"I doubt that."

"Well, he knew Mireille existed—*I* existed?—which puts him ahead of me."

Zaide Romanza was quiet then. Cate took the opportunity to search for the covers as best she could without moving or opening her eyes.

"Bottle-ache," Zaide Romanza said.

"What's that?"

"Your head, your...nausea. When one has enjoyed to excess wine or spirits the way you have, we call it bottle-ache."

"That makes sense. Much more so than 'hangover,' anyway. I'm not even sure where that came from. You know, the etymology or anything." Cate opened her eyes once more and rubbed them. Zaide Romanza seemed neither impressed nor interested. "Never mind. What are you doing here?"

"I told you I would come in the morning. You told me you looked forward to it."

"I was being sarcastic."

"I know," Zaide Romanza said. "I wasn't."

"Apparently." Cate closed one eye because keeping both open was proving to be too much work. "What do you want?"

"I want us to be friends."

Cate laughed and immediately regretted it. She switched eyes. "Thanks for thinking of me, but I'm not someone who *has* friends."

Zaide Romanza sat on the bed. "Neither am I, which is why I believe we would suit each other well."

Both eyes closed again; she couldn't help it. Cate finally located the covers and pulled them up to her neck. "Not while you consider that asshat your friend."

"Asshat?" Zaide Romanza was delighted. "Do you mean Omur?"

"To start."

"He's not my friend."

"You called him that."

"I call a lot of people a lot of things. Very seldom is there actual meaning behind it."

"There's a hell of a recommendation," Cate said. "Be my friend! I lie all the time!"

"Which makes me, I believe, the most honest person you've met," the queen said. "Up, please. Out of bed."

"No. I think if I continue to lie very still, there's a much smaller chance of me vomiting. Could you maybe come back later? Like, when the room isn't spinning quite as much?"

Zaide Romanza stripped Cate of her protective blankets. "No, I'll not come back. You will rise now. We will restore some order to your appearance and—"

Cate cracked open her left eye first, then the right. "Kick a girl while she's down, why don't you?"

"If that's what it takes to get the girl out of bed."

"Is this part of the annoying bullshit you think I'll thank you for later?"

"It is." Zaide Romanza leaned in. "If you don't leave this bed, I shall have the guards in the hall come and pull you out."

Cate propped herself up on her elbows. "That doesn't seem particularly nice."

"I am not here to be nice."

"No, you're here to get whatever it is you want out of me."

"You say that as though you stand to gain nothing," Zaide Romanza said. "I assure you our relationship shall be mutually beneficial."

"What do I stand to gain?"

"Truth."

"I've heard that one before. It has yet to pan out."

"Give me a try."

"How'd you do the fire thing?"

"Did you try it? How did it go?"

Though she could tell it had already healed, Cate waved her bandaged hand. "Really well. Why do you think I'm asking?"

Zaide Romanza smiled. "What were you thinking at the moment of your attempt? Do you recall?"

"I...thought that if you could do it, I probably could."

"That's where you went wrong. If you think you can probably do it, you'll fail. Know you can do it, and you'll succeed."

"Do you moonlight as a motivational speaker somewhere? Some kind of academy for aspiring villains maybe?"

Zaide Romanza smiled again and turned her head. "Bring water for the queen's bath," she said. "Also tea, and something to break her majesty's fast."

Cate sat up. A pair of young, female servants tackling the mess she and Revelin had made the night before stopped cleaning and bowed before exiting through the servants' passage.

"Were they here the whole time?" she asked.

Zaide Romanza slipped off the bed and wandered away. "They were."

"And I was—you let me—?"

"I can assure you they'll repeat nothing they heard here today."

"Because you had their tongues ripped out?"

Zaide Romanza returned with a robe draped over her arm. She shook it out and held it for Cate's convenience. "Their tongues remain intact. My goodness, Mireille, what you must think of us."

Cate didn't move. "I don't think you want to know."

"Oh please. You haven't stopped telling us since you arrived." Zaide Romanza shook the robe again. "If you get out of bed now, I'll have time to show you how to tame fire before the servants return."

Her tone was that of a mother trying to bribe an unruly child with candy. Irritated, Cate folded her arms across her chest. "Could you be any more condescending?"

"Yes."

That was probably true. Zaide Romanza had to be the frostiest ice queen Cate had ever come across, and she had attended some pretty snooty East Coast private schools. That was something to be admired, she supposed. Wouldn't James be having a good long laugh over Cate's irritation at having met her match?

Except that James had been shot through the heart with a crossbow bolt, so he wasn't laughing at anything anymore.

Now she was pissed at more than just Zaide Romanza's tone. Son of a bitch. Cate got out of bed and snatched the robe from the other woman's hands. She didn't have time to put it on before her stomach lurched. She dropped to her knees and vomited.

Zaide Romanza laughed. "You did overindulge, didn't you?"

Cate responded by vomiting again. This time, Zaide Romanza held her hair. When Cate finished, she sat back and wiped her mouth on the robe while Zaide Romanza walked away again. Cate was considering purging a third time when Zaide Romanza handed her a goblet.

"What's in it?" Cate asked.

"Water. I thought you might like to rinse your mouth."

Cate took a sip, swished, and spit the water back in the cup. She set it on the floor and slid away from the vomit. Zaide Romanza reclaimed the cup and carried it off.

Cate stayed on the floor, leaning against the bed for support. "You're a queen, right? Of a country?"

"I am."

"I'm guessing that, as queen of a country, you don't spend a lot of time holding back the hair of puking, hungover girls."

Zaide Romanza sat at the table. "Charmingly put, but you are correct. I don't spend any time doing such...tasks."

"And yet."

Zaide Romanza shrugged. "I told you that you have great value to the gods I serve. I *live* to prepare you for your destiny. There is nothing I won't do for you."

That was a theory just begging to be tested. Cate smiled. "I don't believe in destiny, you know."

"I don't believe that matters."

"No one ever does," Cate said. "Where do we start?"

The side door opened, heralding the return of the servants. Zaide Romanza glanced at them before answering.

"First, a bath, and some tea to cure your bottle-ache."

It was a sign of how bottle-ached Cate was that the idea of tea actually appealed to her. "And then?"

Zaide Romanza smiled. "We have some fun."

———⌘———

James was growing impatient. He shouldn't be. They'd not been in Mairéad long, and Cate had only just arrived. He was closer to her now than he had been in Eluned. There would be more opportunity to reclaim her here. Such anxiety was hardly called for, yet he could not help it. He hadn't had much in the way of patience since burying his parents, but now he could feel it wearing thin to the point where it was nigh on threadbare.

He had to control it. Hot-headedness and rash decisions would do neither him nor Cate any good.

Training with the queen's guard was a start. Rowan worked the off-duty men each day. If not for the setting, James might have been back in the rebel camp. Did Ilya continue to put them through their paces? Were they fighting? Were they still alive?

James was sparring with other members of the queen's guard and considering the state of the rebellion when Cate appeared in the courtyard, surrounded by soldiers and a tall, dark-haired woman James had never seen before. He stared, surprised to suddenly be this close to her.

If he hadn't already known that the true queen of Lira was on the other side of the sea, he would have thought that he was looking at her now, so perfectly did Cate fill the part. He gripped his sword, noting the distance and number of men between them. Too far. Too many. He stepped toward her anyway, and a hand latched onto his arm above the elbow and yanked him down.

"Kneel," Dana hissed.

A quick survey of the courtyard showed James was the only one not already doing so, and he went down on one knee. He had done the same for Dana once, he recalled, and laughed quietly to think that their roles had been reversed. Another obsession with another redheaded noblewoman. How would this one end?

Grooms brought out two horses. The dark-haired woman took possession of a chestnut stallion and allowed one of the guards to help her mount the beast. Cate refused aid and swung herself into the saddle—a man's saddle, James observed, and wondered if that might explain the smile on her face. The dark-haired woman dug her heels into the stallion's side, and the horse bolted toward the palace gate. Cate and the mounted guards followed.

Once Cate and her companions had departed, the remaining men rose. Sword practice resumed, but James looked at Dana, who jerked his head to the left. James walked with him to an emptier spot.

"What is it?" James asked. "Who was that with her? Do you know?"

"That is Zaide Romanza Brollachan."

James could hear the concern in Dana's voice. "Who is that?"

"She's the queen of Feond...and Omur's ally."

"Omur's ally?"

"Aye. What do they want from Cate?"

"The end of the world," James answered. "It's that bloody prophecy of Faolan's. They think she's the second, and I imagine they're trying to recruit her."

"Will they succeed?"

"No," James said. "She's biding her time—waiting for us. She wouldn't align herself with them. She knows what they've done. She wouldn't...No. They won't succeed."

Dana nodded. "I saw her in Eluned, James, and again just now. She did not appear unhappy. She did not appear a prisoner."

No, she had not. James couldn't deny that.

"They won't succeed," he repeated. "I know you have no reason to trust her, and I know I refused to trust the queen when you asked me to, but they won't succeed. She won't let them. I believe that as much as I've ever believed anything."

Dana studied the gate before nodding. "If you say so."

"I do." James looked at the gate as well. "We should go after them."

"There are six men and a servant of the dark gods standing between us and her," Dana said. "To go after Cate now would be suicide."

Dana would be the expert on that. James nodded. "Tonight, then. They've left her alone thus far; they'll do so again. There will be the two guards at the servants' entrance, but we can—we kill them, and we take her."

"What of the prince? What if he's—?"

"We kill him, too, if we have to." James sighed. "Only if we have to."

Dana's resulting smile was crooked, revealing his thoughts on that, but neither of them spoke it as they watched the guards practice their swordplay.

"Even if we can get her out of the palace," Dana said, "what will we do? Where do we go?"

"Home."

"Aye, but we'll have to hide until we have a ship, and once they realize she's gone, that'll be a great deal more difficult. We have no safe haven here, James. We have no allies. Where will we go? What will we do?"

James shook his head. "I don't know."

"We can't do this tonight," Dana said softly. "We have to wait until we do know—for her safety, if not ours. I know you want this done, but—"

"We have to wait," James said. "Aye."

"We need help. We need more people—people on our side," Dana said. "What happened to your lads and the Maoilriain man?"

James laughed. "Lads? They're older than we are."

"Where are they?"

Who knew? They may not have arrived yet. Their ship could have been lost at sea. They could still be in Lira. He would have to go to the harbor to inquire about any recent arrivals.

"I don't know," he said. "Perhaps they're saying the same about us."

"Let's hope so."

Hope. Did he dare?

James smiled. "Aye, let's."

—◈—

At midday, Cate and Zaide Romanza rode out of the palace on two of the most well-bred horses she had ever seen. Zaide Romanza's mount was a stallion, a bright copper-red chestnut with a white blaze down his face. He was poetry in motion. Cate, after being interrogated about her riding skills, had been given a blue roan gelding. Though not as exciting as the chestnut, he was a nice animal with a smooth gait, and Cate found herself with a genuine smile on her face as she galloped along a cliff-side road.

Six guards completed their retinue, armed with blades, bows, and spears, and mounted on high-quality horses. They seemed to have little trouble keeping pace with the chestnut stallion as he abandoned the road at Zaide Romanza's command for the cover of a forest path. That path led to another, darker and narrower. They were forced to slow to a trot and ride single file until they arrived at their destination.

The location Zaide Romanza had selected for their fun would charitably have been described as a cottage in the woods but looked more like a horror movie set. Overgrown vines snaked up the walls, encouraged by the minimal amount of light penetrating the canopy of leaves overhead. Ferns grew on the sides of trees, and the ground was a mixture of dirt and moss. It muffled the horses' hooves and would offer the same protection to anything or anyone else creeping around.

The queen of Feond dismounted smoothly and handed the reins to one of the guards. Cate stayed in the saddle, checking for axe-wielding maniacs. This would be the moment in the movie where the entire audience would be screaming for the character to turn the hell around.

Zaide Romanza removed her gloves. "I'm pleased to find you did not lie about your ability to ride."

Cate ignored the jab. "Why are we here?"

"We can't very well practice our art within the palace walls," Zaide Romanza said. "At least not until you're better at it. Too many potential witnesses, too much risk of disaster. Once your accidental fumbles turn into something less accidental and more deliberate, you can do whatever you want wherever you want."

"What if I don't want to do anything anywhere?"

Zaide Romanza smiled. "You only say that because you don't know what you can do." She patted Cate's leg. "Join me, won't you? There's no reason to be afraid."

It was more likely that Cate had every reason to be afraid, but she'd come this far in her quest for truth. Climbing out of a saddle wouldn't kill her.

Another guard held the roan's head as Cate dismounted. She hadn't worn gloves. The gowns were bad enough; she wasn't about to add to the ensemble. Zaide Romanza had laughed and told Cate she was free to do as she wished. Cate had doubted the validity of that statement as she donned an outfit that looked like a medieval steampunk fan's wet dream.

"You do know we brought along six witnesses, right?" she said, gesturing to the guards. "As they're here to watch us, there's a possibility they'll take notice of our...art."

"They won't notice anything. Like the servants from this morning, they're easily controlled," Zaide Romanza said. "When this day is finished, they shall remember nothing more than the leisurely ride we took."

"Another neat trick," Cate said. "Provided you're into mind control."

"Above that, are you?"

"A little bit, yeah."

"Tell that to your guard back in Lira."

"How did you—?"

"Omur told me. He was quite proud of what you had done. Stopped a man cold," Zaide Romanza said. "Impressive."

"I wouldn't have had to if Omur hadn't set him on me like some kind of brainwashed attack dog."

"Do you always expect the world to play fair?"

"Not for a long time now."

"Smart girl."

"Condescending bitch."

"You're not?" Zaide Romanza looked at one of the guards. "Start a fire."

The guard bowed and went inside the cottage.

"Who lives here? Anyone?" Cate asked.

"Not anymore."

That sounded ominous. "Your doing, I presume?"

"I had someone do it for me," Zaide Romanza said. "One of the benefits of being queen."

"And an evil one at that."

Zaide Romanza made a disapproving sound. "You should be kind to me, or I won't teach you anything."

"Yes, you will. I can be as cruel as I want, and you'll still teach me because it's your purpose in life to prepare me for a destiny I don't believe in."

Zaide Romanza smirked. "You have it all figured out, don't you?"

Not even close. "You know something I don't?" Cate demanded.

"I know a lot of things you don't."

True. And insanely irritating. Cate made a face. "Check out the big brain on Brett."

"What are you saying?"

"I'm saying I'm not impressed."

"Shall I impress you, then?"

"Please," Cate said, "go ahead and try."

Zaide Romanza glanced from side to side. She wasn't checking for witnesses. Considering options, maybe? Upon what would the queen of Feond decide?

The other woman's hands came up, palms facing the sky. Her lips moved, and she muttered quickly and quietly before reaching out in front of her and parting the air. She stretched the air in multiple directions again and again until Cate found herself looking at a floating hole in the world.

Huh.

"What is that?" she asked.

"A portal. It's a—"

"I know what a portal is." Cate squinted at the hole.

"Do you? What a marvelous world in which the goddess placed you."

Cate crept closer to the portal. She could see something—somewhere?—on the other side. A room, just a glimpse of a room and a two-headed dragon tapestry hanging on a wall. The image started to fade, and she looked at Zaide Romanza.

"You opened that?"

"Yes."

"Where does it lead, or go, or...whatever it does?"

"To my home—Feond. I prefer to travel this way, when I can. Sailing is so..."

"Horrible?" Cate finished. "Where else can you go? Other countries?"

"Yes."

"Other worlds?"

"I would not have that power. You might. Or perhaps the two of us together," Zaide Romanza said. "I do not know; we would have to experiment."

Cate snorted. "I am not experimenting with you. I may be a college girl and all, but—"

"What?"

"Nothing. How do you do it?"

"It works best with a person or place you know well enough to see in your mind's eye. The greater the detail, the more accurate the portal will be."

Cate instantly saw home. Boston, Beacon Street, the black front door, and the iron work around the lower windows. She saw the black and white marble floors in the foyer and the vases overflowing with fresh flowers—because her mother always had to have fresh flowers—and Fiona sitting on a couch in the living room, knitting away, while freshly baked brownies cooled in the kitchen.

"Then what?" Cate asked, wiping her cheeks.

"You've already witnessed what comes next."

Tearing a hole in the air with her own two hands. That's what came next. Cate flexed her fingers and looked at the portal again. Could she possibly, *truly* be capable of such a thing?

"Go on," Zaide Romanza urged, waving away her own portal. "Try."

Cate had never been a fan of peer pressure in any form and prided herself on doing the exact opposite of what the other wanted. But this was, perhaps, different. A portal had brought her here. A portal could get her home. How could she not try?

"What were you saying before?" she asked. "When you opened your portal, you were muttering. What was it? A spell?"

"It was not a spell. You do not need spells."

"I must need something."

"Belief. You need belief and nothing else." Zaide Romanza stepped behind her and placed her chin on Cate's shoulder. "Flood your mind with your memories, and command the portal to take you where you wish to go."

Cate raised her hands. Closing her eyes, she conjured the image of the foyer—the floors, the flowers, and Fiona, Daniel, and her mother waiting to welcome her back. She thrust her arms out, her hands mimicking Zaide Romanza's motions.

She could do this. She could go home. The thought made her light, effervescent. She could go *home*—walk right through the front door like she hadn't gone any farther than the damn corner store. She could go home and forget this goddamn world existed. A surge pushed through her, and her eyes flew open to witness the magic at work.

But nothing happened.

No portal. No nothing.

It didn't work. Crushed by defeat, her arms fell to her sides, too heavy to lift again. Her heart broke, and she had to quell a desire to sob. Why couldn't it have worked?

"Where were you trying to go?" Zaide Romanza asked, lifting her chin.

Home. "Away. Far, far away."

"Try again," Zaide Romanza ordered, "but choose a closer location this time—your chambers in the palace, perhaps."

Like she wanted to go there. Cate glanced up and saw a healthy line of smoke coming from the cottage's chimney. "Look—the fire's ready. Let's go play with it."

"Try again first."

"Later, maybe." Yes, she would try again later—when she was alone and could better handle abrupt and severe disappointment. Neither of which applied in that moment.

"Coward."

"Nope. Just stubborn," Cate said. "Shall we go?"

"What do you know of your powers?" Zaide Romanza asked as they walked to the cottage.

"Nothing, really, except for what little you and Voldemort have mentioned," Cate answered. "Oh, and a tiny pegasus saying that I have to use the force. I don't know what it means, but he said it."

"He spoke true."

"Terrific. I still don't know what it means, though."

"It means all of the earth's elements—wind, water, fire, the very air that we breathe—all of them are a force which you will learn to command."

"To do what?"

"Anything you want. Anything you could imagine."

"That's dangerous."

Zaide Romanza pushed open the cottage door. "That's the point, dear."

The house was dark, musty, and slightly terrifying, with a line of iron animal traps hanging from a beam. On ground level was a table, chair, and a straw pallet directly on the floor. All serviceable, but barely so.

"Sad, isn't it?" Zaide Romanza said. "Perhaps we did him a favor."

"You," Cate said. "Not we."

"For now."

Cate glanced toward the door and saw the guard who had started the fire waiting to its left. "Shouldn't he go elsewhere?"

"No. He should stay."

The queen of Feond knelt in front of the fire. Cate, after surveying her options one last time, joined her. By the time she had settled on Zaide Romanza's left, the other woman held a ball of fire in one hand, shaping it with the other.

"Here," Zaide Romanza said. "Take it."

"It'll burn."

"Not if you command it otherwise."

"How do I do that?"

"See it, feel it. Make it what you want, what you need."

"How?"

"You have a mind, don't you? Use it."

"You want me to use my imagination?"

"When you do it, it won't be imaginary."

"You want me to stick my hand in a fire and imagine it isn't burning off my flesh?"

Zaide Romanza sighed and tossed the fire into the hearth. "Help her."

The guard came forward and grabbed Cate's right arm, thrusting it into the fire. She screamed, a mixture of outrage and pain, and threw her free elbow into his groin—once, twice, three times—but the man didn't budge. She screamed again.

"You've mistaken me for someone with patience, Mireille," Zaide Romanza said.

Cate was having trouble focusing on anything other than the pain, but she was somehow still aware that Zaide Romanza had left her side in favor of a dead man's chair.

"Let this show that I am not such a person," Zaide Romanza continued. "Yes, I could wait decades for you to decide you're ready to wear the mantle which belongs to you, but as waiting is so...tedious, I have chosen not to wait anymore."

Cate took short, ragged breaths through both her nose and mouth. Focus, focus, focus. Turn it off, turn it off, turn it off. She could control the fire. She could, she could, she could. She could control the air. She could, she could, she could. See it, do it, turn it off. Turn it off, turn it off, turn it off—

Turn it on them.

Zaide Romanza hummed to herself, almost idly. Cate pushed against the immovable guard before forcing herself to look at the fire eating away her hand.

She could do this. She could.

Slowing her breathing, Cate put her overactive imagination to work.

Fire wasn't hot. It was cold. As cold as ice cream. Iced tea. No—she'd have to think bigger. A walk-in meat cooler. The iceberg that sank the *Titanic*. The entire Arctic Circle. Antarctica. That's what this fire was, and she was in more danger of frostbite than anything else.

Cold, cold, cold. A goddamn three-day blizzard. Just anything but *fire*.

Something pushed out of her, an exclamation point at the end of a sharply spit-out expletive. A barbaric howl shaking the world to its core.

Because that's what she was—a barbarian, a savage ready to smite her enemies and anyone else with the misfortune to happen along her path.

Starting with the asshole holding her hand in a fire.

Putting her free hand into the hearth, she scooped up flames, now as cool as ice. They dribbled down the sides of her open palm, carving little, cold gorges in her skin. She took a moment to register the contradiction before throwing her handful of fire directly into the guard's face.

That made him move. He released her, shrieking and howling. His hands pawed at his face, and Zaide Romanza laughed. The sound caught Cate's fractured attention, and she whirled around, throwing another handful of fire in the queen's direction.

Zaide Romanza caught and squelched the flames. They stared at each other. Cate thought about throwing more fire, just to see if she could burn off the satisfied grin on Zaide Romanza's face. The fire appeared in her flame-blackened hand, and Cate looked at it. It was so damn unnatural, and yet—

The guard caught her eye. The dead guard.

That was pretty unnatural, too.

The fire died, and her skin returned to normal. Untouched by flame.

Zaide Romanza applauded. "Oh, well done," she said, sounding genuinely pleased.

As the only well-done thing in the room was the guard, Cate did not share the emotion. She looked at the queen of Feond. "Well done? I *killed* a man."

"What of it? You'll kill more before this is done."

Cate stared. "What is *wrong* with you?"

"What is wrong with you?"

"There's a dead man on the floor over there because I fried him like a piece of chicken. What am I supposed to do now?"

"There are five others. You could fry one of them."

"Stop it, just stop it."

"I dislike this side of you—this sad, whining girl. I much prefer the other."

"Stop it!"

"*You* stop it," Zaide Romanza ordered sharply. "You are protesting too much; you are fighting too much. This grief of yours, your horror, is false and disgusting. I will not allow you to deny the fact that you enjoyed that power. You were exhilarated by it, as well you should be. What we can do, what *you* can do…" Zaide Romanza waved a passionate hand at the still-smoldering corpse. "That is a human offense, and you are far above that."

Cate wanted to tell Zaide Romanza off. Prove that she was talking out of her ass because Cate was very much human and not interested in the brand of crazy Zaide Romanza was selling. But she kept her mouth shut because as much as she wanted the opposite to be true, she couldn't deny that the power had been exciting. Invigorating. Even though the dead guard had dampened that thrill, there was a piece of her that was purring with contentment.

What the hell was she? It couldn't be human, could it?

Cate looked again at the body and the wisps of smoke rising from her hand. "I don't want to be evil."

Zaide Romanza shrugged. "It's only evil if you lose."

CHAPTER 27

Zoltano had announced a feast that evening, to celebrate his guests from across the sea. Revelin had no desire to attend, but Mireille—or Catherine or Cate—had left the palace at midday on a ride with Zaide Romanza and had not returned until the sun was setting, offering him no opportunity to speak with her. However, as she was one of the honored guests, he had known where he would find her that night, and so Revelin had dressed and gone to the great hall.

He stood alone in a corner, a goblet in his hand, and watched the queen of Feond converse with the woman posing as the queen of Lira. Nearly an entire day had passed since he had become aware of her existence and Haleine's loss. He did not know what to make of it, nor what to do about it, or if he should do anything. He did not even know by which name he should call her. Regardless of the name he chose, she remained Darian's daughter and the rightful heir to the Coileáin holdings. But she was not Haleine. She was not the queen of Lira. Why did she pretend to be?

"Your highness."

Revelin looked away from the two women to acknowledge Adomnan Cathal. The nobleman bowed before joining Revelin in standing against the wall. Revelin returned to his study of Mireille.

"What did you find?" he asked. "Anything?"

"Where would your highness have me begin?"

The rebel or the mercenary? The spy or the traitor? Which was the greater, most imminent threat to the kingdom? Revelin sipped his wine as Mireille laughed at something Zaide Romanza said.

"The Black Wolf," he answered. "Start with him."

"I was able to confirm what the Quatari rebel told you," Cathal said. "Not only is the Black Wolf in Mairéad, he is at court."

At court. His brother had a ruthless mercenary at court. Revelin took his eyes from Mireille and searched his brother's guests. For what or whom he looked, he did not know. Only those who managed to employ the man could make such a claim, and given his methods, no one would admit to such a thing.

"Did any of your sources offer the purpose behind his presence here?" he asked. Cathal's only response was a sigh, and Revelin nodded. "Have you uncovered any evidence linking my brother either to my mother's illness or the mercenary?"

"No, your highness," Cathal said. "I have not."

Revelin drank more wine. "There must be something."

Cathal hesitated before saying, "Is it possible, my lord, that the reason we continue to find nothing is that there is nothing to find?"

Yes, Revelin supposed it was possible that Zoltano was innocent, but was it likely? He looked at his brother, sitting alongside Maddox at the head table, laughing and drinking and eating.

"Who else would do this?" he asked.

"As much support as you and Lord Coileáin secured for your mother after your father's death, there were some who would have preferred to see Zoltano ascend the throne," Cathal said. "Might I suggest we explore those possibilities?"

His tone made plain that he believed pursuing Zoltano any further was a waste of time. Whatever loyalty had made Cathal follow Revelin on this path was drying up. Cathal might have been correct in his belief, but Revelin could not dismiss his own. What would Darian have done?

"Do as you will," Revelin said. "Tell me about Einar. Have you discovered who spies for him within these walls?"

"Not yet, your highness, but—"

Not yet. Revelin stopped listening. His eyes found Mireille and stayed on her. This time, she looked back, a sly half-smile crossing her face. She leaned to whisper some secret in her dinner partner's ear. Zaide Romanza glanced at him as well, her own smile much wider.

"Did you know Darian's daughter, Mireille?" Revelin asked.

"Mireille?" Cathal laughed. "I've not heard that name in years. Darian did not speak of her often. How did you—?"

"He told me about her before he...before he went to Lira."

"I saw her only once, as an infant—but that's all anyone ever saw of that girl, wasn't it? The day she arrived in Parthalan with her mother and sister, I was there. I departed the next day, and I never saw her again." Cathal shook his head as though freeing himself from the memory. "May I ask what prompted this question, your highness?"

Mireille had prompted the question. Back from the dead, beautiful and infuriating, and as thick as thieves with a woman he could never trust. Did that mean he could not—should not—trust her?

"I was only thinking," Revelin said.

"A great deal could have been different had Mireille not died," Cathal said. "But that is always the truth when we speak of the dead, is it not?"

"Should we not speak of them at all?"

"I do not suggest that, your highness."

"Was it so certain, her death?" Revelin asked. "My mother told me her body was never found. Is it not possible that she survived?"

"Your highness, why are you—?"

"Curiosity," Revelin said, watching Zaide Romanza saunter toward him. "Someone comes. Leave me."

Cathal bowed and withdrew. Revelin was relieved to see him go, but Zaide Romanza's continued approach offered him no comfort.

"Revelin," she said when she reached him. "You did not need to dismiss your friend on my account."

He bowed. "Your majesty."

She took the goblet out of his hand and drank from it. "You've been staring at Haleine and me all evening long. Might I inquire why?"

Zaide Romanza did not realize Mireille was an imposter? He supposed he could not judge. He had not realized it, either, not until Mireille had told him.

"I was unaware that you were such boon companions. It surprised me," he responded. "When did this start?"

"About the time that you stopped, I imagine." She drained the cup of its contents and handed it back to him. "Join us, if you wish. We'll happily make room for you."

He shook his head. "I would not wish to intrude."

"You wouldn't be an intrusion. I promise you that," she said. "Come and join us, Revelin. I'll see if I can't broker peace between you."

He looked at Mireille. Her attention was on the men seated at the head table. "We are not at war."

"I'd hate to see your face when you are at war. It must be a frightful thing to behold, if this is what you look like at peace."

Revelin kept his eyes fixed on Mireille. "I said nothing about being at peace."

"Have you ever considered how much simpler your life would be if you'd only let her go?" the queen asked, then laughed. "Well, of course you haven't. That's not who you are. You'll always seek to protect her, won't you?"

Yes. Always and forever, yes. How could she question it? He glanced at the queen of Feond. "I am a servant to the crown, your majesty," he said. "Nothing more."

"I have a crown, Revelin. Perhaps one day you'll serve me."

He lacked a response. Zaide Romanza smiled as though she knew his thoughts.

"Perhaps you already do," she said. "I'll allow you to return to your staring. I would hate to deprive you of your obsession."

There was no response for that, either, and he did not try. He bowed his head as she walked away. When she had rejoined Mireille, he found himself quite unwilling to watch them further and turned to leave. He was nearly out when Eamonn arrived, a guard trailing behind him. As he passed, Eamonn nodded to Revelin, but Revelin barely registered the gesture as he stared at the man who protected his brother.

A man in Maoilriain colors who had no right to wear them.

Dana.

—◦◦◦—

They had returned to the palace with the body of the dead guard in tow and the tale that thieves had done the killing. Zaide Romanza gave an impassioned performance of the danger they were in, and the daring of the man who had sacrificed his own life to save the two queens. Cate stayed silent, feeling nothing and everything all at once, as guards were sent from the palace in search of a roving band of criminals who didn't exist.

Amidst all the madness inside of her, there was a tiny, reed-thin voice offering the opinion that what the queen of Feond claimed to have happened was wrong, that Cate should perhaps *say* something to that effect, and take responsibility for what she had done. That singular, squeaky remnant of her conscience was soon gagged and stuffed into a box that was put on a slow boat to China, for as much as Cate recognized right from wrong, she didn't care.

Because, at the moment, she didn't appear to be entirely in control of herself.

Even later on, at the feast held in Maddox's honor, Cate was sporting a decent buzz. And she had yet to touch the wine.

Maybe 'buzz' was the wrong word. 'Juiced' was better. There was some high-octane shit currently coursing through her veins. There was something wrong with her ears, too, or maybe her head, but somewhere inside of her it was like a television lacking a clear signal had been left on low in the background, filling her with sounds that were anything but ambient. It had been that way since they had left the woods. What other super fun side effects could she expect? Besides wanton murder.

She was spared having to ponder her own question when Zaide Romanza returned and sat next to her, looking like the cat who had eaten both the cream and the canary.

"What did the good prince have to say?" Cate asked, watching him leave the room. "Did he happen to mention why he was staring so damn much?"

"He's obsessed with you."

"With Haleine."

"Someone to whom you bear a rather striking resemblance," Zaide Romanza said. "Henceforth, his obsession extends to you."

Cate grinned. "Fantastic."

A loud noise caused her to look at the head table. Maddox and Zoltano were sharing a boisterous guffaw over a female servant who had dropped her tray. Smart money said they were the ones who had caused the accident.

Maddox came around the table, acting as though he meant to help her recover from her fall, and Cate's whole body tensed when he pulled the girl up and pressed her against his body. The girl struggled to free herself, but Maddox held fast.

"What an ass," Cate muttered.

She rose, intending to set him ablaze—or at least punch him in the teeth—but Zaide Romanza held her back.

"Oh, settle down," Zaide Romanza said.

"He's harassing that girl."

"Yes, and later, he'll harass another one. And probably three or four more after that."

"Not if I have anything to say about it," Cate said, standing again.

Zaide Romanza grabbed her arm. "You don't have anything to say about it."

"Yeah, I do. I have *a lot* to say about it."

"No, you don't," Zaide Romanza said. "Sit down before you make more of a spectacle of yourself."

A quick glance around showed that Cate had attracted even more of an audience than Maddox. Still, she looked at Zaide Romanza and hissed, "I haven't even begun to make a spectacle of myself."

"I am well aware of that, you stupid girl," Zaide Romanza said. "This is how he is meant to behave. He is only as he was made."

As he was made? What the hell did that mean? Cate sat. "Who made him this way? Was it you? You *made* him this way?"

Zaide Romanza shrugged and released Cate's arm. "Omur, specifically, is responsible for Maddox, but I do admit to having taken my turn at the reins."

Cate shivered, gagging silently at the imagery. "Your parents must be so proud."

"My parents are dead."

"Of course they are." Cate looked at Maddox and Zoltano again. They had let the girl go and gone back to their dinner, chortling over their wine.

Made that way. Damn. "What would he have been like if you had left him alone?"

"Not nearly as much fun," Zaide Romanza answered, then rolled her eyes at Cate's less-than-impressed expression. "Don't be like that. It was necessary."

"How could that possibly be necessary?"

"If Maddox were a kind-hearted king, no one would have rebelled against him."

Cate downed the contents of her goblet in one swallow. Carefully, she put the cup back on the table, closing her eyes as the alcohol hit her bloodstream. She shouldn't have been able to feel that so keenly. Would anything ever be normal again?

"You would have learned how to control him," Zaide Romanza said.

Cate opened her eyes. "What?"

Zaide Romanza poured more wine into Cate's goblet. "This would have been your life, had the goddess not interfered. You would have been the one married to Maddox."

Cate snorted as she picked up the goblet. "My mother would've been so proud."

Zaide Romanza laughed into her own wine. "I doubt that. I knew your mother, and—"

"Oh? Which one?"

"I knew the woman who carried you in her womb, but the other—your adoptive mother—her I know."

Know. Present tense. Cate put down the wine. "You know Laura Cole?"

"I do."

"You can't have known her very well. Otherwise, you'd know she's dead."

Zaide Romanza sighed. "Yes, I suppose Laura Cole is dead. But I know the truth behind the one who called herself Laura Cole—someone who is very much alive."

Very much alive. The only thing more impossible than the claim that someone on this side of the portal actually knew Laura Cole was saying that Laura Cole was alive.

"You don't want to lie to me about that," Cate warned through clenched teeth.

"I don't want to lie to you about anything. The woman you called your mother is not the woman you thought her to be. She is something else entirely."

Cate was trembling now. Blood boiling, alcohol evaporating, and whatever force inside of her on high alert. Zaide Romanza's mouth opened, and Cate snapped, "Don't say anything else about her. Don't you dare."

"As you wish," Zaide Romanza said. "When you decide that you are ready to hear the truth, do tell me. Though, I suppose you could ask the pegasus, should you see him again. He'd know better than any of us who she is."

We couldn't leave you with just anyone, Faolan had said, and instead of asking for additional detail, Cate had chosen snark. It was her go-to reaction for most things, but this time it might not have served her well.

Cate stood. "My mother is dead. Laura Cole is dead," she said, enunciating each syllable carefully to avoid any misunderstanding. "I saw her in her coffin, and I saw that coffin put six feet under, and I saw it covered with earth. If I ever again hear you offer an alternative to this truth, I will make you feel pain like you have never felt before. Do you understand me?"

"I do."

Cate walked away, abandoning the feast with the intention of barricading herself in her room where she could lose her mind in private. She only made it into the hallway before something grabbed her arm and stopped her.

"You can't leave," the something said. "We've not yet shared a dance."

Zoltano. Cate reluctantly looked at him. Was he a puppet, too? He was so similar to Maddox that she had to assume he was. Another plaything of Omur's? Was he acting of his own accord at this moment, or was someone pulling his strings?

"Nor will we," she said, prying his hand off her arm. "I'm afraid my dance card is full."

"Dance card?" Zoltano came closer. "What is this jest?"

"No jest. Just truth—I'm not interested in dancing with you. Not here, not now, not ever."

"Come, Haleine." Zoltano backed her against a wall and leaned in. "Let's dance."

"Don't," she ordered. He stopped but didn't freeze like Fionnbar had. Considering the number of witnesses milling around, that was for the best. "Turn around and go away, or I'm going to make a scene."

Zoltano smiled. "I think I would like that very much."

"That's because you're an idiot," she said and turned her head away from the smell of his breath. "A drunk idiot."

"You wouldn't turn away my brother."

"No, probably not," Cate agreed. "Run along, Pinocchio. I'm busy."

This time, he did back off. His bow was only slightly mocking, and she shot him with her fingers before hightailing it out of there.

By the time she made it back to her room, she was tipsy from wine and magic, aggravated over her chat with Zaide Romanza, and energized from her encounter with the crown prince. A dangerous combination.

The servants had already been there, lighting the fire and candles, and setting her table with a bowl of fruit, two bottles of wine, and a pair of goblets.

More wine was the last thing she needed, but her nerves were on edge, and she didn't know how else to calm them.

She was pouring herself a cup when the door opened, and the second son of the queen of Tanuba stepped inside. She raised the wine bottle in salute.

"Hello, Prince Revelin Maoilriain. Come for Round Two, have you?"

Revelin closed the door. "Have you ties to the rebellion?"

Hackles rising fast, Cate placed the wine on the table. Her nerves were like a paranoid dog that could sense unease, and the prince was bursting with it.

"Rebellion? What, like in Lira? That rebellion?" she said.

"Yes. Have you ties to them?"

"No. Well, they kidnapped me, so there's that, but no. I wouldn't say that I have ties to them."

Lie. Cate sipped her wine and hoped Revelin's nerves weren't as intuitive as her own.

"You do not aid them?" he asked.

"They hoped I would, but it turns out that I am not much of a team player."

"You do not aid them."

It wasn't a question this time. Cate shook her head. "No," she said. "Hey, what's with the ninth degree all of a sudden? I thought we were past the interrogation stage of our relationship."

Another lie. A night of drinking did not a relationship make—and they'd only had that much because she had been desperate to *end* an interrogation. If they had a relationship, he was the Spanish Inquisition and she suspected of heresy.

Revelin, however, didn't respond. Whether because he didn't understand what she had said, or because he didn't care, she didn't know, but she suspected the latter. The prince crossed the room to sit on the sofa nearest the fire.

"Would you know their plans?" he asked.

"The rebellion's?" Cate poured wine into the second goblet. "I'm pretty sure their plans these days begin and end with survival."

She carried both goblets across the room and offered one to Revelin. When he had taken it, she positioned herself on the sofa, sitting sideways in order to face him, and bent one leg beneath her, while allowing the other to dangle over the edge.

"What would they do to survive?" Revelin asked.

Kidnapping. Lying. The usual. She shrugged. "What anyone would, I suppose."

"Would they have recruited the Black Wolf?"

"Who or what the hell is the Black Wolf?" Cate asked. "Seriously, I have no idea what we're talking about, or why we're talking about it. Care to clue me in?"

"Would they come here for you?"

She shrugged again and drank some wine. "I doubt it. What good am I to them? I imagine they were glad to be rid of me. Why do you ask? Have they perhaps done something?"

Every molecule in her body hummed. She could hear the fire whispering her name. If she put out her hand, every flame in the room would come to her without her making a sound. Was it the wine? Was it electrifying what it was meant to dull? Or was it the company? She couldn't deny an attraction to the tragedy mask sitting next to her. Perhaps it was the idea that a group of people she thought to be dead and gone were nearby and possibly raising hell. Maybe even on her behalf.

"I do not know," Revelin answered.

"So you came here to accuse me for...what? Fun?"

"I do not know."

"What do you know, Prince Revelin Maoilriain?"

"Not as much as I would like."

"Join the club. We have T-shirts."

"What?"

"Nothing."

She chugged her remaining wine, then reached for Revelin's cup and drained that, too, as she imagined him wearing a tight and possibly wet T-shirt. Revelin's face revealed that he was rather scandalized by the act—and he didn't even know what she was thinking—but the knowledge that he would be much more affected by a magical pyrotechnics show kept Cate from caring. She held out his empty goblet.

"Be a peach and fetch the bottle over here, would you?" she said. "Better bring them both, actually. It'll save you a trip later."

Revelin bristled at the command, and he made no move toward compliance. Cate raised an eyebrow.

"You barge in here—uninvited, mind you—for the second night in a row with an endless string of cryptic questions you won't explain," she said. "The least you could do is bring a girl some wine."

A smile found its way onto Revelin's face, and he took the goblet. "I often do the least I could do."

"If you're going to throw yourself a pity party on my sofa," Cate said, "I'll definitely be needing more wine."

She started to point in the table's direction but felt the magic surging inside of her, so she clenched her fingers into a fist and buried it in her skirts. The molecules were more insistent now, calling and crying for action so loudly that she wasn't sure how Revelin didn't hear it. What the hell had Zaide Romanza done to her?

Revelin rose and walked to the table. "I do not know what to do with you."

That made two of them. "I hear there's a club you can join for that, too."

"You flummox me," Revelin confessed. "I am not accustomed to—"

"Being off balance?"

Revelin nodded and picked up the two bottles. "Yes. Only your sister ever managed to...I loved her very much."

"Sure the past tense is appropriate there, tough guy?"

Revelin didn't respond to that, either, but as he returned with the wine, she decided not to press the matter. He sat down again and poured wine into Cate's goblet. She resisted the urge to snatch the bottle out of his hands and guzzle straight from the source.

"Why do you have to do anything with me?" she said.

"I owe Darian Coileáin a great deal, and I promised I would take care of his daughters."

"Touching, but I doubt that my name came up during that discussion."

Revelin nodded. "Sighle. I swore to look after Sighle."

Cate laughed. "Hell of a job you're doing," she said. "Given that she's on the other side of a large body of salt water doing things that give me nightmares, you've got to be the very best guardian ever. Or, quite possibly, the worst."

"I did leave her with her sister."

"Well, she's not with her sister anymore."

"What would you have me do?"

"What you do is between you and your god. Provided you have one."

"Do we all not have one?"

Cate seemed to have a lot of gods, all vying for her soul. It hadn't worked out that well for her thus far. She shrugged and had more wine.

"That's also between you and your god," she said. "Leave me out of it."

Mistake. Big mistake. The prince studied her thoughtfully. Deep, probing questions were sure to follow, and maybe she would answer that he'd have to pardon her, for she had held fire in her hands and killed a man earlier that day, and was unhinging more and more as a result.

Except she couldn't say that. Couldn't risk it being said, either. She had another swallow of wine—because that would help—and said, "This man you claim was my father—"

"Darian Coileáin."

She snapped her fingers. "That's the guy. Was he a king of some kind?"

"A nobleman."

"Born a nobleman? The latest in a long line of hallowed noblemen?"

"He was the first of his name. His father was a farmer; my father raised him up."

"Okay. I understand why he would owe your father, but how did you end up owing him?"

"Darian Coileáin was a most faithful servant who sacrificed a great deal in the name of my family," Revelin said. "It is only right that I do what I can to protect his."

"The elusive noble nobleman," Cate said. "I have heard tales of your existence."

"I am a prince."

Cate raised her goblet. "And proud of it."

Revelin did not raise his cup. He was staring at her again. Was he waiting for her to say or do something?

"It does not mean anything to you, does it?" he said. "The Coileáin name."

"No, but I bet it's a bitch to spell."

Revelin didn't seem to find her clever. Cate didn't care about that, either, as she transferred the goblet to her left hand in order to write letters in the air with her right.

"Coileáin. Co-lee-ain. Coileáin," she said. "C-o-lee—C-o-l-e-e-ain." She paused when she noticed Revelin's expression. "What?"

"You should know," he said in all seriousness. "You should understand what it is to bear that name."

"I don't bear that name. Neither do you, by the way."

"You are a Coileáin."

"I'm not, though."

Revelin leaned forward and put his hand on her cheek. "You are. Tomorrow, I shall show you."

His touch did something to her—cut through the haze that had been clouding her since her damn hand had gone into the fire. Interesting, odd, and unexpected—nothing else, no one else, had done that so clearly as this. Everything else had only increased the white noise, but the second son of the queen of Tanuba had parted it like the Red Sea.

Another crazy thing in a world where that word had no meaning.

Looking at Revelin through narrowed eyes, she slid closer to him. The movement seemed to startle him, and his hand fell, but she caught it with her own and held it in place.

What was she doing?

"You should go," she said but didn't release him.

He didn't try to leave. "Yes."

"It's probably improper for you to be sitting here with me in a room lacking any sort of chaperone. With or without your hand on my face. This is the kind of place where an exposed ankle is scandalous, so I could—"

Stop. She could stop. She dropped her hand, shocking Revelin back into awareness. His hand fell, and he moved away. They didn't speak nor make eye contact. When the white noise came rushing back, Cate lunged for the wine on the table, but Revelin intercepted her attempt and moved the bottle out of her reach.

She sat back in a huff. "What the hell?"

"I believe you have had enough."

Cate's resulting laugh was a tad on the maniacal side. Would the Wine Police notice?

"I have had enough. You are so right about that. You don't even know how much enough I have actually had," she said. "I should be tunneling out of this place with my goddamn fingernails, but what am I doing? Sitting here, drinking wine when I don't even *like* wine, but that's apparently all anyone ever drinks around here—and why is that? Isn't there anything else? Isn't there any scotch or brandy or whiskey? What about beer, or—I don't know, what else is there? Vodka? You have potatoes, don't you?"

Revelin stood and walked away.

"Where are you going?" she asked. Had he finally had his fill of her particular brand of crazy?

Revelin opened the servants' door. "The queen would like some whiskey," he said to whoever was standing there. "Find someone to fetch it."

"I didn't really want any whiskey," she said as he returned to the sofa.

He sat. "What do you want?"

She wanted Revelin to touch her again. She wanted to hear something other than radio static that sounded vaguely like the shrieking of a man on fire. For some reason, Revelin could do that for her. Would it be wrong to take advantage of that?

She knew what was wrong—killing a man, then hanging around drinking wine while passing judgment on others. *That* was wrong.

Killing someone in self-defense was all right—or, at least, less wrong, maybe—but she had done a lot more than just defend herself. Fricasseeing a man alive went a bit beyond the realm of self-defense.

Which placed her firmly in the murderer category.

She looked at Revelin and chewed on her thumbnail. What was one more wrong to a murderer?

"Mireille? Are you—?"

Before he could finish asking his question, she placed herself in his lap and pressed her lips against his. The din cleared instantly, so when she ended the kiss, she made sure to maintain contact—her forehead against his—as she unbuttoned his jacket. She worked through the other layers of clothing—why were there so many?—to find that very last shirt and slip her hands beneath it. Her fingers roamed over his warm skin, exploring his chest. There were no scars to be found.

"What are you doing?" Revelin asked, his voice tight.

An excellent question, and one without a good answer.

"I'll let you know," she breathed and kissed him again.

———※———

The queen of Feond did not lurk in darken hallways, yet that was precisely what Zaide Romanza was doing. Lurking, lingering, waiting for Revelin outside of Mireille's chambers, in a spot where the light of the torches could not reach.

The queen of Feond should not be made to wait in any capacity, in any locale, but there was nothing to be done about it. Queen as she may be, she served a higher power that did not care what title the mortals had bestowed upon her. Had she been born a scullery maid, a milk maid, a fishmonger's daughter, she would still stand here because her lords wanted Revelin Maoilriain and wanted her to procure him for them.

Their interest in Nathan's second son wasn't new. Omur had long claimed that each of the Maoilriain sons had a role to play in the dark gods' plans, but what Yelsneh and the others wanted him for, she did not know.

Not for the first time, Zaide Romanza wondered what her lords' vision for the future was. They saw everything but shared only what they had to with their servants. What they told her was only a small part, and what they told Omur another. They never told any one soul everything.

She thought perhaps Iollan Iuchar was the exception. Their oldest, most precious servant would certainly be privy to everything his masters knew. He had to understand Revelin's worth. It would explain why he had stayed in his chosen place for so long.

The door opened, and Revelin eased through it. He hadn't taken the time to dress properly before leaving. She smiled as she oozed out of the darkness.

"Oh, Revelin," she said. "What have you done?"

He stopped short and stared. "Your majesty," he said after a moment. "What are you—?"

"Trying not to wake her?" Zaide Romanza asked. "That's kind of you, I suppose. Did you leave her as exhausted as all that? I shouldn't be surprised. I never thought you would lack for stamina."

"I—"

"Was she your first? You're not like your brother; honor means something to you, so you would not have touched Haleine—not before you were wed—but would you have bedded any other women? I suspect not. Your devotion to Haleine would have overruled all else. Tell me, Revelin—am I right?"

He did not answer directly, attempting to regain his decorum. A lost cause, she thought, when one was caught with a half-opened shirt and his jacket over his arm, but she waited patiently as he made the effort and straightened his shoulders. The answer to her question was obvious, but would he admit it? He would, after all, always seek to protect Haleine.

Or, it would seem, her twin.

"I have not now—nor have I ever—bedded the queen of Lira," he finally mustered.

He thought he was being clever. She smiled. "I am certain that is true."

"Jealousy does not become you, your majesty."

"Nor you, Revelin. You should not condemn me for my jealousy when you yourself are riddled with it." She slinked toward him. "I am well aware of what—*who*—caused the schism between you and Haleine. As such, I know what drove you to stick your tongue down my throat last night, just as I understand the desperation which made you lie with that girl in that room this night." When she reached him, she placed her hand on his stomach and slid against his side, resting her chin on his shoulder. "She's not the girl with whom you fell in love as a child. That girl died in Lira, and the one who took her place is a very different sort of creature. Remaining in her company—in her bed—will lead you only to pain and ruin."

"And your bed? Where would that lead?"

Zaide Romanza grinned and rose on her toes to nip Revelin's ear. "Come find out," she whispered before slipping away.

She returned to the shadows and followed them back to her chambers, wondering what the good prince would be doing now. He was always so much fun with which to play; she would hate to lose him. To Haleine, Mireille, or anyone else.

Omur was waiting for her when she arrived. He sat rigid on her sofa, hands on his knees as he stared at the fire. He did not acknowledge her. Unsatisfied, he would claim to be, but he would have felt what Mireille had done in the forest—and that would have delighted their lords.

"Wine, Torin," she said to the servant she had brought with her from Feond. "If you please."

As the young man leapt to the task, Omur's eyes landed upon her. The nicety had not escaped his notice. Torin returned, offering her a goblet, and Zaide Romanza took it without looking at him.

"Thank you, Torin," she said, running her hand along his inner thigh.

She made her way to Omur, selecting a chair angled toward the fire. As soon as she was settled, Torin moved up behind her.

"Him?" Omur said. "Really?"

"Does it matter whom I take to my bed?"

"He doesn't seem to meet your usual standards."

"Pray tell," Zaide Romanza said, "what are my usual standards?"

"Noblemen, not servants."

"As if there's a difference," she said. "I recall you quite happily swiving a little Liran maid not long ago. Whatever happened to her?"

"Maddox flayed her alive," Omur said. "Sabine was a sacrifice that had to be made." He glanced at Torin. "This is an indulgence."

Yes, Torin was that, but as long as he continued to so thoroughly amuse her, she had no intention of giving him up. "Have I not earned an indulgence?" she asked. "Have you not come here this night to tell me how very overjoyed our lords are?"

"They are...pleased," Omur admitted.

"I should think they are a great deal more than that."

He didn't care for her tone. "Whatever small success you had today, we remain far from our goal."

"I am aware," Zaide Romanza said. "Though I must say we appear to be much closer now that Mireille has been placed with me."

Omur glowered at the fire. "What are your impressions of her?"

"I like her. I enjoy her very much," Zaide Romanza said. She felt a sigh building inside her. "But I do not need a bosom friend. I need a monster."

Omur called for Torin to fetch him wine, then gestured for her to continue.

"We've been going about this all wrong," Zaide Romanza said. "Politeness and deference will not get us what we want, what we need."

"What will?"

"The opposite. Somewhere inside that stubborn girl is the being spoken of in prophecy. Iollan Iuchar's descendant—the one for which our lords have waited nearly a millennium—is here now. I *saw* her for the briefest of moments this very day. All we must do is bring her forth permanently."

"I require a plan, not a history lesson," Omur said. "You know how resistant she is. How do you propose to do this?"

"We don't need her to be Haleine; we need the harbinger who will destroy the goddess and restore our lords. The queen of Lira—which ever one of them wears the crown—won't see that done. The darkness inside Mireille will, so we break her down, tear her to pieces. We get to the beast within, and we let it run."

"We'll lose control of her."

"We don't want control of her. We don't want her *in* control. That's what's holding her back—holding *us* back. If we crush the girl, destroy her soul, we win."

"This is not what our lords want."

"This is exactly what our lords want," she said. "They just don't realize it yet."

Omur nodded, ruminating over her proposal. "How do we do this?"

"We don't." Zaide Romanza twisted around. "Torin, fetch me the Black Wolf. You'll find him wherever it is the crown prince is languishing this night."

Torin bowed and exited the room. When Zaide Romanza looked back at Omur, she saw that he was no longer pleased.

"You would trust this to a mercenary?" he said. "To *that* mercenary?"

She shrugged because it would infuriate him. "He's quite capable, I assure you."

"I'm familiar with his work," Omur snapped. "You truly believe he can be trusted with this?"

"We trusted him with Nathan's assassination."

"This is much more important than *that*."

"Yes, it is," she agreed, "which is why we best not make any more errors."

"Then why give this to someone else to do?"

"When she unravels, when she breaks, she will dismantle those responsible," Zaide Romanza said. "I would rather she find someone other than myself to blame. Wouldn't you?"

He would. For a being who had lived as long as Omur had, he was surprisingly wary of dying.

Omur frowned. "If what you plan works—"

"It will."

"*If* it works, we may not survive it."

Zaide Romanza smiled faintly as she stared into the fire. "We were never going to survive anyway."

CHAPTER 28

L ira's princes—the heirs to the throne—were fascinating lads. A smile played on Sighle's lips as she watched the children babble and laugh at their nurses. She had visited her nephews in their nursery many times over, intrigued by these twin boys with her sister's nose and the promise of magic lurking beneath their skin.

It was this promise that brought her back day after day. She would give Garbhan his orders, then make haste to their side to attempt to discover their truth. She had suspected Haleine's sons might have inherited at least some of their mother's abilities—the way Sighle had her father's eyes—but within the babes lay far more than what she had anticipated.

From where that had come she did not have to ponder, for there could only be one possibility. The surprise came from finding it there at all. Charisma and not dying—not dumb luck, but something more. Dana had proved to be a far worthier match for Haleine, but this would not earn him a pardon.

Neither would the children pay the price for their parents' crime. Especially not now that she was aware of their potential. What gifts had been bestowed upon the young princes? Were they already aware of what they could do, as Sighle had always been, or were they as ignorant as the ones who had given them life? Would they act as one, two parts to complete the whole, or would they be opposites, designed by nature to keep a precarious balance? That, Sighle did not know, and could not guess, but endeavored with every visit to discern the answers.

"My lady?" one of the maids said. When Sighle looked at her, she held out the child in her arms. Alain. "Would you care to hold your nephew?"

The two women had accepted her presence readily, assuming Sighle sought to be close to a long-absent sister the only way possible. Each time, they welcomed her warmly, cooing over her as though she were also a babe in their care.

The guard did not. Willem did not trust her. Sighle looked away as he moved into her periphery. He spent every moment of every visit with his hand on his sword, mapping her moves and calculating her motives. He wanted very much to prevent her from returning but could not say why. Only a feeling in his gut guided him, and that would not be proof enough.

"No," she said finally. "Thank you."

The nursemaid nodded and moved away, but Willem stayed and stared. He wasn't even trying to hide his suspicion anymore. From where had it come? Had Mireille gotten to him as well—infecting him as she had the others? With Mireille ensconced in Tanuba, Sighle supposed Bronagh would be the only one with the answers.

Rising from her chair, Sighle left the nursery, Willem's relief at her departure ushering her out the door. The boy guard waited for her in the hall, and together they returned to her chambers. Sighle entered alone to find Bronagh stripping linens from the bed.

"You served my sister," Sighle said, lingering near the door.

The maid did not stop her work. "I did."

"She asked you to serve me?"

"You know she did, my lady. I have told you so already."

Sighle slinked closer. "But how did she tell you? What did she say?"

"She asked me to take care of you, to watch you like"—Bronagh smiled—"an overly protective hawk."

"That does not sound like something Haleine would say," Sighle offered, curious to see the maid's reaction.

Bronagh, to her credit, flinched very little. "She did say that. She also said that no matter how you protested, we were not to give in."

They were not to give in. Could it be? A simple statement, a simple request, uttered by her sister, and the maid was made immune to Sighle's powers. Did Mireille even know what she had done?

Would she now? Sighle was blind to what happened on the other side of the Endellion Sea. Was Haleine? The twins should have been the most closely linked of the sisters, but were they? They had been—continued to be—so resistant to destiny, to the point that Sighle could not be certain they were aware of one another at all.

Closer, closer, and closer still they marched toward their fate. Good soldiers, all of them, getting up upon having been knocked down, and marching on. Could anyone expect anything else from the daughters of a great soldier?

Even Haleine had found her legs, and each day they grew stronger, straighter. She had gone to Loreton and learned Sighle's great secret. What she would choose to do with this knowledge remained a mystery, as Haleine had done nothing yet, but Sighle would be ready when—*if*—Haleine chose to act.

It would take time—Haleine was far from being a threat to her.

Sighle sat in a chair and watched Bronagh put the last of the soiled linens in a basket. "And Willem? Did my sister demand the same of him?"

"No, my lady. Why do you ask?"

"I only wondered. He views me with such suspicion."

Bronagh laughed as she shook out a fresh sheet and laid it over the mattress. "He views everyone that way, my lady."

"Not Haleine."

"No," Bronagh said, struggling to keep a sudden sadness from her voice. "Not Haleine."

"You miss her, don't you?"

Bronagh bowed her head. "Very much, my lady."

The maid's despair was palpable, its bitter taste filling Sighle's mouth. She spat it out. "She'll come back, you know. She won't stay away forever."

That was the truth. Sighle could clearly see Haleine's return to Eluned. She would march straight into the great hall, intending to lay claim to the throne. Sighle did not yet know whether the attempt would succeed, but the answer would come. It always did.

Bronagh smiled at her, a woman unwilling to tell a young girl the truth. "I do hope so, my lady."

—◈—

Faolan did not enjoy the role of coward into which he had fallen, yet he could not bring himself out of it. Not yet. Mireille terrified him, Haleine worried him, and every decision would make the situation worse. Inactivity seemed safest.

Luisiúil was angry; Laorans was angry as well. They could not understand his refusal to move.

You must teach her, they both had said and would say again. *We need her; you know we do.*

He did know that. He had told Haleine the same. They all had, shamelessly promoting their agenda to stifle that of the dark gods. It had to be done, if they were to win. If they were to survive, it had to be done. He did know this. Eventually, he would relent and do what needed to be done, regardless of the cost.

It had been easier to do when he hadn't cared.

Time and time again, he had told Haleine he would teach her, guide her. Time and time again, he had lied. He didn't know how to teach her, nor did he know what to teach her. Somehow, she continued to pretend that he was trustworthy, but the way she had shouted at him upon their last encounter showed that the strain on their liaison was growing greater.

What would happen when he did fulfill those promises? Her powers marked her as something more than mortal, but Haleine's humanity was very much her center. She felt so deeply. If he removed that ability, what would be left?

But he evoked those precious emotions and lied to get her to Loreton. Too easy to do, and she had been aware of his manipulation. In spite of that, she had ridden off, angry and vulnerable, to discover what secret he could not find in the ash of a smoldering village.

He should have followed her, but he returned instead to the rebel camp to find Luisiúil, accompanied by Lorcan, waiting for him in a quiet glen. He settled on an exposed boulder and waited for her to begin.

Why are you here when you should be in Loreton? You continue to avoid her to the determent of our cause, Luisiúil scolded. *We need her; we need her magic, and you are avoiding her.*

Yes, he was. "If I do what you want, it could kill her."

If you do not do what we need, it will kill us all. You brought the other here as a spare, but we both suspect she is lost to our enemy. Haleine is more necessary than ever.

"There's something hunting her. We may not be able to protect her from that."

Then you'd best be sure she can protect herself.

Kynon arrived then, dipping his head in deference to Luisiúil, before turning to Faolan. "The girl calls for you."

"She saw the message?" Faolan asked.

"She did. When she touched the blood, she had a vision of which she would not speak," Kynon said. "But it has agitated her greatly, and now she demands your presence."

"Demands?"

"She requested I tell you," Kynon went on, "that if you do not stop hiding and face her, she shall track down your cowardly self, and you will be sorry for having made her do so."

Luisiúil's vindication and Lorcan's shared satisfaction irritated him, but hearing that Haleine had called him a coward stung. It was the truth—he could not deny that—but he hated that she saw him so plainly.

"We can't have that," Faolan said finally. "Let's go see the queen."

—⦅∿∿⦆—

Haleine remained in Loreton, tending the wounds of those few who had not perished. None of its citizens knew her, and she worked alongside Hanah to bandage gashes, stitch lacerations, set breaks, and apply salves to burns. She hauled water and offered comfort to those who needed it.

After the living had been tended to, she helped lay out the bodies of the dead, coming at length to the boy her sister had killed. Each touch brought her another vision of the deed—Sighle so casually sinking a blade into his belly. Over and over again, Haleine bore witness until tears streamed freely down her cheeks.

When Hanah called for her—using her name and not her title, in an effort to keep her identity secret and safe—Haleine dragged her hands across her face to remove the evidence of her distress. The healer was already too concerned that Haleine was too fragile; if she saw the tears, she would insist Haleine remove herself from Loreton. Haleine did not wish to leave. Aye, she was far too fragile, but she was equally determined to be the opposite.

"Haleine!" Hanah called a second time. "Help me!"

Haleine rushed to the healer's side. On the grass lay a woman, unconscious and bleeding from a wound in her abdomen. Haleine dropped to her knees, and Hanah grabbed her hands and placed them over the wound. Haleine braced herself for a vision—had Sighle done this as well?—but none came. She breathed a small, selfish sigh of relief.

"Here, hold her here. Keep the pressure on," Hanah said, moving away. "They found her in the woods; those bloody soldiers must have cut her down when they had finished with the rest. Damn them all!"

Hanah continued to curse the king's men, but Haleine ceased to listen as she became increasingly aware of the blood oozing between her fingers and of the dying woman to whom the blood belonged.

And she was dying, this woman. Haleine could see it—anyone would—but she could *feel* it as well. The woman's life was fading away, slipping down a bleak hole where it could never be retrieved. Haleine's eyes watered. There would be no stopping it. Hanah would try, Haleine would try, but they would fail because no mortal methods would be enough to reverse what had been done.

The woman's life began evaporating faster and faster. It would not be long now.

"No," Haleine said, pressing harder against the wound. "No, no, no— oh, please, no! Stay here, stay with—Hanah, hurry, please!"

It made no sense, her determination. The woman would die; she understood that. But why should she know that? Why should she accept it? Why should she not fight to keep this woman alive? Others might have told her that one life wouldn't matter to either tally, but Haleine wanted this one life.

She was tired of losing.

She gasped when her palms—still pressed to the wound—began to glow green. The woman's body bucked, and Haleine fell back. Hanah shoved Haleine out of the way and bent over the dying woman. Haleine stayed immobilized where she had fallen, her hands—no longer glowing—clutching her own stomach. Lucius appeared at her side, then knelt behind her, placing his hand on her shoulder.

Hanah straightened suddenly. After a moment, she laughed.

"Hanah?" Lucius asked.

"She's all right." Hanah turned to them. "The lass is all right. Your majesty...you healed her."

Healed? Lucius gripped her shoulder but quickly released her. Haleine leaned forward to look at the woman.

"You healed her, your majesty," Hanah continued. "Look! Her injury is gone...just gone."

Haleine went back to the woman's side. The grass surrounding her was now brown, dead.

But the woman wasn't.

Her heart beat strong, and her face was no longer pale. Apart from a minor scar, the right side of her body was smooth and undamaged. She slept peacefully, and though Haleine did not know when it would happen, she understood that the woman would wake.

She would not die. Not this day.

Hanah hugged her, blessing this miracle, but Haleine didn't respond. She looked at her now-shaking hands. Adrenaline was fading; shock settled in its place. A swell of oblivion worked its way through her body, a wave devouring the sand, and she summoned Lucius before it could overtake her.

When the darkness retreated, Haleine found herself lying on her back, looking through a damaged roof at the stars, the moon, and the thin layer of clouds passing between them and her. The sound of steel connecting with stone dragged her attention elsewhere. She lifted her head, turning to the left. The dull glow of lantern light revealed the remains of an altar. Brighid sat at its base, playing with a dagger.

As Haleine sat up, Brighid gasped and dropped the weapon. "Your majesty! Oh, I didn't—I'm so sorry, your majesty. Are you well?"

Haleine nodded. "The woman—the one that I...Is she well? Did she wake?"

"Aye, your majesty, she's fine. Do you need anything? Food? Water?"

"No, thank you. I require nothing." Haleine glanced at the sky. "How late is it? Is dawn a long time off?"

Brighid shrugged. "Not too long now. Enough time to go back to sleep, if you'd like."

Haleine thought she had spent entirely too much time asleep. "No, I don't want to do that."

Her tone did not go unnoticed. Brighid leaned forward.

"Bad dreams, your majesty?"

Haleine's dreams had not troubled her for some time. She was not sure what that meant—if anything. There had been a time where she had dreamed of Dana—in battle, dying, living—but that had been before she had banished him. Perhaps she would never dream again.

She did not think that likely, though. There had been a dream of her lover teaching one of their sons to ride. She had watched the lesson, looking at both of them with love—*love*, not the hate she had spewed at him upon their last encounter.

She could not imagine how one would become the other.

"No," Haleine said. "When was the last time you slept?"

Brighid shrugged again. "I'm all right, your majesty."

Did that mean the girl had not slept since being awoken in the middle of the night by Haleine's demand to go to Loreton? "You should rest," she said, but Brighid did not appear convinced. Sighing inwardly, Haleine asked, "Where is Lucius? Lurking somewhere outside?"

"Yes, your majesty. I'll take you to him, if you'd like."

"I'm commanding you to sleep," Haleine said, getting to her feet. "I will be quite able to find Lucius on my own."

Brighid bowed her head, and Haleine walked out of the church. Loreton was lit by bonfires. Haleine surveyed them briefly before starting toward the largest. Lucius caught up to her before she reached it.

"Your majesty," he said, "are you—?"

"You have to make them sleep, and eat, and—what else aren't they doing in the name of protecting me?" she blurted. "It is ridiculous that they are charged with that at all. I do not require protection."

"You do require protection, and I will continue to assign my people to that task," Lucius said. "I would never risk your safety by appointing someone incapable of doing it properly. Eion and Brighid are caring for themselves, I assure you. All right?"

Haleine nodded tersely. "Yes."

"Now tell me the true cause of your agitation, your majesty."

She sighed. "I need Faolan. I need him here."

"Does he know?"

Haleine looked to her left where a single unicorn stood secluded in the forest. "He knows."

"Then I am certain he will be here before long."

Haleine was certain he would not, but she smiled and thanked Lucius for his lie.

She spent the remainder of the night working by lantern light to comfort and care for Hanah's patients. She did not stop to rest, no matter how many times Hanah urged her to do so. She did not stop at all until Lucius found her the next morning.

"Haleine," he said.

She looked up from the leg she bandaged. Lucius stood before her, Faolan perched on his shoulder. The pegasus did not speak, protecting his secret from those he did not know.

Dipping her hands into a basin of water, Haleine washed away the blood and stood. She passed Lucius and entered the charred church. Near the altar was a bench, blackened as everything was, but intact. She sat upon it and looked at the ruins until Faolan spoke.

"Haleine?"

"Tell me everything," she said as he landed on the altar. "About the prophecy, about me and my sisters, and the role we are fated to play."

"Sisters?"

"Sighle did this; did you know? She killed that boy and painted those words on the wall outside."

"Sighle? How did—she rode with the soldiers?"

"No."

"Then how—?"

"I don't know how, Faolan. I don't know anything except that when I touched the wall, I saw Sighle's face, and when I touched the boy, I saw her kill him," Haleine said. "Who is she? What is she? What are we?"

"Sighle did this. You're sure?"

"Yes."

"Sighle."

"Yes," Haleine repeated, irritation rising. "Faolan—"

"I don't know," he said. "I don't—the prophecy, Haleine, I've always thought it was you and Cate. I never suspected Sighle would be a part of it."

"Tell me about the prophecy. What does it say?"

Faolan focused on her. "Two from one, they'll come, they'll come. The first from moon, the next from dark. The fate of the world in their hands they'll hold."

She waited for him to continue. When he didn't, she asked, "Is that all? It can't—"

"They'll live, they'll fight, they'll love, they'll die. Blood against blood, light against flame," Faolan said. "Two from your blood will start it all; one from your blood will see it done."

"Whose blood?"

"Yours."

"See what done?"

"The throne of the dark lords will be reclaimed when the rivers run red with the blood of the moon."

"Is that the end?"

"Yes."

She nodded. "From where did this prophecy come?"

"A crone who lives in the wilds of northern Quatara."

"Quatara?" Surely that was not a coincidence.

"Yes."

"How do you know she speaks the truth, that she is to be believed? Might she not be an agent of your enemy seeking to mislead you?"

"The crone is neither good nor evil, and she serves no deity. She is a keeper of magic and prophecy, nothing else."

Haleine wanted to ask how he knew that to be true, but there would be no satisfactory response. There seldom was with him.

"You think I am the first," she said instead.

"I know you are the first," Faolan replied. "I thought your twin was the second."

Two from one. A twin would be a reasonable assumption.

"What do you believe now?"

"I don't know. You tell me that Sighle Coileáin is somehow responsible for this massacre, and I wasn't...I don't know."

"Omur believes my twin is the second."

"That he does."

"Does he know about Sighle?"

"It doesn't appear so."

"What will it mean for Mireille, if she is not the one Omur needs?"

"I can't be certain, but I imagine he would kill her."

"She does have powers," Haleine said. "I believe we have both felt that."

"Yes."

"What are we?"

"Whatever you decide to be, I suppose. Good, evil—you can do anything you want with the powers given to you. That's your choice."

It would seem Sighle had already decided. How had it happened?

"I healed a woman," Haleine said. "Did anyone tell you that? Did you feel that? She was dying; Death had come to claim her, and I stopped it."

"That's powerful magic, a rare skill," Faolan said. "You need to be careful of when and how often you use it."

"Why?"

"Because you're not healing a body—not really," Faolan said. "You're taking life from one source and bestowing it upon another. If you're not careful, that source could be you, or a soul just as innocent as the one you're attempting to save."

"The grass around her was dead afterward."

"And you? Did you not faint? Were you not unconscious?"

"I was."

"You need to be careful," he repeated. "Only use that magic when there is no other choice."

"That woman would have died if I hadn't."

"You should have let her."

"Faolan!"

"You should have let her."

Haleine shook her head. "I won't sit here and listen to you tell me that my life is more valuable than another's."

"It is."

"It isn't."

"It is. I shouldn't have to keep saying it, Haleine. You should know it already," Faolan said. "There will come a time when you are all that stands between the survival of the world and its destruction. You. Not that woman you saved. Not the one you'll try to save next. You. What happens to all the rest if you die for someone who doesn't matter?"

"I won't give up on any of them."

"You will. If you want the rest to survive."

The needs of the many outweighed the few. It was a lesson with which she was all too familiar. Her father had lived by those words, and they had served him well until he had indulged his grief and chased his revenge.

"What good are these damned powers if they're not meant to be used?" Haleine asked.

"Use them all you'd like," Faolan answered. "Just not recklessly."

She laughed. "You wish me to stand between the forces of darkness and the destruction of this world, do you not? I would think that a certain amount of recklessness would be vital."

"Which it is," Faolan said. "But you don't have to be stupid about it."

Haleine stood and walked away.

"I will guide you through this," he called after her. "If you allow me."

"What good will that do?" she asked. "You're only here because of a threat."

"Not just that."

"Yes, that." She turned around. "You're afraid."

"Yes."

"You're afraid for me."

"Yes."

She shook her head. "You can't do both, Faolan. You can't push me to fight, then be afraid of what will happen when I do."

"I know."

"Sighle did this. *Sighle*," Haleine said. "And I don't...I remember when she was born. I doted on her. We all did, the entire household. I loved her; she was loved."

"I don't doubt that."

"How did this happen? How did she become such a monster?"

"I don't know," Faolan said. "I'm sorry. I'm sorry I wasn't prepared for this. For Sighle."

Haleine nodded. "What happens now?"

"I don't know."

She couldn't fault him for that. "What do you know?" she asked, but instead of angry, she was only sad. "Tell me something, anything, that you know without doubt. Tell me something true."

He seemed to consider the question. "We have a long way to go before this reaches its end," was his answer.

Haleine laughed quietly. "Not that we will win this war?"

Faolan looked away. "No."

CHAPTER 29

When Cate woke the next morning, she felt closer to normal. Whatever crazy mojo had been running through her veins the night before had been tampered down, a four-alarm fire reduced to smoldering embers. A current thrummed deep inside, but it was dormant—for the moment at least. How could she keep it that way?

She sat up to stretch, the sheet falling away to reveal her naked body. Naked. Why was she—?

Oh. That.

Covering herself, she looked to the left where she had last seen the equally naked second son of the queen of Tanuba. The pillow held the indentation of his head, but he was gone. A glance around showed he wasn't anywhere else in the room, either.

That was for the best. It wasn't like they were anything—not even friends with benefits. They were barely acquaintances whose next encounter would be the textbook definition of awkward. She had no qualms whatsoever about postponing that as long as possible.

The servants' door opened, and the two women from the day before entered, each carrying a tray—one of food, the other tea. They curtsied, then busied themselves arranging the meal on the small painted table.

"Did Zaide Romanza send you?" Cate asked.

She figured she was due for a visit from the evil queen, if for no other reason than to give Cate hell for her promiscuity, or choice of partner, or bed head or something, but the women declined to answer. They wouldn't even make eye contact as they finished with her breakfast and moved on to the rest of the room. One woman opened the drapes and gathered Cate's scattered clothing while the other brought her a robe.

Cate exchanged her sheet for the robe and took a leisurely stroll toward the table to see what they had brought. Bread, cheese, and tea. The breakfast of champions. She sat and ate while she watched the two women work. Midway through her meal, Revelin arrived, a sword on his hip. That was new.

Cate swallowed. "Good morning, Prince Revelin. I trust you are well."

His brow creased with confusion until he took note of the other two women in the room. He turned to the maids, still in their curtsies. "Her majesty will need to bathe and dress as quickly as possible."

The maids straightened and departed without delay, leaving Cate and Revelin to stare at one another.

Did he want to talk about what they had done last night? She didn't—she never wanted to talk about anything—but what would the prince want? Judging by his body language, he didn't want to talk, either. It was hard to believe the guy could be more stiff and formal, but he managed it beautifully.

"Why do I need to bathe and dress as quickly as possible?" she asked.

"I have arranged to take you home," he said, not looking directly at her.

"That would be quite the feat," she responded. "Where are you really taking me?"

"To your family's estate. To *your* estate. It is yours, after all. With your parents and sister gone, it would belong to you."

"Except that I don't exist here," Cate said. "But sure, let's go take a tour. What could possibly be screwed up about that?"

Revelin looked at her, his face registering her distress. "Do you not wish to know?"

Yes. No. Maybe. She shrugged. "Your questions would be easier to answer if you used contractions once in a while," she said. "No, I want to go. I do. I want to know. Just...let me get clothes and a bath—not in that order, of course—and we'll go."

Could she be more of a babbling idiot? If Zaide Romanza were there, she'd be having a jolly good laugh right about now.

At the thought of Zaide Romanza, Cate asked, "Does anyone else know about this little field trip of ours?"

Revelin shook his head. "I thought it best if they did not."

"Okay," she said. "Why don't you excuse yourself while I get ready. I'll try not to take too long."

Revelin bowed and retreated to the hall. Cate stayed at the table as she waited for the servants to return. Was she really going to do this? Go check out her supposed family home with the former virgin she had taken advantage of not even twelve hours earlier?

Groaning softly, she banged her head against the table. Boy, she sure was racking up the wins. What would she add to the tally next?

After Cate had bathed, and the servants had stuffed her into another absurd, cleavage-happy gown, she walked with Revelin to the courtyard. The day before, it had been crawling with people—noblemen and women, servants, even soldiers in the midst of a training session—but now it resembled a ghost town. Where was everyone? Had Revelin ordered them to be elsewhere?

"No guards?" she asked.

"No," Revelin said. "Only the driver and my man, Darragh, know we are leaving."

His man, Darragh, huh? "Is that safe?"

Revelin touched the pommel of his sword. "I will protect you."

But who would protect him? "So, a driver," she said. "That must mean we're taking a carriage or something, right?"

"A carriage, yes."

They rounded a corner, and a fleet of carriages came into view. Most were nondescript, but there was one that demanded immediate attention. It was larger than the others, painted a garish red with golden accents and wheels.

Cate pointed. "Please tell me we're not taking that one."

Revelin nearly made a face. "No. That is my brother's carriage."

"Are you sure? Because it looks more like a circus wagon."

"Zoltano prefers to travel in comfort."

She laughed. "He travels in something all right."

Revelin helped her into a much smaller and less ostentatious carriage, and they departed from the palace. They sat across from each other, Cate leaning forward to look out the window. Keenly aware of Revelin's eyes on her, she kept her gaze fixed firmly on the city rolling by. It was shimmering, white and bright, with cobblestone streets that looked to be freshly scrubbed. There was no war here, and the city reflected that.

"It's a beautiful city," she said.

"My mother would be pleased to hear you think so."

Cate looked at Revelin. "What's the deal with your mother anyway?"

"The deal?"

"What's wrong with her? I ask because I haven't had the pleasure of making her acquaintance. Is it because she doesn't like Haleine? Is she a recluse? Is she—?"

"She is gravely ill."

"Ill how?"

"She is wasting away. We do not know why."

"But you think you know why," she said. Off Revelin's expression, she added, "It's all over your face. You should never play poker. At least not for money."

"Poker?"

"Not important. What do you think is wrong with your mother?"

"I believe she has been poisoned by a mercenary known as the Black Wolf."

"Ah, the mysterious Black Wolf," Cate said. "Does this mean you're going to tell me about him now?"

Revelin looked away. "He is said to be brilliant, merciless, and willing to do whatever necessary to fulfill a contract."

"Said to be?"

"I have never encountered him, but tales of his exploits have run rampant through court for years now."

"What sort of exploits?"

"Thievery, kidnapping, murder, war mongering," Revelin said. "I am certain there are others."

"So, wait—you think the rebels are responsible? That they—what? Hired a mercenary to poison your mother?"

"I have considered it, yes."

"You're wrong. Poisoning your mother wouldn't do a thing for them."

"I thought you claimed to have no ties to them."

"I don't," she said. "What I do have, however, is common sense. Why would they care what happens over here when they're up to their eyeballs in their own trouble?"

"Their war is with Maddox, and Maddox alone," Revelin said. "Your sister once told me that."

"Did you listen?"

"No."

"How'd that work out for you?"

"We never spoke as friends again."

"Maybe you should listen to me, then."

"Perhaps I should." Revelin leaned forward to look out the window. "We have arrived."

The Coileáin estate was an impressive property, and at the center of it was a massive brown stone castle. Was that what they called it? Maybe it was supposed to be just a house in a country with seemingly endless wealth. There were two turrets in the front and wide stone steps leading to a pair of double doors. The carriage rolled to a stop, and a man wearing a red tunic with a black eagle emblem over his heart opened the door. Revelin climbed out, but Cate didn't move.

"Your majesty?" he said.

Right. She had to get out and walk. She remembered how to walk, didn't she? One foot in front of the other until she was inside a castle that had apparently belonged to a family she hadn't known she had.

Staying in the carriage was growing more appealing by the nanosecond. Revelin offered her his hand. "Your majesty? Are you all right?"

Nope. Definitely not. Cate put her hand in Revelin's, allowing him to help her out and lead her inside. Servants bowed and curtsied to the pair of them, some saying how thrilled they were to see her again. She nodded politely to all of them and smiled but said nothing until she and Revelin were out of earshot.

"How long has it been since Haleine was here?" she whispered.

"I do not know, but it would be more than two years at the very least."

Two years. Okay. She could make that work. A person could change a lot in two years. A person could forget a lot of faces and names; that sort of thing was forgivable. She could do this.

Feeling moderately more confident, she let go of Revelin to explore on her own. The black eagles on their red background seemed to be the Coileáin crest and were found on tapestries and banners everywhere she looked. There were so many rooms—sitting rooms, bedrooms, rooms she couldn't name— and she stood outside of each one without taking a step inside. Though no one would have stopped her from going in and touching everything she could find, she couldn't do that yet. It felt wrong—premature, or something. Regardless, a library at the end of one hall drew her in—she always had been a sucker for those—and she walked along a wall of books, stopping when she saw the first portrait.

A dark-haired man and a woman with auburn tresses stood close together, turned toward one another with honest affection in their faces. Was that what the artist had seen, or had some artistic license been taken?

"Mireille?" Revelin asked quietly.

"Are those my—?" Cate swallowed. "Darian? Rhoswen? Is that them?"

"Yes."

She smiled, tears forming in her eyes. "Sighle looks like him."

"Yes."

"I look like her. I look like my mother."

"Yes. Very much so."

In her sophomore year of high school, she had been assigned a heredity project in biology. Eye color and ear lobes, both attached and unattached, and how parents with brown eyes could produce offspring with blue eyes if they had the right genes. Cate had come home and studied a picture of her and her mother. It seemed the only trait they truly shared was a love of all things chocolate.

"What are you doing, love?" Fiona had asked when she entered the room.

"I must look like my father," Cate answered.

Fiona shook her head. "No, lass—you've your mother's look about you. You always have."

Cate had squinted at the picture, and later at the bathroom mirror, trying to find where her mother's look was within herself. Laura, with her pale skin, dark hair, and ice-blue eyes, was almost a polar opposite of her redheaded daughter. Cate had never seen a picture of her father, but it was hard to imagine that he could look any more different from Cate than her mother did.

But now, as Cate stood in a room that had belonged to a family she hadn't known she had, she could see that Fiona had been right that day. Cate did indeed resemble her mother. Had Fiona always known that Laura wasn't Cate's birth mother? Had Fiona always known that Cate didn't belong?

"Where are they?" she asked. "Where are they buried? Do you even do that here? Do you bury your dead? Or are they cremated, or mummified, or…I don't know—what else do you do with—?"

"They were buried, yes," Revelin interjected, "and they were buried here in Mairéad. I will take you to their graves if you wish."

Cate nodded. "Yeah—yes. Please," she said. "No."

"No?"

"No. I don't know. I just…I don't even know them. I don't know why I should care."

"They are your family."

Maybe a DNA test would say that, but her family was another world away. Daniel and Fiona and Laura—wait. Not Laura anymore. She was dead. Probably.

"Your majesty."

Cate turned and found herself looking at Idwal Kai. The last time she had seen him had been in the rebel camp. That felt like ages ago. How in the world was he standing here now?

"Idwal Kai," she said, slipping back into her accent. "You're—you're here. How did you—?"

"I escaped, your majesty."

"You escaped," she said slowly. "How did you—?"

More movement caught her eye, and she glanced toward it. Gair stood in the doorway, silent and unassuming, and dressed in Coileáin colors. She looked between him and Idwal quickly, then peeked at Revelin. How freely could she talk in front of him?

"You escaped," she repeated, a small smile creeping over her face. "That is—that is wonderful to hear. Were any others able to make the voyage with you?"

"Two came with me, your majesty," Idwal said.

Two. Gair was one, which led her to suspect that Rhydwyn would be the other. They were like the opposite of oil and water, some combination of substances that could never be separated.

"It pleases me greatly to know you are safe," she said. "I have feared for you."

Idwal took her hand. "And I for you, your majesty." He released her and turned to Revelin. "Your highness."

She looked at Revelin, too. "Will you give us a moment?" she said. "He was with my father when he died, and I would like to talk to him about it. Alone. Please."

If Revelin thought the request was odd, he kept it to himself. As the prince left the room, Gair entered and closed the door. Idwal gestured to a sofa, and Cate sat.

Idwal chose a chair across from her. "Are you well, my lady?"

"Yeah, I'm..." Cate trailed off when she saw the second portrait—this one of Sighle and herself. Only it wasn't her, was it? It was Haleine. "I'm fine. What are you doing here with Gair?"

"I told the rebel leader that I would help them get you back." Idwal glanced at Gair and lowered his voice. "I will do as you command, my lady. If you want to go with the rebels, I will continue to help them, but if you wish to remain where you are—"

"You offered to help them?" she interrupted, tearing her focus away from the portrait. "The rebels, after they killed your liege lord and held you captive, you offered to help them."

"Yes, my lady."

"Why?"

"It got me home," Idwal replied.

Home. She surveyed the room, ending on the portrait of her parents. What a foreign concept to her now.

"Get me out," she said, looking away.

Idwal nodded. "The rebel leader is in the city, in the palace, I suspect. I do not know where, and we have not yet been able to make contact with him, but know you are not alone there."

The rebel leader. Did that mean Dana, then? Before she could ask, the door opened and Revelin walked in, Gair stepping quickly out of his way.

"Your majesty," Revelin said, "I do not wish to interrupt, but we must return before we are missed."

She didn't want to return. Being in that damn palace was turning her into something she didn't like and didn't want to be. The last thing she wanted to do was go back to find Zaide Romanza devising a fun, new game to push Cate into becoming more of a murderous monster than she already was.

Did she have to go back? Couldn't she tell Revelin that she would stay here? Sure, the portraits on the wall were incredibly depressing, but the Coileáin estate felt like a safer place to be. Cate looked at Idwal.

"Go," he urged softly. "We will come for you soon."

She nodded. "Hurry, please."

She followed Revelin out of the library. He escorted her through the castle, his hand on her back telegraphing his concern. The people they passed bowed upon seeing them—all except one. Rhydwyn stood near the entrance, just as silent as his brother, and inclined his head slightly when she looked at him. She returned the gesture before Revelin ushered her out the door and back into the carriage.

She had barely sat down before the carriage started to roll. "Something wrong?" she asked Revelin. "You seem a tad twitchy."

"I have not been honest with you."

And the award for least surprising revelation of the millennium went to the second son of the queen of Tanuba. "How so?" she said.

"There are Liran rebels in Tanuba. In Mairéad."

"How do you know?"

"Dana is...here. In the palace. I saw him there last night, dressed as a guard and looking after my brother."

It was true. They were *there,* they had an inside man, and they were coming for her. Were things starting to look up? Dare she think such positive thoughts about possible positive thoughts?

"Wait," she said. "Did you say Dana was guarding Zoltano?"

"Eamonn."

"How many brothers do you have?"

"Two. Eamonn is the youngest."

"Oh my god—you're the middle child! That explains so much!" Cate said. "But it does not explain why you rushed me out of the house you were so determined I visit."

Revelin looked out the window. "I thought I saw...There was a man coming over the wall, and I..."

She smiled. "You don't think Dana came alone."

"I do not."

"Well, you're right about that. He didn't."

That caught Revelin's attention. "What have you seen? What do you know?"

Only things she didn't want to tell him. "Why didn't you raise an alarm?" she asked.

"Excuse me?"

"If Dana's your mortal enemy, and you saw him in the palace last night, why are you telling me—and only me—now? Why didn't you have the other thousand guards in the palace arrest him? Why wasn't he beheaded, or sent to the gallows, or drawn and quartered, or all of the above? Why let him continue to do whatever it is he's doing?"

"Because I do not know what he is doing. He is here for a reason, but I do not know what that is. Haleine told me he was not responsible for the death of my father. You tell me he is not here for my mother, nor for you. If she spoke the truth, if you speak the truth, what is his purpose? Every instinct I have tells me that I should slice him open and let his life slide out onto the floor, that I should have done so when Haleine was alive and I had the chance, but I did not then, and I do not now." Revelin punched the carriage wall. "I do not know whom nor what to trust."

"Sucks, doesn't it?"

Revelin hit the wall a second time. "Sucks?"

"It's hard, with a distinct lack of fun," she explained, "not knowing whom to trust."

"Most have failed to gain yours, but not all," Revelin said. "Who made it past your defenses?"

Cate had a hazy, alcohol-laced memory of the first time this topic had come up. She hadn't wanted to talk about it then; she didn't want to talk about it now, either.

"That hasn't mattered for a while now. He's gone." She leaned back against the seat and looked out the window, the angle giving her a view of the blue, cloudless sky. "It's funny, though. Given how we, uh, first met, and our initial interactions, I never thought he would be someone I could trust. I don't know how it happened, when it happened, but it did. Maybe that's just how it goes sometimes."

"You trusted me with your secret."

"Only because I was dumb enough to tell you the truth to begin with."

"Why did you?"

Because he had been the most genuinely pathetic thing she had encountered in a long time. But she didn't tell him that.

As the palace walls came into view, she looked at him. "About last night...I know we've both been avoiding this conversation, and normally I would keep right on avoiding it, but I think I should—"

Revelin held up his hand. Something outside had caught his attention, and he slid to the edge of the seat. Judging by his body language, what he saw wasn't good.

"What is it?" she asked.

She, too, slid to Revelin's window. Darragh waited in the courtyard with a detachment of guards. An omen? The universe coming to smack her down for having the audacity to think that maybe life was on an upswing?

When Darragh opened the door, Revelin practically threw himself out. "What has happened?" he asked, reaching for Cate. "Is something wrong?"

"It is your mother, your highness," Darragh said. "She is awake and asking for you."

"Awake?" Revelin echoed, squeezing Cate's hand hard enough to make her wince. "Then I must go to her." He looked at Cate. "But first, I will escort you to your chambers, your majesty."

"I promise I can escort myself to my chambers," she said. "Go take care of your mother."

Revelin nodded, squeezed her hand again—this time more gently—and walked away with Darragh and most of the guards. Two were left behind, watching her without actually looking at her, so wherever she went, she wouldn't be walking alone.

She looked at the palace and sighed. She didn't want to go back to her room. Her room sucked. Cate had spent too much time of late sitting, waiting, and notably not doing anything except letting the queen of Feond fuck with her. It was time to try something new.

Besides, there was the question of mothers and verb tense, and of people who were dead still spoken of as though they were otherwise. Her room was not the place she should go.

Omur's was.

"Would you happen to know where I might find Lord Omur?" she asked her escorts. "I have some business to discuss with him."

Neither guard spoke, but one gestured to his left, and she led the way across the courtyard. As they entered a dimly lit passage, her guards stepped closer to her. God, they were paranoid. What did they think would happen?

She was shaking her head when a figure appeared in front of her, and a fist plowed into her face. Head snapping back, she gasped. What the hell? Hands grabbed her arms and yanked them behind her, crossing her wrists and holding them together. No, no, no! This was not happening again. It couldn't be happening again. She was not being abducted for the third goddamn time. It wasn't possible!

She struggled as a rough rope wrapped around her wrists, flailing even as she lost the mobility of her arms. Her legs were free, and she kicked out in every direction she could, making contact with both walls and people without any meaningful results. When she finally remembered to scream, another set of hands shoved a gag into her mouth and tied it securely around her head.

They—whoever they were—dragged her backward. She was disorientated and lost until she saw daylight replacing the darkness. The courtyard. They were taking her somewhere. Made sense, but where?

Once outside, the sun was the only witness to the kidnapping in progress, and it neglected to protest or raise an alarm, while Cate failed at both.

"Put her out."

Cate stopped fighting as she searched for the source of the voice. It wasn't Maddox nor Omur, nor anyone she recognized. To whom did the newest spot on her shit list belong? Two men emerged from the darkened corridor. Zoltano was on the left, and a hooded man on the right.

"Put her out," the mystery man repeated. "Do it fast, do it now."

He passed Cate without looking at her or breaking stride. Zoltano stopped in front of her.

His grin was the last thing she saw.

—◦◦◦—

James rode out of the palace early that day, headed to Odhran and The Thirsty Whale. On his belt was a pouch containing the wages Rowan had given him the night before. Dana had been given an equal share and offered it up, but James told him to keep it. Money was always in short supply and could come in useful. His own coin, however, was marked for the barmaid, with the hope that it would not only pay a debt but purchase him a miracle.

When he arrived, he tethered his mount to a post and went inside the tavern. It was quiet, as he had expected it to be, and he stood at the entrance, scanning the room for Cailean.

"Well," she called from the bar at the back, "if it isn't James the Farmer."

He smiled as he joined her. "Most people call me James."

"What brings you around, James? Bit early for a pint, ain't it?"

He put the money on the bar. "I thought to repay you for your kindness."

"I told you not to bother with that."

"I like to pay my debts when I can."

"Good man."

He shrugged. "I don't know about that."

"Better man than most?" Cailean picked up the pouch, testing its weight. She frowned and dumped the coins onto the bar. "This is too much, James. You've given me far too much."

"Considering I need to ask for more favors, I perhaps haven't given you enough."

Cailean put her hands on her hips. "What is it you need?"

Out of habit, James glanced from side to side, but there was no one within earshot. Cailean put the coins back into the bag, watching him with a raised eyebrow.

"Secretive as all that, is it?"

"No, I—have you any friends down on the docks?" he asked. "Someone who might know whether any ships from Lira have recently arrived? I have some family coming over, and I'd like to know if they're about."

"Why didn't they come with you and your brother?"

"We were separated. Do you know anyone?"

She laughed. "I work in a tavern a stone's throw away from the harbor. Of course I know someone. There's a pair of lads we can ask about your ship. It'll be so easy, you'll be wanting your money back."

James shook his head. "Keep it. Share it with your lads when we're through, and forget I ever asked you anything."

Cailean slid the pouch off the bar. "Maybe not just family, eh?" She pulled a shawl off a hook and wrapped it around her shoulders. "You're an odd one, James, but I like you anyhow. Let's go talk to the lads, shall we?"

Cailean's lads informed him of the arrival of a Liran ship a day earlier. A lord with two servants and no luggage other than their weapons hired a carriage to carry them home, they reported, though they did not know where that was. James thanked them, escorted Cailean back to the tavern, and rode to the palace. Once there, he stopped outside the gates to allow a carriage to pass through.

A carriage carrying Cate. James stood in his stirrups, watching it make its way into the city. Where was she going? Who was with her? Where were the guards? Why would they have taken her anywhere without protection?

James glanced at the palace as he turned his horse in the opposite direction. If only he had taken Dana with him that morning. He trailed after the carriage, following it to the gates of a large manor built from brown stone.

As the carriage passed through the gates, James rode past. He'd have to find another way in. Had he been wearing his Maoilriain colors, he might have been able to gain entrance as well, but there was no telling what he might find inside. Better to find other, less public access.

The grounds were large and well-protected. Perhaps that explained the lack of additional guards. When James finally found a blind spot, he left his horse tethered to a tree and slung his sword across his back before scaling the wall. He landed softly on the other side and started the trek toward the manor. There was some cover, but not enough for him to make it undetected all the way. He got farther than he had thought he would before a guard appeared, sword out. James stopped and put his hands in the air.

"Who are you? What are you doing here?" the guard demanded.

"My name is James ap Seoras, and I'm here to see the queen of Lira. I know she's here. If you give her my name, she'll—"

"If that's true, why'd you come in this way?"

"If you tell her I'm here, she will—"

"He's all right," a new voice said. "Let him pass."

Rhydwyn. James leaned to his right to see him standing in the doorway and nearly broke out into a grin. The guard lowered his weapon, and James joined Rhydwyn inside.

"Bloody hell, it's good to see you," he said.

"She was here, Captain," Rhydwyn said quietly. "She just left."

James nodded. "Where's Idwal Kai?"

Rhydwyn led the way, taking James down a corridor that spoke to wealth and privilege.

"What is this place?" he asked.

"The Coileáin estate."

The *Coileáin* estate? "Bloody hell."

Rhydwyn made a noise in his throat that indicated he agreed.

"Is Gair here?" James asked.

"Aye, Captain."

"Does Idwal Kai know about Dana?"

"No. Not from us, at least." Rhydwyn stopped before an ornate wooden door. "The library."

The what? James followed Rhydwyn inside, his jaw dropping at the quality of the furnishings and the number of books lining the walls. He had never seen so many books in one place in his entire life.

"Captain," Idwal Kai greeted him. "You're here. How did you..."

James stopped gawking and turned. He spotted Gair first and acknowledged him with a nod. Idwal Kai sat on a sofa, and James approached, slowing when he saw the portrait. Bloody hell.

"Over the wall. There's a blind spot along the back," James said, studying the painting of a girl who wasn't Cate but could have been. "Almost made it inside before your men noticed me."

Idwal Kai was slow to smile. "Thank you for bringing that to my attention," he said. "Would you care to sit?"

James saw the second portrait then—this one of Darian Coileáin and a woman who bore a strong resemblance to Cate. Her mother? "No."

"Am I to assume that you are here to discuss Lady Coileáin's rescue?"

"I am. Is this when you have us arrested and thrown into a dungeon?"

"The Coileáin estate has no dungeon, Captain. Were you arrested here, you would either be brought in chains to the palace dungeon or simply killed where you stood."

"Upon which have you decided?"

"I would have killed you where you stood, had my lady not requested to be removed from her current situation."

"Have they hurt her?"

"She does not appear to have been abused, but"—Idwal Kai sighed—"something has frightened her terribly. I cannot say what, but every effort should be made for her swift recovery."

"What do you think I've been trying to do?" James asked, barely containing his annoyance. "Why did you let her leave?"

"She was accompanied by Prince Revelin Maoilriain. He wanted her to leave, and I had to let her go. Without knowing of your whereabouts, I was hardly in a position to countermand anything his highness wanted."

James nodded. "You are now. Get her back here any way that you can, with or without the prince; it doesn't matter which. Do it as soon as you are able. We will take care of the rest."

Idwal Kai stood. "I will not allow you to murder Prince Revelin."

"Nor am I interested in murdering your prince," James responded. "I want only to reason with the man. He can be reasoned with, your prince, can't he?"

"Yes, Captain. The prince is very reasonable. He is a good man."

James was tired of hearing about good men. He turned to leave.

"Where are you going?" Idwal Kai called after him.

"I left something behind," James said. "I need to fetch it."

—◦◦◦—

His mother was awake. Not only that, but she was sitting up in bed, partaking in a simple meal and talking quietly with her youngest son.

Revelin stood in the doorway, watching his mother with a mixture of relief and concern. The physicians and nurses and servants were calling her sudden recovery a miracle, a gift from God above. He did not share their views, but without evidence to the contrary, he was forced to keep his opinion to himself.

Indeed, it could have been a miracle. What other explanation existed? Cathal had found nothing, after all, and had only worked off of Revelin's suspicions. His *instinct*.

Though that was all he had, he trusted it more than what he could see. Someone had done this to his mother. Why it had been done, why it had now been ended, he could not say.

Haraszty looked at him and smiled. She waved him over, and he obliged. When he reached her, he kissed the top of her head and took her hand in his. Haraszty clasped the other.

"It is good to see you recovering, Mother," he said. "You frightened us immensely."

"Nonsense." Haraszty set aside her tray, and a servant promptly took it away. "You are more than capable of caring for this kingdom. I'm sure you barely noticed I was gone at all."

"We did," Revelin insisted. "There has been a distinct lack of mirth within these walls."

"We'll change that soon enough," Haraszty sniffed. "But tell me—where the devil is Zoltano? The nurses told me he has been in the palace, but I've not seen him. Is he here? Why has he not come?"

Revelin did not know where Zoltano might have been but did not doubt that the devil kept the crown prince company. Had his brother turned tail and run? Or perhaps he was hiding somewhere deep in the bowels of the castle, concocting a new scheme to claim the throne.

Provided the first one had failed.

Revelin looked at his mother. Did she suspect her eldest son in any manner?

"I believe he is hunting boar today," he lied, lest Haraszty did not. Eamonn's head turned at the falsehood, but he did not call his brother out.

"You send him here when he returns. I would very much like to speak with him. Now go away, both of you," Haraszty ordered, waving them toward the door. "I'm exhausted, and there is no reason for either of you to hover over an old woman while she sleeps. You may return after I've rested."

Eamonn stood, and together they left their mother's rooms. Once out in the hall, Eamonn placed himself in Revelin's path.

"Our brother is not hunting," he said. "Why did you lie?"

"Our brother is always hunting," Revelin replied. "I only lied about the boar."

He walked away, debating whether to summon Cathal, but found himself moving toward Mireille's chambers. What would Zaide Romanza say about that? The answer bothered him, but he did not alter his course.

He slowed as he approached the doors. No guards stood where there should have been two. Was she not there? Where else would she have gone?

Perplexed and concerned, he went inside to find Zaide Romanza sitting at the table, facing him.

"What are you doing here?" he asked. He did not bow.

"Waiting for you. I thought you would come here after you had finished with your mother. I see I was not wrong."

"Where is Haleine?"

Zaide Romanza sighed. "I'm afraid she isn't here anymore. She's gone."

"What have you done to her?"

"Why would I do anything to her? It's terribly insulting that you should accuse me of such a crime."

"Crime?" he echoed. "Where is she?"

"I've been sitting here, waiting for you, so that you might hear it from me and not—"

"Hear what?" Revelin demanded. "What has happened?"

"Haleine has left."

"With Maddox? They have gone back to Lira?"

Zaide Romanza stood. "With Dana. She has run off once again with her lover and his followers," she said. "Did you know they were in the palace? Masquerading as guards, apparently. It's quite a scandal."

"No, I did not know." It was his second lie of the day. He shook his head. "No, this is not right. It cannot be. She would never—"

"There you go again, putting Haleine ahead of everything. Even the truth," Zaide Romanza said. "There are witnesses, Revelin. There are dead men in the courtyard. The Liran rebels came for Haleine—they came *here* for her—and she went with them gladly."

She was wrong. She had to be wrong. Mireille never would have gone willingly with the rebellion. She had no ties to them—apart from her kidnapping. Why would she ever go with them willingly? If they indeed had her, they had taken her by force. Because he had given them the opportunity.

"You must excuse me," he said, walking away. "I must tend to this matter. Thank you for bringing it to my attention."

"She does not love you, and she never will," Zaide Romanza said. "Do yourself a kindness, Revelin, and let her go."

"This is not about Haleine."

"I never claimed it was."

"Have a care, your majesty," he said. "You will not always be able to play me for a fool."

Zaide Romanza laughed. "I've never done anything else."

He did not respond as he left the room.

The courtyard was empty no longer, filled almost past the point of capacity, but a path opened for Revelin, and he followed it to the dead men of which Zaide Romanza had spoken. Their throats had been cut, their life's blood seeping into the cracks between the cobblestones.

Dana would have known that she was not Haleine. If he had been the one to take her.

"Your highness," Darragh said.

"You should have sent for me immediately."

"My lord, you were seeing to your mother. I did not wish to distract you from that."

Distraction. Yes, there had been an endless amount of that of late.

"The queen of Feond told me that the Liran rebels are responsible for this," Revelin said. "That they claimed Haleine, that she…allowed them to do so."

"It appears her majesty spoke true, I am sorry to say. Lira's queen clearly has announced where her allegiance lies. I have found no one who tells another tale."

But Lira's queen had not done that. Haleine was not the one they had taken. It had been Mireille, and she had no allegiance to the rebellion. Or so she had claimed. Would she have lied to him?

Revelin turned from the dead men, his eyes sweeping over the courtyard. They stopped when they reached the spot where his brother's carriage normally sat. It was empty now.

"Has the crown prince gone somewhere?"

"Gweneria, my lord."

"Who with him?"

"A small number of guards. As the Liran rebels have infiltrated our walls, he only took those men most loyal to him."

"Did anyone else travel with him?"

"Another man, your highness. No one seems to know who he might be."

Revelin knew who he was. "You asked?"

"I thought you would want to know."

"Indeed," he said. "Have you sent men to track the Liran rebels?"

"Yes, your highness."

Revelin nodded. There was nothing left to ask, only one thing more he needed to see. He took one last look at the dead men before turning toward the soldiers' barracks.

Dana lay on his thin mattress, looking at the bunk above him while his fingers drummed an erratic beat on the flask resting on his chest. The contents didn't interest him. Progress, he supposed.

The barracks were loud and crowded as men came and left. Both he and James would stand their watch later in the day, leaving their nights open for a rescue they had yet to attempt. Neither of them had planned on Revelin's continued involvement. Dana should have considered that possibility sooner. If he were Revelin, surely he would have done the same.

James walked into the room and made his way to his bunk. Dana didn't know where he had gone or what he had attempted to do. Although the hate James bore him seemed to have lessened immensely, James was still shutting him out of most of his plans. Now, however, James moved with a renewed energy. Something had encouraged him greatly. When he caught Dana's eye, his vigor faded a bit, but James nodded. Dana nodded as well—though he didn't know why—and as James unbuckled his sword belt, Dana returned to staring at the bunk. Would James ever trust him again? Should he?

The barracks fell into sudden silence. Dana looked to his left to see Revelin. Everyone who wasn't James or himself had knelt and bowed their heads. Revelin didn't seem to notice them, nor the fact that James remained standing, as his eyes were fixed on Dana. Dana glanced at the sword strapped to the prince's side, then looked at his own sheathed blade resting against the end of the bed. It was too far away to be useful, even if it would make a difference against the number of men in this room Revelin held at his command, but when his gaze reverted to Revelin, the prince gave a subtle shake of his head and touched the shoulder of the man nearest him.

"Leave," he said.

Soon every man had filed out except for Dana, the prince, and James. James stayed by his own bunk, his sword drawn and held at his side. He slapped the blade lightly against his leg. He wanted Revelin to see it. Dana should have called James off but decided against it. He, too, wanted Revelin to see it.

"You will go as well," Revelin said to James.

"No." Dana sat up and slid off the bed. "He will stay."

Revelin nodded. "She said you did not come alone."

She knew they were there? That was a surprise, as was the revelation that she had told Revelin of their presence. What else might she have told him?

"They have taken her," the prince said before Dana could ask.

James's sword stopped moving.

Revelin looked at the floor. "They have taken her and blamed you for the act. But as you are here, and she is not..."

Dana waited, willing James to do the same.

"North of here," the prince continued, "about two days' ride is Gweneria. My brother has a holding there—a fortress—and it is there they would have taken her."

"They?" Dana asked.

"My brother and his mercenary. The Black Wolf."

The Black Wolf? The name meant nothing to him, but Dana supposed that didn't matter at the moment. He nodded. "Guards?"

"Very few. They know you have gained access to the palace and are wary of having included you or any of yours among their number," Revelin answered. "But the Black Wolf...by all accounts, he is vicious and dangerous, perhaps more so than my brother. He should not be taken lightly."

"He won't be," Dana said.

Revelin nodded and lifted his head, resolve showing on his face. "Take horses from the stable. Tell the grooms you carry a message from the queen to her son. They will not question you, and they will make sure you have the supplies you require." He held out a sealed piece of parchment. "You will have to ride hard to catch them. I do not know what they...Of course I know. Hurry. Please."

Dana looked to James, but James was already moving. He sheathed his sword, gathered his belongings, and snatched the letter from Revelin's hand. He walked out of the barracks, leaving Dana alone with the prince.

They stared at each other, but Dana broke quickly. James would leave without him if he took too long, so Dana collected his cloak and sword and moved toward the door. Before exiting, he looked back at Revelin. The prince hadn't moved.

"You do know, don't you?" Dana said. "You know she isn't Haleine?"

Revelin didn't turn around. "I do remember it from time to time, but I find it matters not. I have lost them both."

"Not yet," Dana said.

Leaving the barracks, he rushed toward the stables. He hadn't gotten very far when something forced him, face first, into a wall. His arms were thrown out wide, causing him to drop all he carried. He struggled to free himself, but nothing physical held him. It could only be magic. Which meant it could only be Omur.

"Going somewhere?"

He had been wrong. It wasn't Omur; it was Zaide Romanza. Dana didn't respond to her question, focusing on regaining control of his body.

"You've only just arrived," she said. "It would be rude to leave so soon."

He had almost twisted the fingers of his right hand into a fist when the magic holding him let go. He turned quickly and searched for his sword.

"Looking for this?"

The sound of steel dragging on stone made him look at the queen of Feond. She stood in front of him, holding his sword and watching its tip move across the floor.

"We've never been properly introduced, but I trust you..." She looked at him, tilting her head to the side. Smiling, she took a step closer. "So you're what happened to her."

"I won't have you talking about Haleine."

Zaide Romanza looked at him in amused disdain and raised her hand, palm facing him. He was soon flush with the wall again, this time his arms pinned at his sides. Her fingers curled inward, and Dana slowly lost his ability to breathe. As her magic choked him, he gasped for air, desperate to claw at his throat, but helpless to do anything but die. When he thought that might happen, she opened her hand, and he fell to the floor. He rested on his hands and knees, taking ragged breaths.

"I was not referring to your whore, but do keep in mind that I will talk about whomever I'd like whenever I'd like," she said. "After all, I trust you know who I am."

Dana used the wall to help him stand. "Do you expect me to bow?"

"That won't be necessary. It's not your homage which interests me."

"Dare I ask what does interest you?"

"A man who's done all that you've done afraid to ask a question? I have to wonder why she was so willing to sacrifice so much for you."

Dana didn't respond.

"That time I did mean your whore," Zaide Romanza said.

"She isn't my whore."

"Maybe not anymore."

"She's not anything anymore. She's dead."

"And you're a liar, amongst other things," Zaide Romanza said. "It's no matter. You best be running along. They'll kill her twin if you don't get there in time."

"You care about that?"

"You'd be surprised by what I care about," she said. "Happy hunting."

Zaide Romanza tossed the sword to him, and he caught it. He stayed frozen in that position until she was gone from sight. Then he grabbed his cloak from the floor and ran in the opposite direction.

When Dana reached the stables, James waited in the saddle of one horse, holding the reins to a second.

"Where the hell have you been?" he demanded as Dana claimed his mount. "What happened?"

Dana glanced at the palace before pulling himself into the saddle. "I have no idea."

CHAPTER 30

Her head hurt. Again. Still? That detail probably didn't matter much. It wasn't like she could remember the last time her head didn't hurt. Though her eyes were open, it was dark. A scratchy, heavy bag, a sack, a hood—she didn't know what they might have called it, but they'd put a goddamn *bag* over her head. Just in case the ropes around her wrists—now tied in front of her—and the gag in her mouth wasn't humiliation enough. Fuckers. It was possible that they just didn't want her to know where she was, but the joke was on them because Cate wouldn't have known that even with a map, a compass, and someone with the ability to read both.

Her gown was gone, leaving her in the sleeveless slip the maids had put her in that morning. Her shoes were gone, too, so her feet were bare but not cold. They were moving, rolling along at a good clip. A wagon, then, or more specifically, a carriage, as she didn't feel exposed to the elements.

There was also the involvement of Prince Zoltano Maoilriain, whose flamboyance would have made Liberace jealous. Forget keeping a low profile following the brazen daylight kidnapping of a noblewoman—they were probably riding around in the goddamn royal carriage, a portable Versailles, to prevent his highness from experiencing any sort of discomfort while committing a felony. Not that felonies were a thing here.

She hated it here.

Zoltano was talking, using a surprisingly quiet voice for a man who likely had never spent so much as a minute being considerate to another soul—living or dead—as he discussed their destination. Gweneria—that's where they were headed. She didn't know who or where or what that was, but having a name to work with was bound to be better than not knowing anything.

At least that's what she would keep telling herself. It was important to maintain one's delusions in times like these.

The mystery man joined the conversation and gave Gweneria a second shout-out. Talk of a lowered number of servants and guards followed, making her suspect Gweneria was a place, not a person, and she made a note of it.

Everything she learned, no matter how minor, could help. Would help. Because knowledge was power. But now that she thought about it, she did have other powers. Actual powers. Active ones—the kind that could cause bodily harm to others. She'd frozen people in their tracks, held fire in her hands, and *killed* a man. Of course, she had had full, unhindered use of her hands and eyes and mouth when she'd done those things.

Huh. Maybe they weren't concerned about her knowing where she was.

Did they know who she was? Zoltano didn't—she was fairly convinced of that—but Mystery Man might. He was, after all, a mystery.

"What about her?" Zoltano said when the carriage had come to a stop.

"I'll deal with it," Mystery Man replied.

It? He'd deal with *it?* Was Mystery Man within kicking range? Her legs were still free, and he had earned his most sensitive areas a date with her foot. Multiple dates with her foot. And any sharp objects she happened to come across.

The carriage rocked as Zoltano exited, but Mystery Man didn't move. How was he planning to deal with it?

"Do you think you can walk?" he asked.

Was he speaking to her?

"I know you're awake," he said. "Are you able to walk?"

Was he seriously expecting an answer? Had he forgotten the part where someone had gagged her?

"Nod, if you believe you are able."

She could walk. Her head may have hurt, but her brain wasn't scrambled this time. Her legs and stomach and all the rest seemed fine; walking shouldn't have been a challenge. But she didn't nod. To hell with him. She wasn't about to make life easier for that bastard. Screw him. Let him drag her every step of the way.

"Very well," Mystery Man said.

Dragging her out of the carriage, he tossed her over his shoulder. Outside gave way to inside. Gweneria, or a way station in between? Wherever they were, it was loud with conversation and laughter and smelled like piss and stale ale. A tavern? Mystery Man moved farther into the room, whispers chasing after him. There wasn't a single mention of the bound and hooded woman he carried over his shoulder, just a single word. *Wolf,* they said. Wolf. Was her mystery man the same mercenary Revelin suspected of poisoning the queen? Was he the Black Wolf?

The noise fell away as Mystery Man climbed stairs and entered another room. He carried her across a wooden floor and dumped her onto it before walking away to confer with an unseen presence too softly for Cate to hear what was said. When he came back, he lifted her and a second pair of hands held her sides as Mystery Man raised her arms above her head. Metal was introduced—a hook, she realized, as the hands drew away, and she remained upright, her arms suspended and her feet grazing the floor. The hood was pulled from her head, and she looked at the man standing in front of her—lithe and blond—with the hood in one hand and a wine bottle in the other. She looked the longest at the wine.

Well, that could only lead to good things.

Mystery Man examined her face and dropped the hood to pull the gag from her mouth. "Does it hurt very much, your head?"

Not as much as her arms and shoulders soon would be. They already ached, and her tenure on the hook was only just beginning. Her fingers scraped the metal, searching for—and failing to find—a way to alleviate some of the pressure.

"If I say no, will you have Zoltano hit me again?" she asked, not bothering with the accent.

"Mayhap I'll do it myself."

Her lack of accent didn't faze him at all. More evidence that he knew more than most.

"I doubt that," she said. "You don't strike me as the type to get your hands dirty."

"I do when necessary."

"Which is why you ordered the crown prince to put me out in the first place."

Mystery Man shrugged. "He would have done it anyway. Your head?"

"Why do you care? What do you want from me?"

"It's not what I want that you should concern yourself with."

Cate nodded. "I guess that makes you the mercenary. The Black Wolf."

"I am he, yes."

"With a name like that, I thought you'd look different."

The Black Wolf nodded. "Most people do."

"Where'd that name come from?" she asked. "You didn't give it to yourself, did you? Maybe you don't know this, but giving yourself your own nickname is incredibly lame."

"You're not trying very hard to hide who you are," the mercenary remarked.

"Don't see the point in that. You obviously know I'm not Haleine, so…" Shrugging as best as she was able, she promptly grimaced. She wouldn't be trying that again.

The Black Wolf smiled. "I truly do appreciate your lack of fear. It's…refreshing."

"Don't see the point in that, either."

The mercenary took his wine and sat in a chair across from her. He pulled the cork from the bottle with his teeth and spat it onto the floor. "You will."

Maybe. At the moment, she was too pissed off for any other emotion to get any play. Cate didn't mind; she preferred it that way.

"Do you have a name?" she asked. "Like, an actual name?"

"I have several."

"One for every personality?"

The Black Wolf drank straight from the bottle. "Perhaps."

"What's the name your mother gave you?" she said and took note of the flash-in-the-pan change in his expression. "You do have a mother, don't you? I assume you weren't grown in a lab or anything."

"I had a mother once," he said, "but she has been gone for quite some time now."

Something she had in common with Mercenary Guy. How unexpected.

"What did she call you?" Cate asked.

"Her darling boy."

"Isn't that adorable. Tell me, darling boy, are you planning to have your way with me?"

"Not in the manner in which you now imply," he answered. "I hate to be obvious."

"I don't think your employer shares that trait."

He tilted his head and stared at her intently. Perhaps checking out the bruise Zoltano had undoubtedly left on her cheek? Wondering how long it would take for both shoulders to dislocate themselves?

"The crown prince is not my employer, but you're quite correct about his character," the Black Wolf said. "More's the pity for you, of course."

Cate registered the pity comment but focused exclusively on the first statement. "Zoltano's not your employer? He didn't hire you to do this?"

"No."

"But he hired you to poison the queen and put him on the throne?"

The Black Wolf laughed into his wine. "Is that what Revelin believes? Oh, the poor, ignorant fool."

"I don't hear you denying it."

"You just did. Pay attention, my lady; I'd hate to be disappointed in you."

Cate made a face as she dragged her toes across the floor, hunting for a bit of leverage. "Yeah, wouldn't that be a tragedy."

"If I had been hired to put the crown prince on the throne," he said, "we would no longer be calling him the crown prince."

"If not the employer, what is he?" she said. "Your playmate? Your partner in torture?"

The Black Wolf shook his head and drank some more wine. "Part of the job. A tool of the trade, if you will."

Oh good. Something else to not think about.

"Who did employ you, and what do they want?" she asked.

"I think perhaps you already know the answer to both your questions."

Omur. It was the only possibility that made even the smallest bit of sense. Why he would bother to hire a mercenary to orchestrate the kidnapping of someone he was already holding hostage, Cate didn't know, but he was the only one besides Zaide Romanza who wanted anything out of her, and Zaide Romanza wouldn't have resorted to this. Not when she was having so much damn fun twisting Cate around on her own.

"What does he think you'll be able to do that he couldn't?" Cate asked.

"Get him what he wants."

"He can't have told you what that is."

"What makes you so sure?"

"He didn't tell you because if he had, you wouldn't have accepted the job because there's no way to be successful," Cate said. "But you go ahead and dream your impossible dream. Don't let me stop you."

"I never let anyone stop me."

"Until now," she said. "He wants my soul."

The Black Wolf smiled. "You still have one? How quaint."

"Yeah, you're a real bad ass, I'm sure."

"Would you like me to show you how bad I can be?"

There was a glint in his eye that convinced Cate she didn't want to know the extent and depth of the Black Wolf's evil nature, but she couldn't help but answer, "Only if you want the favor reciprocated."

The smile broadened. "It is such a shame that we've had to become acquainted under these particular circumstances," he said. "In another life, I think we could have been great friends, if not more."

Cate snorted. "Oh, no doubt."

"You don't agree."

"Gee, what gave it away?"

The mercenary laughed but didn't respond. The conversation ended, and Cate looked away from her captor to evaluate her surroundings. No windows, and only the one door at the far end of the room. Dark wood made darker by lanterns and candles that should have done the opposite. The furniture was beyond minimal—just the chair in which the Black Wolf sat and something she thought was supposed to be a bed built into a corner. No amenities worth speaking of. Nothing useful in facilitating an escape. Not that it mattered when she was suspended from the goddamn ceiling.

"Weylyn Lann," the Black Wolf said.

Cate looked at him. "What?"

"My name. The one my mother gave me. Weylyn Lann."

She blinked, unsure what to do with this information. What angle was he running? Trying to make her like him? Trust him? "I think I like your other name better."

He grinned. "As do I."

"Are you lying to me? About your name?"

"Possibly," he said. "I don't suppose you'll ever know."

"No, I suppose not."

He sighed. "You may want to at least consider being frightened."

"Guess that whole refreshing thing's over for you now, huh?" she said. "What's the matter? It didn't fit into your diabolical scheme?"

"My diabolical scheme remains intact."

"Well, don't be shy. Tell the audience how you're planning to extract from me my soul."

Weylyn Lann drank more wine and looked at her for a long time. It was so quiet, she could hear the revelry downstairs. Was the crown prince a part of it?

"Have you ever been to Gweneria?" Weylyn Lann asked finally. "It's a lawless place—largely ignored by the ruling family, apart from their psychotic firstborn—and over time, that wildness has trickled down to the areas surrounding it. If I wanted, I could find no shortage of men and women willing to have their way with you. They would line up for days just for the chance to taste that lovely white flesh of yours. Noblewomen are scarce that far north, you understand. You would be a rare treat."

"Like Beluga caviar," Cate said, hoping beyond hope that her voice wouldn't betray how inordinately freaked out she was. "Not that you would know what that is."

"You don't need to keep playing this game," Weylyn Lann drawled.

The hell she didn't. If she didn't keep playing, she was just one completely screwed girl suspended from a ceiling, counting down the minutes until the gang rape began. Until she figured out how to either get her hands free or vaporize people using nothing but the powers of her mind, sarcastic bantering was all she had; it kept her grounded, kept her present, and kept the panic and terror building deep inside her from boiling over past the point of no return. So she'd keep playing. Like her life depended on it.

"You should take your own advice," she said, "because if you keep playing this game, you'll be sorry."

Weylyn Lann drank again. "I'll be rich."

"And that's your guiding star?"

"Easier than morals, I find. More lucrative, too." He let out a brief, unenthusiastic laugh, followed by a deep sigh. "But despite my best judgment, I find I do like you, my lady, so please allow me to offer you some advice."

"Never hit a man with a closed fist? Never get involved in a land war in Asia? Never wear white after Labor Day?"

Weylyn Lann's mouth quirked with another smile. "Give him what he wants. Now. Or yesterday, if you can find a way to accomplish that."

"Angling for a bonus, are we?"

His eyebrows furrowed. "Angling to avoid doing what I'm going to do to you."

"Thanks for the concern, but I'm not overly inclined to do you any favors."

"The favor would not be for me," Weylyn Lann said. "The crown prince will make his way here before long, and as we've previously discussed, he's quite interested in being obvious. And cruel. He won't mar your face further, though, should that offer you some small comfort. He likes his girls pretty— from the neck up, at least."

Her stomach was tying itself into knots, repeating the action over and over. What would happen when she ran out of stomach?

"Be that as it may," she said, "I'm not giving up my soul."

"Do you believe you will possess it still when he is done with you? When *I* am done with you?" Weylyn Lann asked. "Mayhap you're not as smart as I took you to be. Bravado can carry you only so far, my girl."

"I'm not your girl."

"Not yet anyway. But perhaps when the crown prince is done with you, and the people of Gweneria have had their fill..." Weylyn Lann shook his head. "No, not even I would have you then. By then, you would assuredly be more animal than anything else, and I've never been interested in bestiality."

"You know what? I've changed my mind," Cate said. "Let's be best friends."

Weylyn Lann snorted as he took another drink from his bottle. He held it out to her. "Would you care for some? It might make the night to come more bearable for you."

She looked at the bottle. Was he serious? Should she take him up on that? Was she serious? Would it somehow be granting permission? God, she wanted to be anywhere else at that moment. She wanted to throw up repeatedly and cry her damn eyes out. She wanted to beat Mercenary Guy to death with his own stupid smile. Or a crowbar.

"Is that why you're drinking?" she asked.

He smiled again, but his delight was gone. He turned the bottle upside down, and together they watched wine spill on the floor. When he had shaken out the very last drops, he smashed the bottle against a post and came at her with the broken jagged top. He pressed it under her chin, and the glass sliced into her.

"Do not mistake my fondness for you as anything other than a passing amusement," he snarled. "I will see this job finished. I will do anything and everything I must to get from you what my employer wants. You tell me he requires your soul, so that is what I shall provide. If I had a way to extract your soul from your cold corpse and present it to my employer on a bloody gold platter, I would shove this bottle through your heart this very instant. But since I have not yet found such a way, I shall have to settle for this."

He drove the jagged end of the bottle into her left thigh. Cate wasn't prepared for it and screamed, but even if she had known what he would do, she still would have screamed.

But she wouldn't do anything else. She wouldn't give him anything else. Even if her entire body called for tears and capitulation, he wouldn't get it. Not from her. Fuck him. She wouldn't give him anything. She wouldn't, she wouldn't, she wouldn't.

Don't cry. Don't think. Don't do anything.

Weylyn Lann pulled the bottle out and dropped it on the floor. "I'll see you and your soul in the morning," he said, backing away. "If you're both still here, that is."

Cate stared at him until he left the room. When the door closed, she dropped her head, squeezed her eyes shut, and gritted her teeth as she fought the urge to scream again.

Don't cry. Don't think. Don't cry. Don't think. Don't cry. Don't think. Don't—

The door opened again, and Cate could sense the crown prince's malice before he took a step toward her. A tool of the trade. Goddamn.

Stop it. Don't do that.

Don't. Just—don't.

———

Before Haleine had left Loreton, the soldiers attacked another village—this time Rushwick in the southwest—and left another message. No one had seen them leave the palace. No one had seen them on the roads. No one had seen them arrive, nor depart, but the damage done could not be denied.

Haleine had traveled there as well—though both Faolan and Lucius desired her to go instead to the relative safety of Enimode—to touch the blood and confirm her suspicion that Sighle had done this, too.

"I'll return to the palace," she said later in the privacy of the forest, Faolan and Lucius her audience. "I'll return to the palace and order the soldiers to stop. I am their queen. They'll have to listen to me."

"Everyone in the palace believes you're in Tanuba with the king. How will you convince them of the truth?" Faolan asked. "Even if they do believe you're Haleine, how do you explain the absence of Maddox or Omur, or any of the other people who also sailed to Tanuba?"

"I'll tell them something. We can think of something."

"What about Sighle?" Faolan asked. "She doesn't have to listen to you, and you can't make her listen. It seems painfully obvious that she's stronger than you. Than all of us."

"What am I supposed to do? Stand by and let them raze another village? If you want me to sit meekly in a farmhouse, you have to stop them. If it can't be done on the road, you have to get ahead of them, and without me in the palace to help you, you'll never be able to do that," Haleine argued. "She wants me. For whatever purpose, Sighle wants that. She's written it on the walls in blood, Faolan, and she won't stop until—"

Haleine gasped and jerked back, her hand cupping her chin as a sudden, burning pain tore her skin.

"Haleine?" Faolan asked, cautious.

She pulled her hand away, blood dripping between her fingers. Lucius rushed forward and examined her hand before forcing her head back.

"There's no cut," he said. "From where did the blood come? How did you—?"

Haleine screamed as pain exploded in her left thigh. She fell to the ground, leaning to her right and clutching her leg, tearing at the fabric covering it to find the source. Lucius called for Faolan before collapsing at her side. He reached beneath her skirt and straightened her leg while pushing up the fabric. The air only made the pain more intense, and she lashed out, struggling to protect her skin. He misinterpreted her actions, raising his hands with his fingers spread wide, and offering apologies for his offense. She wanted to tell him he was wrong, that no slight had been committed, but the pain pulsing through her was too powerful to allow for anything like the forming of words. Shaking her head, she dragged herself away until she was backed against a tree, her hands pressed into the ground.

"Faolan, help her!" Lucius barked. "Stop this!"

"Find Hanah. Bring her here," Faolan said, and Lucius bolted toward the village. "What's happening, Haleine? Is it a vision? What do you see?"

An invisible fist hit the center of her stomach, and she pitched forward, laying her forehead against the ground. Faolan called her name—now sounding concerned—but as the assault continued, she ignored him and covered her head with her hands. It did nothing to shield her.

She swayed and fell on her side, closing her eyes and curling inward, but that did not protect her, either. Her body continued to sustain abuse—hitting, kicking, cutting—and scream after scream left her lungs until they burned as badly as her skin.

The deluge stopped suddenly, and Haleine dropped onto the uneven planks of a wooden floor. Trembling and gasping, she opened her eyes and saw her twin—lying naked, bound, gagged, bruised, and bleeding—just out of reach.

"Oh," Haleine breathed. "Oh no."

She heard footsteps—slow, heavy, menacing—and her arm shot out, fingers stretching, desperate to reach her twin, but the same force that had brought her here to witness such a sinister act jerked her away. Haleine screamed as she was dragged back, hands still trying to get to her sister, and did not stop until she landed on the ground.

Fingers digging into the dirt, she struggled to sit up. She had almost succeeded when the need to vomit overtook her. Afterward, her body buckled, her elbows barely able to keep her head and chest off the ground.

Cool hands touched her cheeks, and she became aware that she wasn't alone. While Faolan and Lucius yelled at one another, Hanah had gotten on the ground in front of Haleine, and she looked into the healer's terrified eyes. Hanah opened her mouth, but her question did not leave her lips before Haleine crumbled once again. She dropped her head in Hanah's lap and sobbed.

The shouting stopped, everything stopped, as they stared at her. Hanah stroked her hair and said, "She's colder than ice, Lucius. Fetch a blanket. Fetch two."

"Haleine," Faolan pressed, when Lucius had run away, "you need to tell me what happened."

"For Laorans's sake, leave her alone," Hanah snapped.

"I can't," he said. "Haleine, what did you see?"

"Where is she?" Haleine turned her head to locate the pegasus, finding him perched on a tree branch. "Where is she, the one you called my sister. Mireille or Cate, or whatever name you use for her—where is she?"

"What did you see?"

Haleine pushed herself up. "Where is she! Where is she! Where is she!"

Behind her, Hanah stood but did not call for Haleine to back down. The healer was angry as well; Haleine could feel it leeching into her own, and she grabbed hold of it and carried it with her.

"Where is she?" Haleine demanded, her voice low and raw.

"Tanuba."

"What is happening to her there?"

"You tell me. What did you see?"

The image of her sister, trussed and damaged, replaced Faolan. Haleine was returned to the room where the violence had occurred and stood over her sister's body. Was Mireille still in there?

"You do not know what they've done to her," Haleine said when she was once again in the forest.

"I think I might now."

"They are *torturing* her, Faolan."

"So I gathered."

"Why? Why did you let them do this?"

"I didn't *let* them do anything."

"This is happening because of me," Haleine said. "They're hurting her because they believe she is me."

"If they thought that, she would already be dead," Faolan said. "They're perfectly aware of who she is."

"Then why?"

The pegasus looked away. "She won't give in."

She wouldn't give in. Haleine went to her knees. Sighle needed to be stopped, Mireille needed to be saved, and Haleine was helpless to do either.

Helpless, powerless—that was all she was, all she had ever been.

"Your majesty?"

Lucius had returned. He stood behind her and draped the blanket Hanah had requested around her shoulders. Haleine nearly laughed at the absurdity of it all, and then did laugh at the absurdity of her own actions—or lack thereof.

Mireille wouldn't give in. They would torture her, rip her, break her, and she wouldn't give in. When had Haleine ever done as much?

Haleine stood, letting the blanket slip away. "Can we do anything for Mireille? You and I, and the unicorns, and the people here and now," she asked Faolan. "Can we save her?"

"No, her survival depends upon her," the pegasus said. "It will depend upon Dana and James. They will do everything they can—I know they will—but we can do nothing for her."

Haleine nodded. Then she would stop Sighle. Some way, somehow, she would do that.

"Very well," she said and walked away.

Lucius and Hanah scrambled to catch her, ever reluctant to allow their queen to walk alone. Faolan, however, stayed behind.

"Where are you going?" he called after her.

She did not look back. "Eluned."

—∽∾∾∿—

Revelin stood on a balcony facing north. Two days had passed since Zoltano and the Black Wolf had taken Mireille. Two days had passed since he had sent Dana and his companion after her. One day since the king of Lira and his man had departed for their home. One day since Zaide Romanza had left as well.

Days had come and gone, and Revelin remained motionless through them all. How many days would he continue as such? How many more days would go by before he discovered what had come to pass in Gweneria?

Perhaps he should discard with the illusion of searching for Dana where he already knew the rebel leader did not hide. Perhaps he should dispatch men to go to Gweneria directly. Or go himself. It would be safe to leave Mairéad now. With Zoltano and his mercenary gone, Haraszty would be safe.

"You're worried about Haleine, aren't you?" Eamonn asked, joining Revelin at the rail.

Revelin nodded. "I am."

"You shouldn't be," Eamonn said. "For a second time, her husband has denounced her and named her a traitor to the crown. Not only that, but she betrayed you."

Revelin looked at his brother. "Betrayed me?"

"She aligned herself with the man who saw our father murdered."

Yes, Haleine had done that, but she had also claimed that Dana had played no role in Nathan's death, apart from scapegoat. The truth of that was undetermined, but what was certain was Mireille's innocence.

"No, she did not," Revelin said. He should have gone to Gweneria himself. He should not have sent Dana. He sighed. "I must leave for a time."

"I'll go with you."

"No, you need to stay here to keep our mother safe."

Eamonn scowled. "You treat me as a child. You shouldn't."

"I have charged you with safeguarding the queen. That is hardly something one asks of a child."

"I can do more than that. I can help you, if you'd only let me."

Revelin shook his head. "There is nothing with which to help."

Leaving his brother standing alone, Revelin went to the library where he found Darragh sitting behind the desk. His advisor immediately stood and bowed.

"Your highness," he said. "What may I do for you?"

"I need to go to Gweneria. I will require men to accompany me," Revelin said. "Only the very fastest, Darragh. Time is of the essence."

"May I ask why you—?"

"I have business with my brother," Revelin said. "Assemble the men."

"Of course, your highness."

"Summon Adomnan Cathal as well. I should like him to come along."

"Yes, your highness."

"We will leave today."

"Today?" Darragh echoed. "I do not know if—"

"Today," Revelin repeated. "Make it happen."

Darragh bowed his head. "As you wish, your highness."

Revelin rode out of Mairéad as the sun was reaching its midday position. Behind him rode a detachment of ten guards, and on his right was Adomnan Cathal. Darragh had told him only of Revelin's desire to speak with his brother. If Cathal suspected another purpose, he had not yet made mention of it.

How much to tell him? Could Revelin divulge Mireille's secret? He had promised to keep it for as long as she required, and she had never told him otherwise. Could he confide in Cathal the true reason they rode to Gweneria? The court believed that Haleine had absconded with the Liran rebels, with her lover. What did Cathal believe? Only Revelin seemed to be aware of the truth, but he badly desired a confidant.

They stopped for the night at Cathal's northernmost manor, and it wasn't until Revelin sat at a table eating dinner with his ally that his decision was made.

"Thank you for accompanying me," he said.

"I am happy to serve the crown in any capacity," Cathal responded, "but might I inquire, your highness, as to the purpose of this journey? I trust you would not have requested my presence if your task was simply to speak with the crown prince."

Revelin looked into the bottom of his goblet. "Perhaps I merely enjoy your company."

"That would be a great honor, if only it were the truth."

Revelin nodded, set down the goblet, and broke the promise he had made. "Mireille Coileáin is alive."

Standing, he walked to the tall windows that overlooked fields bathed in moonlight. In the reflection, he could see Cathal struggling to reconcile Revelin's disclosure.

"She's...alive? Mireille is alive? When you asked about her, you—"

"I already knew, yes."

"How—where has she been all this time?"

"She would not say."

"How long have you known?"

"Since the night Maddox arrived in Mairéad."

Revelin looked at Cathal directly, watching for the realization to cross the nobleman's face.

"Haleine. It wasn't Haleine," Cathal said once it had. "Has it been Mireille the entire time?"

"Yes."

"What has become of Haleine?" Cathal asked. "Do you know?"

"Haleine is dead." Revelin uttered the phrase without feeling. "Mireille assumed her identity to keep herself alive, and I kept her secret when she requested I do so." He laughed. "Until now, that is."

"To keep herself alive," Cathal mused. "What threat does she face that she would need to do such a thing?"

"She would not tell me."

"Why break her confidence now?"

"Because my brother took her."

Cathal shook his head. "Your highness, witnesses say the Liran rebels took the queen—they took Mireille—and she did not fight them. They say she went with them willingly."

"If there were witnesses at all, they were wrong," Revelin said. "She did not go with the rebels. My brother took her. He is what threatens her now."

"May I ask how you are so certain?"

"That, I will not divulge. The rebels are not important."

"If they came here for her, they matter a great deal."

Whatever happened in Gweneria would be over soon, if it was not already. Perhaps Dana and his companion would free Mireille; perhaps Revelin would see their heads on spikes atop the fortress walls. He truly did not care which, so long as Mireille was safe.

"They do not." Revelin returned to the table and sat. "Mireille is all that matters."

"Posing as the queen of Lira will not protect her any longer."

"Then we will have to do it," Revelin said. "For Darian."

Cathal nodded and raised his goblet. "For Darian."

CHAPTER 31

The fortress in Gweneria was a menacing structure of iron and stone. Dana sat on his mount and examined it from the safety of the forest. It appeared to be not only unguarded but also deserted. If it hadn't been for the fresh carriage tracks, Dana would have thought that Revelin had misled them.

Dana glanced at James, who hadn't spoken a single word since their departure from Mairéad. "What do you think?"

"I think we carry a letter from the queen to her son," James said and nudged his horse forward.

They were able to ride right into the bailey. James slid from the saddle, holding his mount's reins as he looked at the keep itself. Dana looked away as a gray-haired man limped toward them. He carried no weapons and was likely not a threat, but Dana alerted James to his approach anyway.

"What are you doing here?" the man asked when he was close enough to be heard without shouting. "No one should be here."

James held up the letter Revelin had given them. "We carry a letter from the queen to her son."

"No one should be here," the man repeated.

"Well, we are," James said. "Where will we find the prince?"

The man shook his head. "He's inside, but he's...The Black Wolf won't let you pass."

James tucked the letter in his belt. "Where will we find the mercenary?"

"He won't let you pass."

"That's my problem, now, isn't it?" James said. "Where do I find him?"

The man took possession of James's horse. "You go on inside. He'll find you before you've gone too far."

As James walked toward the fortress, Dana dismounted and handed off the reins.

"Shall I keep them saddled?" the man asked. "Do you mean to depart as soon as your message is delivered?"

Dana nodded. "Please."

He quickened his pace to hurry after James. One of the double wooden doors had been left open, and Dana carefully slipped through. Once in the darkness of the entry, he drew his sword. The shadows gave way to a large room with hallways leading to the left and right. A flight of stairs sat in the center, but James was already disappearing down the right hall. Dana followed. There were a few doors that opened into small chambers, each devoid of life. No guards, no servants, no mercenaries, no Cate. The door at the end of the hall led to a garden, overgrown and forgotten.

"There's nothing here," James muttered. "No one anywhere."

"They're here somewhere," Dana said. "We'll keep searching until we find them."

"We haven't seen a single soul yet. Not even the damned Black Wolf. Wasn't he supposed to find us?"

"Not if we're hiding in a garden. Come on."

They returned to the center room. James stopped and surveyed each option. He gestured to the left corridor, and Dana nodded. They'd only taken a few steps down it when a voice stopped them.

"Here already, are you? Prince Revelin wasted no time at all. Interesting, that."

Dana and James turned to see an unarmed man standing at the foot of the stairs. It wasn't the crown prince, nor was he wearing Maoilriain colors. The Black Wolf, it would seem, had found them at last.

He walked toward them, stopping just out of a blade's reach. "Which one of you is Dana?"

"I am," Dana said.

"I've heard so much about you, and I must admit I have long hoped that our paths would one day cross." The Black Wolf looked at James. "But you, I don't know. No one mentioned you."

"I'll live," James said. "Where is she?"

"She is above stairs with the crown prince. Last door on the right. It's locked, so you'll be needing this."

The Black Wolf tossed something at James. He caught it instinctively and opened his palm to reveal a key.

"There are, naturally, a few guards standing between here and there, but you seem like a strapping young lad, so I'm sure you'll do fine," the Black Wolf continued. When neither James nor Dana moved, the mercenary added, "I'd hurry, if I were you. The crown prince has a right interesting reputation with women. He does love to hurt them, and I'd think you'd want to spare the lass that experience a second time."

A second time. Dana's stomach clenched. "James," he said, not taking his eyes from the Black Wolf, "why don't you go on ahead and find your girl. I'll take care of this."

"Are you—?"

Dana readjusted his grip on his sword. "I'm sure."

James hesitated a moment longer before he edged his way around the Black Wolf and ran for the stairs. The mercenary made no move to stop him.

"Alone at last," the Black Wolf said, watching Dana with curiosity and amusement in his eyes. "How shall we occupy the time before your boy returns? *If* he returns, I should say."

"He'll return."

"Ah, faith. I do find that a terribly strange concept, but I suppose that sort of thing comes easily to someone like you."

"Someone like me?"

"Someone who fights against the evils of this world. Someone who cares. How exhausting caring must be."

"And you don't care."

The Black Wolf shrugged. "There's no profit in that."

"I snapped the neck of the last person who said that to me."

"How intimidating. My knees are simply quaking with fear."

"Why did you tell us where she is?" Dana asked. "Why give him the key?"

"I want you to take her back," the Black Wolf said. "Whatever is left of her, I want you to have."

"Why?"

"My employer wants something from her, and I can't imagine he'll have much luck getting it from a corpse," the Black Wolf answered. "Though given her penchant for stubbornness, her corpse might make things easier."

"Who is your employer? What does he want from her?"

"You'll have to ask her that and pray she retains the ability to answer. There really is no telling what the crown prince will do to her," the Black Wolf said. "But if you happen to see her again, please do tell her how much I enjoyed her company. She was truly a delight."

The Black Wolf offered Dana a short, mocking bow before turning for the entry. Dana glanced between the doors and the stairs, then sprinted for the doors, placing himself in between them and the mercenary, his sword ready.

The Black Wolf sighed. "What are you doing? Why aren't you rushing the stairs? I wasn't lying about wanting you to take her. Nor did I lie about the guards. I may not want to stop you, but they will. And beyond them lies the crown prince himself—a master swordsman, if ever there was one. I don't believe he will take too kindly to having his sport interrupted. If I were you, I'd be running along now. Your boy's likely in trouble, and there's no need for us to draw weapons on one another."

When Dana looked at the stairs again, the Black Wolf moved forward, crushing him against the doors. His sword clattered to the floor as his brain registered a sharp and rapidly spreading pain in his side. The Black Wolf drew away, holding in his hand a small dagger, red to the hilt with blood.

"Of course, want and need are two very different things," the mercenary said, letting the weapon slip through his fingers. He nodded at Dana's side as he walked away. "Good luck with that."

—✺—

oh god oh god oh god

It was the only thing she could think, yet every time she did, another small part of her sniffed in laughter because why would she ever think

oh god oh god oh god

when she wasn't even a religious person? She didn't believe in a higher power at all, and on this earth, there were several gods—some of which Cate was fated to serve, and a goddess who wanted Cate to serve her—but since all of them were content to let her

oh god oh god oh god

she'd stick with the one who didn't seem to exist in these parts. It wasn't like it mattered. Wasn't she already in hell? So far down the goddamn rabbit hole that no one could get to her now? And if anyone did manage to come this far, what would there even be to find? Just a pile of dirt and crawling insects and her bones stripped clean lying amongst them.

oh god oh god oh god

Someone smelling distinctly of Wolf had gathered those bones, dusted them off, and reassembled them in the form of a person. When this had happened, she didn't know. Time was a fluid thing, now more than ever, and she was simultaneously everywhere and nowhere—on the floor of rolling Versailles; on the floor of a room above a tavern, dangling from a hook in the ceiling; sunbathing on a white sand beach; in a man's arms, her hands tied; in a man's arms, her arms around his neck.

Hands, hands everywhere—on her, *in* her—scarring and desecrating places they hadn't the right to touch.

oh god oh god oh god

Her skin was gone, just gone—poof!—nothing but nerve endings remained, overloaded and choking on every salt-coated malfeasance carved, scorched, branded into it. It was fire, it was ice—a choir singing a dirge, a roast abandoned in a flaming oven. A sickly-sweet, retching ejaculation strangling its host until drowning on air alone.

oh god oh god oh god

Someone had put the gag back in her mouth and the hood back on her head, or maybe she was just dumb and blind. Not deaf, though, because she heard—had heard?—Zoltano speak.

"Is she dead?"

A kick to her ribs followed—had followed? It hurt, but the pain was so insignificant that it merely drifted away like a lost balloon.

"No," Weylyn Lann replied—had replied? "She lives."

His voice was calm, quiet. She hated and envied it all at once. Her head was a cacophony of noise, noise, noise, and none of it made sense. Screaming, crying, wailing, shrieking, growling, laughing, sobbing, and running beneath that was an entire orchestra—woodwinds and strings and brass—tuning up along with a steady thump like someone was playing a bass drum somewhere inside her brain. If she tried to speak, it would only come out in shrieks. Glass would break, dogs would howl, and she would do both.

Wherever she was—*whenever*—hysterical laughter bubbled up inside her. It came out in loud, painful gulps that disappeared into the ether.

Was she here and now, or there and then?

The answer came when time abruptly rebooted and dropped her on a stone floor.

Now. This was now.

She had to hold on to it and find a way out.

Someone yanked up her arms and untied the ropes binding her wrists before dropping them and walking away. Something somewhere inside her perked up and took notice, recognizing the opportunity before it. She needed a moment to convince her arms to move and her wrists to bend, and another moment to make them work properly enough to pull off the hood and remove the gag.

Now for her legs. They were more reluctant to work than her arms. The wound the Black Wolf had inflicted upon her oozed blood and pus, and the thin fabric of whatever they had dressed her in stuck to it. Every time her leg moved, the fabric would tear off. That hurt, too, a little burst of misery joining forces with the rest of the pain radiating from every part of her body, but she dismissed it and continued to work and kick her legs in any direction they were willing to go.

Eventually, the left found purchase on the stone and propped her up. The right followed, and slowly, her body rose until Cate was standing—albeit unsteadily—on her own power for the first time in...How long had it been?

"Going somewhere?"

Zoltano. A banshee screech formed inside her lungs, swirling in perfect hurricane formation, but she would not let it free. Instead, it fueled her as she turned to face her tormentor.

Hold on. Find a way out.

He stood at the other end of the room, removing his sword belt and dagger, laying them on a table. His gloves and coat came off next, followed by his boots.

Hold on. Find a way out.

"You shouldn't have untied me," she said, her voice like gravel dragged over glass.

He pulled his shirt over his head and dropped it on the floor. "Going to fight me, are you?"

"Going to kill you."

Zoltano grinned. He unlaced his breeches and lowered them enough for her to see he wore nothing underneath. "Bold words."

Hold on. Find a way out.

"Only kind I know," Cate said. "Why waste time with anything else?"

His smile widened. "This will be fun."

"Just not for you."

He moved forward, a panther stalking its prey. "Oh, I don't know about that. I am planning to fuck you in places and ways you've never envisioned."

He was growing closer, but she didn't move. She wasn't sure she could, at least not with anything resembling grace or even basic skill. But she had one thing that could possibly compensate for her lack of mobility. If she could locate it. It had to be there somewhere beneath the layers of pain and confusion. It had saved her before; it could save her again. She only needed to find it.

His hands landed on her shoulders, pulling her toward him. She brought up her own arms and broke his hold, then pushed him away. He staggered back and chuckled, more entertained by her efforts than affected by them, and the sound cut her to the quick. A fuse was lit, and she smiled as it worked its way through her.

There it was.

"Something amusing you?" Zoltano sneered.

Grabbing her arms, he slammed her against the nearest wall. Cate cried out as the air was forced from her lungs.

"Just imagining all the ways I'm going to hurt you," she said once they had recovered.

"After last night, I wouldn't think you would need to imagine anything."

She forced her knee up between his legs. When in doubt, hit them where it would be sure to hurt. He howled and let go of her as he folded in on himself.

Cate slipped to the floor. "Of course you would think that. You don't have the brain power for anything else. You're just some big, dumb animal. A...thug, some stupid thug whose only talent is vio—"

Zoltano put his fist in her face, and her head bounced against the wall. An entire galaxy of multi-colored stars overwhelmed her vision.

"Violence," she gasped, and a sound that might have been laughter followed the word.

He responded with a snarl as he grabbed her hair and the gag around her neck. Dragging her away from the wall, he lifted her into the air. She was flying then and landed hard on her left side. Bones rattled, and the wound on her leg convulsed with pain. Tears overtook the stars, and she wept against the stone.

Was this it? It could be. The end, *her* end, her way out. All she had to do was stop fighting, let him win, let go, and drift away. Would there be anything beyond the black? No heaven—not for her anyway, not with all she had done on either side of the portal. What did that leave? Purgatory? Hell?

Maybe she was already there. Maybe she had died on the floor of a room above a tavern smelling of piss and puke, and now she was condemned to spend eternity trapped in this room with this man.

Except that was a terrible fate. So...screw that. Why should she do any of that? Let that bastard win? Let any of them win? Give in, give up, let go— what kind of plan was that? No. Hell no.

She was going to live. Or, failing that, she would at least take this bastard down with her.

Capturing her ankle, Zoltano pulled her to him. Cate flopped onto her stomach and closed her eyes, not fighting, only waiting for her moment. It was coming. She could do this.

"You're not done already, are you?" he asked. "I thought you would give me more of a challenge than this. You were so feisty before. What happened?"

He flipped her over and spread her legs. Kneeling between them, he shoved his breeches down. Cate gasped, feeling the energy—*magic*—flowing freely, coursing through her blood, and took a swan dive into the center of it.

She opened her eyes and smiled. "Time's up."

Hands rising, she used that magic to propel him away. He soared across the room and hit the wall. As he slid to the floor, she got to her feet, not feeling anything but the power surging through her.

She walked toward Zoltano. What to do with him? How long to make it last? Maybe she should do to him what was done to her. Would he enjoy that? Would she?

Zoltano was now the one gasping and hurting. He stared at her. "How did you—?"

"Told you you shouldn't have untied me."

He growled and stood. She'd ruined his game, complicated his day, and for that she would pay.

But every time he came at her, she shoved him back and closed the distance between them.

"Bitch!" he spat when they were face to face.

"What's the matter?" she asked, thrusting her hands forward. This time, they went through his skin, coming to rest deep inside him. "Not having any fun?"

She pulled her hands out—bringing with her whatever body parts her fingers had latched on to—and he stood a moment longer, stunned and witless, looking at his insides in her bloodied hands. Then he buckled and went down like a puppet whose strings had been severed. He landed first on his knees, then fell on his back, his now-vacant eyes fixed on nothing.

The withdrawal was almost immediate, the power evaporating as rapidly as it had appeared, leaving her human, mortal, and hurting. She collapsed, falling on top of the man she had killed, and rested there, soaking in his blood and guts until her brain recalibrated.

As soon as it had, and she realized where she was and what she was doing, Cate dragged herself in the opposite direction—lungs burning, ribs aching, legs and head throbbing—and didn't stop moving until her back hit a wall. The contact made her scream, but she forced the sound back down.

She couldn't let him hear. Him, them—whoever was out there—the Black Wolf, the guards, the scores of men and women who had lined up for days just for the chance to taste her lovely white flesh. It was neither of those things now, but they probably wouldn't care. They would only add their own marks to the grotesque canvas her body had become while the Black Wolf stood idly by, waiting for the remains of her soul to be shaken free.

The red wouldn't stop them. Nothing would stop them. That word had no meaning in these parts.

Away. Away, away, away—she had to get away. Out of this room, this castle, this country, this goddamn world, and her skin. She had to get out of her skin. It was itchy and tight, and she clawed at her forearm with unsteady fingers, wanting, needing, to peel it off. Touching him, wearing him, she couldn't do it anymore.

A noise sounded, and her fingers froze as her head snapped up to survey the room. Zoltano was still dead, and she was still alive. There was no other threat, nothing else to be seen.

Except for the door on the other side of the room and the table next to it, complete with the glint of shiny metal resting on top. The corner of her mouth twitched.

Hold on. Find a way out.

Her legs still wouldn't work, so she dragged herself across the room, stopping often to catch her breath, work through some pain, and cry. By the time she reached the table, she was drained and useless and was forced to rest before attempting anything else. She lay on her side, fighting to keep her eyes open. It was a losing battle, and they soon slid shut.

She could rest for a moment. That would be okay.

How long that moment may have lasted, she wasn't sure, but more noise—loud and angry—woke her. Where was it coming from? Was that in her head, too? Had the orchestra dissolved into a street fight? Panting heavily and crying once more, she rolled onto her stomach, pressed her forehead to the floor, and covered her ears with her hands. It blocked nothing; she heard and felt everything. It was too much, much too much, and was silenced only when the smallest sound broke through.

A click. A key in a lock.

No no no no no.

She forced herself up, putting her back against the wall for support. Stretching well beyond her body's appreciation, she felt along the tabletop for a weapon. She found the sword first, its unsheathed broad blade nicking her palm. No, not the sword. That would be too big, too heavy. She hadn't been able to hold one even when she hadn't been bruised and bleeding and broken. That would never work. But there had been a dagger, too. She could manage that. Where was it?

Once located, she pulled it toward her and allowed it to clatter on the floor. She had to rest again before bringing the dagger to her side. It was still in its sheath. Her fingers ran over the single strip of leather holding the blade in place, but they shook too badly to do anything else. She leaned over, lowering herself until her nose grazed the sheath, as though the proximity might help.

But it did help—or perhaps it was just sheer determination that she be armed when the Black Wolf came. Whatever the reason, she removed the tie and wrapped her fingers around the handle.

"Cate."

She hesitated. Her name. That was her name. Not Haleine. Not Mireille, but *Cate*. Far away and muffled—probably some kind of trauma-induced hallucination. She ignored it as she pulled the dagger free.

"Cate?"

James. Was that...God, it was James. How was that possible? Was she...dead? Had she died? After all that had she fucking *died*? Was he a ghost here to escort her into the afterlife? Of course it would be him. He just couldn't stop drawing the short straw, could he? Lifting her head, she watched him approach.

Something inside her broke. Relief, she thought, though she couldn't be sure. Maybe it was just that scream from before. It pushed against her, stretching her skin and moving her bones, as it searched for a way to be free. She pushed back, unwilling to let it go.

"Cate," James said. "Oh Cate."

Why did he say her name like that? The pressure in her chest worsened, making it harder to breathe, and every step he took made it worse. By the time he crouched in front of her, she was barely getting any air at all. Leaving the dagger on the floor, she sat up, keeping her back against the wall.

He smelled of sweat and death—or perhaps that was just her—and he wore the colors of the Maoilriain queen. Why was he doing that? How? His hands were caked with grime and blood. A fresh cut tattooed the side of his neck. It wasn't bleeding badly, but it was bleeding.

He wasn't a ghost. He wasn't dead. Which meant she probably wasn't, either.

He reached for her. Moving back was impossible, so she leaned to her right to avoid his touch and wrapped her arm around her torso.

"About time you showed up," she said.

Her voice was thick with emotion as her relief struggled for release. James heard it—how could he not?—but what would he make of it? Dropping his hand, he nodded and glanced at Zoltano's body. What would he think of that?

"I see you managed to keep busy," he said.

She nodded. "You know me. I do hate to be bored."

More hysterical laughter was building up inside her. It combined with the relief and threatened to drown her where she sat. The effort of keeping it contained choked her. Shit, she needed to get control. She couldn't do this; she couldn't *be* this girl, this goddamn victim.

James looked back at her. What was he looking at? Her eyes widened slightly. Shit, what *was* he looking at? She glanced down to see a thin slip, torn in inconvenient places and soaked with blood. Covering her chest with one bloodstained hand, she used the other to hold the skirt together.

James turned, searching the room. He reached for the shirt Zoltano had discarded on the floor.

"No," she said.

Another look, more pity.

Fuck his pity.

"No," she repeated.

He left the shirt where it was and walked out of the room. When he came back, he carried something over his arm. A cloak, a deep emerald green with gold trim. A guard's cloak. Okay. That was okay. They hadn't done anything to hurt her. They hadn't done anything to help her, either, but that was okay. She could handle that.

She slid out from the wall to allow James to drape the cloak around her and pulled it tight, her fingers fumbling and failing with the fastenings. He leaned in to do it for her, and though he didn't physically touch her, his proximity still made her throat close up. She pressed her hands into the floor and turned her head, gasping for breath as inconspicuously as possible.

"Can you stand?" James asked, settling on his haunches.

"Of course I can stand." She pushed off the floor, using both the wall and table for support, but her legs wouldn't cooperate and she went back down. "Just...not right now."

"It's all right. I can carry you."

"I don't want you to."

"Let me help you."

He made another move toward her, and she held up a warning hand. "I don't want you to touch me."

No, if the sound of his voice was crushing her like this, she couldn't possibly entertain the idea of physical contact.

"We can't afford to wait."

She closed her fingers into a fist and let it fall. He didn't know what was inside her. He couldn't feel it growing more potent with every breath. He didn't comprehend what she could do, nor what she had done. Even though he could see it, he didn't understand.

"I'm sorry. Am I holding up your big, daring rescue?" she asked. "How rude of me."

"I'm picking you up."

"Do it, and I will set you on fire using nothing but the power of my mind."

"Have at it, then."

He moved to her side, draped her left arm around his shoulder, and scooped her up. The motion was quick and smooth, forcing Cate to wrap her other arm around his neck to keep from slipping. As he stood and carried her to the door, she glanced back at Zoltano's body. Anger and fear boiled over before she could control it, and a single choking sob bubbled up from within and escaped from her throat. She hid her face in James's clothing and tightened her hold on him.

"You're all right," he said. "It's over."

She wasn't all right, and it would *never* be over. Why didn't he understand that? Why didn't he realize there would always be something else—someone else—coming for her? They wouldn't let her go. None of them would ever let her go.

"You're wrong," she said.

—⟳⟳⟳—

Inside James, anger, relief, and frustration all vied for position, violent and crashing like thunder and lightning.

Cate was somehow quiet as he carried her through the equally silent hall. Dead men made no noise, and no one else had appeared.

There had been six of them, standing in three pairs of two, spaced evenly between the top of the stairs and the room at the end of the hall. The first pair fell easily. They had seen his colors, perhaps recognized his face from the barracks, and had done nothing to hinder his approach. James moved in close and killed them both with a dagger before a sound could be uttered.

The rest were more of a challenge. His purpose and betrayal had been exposed, and they came at him. Three rushed him while the fourth stayed back to guard the last door on the right. The narrowness of the hall helped James, prevented them from taking him on all at once. It didn't matter, though—even if the three could have attacked simultaneously, they would have lost. Their blood was high, their emotions scattered, while he had benefited from a singular purpose: Cate. Get to Cate.

The path to doing so was clear and simple—get through the door, get through the crown prince, and get to Cate. He had been so calm and focused, there could have been twice as many men, and he still might have prevailed.

Now that he had Cate in his arms, however, the emotion reigned unchecked, pouring out like an oversaturated dam after a bout of heavy rain. But she was quiet—so quiet. Bloodied—so much goddamn blood—and bruised, and God only knew what else—was it any wonder?

"Are you here alone?" Cate asked, her voice treading dangerously close to a whimper. She shook her head. "No, that's crazy. Who's here with you? The Bobbsey twins?"

He supposed that meant Rhydwyn and Gair, but he answered, "Dana."

"You brought the drunken deadbeat back to life."

"Not me."

"I'm sure," she said. "Where is he?"

An excellent question. Would Dana and the Black Wolf have fought? If so, who might have won? When they found Dana at the bottom of the stairs, propped awkwardly against the wall, James still didn't know the answer. Dana's sword lay at his feet, and his hand held his right side. He looked up at the sound of footsteps but made no other effort. Perhaps he couldn't. Before James could ask, Dana picked up his sword and used it to help him stand.

"You found her," Dana said.

James nodded, his eyes taking in the blood on Dana's clothing. He scanned the rest of the alcove and found no sign of another living soul. "Where's the Black Wolf?"

Cate hissed softly but not quietly enough to avoid being heard.

Dana stared outright at Cate. "Gone."

"Dead?" James asked.

"Gone. Just...gone."

"In a puff of smoke?" Cate asked dully.

Dana continued to stare. "On a horse. I think he stole ours."

"He's not here?" James asked.

"Not anymore."

James nodded. "What happened to you?"

Dana looked at the floor. "Want outweighed need."

James examined the trail of blood leading from the doors to the stairs. "How bad is it?"

"Barely a scratch."

Too much blood for that to be true. "Liar."

"Aye, well," Dana said, "what are you going to do about it?"

What could he do? James sighed. "Nothing."

"I'll survive; it's not my first stab wound."

"Aye, but—"

"We should go," Dana said, walking away. His injury showed in his gait. "Revelin will have sent reinforcements."

"Aye," James said. "We'll have to find a wagon or a carriage we can use. She can't ride."

"Yes, I can," Cate said.

"No, you can't," James responded. "You can't ride, you can't walk—you can't even stand."

"Oh, I'm sorry. Did you need me to stand on the horse's back? I didn't realize we were doing a circus act."

"You can't ride or walk, and you know it," he said. "Stop fighting me for the sake of fighting me."

She sank deeper into his arms. "Where's the fun in that?"

"Does everything have to be fun?"

"It would make for a refreshing change of pace."

He laughed until he heard her sharp intake of breath. "Are you all right?"

She sighed. "Oh, for fuck's sake, stop asking everyone if they're all right. None of us are all right."

He said nothing more as he carried her from the fortress. By the time they reached the stable, her breathing indicated that she had fallen asleep. Dana and the man who had approached them upon their arrival worked to hitch a pair of horses to the crown prince's carriage.

James stopped. "What are you doing?"

Dana glanced up. "It's fine. He won't say anything. Nothing they won't already know anyway."

"I'll drive you to Odhran and buy you what time I can," the man said.

"Why?" James asked. "You know who we are and what we've done. Why help us?"

The man gestured to Cate. "I help you to help her. The lass deserves better than what would've happened here. She's a good girl. Always was."

They would have to take the risk, he supposed. It would be all right. The man was hardly a threat. James nodded and looked at Dana. "The crown prince's carriage?"

"Will he be needing it anymore?" Dana asked, then shrugged. "It's the only one here."

The only one? Gweneria may not have been an active fortress, but neither had it been abandoned completely. There should have been more available to them. Where had it...The Black Wolf. That bloody mercenary had forced them into this—made sure two of their number could not travel any other way, then offered them only one way to get out.

"No one will dare stop it," Dana said. "At least not until they know what's happened here, and they won't know that until we're lost in Odhran or—goddess willing—on a ship bound for Lira."

"The prince knows what's happening here," James said. As did the Black Wolf.

"Revelin won't act on it," Dana said. "He wants us—*me*—dead, but he won't seek that out. Not while he believes her life hangs in the balance. This is the best way, James."

James looked at Dana's bloodstained clothing. Considering that neither Cate nor Dana could sit a horse, it was the only way. He nodded again and looked at the driver. "Can you avoid the roads the queen's men would normally travel?"

"Aye, it can be done, but not easily," the man answered. "It will take longer to get to Odhran that way."

Better it take longer than to run afoul of the queen's men. Dana may have believed that the prince wouldn't act, but James wouldn't.

"Do it," he said, stepping toward the carriage.

The man opened the door, and James carried Cate inside. The bench seats were far wider than normal, and he carefully laid her across one of them. As he pulled his hands free, she woke, groaning and writhing until she was situated on her side and looking at him.

He crouched down. "I'm sorry. I didn't mean to wake you."

"I didn't mean to fall asleep," she said. "What's going on?"

"We're taking you out of here. We're taking you home."

"Not my home."

"Aye." He pulled back. "I'll go help them, and we—"

"James," she said, reaching for him, "don't—don't go, okay? Could you...I know I said I didn't want you to touch me, and I may have threatened to set you on fire, but could you maybe…maybe just stay where I can see you? Just for a while?"

He didn't answer right away, looking at her reddened fingers ensnared in his clothing. He shifted to maintain his balance, and Cate's hold tightened.

"Please, James," she whimpered, "don't make me say it again."

"A-aye," he stammered. "I-I'm so sorry I let this happen."

Her hand fell. "I don't need you to be sorry. I need you to sit with me."

He nodded and fumbled to unbuckle his sword belt. Leaving the weapon on the floor, he sat next to Cate. She slid along the seat and laid her head on his leg. Her hand landed above his knee, fingers digging into his skin. Her hair obscured her face, so he focused on her hand. When her grip relaxed, he knew she had fallen back to sleep.

What had they done to her? He was torn between pleasure that she had killed the crown prince and fury that he hadn't been able to do it himself. But he had seen what she had done. Killed a man with her bare hands in a way James had never considered possible. What had the crown prince done to drive her to such an extreme?

"Asleep?"

James lifted his head. Dana hovered at the carriage door. He put the saddlebags containing their remaining supplies on the floor. At least the Black Wolf had left those behind.

"Aye," he said.

Dana nodded. "I'm surprised she survived it."

"Why? She's not the queen." James rested his hand lightly atop of Cate's auburn curls. He could feel Dana's stare but did not meet it.

"No," Dana said, "she isn't."

"Are we ready to leave yet? Or has something else gone wrong?"

"We're ready," Dana said. "I'll sit with the driver and make sure he's taking us where we want to go."

As though either of them would know that. James nodded anyway as Dana closed the door and scrambled up to the driver's seat. The carriage lurched forward, and James checked to see if Cate had stirred. She hadn't, so he relaxed against the seat and closed his eyes to wait.

chapter 32

More disconcerting than feeling her twin's pain was the moment when it stopped. A smattering of bruises arrived in its place, including one across Haleine's cheek. Hanah had gasped upon seeing it and accused Lucius of pushing their queen too hard during training, but it hadn't been him nor anyone else in camp. They weren't Haleine's bruises at all.

They were Mireille's.

But the link between them remained severed, so there was naught for Haleine to do but trust in Dana and James while continuing on to Eluned. No offer of a mount or tunnel had been made—Faolan's way of delaying her—but she did not care. She would walk to the city if she had to. Lucius matched her step for step, every breath spent begging her to reconsider.

"Please, your majesty," he said. "Please, turn back."

She didn't know how she could. Each day she delayed only endangered another village, more lives. Cinna had been the beginning, and she would see that Rushwick was the last. Never before had her path to ending those massacres been so clearly defined: turn herself over to Sighle, or more would die. The choice was simple. No matter what Faolan claimed, her life wasn't worth more than any other, and Haleine did not want anyone to die for her nor because of her.

Not again. Never again.

It had to be this way; she had to do this. Nothing would turn her back—not before her sacrifice was made.

"Haleine," Faolan said.

He had stayed behind in Rushwick, a coward to the core. He had done this—primed her to make this choice—and now could not bear to witness its end. What had brought him out? What plea did he intend to make?

"I will not be dissuaded," she said, pressing on.

"There's been another attack."

She turned. Faolan perched on Lucius's shoulder.

"What village?" Lucius asked.

"Hythe," Faolan answered. "In the west."

Rushwick wouldn't be the end after all. Already had she failed. Haleine looked from Faolan to Lucius, Eion, and Brighid flanking him. Behind them were more—men and women whose names Haleine hadn't learned.

"You should go, all of you, and do what you can to help. I can do this on my own," she said, but no one moved. She looked at Lucius. "That is a command. Do as I say."

He gave her a wry smile. "Not this time, your majesty."

"Lucius—"

"We are rebels, your majesty," he said. "Do not forget that."

She sighed. "At least send the others. They can do more good in Hythe, and you know it."

Lucius looked over his shoulder. "Get yourselves to Hythe. Help however you can."

The nameless men and women slipped away until only her devoted cadre of guards remained. She could feel their determination to stay with her. They wouldn't be deterred, either.

"You should go as well," Faolan said. "Hanah could use your help."

Haleine looked at him. "Oh yes, you would much rather I go there, or anywhere other than—"

"Than the belly of the beast?" he finished. "Yes, I would much rather you avoid going there."

She shook her head. "I have avoided that for too long. It ends now."

"You think it will end if you do this?" Faolan asked. "You think if you forfeit your life that Sighle will be satisfied?"

"I don't know what will happen," Haleine said. "I only know it won't stop should I choose to stay away. She'll keep doing this, Faolan, until this country and those within it are nothing but smoke and ash. I don't intend to stand by and let it happen."

"Haleine—"

"No," she stated flatly. "There is nothing more to be said, no new argument to be made. I will return to Eluned, and I will face my sister."

"She'll know you're coming."

"Good."

"She's prepared for this encounter," Faolan warned. "You're not."

"Yes, I am."

"You're not," he said. "There must be a better way to approach this, Haleine. A smarter way."

"If there is, it won't be discovered here," she said. "I'm doing this, Faolan. Regardless of the consequences."

"Allow us to go with you," Lucius said.

"It is too dangerous," Haleine said. "Until I know what she is and what she wants, I'll not put any of you in her path."

"Until we know what she is and what she wants," Lucius countered, "you should not go alone."

"If you do this, if you come with me," she said, "you could die."

Lucius looked at Brighid, then Eion. "We stand with you, your majesty. Regardless of the consequences."

Haleine felt their resolve strengthen. It made her heart hurt. She nodded. "As you will."

———❧❧❧———

James had been watching the sun drop lower and lower in the sky when the carriage came to a halt. Cate woke suddenly, raising her head and gripping his leg hard enough to make him flinch. A scream was on her tongue, but she choked it back.

"It's all right," he said. "You're safe."

Another moment passed before she pushed off him. She didn't appear comfortable, supporting herself with an elbow while keeping her other arm wrapped protectively around her ribs. He wondered—and not for the first time—about the full extent of her injuries.

"Sorry about your leg," she said.

He rubbed the area. "No matter. Are you—?"

"If you ask if I'm all right, I will set you on fire using nothing but the power of my mind," she warned. "Where are we? Why did we stop?"

"I don't know." James glanced at the roof. "Dana will be along to tell us."

The first face to appear belonged to the driver. "The horses require rest," he said, "and your friend requires care."

The driver disappeared from view, and James looked at the roof again. He wasn't surprised to hear it, but what would he be able to do about it?

"Who was that?" Cate asked.

She was trying to keep panic out of her voice. He could see her forcing it down like she had her scream. What would he do about that? What *could* he do about that?

"The driver," he answered. "He's helping us. He thinks...he thinks you're the queen."

Cate nodded. "Good. Let him."

"I intend to." James reached for his sword. "I need to help Dana. Will you—?"

"I'll be here."

He slid away slowly, waiting to see if she might change her mind, but she was quiet as she settled on the carriage floor. He stayed near the door a moment longer, but she didn't look at him.

Outside, the driver was already unhitching the horses, and James took in their surroundings. They were in the forest; the road was nowhere to be seen.

"Where are we?" he asked.

"Off the road as far as the carriage will go. I'll cover the tracks, so none who pass will notice," the driver said. "This is a good place to stop for the night. There's cover, a stream close by, and the possibility of food."

James nodded. "No fire."

"Seasons are changing. It'll be cold without one."

"We'll survive. No fire." James moved to the other side of the carriage where Dana sat on the driver's bench, appearing as though he should already be a corpse. "You look awful."

Dana smiled and accepted James's help in getting down. "I did get stabbed, you know."

"Aye, I know. Remind me how it is you're not dead yet."

"Either very good luck or very bad."

"If you ever work out which, be sure to tell me."

"You'll be the first."

James helped Dana over to a tree, and Dana grimaced and groaned as he leaned against the trunk and sank to the ground. James knelt, untying and lifting layers to expose Dana's tunic and the wound which lay beneath. He carefully unwrapped the fabric Dana had used to bind it. At his first sight of the injury, James was tempted to swear both loudly and profusely. Dana was more of a liar than he had anticipated.

"We need something else to..." James looked around. "The man said there's a stream somewhere; we can at least clean it. Maybe there's some moss or birch bark, and we can hold you together a bit longer. I'll go—"

"I'll go," the driver interrupted. "I need to bring the horses there, and you're needed here, I think."

Dana gestured with his chin, and James glanced over his shoulder to see Cate lingering in the carriage's doorway.

"Your majesty," he asked, "are you—?"

"I'm fine," she said, accent firmly in place.

Her noble demeanor disappeared as the driver grew farther away. Shoulders slumping, she sat on the carriage floor, leaning heavily to her right. She nodded toward Dana. "The Black Wolf do that?" she asked, her accent gone.

"Aye."

Cate nodded again. "That guy's such a dick."

Dana looked at James, the question in his eyes, and James shrugged. He stood and returned to the carriage. "Could you please hand me those bags on the floor behind you?"

Cate looked at them but made no move to pick them up.

"Can you?" he asked. "I'm sorry, I didn't—"

"My arms aren't broken."

She bent back, dragged a bag to her, and threw it in his direction. As he caught it, he took note of her scowl and her free arm wrapping around her belly. Her ribs, then. Would she admit to it?

"What *is* broken?" he asked.

Cate threw the second bag at him, harder than the first. "Your friend over there. You should do something about that."

Taking both bags to Dana's side, James knelt again, motioning for Dana to expose the wound.

"Ribs," Dana murmured. "Her ribs are—"

"Aye." James removed the wineskins from each bag. "What did he use?"

"Small blade, concealed in his—bloody hell," Dana spat as James poured the last of their water over the wound. "Have you been taking instruction from Hanah?"

James set aside the wineskins and inspected the wound. "You should be so lucky. If I had, I might know what to do with you now."

"I'll be fine."

Dead was more likely. The injury could have been worse, but it was far from minor. There was no telling what the Black Wolf might have hit with his knife, and given the resources available to them, James would be surprised if Dana survived the night.

"Aye," James said, searching for the driver. "Where is that man? I need water."

"I'll get it," Cate said. She now sat on the ground, resting her head against the carriage.

"How will you do that?" he asked. "You can't walk."

"I'll manage."

"You don't know where it is."

"Neither do you." Using the carriage for support, Cate stood and took unsteady steps over to them. She put one hand on his shoulder and gestured to the wineskins with the other. "You can't guard us both all of the time, James, and I can take care of myself. So why don't you stay here with the human pincushion, and I'll go get some water."

He put the wineskins in her hand, and she headed into the trees. Aye, she could take care of herself, but what would be the cost?

Dana laughed. "I like her."

James sighed. "Shut up."

"You should know," Dana said, coughing through a grin, "the Black Wolf, he..."

A growl rose in his throat, and James swallowed it. "What about him?"

"He wanted us to take her...to take her back. Whatever was left of her, he told me, he wanted us to have. We're doing just what he wants. *How* he wants it, too."

James nodded. He was already aware of that, but since he had Cate, he didn't care at the moment. There would be time enough later to work out the Black Wolf's game. When Cate recovered, she could help him thwart the man. She'd enjoy that greatly, James suspected.

"He also said"—Dana winced—"said it wasn't done. His employer still wants her. They'll try for her again."

"Then they'll have to go through me."

"They'll kill you."

"They can try," James said. "Now put your damn hand over the hole in your side and see if you can stay alive until she gets back."

Dana did as he was told while James went in search of birch bark. He cut a few sizeable strips from the first trunk he encountered and headed back. The driver had returned and was tethering the horses. Dana was either dead or asleep against the tree, an offering of moss resting in his lap. The wineskins were next to him, but Cate was nowhere to be found.

"Did you see the queen?" James asked.

"Aye, she requested I bring those wineskins back for you," the driver said. "She's down at the water, washing."

Washing. Aye, of course. The blood—she'd been covered in it. He should have taken the time to deal with it before they had left Gweneria.

He stalked over to Dana, crouching to thrust his fingers beneath Dana's jaw. After reassuring himself that Dana hadn't yet died, James eased him onto his back and did what he could for the wound. It wasn't much, but it was, perhaps, better than nothing.

Cate hadn't returned by the time he finished. Knowing the remaining light wouldn't last much longer, he wiped his hands on Dana's cloak and went after her.

She sat at the water's edge, naked from the waist up. James stopped to stare at her back and the damage that had been done to it. The shock wasn't from knowing she was hurt—he had been well aware of that already—but her back...They had...Letters—there were *letters* carved into her skin. A name.

The crown prince had branded her.

"Oh God," James said involuntarily. "Cate."

She jumped and glanced over her shoulder before covering her body with her cloak. "What are you doing here? Go away!"

He took a few steps more. "I came to make sure you were all right."

"Well, I am. Leave me alone. I just needed a minute, for crying out loud. I just need a damn minute."

"You need a doctor—that's what you need," he said. "You need…Why didn't they heal, Cate? Why aren't they healing? Your body can do that; I've seen it, so why not this time? What happened? What did they do?"

Her shoulders sagged, and her body trembled. Was she crying?

"Cate?"

"Just leave it alone," she pleaded. "Just leave me be. I'm all right."

"No, Cate, no. You're not all right, and I'll not leave it alone. Your back, it's—"

"It's nothing."

"It's not nothing." He crept close enough to gently touch her shoulder. "What does the rest of you look like?"

Cate stood and faced him. "The rest of me is fine."

"I don't believe that," he said. "Will you show me?"

Her face contorted in a mixture of shame and outrage. "No."

"Please, Cate? I only want to—"

"No. I am saying no. Do you hear it? Does it register with you?" she demanded, her voice tight and on the verge of breaking. "No, James. I am saying no. I will not show you anything. My body is my business. It is not yours, and you will stay out of it because I am saying no."

He should walk away. He should do what she had asked of him and walk away and leave her alone. Give her a damn minute—whatever that was—and more. She deserved that, and it made him sick to do it, but he said, "Your injuries, Cate, if they go untreated, they'll—"

"What are you going to do? Force me to take off my clothes?" she challenged.

James stepped back. "No. God, no. I would never do that."

She nodded, tears in her eyes. "You have to leave, okay? Give me a minute. I just…I just need a minute."

She turned, not waiting to see if he obeyed. He left—how could he possibly stay?—and went back to their small camp, leaving her to repair her shattered dignity.

He checked Dana's wound again, then worked on any task he could find, desperate to keep his anger and shame from overflowing. He should have gotten to her sooner. Why hadn't he done that? Why hadn't he found a way to do that? He should have done something—*anything*—to spare her. Tear down the palace walls brick by brick with his bare hands, murder the entire royal family and anyone who tried to stop him—anything. Just something more. He should have…

He should have never brought her here.

When Cate finally returned from the stream, she wouldn't look at him. She didn't look at anyone else, either, as she sat, knees to her chest, on the ground near the carriage. The driver offered her some of the dried meat that had been in the saddlebags, but she refused him, and the man retreated, looking pointedly at James.

With some reluctance, James approached her. "Would you be more comfortable in the carriage?"

Cate tucked her cloak around her bare feet. James untied his own cloak and slipped it off his shoulders, but before he could offer it to her, she pointed to Dana, lying on his back, asleep and shivering.

James held out his wineskin. "At least have some water."

She took it, and he crossed the camp to drape the cloak over Dana. When he came back, the wineskin was on the ground.

"Did you have any?" he asked, and she shrugged. "I don't suppose you'll eat anything, either."

She shook her head.

He crouched in front of her. "I know we don't have much, and it's not, perhaps, what you're accustomed to, but you have to eat something."

"I don't have to do anything," she said, her tone deadly.

James rocked back. "Are you...Cate, I'm sorry to ask again, but what did they—*he*..."

He couldn't finish the question, and Cate didn't answer. She eased onto her side, pulling the cloak tight, and tugged the hood over her head. James sat beside her, watching for the moment when she let go of the demons in favor of sleep. After it came, he walked away.

He took the first watch himself, walking the camp perimeter in the light of a cloud-filtered moon. Partway through the night, the driver relieved him, and James settled on the ground near Cate. Eyes heavy, he looked at the stars until he fell asleep. When he woke, the sun was rising, and he lay on his side. Cate had molded her body to his back. Fingers grasping his tunic, she cried softly into the space between his shoulder blades.

What had they done to her? How had they managed to disarm her so completely? As desperate as he was to understand, he willed himself to stay immobile and relaxed. She needed this release—he at least recognized that— so he stayed as he was, as she needed him to be, and let her cry.

Her tears came to a sudden stop when someone else in the camp moved. James assumed it was the driver, but Cate wouldn't care who it was, and she pulled away, taking several deep breaths. A sharp jab to his kidney followed. James yelped before twisting to look at her.

"Sorry," she said, drawing farther away. "Spasm."

He nodded as he got to his feet. The driver was tending to the horses, but Dana hadn't moved. James approached with apprehension.

"Is he dead?" Cate asked.

James couldn't tell. He carefully picked up Dana's wrist to check for life. "No," he said after a pulse had been found.

"Well, that's something, I guess. Maybe. I don't know." She laughed a little and sighed. "So, what's the plan?"

James pulled the cloaks off Dana to check the wound. "We go home."

"Not my home," Cate murmured.

James glanced at her but didn't comment. He removed the moss from Dana's side and pressed his face into his sleeve at the smell. How was Dana still alive? Surely any other man would have been dead long before now.

James looked at the driver. "How far are we from Odhran?"

"We covered a fair amount of ground yesterday, but if we continue to avoid the main road, it will take the better part of two days to get there."

Two days. Two more days. Could Dana survive that long?

Cate stood. "Why are we going to Odhran?"

James poured water over the wound and prodded it warily. Dana still didn't wake. "That's where the ships are."

"Yes, but shouldn't we go to Mairéad first?"

James shook his head. "There's nothing in Mairéad."

"Except help."

"Who will help us?"

"Rhydwyn. Gair. Idwal."

"Idwal Kai?" James asked. He glanced at the driver, then returned to Cate so he could continue without being overheard. "Idwal Kai cannot be trusted. Not with this."

"Dana is dying, James. He should already be dead. I know it, you know it, he knows it, and I'm pretty sure the damn horses know it," Cate said. "This is beyond moss and bark and mud now, so unless your master plan involves letting him die, we're going to need some better resources."

"Idwal Kai belonged to your father."

"Now he belongs to me."

James looked at Dana. Cate hadn't said anything untrue, but returning to Mairéad and remaining in Tanuba any longer than necessary would put her at risk. But could he allow Dana to die? It might not matter. Mairéad was just as far away as Odhran was. Dana might be dead before they reached either location.

"If you're going to let him die," she said, "you should do it here so we can be on our merry way and not have to lug around a corpse while we try to make an inconspicuous escape."

"Of course I don't want to let him die, but if doing so allows me to keep you safe—"

"Fuck that." Cate turned toward the driver, once again becoming the queen. "Do you know where my family's estate in Mairéad is?"

"Aye, your majesty."

"Bring us there."

"Aye, your majesty," the man said and set to work hitching the horses to the carriage.

Cate looked at James. "You should help him."

He smiled. "Aye, your majesty."

She raised her hand. Her fingers were curled into a fist until she extended only the middle one.

"What is that?" he asked. "What are you doing?"

She dropped her hand. "I hate this place. Go help the man already so I can get the hell out of it."

"Why are you so determined to keep Dana alive?"

Cate looked at Dana's dying form. "None of your damn business."

———⟆⟆⟆———

When they arrived at his brother's stronghold, there were no heads adorning the walls, but there was a blood trail leading from the living quarters to the stable. Revelin studied it as he slid from the saddle.

"Check the stable," he commanded.

The captain divided his men, five going to the stable. The rest surrounded Revelin as they made for the fortress, their weapons drawn.

Revelin was made to linger outside while the others cleared the remaining rooms. With him waited Cathal and the two men charged with Revelin's protection. When Revelin was allowed through the doors, the first thing he noticed was the blood smeared across the floor. There was not as much as he had expected to find. To whom might it belong?

"Search every room. Find the crown prince," he said softly. "And the queen."

At the captain's request, Revelin and his guards remained in the alcove. Cathal stayed as well. The guards took up position around him while Revelin stared at the blood. All who had come to this castle had done so with violence in mind. Zoltano and the Black Wolf likely had thought to torture her, murder her, and if Dana and his companion had arrived in time, they would have had to fight for her life, as well as their own. Whatever might have happened within these walls, the absence of anyone—servants or his brother's own guards—did not lead him to believe that Zoltano lived.

"Your highness," the captain said, "you should come."

Revelin looked away from the blood. The captain stood at the top of the stairs, a grave look upon his face. "My brother?"

"Yes, your highness."

Revelin nodded and made his way above, Cathal and the two guards trailing after him. When they reached the top, Revelin looked at his shadows and told them to stay behind. The guards obeyed; Cathal did not.

Passing the bodies of Zoltano's fallen guards, the captain led Revelin into a room at the end of the hall. His brother's sword lay unsheathed upon a table, next to a discarded coat. A dagger was on the floor, alongside a shirt and pair of boots.

Then, Revelin saw his brother.

Though he had expected to see Zoltano's corpse, he had not anticipated the manner in which his brother had died. Revelin's stomach turned in on itself, and his hand covered his mouth.

What had Dana done?

"I'd say the rebels found her," Cathal said. "Wouldn't you, your highness?"

"What of the queen? Haleine?" Revelin asked the captain when he thought he might not vomit. "Have you found her?"

"No, your highness," the captain answered. "There is no sign of her."

Unless the blood on the floor below belonged to Mireille, they wouldn't find one. Dana had her now. Where might they have gone? Off to find a way back to Lira? A ship would be needed for that. He could send men to every port in the country and search every ship until they were found. Unless, perhaps, they were already gone. He had delayed so long in traveling to Gweneria, it could have been too late. They were already lost in the wilderness. It was possible, though not likely, that they had already set sail. He did not imagine he would see them again.

Did he even want to find them? What would he do? Kill Dana and the other, and take Mireille back?

No, he couldn't do that. He couldn't bring Mireille back to court. As long as Haleine was believed to be a traitor, Mireille wouldn't be safe there.

"Your highness?" the captain said.

"What of the mercenary?" Revelin asked. "The Black Wolf. Have you found any sign of him?"

"No, your highness."

Revelin nodded and looked at his brother. "The queen will need to know what has happened to her son. Prepare his body for transport back to Mairéad."

"Yes, your highness."

He left the room and did not stop moving until he was outside. He braced himself against the castle wall and gulped fresh air, attempting to neutralize the toxicity of his brother's death. Cathal and his guards stood nearby, none of them speaking until Cathal muttered, "Your highness."

Revelin straightened and faced one of the men the captain had sent to the stable.

"The crown prince's carriage is gone," the man reported. "Shall we send men to track it?"

Had Dana been foolish enough to steal his brother's gaudy carriage? Suppressing a sigh, Revelin nodded and watched four men depart. If the rebel leader had been that stupid, he hoped—for Mireille's sake—that Dana at least had sense enough to abandon it as quickly as possible.

He looked at Cathal. "Send a man to Mairéad to tell Darragh—and only Darragh—what has happened here. Arrangements need to be made, and he...Make sure the messenger understands that no word of this is to reach my mother or brother's ears. I will tell them myself upon my return. They should hear it from me."

"At once, your highness," Cathal said. "As for the rest of us, it is much too late in the day to make it back to my estate before nightfall. Might I suggest—"

"We will find somewhere else to go, or we will camp in the forest. I will not stay here," Revelin said. "Tell the men to work quickly. I should not like to be here any longer than I must."

"Yes, your highness."

When the men brought out his brother's body, Revelin waited in the saddle. The shroud-wrapped corpse was placed in a wagon requisitioned from a nearby farm, and two of the remaining soldiers climbed onto the seat.

"You do realize what this means, don't you, your highness?" Cathal said as they trailed after the slow-moving wagon. "The throne will now rightfully be yours."

Revelin gave Adomnan Cathal a sidelong look and said nothing.

CHAPTER 33

When the carriage finally arrived at the Coileáin estate, both the sun and Dana were dying, and Cate was only certain that one of them would be around the next morning. She left an unconscious Dana on the seat and moved to the door, but one of the servants beat her to it. He opened the door and offered her his hand. Still sore and unsteady, she accepted.

"Is Idwal Kai in residence?" she asked.

"Yes, your majesty."

She nodded. "Fetch him."

As the servant bowed and disappeared inside, James climbed down from the driver's bench. He looked in on Dana, then stared at the manor and the stream of people coming out of it.

"We shouldn't be here," he muttered.

"It'll be fine," Cate said as Idwal, followed by Rhydwyn and Gair, appeared.

Idwal's eyes widened, and he rushed to her. "My lady, it is so very good to see you. I thought—"

"We need your help," she interrupted. She could imagine what he thought. She didn't need to hear it. "And your discretion."

"Anything you require, my lady."

Glancing at an unresponsive James, she stepped aside, gesturing to the carriage. "He needs a physician. One who won't…"

Idwal looked inside the carriage. "You needn't worry about that, my lady. There are not many who would recognize him here. They may know his name but not his face."

"Omur does. Maddox. Revelin. Probably Zaide Romanza, too," Cate said.

"They have gone; all of them have gone. Only Prince Revelin remains in the country, and he has gone to Gweneria." Idwal nodded toward the carriage. "He will go unnoticed here. You all will."

"No one can find out we're here," Cate said. "No one."

"Not a single soul within these walls would say anything that would put you at risk," Idwal said. "I promise you that."

She would have preferred him not to have used that word. Too much weight came along with it, and she couldn't breathe correctly as it was. But she nodded and looked at James. "All right?"

James offered a curt nod, and Idwal summoned two men. The first was sent to find the physician. The second was tasked with providing a room for Dana. James, Rhydwyn, and Gair carefully brought Dana out of the carriage and followed the second man inside. Idwal held Cate back, his hand on her elbow.

"Will you require the physician's services as well?" he asked.

"No," she said, shaking her arm free. No way in hell was a complete stranger putting his hands on her. "I'm fine."

"I beg your pardon, my lady, but you clearly are not."

"You don't know what I am," Cate said. "Show me where they went."

Idwal didn't move. "I will find someone else for you. A woman, if you wish."

"I'm fine."

How many times had she said that lately? She wasn't sure, but it was getting harder and harder to make it sound convincing. The look on Idwal's face proved that she'd utterly failed this time, as sadness and disappointment jockeyed for position in his eyes. Fuck him. He didn't get to judge her. Anger propelled her away, and tears threatened to expose her as she entered the manor.

Once inside, she searched for a sign of James, but there were only servants rushing around in various directions. Where should she look? This was her family's house—*her* house—and she had no idea where she'd find anything except a pair of portraits depicting a life of which she had never been a part.

"My lady?" Idwal said.

He stood nearby but not close enough to touch or be touched by her. Smart man. She was becoming more and more like a ticking time bomb stuffed with fear and fury that could cut someone to ribbons just as effectively as nails or crushed glass. It was certainly shredding her.

She looked at him. "Show me where they are. Then find me a room and a bath."

Idwal bowed. "Yes, my lady."

They had put Dana in a little room at the end of a hall in the opposite direction of her father's library. She thought about complaining and demanding something better, but another look indicated that, as small and simple as it was, the space was equipped as a sickroom, so she kept her mouth shut and hovered outside the door, watching James strip Dana of his clothing. Servants brushed past her, murmuring apologies, as they brought more light, water, rolls of bandages, and whatever else had been needed or requested. The physician arrived next, but instead of passing her by, he stopped.

"Your majesty," he said, "are you—?"

"You're here for him," Cate said, pointing to Dana. "Do your work."

James turned at the sound of her voice, looking as though he'd forgotten she existed. She left the doorway and stood in front of the window at the very end of the hall. The sun was just about gone, and Cate wanted to go with it. Melt into the ground and disappear.

"Cate?" James said.

She looked at him. His shirt and pants appeared to be made entirely from other people's blood. "You need a change of clothes."

"I don't have—"

"Idwal will find you some," she said. "How's Dana?"

James shrugged. "He's still alive."

"They'll make sure he stays that way," she said. "At least they better."

"Why do you care if he lives or dies?"

How much did she not want to answer that question? Cate took a deep breath and held it a moment before exhaling slowly and angling herself toward the window. She could ignore him. Say something stupid and snarky, and keep doing it until he walked away. She'd done it before; she could do it again.

But she didn't want to.

"I don't want to be who they say I am," she answered. "*What* they say I am."

"What do they say you are?"

A young girl interrupted then to announce that Cate's room had been prepared.

"Saved by the bell," Cate said, patting James's arm as she passed. "Sorry, cowboy. Better luck next time."

———

James watched Cate walk away. He didn't want to let her out of his sight but didn't seem to have much choice. He glanced at Gair, lurking behind him. Should he send Gair after her? Or should he go himself?

"Captain?" Idwal Kai said.

James looked at him. From where had the man appeared? "Don't call me that."

"It is what your men call you, and a title you have earned, I think."

"Don't call me that," James repeated. "What do you want?"

"I am grateful to you for having returned my lady to her home."

"It's not her home," James said as Cate vanished from sight.

"Her family's home," Idwal Kai amended. "Regardless, I am grateful that you have saved her. As such, I am—*we* are—indebted to you. The entire Coileáin household is at your service. Anything you need—"

"You've already done enough."

"I understand your reluctance to accept our aid—"

"Do you?"

"I serve the Coileáin name," Idwal Kai said more forcefully, "and if my lady chooses to help you, then so do I."

"Tanuba is our enemy."

"I am not. Not anymore. I hope you will remember that."

James gestured down the hall. "Where has she gone?"

"My lady requested a bath and a place to rest."

"Where is she?"

"The lord's bedchamber, Captain," Idwal Kai said. "I do not hide her from you. If you like, I will bring you straight to her door."

James looked between the empty hallway and the sickroom. It would be dangerous to leave Dana alone in the hands of an enemy, and Cate had proven time and time again that she could handle herself. But something had happened to her, and he was reluctant to leave her alone for long.

"I'll go," Gair offered.

James nodded. "Keep as much distance as you can. She won't like...I'll relieve you later."

"Aye, Captain."

Stopping a passing servant, Idwal Kai instructed the lass to bring Gair to the queen's chambers. "We can provide the same for you, Captain," he said then. "A bath, a bed, a change of clothing."

James glanced at his tunic. Cate had commented on that as well. "Later."

"Of course," Idwal Kai said. "I don't suppose you would tell me what occurred in Gweneria."

"I don't suppose I would."

"I could better protect her, you—all of you—if I knew."

That was probably true. Mistakes had been made in their haste to leave the fortress—including the involvement of the driver. James didn't know what had become of him nor the carriage they had stolen. And theft was the least of their infractions against the royal family.

"I will find out soon enough," Idwal Kai said.

That was true, too. None of them could risk being in Mairéad when that time came. Cate had killed Tanuba's crown prince, and James would be damned before he allowed any of his to take the fall for that.

"Captain," Rhydwyn said from the sickroom door. "He's awake. He's asking for you."

James looked at Idwal Kai. "Thank you for what you have done for us."

"I am not your enemy."

They would see. James nodded and returned to the sickroom. Everyone had gone, except for Dana on the bed and a pretty, young maid sitting on a stool at his side.

"Give us a moment, please," he said to her.

She curtsied and left. Rhydwyn moved in front of the door, and James dropped onto the stool.

"Still alive," Dana said.

"You, too."

"That girl curtsied to you."

"I saw."

"Wager you never thought that would happen."

"No. Not in this lifetime."

Shifting, Dana nodded and grimaced. "Where are we?"

"Mairéad. The Coileáin estate."

"What?" Dana attempted to sit up, but James pushed him back down. "Why? Why would you ever—?"

"You were dying."

"You should have let me die."

"Cate wouldn't let me."

Dana's mouth formed a reluctant smile. "Glad to hear you were on the right side of things, if not the winning side."

"We should be used to that by now."

"Aye." Dana lifted his head. "Are we alone?"

James glanced over his shoulder to make sure Rhydwyn was in place. "Aye."

"The crown prince. Did you…"

James shook his head. "Cate."

"Cate?" Dana looked away. "Tell them I did it."

"I'm not telling them that."

"I'll tell them."

"Don't be an idiot; no one is telling anyone anything."

"They'll find out before long," Dana said. "Our host will realize we are responsible."

"I know," James responded. Considering they had arrived in the crown prince's carriage, their host likely already suspected.

"They won't care who did it, or why."

"I know that, too."

Dana looked at James. "Then you know you can't stay here. Leave me behind. Take her and go. Now. Do it now. Get out of Mairéad; get out of bloody Tanuba. Take her back to Lira, and keep her safe."

"I don't think she'd be willing to leave without you."

"Convince her."

James laughed quietly. "You obviously don't know her."

"If she won't go willingly, hit her over the head and carry her out of here."

"No. I'm not doing that. It's not an option."

"Neither is staying here. You have to do something, James."

"And I will," he snapped. "Dammit, Dana! Trust that after all I've done to get her back that I'll do even more to keep her safe."

"I'm sorry. I just...I want it to be worth something, my life." Dana sighed. "I thought I was done. I thought I was free, that I had done what I was meant to do. My life was supposed to be given in the goddess's service, and when I closed my eyes in the forest that night, the last thing I saw was you and her, and I thought it was finally over," he said. "How disappointing it was to wake up here."

James stared at the man he had once considered a brother. How had they come to this?

"Why does she care?" Dana asked. "What is my life to her?"

"I don't know," James admitted. "But it does matter to her, so you should rest. The sooner you can travel, the sooner she'll leave."

Dana nodded and closed his eyes. James didn't wait for him to fall asleep before departing. He walked out of the room, finding both Idwal Kai and the physician standing opposite the door. James looked at them briefly before pulling Rhydwyn back inside.

"I'm going to watch over Cate," he said softly. "You and your brother will need to take turns guarding Dana. One of you must always be in the room with him. Always. Be mindful of what he says and who he says it to. If he ever mentions Gweneria or the crown prince"—James sighed—"knock him out, or do whatever you have to do to stop him from saying more."

"Aye, Captain."

James thanked him and returned to the hall to confront the physician. "Will he live?"

"Provided he stays free of infection and fever, I think so," the physician answered. "However, his recovery will take time."

"How much time?"

The physician shrugged. "It is hard to say. So much depends upon the patient. If he was strong and healthy before this—"

"If he wasn't?"

The physician didn't answer right away. "It may take longer," he said carefully. "But that injury is days old already and your man is still alive, so I believe there is much cause for hope. I will do all I can to help speed the process along."

James involuntarily rubbed the spot on his chest where a crossbow bolt should have killed him. He caught Idwal Kai watching and dropped his hand.

"Thank you," he said to the physician. "I won't keep you any longer."

The physician offered him a perfunctory bow and returned to the sickroom, leaving James alone again with Idwal Kai.

"Captain?"

"I'd like that change of clothes now," James said, "if it's not too much trouble."

Idwal Kai bowed his head. "Of course."

The room must have belonged to her parents in another life. She had thought Idwal would have stuck her in a guest room or something, but with her parents dead and Idwal believing Haleine to be the same, Cate supposed she would be the de facto lady of the manor and, as such, would have the best chamber for herself.

If it wasn't the manor's best chamber, her family was more loaded than previously thought. It was well-appointed, much like her accommodations in the Maoilriain palace had been, filled with an impressive range of quality furnishings, rugs, tapestries, and a massive fireplace.

But unlike her previous rooms, there was no bathroom. A wooden tub had been brought in for her use, and the two men who carried it had been banished immediately after setting it down—something she suspected had been Idwal's command. It was supposed to have been a gesture of kindness, a consideration for what he was assuming she had been subjected to. Every other person in the room was female because that was supposed to help her, too, supposed to make her feel safe.

But it didn't.

She carefully examined each female attendant, guessing that at least one of them was a doctor, or whatever a female doctor was called in this world. The title didn't matter. She didn't want a doctor, regardless of gender. She didn't want to be poked and prodded and asked questions she wouldn't want to answer.

There were five of them—one slight girl, younger than Cate, who looked more like a timid mouse than a teenage girl, and the rest older, each with a worldly-wise look about them. She would have dismissed them all, but she wasn't entirely convinced she could get undressed without help.

"You four can go," Cate said. "Minnie will stay."

The attendants looked amongst themselves in curiosity and confusion until Cate pointed her out. Minnie's face flushed, and three of the four remaining women curtsied and left the room.

The fourth looked at Cate sadly. "Will you allow me to—?"

"No," Cate said. "Tell Idwal he should stop what he's doing."

"He is only concerned for you, your majesty."

"And he should stop it. As should you."

The woman bowed her head. "As you wish, your majesty."

Wishing was a useless thing, but Cate didn't say that. She pointed to the door, and Idwal's medicine woman reluctantly walked through it.

Cate looked at Minnie. "Later, either she or Idwal Kai will ask what you saw, and you will tell them you saw nothing. You will tell them that my skin is unblemished. You will tell them there isn't a single bruise, welt, cut, or *any-thing* over which they should concern themselves."

"Will that be the truth, your majesty?"

"No," Cate said. "But if you tell them the truth, I will have you punished."

That was a lie. She would never do something like that. Maybe she'd glare disapprovingly, but that would be innocuous so long as she hadn't suddenly developed the ability to kill with such a look. But Minnie didn't know that, and the color drained out of her face. It made Cate feel like an even bigger jerk, but what else could she do? She had to protect herself by whatever means necessary. That had always been the case. It was just as true now as it had been when she'd been dismantling Zoltano from the inside out.

"Do you understand?" Cate asked.

Minnie nodded feverishly. That didn't necessarily mean the girl understood, but she would be familiar with punishment—and in this fucked-up world, that was something to be avoided at all costs.

"Good." Cate shed the cloak she'd been wearing since departing Gweneria. "Help me undress, please. I don't want the water to get any colder."

"Yes, your majesty."

"You don't have to call me that," Cate said, now shedding her accent. "I'm not actually the queen."

"Yes, your majesty."

Cate nodded. "We'll work on that."

As there wasn't much left to her clothing, it didn't take long for it to end up in a puddle on the floor. Minnie helped her step out of it and noticed for the first time what Cate had been talking about.

"Oh, your majesty," she breathed as she took in the sight of Cate's battered body. "What have they—?"

"Ignore it."

"I can't do that!"

"You can, and you will."

Cate stepped into the tub. The hot water was welcomed and torturous all at the same time. Cuts and burns stung, while her leg throbbed and twitched. She sat before it could give out, then leaned forward to pull as much of her back out of the water as she could. Perhaps a bath was a bad idea.

Gripping the sides of the tub, she swooned and fought not to swoon. If she passed out, Minnie would call the medicine woman and the doctor and everyone else, and they would see—they would *all* see—what Cate most wanted to keep secret.

"Your ma-majesty," Minnie stammered. "I-I—"

"I need you to focus," Cate said in between ragged breaths. "And not on my body. Just...help me with my hair, please."

Minnie did as she was told and carefully washed Cate's hair. When she felt able to sit upright without support, Cate claimed a sliver of soap and ran it over her skin. She had washed off the blood in a stream in the woods, but she could still feel it—the blood and everything else she had pulled out of the crown prince. There wouldn't be enough soap in the world to make that disappear.

"You look as though you've traveled for days," Minnie said after a while. "It must feel good to be clean again."

It wouldn't matter how many baths she took, Cate wouldn't ever feel clean again. "I'm finished," she said and braced herself against the tub to stand.

Drying off was an excruciating experience that left Cate drained and trembling. Minnie helped her put on a robe, then escorted her to a backless chair. Cate sat, slumping to the right, and pulled the robe around her body as tightly as she could tolerate. As Minnie combed out her hair, Cate slowly pulled up the left side of the robe until the Black Wolf's wound was visible. Given her current myriad of issues, how bizarre that it should be this injury about which she could not stop thinking.

It was bad. Red, angry, infected. A microcosm of her entire life.

"My lady?"

Cate looked up. Minnie stood in front of her, hands hovering over the wound as though trying to screw up the courage to stick them in an active bee hive.

"Ignore that, too," Cate said, putting the robe back in place. "You never saw it. It's not there."

"You can't ignore that; you can't ignore any of it," Minnie said, a little backbone creeping into her voice. "You shouldn't. Your leg is…"

Her leg was, truthfully, the least of her problems, and Minnie had to know it. But saying that aloud would lead to a question concerning the laundry list of Cate's other problems, and there was no way she was opening that door.

"Do you know how to treat it?" Cate asked. "You, and no one else?"

"Yes, my lady."

"You alone can treat this? You don't need to ask for help or advice or anything?"

"Yes, my lady, I can do this on my own," Minnie said. "There will be no need to involve anyone else."

Cate nodded. "Have at it."

Treating the wound on her leg involved hot water and wine—not to drink but rather to pour over the wound. Cate looked away as Minnie worked, not wanting or needing to see the process. Pain stabbed through her again and again, but she studied the tapestries in an effort to ignore it.

The pain lessened only slightly when Minnie moved on to Cate's wrists, applying a thick salve to the damaged skin before wrapping each with linen strips. They sat on Cate's thighs then, heavy, weighted down. Little anchors to keep her from moving on.

"Your back now," Minnie said. "If you lie on the bed, I will—"

"Can you read?"

"No, my lady."

Cate nodded and stood. "Okay."

She laid on her stomach on the bed and hid her face in a pillow. As Minnie worked, Cate concentrated entirely on not crying her eyes out. Uncontrollable sobbing would come later—she wouldn't be able to stop it— but she would rather not have an audience for the event, if it could be avoided.

Minnie touched her arm. "Can you sit up?"

Could she? An excellent question. Her entire body felt like one overstimulated nerve, raw and quivering, incapable of doing anything. But she pushed herself up, keeping her weight on her elbows, and Minnie gingerly lifted her the rest of the way. Standing came next, and Cate was forced to hold on to the maid's shoulders until her head stopped swimming and her legs stopped shaking.

"Almost done, my lady," Minnie assured her. "Raise your arms, please."

Cate obliged, resting her too-heavy wrists on top of her head, and allowed her caregiver to imprison her chest and torso in a bandage cocoon. When Minnie finished, Cate looked down at her handiwork. "Is all this really necessary?"

Minnie held out a robe. "Yes."

Who was she to argue? Cate accepted the robe and tugged it over her shoulders.

"You didn't cry out," Minnie said, washing the blood from her hands. "I thought you might. Most would, with injuries such as those."

"I gave that up. Seemed the sensible thing to do."

Now Minnie looked sad. Cate hated seeing it.

"Are there any clothes in this place?" she asked. "Or should I make something out of the drapes?"

Minnie's eyes darted toward the windows. "Of course there is clothing. What would you like?"

"Just something to sleep in for now, a shirt or a tunic or something— nothing too nice because I'll only bleed through it," Cate said. "But tomorrow, I'll need something else. Trousers, if you can find them. Pants, leggings, tights—whatever you call them, I'll need a pair."

"Trousers wouldn't be appropriate," Minnie squeaked.

"Even better," Cate said. "Clothes. Now."

She was being a bitch. Maybe she had a right, maybe she didn't, but either way she would keep doing it until she figured out how to put herself back together. *If* she could put herself back together. Maybe she was like a shattered crystal vase—just a collection of tiny, little shards that would never fit back together again.

But James and Idwal and Minnie and everyone else would keep trying to do just that, regardless of how it destroyed them.

Minnie brought her a black tunic, and Cate slipped it over her head, then pulled the robe back on. The combination of fabric felt too heavy on her back and rubbed uncomfortably against the wall of bandages, but it was better than being exposed. As the men were summoned to remove the tub, she settled on a sofa near the fire. Minnie brought over a tray of food and wine—neither of which interested Cate in the least, but she took a slice of bread and tore off pieces to throw into the fire when the maid wasn't looking.

"Would you like me to stay with you this night, my lady?" Minnie asked.

"To do what? Watch me sleep?" Cate said. "No, that's creepy. I'd rather be alone, please."

That was an overstatement. Being alone sucked, but neither could she stand to be around anyone. Almost anyone. That sucked, too.

Minnie nodded. "I'll come back later, then, to change your bandages."

"Change the bandages?"

"Yes, my lady. It should be done—"

"In the morning," Cate interrupted. "You can come back in the morning and do whatever you want then. Not before."

Minnie curtsied and departed without another word. Alone at last, Cate looked at the bed, illuminated by the light of a lantern. Should she give sleep a try?

Deciding that she should, Cate returned to the bed, pulled back the covers, and eased beneath them. Lying on her back or stomach was impossible. Her sides weren't much better, but that pain was more tolerable than the rest, so she lay on her side, facing the door, and angled her head toward the ceiling.

There was nothing painted there—no knots, no angels—but Cate saw plenty. Zoltano. Weylyn Lann. Ropes and hoods and broken bottles and flames and knives and—

She rolled onto her other side and stared at the wall, only to find the same movie showing on a different screen. She tossed the covers over her head, but it was too much like that stupid hood. Throwing the blankets off completely, she curled into the tightest fetal position she could manage, her eyes squeezed shut.

That didn't last long, either, as her eyelids had gotten the same distribution deal as the ceiling and the walls. She got out of bed, pulled the covers to the floor, and went in search of the wine. She'd drink until she passed out. Dreamless sleep would be a thing of beauty, and it wouldn't matter if her head hurt in the morning because her head would hurt anyway.

Taking the wine off the tray, she brought it to her lips, but the moment her nose caught the scent, her stomach lurched, and the bottle slipped through her hands. She could feel him now—his hands, his breath roaming her skin, the taste of him in her mouth, the moment when he—

She fell to her knees and retched repeatedly, her body ripping and tearing with each heave. By the time it stopped, her eyes watered uncontrollably; each swipe of her hand only cleared the way for more tears. Would she ever stop crying? Or had they broken that, too? Ruptured a tear duct or twenty so that she would perpetually leak salt water from her eyes?

She pounded the floor. Fuck, fuck, fuck, fuck, fuck!

Control. She needed to regain control. But how could she possibly do that? Things were decidedly *out* of control, unraveling faster and faster. So fast that she didn't think she could stop it. Maybe she shouldn't stop it. Why bother being in control? Why bother with anything?

No. Bad plan. Bad place to go.

One thing. Was there one thing she could control? That was all she needed—just one thing, no matter how minor. She only needed to know there was something.

There had to be *something*, right?

The sound of a log crumbling in the fireplace caught her attention, and she looked at the flames. There was always that. The girl who could hold fire in her hands was a girl who didn't feel pain. That girl didn't feel *anything*.

Which would make a delightful alternative to her current self.

But she didn't go near it. Delightful, yes, but also dangerous, deadly—and there would be no telling who would pay that price. James? Rhydwyn? Gair? Someone else? No one here deserved that. If she was going to implode—and that happy event did appear to be pretty goddamn inevitable—she'd do it without taking anyone else down with her.

Defeated, she crawled back to bed and lay in the center of it. If there was no place for her to go but crazy, she could at least do so on a feather mattress.

But despite her utter exhaustion, sleep continued to be an elusive bitch. Cate slipped in and out of it like a ghost might walk through walls, falling asleep only to find herself trapped once again with Zoltano and Weylyn Lann. She'd claw her way out of the dream, find herself back in that strange bed, and have to start all over again.

She should have asked for pants to sleep in. Why hadn't she thought to do that? She should've asked for those—or a suit of armor. A big one, large enough that she could curl up inside its torso, like a hermit crab inside its shell.

But that was stupid, wasn't it? She was safe now. Safer, anyway. Zoltano was dead—exceptionally dead. She had seen to that. Eviscerated the asshole with her bare hands. Hard to come back from that. Downright impossible, even.

But there was still Weylyn Lann. The goddamn Black Wolf wasn't dead. He was out there somewhere—probably drinking wine straight from the bottle and grinning over some joke only he could hear, while he crafted the next phase of his plan to reclaim the tattered remains of her soul.

Unless she was already in that next phase. Weylyn Lann prided himself on reputation. He did what had to be done to fulfill his contracts. Why would he have allowed James and Dana to walk out with her while he rode away on a horse? He wouldn't. Swords would have been drawn, threats would have been exchanged, and Dana would be clinging to life in a dark, little room in a manor that used to belong to an enemy.

It belonged to her now, and there were lines and lines of people who would work to make sure she stayed safe. They'd give up their damn lives if they had to, in order to protect hers.

But she didn't want them to do that.

She sighed. Maybe sleep was a bad idea. Not dreaming would make one crazy, but she had gotten a decent head start down that road already. It wouldn't matter if she skipped a night.

Abandoning the bed, she headed for a window where moonlight was peeking around the drapes but soon tripped and fell. Landing on her bad leg and jostling damaged ribs, she lowered her head to the floor, fighting the need to whimper and cry.

"Cate?"

James. Of course it was James. She pushed herself up to see him slouching in a chair, his outstretched legs responsible for having brought her down. Using the arm of the chair to help her stand, she asked, "What the hell are you doing here?"

He ran his hand over his face. "I have to keep you safe."

"Well, aren't you doing a bang-up job," she said, returning for the lantern. "And I do mean that literally."

"I didn't mean to frighten you."

"Did you mean to break my ankles?"

She took the lantern off the bedside table and twisted the little knob to increase the light. When she turned around, it was bright enough to see James examining her legs.

"You can relax, cowboy. That was hyperbole," she said, carrying the lantern back. "Why are you here? Is Dana dead?"

"Not when I left him."

"Shouldn't you be sitting in the dark in his room, then?"

"Rhydwyn and Gair are taking it in turn."

"So you can be here."

"Aye."

"So you can keep me safe."

"So I can try."

Cate nodded and sat in the chair across from him, setting the lantern on the floor.

"Though I fear," he continued, "that I am much too late."

Why had she fetched that damn lantern? She should have left it right where it was because now there was more than enough light for James to see her face. She tried to stay expressionless, but the more effort she put into it, the more she felt her façade cracking, as her body filled with tears she wouldn't let free.

"I know what you claim, that you're fine, that they..." James shook his head and looked toward the window while his hands formed and reformed fists. He sighed. "I know what you want to be true, Cate, but it isn't."

No, it wasn't. Tears were spilling over, but she didn't dare to wipe them away. She didn't want to draw attention to it.

"Will you please tell me what they did to you?" James asked.

No, she couldn't. She just...couldn't. The words to describe it may have existed, but they weren't anything she could—or would—ever say. How could she tell him what they had done—what she had let them do? How could she tell him that she hadn't stopped it?

"Cate?"

She could barely look at him when she whispered, "You don't need me to tell you. You already saw what they did."

"There's more, though, isn't there?"

She drew her entire body into the chair and made herself as small as possible, ducking her head and covering it with her hands. Too soon. Too much.

"I'm sorry," he said. "I'm sorry, I shouldn't have—"

"They didn't..." Her fingers clutched at her skull. Hold on. Find a way out. "Not what you're thinking. They didn't...He was drunk—Zoltano was too drunk, and he couldn't..." Why was this so hard? She was only telling him what *didn't* happen. She shook her head and looked at James. There was nothing to do but power through it. "They didn't rape me. The Black Wolf was only interested in a mindfuck, and Zoltano was too drunk. So they found other ways to entertain themselves, but they didn't...They didn't do that."

James closed his eyes; his hands clenched and stayed that way. A need to vomit was growing inside her, so Cate pushed out of the chair and walked away. She didn't have anywhere to go, but being in motion had to be better than not. Sharks never stopped moving, and they were the bad asses of the ocean. So that's what she would be. A motherfucking great white shark.

"I'm sorry," James said. "I am so sorry, Cate."

He couldn't do that. Couldn't *say* that. The emotion—the despair—behind his words pushed into her like a bullet—no, like an entire burst of them from some kind of machine gun, piercing every vital organ and leaving her to bleed out. She pulled her robe tight against her body, as though that would shield her from anything, as though that would keep her contained.

As though that were something she wanted.

"If I had known," James said, "if I had thought that this would happen, that it *could* happen, I never would have—"

"You never would have *what*? Brought me here?"

"Aye."

"You would have let the world burn?" she asked, knowing full well that could still happen. But she couldn't tell James that, either.

"I don't know. Maybe."

"Don't. Don't say that. You don't mean it."

"Don't I? Isn't the world already burning? Maybe it can't be saved, not by me, not by anyone," James said. "But you? If I hadn't...I could have saved you."

Cate slid to the floor in front of the fire. Screw being a shark. That was just another dumb idea in a long line of dumb ideas. She'd be a stone instead. You couldn't hurt a stone. You could smash it into pieces, but you couldn't hurt it.

She was shaking again as she brought her knees to her chest. Her arm wrapped around her torso, and she looked at the bandages around her wrist.

Her nails dug into the linen, tearing away piece after piece, until a hand on her arm stopped her.

"Don't do that," James said softly.

She looked at him, kneeling in front of her. When her eyes dropped to his fingers encircling her arm, he released her.

Cate resumed the destruction of the bandage. "I shouldn't have let her do it in the first place."

"She was only trying to help you."

The bandage gave way, and Cate threw it in the fire. "I don't need her help. I don't need your help, either. I don't need anyone's help. I can take care of myself."

"Aye, I know you can," James said. "I don't believe a soul exists that would disagree with that, but Cate...mayhap you don't have to."

Yes, she did. Cate tore at the remaining wrist bandage until James sat beside her and took her arm. Placing it on his leg, he carefully unraveled the bandage himself.

"It doesn't have to be me," he said as he worked. "If you prefer someone else—your maid, or—"

"No. No one else," she said. Too many people had already seen. She wasn't about to add to that number. She shook her head. "Stay if you want; I don't care. It doesn't matter to me."

"Well, then. If it doesn't matter."

"It doesn't."

He removed the rest of the bandage and gathered it in his hands. When he offered it to her, she pointed at the fire. He tossed it in, and Cate watched it burn.

James watched her. "Do you mean to remove the others?"

As that would entail the removal of her clothes, she shook her head and laid her arm across her knees to study her wrist. The damage seemed lessened in the firelight, bruises and lacerations becoming nothing but shadows.

"How do I help you?" James asked.

Her arm fell to her side. "You don't."

"I don't accept that."

"Good thing I don't care what you accept or don't accept."

"Cate," he pleaded.

"Let me pretend," she said. "Just for a while."

He didn't care for that suggestion, and there was no reason why he would. It didn't involve actually *doing* anything. There wasn't anything physical to take his mind off of how miserable the situation was. Nothing to do, no one to hit.

"Cate—"

"Worry about Dana. Worry about Lucy and Ethel—"

"Who?"

Cate shrugged. "Rhydwyn and Gair. Worry about them, or how we'll get back to Lira, or anything else. Just not me. Not...this."

"I don't know if I can do that."

"Then keep it to yourself. I only want to forget."

"Can you?"

"No. That's where the pretending comes in," she said. "Just let me do that, all right?"

James nodded. "All right."

They fell quiet then and sat side by side, watching the fire.

"You should sleep," he said after a while.

"Can't. I haven't been doing so well with my eyes closed."

"You slept in the carriage and later in the forest," he said. "Why not here? Too comfortable?"

She smiled. "That must be it. No other common denominators to be found there." She looked at James and slowly uncurled. His clothes were different—clean and blood-free—and his face was freshly clean-shaven. "Idwal found you new clothes."

"Aye—Coileáin colors. First Maoilriain, and now this." James pulled at the tunic. "I hardly remember who I am anymore."

No, she hardly remembered who *she* was. He was easy. "You are James ap Seoras, the defender of good and vanquisher of evil."

James laughed, and the vibrations traveled through her body. It made her ribs hurt, but the sensation felt good. Warm. She put her hand on her stomach to hold it there.

"It doesn't matter whose colors you might be wearing," she continued, "you're still a white hat."

"Am I?"

"You are." She sighed. "You're also the common denominator, you know."

"That phrase again. What does it mean?"

"It means something—a factor—that's shared among all members of a specific group."

"Well, that..." James laughed again. "That explains nothing."

"When I slept in the carriage and later in the forest—you're why I could do that. *You* are the common denominator to me being able to close my eyes."

A long pause followed her disclosure. Cate was too afraid to look at James and focused hard on the fire. She shouldn't have said that. She shouldn't have said anything. What was wrong with her? Forget that—what *wasn't* wrong with her?

"Why?" he asked. "How could that possibly be true?"

Cate shrugged again. "If you're here, I'm not there."

Another long pause. Tears reformed in her eyes. This time, she did wipe them away. It didn't matter anymore.

"I'm here now. I'm not going anywhere," James said. "If you need to sleep—if you need *me* to help you sleep, I'll—"

"You'll what? Stop whatever you're doing to be my human security blanket? My goddamn body pillow?"

"If that's what you need, aye."

Was that what she needed? How could she tell? She could go from being completely numb to weepy to face-melting angry and back again in under a minute. How many times had she threatened to set James on fire? How many of those times had been followed with an immediate and desperate request for his company?

She shook her head. "You shouldn't—I don't—I don't deserve that. You. This. Whatever this is, I-I didn't earn it, I—"

"Cate?"

"I let it happen," she blurted. "I-I couldn't stop it. I didn't stop it— *them*—I-I let it happen and I-I didn't do anything. I stopped fighting, I stopped, and I-I should have...done something, fought harder—*something*— and I-I didn't do anything."

"That's not true. You did something." James's voice was tight, more so than before. It was an elastic stretched to the point where breaking was inevitable. "You survived."

A tear-soaked laugh escaped. "You say that like it matters."

"It does matter. You survived, Cate. That's everything."

"You believe that? You?"

"Aye, me," he said firmly. "It is everything, and you did that, Cate. You survived."

Had she, though? Had she really? It didn't feel that way. It felt more like she was a sandcastle built too close to an incoming tide. She shook her head and started to tell him how wrong he was about that, about her, but she cried instead, and this time there was no stopping it. Floodgates broke open, sobs wracked her body, and she fell forward. He caught her and wrapped her in his arms. Part of her wanted to push him away, but a larger part didn't have the energy, so she leaned into him and cried.

CHAPTER 34

The addition of the wagon and his brother's body slowed their progress back to Mairéad. The first night, Revelin forced them to make camp in the woods, every man questioning why their prince had driven them from the shelter of the fortress to spend the night in a cold, damp forest. They kept their complaints to themselves, grumbling beneath their breath when they thought he could not hear.

Cathal stayed close, to the point of hovering. He hadn't spoken to Revelin since their departure from Gweneria when he had made mention of Revelin's change in status. Of course Cathal would mark that. He likely thought that he could be to Revelin what Darian had been to his father, or what Darian had been to Revelin himself. To be the king's most trusted man, his advisor, was a most profitable position. Look at all that Darian had built with it. Cathal hardly needed wealth—his family was near as wealthy as the Maoilriains—but perhaps he craved the position. Powerful men would fear him, and others would bow and scrape to serve him. To hold the king's ear— that was something to which all noblemen aspired.

Revelin spent that first night sitting on the ground, his back against a tree and his eyes on the wagon in which his brother's body lay. Having the king's ear was not something to which only noblemen aspired. His own sons might aim for the same honor.

The next morning, they broke camp and continued their sluggish march toward Mairéad. The men he had sent to track Zoltano's missing carriage found them, but the carriage and those who had stolen it remained lost. By the time the day had turned into night, they were able to reach Cathal's estate. The men were cheered by the improvement in their accommodations, but Revelin paid them little mind as he escorted his brother's body to its temporary resting place.

"If we depart early and ride hard, we will reach the palace tomorrow," Cathal said later that night, as the two of them sat alone at dinner.

Revelin nodded. He wanted this journey to end as much as the rest of them. "Then we will," he said. "But there is no need for you to accompany us. You are already home."

"If that is what you wish, your highness," Cathal said. "I can continue on, if you require it, or merely just desire it."

"No," Revelin said. "I will not need you now."

Indeed, the rebels were gone—or would be soon—and his brother was dead. It would seem that all threats to his kingdom had been subdued. There was no reason for Cathal to continue on, and Revelin found he needed the nobleman to stay behind. Yes, he was now the heir to the throne currently held by an ailing woman, and another heir in similar circumstances would be gathering close those he could trust, those he could use. But Revelin would not. Not yet. He wanted to distance himself from any sycophantic behavior for as long as he could.

In accordance to Revelin's command, Cathal roused the men well before dawn but stayed behind when they rode out. Revelin kept them moving as quickly as possible. By the time they reached the palace gates, night had long since fallen. Revelin rode into the torch-lit courtyard to find Eamonn waiting. His younger brother held the horse steady as Revelin dismounted. Together, they watched the wagon pass.

"Who is it?" Eamonn asked.

He would take the news hard. There had been an affinity between Eamonn and Zoltano of which Revelin had never been a part. Of which he had never wanted to be a part. But he did not relish the idea of Eamonn in pain.

Revelin motioned to an idle groom to take possession of the horse. "Our brother."

Eamonn stared at Revelin in disbelief. "No."

"Eamonn, I—"

His brother turned and ran toward the wagon. Revelin pursued, catching him at the wagon's side. Grabbing Eamonn's hand as it reached for the body, he said, "Do not look. You do not want to see."

Eamonn pulled free. "Yes, I do!"

"No, you do not."

"What does that mean? What was done to him?"

"You do not want to see," Revelin repeated. "Neither does our mother. Promise me you will not look. Promise me you will not let her see."

Eamonn looked again at the shroud concealing their brother's body and nodded. "I promise."

It was a pledge too easily made and would be, Revelin assumed, broken in the same manner. He thanked his brother anyway and looked at Darragh, waiting nearby.

"Did the messenger find you?" Revelin asked.

"Yes, your highness." Darragh glanced into the wagon. "The arrangements are already underway."

"See that it is immediate," Revelin said. "No fuss, no fanfare. My mother will require some ceremony, but this is to be done as quickly and quietly as you can manage."

Darragh nodded. "Yes, your highness. I will see it done."

"A messenger?" Eamonn asked. "You sent a messenger?"

Revelin closed his eyes for a moment. "Yes."

"With word of our brother's death?"

"Yes."

"Why weren't we told? Why was he"—Eamonn pointed to Darragh—"told of this and we were not?"

"I wanted to be the one to tell you," Revelin said. "I did not want you to hear it from anyone else."

Eamonn shook his head. "I should have been told."

"I am telling you now."

"What happened to him?" Eamonn demanded. "How did he die?"

"He was murdered," Revelin answered. He could not lie about that. When Eamonn did go back on his promise and look at Zoltano's corpse, the manner of death would be quite obvious.

"By whom?"

"I suspect it was Dana," Revelin said. That, at least, was the truth. He looked to Darragh. "Has there been any sign of the Liran rebels?"

Darragh shook his head. "No, your highness. It is as though they have all but disappeared."

Perhaps they had. There was no telling of what that man and those who followed him were capable.

"The guards at the north gate reported that the crown prince's carriage came through yesterday, but it has not been seen since," Darragh said. "The horses, however, were sold at market by unknown men. No one has admitted to recognizing or even seeing their faces."

"Those bloody rebels," Eamonn said. "How did we allow them to come here a second time and kill another member of our family?"

"Eamonn," Revelin said, "you must—"

"Don't tell me what I must do," Eamonn snapped. "As if you would know such a thing. You do nothing, Revelin. You stand aside and let it happen and won't even comment on the pieces. You always do this. Our brother lies *murdered* in a manner so horrific, you'll not allow us to see, but you do nothing to avenge it."

"Revenge will serve no—"

"Revenge?" Eamonn shouted.

The entire population of the courtyard stopped to stare at the two brothers. Darragh drifted back, looking uncomfortable.

"Revenge?" Eamonn repeated. "These men—these bloody men—they came here and killed our father, and now they have killed our brother. We should be hunting them down; we should be driving them off the edge of the world, but you'll only stand there and let them get away with it. Again."

Eamonn spat on the ground in front of Revelin and looked at Darragh. "Double the patrols. Triple them," he ordered. "Send every man we can spare. Raise men from the nobles and send them as well. Tell them to hunt these dogs down and drag their bodies back here. I want their heads for our wall."

Shocked, Darragh looked at Revelin.

Revelin dragged his hand across his mouth and sighed. "We will not find them. They most likely took a ship out of Odhran and are well on their way back to Lira by now."

"Then send faster ships to run the others down. Search them all until they're found!" Eamonn exclaimed. "Revelin, you can't ignore this!"

Revelin knew that all too well, but while Dana had Mireille, he would not touch them. It would be the only way to keep her safe. As long as she was known as Haleine, and as long as Haleine was known as a traitor, she couldn't come back to the palace. But neither could Revelin explain this to Eamonn. His brother would never understand why Revelin was willing to let the rebels go free. He would not understand why Revelin wanted to protect Mireille.

Silently, Revelin counted the number of days he had been gone. There was every chance that Dana, his companion, and Mireille were already out of reach. He could not very well tell Darragh to have the men stop searching for them, but would it endanger Mireille if Darragh were to do what Eamonn had requested?

"Scour the land," Revelin said to Darragh. "Have men go to the harbor in Odhran and question dock workers about ships that have recently departed. If the rebels are found, they are to be brought here alive."

"Alive?" Eamonn was incredulous. "Why would you ever want them alive?"

"I want their confession," Revelin said. "Darragh, you have work to do."

Darragh bowed and walked swiftly from the courtyard. Revelin took his brother by the arm and drew him away from the growing crowd of spectators.

"You are angry, and now you are grieving all over again," he said. "But neither of these are reason enough to excuse such reckless behavior. You do not think, Eamonn, and you are not controlling either emotion. A man who cannot is easy prey for his enemies."

Eamonn pushed him away. "What should I do? Nothing?"

"Yes. Please," Revelin said. "Please do nothing. I will take care of it. I will."

"Because you don't feel?"

"I feel a great deal. But I do not allow it to rule me."

"No, you only allow Haleine to rule you." Eamonn laughed. "How many other lies do you tell yourself?"

"Eamonn, I—"

"Is that why you won't hunt them? Is *Haleine* the reason you're allowing murderers to go free?"

"Not Haleine, no."

Eamonn nodded. "Another lie."

"I swear Haleine is not involved in this."

"She's involved in everything you do," Eamonn said. "You just don't realize it yet. You probably never will."

He walked away, running his hand along the wagon as he passed, and disappeared into the stables. Revelin went in search of his mother.

He found her in the solarium and dismissed her attendants. Holding her hand, he did not prolong the announcement, only stated the fact plainly. She did not cry as she inquired as to the manner of her firstborn's death, nor when Revelin answered that her son had been murdered. A mere nod followed his claim that the perpetrators would be found and persecuted, and a sigh was the sole indication that he had delivered tragic news.

"A funeral," Haraszty said. "There will have to be a funeral."

"Darragh is working on the arrangements."

Haraszty's eyes widened. "Zaide Romanza will have no idea what has happened! She needs to be told right away. Oh, that poor girl."

Revelin did not think that was an apt description of Feond's queen, but Haraszty was blind to Zaide Romanza's true nature. Zaide Romanza was careful to keep it hidden from his mother.

"What will she do?" Haraszty sighed. "That poor dear. There's been so much loss."

"I will take care of it," Revelin assured her. "I will take care of everything."

Haraszty shook her head. "She's here no longer. She's gone home."

"Letters can and will be written," he said. "I will see to it."

Haraszty nodded again. "I will write to her as well," she said. "Does Eamonn know?"

"Yes. He was in the courtyard when we arrived."

"He shall take this hard."

Yes, he would. Revelin would have to find someone to watch his brother to make certain he would not come to harm. If Revelin was to be the heir, then Eamonn was closer to the throne than ever. Any reckless behavior could not be tolerated.

"I will see to it," Revelin said.

Haraszty gripped his hand tightly, and he allowed her to do so, pleased to have a moment to indulge his own anguish.

"Your brother's passing means you will inherit the throne upon my death," Haraszty said.

It was not the first time that fact had been stated. And as it had before, it hung oddly in the air, as though it did not belong there at all.

"You will not die for years," he said.

"I fear not. Indeed, I have lived too long. I am an old woman who has outlived both a husband and a son," she said, "and I do not wish to be strong any longer."

"Strong is what you are, who you are. You cannot deny nor ignore that."

Haraszty released his hand. "What I can do is relinquish the throne to you. When the mourning period has ended, I will step down and you will wear the crown."

No one would argue with her decision. The majority of noblemen would be thrilled by the announcement, and those few who had backed Zoltano would have no choice but to accept Revelin, but he did not want the crown. Though he could not explain why to anyone's satisfaction, he believed Eamonn—once his sorrow had been processed—would be better suited for it. Eamonn would have what Revelin lacked.

Despite being born a third son, Eamonn had assumed he was meant to be king one day. Revelin never had. With a healthy father and an elder brother, it was not an unreasonable supposition.

But reason had been discarded, and the second son was meant to wear the crown. Revelin had taken on the care of the kingdom in the wake of his father's death, but the crown itself was an onus that he did not want.

Neither could he allow his hard-headed and grief-stricken younger brother to carry that burden. Both Eamonn and the kingdom would suffer for it.

Revelin stifled a sigh and bowed his head. "I shall rule as you and Father have taught me."

—◦◦◦—

She cried until she couldn't possibly have had any liquid left inside her. James held her, arms and legs aching and cramping, until she slipped through his arms—as though liquid herself—and lay in a quivering heap on the floor. Eventually, she laid her head on his leg and fell asleep, so James was sitting on the floor, his legs stretched toward the fire, when a knock came at the door.

Unwilling to disturb Cate, he ignored it, and the knocking continued. It couldn't have been Rhydwyn or Gair—they would have entered by now—

which left no one James cared about. Finally, someone came inside and carefully made their way over to him.

"Captain," Idwal Kai said.

"Later," James responded.

"It's rather—"

"Later," he repeated with more force but not volume. "Whatever it is, it can wait."

"I'm afraid it can't."

James looked at Idwal Kai, who was staring at Cate. "What is it, then?"

"Is she—?"

"She's fine. What's so urgent that it can't wait? Dana? Is he—?"

"No, no, Captain, he lives, but...I have received word from the palace that the crown prince is dead."

Prince Revelin had made excellent time. James looked at the fire. "Have you?"

"Murdered in Gweneria. Most gruesomely, I am told."

"Was he?"

"Captain, I—"

"Where is the carriage?" James interrupted. "The one in which we arrived?"

"Being dismantled. There will be no trace of it when they're done."

"The horses?"

"Sold at market by hooded men," Idwal Kai said. "It will be assumed that they are you, but—"

"They would think that anyway," James finished. "What of the driver?"

"In the kitchens, eating stew, I believe. He is not a threat to you. He once served Lord Coileáin and would do anything to aid his daughter. He won't give you away."

How was everyone so damn loyal to a dead man? James shook his head. "Convenient, that."

"Fortunate."

Aye, it was fortunate, which would suggest that it was not to be trusted. James looked at Cate. After a moment, he nodded and reached behind him for one of the small, square pillows on the sofa. Gingerly, he lifted Cate and slid out from underneath her, leaving the pillow in his place. He stood and walked toward the door, Idwal Kai following.

"How long do we have?" he asked when they were far enough away not to rouse Cate.

"Captain?"

"You received word about the crown prince. I assume you sent word back about us. How long do I have to...How long?"

"Perhaps you don't understand, Captain, but I've been working to *hide* you. Unless my lady orders me otherwise, I have no intention of allowing anyone to discover your presence here."

"You don't care who is responsible for the death of your crown prince?"

"I do not."

"Why?"

"Because she is not fine," Idwal Kai said, nodding in Cate's direction, "and I suspect you are the reason she is still alive."

"She's still alive because she's the strongest bloody person I have ever known. I had nothing to do with that."

"But you're keeping her that way. She has let no one near her, no one save you," Idwal Kai said. He sighed. "I do not know what madness she has endured. I do not know why the crown prince was involved, nor why he would...I do not know."

"That's right," James said, more sharply than intended, "you don't."

But he did. God help him, he did.

"Do what you will, Captain, but please understand that you are safe here—all of you," Idwal Kai said. "For as long as you want. Or need."

James followed each step Idwal Kai took out of the room. After the door had closed, he continued to look at it. He stood paralyzed with indecision. The burden was making him crack; he could feel it running down his center, but it was imperative that he remain whole. Cate depended upon him, as did Dana. He had to find a way to keep shouldering the weight.

"I killed him. Zoltano—I killed him."

James turned. Cate had moved to the sofa, sitting sideways at the far end, her knees drawn to her chest.

"I know," he said.

"He wasn't the first."

That, James hadn't known. He walked toward her, moving slowly, wary of startling her, but Cate's attention was on the fire.

"I remember the first man I killed," he offered, sitting at the other end of the sofa. "It's not something easily forgotten; I don't believe I ever shall. It makes a mark on you, a scar, and you carry it with you for all your life."

"Did he deserve it?"

Had he? Tilting his head back, James suppressed a shudder as he recalled the sword thrust that had stolen the light from a stranger's eyes. No, he would never forget.

He sighed. "Probably not. But there we were, pitted against one another on opposite sides of a war neither of us had begun, and if I hadn't killed him..."

"He would have killed you," Cate supplied.

James lifted his head to find her looking at him. "Aye."

"Does that make it easier?"

"No. Nothing will do that."

"Not even time?"

"Not so far."

Cate nodded. "Why didn't you tell him?"

"Tell who what?"

"Tell Idwal that I killed Zoltano."

"Why would I tell him that?"

"It's the truth."

"He doesn't need to know."

"He thinks you did it."

James shrugged. "He thinks Dana did it."

"Which he didn't," Cate said. "Neither did you. Idwal should know that."

Perhaps, but he wouldn't hear it from James. Keeping that secret felt like his only sure way of protecting her.

"Why does it matter?" he asked. "You heard him; he doesn't care who did it."

"I care. I'm the one who killed him. I'm the one who...*I* killed him. No one else should take the blame for that."

"Cate, what you did...What *he* did—"

"We're not talking about that."

Uncurling, she slipped off the sofa and slid across the floor, stopping in front of the fire. She sat with her back to him, shoulders hunched and body trembling.

"He deserved it," James said, leaning forward. "What he did to you...He deserved what he got in return. He deserved far worse. God help me, I would have—"

"I didn't need you to," she blurted, her anger palpable. "I *don't* need you to."

"I know," James responded just as quickly. "No one thinks you weak, Cate. No one."

"Fuck what they think."

There didn't seem to be anything to say to that. He didn't try, as he rested his elbows on his knees and waited for her to guide him.

"God," she said finally.

"What about him?"

"Before...you said 'God.' You said, 'God help me.'"

"Aye. What of it?"

Cate turned, allowing him to see her in profile. "You meant 'goddess,' didn't you?"

"No."

"Isn't the goddess the foundation of your cause or whatever? You all live to serve the goddess?"

James fought the urge to laugh and settled back. "Faolan likes to think so."

"That's not true. As long as you're doing what he wants, he doesn't give a shit to whom you might say your prayers."

"I'm not in the habit of saying prayers to anyone."

Cate shrugged. "I didn't mean that literally or anything; it's just an expression. I can't imagine Faolan cares at all if you pray or not. Hell, he probably prefers someone more agnostic; it would make things easier for him. Less complicated that way."

James wasn't sure what she meant, and neither was he inclined to ask for further explanation. He nodded, though she couldn't see him doing it.

She faced him. "It's interesting, your lack of religion."

He found it to be far less interesting than she; it wasn't a conversation on which he was keen, but she did appear more relaxed now—or perhaps merely distracted. Either way, he decided to continue.

"Is it?" he asked. "How so?"

"Well, it's not interesting in a launch-a-full-scale-investigation kind of way. More...unexpected." She shrugged again. "Didn't your mother ever make you go to church? The whole family go share a bench and listen to someone preach about the evils of—I don't know—strong-willed women or independent thought or something?"

He laughed. "Who had the time? We had a farm to run," he said, then chuckled again. "Did your mother ever do that? Take you to church?"

Somehow, it had been the wrong question to ask. Any respite, any diversion, their talk had offered her evaporated instantly. She looked at him, eyes expressing a range of emotion he couldn't name.

"No. No, she didn't," she answered, turning back to the fire. "We have to get out of here. Tanuba, I mean. We need to get back to Lira."

James leaned forward again. What had caused the change of topic? What had altered her willingness to be in Mairéad? He wanted to ask but doubted she would answer.

"Is it Idwal Kai? Do you not trust him? Do you think he's a threat?" he asked instead.

"He's not the threat. Stop trying to see threat there. Idwal's intentions are good, and he will work to protect us—me, at least, and by extension, you—but intentions might not make a difference if he's motivated."

He? Did she mean the Black Wolf? Omur? Someone else? How could he convince her to tell him?

"It was right of us to come here, I think; Dana would have died for sure if we hadn't," she said. "But someone sent Idwal that message. They sent it to

Idwal—someone who's not that important—which means they had some other reason for doing it. Maybe it was a warning."

"To protect us?"

Cate shrugged. "Maybe to inform us that they know we're here. If we stay too long, it will put everyone in danger. I don't want to do that."

"Neither do I."

"We go, then. Sooner rather than later."

"Aye, but Dana's injury—I believe if we were to put him on a ship as he is now that he would be dead before we reached Lira."

"We could leave him here. Idwal will send him home when he's well."

"If that's our only plan, we should have let him die in the forest," James said. "I won't leave him here unguarded."

Nor would he leave Dana here in Cate's absence. She was the only reason they were welcomed at all. She might have trusted Idwal Kai, but James would not. Dana had killed the man's last master, and Idwal Kai wasn't likely to forget—or forgive—that.

"It will probably take some time to find a ship to carry all of us to Lira," Cate said. "Maybe he'll be stronger by then."

"Do you mean to pay for passage?"

"You don't think all of us could stowaway in the cargo hold, do you?"

"Not successfully."

"Okay, then. We'll hire a ship, and—"

"Money," James said. "As not all of us are able to work for our passage, we will require money, and all we have are Dana's soldiering wages. It won't be nearly enough. Or, if it is, I would not like to embark upon that ship."

Cate turned. "Maybe you didn't notice, but I'm kind of rich. There are a couple of candelabras in this room alone that could pay for passage for five people. I'm sure we could work something out with someone."

James glanced around the room. There was an immense amount of wealth everywhere his eyes settled. There was more than enough to hire a ship. There was more than enough to purchase the damn vessel outright if she wanted.

"What's the matter?" Cate asked. "Do you have a problem with women paying for things?"

He looked at her in exasperation. "No. I am, however, reluctant to accept money from an enemy."

"Didn't you just say that Dana had soldiering wages?" she said. "Where did those come from? Oh wait—that's right. Your enemy."

"That is different."

"It really isn't. Besides, it's my money. *This*"—she waved her hand vaguely—"is my money. So unless you're saying that *I'm* an enemy, your argument is invalid." She waited a moment before adding, "Do you think I'm an enemy?"

James cracked a smile. "I can never tell."

Cate smiled as well and looked back at the fire. "Me neither."

"Aye, well, we'll start searching for a ship in the morning."

"Idwal could help with that."

"I'd rather not involve him, if we don't have to."

"He's not evil."

"Perhaps not, but he is connected to those who are. Keeping him ignorant to our plans will help keep us safe," James said. "It could also be the only thing that keeps him safe."

Cate whipped around to look at him. James held up his hands.

"I'm not threatening him," he explained. "I just...There are people hunting us, Cate. Their crown prince is dead, and they know it. Not only that, but there are people after you specifically. If Idwal Kai begins making inquiries about a ship to Lira and our pursuers hear about it, they'll—"

"They'll go after him to get to us," Cate finished. She sighed and ran a hand through her hair. "Okay. We'll leave him out of it. Tomorrow, you can take your groupies to the harbor and make some discreet inquiries about getting us the hell out of here. I'll stay with Ken Doll."

"Do you mean Dana?"

"Yes, Dana."

James nodded. "You should know...he wants to confess to Zoltano's murder."

"Why would he want to do that?"

"Perhaps he thinks he's going to die anyway, or maybe he wants his death to have some noble purpose," James said. "The reason doesn't matter. I won't let him—nor you—take the fall for that."

"How will you keep him from saying anything?"

"Rhydwyn or Gair will handle it. They'll make sure he confesses nothing."

"How will they do that?"

"However they have to."

Cate smiled again. "That could delay his recovery."

"Then he best keep his mouth shut, hadn't he?"

She laughed as she made her way back to the sofa. She stayed on the floor, folding her arms on the cushion. Laying her head on top of them, she looked at him.

"Thank you for doing this—all of this," she said. "Tonight, last night, the nights before...I don't even know how many nights there were, but it's a lot of insanity, and you're bearing it nobly."

He shrugged. "Anyone would."

"Be insane, or sit with the insane person?"

"The latter, but you're not insane, Cate."

"I think you'd be surprised. On both counts."

James nodded toward the door. "How many people out there would have sat here with you tonight if you had allowed it?"

"Doesn't matter. I didn't allow it."

"You let me."

"You snuck in during one of the few and far between moments when I was actually asleep."

"You allowed me to stay."

Cate made a face. "Only because I'm using you as some sort of weird, reverse-totem, anchor-type thing."

"I don't know what that means."

"In lies the hilarity."

"You're not laughing."

She shrugged. "Guess it's not that funny."

—◦◦◦—

It wasn't funny. Nothing was funny. She hated being such a goddamn train wreck.

How could James possibly consider her a survivor? Was that another word for which he lacked a proper definition? Did it mean something different here? It didn't seem as though she was doing much surviving at all. Crying— she sure was doing a lot of that. Was that surviving? Or maybe it was the part where she was clinging to James as though he were a flotation device and she adrift at sea. Yes, the perfect combination of weak and pitiful was she.

She hurt, too. Just...*hurt*. There wasn't a part of her that didn't ache or throb, or wasn't bruised or bleeding or broken. Her body wasn't healing, either. James had been correct in his observation that first day in the woods. *What did they do*, he had asked, but she hadn't had an answer. The truth was, she didn't know. It tasted like salt. On their blades, their hands, everything— it had been rubbed into every place they broke skin. She didn't know if it had been salt, or a mixture of things that just happened to taste like salt, or even her own goddamn brain making shit up. Maybe she was only remembering tears.

But regardless of what it was—or wasn't—whatever they had done had disturbed the accelerated healing powers she had enjoyed on the other side of the ocean. Another thing broken, and this one meant that she had to live with some asshole's name carved into her back.

Well, she probably would have to live with that one anyway.

Another storm surge of salt-flavored shame was rising fast. If history had taught them anything, it was that she was about thirty seconds away from crawling on that couch, laying her head on James's leg, and crying until she passed out from sheer exhaustion.

And he would let her do it. He would sit there all damn night and let her cry. Whether it was guilt or genuine caring, or some twisted combination of the two, Cate couldn't tell, but the reason didn't matter. She couldn't keep letting him do it.

Although she was adverse to the concept of sleep, it didn't mean that James was. In fact, she thought he was more in need of some shut-eye than anyone she had ever met. For one reason or another, he'd stayed awake for more than one night on her behalf, and now he was doing it all over again because she was a goddamn mental case. It wasn't fair that he should have to handle all of her fucked-up emotional baggage. No one should have to suffer like that.

"You should get some sleep," she said. "You won't get very far in your ship-hunting mission otherwise."

"What about you?"

"I'm not planning to hunt ships in the morning, but I'll sleep if you sleep."

"Will you?"

"I'll try."

James nodded. "All right."

She stood and adjusted her robe before holding out her hand to him. "Come on."

"Where are we going?"

"There's a perfectly good bed over there. Unless you're jonesing to sleep on the floor, we should take advantage of it."

James looked at the bed. "Are you sure you want—?"

"I'm sure."

"Idwal Kai wouldn't like it, if he were to see."

"All the more reason, then."

When he took her hand, she pulled him up. After recovering his sword, he followed her to the bed. She settled on her side and watched him disarm.

James laid his sword on the floor beside the bed. He set a dagger on the mattress before kicking off his boots. Though the sword was carefully arranged on the floor, he left the boots where they had fallen and—with a hint of reluctance—placed the dagger underneath a pillow.

"Isn't that a dangerous place to keep that?" she asked.

He smiled. "Just in case."

Cate nodded. "Have any more of those?"

The smile disappeared. "We'll get you one in the morning."

He bent at the waist, and she heard the rustle of the blankets she had pulled to the floor earlier. When James straightened, she said, "No. Leave them down there, please."

"You won't be cold?"

"Temperature isn't the problem."

Another nod, another quick look that suggested she would have been better off dealing with the blankets. But he dropped them and settled on the bed, the dagger-concealing pillow beneath his head. He looked at the ceiling and shifted his position in an obvious attempt to get comfortable. Was it the mattress or the company giving him the most trouble?

He stopped fidgeting and looked at her. "Doesn't it hurt, lying like that? Your ribs are broken."

"They're not all broken," she answered. "Some are probably just cracked."

"Which still hurts."

"Not as much as other things, maybe."

He nodded. "Aye."

He was watching her with those sad eyes again. Maybe he didn't realize he was doing it. Cate looked away, unable to take the pity any longer.

The moment destroyed, James rolled from one side to the other but settled on his back again with a heavy sigh. "How does anyone sleep on something so bloody soft?"

She smiled, tears once again sliding down her face. "You get used to it."

"I thought my bed in the barracks was the nicest one I'd ever had, but this?" he said. "This is what you're accustomed to, and I made you sleep on the ground."

"You didn't make me sleep on the ground. Nobody makes me do anything."

The second part of her declaration sounded much weaker than she had intended. James glanced at her, and she knew he had heard it, too.

"No," he said, "they don't."

He was still a terrible liar, but Cate appreciated the effort.

chapter 35

t some point during the night, Cate had—much to James's relief, she was sure—cried herself to sleep. The dreams that followed were the usual terrible sort, and she woke suddenly at the sound of a door opening. Her mind remained trapped in a room above a tavern, and though her eyes told her she was no longer there, she fought to break free, pushing against the solid bulk of James's chest, waking both him and her injuries.

James sat up and caught her arms above the elbows. "Cate, Cate, it's all right. It's all right, Cate—you're safe. Cate, listen to me, look at me—you're safe."

She gripped his arms. Safe. She was safe. The exact truth of that statement was debatable, but she couldn't deny that there were significantly fewer threats in this room. As the panic abated, she nodded and pulled away.

"Sorry." She looked at Minnie, standing near the bed with a tray in her hands. "Sorry."

James watched her with concern, poised to intercede should she again demonstrate how badly deteriorated her mind had become, while Minnie appeared downright mortified. When Cate worked out the reason why, she laughed until the aching of her ribs became too much.

"No need to look so scandalized, Minnie," she said. "We're all adults here."

James glanced between her and the maid. Catching on to Cate's meaning, he let out an exasperated breath and got out of bed. "Bloody hell."

"I-I didn't bring food for two," Minnie squeaked.

James took the tray from her hands. "Nor should you have."

Cate grinned. "You can go, Minnie. My houseboy will see that I eat."

As Minnie curtsied and disappeared, James set the tray in front of her. "Your houseboy?"

She laughed. "Just having some fun."

James released his second sigh of the day and retrieved his boots and weapons. Cate examined her breakfast, finding none of it tempting.

"I need to look in on Dana," James said. "Will you be—?"

"I'll be fine," she said. Given what he had endured the night before—and the nights before that—she owed him a serious response. She owed him a hell of a lot more than that, but answering serious questions seriously was a decent start. She waved him off. "Go do what you need to do. Happy ship hunting."

James, however, didn't leave. "Come with me, if you want," he said. "Rhydwyn and Gair can tend to Dana. You and I can hunt ships."

How pathetic did she look? It must have been bad if James wasn't willing to leave her alone in a well-guarded castle.

"You're just afraid to leave me behind," she said.

"Aye, very."

It would feel good to do something, she supposed. Better than sitting alone in a room all day with nothing to do but think about things she didn't want to think about.

"Well, if it'll alleviate your fears," she said, "I'll go."

James hid a smile as he buckled his sword belt around his waist. "Good."

"I, uh, I told Minnie that she could..." Cate rubbed the back of her neck. "I'll need some time."

"Take all you need," he said. "When we do go, we can't tell Idwal Kai what we're doing."

"Is that possible?"

"The man's not a god."

"It can be hard to tell sometimes who is, or is not, a god."

"Idwal Kai is not a god," James said. "If you want to keep him alive, you can't tell him what we're doing."

"Then I'll tell him something else," Cate said as James headed for the door. "I'll find you when I'm ready."

"I'll be with Dana."

She nodded. "If Minnie's lurking around out there, send her back in."

James slipped out the door, and a moment later, Minnie returned. She stopped in front of Cate, eyes fixed on the floor.

"You might not have noticed because you had your sin-detector goggles on, but we were both fully clothed," Cate said. "We didn't do anything but sleep."

"You're not wearing trousers," Minnie said.

Cate slid off the bed. "Well, that would have been inappropriate," she said. "But now that we're talking about pants yet again, I need some. After you finished with"—she gestured to herself—"this, I will need some pants. Pants, shirt, cloak, boots, probably something to cover my hair—that kind of thing."

"Why do you require these things?"

"Because I have a costume party to attend and thought I'd go dressed as a member of the Fellowship," Cate said. "Why do you think, Minnie? I need to leave this room today, and not wearing any pants might attract some un-wanted attention."

"What do you intend to do today?"

"Thought I'd head down to the docks to see what kind of action I can find."

It was, technically, not a lie. It also had the benefit of horrifying the maid and giving Cate's mood a much-needed boost. That wouldn't last, but she'd hold on to it for as long as she could.

"Action?"

"There's bound to be a bar fight or two I could get into," Cate said. "Not that I have any qualms about starting my own, if things prove to be slow."

Minnie looked more aghast now than she had upon seeing James in Cate's bed. "You...you want to get into a bar fight?"

"Oh, at least one. I was thinking more like three. That sounds good, doesn't it? Three nice tavern brawls."

"Three tavern brawls?"

"Well, yeah. You need the first to get the feel of it, the second to really cut loose, and the third—"

"*Three* tavern brawls?"

Cate smiled. "I'm teasing you, Minnie. There are no bar fights nor tavern brawls in my immediate future."

"Just your immediate future?"

"I like to keep my options open," Cate said. "Look, I'm not going to tell you—nor anyone else—what I'm doing today. What I will say is that you can't tell anyone I've left this room—and that includes Idwal Kai. Instead, you will tell anyone who does ask that I'm asleep and don't wish to be disturbed."

"But Lord Kai—"

"Lord Kai takes his orders from me," Cate said. "Ask him, if you want. He'll tell you."

"That is not necessary, my lady."

"Does that mean you'll help me?"

"Yes, my lady," Minnie said. "Allow me to change your bandages, then I shall find and do all that you require."

Cate nodded and removed her robe. "Let's get started, then."

The cleaning of her wounds and changing of the bandages was somehow more excruciating than the last time. Cate gritted her teeth to keep the tears at bay, but they spilled over anyway. Minnie said nothing about them as she finished and walked away. Cate headed for the nearest corner and leaned into it until self-control had been restored.

When she turned around, she found Minnie had laid a series of garments on the bed: a rich red cloak, a linen shirt, brown leather pants and bodice, and a dark green scarf. Cate crept closer and fingered the scarf.

"Were these...Did these belong to my parents?" she asked. "My mother?"

"Yes, my lady. All save the trousers." Minnie smiled. "Your mother did not wear them. Would not."

Cate nodded. "She'd be disappointed in me, huh?"

"No, my lady. I believe she would have been rather proud."

That wasn't possible. What was there to be proud of? Murder? Mayhem? Incessant crying? Oh yeah—just so much awesome from which to choose. Cate could feel tears pricking at her eyes again and pointed to the cloak to distract her.

"That won't work. I need something more understated," she said. "Have anything in black? It's much more slimming."

Minnie carried the red cloak away. "You're quite thin enough already."

Cate reached for the pants and stepped into them. "Yeah, well, starving yourself can have that effect."

Minnie returned, a black cloak draped over her arm. The look on her face was miserable. "How do I help you, my lady?"

"Boots. I need boots."

"I didn't mean—"

"I know what you meant," Cate said. "Just...find me some boots. Please."

Minnie nodded. "Yes, my lady."

The maid didn't speak again, communicating in gestures, as she helped Cate prepare. Though an apology sat on the tip of her tongue, Cate stayed silent as well. Every time she tried to talk, the words only sat in her mouth, refusing to do anything else.

When Cate was dressed, Minnie wasted no time in heading for the door.

"Hey. Wait," Cate said, and the maid stopped. "You don't have to worry about me. I'll be fine. And even if I'm not..." She shrugged. "It doesn't matter."

"That is why I worry," Minnie said. "Do take care of yourself, my lady."

She walked out of the room. Cate looked at the closed door for a long minute, then grabbed the cloak off the bed and made her way downstairs.

James and Gair stood outside of Dana's room. James, leaning against the wall and glaring at the bricks opposite him as though they had done him wrong, noticed her first. He hit Gair lightly across the chest and jerked his thumb in Cate's direction. Gair glanced at her, then walked away, nodding at her as he passed.

"Did you handle the maid?" James asked when she reached him.

"Yeah, she'll cover for me. Not happily, but she'll do it."

"Good." He took a dagger from his belt. "Here."

A smile tugged at her lips as she accepted the weapon. She knew less than nothing about weapons or their construction, but it felt right in her hands. Good. Solid. She ran her fingers over the eagle's head pommel and removed the dagger from its leather sheath.

"Where did this come from?" she asked.

"The Coileáin family has an excellent armory."

"Did you steal this?"

He shrugged. "I suppose that depends upon you. Didn't you tell me all this was yours?"

She laughed. "You stole this."

"Are you familiar with its use?" James asked, removing his cloak and dropping it on the floor.

"I know what end to stick someone with."

"That's something, then. If they're not wearing armor, aim here." He poked his ribs, then took her hand and put it against the same spot. "Do you feel the space between the bone?"

How good did he think her aim was? "Yeah."

"Aim there. Thrust up—toward the heart, aye? Understand?"

"Yeah."

James nodded. "Try it."

"What?"

"Try it. I'd appreciate it if you didn't actually stab me, but try it," he said. "Understand the weight of the weapon and the motion of the act."

"James, this is—"

"Try it."

She obliged, slowly swinging the dagger the way he had showed her. He made her do it three times before he was satisfied.

"Aye, good," he said. "Remember that."

"What if they are wearing armor?" she asked, afraid of what demonstration the answer would inspire. "Or, if I'm, say, a complete novice who has little to no chance of actually hitting that tiny, tiny target in the heat of the moment."

James stepped back, looking at her in something resembling surprise. After a moment, he nodded. "Aye. I sometimes forget that you're..." Sighing, he took her dagger-wielding hand, maneuvered it into position, and pressed it against his neck. "Here. Understand?"

She nodded. The neck would be an easier target.

"Eyes are always a good choice as well," he said.

He wouldn't make her practice that, would he? Not willing to find out, she twisted her wrist to free herself from his hold, cutting his neck in the process, and he hissed.

"Sorry," she said, looking at the fresh scratch on his skin. "I didn't mean—"

"No matter," he said, wiping away the blood. "Strike anywhere you can. Anywhere there's flesh, aye? Across the hand, the face—anywhere. It'll hurt, and give you time to get away."

Escape wasn't necessarily her primary objective, but admitting that was probably a bad idea. "Okay," she said.

"Are you ready, then?"

Tucking the dagger into her belt, Cate looked at the red mark on his neck. "As I'll ever be."

James gathered his cloak and led the way through the castle. Cate walked behind him, her eyes on the floor. It wasn't until they were in a corridor empty of people that she stepped up next to him and spoke.

"Where did Gair go?"

"Into the city," James said. "He'll meet us there."

"Is he going with us to Odhran?"

"Aye."

"Why isn't he here with us now?"

"Idwal Kai is aware that Gair and I intend to ride out today, and he doesn't care what we do so long as he believes you are here and safe," James said. "If he happens to witness our departure and sees three of us, he may take us for liars."

"We are liars."

"Aye, well, let's hope Idwal Kai doesn't know that," he said. "You and I will ride out together, and once we...Can you ride?"

"If I had a nickel for every time we had this conversation, I'd have—"

"Cate," James said. "Can you ride?"

She looked away. "I don't know."

He nodded. "We'll take it slow."

Thank all the gods she didn't believe in that he hadn't changed his mind about her tagging along on this trip. She had spent too much time doing nothing. Having a mission felt good, so even if she ended up dying of internal bleeding, it would be done in the pursuit of something. Whatever happened, she would stick it out.

Once outside, James directed her to wait in the shadows against the castle wall. She obeyed, her hood pulled low to conceal her face. When James returned with two horses, she ceased skulking and pushed off the wall. He boosted her into the saddle of the first horse, and she settled with a grimace of pain. Damn, her body was already unhappy. Her ribs especially wanted her to turn tail and run—well, maybe shuffle—back to bed.

James put his hand on her leg. "All right?"

"I'm good," she said, reaching for the reins.

He didn't believe her but pulled himself into his own saddle, and they rode through the gates, unchecked by the on-duty guards.

The Coileáin castle was out of sight when they located Gair in the city. No words were exchanged between them as James gave him his own mount and rode with Cate. Mindful of her back and ribs, she sat behind him, her arms around his waist.

"All right?" James asked when the splendor of the city gave way to a wide and dusty road.

She wasn't. Her ribs were planning a full-scale revolt that the rest of her body wholeheartedly supported. But she nodded and answered, "I'm good."

The city had disappeared from view when they came across the first of the roadblocks. Men in Maoilriain colors rode in groups of two and four, stopping anyone who crossed their path. Both James and Gair slowed their mounts but did not stop.

"Captain?" Gair said.

Don't stop us, Cate thought as she looked at the soldiers. *Don't stop us, don't stop us, don't stop us.*

She continued her silent chant, her heart skipping a beat when a quartet of soldiers waved them down. As they approached, James threw back his cloak to reveal his Coileáin colors. Gair followed his example, and the leader waved them through.

They had cleared two more roadblocks before the dirt road turned to cobblestones. Odhran. It was a closely packed area with little to no space between straw-roofed buildings—or groups of soldiers patrolling the streets. It was almost as if someone had murdered their crown prince.

James didn't seem concerned as he rode up to a building whose sign read *The Thirsty Whale.* A tavern, perhaps? A home away from home for sea captains, maybe. Was this where they would find a ship?

James slid from the saddle and reached up to help her, but the idea of his hands on her ribs made her flinch, and she dismounted on her own. After tethering the horses to a post, James led the way inside.

It was definitely a tavern, and Cate stopped short just inside the door as the scent of smoke and stale beer stung her nose. James gestured for Gair to hang back. After searching for and failing to find a staircase, Cate followed him to the bar at the back—and the pretty, well-endowed brunette working there.

"James the Farmer, back again," the brunette said, catching his sleeve with her fingers. Her hand dropped when she noticed Cate. "Who's your friend?"

"Cailean, this is Cate," James said. "Cate, Cailean."

Cate smiled as she lowered her hood, leaving the scarf covering her hair in place. "Hi."

"What's that accent?" Cailean asked. "I've never heard it before. Where are you from?"

"Boston."

Cailean shook her head. "Never heard of that, either. Is it far away?"

"You have no idea."

Cailean looked at James. "Are you here to drink or to ask for more favors?"

"Favors, I think," Cate said. "But I wouldn't turn down a beer, if you're offering."

That earned her an odd look from Cailean—but did gain her a pint. Cate thanked her, and Cailean started to turn back to James, but something else caught her eye. She sighed.

"I've a customer, but don't run off, eh?" she said. "I want to talk to you."

James nodded. "We'll be here. I need to talk to you as well."

As Cailean walked away, Cate sampled her beer and made a face at the bitter taste. "Do you have a barmaid in every port?"

"A barmaid in every port?"

"Is that the first thing you do when you land somewhere new? Sniff out the local watering hole and cozy up to whoever's pouring drinks?"

"What are you going on about?"

"Is there a barmaid in this world with whom you aren't friendly?" Cate asked. "Cailean, Orla—"

"Orla's friendly with Dana. She merely tolerates me."

"Cailean does more than tolerate you. She likes you."

James turned and leaned against the bar, his eyes following Cailean's movements. "I suppose so. She's been quite helpful."

Cate smiled. "No, I meant she'd like to see you naked."

"What?" James looked at her. "She—what?"

"She'd like to see you naked. She'd probably like to do other things involving you, too. Sex-type things, if that wasn't clear."

"Aye. Thank you for explaining."

"No problem. Hey, go for it, right? Why not? You're single, she's cute." Cate shrugged. "Just wear some sort of flotation device if you do. You don't want to drown in those things."

James turned around. "Are you drunk? How much of that ale have you had?"

"Not nearly enough," she responded. "But, you know, now that I'm thinking about it, there are probably far worse ways to go than death by buxom barmaid."

He sighed. "Are you enjoying yourself?"

"A little bit, yeah." She drank more ale and gagged. "Goddamn, that's terrible."

"Don't drink it," he said. "Why did you tell Cailean where you're from?"

"What will she do with that information? Knowing where I'm from hasn't done you any good."

"You are supposed to be hiding."

"Which is why you brought me to a tavern in a town crawling with armed men looking for us."

"That's not why." James shook his head. "Just be quiet and drink your ale."

As Cate laughed into her mug, Cailean returned. She bustled behind the bar, pulling out a tray and a pair of pewter mugs.

"Where have you been?" she asked, filling the first mug.

"What do you mean?" James said.

"Rowan came in, told me you and your brother had disappeared—that you deserted. Why would he think that?"

"Possibly because we did," James answered. "Cailean, we need your help."

She filled the second tankard. "You're a deserter. I'd say you need someone's help."

"We have to find a ship—"

"Do I look like a harbor master?"

"—that will carry five people to Lira. I thought maybe you could—"

"Lira? Why would you want to go back to Lira?" Cailean put the second mug on the tray and reached for a third. "Didn't you come here looking for a new beginning away from Lira?"

James hesitated. "I haven't been honest with you."

"I actually worked that out on my own." Cailean looked at Cate. "What have you to do with this?"

"I'm the money," Cate said. "Can you think of anyone who could help us secure safe passage? We can pay."

Cailean looked at James. "With what? Your wages?"

He shook his head. "You know those are already gone."

"What, your brother's wages? That won't be nearly enough."

"No, but we can pay," James said. "You, and anyone who aids us. We have money. You needn't worry about that."

She laughed and picked up her tray. "That's not my worry."

She walked off again, and this time Cate watched her. The barmaid stopped at a table in the center of the room and flirted with the three men sitting there as she served their ale. One of the three paid her no mind, his focus on Cate. She broke eye contact first and glanced at James.

"We should go," she said.

The man stood and walked out of the tavern. He didn't notice Gair slip out behind him.

"Cailean will help us," James said.

"Before or after the soldiers figure out we're here?"

"She'll help."

As Cailean circled back to the bar, Cate said, "Well, work your magic fast because I think we've been made."

"Made?"

"Discovered."

James looked at the spot where Gair was no longer standing. "Aye."

Stepping behind the bar, Cailean reached for another tray and set it in front of them. "Soldiers from the palace have been all over town, looking for something. I thought I might see you—of course, I didn't—then Rowan came in and told me you were gone." Cailean paused and reached for more mugs. "Are you the one they're looking for, James?"

He didn't answer as he surreptitiously reached for Cate's wrist and gripped it tightly, fingers wrapping around unhealed rope burns. She swallowed an involuntary whimper and sidled closer to him, ready to move when he did.

"It's you, isn't it?" Cailean said. "They're searching for you. Because you're a deserter."

"That's not why," James said, glancing over his shoulder.

Cate looked, too. Gair stood by the door, making a subtle gesture that she interpreted to mean that danger was nigh. James responded with some hand jive of his own and turned back to Cailean.

"Thank you for all you've done to help me. I'll never be able to repay you properly," he said. "Except maybe to tell you this: when they ask you about us, convince them you know nothing. It'll save your life."

Before Cailean could respond, James pushed off the bar, taking Cate with him. She put herself in neutral and allowed him to get her out of the tavern and into a narrow, shadow-filled alley. One alley led to another, and James released her midway through. While he trotted on ahead, she sank to the ground next to a barrel. Breathing was difficult, and Cate loosened the clothing around her neck. Why had Minnie insisted upon so many damn layers? She ducked her head, keeping the wrist James had grabbed in the air.

He came rushing back. "Cate, we have to...What's wrong?"

"I need a minute. Maybe two."

He crouched in front of her. "I grabbed your wrist. I'm sorry—I didn't think."

"I'm fine." She lifted her head. "What happened to Gair?"

"Don't worry about him. He'll make his own way back to Mairéad," James said. "It's you we have to worry about. If you can't walk—"

"I can walk."

James snorted. "Prove it."

She flipped him off. "What's your plan? You can't carry me all the way back to the city."

"We can't sit in this alley all day, either."

"I don't need all day. Just part of the day. A small part of the day."

Something crashed at the other end of the alley, back the way they had come. Head snapping to the left, James stood.

"Make it smaller," he said, his hand on his sword.

As he went to investigate, she reached out, searching for the top of the barrel. Pushing against it, she lurched to her feet.

"All right?" he said when he returned.

She nodded. "What was it?"

"Bloody cat."

"Do you have a plan to get us out of here in one piece?" she asked. "Good, bad, or in between?"

"Not yet."

The distinctive sound of marching caught their attention. James backed her against the wall, shielding her with his body. The friction of the rough building material rubbed against her back, and she leaned into James to alleviate the pressure, grasping his cloak to maintain her balance.

"Did I hurt you?" he asked when the marching had faded.

"No." She released him and glanced toward the street. At the end of it, a lit lantern swayed in the sea breeze. Maybe she could do something with that. "Did Gair take both horses?"

"He would have only taken one. The other he would have left, in case we could get back to it."

She nodded. "Go get the horse, and bring him here. I'll—"

"I can't get the horse. It's too exposed. The soldiers will—"

"I'll get their attention."

"Like hell you will! You're not using yourself as bait."

"I don't intend to use myself as bait. I'm just going to get their attention."

"How?"

"Okay, do you remember that day in camp, a million years ago, when Faolan was telling me all about my magic powers, and I told him he was wrong?"

James stepped back. Wary. "Aye."

"Well, he wasn't. He was right; I have powers. Like, crazy serious magic, and I don't want to get into all of the details right now—or ever, really. Just know I intend to use that magic," Cate said. "It'll get their attention. It'll get *everyone's* attention. And while they're all distracted, you'll get the horse, and we'll get the hell out of this town."

James nodded. "Did you use your...powers on Zoltano?"

"You really want to have this conversation now?" she asked. Off James's look, she added, "Yes."

"On the other man you killed?"

"Yes."

James glanced at the street. "Do you mean to kill anyone now?"

She swallowed. "Not intentionally."

"It's a risk."

"As is staying in this alley, but if you have another plan, I'd love to hear it."

After a moment, he sighed. "I don't have another plan."

"Great. Poke your head out there and tell me which building appears as though it would be least likely to have people in it."

"What are you going to do?"

"Provide a distraction," she said, waving him away. "Now, go."

Cate followed him to the edge of the alley, dragging her fingers along the wall. He cautiously peered around the corner but turned back almost immediately. He flattened her against the wall, his head angled toward the ground at her feet. After four men in Maoilriain colors passed by, James pulled her to the other side of the alley.

"That one there." He pointed. "Two buildings down. It looks as though it might be a warehouse."

"Might be?"

"Far fewer windows than the others," he said. "That's the best I can do without looking inside each one."

Cate nodded. "That's the one, then."

James slipped off his cloak and unbuckled his sword belt. He handed both to her, and she took them reluctantly.

"Won't you be needing the sword?" she asked.

"No. They're looking for two people—a woman and a man, and that man has a sword."

"Won't it be weird for a Coileáin man to be walking around without one?"

"If anyone asks, I'll tell them I'm a bloody clerk or something," James said. "Just don't lose it."

"I'll do my best," she said. "No matter what you hear, keep going. Don't turn around, don't look. Just—"

"Get the horse, aye. You've mentioned it enough that even I figured it out."

"Great." She shoved him onto the road. "Now do it."

He stumbled a few steps and whirled around to fix her with an irritated glare. She jerked her thumb in The Thirsty Whale's direction. Adjusting his clothing, he stormed off, his gait relaxing with each step.

When he had disappeared from view, she leaned the sword against the wall and focused on the lantern and the warehouse-like building. Could she manipulate the fire from a distance, or would she have to expose herself to accomplish it?

At any rate, she needed more fire. How could she get it to grow? What powered the lanterns? Some kind of oil, most likely. If she could increase the amount of fuel available, she could increase the amount of fire. In theory.

Whatever she was going to do, she had to do it soon. More soldiers were marching her way, and there would be still more behind them. No time for trial and error. She would have to rely upon belief.

Which was truly a terrible plan.

But it was the only one they had, so she would have to make it work.

She focused on the lantern, imagining a turning knob on its side. The flame grew in small increments, and she twisted her wrist quickly to see what would happen. Flame burst through the top, and she backed off. Okay. Good. That worked.

Now for the real test: could she pick it up? Could she move it?

Using every last bit of concentration she possessed, she flicked her wrist, causing the flame to bounce on its base, and smiled.

The soldiers continued to advance; she couldn't wait much longer. She had to do it right in front of them. Boosting the flame as high as it would go, she twisted her wrist toward the warehouse, and the fire leapt to the straw-covered roof. It quickly took hold, expanding without help. Once the soldiers noticed, they'd have to deal with it. Everything in this town was so close together and capped with flammable materials. If they didn't act, they'd run the risk of losing the entire town. They wouldn't allow that to happen; they couldn't.

A single voice called out the first alarm, a panicked cry quickly taken up by others. Cate peeked around the corner to see soldiers and townspeople gathering and organizing. People ran toward the fire; no one ran away. A glance in the other direction showed a lone man in Coileáin colors riding a horse down the street. Throwing on his cloak over hers, Cate pulled a hood over her head, slung the sword across her back, and left the safety of the alley.

When she reached James, he held out his hand and she took it, allowing him to pull her up. As soon as she was settled behind him, he turned the horse in the opposite direction and spurred him into a quicker gait.

As they raced out of Odhran, Cate resumed her mute chorus—*don't stop us, don't stop* us—and continued it all the way back to the city. Did it make any difference? Perhaps it was only the Coileáin colors keeping any passing soldiers from giving them more than a momentary glance, but she didn't want to risk it. It was safer to keep chanting.

She stopped once they were ensconced within Mairéad's walls and found Gair waiting not far from the Coileáin estate. He was visibly comforted to see them approach. Cate felt James's own relief as he brought their horse alongside Gair's.

"He's waiting," Gair said.

James looked toward the estate. "Idwal Kai?"

"Aye, Captain."

Cate glanced between the two men. "And?"

"You are supposed to be sleeping in your chamber," James said. "If he discovers you with us here and now—"

"Never mind." She slid from the horse's back. "You two go on ahead. I'll get myself back in."

"How will you do that?" James asked. "Start another fire?"

"Are you volunteering to be kindling?"

She carefully removed the sword and handed it to him. After tossing him the cloak, she walked away, irritation dulling any pain. A moment later, the boys rode past. The gate guards stopped them briefly but allowed them to pass.

As she neared the entrance, she resumed her chant—*don't stop me, don't stop me*—but it didn't really matter if it worked. Nothing would happen if they discovered her because she was the lady of the manor. Her wishes were their commands. She'd explain how she had elected to go for a walk. Alone. In a strange city. Where she was being hunted. Idwal would probably frown deeply at her poor decision-making skills, but he couldn't do anything else.

None of them could.

With that very true thought in mind, Cate stopped skulking and walked confidently to the gates. The guards didn't so much as blink as she passed. Neither did anyone in the courtyard.

Not even James saw her. He stood with Gair, being interrogated by Idwal Kai. His eyes ran over her more than once but never registered her presence.

Maybe it wasn't just the Coileáin colors.

As she left the courtyard, she allowed the magic to ebb but kept her hood up until she walked back into her room.

Minnie rushed her. "Where have you been? I was so worried, my lady."

Easing past the maid, Cate removed her cloak. "Did Idwal Kai come by today?"

"Yes, once in the morning, and once again at midday," Minnie said, reaching for the cloak. "I turned him away both times, telling him you were asleep, but he will return. He's quite concerned."

Cate pulled the scarf from her hair. "The next time he shows up, you can let him in."

"You should allow me to tend your wounds as well."

"If you want."

"I want to," Minnie said, carrying away the cloak.

Cate sat on the edge of the bed to kick off her boots and unlace her bodice. "Have you told anyone? About me? About what's wrong with me?"

Minnie stopped, her back to Cate.

"If you have, I won't punish you," Cate said. "I never should have threatened that. You."

Minnie turned. "You commanded me not to speak a word of it, so I have said nothing."

Threatened. Commanded. Funny how much those felt like synonyms. Cate nodded and removed the bodice. The dagger followed, and she held it loosely as she stared at the floor.

"From where did the dagger come?" the maid asked.

Minnie's feet in their soft-soled shoes appeared in Cate's view. She studied them, then lifted her head. "The dagger fairy."

The maid held a basket overflowing with medicinal supplies. Cate sighed, tossed the dagger onto the pillow, and gingerly shed her shirt. After the old bandages had been removed, she settled on her stomach. Dragging a pillow to her, she clutched it with one hand while the other grasped the dagger.

"Did you find what you were looking for today?" Minnie asked as she cleaned the wounds.

Cate pressed her face into the pillow, trying to focus on anything other than the sound of her skin ripping and tearing all over again. Would stabbing the mattress a few dozen times be enough of a distraction? Maybe she should go for an even hundred. "No."

"Will you search for it again tomorrow?"

"Not sure yet. Maybe."

Someone had to. They still required a way to return to Lira. James needed to get back to the fight; she needed to have a discussion with the pegasus. A ship would be imperative in accomplishing both those goals, so someone would be harbor-bound in the morning.

But it would have to be someone who wasn't her. As much as she hated to admit it, her body was not equipped to deal with another jaunt through Odhran. James wouldn't complain about that, but neither would he want to leave her behind. That left Rhydwyn and Gair. She hoped they were up for the challenge.

"I heard there was a fire in Odhran today," Minnie said. "Did you see it?"

See it, started it—whatever. "How did you hear about that?"

"Lord Kai received word."

"Lord Kai receives a lot of words. Quite promptly, too."

"He is lord of the manor until a Coileáin returns," Minnie said. "Though you are in residence, Lord Kai ordered that we keep your presence secret, that we tell no one you—nor your companions—are here."

"And because he's the lord of the manor, he's automatically kept apprised of what's happening in the kingdom?" Cate asked. "Even if he's not actually a Coileáin?"

"Yes," Minnie said. "The Coileáin name is a powerful one in Mairéad."

"Because of my father?"

"Yes, my lady."

Someone knocked. Minnie washed her hands and dried them on her apron as she went to answer the door. Cate pushed up and put her shirt back on. Guess they would finish later.

"It is your...houseboy, my lady," Minnie said.

Cate laughed. "Let him in."

James strode into the room. When he located her, still sitting on the bed, his entire body relaxed. She smiled. Had he thought she would disappear?

She looked at Minnie. "Will you give us a moment?"

The maid curtsied. "Yes, my lady."

"Thank you, Minnie," James said as she departed.

Cate reached for her dagger. "That's not her real name, you know."

"What is?"

Shrugging, she headed toward the fireplace. "It never occurred to me to ask."

"Well, I'm sure she believes my name to be 'houseboy,' so perhaps we're even."

"If anything, she believes that's your position," Cate said, perching on the edge of the sofa. "Not your name."

James sat at the other end. "I'm not your bloody houseboy."

"I know. It's just funny."

Cate stood, her ribs angry enough after a day spent riding and running that sitting was uncomfortable. She limped back and forth in front of the fire, holding her sides lightly.

"I didn't see you come in," he said.

"You weren't supposed to," she replied. "What did Idwal want to talk about?"

"You."

Cate nodded. "What did you tell him?"

"What do you think?" James said. "You're hurting. I should call your maid back."

"Don't. Please."

He leaned forward. "She could help you—or summon someone who can. They could lessen the pain, if nothing else."

She stopped pacing. "I don't hurt anymore."

"Cate—"

"The ship thing's not going to work, is it?"

James's expression showed he did not approve of the change in subject, but he didn't push her on it. "I don't think so," he said. "The number of soldiers will only increase. Captains will be less willing to take on strangers heading for Lira, and we wouldn't be able to trust any who would. It would either be a trap, or they'll take our money, slit our throats, and dump us in the sea."

"Also a trap."

"Aye."

She sat next to him. "It's because I killed Zoltano. I shouldn't have—"

"His death is the only way it would have ended, Cate. The only way."

Not the only way. But she wasn't interested in having that conversation again. She stood and resumed pacing. "If we can't get a ship, we'll just have to go another way."

"Off a bloody island? What other way is there?"

She faced the fire. "Remember the magic? The *whatever* that got us out of Odhran?"

"Setting a fire won't get us back to Lira."

"I'm not just a pyro. I can do other things, too."

"Like make your way through a crowded courtyard unseen?"

"Like that, yeah."

"Your magic can get us off an island?" James asked. "It can get us back to Lira?"

"Right to your very own front door." She shrugged. "Well, if I do it correctly."

"What does that mean?"

"I've never actually done it successfully before—I tried, I failed, but it's different now. *I'm* different. It'll work. I can open it."

"Open what?"

"A portal."

James was quiet. She glanced at him over her shoulder.

"Is it safe?" he asked, and she laughed. "I'm serious, Cate. Is it safe?"

She shrugged again. "You've traveled through portals before, and you seem to be okay."

"Is it safe for *you* to attempt this?" he asked. "Are *you* strong enough?"

"I'm the strongest bloody person you know, aren't I? Which is, by the way, tremendously sad for everyone else you know."

"Are you strong enough?"

She turned, revealing a crackling ball of fire in her hand.
James shot to his feet. "Bloody hell, Cate! What are you—?"
"Yeah," she said, "I'm strong enough."

chapter 36

In the end, Haleine traveled to Eluned with Faolan, Lucius, Eion, and Brighid. There were others as well, gone on ahead or guarding her back. Either Lucius or Faolan had assigned them in secret, believing she wouldn't know of their presence. Haleine said nothing of it, allowing them to take whatever precautions they desired. Arguing was futile; it would only waste more time. Sighle only seemed interested in Haleine. Perhaps she would ignore the rest.

When the city came into view, Haleine's chest tightened. Faolan's own anxiety spiked, and she glanced at him, hovering on her right.

"You should not go through the main gates," she said.

"Neither should you," he returned. "Fortunately, there's a way to avoid doing so."

He led them away from the city, its gates and guards, and back into the shelter of the forest, stopping at a secluded spot along the city wall.

"Here," he said to Lucius. "Press here."

Lucius placed his hand against the stone. After a short delay, a section of the wall opened.

"How did you know about that?" Haleine asked.

"Bronagh," Faolan answered.

Bronagh? Haleine had expected to hear him offer credit to Laorans, or to magic in general, but to her maid? To hear her name at all was a shock for which Haleine was unprepared. When was the last time Bronagh's name had crossed her mind?

"She showed this to you?" Haleine asked.

"It's how we got you out," Faolan said. "It's how we saved your life."

Why would he say it like that? Did he want to make her feel more guilt? Did he not think she carried quite enough already? What did he hope to gain?

"It was just the truth, Haleine," Faolan said. "I don't hope to gain anything from that."

"Liar."

"Not this time," he said. "Be careful in there. Please. You don't know what's waiting on the other side."

"You're not coming," she said.

She didn't know why she should be surprised. He was only doing as he had always done. Not waiting for it to be stated or defended, Haleine turned and followed Lucius through the door.

Sighle's magic stopped her almost immediately. Speaking in whispers, it pushed against her, seeping into her skin and curdling her blood. Haleine stepped back, her hand covering her mouth as her stomach lurched. Was this the reason Faolan had stayed behind?

"Your majesty?" Lucius asked. "Are you—?"

"Fine," she spat, lowering her hand. "I'm fine."

Spindly threads of magic only she could see or feel obstructed the path, but she pushed through them without hesitation, allowing them to do nothing more than caress her body as she passed. Webs became walls as they neared the palace. More than just stone, they were barriers she could not penetrate. Once, she had used her bare hands to tear down a shield created by an evil man.

She would not be able to do that now.

What had Sighle done? How would Haleine ever counter it?

You know how, the whispers responded.

"The palace is this way, your majesty," Lucius said.

"Not the palace," she said, looking at him. "We can't go there yet."

No one questioned her. They merely turned away and walked into the open streets.

Though Eluned had been Haleine's home for some time now, she had seen very little of it, and never had she walked amongst its people like this, with only a hood to hide her identity. Lucius stood close to her, his hand lightly on her back. Eion trailed behind them, while Brighid walked in front. Their progress was slow, as the streets were crowded, but Lucius ably guided her through them.

As the palace loomed over them, large and threatening, Sighle's whispers grew louder. There was no need to ask if the others could hear them; her sister's chant was for Haleine's ears alone. The words were intelligible, but the spite fueling them was clear enough, and Haleine looked at the ground.

How had this happened? How had her sister become this...thing? How had Haleine never known before?

You weren't meant to know before, the whispers answered. *You weren't ready to know.*

"I'm ready now," Haleine murmured.

Then come and find me. If you dare. If you can.

The chorus of whispers ceased as Lucius's arm snaked around her waist and pulled her close. Lifting her head, Haleine saw what had made him stop.

Maddox stood on the wide wooden platform used for public hangings, whippings, and beheadings, but no prisoners awaited execution. Only Omur accompanied him, hands concealed in his scarlet robes.

Lucius released her. "We need to leave."

"No," she insisted. "We will proceed."

"My wife, your queen," Maddox began, his voice loud and clear, "has abandoned you."

"Please, your majesty," Lucius muttered. "We must leave."

Haleine shook her head. If Maddox was speaking against her, she would witness it.

"As I understand it, many of you believed her to be your protector, your savior," Maddox continued, "but if she ever was that, if she ever brought you hope, know it is over now."

An urge to shout the truth took over her sensibilities. She had abandoned her people—she could not deny that—but she was here now, and she had come to fight. Never again would she back down. She stepped forward, but Lucius snared her elbow and held her back.

"Don't," he whispered in her ear.

"She is gone—killed while betraying her crown, her duty, you," Maddox proclaimed. "The queen has died a traitor, and any who insist upon speaking otherwise will follow her to the same end."

"Why would they say that?" Haleine seethed. "Why would they announce it in this manner?"

"They believe you are dead, your majesty," Lucius said.

"But Mireille! Omur intended for her to take my place. Why would he ever—?"

"Perhaps that is no longer his plan. Perhaps..." Lucius hesitated. "Perhaps she is the one who has died."

Mireille dead. It could be the truth. Hadn't Haleine thought so herself? Hadn't she stood over her twin's body, questioning if Mireille was even in there? Her twin could very well have died on that wooden floor in Tanuba.

Haleine looked at Omur. Had he killed her?

Omur's head swiveled in her direction, and they locked eyes. The corner of his lip curled into a sneer. Lucius swore and dragged Haleine back.

"We're leaving," he said, his voice marked by an uncharacteristic roughness.

Haleine struggled against him. "I'm still the queen, and I am very much alive! We can—"

Lucius pulled her into an alley and pressed her against a wall. "Aye, you are the queen, and you are very much alive, but you've been publicly named a dead traitor," he said. "You're not setting foot in the palace with only the three of us to protect—"

"There are more than three of you," Haleine hissed. "I don't need—"

"You do," Lucius responded. "It was dangerous enough when we faced only your sister, but now Omur also stands in the way. We are not taking another step forward."

Haleine shoved him. "Backing away, running away—do we ever do anything else?"

"We will come back, your majesty—I promise you we will," Lucius said. "When we do, you will have an army at your back, and a proper strategy in place. But now, in this moment, we must retreat."

Finally, Haleine relented and followed Lucius out of the alley. Sighle's laughter chased after her.

—⟨∅∅⟩—

Sighle did laugh as her sister turned tail and ran. How easily she gave up. She was starting to fight, though, and Sighle looked forward to the day when Haleine returned with her guard's promised army at her back. Would Haleine rise to the challenge? How long would she take to figure out how?

As eager as she was to find out, Haleine was not, at the moment, her most pressing concern. Omur was. Leaving her sister to her fleeing, Sighle turned her attention to the mage.

He had arrived in the dead of night, his oblivious puppet in tow, by magical means, and not the ship on which he had sailed away. Whatever had prompted his swift return, he was not concerned that anyone would either notice or question how it had been achieved.

Indeed, he had only one thing—one name—on his mind: Mireille.

Sighle had watched as he had his puppet declare Haleine dead, unable to tell if he believed it or just wished it. That night, after the castle dwellers had retired to their beds, she drifted to his chamber to coax the truth out of him.

She slipped inside and closed the door quietly, watching him pace and fret.

Mireille, Mireille, Mireille. She was everything to him.

"I thought you'd be gone longer," Sighle said. "I'm pleased you weren't."

He looked at her, eyes flashing, furious and hungry. "What are you doing here?"

"I missed you terribly. Haven't you missed me?" Innocent, fragile—that's what he liked. He wanted to prey on her. "Don't be cruel," she pouted when he stayed silent. "Tell me you missed me."

"I did not."

Liar. There may have been some small part of him somewhere that felt so, but the whole of his body yearned for hers. A human made more centuries ago, but still human at the core. It would ruin him. Did he know?

"If that's the game you wish to play," she purred, slinking in his direction, "tell me what's become of my sister, and I'll go."

"Your sister."

He nearly asked about which one she was inquiring before his mind started whirling, shuffling through possible responses.

"You remember her, don't you?" Sighle asked. "Irritatingly lovely, red hair, called queen?"

Reckless, so reckless. Taunting led to agitation; agitation only complicated things that were already complex enough on their own.

"They won't call her that anymore," Omur said.

How proud he was of that. Sighle pressed herself against his chest and looked at him. "Why?"

"Didn't you hear the king's announcement?" he asked, making no attempt to move away. "Haleine is dead."

He knew. He, too, had seen her amongst the crowd. Sighle could see it, feel it without trying. She loosed her magic, wrapping it around him before asking her next question. "What of Mireille? What have you done with her?"

"Gave her to the wolf," he answered without hesitation. "The Black Wolf."

The Black Wolf? What—who—did that mean? Sighle put her hands on his cheeks and peered into his eyes. A man, blond and blue-eyed, looked back at her.

Her hands fell. "Human? You gave her to a human? Why?"

"To get to Mireille."

Because he suspected—wrongly, Sighle thought—that Mireille and Cate were separate entities sharing one body. That one was imprisoned inside the other, and he could think of only one way to change that.

"You could have done the torture yourself. Why entrust it to another?"

"Mireille will kill the one responsible. I don't want that to be me."

Yes, Mireille would do that, and Omur feared death more than anything. He would be eager to avoid endangering himself.

"She will kill you anyway," Sighle said, not realizing it was the truth until it had been spoken. She could see it—no flames, no weapons. A clean death, but one still terrifying for someone afraid of dying.

She broke away, tired and disgusted. He had always been that way, but never before had it rankled her so deeply. She allowed the magic to lapse and walked away.

"You're not leaving, are you?" Omur called.

"I don't wish to play anymore."

"Why not?"

She put her hand on the door's latch. "My sister is dead; I need to mourn her."

Omur scoffed. "What good does mourning do?"

She looked at him. "I will miss you when you're gone."

Omur's brow creased with confusion. "I don't intend to go anywhere for a very long time."

"Neither did my father," Sighle said. "At least you'll fare better. Not that you deserve it."

Wiping his memory, she walked out.

She had not made it back to her chambers before Mireille's return shoved her onto her knees.

It had not been a gradual thing but rather sudden—a loud noise in a vacuum of silence. Magic had brought Mireille back, and all at once Sighle felt what had been done to her. There was no mistaking the animalistic rawness of her pain. Mireille was a wounded beast caught in a trap, chewing off her limbs to survive and bleeding out because of it.

This was the woman who could bring an ancient prophecy to life. This was the woman who would turn the rivers red with the blood of the moon. The dark gods would revel in the destruction she wrought.

Tears filled Sighle's eyes as she bore witness to that waste, but they did not fall until she smiled.

The end of the world was a beautiful place.

How very close they were to it.

———◦◦◦———

Cate's portal opened in the center of his family's land, in a field that should have been growing wheat. James and Rhydwyn, Dana supported between them, had stepped through first. Gair followed, and Cate came through last. She had not taken two steps before collapsing, and the black hole through which they had passed closed. Gair lifted Cate to her feet, and together they walked to the cottage.

It felt strange to be coming home, and James's chest swelled with an unfamiliar emotion. Relief? Happiness? He couldn't say.

Sarai came out of the barn and spotted them immediately. Initially wary, her concern faded as her expression flashed with recognition. She ran to meet them, her hand just grazing James's arm as she assessed Dana's condition.

"In the barn," she said. "Take him there, and I'll—"

"Is Faolan here?" Cate interrupted.

Taken aback, Sarai looked at Cate. "Aye, in the cottage with the queen."

James watched Cate march away. What did she want with Faolan?

"Gair," he said as Cate disappeared inside. "Take Dana."

When James entered the cottage, Cate stood staring at the now-healthy queen of Lira, who sat at the table, Faolan in front of her. Brighid hovered near the fire, eyes darting from one sister to the next.

The queen rose slowly. "Oh, Mireille, you're—"

"Your lover's dying out in the barn," Cate said, her tone rude and abrupt. "You probably want to watch or something."

The queen stared a moment longer before walking out, Brighid on her heels.

Cate settled in the chair and looked at Faolan. "Where is Laura Cole?"

"I would think you'd already know where she is," the pegasus replied. "You buried her."

"I don't know what I buried. Where is Laura Cole?"

"She's dead. You know that."

"The only thing I know is that you are nothing but a walking, talking, flying lie." Cate slammed her fist against the table. "Dammit, Faolan! Where is she?"

"Everything they told you was nothing but a lie."

"Ask the pegasus; he'll know. Ask the pegasus; he'd know better than any, they said, so here I am, asking the goddamn pegasus," Cate snarled. "Where is Laura Cole?"

James laid his cloak and sword on the table behind the pegasus, then checked the cottage to ensure they were alone. No one else needed to witness what was to come. Wherever Cate's questions would lead, the fewer people exposed to it, the better.

"I don't know what they told you, Cate," Faolan said, "but—"

"The truth. They told me the truth."

"I doubt that."

"Oh, do you? What would you even know about the truth?" she asked. "You've done nothing but lie to me since I showed up here."

"Cate, I know how you—"

"If the next words out of your mouth are any kind of attempt to acknowledge my feelings at this moment," she said, "I will set you on fire and burn you alive."

"Yes, I lied—*we* lied—but there were reasons."

"Because I'm evil?"

"You're not evil," James interjected.

The look she gave him chilled his blood. "That remains to be seen." She turned back to Faolan. "Doesn't it?"

"It does," the pegasus conceded.

"It doesn't!" James exclaimed. "She's not evil—you're not evil, Cate!"

"You didn't tell him," she said to Faolan.

"I did. I told him this was a possibility—a probability," the pegasus replied. "But he chose to believe in you, in your inherent goodness."

Cate nodded. "Everyone makes mistakes."

"Yes," Faolan said, "they do."

"Bloody hell, this is madness," James said, but they continued on as though he wasn't even there.

"You think yours was bringing me here in the first place," Cate said.

"Yes, I do."

"Then why do it?"

"The goddess wanted you brought here, so I brought you here."

"And after they...Why try to save me?"

"The threat of leaving you with them was too great. We couldn't risk them keeping you alive."

As Cate nodded, James sputtered another protest—that had not been his motivation—but was silenced when she held out her hand. Try as he might, he couldn't utter a single sound. He had been struck mute. He glared at her, but the look went unnoticed.

"That wasn't the only reason, was it?" she asked Faolan.

"The goddess wanted you safe."

James watched Faolan. The pegasus sounded so sullen. He didn't want to have this conversation. Why?

"Why would your goddess want that?" Cate asked. "I'm fated to destroy her and everything she holds dear—and you're convinced I'll do just that—so why would she want me anywhere near this world? How does she know what I will or will not do? Why would she think I'm anything other than...Oh."

Cate's hand fell, freeing James from the magic which stifled his voice, but the expression on her face left him speechless. What had Faolan done?

"Cate," the pegasus pleaded, "don't do this."

"Call her," Cate said. "Call her, summon her, or do whatever it is you do to get her to grace us with her presence, and do it now."

"Laorans has no earthly form."

Cate laughed, the sound hollow. "Oh, I think she does. Summon her."

"It's true. She—"

"It's *not* true! It's not *true*! How do you do that? Just...*stand* there clinging to such an obvious lie? What do you think will happen?"

"Nothing I wish to experience firsthand."

"Call her."

"No."

"Call her."

"You don't want this," Faolan stated flatly.

"*You* don't want this," Cate corrected. "Call her."

"No."

"Fine. I'll do it myself," Cate said. "I opened a portal between countries; I can do *this*."

"I have no doubt that you can do this," Faolan said. "But you shouldn't. I don't want—"

"Why should I care what you want?" she asked. "Give me one reason. Just one. Go ahead—it'll be funny."

"Cate," James said, fear filling his gut.

"You shouldn't be here," she responded. "Go watch your friend die."

He shook his head. "I'm not going anywhere."

"Another mistake. You have to be careful about making too many, James," she warned. "You never know which one will get you killed."

Bloody hell. James exhaled heavily.

Cate stood, keeping her hands on the table, and leaned in, eyes fixed on Faolan. "Last chance."

"Yours, too," Faolan said. "Don't do this."

Pushing off the table and knocking over the chair, Cate screeched, "Laorans! Show yourself! Where are you?"

"I am here," a woman answered.

The door and shutters slammed shut. The fire went out, engulfing the cottage in an unnatural darkness. A luminous ball of light appeared in the corner—the opposite of the portals through which James had traveled—and from it emerged a pale, dark-haired woman who seemed to glow. She was a stranger to him, but James knew who she was. That voice was impossible to forget.

"Mireille," the woman said.

Cate whirled around. Eyes wide and bright, she shook her head and backed up until she came against the wall. "No."

"Laorans," Faolan said, "you shouldn't have—"

"Shut up." Cate threw her arm out in his direction.

The pegasus stopped talking, stopped moving, stopped...everything. James stared at the sight. What had she done to him?

"Release him," Laorans said.

"No."

"Mireille, I—"

"No," Cate repeated. "No. Just...no. You don't get to...to talk to me like that while *looking* like that. Like her."

"There is no other way for me to look," the goddess said gently. "You requested the truth, Mireille. This is it."

Truth? What truth? James looked between Cate and Laorans—a bloody *goddess* standing before him. Whatever the truth might be, it was tearing Cate apart. And he could do nothing to stop it.

"This is worse. It's worse to see it—you—*this*. It's…" Cate laughed and pointed to Faolan, but he remained motionless. "He was right—who knew that was possible, huh? But he was—I did not want to do this; I should not have done this because now all I feel is…"

"You must feel betrayed," the goddess said.

"You think?" Cate said. "I cried for you. I cried so much. You were dead, I saw you—your body; I saw it, I buried it, and I cried."

"I know this, Mireille, and I am sorry. It broke me to leave you, but it could not be helped."

"Let's say that's true. Let's say that for once you're not lying, that faking your death had to be done," Cate said. "You didn't have to lie about who you were, who I was—*what* I was. You could have prepared me, taught me, done *something*, but all you did was lie."

"I only ever meant to protect you."

"Then where were you when I was being tortured? When I was…Where were you then? Why didn't you want to protect me then?" Cate challenged. "You're a fucking *goddess*, aren't you? If you wanted to protect me so badly, why—?"

Tears overtook her; her body caved in, and she lay in a heap on the floor. James had witnessed her sobs too many times. It never became easier. Were they alone, he could have done something—gone to her, held her while she cried, comforted her in any way she would allow—but she wouldn't want it here. Not like this. He stayed where he was and watched the goddess glide toward Cate.

"Mireille," Laorans said, "please understand—"

Cate's head snapped up. The blue drained from her eyes until they were gray. She rose gracefully and took her first determined step. Her intention was violence. James's heart stopped upon recognizing it.

"No!" he yelled. "No, Cate, no!"

Rushing across the room, he grabbed her arms and pushed against her to force her back, but she broke his hold and shoved him with enough strength to lift him completely into the air. He hit the wall with a loud crack and slid to the floor, stunned and hurt.

The door opened, Rhydwyn and Gair flooding in. James lifted a weak arm in warning, but Rhydwyn didn't notice as he stepped in front of Cate. There was the flash of a dagger, then Rhydwyn went down hard, a moan of pain leaving his lips. Cate threw the blade into his thigh and marched on. Gair took his brother's place and was thrown through the opposite wall. The cottage filled with sunlight as Gair disappeared from view. No one else had arrived, leaving no barriers between Cate and the goddess.

Cate's hands were at her sides, fingers outstretched with some magical force—lightning?—crackling in the spaces between. As her hands rose, James fell forward, aching and breathless, but it didn't matter. If he had to, he would drag himself the entire way. She had to be stopped, and he had to be the one to do it. There was no one else.

"Cate, don't," he croaked.

She didn't hear him, or perhaps she ignored him, as she thrust her arms toward the goddess. The lightning between her fingers shot through her palms and hit Laorans. James had never heard a deity scream before—had never known that they could—and covered his ears to muffle the toxic sound.

"Mireille!" the queen exclaimed, grabbing Cate's arms and shoving them away.

The energy Cate had channeled into the goddess slammed into the damaged wall, causing it to shatter completely. James threw himself over Rhydwyn to shield him from debris.

"Stop this now," the queen commanded. "This is not what we do."

James twisted to see the two sisters facing one another. The goddess had disappeared, and Cate looked at her twin with gray eyes dimming darker. Did the queen notice?

"No," Cate responded in a voice that was not her own. "This is not what *you* do, and you will lose because of it."

"Mireille, please—"

Cate held up her hand, and the queen stopped, her arm outstretched, reaching for her twin.

James slumped. "Cate."

She turned her head in his direction. "Cate doesn't live here anymore," she said and vanished in a ring of fire.

Part Three:
Reckoning

CHAPTER 37

First things first: assess the situation and identify priorities. James was not a priority. Every breath he took rippled pain through his torso, but he could breathe and move and think; therefore, he was not a priority. Rhydwyn was. Check for life, check for injuries. Only James already knew what he'd find, didn't he? A slash across the chest, a dagger in the thigh. He had watched it happen and hadn't done anything to stop it.

Her.

The dagger had fallen out, and the wound it had made wept blood, but James only gave it a passing glance as he tore Rhydwyn's shirt along the line she had made. The injury beneath it seemed deeper than it should have been, but it was not deep enough to kill so long as the bleeding was controlled. Pulling his cloak from the table, he pressed it against the wound. Stop the bleeding, and Rhydwyn could survive. Would survive.

"You'll live," he told Rhydwyn, and the man's eyes closed.

Now for Gair. Keeping his hands on Rhydwyn's chest, James twisted—bones and muscles protesting—and saw Gair standing unsteadily amidst chunks of what had once been a wall. A thin line of blood made its way down the right side of his face. He, too, would survive.

"What happened here?" Sarai gasped from the door. "Oh God! James, what..."

He turned to her, and Brighid behind her, and watched his grandmother sink to her knees. Was it the sight of her home—a place that had withstood generations and attacks from the king's men—falling down around her ears? Perhaps it was seeing the queen standing so still she could have been carved from stone. James glanced at her. Would that change? Would it kill her? Did he care?

Sarai crawled toward him. "James, what happened?"

Cate. Cate had happened. She had become the thing Faolan had feared, the thing that James believed she never would. But he couldn't say it out loud.

He looked at Gair. "All right?"

"Aye, Captain," Gair responded, eyes on his brother. "Is he—?"

"He'll survive," James said. "Help me move him to the bed."

Together, they lifted Rhydwyn and carried him to the other room. Sarai and Brighid—carrying the basket of medicinal stores—followed. Carefully, they laid him down and backed away to allow Sarai and Brighid to work.

James pulled Gair aside. "Find Lucius and Eion. Bring them back here."

"They went to fetch water," Sarai offered, examining Rhydwyn's wound.

"Then hurry them along," James said.

Gair nodded and left, breaking into a run once outside. James hovered between the rooms, taking in the damage, focusing for a time on the perfect circle burned into the floor. They wouldn't be able to stay there. They would have to leave.

"What happened?" Sarai asked again, her voice more composed. "Where's the other one? Cate. Where is she?"

"Gone," he answered.

"They took her?"

The image of flames engulfing her had scorched his brain; it was difficult to see anything else. James shook his head. "She took herself."

He stepped into the common room, the still-frozen queen drawing his attention once again. He looked from her to the immobile pegasus. What would he do about that?

"James," Dana said, "what...what happened here?"

James turned. Dana stood in the doorway, his arm braced against the frame, but not because he lacked the strength to stand unaided. How was he not bleeding to death?

"You're alive," James said.

"I am."

"How?"

"I don't know. Magic?" Dana said. "What happened here?"

Cate. Cate had happened. The answer was the same, and he gained nothing by concealing it. Gair would be telling the tale to Lucius, and Rhydwyn would say the same when he woke.

"Cate," James said. "It was Cate."

But, at the same time, it hadn't been. Her eyes, her voice—they had belonged to someone else. How that was possible, or what it might have meant, he couldn't say. Maybe it meant nothing.

"How?" Dana asked.

James sighed. "I don't know. Magic?"

"Why?"

"We lied to her."

Dana came inside, glancing at Faolan as he made his way to the queen. He stood in front of her and put his hand on her cheek. "We can't stay here," he said, letting his hand fall.

James looked past Dana, seeing sky where there should have been wall. No, they couldn't stay there.

"Cate could come back," Dana continued. "If she was angry enough—*powerful* enough—to do this, she could come back and do worse. We can't stay here and—"

"She's not coming back." James limped toward the door, pain infusing each step. "Stay here and keep watch. I need to—"

"—come here," Faolan said.

James stopped to look at the pegasus as he swayed and fell on his side. James had never seen him exhibit any sort of true weakness, and to witness it now sent a new pang of concern through him.

"Faolan?" Dana asked.

Faolan lurched to his feet. He stood for a moment before crumpling again, this time tucking his legs beneath him. "What did she do?"

James fought off another sigh. "She...she froze you and the queen, threw me across the room and Gair through a wall, stabbed Rhyd—"

"What did she do to Laorans?"

"I don't know. I've never seen anything like it," James answered. "She hurt the goddess—that much is clear—but what or how...I don't know."

"Someone should stay close to Haleine," Faolan said. "She'll be weak when she—when the magic's run its course."

James looked at the queen. "So she'll..." What? What would she do? Wake? Was that the proper term? Was there such a thing? He shook his head. "She'll be all right?"

"Eventually."

Not especially reassuring, James noted. He glanced at the door as Lucius, Gair, and Eion came through it. Lucius and Eion stopped short to stare at the queen. Gair did not.

"Where's Aaron?" James asked. "He's not with you?"

"He's on watch in the village. At the church," Lucius said, distracted. "Will she..."

James nodded. "I'll fetch him."

Lucius stopped staring. "Fetch him? For what?"

"Pack whatever you can, whatever we can use," James said as his grandmother came out of the bedroom, wiping her hands on her apron. "There won't be room for everything."

"You mean to leave?" Sarai demanded, then smiled at Gair when he stepped forward. "Your brother will live. He's resting now."

"I mean for all of us to leave," James said. "We can't stay here."

Sarai's expression cracked. "You want me to leave my home? This place where I have spent all my life—where *you* have spent all of yours—you want me to abandon it?"

"Aye. What's left of it." James looked at the floor to gather himself, the bloodied dagger with the eagle's head pommel catching his eye. He sighed.

"James?" Dana said. "Are you—?"

"Dana will stay with the queen, and Gair will stay with his brother," James said. "The rest of you make sure we can leave just as soon as they can be moved."

He snatched the dagger off the floor and walked out before any argument could be made, but Dana came after him, calling his name. James continued on, not stopping until Dana grabbed his arm and pulled him back.

"Are you all right?" Dana asked.

No, he wasn't. Of course he wasn't.

"Go back to the queen. She needs you," James said, walking away. "I don't."

———✦———

As James limped toward the village, Dana returned to the cottage and hovered outside the door. Lucius and Eion had gone, leaving Sarai and Faolan to act as Haleine's guardians. The pegasus hadn't moved, but Sarai was sorting items from a wooden chest.

She looked at him with shiny, bright eyes. "Where did you go? You were meant to be here, watching over the queen."

He stepped inside and glanced at Haleine. "She doesn't want me here."

"She doesn't know you're here. She doesn't know any of us are here."

"You can't be sure of that," Dana said. "One of the others can do it."

Sarai stood. "Do you know how it is you're not dead right now?"

"Magic."

"Aye, that's without doubt, but do you know who brought you back?"

"One of the unicorns, I suppose. She's done it before."

"The queen. It was the queen," Sarai said. "She swept into the barn, took one look at you, and ordered us away. She knelt at your side, apologized to me for what she was about to do, and healed your wounds with naught but her bare hands. The *queen* saved *you*."

Haleine had saved him? Haleine had used magic to save him? Dana looked hard at Sarai, wanting to call her out for her lie, but she had never spoken a false word to him, not once in all of the years he had known her.

He turned to Haleine. "Why?"

The question hadn't been for Sarai, but she answered, "You were dying, lad."

He would have thought Haleine would have preferred that. Him dying, him dead. Easier that way, wasn't it?

"She apologized?" he asked.

"Aye, as though such a thing were necessary when saving one of my lads." Sarai sighed. "I cannot claim to understand any of it—nor do I wish to—but I do know that you are alive now because of that girl."

Dana smiled. "That girl is your queen."

"Aye, she is. She's yours, too," Sarai said. "Now get yourself to her service."

His smile faded. "Wanting me alive and wanting me at her side are two different things, Sarai. The last time we spoke, she…"

Sarai nodded and crouched to scoop up a pile of quilts. "Well, don't just stand about—help me. I've got a queen to look after."

"You will come back here," he said. "It's not lost forever."

"Don't be telling me lies, lad," she said, thrusting the quilts into his arms. "Just carry these out to the wagon."

"Aye, Gran," he said.

She patted his cheek. "You're a good—"

"—don't do this!" Haleine blurted.

Dana turned to see Haleine collapse to her knees. He stood frozen, useless and dumb, as Sarai knelt at Haleine's side. She leaned in, speaking quietly while her hand rubbed her queen's back. When Haleine began to cry, Dana left the cottage before he could be seen.

Faolan followed, landing on his shoulder once they were outside. Lucius and Eion were hitching a pair of horses to the wagon. They ignored him as he approached. Going around to the end, Dana saw that someone had already dropped a few baskets of food and other sundries in the wagon's bed. As Faolan abandoned his shoulder for the driver's bench, Dana set down the quilts. He moved the baskets to the far end and carefully spread out the blankets to cushion the remaining space for Haleine and Rhydwyn.

"What else needs to be done?" he asked when he had finished.

Lucius looked at him. "Horses need to be saddled. All of them."

"All of them? What about—?"

"The unicorns are gone," Lucius said.

Gone? Dana looked at Faolan. Had they been affected as well? What had Cate done?

"Where are we?" James demanded, stalking up to them.

Lucius turned to James, but Dana watched Aaron, the boy's eyes wide with shock as he skirted the wagon and made his way to the barn. Once he had gone inside, Dana joined Lucius and James.

"We're going back to camp, aye?" Lucius said, and James nodded. "Then I'll send Eion to make sure the tunnel entrance is clear."

"We won't be able to use the tunnels," Faolan said. "The magic, it's…gone. We'll have to use the forest paths."

"What about the camp?" Lucius asked. "What about their defenses?"

"Also gone," Faolan said.

"Has she been there?" Dana asked. "Has Cate ever been to the camp?"

James looked at him, seeming surprised to see him. "Aye. She was there."

"Faolan," Dana said, "can you get a message to camp?"

The pegasus was slow to respond. "I believe so."

"Tell them to start packing," Dana said. "We have to move the camp somewhere safe. Some place Cate's never been."

Both Lucius and Faolan looked to James for approval, but James glowered at Dana and said, "She wouldn't go there."

"You're willing to risk all those lives on that belief?" Dana asked.

"Don't ever talk to me about risking lives," James seethed.

He stalked toward the cottage, Lucius trailing after him. Sighing, Dana went to the barn to ready the other mounts.

He and Aaron had brought out the last horse when James and Gair left the house, Rhydwyn between them. They half-carried him to the wagon and lifted him inside. Lucius emerged next, Haleine in his arms and Sarai on his heels. Brighid was last, holding Sarai's medicinal supplies.

Lucius carefully laid Haleine in the wagon, then helped Sarai and Brighid to climb up. As Gair and Aaron settled on the driver's bench, James closed the back of the wagon.

"Riders up," he said. "We're leaving."

They departed before the sun had set, making for camp as quickly as they could. Lucius and Eion acted as advance guard, while James was alone at the rear. Dana rode alongside the wagon, watching its occupants from the corner of his eye.

No one spoke, all choosing to scrutinize their surroundings, as though at any moment enemies might burst out of the trees. But the woods stayed silent, and Dana was left to contemplate the question of his continued existence.

He was alive.

Though it felt foolish, he repeated that fact to himself frequently. He didn't quite believe it.

He was alive when he should have been dead.

Dying was a slow process, taking much longer than it should have. For days, he had lingered between life and death, trying desperately to surrender to wherever death would leave him.

But when the fog cleared, he had opened his eyes to see the rafters of a barn he had looked upon so often before. Not only had he somehow cheated death yet again, he had crossed an ocean and returned to Enimode.

Returned to chaos, wrought at the hands of the woman he had journeyed to Tanuba to retrieve.

Faolan had talked about magic before, and Dana was no stranger to the turmoil it could cause, but this...the repercussions of Cate and what she had done seemed to be something else entirely.

They traveled until it became too difficult to see. The moon offered no assistance, so the decision was made to stop for the night. A suitable location was discovered, and lanterns were lit, their light kept low. James barked out assignments to all, save Dana. He drifted away to help Aaron tend to the horses, while keeping an eye on those in the wagon.

The camp quickly came together, sparse but functional, providing shelter for the wounded and some sense of protection for the rest. After a meal more meager than the camp, James sent Lucius and Eion to take the first watch. Brighid sat, sharpening a dagger blade. Aaron had settled near the horses, and Gair took up position by Sarai and her charges. Dana kept apart from the rest, sitting on the ground with his back against a tree, and watched James, who hadn't yet stopped moving.

"You should rest," he suggested when James roamed within earshot.

James stopped and looked at him. "You're the one who most recently came back from the dead. You rest."

Most recently? "If you don't rest, you'll fall over," Dana said. "That won't do anyone any good."

"Do you honestly mean to lecture me on the importance of maintaining one's health for the benefit of others?"

"Not a lecture. Just an observation. Aye, I abandoned you, but you don't have to do everything alone, James. Let someone help you carry this burden. Lucius, for example, or"—Dana hesitated—"me."

"You?" James laughed. "They'll not follow you anymore. Don't you understand that? You ruined that, Dana. Everything we worked for, every-thing we lived for, *died* for—you destroyed for a suicidal whore who can't stand the sight of you. You left them; you left *us*, and now we must finish alone what you started. And we will. But it's over for you, Dana—your time is over. No one wants you to do anything anymore—especially lead."

"I'm not looking to lead. Only to help."

"You can't help." James looked away. "You could leave during the night. No one would care. No one would stop you."

"Sarai might."

"She might not."

Dana nodded. "Also a possibility. I'd like to stay, though. If you'll let me."

James grunted and glanced toward the wagon. "Of course you'll stay. You're found now, aren't you?"

"It doesn't have anything to do with Haleine."

"Doesn't it? Everything you do is for her, or because of her."

"I left her, too, remember? I left her to go to Tanuba with you to find your girl, and—"

"She's not my girl."

There wasn't much conviction in his voice. Dana smiled and ducked his head so James wouldn't see.

"Just as well, that," Dana said. "It won't end well with her."

"She's not what you think."

"You say that, but I know what I've seen," Dana said. He was treading dangerously, on the thinnest of ice; if he kept pushing, James would force him to leave for sure. "She cuts a miserable, bloody swath through wherever she is, through whomever she comes across, and—"

"You're wrong about that. Her."

Dana stood. "You were wrong. You were wrong about her, and you're wrong now not to move the camp to safety. James, if Cate—"

"She's not coming back."

It wasn't the first time James had stated that opinion. The conviction he had been lacking earlier was now overwhelming. How was he so certain? What wasn't he saying?

"Why do you think we're safe?" Dana asked. "Where do you think she went?"

James looked into the darkness. After a moment, he shook his head. "I have no idea."

———❦———

Melancholy was not an emotion with which Zaide Romanza was familiar. It was a human thing, and a worthless one at that, which meant she had no use for it. Though she was, regrettably, human, she never had been prone to fits of gloom.

Until now.

She slouched on her throne as the sadness worked its way through her. It had followed her from Mairéad to Eacha Donn and indicated no intention of abating, no matter what she drank or whom she took to her bed.

Never had she believed that serving her lords could leave her so bereft. Perhaps her disposition would have been improved had she not liked Mireille as much as she had.

Of course, it might not have been Mireille at all. The revelation about the Liran rebel leader might have been to blame.

Idris Fein had never been a man to stray. Even when without a wife—as he had been so frequently—he did not avail himself of any woman. Chambermaids, whores, and eager noblewomen all placed themselves in his path, but the king had no interest in any of them.

Except one.

Zaide Romanza had been a young child when it happened, still mastering the art of proper speech, but she was old enough to be aware and watching.

She had seen her father with the maid.

She was beautiful, the maid. Zaide Romanza could recall that. Soft and sweet with her golden hair and fair skin, the maid had been walking, breathing sunlight in which Idris Fein had basked. Kissing, touching, tasting—Zaide Romanza had seen it all. She witnessed their courtship without understanding what they did or what it meant—except that her mother frowned and the court whispered whenever the maid entered their sight.

One day, the maid disappeared. Without word or warning, she was gone, and the court spoke as though she had never existed at all.

As Zaide Romanza grew older, she reached the conclusion that her mother had banished her husband's lover. An admirable act, to remove a threat to one's position, and Zaide Romanza approved of what her mother had done. She hadn't thought about the lost chambermaid since.

Now she was at the forefront of Zaide Romanza's mind. How large a debt was owed to her mother's memory? Her actions had safeguarded her daughter's future.

True born or bastard did not matter in Feond. If claimed by his father, a bastard son would inherit what an elder, legitimate daughter would lose—even if that daughter were a princess. A bastard son could sit the throne and rule, if it were his father who had worn the crown before him.

But Zaide Romanza didn't want a bastard on the throne. The crown was meant to rest upon her head, and she had worked her entire life to make sure she remained her father's sole heir. She thought she had been so thorough, so careful.

But not careful enough, as it was.

What to do with her newfound knowledge? Ignoring it would be best; he seemed unaware of his parentage, and the only others who would know were long dead.

It was possible the maid was alive, that she had raised her irritating boy in some Liran hovel. It was equally probable that she had died in childbirth, or of sickness, or in one of the village massacres of which Omur was so fond. Truly, it was a waste of time to contemplate whether the maid lived. She did not matter. Only the fool to whom she had given birth did.

Perhaps she should have killed him in Tanuba, used his own sword to end his miserable existence. Had it been a mistake to let him go?

No. Alive or dead, he wasn't a threat. He could not hurt her. He could not take anything from her she did not wish to surrender.

"Your majesty?"

Zaide Romanza looked at Torin, standing before her with his head bowed. Another man—one of her guards—stood next to him, mimicking his posture. "What is it?"

Torin kept his head down. "Word has come from the city gates. The men there say a storm is coming."

Zaide Romanza looked at the guard. "A storm is hardly an unusual occurrence here."

"No, yer majesty," the man said.

"Why, then, do you feel the need to warn me about this one?"

"Beggin' yer pardon, but this is no usual storm, yer majesty," the guard replied, daring to look at her. "This storm be different. Unnatural. It's..."

"What?" she demanded, seething with impatience.

"Evil," the man spat.

Evil? Her irritation fell to heel, intrigue rising to take its place.

After assuming the throne, she had made no effort to conceal her gifts in her own court. It was not an option wherever she went, and she was determined to live as she wanted in her own home. Those who served her had adjusted to the change but were wary. Many considered her evil, but seldom did they employ that word, so fearful were they of tempting the wrath of their queen. To hear it now, and in the description of a storm, was most captivating.

She straightened. "An evil storm? Well, that would merit our attention."

Both Torin and the guard looked at her, unsure of her tone.

"Your majesty?" Torin asked.

"How do you know this storm approaches?" she inquired.

"We've been watchin' it, yer majesty," the guard responded. "It's been buildin' and buildin', and the clouds...I've stood on that wall for thirty years, yer majesty, and I ain't never seen anythin' of the sort. Now it's movin' this way, and—"

"From which direction does it come?" she interrupted. "North? South?"

"East, yer majesty. It comes from the east."

From Lira. Zaide Romanza glanced at the windows on the east wall. Could it be? Why didn't she feel it—*her*?

"When do you expect this storm to—?" She stopped when the entire hall shook as though the earth itself had split in two. "Never mind."

The doors flew open, rattling the stone walls surrounding them. Her nobles and servants cried out, scurrying to the corners. Zaide Romanza could feel the power before Mireille entered and was on her feet when the woman came in. The sight of her made Zaide Romanza weak with pleasure. Mireille was wild, her eyes black holes. *This* was what they had wanted, needed, all along.

"Well," Zaide Romanza said as Mireille approached, "do come in."

chapter 38

When the goddess had come under attack, Omur had been with Sighle. Upon having realized that her sister's death meant there was naught but him to protect her, she had come crawling back, offering herself to him. He took her gladly; he enjoyed her.

Their reunion had been interrupted by magic—Mireille's magic, he quickly realized. It dropped into him like a heavy weight and spread through his body. Warm, invigorating—Omur closed his eyes and imagined he could taste it on his tongue. The goddess's hurt was a delectable morsel.

The last time the goddess had been so weakened, Omur had only felt it when he was nearly upon her followers. This time, however, it had sought him out. What had Mireille done?

He abandoned the bed, leaving Sighle behind. She stirred but made no complaint about his departure. Instead, she hummed softly to herself. He smiled as he made his way to the balcony doors.

He looked at the night sky where a brightly burning moon should have been. The orb that had taken its place was a drab thing, acting as confirmation that Mireille had done him a great service. The Black Wolf had performed his task well.

The rebellion could be destroyed now. Nothing stood in his way. They had outlived their usefulness, and he would be glad to see them gone. He could kill them all and wipe them from the face of the earth, leaving his lords free to have everything they desired.

Behind him, Sighle was absently singing. She had taken to doing so ever since the announcement of her sister's death. He hadn't cared before, but it cut into his concentration, and he shook his head irritably.

"*There once was a lad, a brown-eyed boy, who loved a girl so fair,*" she sang. "*He went to the ends of the earth for her, but never did she care.*"

"Hush," he commanded, but she continued to sing.

"*There once was a lass, with hair red like flame, who loved a brown-eyed boy. Her life she would give in protection of his, and in that he took no joy.*"

He glanced at her. "Would you cease?"

"*Oh, what would they do, these two, these two? Oh, what would they do, these two? When to die is to win, and to live is to lose—oh, what would they do, these two?*"

"I said, stop!"

Sighle sat up and leaned toward him. "I thought you'd be cheerier. You usually are, afterward. What's wrong? Didn't I please you?"

"I'd be more pleased if you would stop your prattling."

"Yes, you'd rather I do something else with this mouth, wouldn't you?"

Omur narrowed his gaze. "You may leave. I have no more time for you this night."

The girl pouted. "I've displeased you."

He shook his head and looked away. "We are not playing this game again."

"Who's playing? I just...Quick it will be—no time to play. She doesn't like it, so no delay."

"Oh, cease with your rhymes and—" Omur stopped. What had happened to her voice? Her singsong tone was now rapid and guttural. What game was she playing? He turned to look at her.

"One by one, they come, they come."

The song had become a chant. Omur walked back to the bed. She lay in its center, arms flung out to either side. Her now-vacant and black eyes stared at the ceiling. Sighle was gone; something else was in her place.

"Who comes?" he asked.

"They come," Sighle—or the thing inside her body—intoned. "One by one, they come, they come, one by one, they come, they come; one by one, they come, they come—"

"Who speaks to me through this girl?" he said. "Tell me your name."

"She'll come to you; in division is your fall. When she rises, the end is near, for her power is your all."

"Enough with your rhymes," he said. "Tell me who you are."

"So many am I. How to choose? Can't—I am all. Mother, lover, sister, friend or foe, and whore. Infant child, stupid girl, cheerless woman, ugly hag, and more."

"Not your host. You."

"Not your host. You." Sighle's head snapped in his direction, her blank, dark eyes focusing on him as she rose. She walked on her knees to the edge of the mattress and faced him. "Bothersome man, bothersome questions. Close-minded, future-blinded. Doesn't pay attention, doesn't ask what he should."

"I'm not a man," he said. "Name yourself and leave this girl."

"Can't leave, never been," Sighle sang. "And the worm between your legs, and the lass in your bed make you more man than human. A dead man. Fucking. A fucking dead man."

He grabbed the girl by the throat and forced her onto her back. Straddling her, he said, "You have no power here. Name yourself. Are you friend or foe?"

"Friend or foe, she doesn't know," Sighle said, speaking as though he wasn't crushing her trachea. "Doesn't change what's to come. She's to come—can't stop it, like the setting of the sun. It's done." Her arms came up, and her hands clapped together in front of his face. "Three to one and back again; you can't leave where you've never been."

"Who are you?" he demanded, choking the girl beneath him.

"Mystic hypocrite. Soothsaying charlatan. Harbinger. Destroyer!" she screamed. "Destroyer her name shall be, and she shall come for thee!"

"Leave this flesh, abandon these bones," Omur ordered. "You have no power here. I am—"

Her hand latched onto his throat, and he could no longer speak. He gagged and sputtered, releasing her to pull at the hand choking him, but she did not falter. Slowly, she pushed him back, off the bed, and onto the floor. They stood face to face.

"You have no power here, and I am more than all-powerful," she said, malice dripping from her voice. "I am power."

She shoved him, and Omur flew through the air until he struck a wall. He fell forward onto the floor and pushed himself up in time to see Sighle release a delicate, little sigh before collapsing, as though in a faint. He waited to see if she would rise again, but when she failed to move, he crawled to her side and examined her without touching her. Her chest rose and fell at a regular interval, and color was returning to her cheeks. She appeared to be simply sleeping, and the demon that had possessed her was gone again.

Destroyer her name shall be, and she shall come for thee!

The girl's warning. From where had it come? Yelsneh would have spoken to him directly and would not have employed such childish rhymes. He supposed that left only the girl herself.

He had long suspected that Darian Coileáin's youngest daughter would contain some skill. Her sisters certainly did; there was no reason to think the third would be different. Omur had waited for a sign to confirm his theory, but the girl had shown him nothing, forcing him to consider the possibility that he had been mistaken—that the girl was just a girl and nothing more.

He wouldn't need to consider it any longer.

But to whom had she been referring? The safest answer was her sisters. One of them would come to kill him. Perhaps both of them would try to kill him. Sighle had called him a dead man—who would succeed?

Mireille was the likely culprit. Zaide Romanza's plan had been a terrible risk, and if she was aware of what had happened in the days since Mireille had been given to the Black Wolf, she wasn't sharing that knowledge. But what was certain was that Mireille—wherever she had been, whatever had happened to her there—had come close to killing the goddess. Now, perhaps, she would come for him.

Destroyer her name shall be, and she shall come for thee!

Sliding his arms beneath Sighle's limp body, he carried her to the bed and laid her upon it. He stood at her side, stroking her hair, waiting for her to emerge from her slumber. When she opened her eyes, they were hers again.

"Do we play now?" she asked, her voice lethargic. "But I'm so tired."

"No." He ran his thumb over her lips, and they parted. "We do not play."

She nipped him, and he drew away his hand.

"Stop that," he scolded. "Be a good girl and tell me what happened."

"I bit you."

"Before that."

She licked her lips. "I asked what you wanted me to do with my mouth. Did you answer?"

"Are you certain that is the first thing you recall?"

"Yes." She frowned. "Why?"

"No reason, merely curious. Your grief has made you faint. You need to rest now," he said. "But I shall return later."

"My faithful dog."

"Your master."

Sighle smiled drowsily. "Oh yes, master and slave are we."

Her eyes closed, and Omur walked away. She was softly singing again, and he stopped to listen.

> *A lost little lass alone in the wood came*
> *across an evil thing made of horns and*
> *teeth and smoke.*
>
> *'Come with me now,' the evil thing said,*
> *'I'll bring you some place where you can*
> *rest your head. Then later shall we go to*
> *my kingdom below, for I need a queen,*
> *and you will share my throne.'*
>
> *Oh, how she cried, that lost, little girl. Oh,*
> *how she cried, that little girl who died.*

The girl ran away, just as fast as she could,
but there was no escaping from the evil in
the wood.

'I want to go home,' the lass wept and
cried. But the evil thing, he laughed and
said, 'My dear, you've already died.'

Oh, how she cried, that lost, little girl. Oh,
how she cried, that little girl who died.

The words gave way to idle humming, and Omur opened the door. "How does it end, your song?" he asked, not quite sure why he cared.

"No one knows."

"Not even you?"

"The song's not over yet," Sighle replied. "But I'll sing the ending for you when it comes."

"You do that, lass." Omur slipped out of the room, a smile on his face.

———⟪∾∾⟫———

Sighle lay on the bed, tracking Omur's movements. When he entered the king's library, she slid off the bed and walked to the balcony.

She felt as worn out as the moon appeared, but her exhaustion was nothing compared to what Mireille had done to the goddess—to her own twin. Sighle had been aware of it long before Omur had, and only she understood the true extent of the damage done.

Close. They were so very close.

Omur could indeed wipe the rebellion from the face of the earth. The goddess was frail enough, and her servants had been weakened along with her. Nothing protected them. He could crush every last one. It was possible that he would not fail this time.

She really should have allowed him to do it.

But as close as they were, as near to falling as Mireille was, she was not there yet. No matter how unlikely Sighle thought it to be, Mireille could still make the wrong choice. As easy a task as exterminating the rebellion would be, to do so at this time would be, perhaps, counterproductive. Her sister's actions had been only a response to the perfidy of the goddess who had spent years masquerading as her mother. Good remained within Mireille's soul—in the form of her brown-eyed boy. He had saved her from the monsters and hid her tears in his skin, and she now carried a piece of him with her. If he were to die, there would be no telling how she would react. Try as she might, Sighle remained blind to that. There was no way to be certain what Mireille might do.

Until there was, until Sighle did know without doubt, the brown-eyed boy would remain untouched, his rebellion along with him.

Sighle left Omur's chambers, looking at her guard as she passed. All that Mireille had done in Enimode had broken the protection she had bestowed upon her servants. Sighle had felt it break, heard it snap like a twig, and found herself once again able to dismiss Bronagh and the boy guard with a wave of her hand. Out they had marched, and Sighle had commanded the one remaining guard to bring her to Omur. Though Mireille had instructed him not to, he obeyed.

How devastated he would be if he knew that he had done precisely what Mireille had forbidden him to do. She had threatened him so nicely, and he had been afraid ever since.

Would Mireille remember the promise she had made to him? Would she even care that her mandate had been broken? She did, after all, have other things to worry about now.

When Sighle slipped into the king's library, Omur and Garbhan stood bent over a table, discussing a map and where upon it the rebellion might be found. She stepped between them and ran her hand across Garbhan's broad back. How she loved the strength of him.

She continued to touch him as she listened to their conversation. What was to be done about the rebellion? How could they best take advantage of Mireille's gift? Perhaps Sighle should have told them, but the rebellion didn't matter. They were ineffectual bumblers whose greatest assets had been the goddess and Mireille herself. But Mireille had taken both those resources away, rendering the rebellion to be nothing more than children playing at war with a pair of sharpened sticks.

The brown-eyed boy remained stubborn, even after all Mireille had done. He still wanted to believe—*needed* to believe—that Cate was good and that his cause would not fail.

He didn't know it, but he was right. His cause would not fail, but not through any determination of his own. Neither would his resolve be enough to save Mireille. Yes, there was good deep inside her, but it would not last. It could not. The magic would erode it like water on metal. The more Mireille partook, the quicker it would happen. She may have realized the truth of that, but she would press on regardless. The magic would ease her pain, and she was in great pain. She'd do anything to make it stop, including surrendering her soul.

When that happened, fire would rain from the sky, and the dark gods would have what they had long wanted.

But for now, Sighle would wait.

She touched Omur. "You will do nothing," she said. "You will stand down."

—◦◦◦—

Cate woke up on her stomach, head on a pillow, arms tucked beneath her, and her fingers grazing her face. Her wet face. Great to know she'd been crying again. Opening her eyes revealed nothing but darkness, and she took advantage of it to clear her eyes and cheeks of any lingering tears.

That task completed, she took stock of her situation. Or as much as could be determined without moving.

The pillow was nice, soft and clean. There was a blanket or two covering her from the hips down. Her back was exposed to the open air, but it wasn't completely bare.

Rolling on her side, she winced at the ache in her ribs and pulled the covers to her nose. The weight of the fur made it difficult to breathe, forcing her to shove the blankets away. Self-inflicted asphyxiation wouldn't solve her problems.

Would it?

Too early to tell.

A global positioning system would settle the mystery of where she was because she couldn't even begin to guess. She remembered pulling a Carrie, leaving Enimode in an über-rage, and—and what? There was nothing after that. Nothing until now.

She lifted her head to listen for clues, but there was no sound apart from a burning fire. So, she was some place with decent bedding and heat. Two things not to be discounted, but the more information she had, the better.

However, as acquiring that information would require her to leave her nest, she laid her head back on the pillow and listened to her heart beat. It seemed amplified somehow, confirming the fact that she was alive. Another good thing to know, she supposed. There had been doubts.

The drapes on the left side of the bed parted, flooding the dark space with light, and Cate peeked over her shoulder at the queen of Feond.

"Awake at last, are you?" Zaide Romanza said. "How do you feel?"

How did she feel? What a dumb question. Cate looked away.

"I must say, Mireille, you do know how to make an entrance."

Did she? Good. Or, more likely, bad. If it had impressed Zaide Romanza, her entrance probably had involved more than confetti cannons and a kick-ass walk-up anthem.

"Do you not remember it?" Zaide Romanza said. "Such a shame. I've never seen its equal."

Swell. Cate rolled onto her stomach and pressed her face into the pillow. Perhaps it was time to reconsider her stance on self-asphyxiation.

Stretching out on the bed, Zaide Romanza rested her head on Cate's shoulder. "Do you want to tell me what happened?"

No. Hell, no.

Zaide Romanza rubbed the small of Cate's back in a tight circle. "Do you want to tell me how it happened?"

Even less. What would she have said? It hadn't been planned; she hadn't known what she'd been doing. She still didn't.

"They said you'd run off with the rebellion," Zaide Romanza continued. "I thought perhaps—"

"Stop talking," Cate murmured. "Stop...everything."

Zaide Romanza froze in place, just as Fionnbar and Faolan and Haleine had done. Cate eased away, leaving Zaide Romanza behind.

The drapes shielding the right side of the bed parted without her laying a hand upon them—more magic she could neither control nor explain. She slid off the bed slowly, feet searching for the floor. When it was found, she walked on her toes to the end of the bed and used the post for support until she could be sure her legs would function properly.

She wore a low-cut slip—soft, gauzy, and white—that came down to her ankles and left her back exposed. Who had dressed her? Had it been Zaide Romanza? A servant? A pair of servants? More? Shit, how many people had seen?

Removing one hand from the bed post, Cate gingerly felt her back and the bandages someone had laid there. They were fused to her flesh, soaked through with whatever had come out of her body. Grabbing the stiff edge of one sodden linen strip, she ripped it off, swearing as she did so.

Panting and crying yet again, she crumpled the bandage into a ball and looked around the room. It was small and simply furnished—a sickroom, equipped only with the bare essentials.

One of those essentials was a fireplace, and she pushed off the bed, bandage in hand, and stumbled over to it. Sinking to her knees in front of the hearth, she watched the flames grow larger, angrier, without anyone stoking them. When she threw the linen into its center, it howled and sputtered and devoured her blood. She contorted her body to remove each bandage and fed them to the fire one by one. Her skin was left raw, bloodied, and throbbing.

She lowered herself to the floor, stretching her arms out toward the fire, and rested her forehead on the stone.

What the hell was she going to do now?

"Why did you do that?" Zaide Romanza demanded.

How had she gotten free? Had Cate done something to release her, or had Zaide Romanza done it on her own? Was there such a thing as time-release magic? Was there even anyone around who would know the answer?

Cate sat up and looked at the queen of Feond, then at the window behind her. "They're called personal boundaries. Learn to respect them."

Zaide Romanza pushed off the mattress. "You allowed the prince in your bed."

Cate stood and walked to the window. "Did he tell you that?"

"He didn't have to."

The view was of nothing but the courtyard and the queen's various soldiers and retainers milling about. Cate leaned in to study them.

Zaide Romanza joined her. "You shouldn't have removed your bandages. You're bleeding all over my nice floors."

"They're not that nice."

Sighing, Zaide Romanza leaned against the wall to the window's left. "You should tell me why you're here. What brought you to my gates?"

Cate found the gates. Or what was left of them. They appeared to have had an unfortunate run-in with the Kool-Aid Man.

"Where did you go when you left Mairéad? What happened to you?" Zaide Romanza pressed.

"You say that like you don't already know."

"I don't, Mireille. I swear it, and you know I have never lied to you."

She didn't actually know that at all. Zaide Romanza could have been the diabolical mastermind behind everything. If she was, she would never admit it easily.

Cate motioned to the scene below. "How many did I kill?"

Zaide Romanza shrugged. "A fair few, but they would have died anyway. It hardly matters."

A fair few. She sure was raking up the body count. "They could have died from old age, peacefully in their sleep, surrounded by loved ones, and not—"

"No one has that option anymore," Zaide Romanza said. "Not even us."

Live fast and die young. It wasn't a good enough excuse—nothing ever would be—but Cate nodded and said, "Did you do this? Did you hire the Black Wolf, bewitch Zoltano to...Did you set this up to get—?"

"I have done nothing, Mireille. Tell me what Zoltano has to do with any of this."

"You didn't hear? I killed him."

Zaide Romanza stepped forward. "You what?"

Now that she had said it, Cate could see it, feel it, and smell it all over again. The sensation of his innards in her hands had felt so damn good. "I killed him."

"Why would you—is he the one responsible for..." Zaide Romanza gestured to Cate's body.

Did she really think someone else had carved his name into her back? Folding her arms across her chest, Cate looked at the other woman. "Don't play stupid."

Zaide Romanza shrugged. "I'm not playing anything. I simply don't like to assume."

"No, you like to force the issue."

"I can't deny that," the queen of Feond said. "But with Zoltano...you have my gratitude. You have saved me from a most unpleasant marriage."

Zaide Romanza had been engaged to Zoltano? Had that been mentioned before? Cate supposed it didn't much matter now. "As I should. Your betrothed was a bigger asshole than Maddox."

"To hear your sister's tale, the opposite was true," Zaide Romanza said. "But then, Zoltano never did play with her the way he played with you."

"Played?"

"That's what it was to him."

"He's not playing anymore."

Zaide Romanza cocked her head. "How did you do it?"

Cate turned from the window. "Painfully."

"I am pleased to hear it. Come, Mireille, humor me. Regale me with the tale of how you disposed of the man I never desired to marry."

"No."

"You gain nothing by keeping it secret. I shall only find out on my own."

"Sounds like a terrific plan. You should get started on that."

Cate crossed the room again, this time intending to bleed all over Zaide Romanza's nice furniture. The room lacked choices—only the bed and the fireside chair offered seating. She selected the chair and looked at the two-headed dragon tapestry hanging over the mantle. Welcome to Feond.

"This is all you will offer me?" Zaide Romanza asked, staying out of Cate's sight. "Zoltano tortured you, you killed him, then came running all the way here just to tell me what you'd done?"

"Yes."

"No. You're lying. There's something more; there must be. What else could have—oh." Zaide Romanza paused. "Did you discover the truth?" she pushed softly. "About Laura Cole?"

There was no Laura Cole. There never had been. What did that mean for her daughter? Cate stared at the fire and stayed silent.

"You should have let me be the one to tell you," Zaide Romanza said. "It would have been kinder."

It was cute that she thought there was a kind way to tell someone their entire life had been an elaborate, manufactured lie.

"It doesn't matter anymore," Cate said. "It's in the past, and I'm not interested in the past."

"What does interest you? The future?"

Cate didn't know. The future was too vast, too overwhelming to consider at this juncture. There would come a time when the issue would be forced, regardless of her personal feelings on the subject. But that time wasn't now, and she was strongly considering ignoring it for as long as she could.

"Revenge," she answered. That would please her host. Besides, she couldn't dismiss the possibility entirely. Revenge could be a very fine thing, and there were a few souls somewhere out in the world to which she owed pain. A lot of pain.

"Upon whom?"

"Everyone."

Though Cate wasn't looking at the queen, she could see Zaide Romanza's smile.

"I can help with that," Zaide Romanza said.

"I don't want your help. I want to do it myself."

Zaide Romanza's smile broadened. "Even better."

The pleasure in the other woman's voice sickened Cate. New waves of nausea rolled through her stomach.

"What's the deal here?" she asked.

Zaide Romanza moved in front of the fireplace. "The deal?"

"Am I a prisoner? Am I *your* prisoner?"

"Do you look like one?"

"I haven't looked like a prisoner for a while now, but looks are typically deceiving."

"You are not a prisoner," Zaide Romanza said. "Not mine, nor anyone else's."

It didn't feel like a lie, but Zaide Romanza was an expert at concealing the truth. Cate would have to wait and see.

Zaide Romanza sighed. "Need I remind you, Mireille, that you came to me. *You* destroyed my gates, *you* killed my retainers, *you*—"

"Thought you didn't care about that."

"Well, they were very nice gates."

"I was talking about the people."

"I know."

They stared at each other. Cate broke first and gestured to the door. "What's on the other side?"

"A corridor."

"Who's standing guard? How many are standing guard?"

Zaide Romanza arched her eyebrow. "Do you believe you require guards? I would think you were perfectly capable of protecting yourself."

"No one's out there?"

"Not a single soul."

"I could leave this room if I wanted?"

"This room, this castle, this city, this country," Zaide Romanza said. "I'm not sure how else to say this so that you might understand it, but you are not a prisoner."

Cate thought about that. Not a prisoner. Could it be?

"While you contemplate the validity of my claims," Zaide Romanza continued, "might I make a small request?"

Cate looked at her host, suspicion oozing from every pore.

"Allow me, please, to summon someone to tend your wounds," Zaide Romanza said. "Neglecting them serves no purpose."

It served some purpose. It just wasn't one Cate could—or would—explain to anyone's satisfaction.

"I don't..." She sighed. "No."

By her count, five people—including the asshole responsible—had seen the full extent of what that asshole had done. It was five people too many, as far as she was concerned, and she didn't want to hand out any more membership cards than necessary.

"You only weaken yourself," Zaide Romanza said. "It is essential to stay strong, if you wish to survive."

Did she? Did she wish to survive? Aaron had asked her the same question once—did she want to die? She hadn't known then; she was less sure now.

Cate focused on the floor. "I don't want anyone else to see," she admitted. "I don't want anyone else to know."

She braced herself for the mocking that would be sure to follow such a confession. Being openly afraid, vulnerable—cowardly—was just begging for a mountain of ridicule to be dropped on her head.

But Zaide Romanza only said, "I have in my service a healer who is blind. She is the one I summoned to tend to you when you first arrived."

Six people, then.

"Did you do the blinding?" Cate asked.

"Not in this instance," was the queen's answer. "Shall I fetch her? I assure you she'll see nothing."

"She'll feel it."

Zaide Romanza shrugged. "If you prefer, I could tend to you myself."

Cate sighed. "Send in the healer."

"As you wish."

Zaide Romanza left the room. When the door opened, Cate could see no burly men loitering in the hall. Maybe they were lurking around a corner. Lull her into thinking she was free, only to spring the trap and snare her when she dared to venture out. But unless she wanted to spend the rest of her existence in that room, she'd have to risk it sooner or later.

Zaide Romanza returned, carrying a basket and leading a petite woman with opaque eyes. Together, they crossed the room and stopped in front of Cate. She smiled to see the queen of Feond playing servant. When Zaide Romanza caught her amusement, she scowled, dropped the basket into Cate's lap, and walked out again.

Cate looked at the healer with a mixture of curiosity and misgiving. "What's your name?"

"Rhona, my lady."

"Were you born blind?"

Rhona smiled. "No, my lady."

"When did you lose your sight?"

"About eighteen years ago."

"How did you lose your sight?"

"That has never been determined. I was in the forest, gathering plants for my work, when a storm came through. I took shelter against a tree, huddled in my cloak, but when the storm had gone again, it had taken my sight with it."

It didn't clear Zaide Romanza. But neither did it implicate her. Cate nodded. "Okay," she began. "Recently, I experienced…some trauma. I believe you might already be familiar with the damage done."

Rhona bowed her head. "Yes, my lady."

"When I woke, I tore the bandages off my back, but if you could help, it would be appreciated. I won't tear them off again."

"I will do all I can, my lady."

Cate stood, placed the basket on the chair, and turned her back to Rhona before reaching behind her for the healer's hand. She put it on her waist and braced herself for the examination. Rhona's hands moved lightly across her back, as though Cate's skin were a book written in Braille. It hurt, but not nearly as much as anticipated.

"Why did you remove the bandages?" Rhona asked.

"I didn't know who had put them there, or why," Cate answered. "Can you see anything at all?"

"I can assure you, my lady, that my blindness will not affect my ability to treat your wounds."

"Not why I'm asking."

"Why do you ask?"

"A storm stole your vision. One doesn't hear that every day," Cate said. "So, can you? Can you see anything? Shapes? Colors? The future?"

Rhona chuckled. "Perhaps I shall tell you, if you divulge to me how you received these wounds."

Cate smiled. "I didn't want to know anyway."

"Why did you ask?"

"Just making small talk. I love small talk. Especially with strangers."

Rhona laughed again. "I'm not entirely convinced that you're telling the truth."

"Skepticism is always wise."

Rhona's hands fell away, and Cate turned around to await the prognosis.

"The wound needs to be cleaned," Rhona said. "It...I'm afraid it will hurt a great deal."

Not as much as other things had. "Don't worry about the pain," Cate said. "I can take it."

"Some wine would make it easier to bear."

That's what the Black Wolf had said, too. She hadn't taken him up on that offer, nor could she accept Rhona's. The last time she had even *smelled* wine, she had vomited all over the floor. She wasn't looking to put on an encore performance.

"No," she said, "thank you."

"Are you sure? I shall mix it with—"

"Yeah, I'm sure. No wine."

"Tea, then."

"I don't need anything. I'll be fine."

Rhona nodded thoughtfully. "At least lay on the bed while I treat you. It will be more comfortable for you, as well as—"

"I don't care about that, and neither should you," Cate interrupted.

"—being easier for me," Rhona finished, exasperation evident in her voice. "It will be easier for me if you were to do this."

Cate offered Rhona a crooked grin that went unnoticed. "Why didn't you say so?"

She helped Rhona over to the bed, then went back to fetch the basket. After arranging the items inside on a bedside table to the healer's specifications, Cate climbed onto the bed, settling on her stomach. As advertised, the cleansing process was a slice of hell that left her in tears. She wiped them away, grateful Rhona couldn't see them.

"You'll have scars, I'm afraid," Rhona said, applying salve and bandages.

"Yeah, I've known that for a while now."

"When did this happen, my lady?"

"I don't...I'm not sure. A few days? A week, maybe? Not much more than that, I wouldn't think, but everything's been so...It's been difficult to keep track."

Rhona made a quiet noise of understanding and gently patted Cate's shoulder. "I have finished for now, my lady. Avoid lying on your back, and try not to allow anything to come into contact with it."

"Will do."

Cate pushed herself up, moving carefully in deference to Rhona's work, but the healer's hand shot out. When she had located Cate's shoulder, she pushed down firmly.

"No, my lady. I can find my own way out, and the servants can retrieve my things at a later time," she said. "Your body is demanding that you rest, and so am I."

Her body had also demanded that she blow a hole in the woman she'd once called her mother. Cate didn't mention that as she relented to Rhona's wishes and laid back down.

"I shall return in the morning to clean the wound and change the bandages again," Rhona said. "Please, my lady, don't remove them this time."

Cate watched Rhona feel her way to the door, and despite her earlier claim, she said, "No promises."

chapter 39

The magic that had bound Haleine had been equivalent to being under thickened water. She floated, suspended weightless and trapped. Struggling to reach the surface did nothing; she was tethered to an unseen stone.

When it finally released her, there had been a single gulp of fresh air before she had been plunged back into her own body, as weak and ill as she had ever been in all her life.

Faolan had been similarly affected, she suspected, though he had not spoken of it. Whether he was unwilling or unable to do so, she did not know. Like her, he would require time to recover.

They rode together in the back of a wagon, watching Sarai tend the wounded man. Her twin had been responsible for that. Haleine knew it instinctively, though none had said it. Sarai uttered multiple assurances that he would live, perhaps as much for herself as for the man who had fallen prey to Mireille's fury.

"Will he truly recover?" she had asked Sarai quietly that first night. "You are not lying for the sake of him and his brother?"

If he were dying, she could attempt to save him, bring him back, as she had Dana or that woman in the village. Faolan would not like it, but saving this life could restore some balance to the evil done by her sisters. One life would not make it even, but it would only be the beginning.

"Aye," had been Sarai's response. "He will live, your majesty. You needn't fear for his life."

It was not just his life for which Haleine feared, but she had not said so.

She stayed the entire night in the wagon, covered by a blanket Sarai had given her, and looked at the stars. She had done this before, contemplating the fate of her sisters and vowing to find answers. She was no nearer to a single one.

Perhaps there were no answers, and searching for them was nothing but a waste. There was no guide, no map for her to follow. They knew nothing of stars but had given them a name and a purpose. Haleine could do that with herself, her sisters, their destiny, their legacy.

What a legacy it was. Faolan had told her that their magic had been passed down through her father's line, that he didn't know how far back it went. Haleine was inclined to believe him, but she could not recall a time in which Darian Coileáin had demonstrated that he was anything other than a mortal man.

Had their father been aware of what he had passed down to his daughters? Why had his children been made to suffer this curse? If the magic had been passed down from one Coileáin to the next, why had the magic chosen to reveal itself within her generation?

Because it had chosen her. It had selected Mireille and Sighle as well—Haleine believed that as much as anything—that this damned magic was a living thing inhabiting their bodies and souls. It corrupted and killed. Sighle had lost the fight, as had Mireille. Would Haleine lose as well? Was it inevitable? She had attempted to use the magic only for good—freeing the unicorns, saving the life of a dying woman, saving Dana—but perhaps it wouldn't matter.

Haleine had no more answers nor solutions when dawn finally came, bringing an end to the miserable day before. Their small band swiftly prepared for departure, breaking their camp and leaving no indication that they had ever been there.

She rode in the back of the wagon, studying her escorts. They were not pleased to have Dana back among their number. Why she should know it so certainly, feel it so keenly, could only be magic. How intrusive that she be privy to what had not been spoken. She looked from one to the other, finding the same sort of anger in each of them, before turning to look at Dana himself. He rode alone at the rear, searching the trees for enemies. There was no anger to be found within him, only sadness.

Upon their arrival to the rebel camp, they were met by a woman bearing a resemblance to Lucius. He slid from the saddle and embraced her before opening the back of the wagon. He helped Sarai and Brighid out, then reached for Haleine.

"All right?" he asked, setting her on the ground. When Haleine had nodded, he said, "Your majesty, this is my sister, Ilya. Ilya, may I present to you the queen of Lira."

Ilya examined Haleine with a critical eye, then scanned the rest of their party. "Where's the other one? Cate—where is she?"

All movement among them stopped. James broke it quickly, stalking to the back of the wagon.

"Not here, not now," he said. "Take the queen to a tent. We'll talk after Rhydwyn is taken care of."

"What happened to…" Ilya's eyes settled upon Dana, and a fresh rush of resentment filled Haleine. "James, what is—?"

"Not here, not now!" James exclaimed, helping the injured man out of the wagon. "Bloody hell, Ilya, get her out of sight!"

Lucius put his hand on Haleine's back and led her away. Ilya walked at her side, while Brighid and Eion followed behind.

As they moved through the camp, its residents paused to look at her and her guards. The last time Haleine had been within the rebel borders, Dana had brought her. Her appearance had been a surprise for the people there, her relationship with the rebel leader a revelation. She had not been entirely welcome by a great many of its residents. Would that have changed?

None spoke nor approached. The occasional person called a greeting to Lucius. She glanced at him. He had been away from the camp for so long, and all because of her. Did any part of him resent her for it? Did Ilya?

"In here, your majesty," Lucius said, gesturing to a tent.

Brighid and Eion stayed outside, but Lucius and Ilya followed her in. Ilya lit a lantern and set it on a map-covered table. Lucius waved to the chair at its side, and Haleine sank onto it.

"What happened?" Ilya asked, lighting a second lantern. "Why is Dana here?"

"I don't know," Lucius said. "Wait for James. He'll explain everything."

Would he, though? Haleine didn't doubt that he would possess the answers. He had been with her sister the longest. He would know what had happened and what had gone wrong.

But would he tell them?

James arrived at last, Faolan and Dana coming in behind him. Faolan perched on the table, but Dana stood, head down, in a corner to her left. He had been skulking behind her ever since they had left Enimode, as though she might not be aware of his presence if he merely avoided her eyeline, but she was more aware of him than anyone.

"For the love of Laorans," Ilya cried, "would someone *please* tell me what has happened? Our defenses are lost, the unicorns are all ill, you two"— she motioned to James and Dana—"are supposed to be in Tanuba recovering the queen's twin, but you're here and she's gone, and the queen's sitting in this tent. What happened?"

"There was an attack on Laorans," Faolan said.

"An attack?" Ilya said. "By Omur?"

Faolan looked at James. "Cate."

"Cate?" Ilya turned to James. "Where is she now?"

James didn't offer an answer, but Dana did.

"We don't know."

The sound of his voice was poison to Haleine's soul. She closed her eyes.

"We don't know where she is, nor what she might be doing there. But there is no mistaking what she's done," Dana continued. "Destroyed the farm, injured Rhydwyn and Gair, attacked Faolan, the queen—attacked the *goddess.*"

Haleine looked at Dana. He was so irate with Mireille. Why? Because she had destroyed the closest thing he had ever had to a home? Because she had damaged his cause?

"Why? Why would she do that?" Ilya asked. "Why would she hurt Laorans? Why would she want to?"

Because they had tortured her. Haleine glanced at James and found him already looking at her.

"What about Loreton and Rushwick? Hythe?" Ilya asked. "Is she responsible for them as well?"

James looked at Ilya, unaware of what had transpired in Lira during his absence.

"No," Lucius responded. "That was the queen's other sister."

Haleine laughed, attracting the attention of all, and dropped her head in her hands. Her audience remained rapt and silent as her jollity mixed with tears.

"For God's sake," James said, "someone fetch Hanah."

Someone left—not Dana, as she could still sense him—and Haleine lifted her head, gulping air, attempting to regain control.

"No, no," she gasped. "Please, no. There's no need"—she laughed again—"I'm sorry; I don't understand what is wrong with me."

Another peal of devastating mirth bubbled up, and Haleine clapped her hands over her mouth to stop it. As tears ran over her fingers, she shook her head and looked at the others. Ilya had left, and those who remained were helpless in their bewilderment—except for James. He was irritated at both her and his own presence there. He would bolt soon—she was astonished that he had come at all—but there had to be a way to make him stay and tell her about Mireille.

"What was Ilya talking about?" James asked, ignoring Haleine's ongoing hysterics. "What was done in Loreton and Rushwick and Hythe?"

"A group of the king's soldiers razed them to the ground," Lucius said. "A message, written in blood, was left in each village, demanding the return of the queen."

James's face creased with confusion. "But both the king and Omur—"

"It is my sister, Sighle, who is responsible," Haleine interjected, any trace of laughter gone. She straightened and looked at James. "It would seem that both my sisters are monsters."

No one said anything. Only James appeared to consider an argument.

"They need to be stopped before they can do more damage," Haleine continued. "In order to do that, we will need to find Mireille, as well as a way to get to Sighle." She looked at Faolan. "How do we accomplish this?"

"I don't know," Faolan answered.

"Then find out how."

The pegasus understood that he had been dismissed but did not fight her on it. He unfolded his wings and flew out of the tent.

"Your sisters are not the only threat," Lucius said.

"No, they are not," Haleine agreed, "and it may well be that those other threats are searching for us now. There is an excellent chance that they are well aware of the goddess's predicament and, by extension, ours. You should make certain that these borders are secure."

Lucius hesitated, not accepting his release as readily as Faolan. He looked between her and James, reluctant to leave her unguarded. Habit, perhaps, or was he concerned what would happen if he left?

"Lucius, you may go," Haleine said, and he reluctantly obeyed. She turned to James. "Please, will you tell me what they did to her?"

His head snapped toward her, anger flaring in his eyes. Haleine sat rigid and studied him. He had not said so much as a word to her, but neither was there a reason he would. He did not care for her—he despised her. She could not demand anything from him.

"Please?" she implored. "Will you tell me all you know?"

He settled somewhat, his mouth working as he considered her request. "All I know?" he said. "Farming included?"

Whether a jest or simple spite, Haleine could not tell. She made no remark upon it, only waited to see what he might do next.

"You should ask your questions to the pegasus," he said.

"I am asking you."

"Why?"

"You went to Tanuba to bring back my sister. Faolan didn't."

James turned to leave. "Dana went. Ask him."

Haleine shot to her feet. "Wait, please!" she cried. "James, please."

He stopped and looked at her. "What do you want to know?"

"What happened in Tanuba? What did they do to her that made her...What did they do?"

"That remains a question for Faolan."

Haleine shook her head. "He was not in Tanuba."

"It started long before then," James said. "You ask Faolan, or you ask your goddess. You don't ask me."

"I know they tortured her."

"And you want to hear about it?" he demanded, livid all over again. "You want to hear everything that was done to her?"

"I don't want to, no, but if it helps explain why—"

"If you want an explanation, you'll have to talk to the pegasus."

"Why won't you tell me what they did to her?"

"She wouldn't want me to."

"Are you truly so devoted to her? She destroyed your home."

James shrugged. "A cottage."

"She injured your men. You as well, I believe."

"They'll live," he said. "You don't have to tell me what she did. I was there; I witnessed it all, but it changes nothing. She wouldn't want me to tell you anything, and even if she did, I wouldn't."

"Because you loathe me so much?"

"Because it's not mine to tell," he responded. "You flatter yourself if you think I spare any feeling at all for you."

"I apologize, then. I did not intend to offend you," she said. He walked away without further comment, and she let him, adding only, "Your loyalty is admirable."

James grunted. "I'm so glad you think so."

There was no mistaking the spite that time.

After he had gone, she returned to the chair and studied the maps until the weight of all that had happened began to suffocate her all over again. Resting her elbows on the table, she placed her head in her hands. Tears she didn't want to cry dripped from her nose and chin onto the parchment.

"Your majesty?" Dana said.

She had forgotten he was there. Her fingers snagged her hair briefly before she lowered her hands and looked at him, making no effort to wipe away her tears. He stood near the tent's entrance, healthy and whole, his head angled toward the ground, and his hands clasped together behind his back.

"Do you know what they did to her?" she asked.

"I do not. I'm sorry."

She nodded. "No matter."

"Your majesty, I..."

"Yes?"

"Sarai tells me I have you to thank for saving my life." When she failed to respond, he went on. "I'll not be staying here; you won't need to see me further. I wanted only to thank you for your care—your pity."

"It wasn't pity," she said both quickly and quietly. He raised his head. "Nor should you leave. There is still a war to be won, and the goddess will require all her servants."

As they looked at each other, a weight dropped through her heart. Would it ever be easier, talking to him, seeing him? Would she ever be able to look at him without feeling as though she were collapsing inside?

Dana bowed. "Whatever the reason, I thank you for it."

—◈—

It rained the day they buried his brother.

Revelin Maoilriain, the newly anointed crown prince of Tanuba, stood in the center of the room in which his father had been murdered so long ago and gazed at the rain instead of his brother's coffin. Weak from illness and grief, Haraszty stood at his side, clinging to his arm for support. He bore her weight easily, but Revelin did not grieve. He felt nothing.

He should be outraged that someone had so gruesomely murdered a member of his family. It had been more than murder, truly. However, Revelin could not muster the appropriate emotion. When Nathan had died, Revelin had wanted to commit a murder of his own, but now there was nothing. He knew who had done this, and why it had been done. But he did not care.

His mother tugged on his sleeve, and he helped her kneel. As she prayed, he sank to his knees and bowed his head but did not recite the words she spoke. When she whispered the final word, they returned to their seats. He sat beside her as the priests in their multicolored vestments came from the corners to perform the ceremony.

Later, after he had seen Zoltano's coffin interred next to their father, he sat with his mother in her chambers. Neither of them spoke, and Revelin was grateful Haraszty was bearing her anguish so privately. He did not wish to offer comfort over the loss of her eldest son. She did not know all that Zoltano had done to harm her. She did not understand that she was safe now that he was gone.

"Eamonn," his mother said. "Where is he?"

"I do not know."

"He should be found. Looked after."

Eamonn hardly needed looking after. He was old enough to sit on the throne in his own right; he was old enough to stand this trial unsupervised. But that was another conversation Revelin did not wish to have.

"I will see to it," he promised.

"I know you will." She sighed heavily, and he looked at her. "I have something I need to discuss with you."

"Yes?"

"You will be king soon, and you are in need of a wife."

"I do not wish to marry," Revelin responded. He had no desire to be king, either, but there was nothing to be done about that.

"What does wishing have to do with anything?" Haraszty said. "As king, you will need heirs, and for that you will need a wife. A proper wife—not an adulterous traitor."

Neither of them had discussed Haleine with the other. There hadn't been the opportunity before, but now there seemed to be little need.

"She was not a traitor then," Revelin said. "Just the girl you chose for me."

Just the girl he had loved. Eamonn would have argued that his love was hardly in the past, but Revelin thought perhaps his brother was wrong.

"Now I have chosen someone else for you."

The iron in his mother's tone nearly caused Revelin to flinch. He straightened and looked away. Which nobleman had purchased his mother's favor? Did Cathal have daughters? Revelin could not recall.

"Who?" he asked, steeling himself for the answer.

"Zaide Romanza."

His eyes shot back to his mother. "No. I will not marry that woman."

"You most certainly will," Haraszty said. "The girl needs a husband—a king—and you need a wife. One with her own country is unquestionably more appealing than one without."

"Mother, I never wish to disobey you, but—"

"There you go again—wishing."

"—I cannot marry Zaide Romanza," he finished. "Please, Mother, I beg you to reconsider."

"What is your aversion to the girl? She is neither ugly nor stupid."

"She was betrothed to my brother."

"Yes, and now that brother is dead. Betrothed is not married, as you well know," Haraszty said. "I don't understand why you are protesting this. Zaide Romanza will have you; she has always liked you."

She liked to make him feel the fool. Yes, she would have him—with open arms, she would welcome him—much in the way a cat would enjoy a mouse.

"Your father wanted this," Haraszty said. "He wanted an alliance between our countries—between our families. Your marriage would achieve this."

"We have no need of another alliance," Revelin said. "The one with Lira has done quite enough damage on its own."

Haraszty gathered herself, placing her hands in her lap. "If you do not consent to this marriage, Eamonn will do it."

Revelin's blood ran cold. Eamonn married to Zaide Romanza? That would be far worse than cat and mouse. It would be a hawk and vole, an ant and the boot which crushes it. If Revelin allowed such a union to take place, it would not be long before there was another funeral to plan.

"You cannot do that," he said.

"Can't I? I was the queen, the last I checked," Haraszty challenged. "Do not fight me on this. I will have one of my sons married to the queen of Feond—I will have it, Revelin, and nothing will alter this desire. I do not care which one it is, so I will allow you to make the decision. You will choose which son it will be."

That was not a choice at all, and his mother knew it. Revelin looked away again.

"I will marry her," he answered.

"Yes," Haraszty said, "you will."

The ensuing silence was strained. Revelin stared at the wall until he could take it no longer. He stood. "I should find Eamonn."

"One thing more, Revelin," Haraszty said, and he looked at her. "There's a ship leaving Odhran for Feond in the morning. Do be on it. Your bride is expecting you."

He forced himself to bow. "As you wish, your majesty."

He walked out of the room and sent the waiting attendants to take his place. He wandered through the somber corridors until he found his younger brother in the great hall, keeping the company of the younger noblemen and the elders' sons. The wine and whores were plentiful, but unlike any of Zoltano's gatherings, the tone was muted and solemn. Eamonn slouched in a chair away from the others, a bottle of wine in one hand and a half-naked girl on his lap.

"Come to join us?" Eamonn asked as Revelin approached.

"I think not," Revelin said.

The girl in Eamonn's lap slid off, but he caught her wrist and stopped her with a shake of his head. She settled back into place, keeping her eyes adverted and her hands plainly in Revelin's view.

"What does bring you here?" Eamonn asked.

Revelin glanced at the activity surrounding them. "Our lady mother believes you need looking after."

Eamonn smiled, his expression becoming unfriendly. "Does she? But I wasn't the one who fucked the queen of Lira."

Revelin stood frozen with shock. What had Zaide Romanza done? She had to have been the one to spread the tale; she was the only one, apart from Mireille herself, aware of what had happened that night. Who else had she told?

The girl looked at Revelin, curiosity written across her face, until Eamonn lightly slapped her thigh.

"No, you were not," Revelin choked out finally.

"Is there anything else?" his brother asked.

"No," Revelin said, walking away. "There is not."

"Enjoy Feond," Eamonn called after him.

His family had been given a tent to share, but James did not join them there. He saw them settled, then went in search of Ilya.

She sat on a log near the fire burning in the center of camp. When she saw him coming, she slid over to make room for him. He took the seat, leaning forward to rest his elbows on his knees.

"So," she said.

"So," he echoed. He focused on the ground, careful not to look at the fire. Every time he did, he could only see Cate disappearing from Enimode.

"I don't know what to do," Ilya confessed. "I don't know what we can do."

"Start with the soldiers," he said. "The ones who attacked Loreton and Rushwick and Hythe. What do we know about them?"

"Not enough," she responded. "We haven't even seen them. Nobody sees them until it's too late. They're bloody ghosts. Bloody, vicious ghosts."

James nodded. "What else?"

"The queen claims her sister, Sighle, is at their head. Faolan tells me that Sighle is little more than a child, but they believe that she somehow takes control of these men and forces them to do her will."

James ducked his head and rubbed the back of his neck. Another damned obstacle. More bloody magic. It never ended. "Why?" he asked. "What does she want?"

"She seems to want the queen, though we don't know why."

He straightened. "Let her have the queen, then. Maybe it will help."

"We can't do that."

"Why not? She's not doing us any good, is she?"

"Faolan would have us believe so."

"Faolan lies more often than not."

"Aye, but does he lie about this? The queen has done great things for us."

"Any of them recent?"

Ilya smiled. "You don't like her much, do you?"

"I don't like her at all," James said. "But if she could do *something* to end this quagmire—"

"Quagmire?"

James shrugged. "Cate said it."

Ilya's smile faded. "Are we in danger?"

"Aren't we always?"

"Are we in danger from her? Is Cate a danger to us?"

Was she? Everything in Enimode had escalated so quickly. One moment, she had been Cate, and the next...He didn't know who she was. What she was. Those eyes, so dark and cold—they hadn't belonged to her.

Had they?

Cate doesn't live here anymore.

"James?" Ilya prompted.

He looked at the fire and watched Cate melt into flame again and again. "She's not coming back."

"But you want her back, don't you?"

No. He wanted to know where she had gone, if she was safe. Had she found a way home? That would be best. He couldn't have her amongst them anymore. The threat was too great. To them—and her.

"What good has Cate done us?" Ilya asked. "She attacked the goddess and left us defenseless. What is that, if not evil?"

Evil. They used that word so often, as though it were an absolute. Hadn't Faolan committed some evil acts? Hadn't James himself done the same? Were any of them truly innocent?

"She brought us Emrys, and he has kept us alive," James said.

Should he hate her or pity her? Why didn't he already know? She had attacked Rhydwyn and Gair; she had attacked him. His back was a mottled array of bruises and his home a broken, abandoned structure. Hating her should have been easy, yet he continued to defend her. Against Ilya, the bloody queen, Dana. But despite his protest, part of him did recognize Dana's words as truth.

It would not end well with her.

But it wouldn't end well with any of them. War had that effect on a soul.

"And then she attacked the goddess and left us for dead. I believe one quashes the other," Ilya said. "What happened to her, James? How did she go from helping us to killing us?"

Will you tell me what they did to her? the queen had asked. *What did they do that made her...*

"Is anyone watching the palace?" James said.

Ilya sighed. "We've had people in the city since you left. They watch the palace day in and day out, but no one's ever seen the soldiers. Night and day, we're watching, James, and we haven't seen them once."

"What about *in* the palace? Do we have anyone there?"

"Not anymore."

"Then we need to change that."

"Faolan tells me that's not likely to happen."

"Why not?"

Ilya shrugged. "Something about a wall made of magic—like our defenses, I suppose. Faolan says Sighle has sealed us out of the palace."

The wall was still up, then. Perhaps it never had anything to do with Cate at all. James nodded. "We'll have to enlist the aid of someone who's already in there."

"Who would help us? Who's left?"

"The queen's guard," James said. "Willem."

"Why would he help us?"

"Because we have the queen, and he wants her back."

"They announced her death in the city. He likely believes she's dead."

"Then it's a good thing she's alive."

Ilya looked over her shoulder. "How will we make contact? We can't get into the palace, and we can't very well send the queen into Eluned."

James thought they would do exactly that, but he lacked the energy to argue with Ilya about it. He stifled a yawn. "I'll work it out."

"Well, do it in the morning," Ilya said. "You're about to fall asleep on your feet. Go do it lying down somewhere. We can make a plan later."

He didn't argue that, either, as he took his leave and wandered to the edge of camp. Sitting at the base of a tree, he dozed sporadically against its trunk, dreams plagued by visions of Cate vanishing and the queen beseeching him for answers. *Will you tell me what they did to her?*

Why did she ask? Why didn't she already know? James could recall Cate admitting to feeling her twin's pain. She bore a scar over her heart from a wound the queen had inflicted upon herself, and the queen had the same bloody bruise on her cheek that Cate did. Did she have the rest of it as well? The welts, the burns? Did she have the crown prince's name carved into her back?

What would he do if she did?

He stayed awake the remainder of the night, watching the sky when it began to lighten. As the camp stirred, he abandoned his solitude and went first to Hanah's tent to check on Rhydwyn. There, he found his grandmother working alongside the healer making bandages. They looked at him in unison, but only Sarai smiled.

"Your man's alive," Hanah said, her tone irritated. "He'll recover nicely."

What had her on edge? Had he done something? Was it Cate? Did Hanah blame him for it?

"I see you brought Dana back with you," Hanah said.

Was it that which bothered her so? "He brought himself back," James said. "How fares the queen? Have you seen her?"

"Why are you asking me that?"

"I just want to know if she's all right. Is she injured? Is she…" he hesitated. How could he pose the question without admitting his purpose?

"She's fine." Hanah jabbed a forceful finger in his direction. "She had better stay that way, too."

"I have no intention of putting the queen in danger," he lied, then looked at his grandmother. "All right?"

Sarai nodded. "Find your brother some useful employment, won't you? He's a bit lost."

That was hardly surprising. James nodded. Returning to the center of camp, he approached Eion, standing guard outside of the queen's tent.

"Is she alone?" James asked.

"Aye, Captain," Eion replied. "If you wish to speak to her, I'll—"

"Why do you have to do anything?" James asked. He laughed when he realized the answer. "Did Lucius tell you I wasn't to be left alone with her?"

Eion avoided looking at him. "Not that exactly, Captain, but..."

Bloody hell. James pushed onward and walked into the tent unannounced, Eion following. The queen, sitting at the table, looked at them in surprise. She had been crying; the stain of tears marred her face, but James focused on her bruise. Were there others? Were there scars?

"It's all right, Eion," she said, rising. "You may go."

"The bruise on your cheek," James said when they were alone. "How did you come by it? Who struck you?"

Her hand came up to touch the bruise, but she didn't speak.

"Why ask what happened to her?" he continued. "You feel each other's pain, don't you? I know she has felt yours."

"I was struck here first"—the queen gestured to her cheek—"but no one had laid a hand on me. Then came the cut under my chin. There was no mark, just blood, and..." She stopped, rubbing her thigh with one hand while covering her mouth with the other.

"What?" James pressed.

"I saw her. Bound, gagged, naked, beaten, bleeding," the queen said. "You won't believe me, but I tried to intervene. I tried to help, but I couldn't reach her; I couldn't stop it. I was pulled away—dragged away—and then I was in the forest, and she was gone. I saw nothing else; I felt nothing else." The queen looked at James. "But I do not believe her torture ended there."

It hadn't, but James said nothing about it. The queen nodded as though she had expected his silence.

"However, to answer your question—your first question," the queen said, "I believe whoever struck her, struck me."

"You don't...You don't know who took her? Who hurt her?" James asked. "You never saw them?"

The queen shook her head. "I suppose that is not yours to tell, either."

Would it be a betrayal to tell her? Would Cate want her twin to know? He couldn't imagine that she would.

"I thought so," the queen said when he neglected to offer a response. "Then perhaps you might consider explaining what drove you here so abruptly this morning when you cannot tolerate my presence."

"You lied," James said. "I wanted to know why."

"You only thought I lied, but I did not."

"Perhaps not this time."

The queen nodded. "You're quite protective of her."

"I brought her here. Am I not responsible for her?"

"Do you feel responsible for what she's done?"

"For what was done to her," he responded before he could stop himself.

The queen smiled. "You don't believe she's evil."

That word again. James shrugged. "I don't know what I believe."

She returned to her chair. "That wasn't a question."

He left before she could ask one and pushed out of the tent, stalking away. Dana immediately fell into step with him.

Dana glanced back at the queen's tent. "Is she all right?"

As smug and superior as ever. James sighed. "Why are you here?"

"I told you I wanted to stay. I want to help."

"Ilya wants you gone. She's not the only one, either."

"The queen requested I stay," Dana said, and James stopped to stare at him. "She says the goddess requires all her servants, myself included. I suppose a disgraced soldier is better than none at all."

James wasn't convinced that was true. "I suppose stranger things have happened."

"I'll do whatever you may want. I'll follow your every command. Ilya's, too."

"What if I command you to leave? What if Ilya commands it?"

Dana looked uncomfortable as he said, "I think the queen would outrank you both."

"You should tell that to Ilya. She could use a good laugh," James said, then shook his head and walked away. "If the queen wants you, the queen can have you. Let her issue your commands."

Dana fell back, but James continued on until he reached the edge of camp where Faolan, Lorcan, and Luisiúil waited. Faolan stood on a boulder, looking healthier than the day before. The same could not be said for the unicorn mare. Luisiúil had lost her sheen entirely. However the attack on Laorans had affected her, it was obvious that she was far from recovered.

"James," Faolan said, his tone flat.

"When will the walls be restored?" he asked.

"Soon enough."

"They must know," James said. "Omur, the queen's other bloody sister—all of them. They must know that we're weakened, that we're sitting here unprotected."

"Yes, but—"

"But what? We need protection."

"I realize that, but we need more time. Cate did this—"

"*You* did this," James interrupted. "You and your goddess. If you hadn't lied to her, *blindsided* her—"

"It would have happened in some other way," Faolan said. "This is who she is. This is what she does."

"And you're so certain because some ancient prophecy named her an agent of evil."

"She was not specifically named. Neither of the twins were, but—"

"But you're quick to condemn her, and you're never wrong."

"Seldom wrong," Faolan corrected. "And I'm not wrong about this."

James walked away. "We'll see."

"We already have," Faolan called after him. "It's time you accept that."

Was it? Should he give in and join the ranks of those who stood against her? Dana and Faolan and all the rest who had dismissed her—should he be one of them? Was he as blind as Dana claimed him to be?

Cate doesn't live here anymore.

He made his way to the training field where Ilya was putting people through their paces—Aaron included. The last time James had seen his brother with a sword, he had been easily disarmed, but watching him now showed his skill had much improved. Had Lucius been training him?

James considered joining them. It might feel good to hit something, but if that was what he wanted to do, he'd be better off finding a tree or a boulder to act as a sparring partner. Safer that way.

"Captain."

James glanced from one side to the other and found Iestyn standing on his right. "Still here, are you?"

Iestyn nodded. "No other place to go, so Mam said we'd stay. We've been helping."

"I'm certain you have." James gestured to the swordplay. "Have you been practicing what you were taught?"

"Aye, Captain."

"You don't need to call me that, Iestyn. My name is James."

"Aye, Captain," Iestyn said. "But Da taught us to call men by their title. He said names were given, but titles were earned. If a man had one, we were to use it. I know he's dead, but I—"

"It's all right. Call me whatever you want," James said. "Iestyn, when we came across your family on the road that day, from where had you come?"

"The city," the boy answered. "Da worked in the king's stables, and Mam in the laundry."

"You've been in the palace?"

"Aye."

"Why did you leave?"

"Da didn't think it was safe. He wanted to go somewhere else. The king," Iestyn said, looking at the ground, "Da was afraid of him."

James nodded. "He was right to be."

Iestyn glanced up. "Are you afraid of the king?"

"I was once."

"But you're not now?"

No, he had since learned that there were things much worse than Maddox Aelhaeran.

"Not anymore," James replied. He sighed and called Ilya's name. When she looked at him, he said, "We have to move the camp."

Chapter 40

Her accommodations lacked a decent view of the sunset, but Cate stood at the window every evening to mark the passing from day to night. It was a countdown, a starting pistol, heralding the next run of the gauntlet, and as soon as the sun had disappeared, she settled on the floor in front of the fire and stared into the flames.

The name of the game: survive the night.

She had been playing for…How long, now? Fingers grasped for the sliver of silk torn from the bottom of her slip. Seven knots. Seven sunrises. Seven sad, little trophies from seven sad, little triumphs.

The winner and still loser: Catherine Mireille Cole.

If that's who she was anymore. Cate with a C, Mireille with the easy evil grin, or someone else entirely. Who knew which one? Not her. Hell, she didn't even know if she was a who anymore. Maybe she was a what, an it. The last seemed most likely. That was a common theme among the commoners, after all—fear the monster in the corner room. Tread lightly, lest you be eaten.

If only their goddamn emotions had the same sense. Or just general decency. They were grieving; she got it—she *really* got it—but couldn't they at least do it somewhere she couldn't *feel* it?

And feel it she did—like everyone had been given their very own Cate-shaped Voodoo doll and a lifetime supply of pins. It was familiar, their grief—she had mourned the loss of Laura Cole once—but there was just so damn *much* of it.

Night was the worst. At night, they had nowhere to be, nothing to do, but indulge their sorrow. It burrowed into her bones, carving out a home, and the more it clawed, the deeper it cut. This was more, much more, than the mark, the scar James had told her she would carry for all her days. This was a gorge running straight to her soul—through her soul—or whatever was left of it. If any did remain, it had to be pretty tarnished by now. Black beyond repair.

As well it should be.

Theirs was a pain she had earned, a pain she deserved.

But how was she supposed to live like this?

The previous seven—seven, right? She checked the silk again. Yes, seven—nights had provided no solutions. Any attempts to block out the invasion—hands over her ears, pillows over her head, hiding beneath the bedding, crawling under the mattress—made no difference.

Neither had her own pain. Her fingernails couldn't scratch deep enough, the stones surrounding the fireplace weren't sharp enough, the nails holding up the tapestries wouldn't budge. Holding her hand in the fire only tickled. Not even lying on her back on the stone floor, or digging at the Black Wolf's wound helped. Nothing had been enough to puncture their angst.

If her own pain was the key to relief, she would need something more to get the job done—something that obviously wasn't in her room. But leaving…she couldn't do that. Not yet. Maybe not ever. As bad as it was inside, being out amongst those she had wronged would be so much worse.

So there she would stay.

The past few nights had been spent sitting in the corner, feeling everything they threw at her, and crying—just so much crying. Her eyes were raw and aching with the effort. Keeping them open hurt, but closing them wasn't much of an improvement.

She needed a reprieve. A distraction. Constant distraction. That's what the others did during the day—threw themselves into their work and occupied their mind—the mind. *Her* mind was the problem. Not her ears, not her heart, not whatever was lurking beneath her skin. Her mind.

Keep her mind occupied. She could do that. Try it, at least. Her brain was a big bag of useless information. She had no head for languages, but she could sing—if slightly off-key—the entire Stephen Sondheim songbook. Others, too. Probably not many people knew the goddess was a Broadway fan. Cate had grown up listening to them all. Over and over again. Never once had she thought something useful would come out of it.

It wouldn't be a perfect fix, but it could help. Take the edge off, if nothing else.

And it wasn't like she had any other ideas.

She lay on her side and began to sing softly—no, she could still hear them. Quiet wouldn't cut it. She would have to be louder—as her fingers tapped the beat against the stone floor. When the first song ended, she started the next and continued on until her throat was too parched and her voice was too hoarse. Then, she sang silently until Rhona interrupted.

"My lady?" she called. "Are you here?"

Cate lifted her head. Why was Rhona there? Was it morning already? She looked toward the window. Sunlight. Guess that made it official, then. Her winning streak continued.

She sat up. "Here. I'm over here. By the fire."

"You sound tired," Rhona said. "Did you sleep at all?"

No. No, she hadn't. She didn't seem to do that anymore. To *need* that anymore. But she couldn't tell that to Rhona. "I, um, I just"—her fingers fumbled to tie another knot—"I had a bad dream."

"I can brew a tea to help you sleep."

Somehow, Cate didn't think it would be that simple. She stood, silk clutched in her fist, and looked at Rhona waiting by the bed. "Don't worry about it. They don't happen that often."

"There is no shame in accepting aid, my lady," Rhona said.

"I'll keep that in mind," Cate replied, making her way to the healer. "We should get a move on. Zaide Romanza will be here soon. You know how she feels about being kept waiting."

Feond's queen had put in an appearance every morning following Rhona's ministrations, bringing a meal Cate wouldn't eat and asking how the revenge plans were coming along. Cate would decline to answer and stare at the dragon tapestry on the wall until Zaide Romanza got bored with the silence and left. It generally didn't take very long, leaving Cate free to spend the rest of her day trying to work out how to survive another night.

Maybe she could sing *and* dance.

Zaide Romanza arrived just after Rhona had gone. Cate had already assumed her normal position—sitting on the edge of the bed, leaning against the post—and was deep into her study of the two-headed dragon.

"I've had a chamber prepared for you," Zaide Romanza said.

Wait—what? Cate stopped leaning and looked at the other woman. Where was the question about revenge? Where was the breakfast tray?

"A chamber?" she asked.

"Yes," Zaide Romanza said. "One more fitting for someone of your status."

Her status. Cate could only imagine what Zaide Romanza meant by that. Actually, she didn't have to imagine anything. The mentally unstable, magically inclined, revenge-seeking freak would have a different chamber. The question was, would it be dungeon-side or penthouse?

"Where might this chamber be?" Cate asked.

Zaide Romanza smiled. "You'll find out," she said. "Come along."

Omur had said that to her, too, once—and look how *that* turned out—but Cate followed Zaide Romanza through the halls, once again making note of exits and guards. While the walk was not completely guard-free, there were far fewer men in Brollachan colors than Cate had expected to find. The number only decreased as they climbed one flight of stairs and then another. The penthouse, then. What would that be like? Champagne and caviar? A Rapunzel-style tower in which she would be trapped?

"Here we are," Zaide Romanza said, opening a set of doors and gesturing for Cate to go inside.

She did, warily, and surveyed the room. Glass doors leading onto a balcony, gorgeous furniture including a gigantic bed, tapestries, rugs, furs—oh shit.

She had seen this room before. Her eyes traveled back to the bed. She had huddled there, crying, until...*Shit.* The knotted silk slipped from her fingers.

"Something wrong?" Zaide Romanza asked.

Cate glanced back and forth between the bed and the balcony. "Everything's fine."

"Is the chamber not to your liking?"

"No, no—the room's great."

Just perfect for being mauled by hell hounds.

"If you're sure."

"I am."

Zaide Romanza nodded. "Allow me to order a bath for you, and—"

"No. Don't bother."

"Don't bother with a bath? I don't mean to be rude, but—"

"That's a first."

"—there are hogs with a more pleasant scent," the queen of Feond finished. "Might I suggest you take me up on my offer."

Cate looked at the balcony again. "Not today. Tomorrow, maybe, before Rhona comes."

"If that is what you want."

"It is."

"I'll leave you to get settled, then," Zaide Romanza said. She pointed to a wooden chest at the foot of the bed. "You shall find clothing in there. Should you require help dressing—"

"I won't."

"Suit yourself."

"I intend to."

As Zaide Romanza backed out of the room, Cate took hesitant steps toward the glass doors and the balcony onto which they led. The hell hounds had thrown themselves through those doors to get to her. But they weren't there yet, so she stepped outside.

A gorgeous vista spread out before her—a great silver lake, a dense green forest, and the snow-capped, jagged mountains behind them. But no hell hounds. Yet.

Cate went back inside and sat on the bed. At least it was quieter in this part of the palace; her head wasn't nearly as busy and full now. Fewer people had a reason to be in this wing, she supposed. Servants only came around when they were summoned, maybe. Whatever the reason, she could almost breathe normally. The peace and quiet might be worth running the risk of a hell hound encounter.

Except, no. It wasn't. Cate wrapped her arms protectively around her stomach. Nothing would be worth that.

She glanced at the wooden chest. It was probably full of intricate gowns that would require a small army to help her dress. If she hadn't been wearing the same damn thing for more than a week now, she wouldn't have bothered, but there was something appealing about clean clothes, and perhaps even that bath she had declined earlier. She'd need to call for servants, but that was all right. Maybe one of them could untangle the rats' nest that was her hair.

She laughed. How quickly had she grown accustomed to having servants help her bathe, or dress, or just brush her damn hair? In her other life, she'd been extremely well off—rich, some would say—and though she had grown up with Fiona as a caregiver, she had still been self-sufficient. Laura had in-sisted on—

No, not Laura. Laorans. Laura didn't exist.

Which meant her daughter didn't, either.

Sliding off the bed, Cate opened the chest. She pulled out a few items and examined them before breaking into a small, guarded smile. Apparently, an unexpected benefit of hiding out in Feond would be the clothes. The wardrobe was composed of soft, clean garments that bore no resemblance to a dress. Shirts, leather bodices and vests, breeches and leggings. She grinned, then promptly laughed again. How sad was it that the possibility of pants had become so damn exciting in her life?

But she slipped on a pair of leather breeches, reveling in their comfort and simple protection, then pulled on a shirt and hooded leather vest. To the trunk's left, two pairs of leather boots—one black, one brown—rested along-side silky, blue ballet-like flats. Cate ran her fingers over the flats before choosing a pair of boots. They, like everything else, fit perfectly.

Why was that? Had they taken her measurements while she was uncon-scious? How long had it all been there? Had Zaide Romanza been expecting Cate to show up on her doorstep one day? Had the plan always been for her to end up in this room?

Cate looked at the balcony doors. Something had planned for it. Some-thing had wanted her here.

Perhaps it was time to test that whole not-a-hostage theory.

Putting on a cloak she found in the trunk, she wandered through the castle, singing silently to herself and avoiding eye contact with anyone she passed, until she found an exit.

The courtyard was crowded, too many people with too many feelings, and Cate leaned against the castle wall and pulled the hood over her head.

Songs weren't cutting it; she needed something more. A wall, a shield, a Cate-sized hamster ball to protect her on all sides. Or, at the very least, a less populated area.

Where was the nearest exit?

Appraising the courtyard, she saw the stables first, then another building that was probably the soldiers' barracks. On the opposite side was a gap in the stone wall circling the palace. They hadn't replaced the gates yet. The hole was guarded by five men on the ground and another five standing on the wall walk. What would they do if she passed by? Stop her, or run for cover?

Only one way to find out.

She pushed off the wall and headed for the stables. Lowering her hood, she walked down the center aisle, evaluating her choices, as everyone with the ability to flee scattered out of her path. Her reputation preceded her, then. Good.

There were a number of beautiful stallions—because Zaide Romanza had a thing for those—but Cate bypassed them all, stopping at a stall housing a silver-gray mare. The horse met her at the door, thrusting her nose in Cate's direction.

"Are you searching for treats or evil?" she asked. "Because I don't have any of the former, and the jury's still out on the latter."

Except that the jury couldn't have been deliberating any longer. Not with everything she had done.

"Hey," she said, "let's go for a ride."

It didn't take long to find what she needed to saddle the mare. It took less time to leave the castle. The guards did absolutely nothing as she rode through the city and into the thick forest surrounding it.

It felt good to be riding. It felt good to be free of *people*. The farther she rode, the fewer people who were around, the clearer her mind became. Hell, maybe she would never go back. She'd just take her sweet little mare and ride away as far as she could. Feond was pretty enough; the view would never get old.

And there she was—planning to run away yet again. Maybe it was a sign. Maybe it was a cop-out. Maybe she needed to turn around and make a stand. Take that power everyone was so damn obsessed with and use it against them.

Bet none of them would see that coming.

But in order to do that—or anything else—she had to stop ignoring it and hoping it would go away. She had to learn exactly what she could do and how to control it. That was the important part—control. Considering people were dead because of her, it was well past time for that, but perhaps she could prevent it from happening again.

With that in mind, she rode deep into the forest until she found a clearing of grass and wildflowers. Dismounting, she left the mare to her own devices and moved into the center of the field, shaking out her arms.

How did she do this? Where did she begin? Was there a proper procedure for exploring one's magical powers, and if so—what was it?

Maybe she could review what she already had done, and go from there?

She laughed. Oh yes, wasn't she proud of each and every one of those things. That guy in Tanuba whose name she hadn't known, and Zoltano, whose mangled body she had left behind. Word of his untimely demise had gotten back to Mairéad, so someone had to have found him. Who had it been? The Black Wolf? Idwal Kai had said he received word from the palace. Had Revelin gone to Gweneria? If he had, had he done it for her or his brother?

Shit—why did it matter? The relevant thing was that she had killed Zoltano, too. Turned him into performance art, even.

Then there was Enimode, where everything had gone horribly, *horribly* wrong. Laorans—*Laura*—she had meant to do that. Not some small part of her, either, but all of her had wanted to tear the goddess limb from limb. Rhydwyn, Gair, *James*...that she hadn't wanted to do. That she had *needed* to do. Laorans was their goddess, the one none of them worshipped, but they wouldn't have just stood there and watched.

It had to be done, what she did.

But it didn't have to be done; it didn't, and she would never be able to convince herself otherwise. James wouldn't have agreed, either.

Was he all right? Physically, at least? What about the other two? They were only guilty of blindly following James wherever he went and in whatever he did. It wasn't, perhaps, the best way to live, but they didn't deserve to die because of it.

Not that she had intended to kill them. She had only meant to stop them, to get them out of her way, but that didn't mean she hadn't inadvertently killed them or someone else as part of her mission to murder a goddess. Look at what had happened in Feond. A fair few had died because they had been in the wrong place at the wrong time. Had she killed anyone in Enimode?

Cate, James had begged. *Don't.*

And she had looked at him, through him, and replied, *Cate doesn't live here anymore.*

Because she was an asshole incapable of saying anything normal—or of doing anything that wouldn't lead to another's agony and pain. She was a stupid, selfish bitch who was mean for the sake of being mean. A goddamn murderer who should be locked up in some dark dungeon miles upon miles under the ground.

James would concur with that assessment. How could he do anything else?

And then there was Haleine. Cate had hurt her as well. Frozen her like a casualty of an out-of-control game of freeze tag. Her twin was probably recovered by now; Zaide Romanza had been released from the same magic, so Haleine would have been, too. She'd be free to take her rightful place as Faolan's favorite girl—the savior of the entire goddamn world—and Cate could go back to being...

Nothing. She could go back to being nothing. Not that she had ever wanted to be anything other than normal. But normal was a ship that had long since sailed.

She collapsed in the grass and drew her knees to her chest. Folding her arms on top of them, she pressed her face into the crook of her elbow. Dropping her right hand, she formed a fist and hit the ground. It bounced, its only impact a slight dent in the grass that disappeared almost as soon as her hand came back up. Just what should have happened when one casually punched the ground. It was a solid object. To pass through it wasn't normal.

But she wasn't normal, either. Not by a long shot.

Besides, Zoltano had been solid, and she had found a way around that easily enough. Of course, when she had done that—when she had done *all* of it, she had been angry—not angry; no, angry was too insignificant a word. What would cover it, if not that? Enraged, incensed, riled? Irate. Furious. Livid. Outraged? No. None of those were right.

Wrathful.

That came closer.

Cate unclenched her hand and ran her fingers through the grass before pressing her palm into it. Still solid. Lessening the pressure, she imagined the spot beneath her palm was softer than the rest of the ground. It was mud. Quicksand. Not quicksand. Mud, though. That would work. It was mud, and her hand could slip through it, as though it were pudding. She rubbed the grass in a counterclockwise circle before lifting her hand entirely and driving her fingers toward the ground.

They slipped past the grass and into something with the consistency of tapioca. She grinned as she wiggled her fingers in the muck but pulled them out as soon as she felt the earth hardening. She looked at them, black with mud, and shook her hand until the bulk of the dirt had fallen away. The ground itself appeared untouched.

Interesting.

She continued her experiment—not encouraged by her success, just resigned to it. Pandora's Box had been opened, the evil had been released, and she was the one responsible for the mess. She had to contain it, control it, understand it.

Cate moved, twisted, and played with everything in sight. She levitated rocks and threw them with a flick of her wrist. Leaves changed to whatever color popped into her mind. A fox happened into the clearing, and she froze him. Closing her hand into a fist, he shrunk in size, becoming no larger than some tiny toy breed of dog. When she opened her hand, the fox returned to normal and bolted from the clearing as quickly as he could.

It was wrong that she could do this—just think something and have it happen—but there it was, all the evidence laid out before her. The more she did, the more she could do, too. One skill set only unlocked another. It was rapid fire, a runaway train with a faulty brake headed downhill.

How would she ever stop it?

When she decided she had had enough practice for one day, she gathered up her mare and rode back to the palace. Zaide Romanza waited in the bailey, and this time, when the queen asked about Cate's plans for revenge, Cate answered, "I'm working on it."

—◦◦◦—

The night was surprisingly emotion-free—another apparent perk of her new digs—and for the first time since her arrival in Feond, Cate felt almost normal when morning broke. She needed more than a knot in a now-lost strip of silk to commemorate the achievement, but settled for lounging in her luxurious new bed and watching the sunlight stream through the balcony doors.

What time of day had the devil dogs come for her? Not morning, she didn't think—at least not early morning. The light in her vision hadn't been as bright as this. But it had been daytime. A lunch date, perhaps, or afternoon tea with the hounds of hell. She could hardly wait.

Would today be the day they killed her? Would she care if it was?

A cloud of concern heralded the arrival of the servants. They entered the room, chattering like a gaggle of geese, talking over one another as they arranged the breakfast they had brought. Cate glanced in their direction. What was with all the damn noise? They hadn't uttered so much as a single syllable in her presence before, so to be privy to their conversation now was—

They weren't speaking. None of them. She propped herself up on her elbows and stared. Not one mouth was moving, yet...she could *hear* them.

Don't spill—Be careful with—Don't look—the tea—be careful—My son—at her—She killed—Don't spoil the—a bath—dead because of—the breakfast—my husband—Will she want—Don't make—of her—my son—careful, so careful—Be careful—

Don't look at her.

Don't.

Shit. Was she hearing thoughts? Like, specific thoughts? Was that even possible? As she was clearly listening to multiple running monologues that nobody was actually speaking out loud, she had to consider that it was. It was either that or Zaide Romanza had some truly exceptional ventriloquists in her service.

Cate sagged against the pillows, then reached for another to press over her face. Where would it end? What if it didn't end? What if there really weren't any limits to what she could do?

Self-asphyxiation was looking better and better all the damn time.

She whimpered into the pillow. Thoughts weren't as invasive as the emotions, but the combination of the two was entirely too much. Why were they still there? How long did it take to lay out a meal she wouldn't even eat?

Throwing the pillow aside, Cate rolled out of bed. The servants jumped and shied away, even though they were on the other side of the room. Their fear was an ice pick to her brain that stopped her in her tracks. One of the women stepped forward. This time, her mouth moved, but Cate couldn't hear anything over the others' terror.

She shook her head, pressing her hand against her temple. "Finish what you're doing and get out," she said. "Please."

Escaping onto the balcony, Cate leaned on the railing until the room—and her head—had cleared. Once it had, she sat with her back against the palace wall and ducked her head, covering it with her arms.

She could *hear* thoughts. She could hear *thoughts*. How could she make it stop?

"Still moping?" Zaide Romanza said.

How had she managed to sneak in undetected? What the hell good was this power if it couldn't recognize the approach of genuine threats? Cate lifted her head and indulged in an eye roll as she looked at the queen of Feond standing on her right. "Go away."

"We need to talk first."

"I doubt that," Cate said. "You know, I could throw you off this balcony using nothing but the powers of my mind."

"I could return the favor. What of it?"

"Just thought it should be said. In the interest of full disclosure and all that." Cate shrugged. "I'm mentally unstable and morally ambiguous. That combination might not work out so well for you."

"You may be wrong about that," Zaide Romanza said. "What did you do in the woods yesterday?"

"Became one with nature."

"Manipulated it, I think you mean."

"If you already knew the answer, why did you ask the question?"

"I was curious what you would tell me. You've been so secretive since your arrival. You weren't like this in Tanuba."

Funny what days of torture would do to a person. Cate's jaw clenched. "Well, I'm like this now," she said. "Is my attitude what you wanted to talk about?"

"No. I wanted to talk about the arrival of my betrothed. He'll be here any day now."

"Didn't I kill him?"

"You murdered my first intended," Zaide Romanza responded. "I thought you might care about the second, as he is the man with whom you most recently shared a bed."

Cate blinked. "You're marrying Revelin."

"Lovely to hear you didn't fuck anyone else."

"No need to be crude."

"No? It's what you seem to respond to."

Cate was tempted to respond with a crude hand gesture, but it was too easy. She looked away. "When's the big day?"

"That has yet to be determined, but I do hope it won't be a long engagement."

"You actually want to marry this brother."

"Yes, I admit that I have a weakness for Revelin. There's something about him—his innocence, his...gullibility that I find irresistible."

Innocent and gullible. That was a fair assessment. "Sounds like the foundation of a great relationship," Cate said. "Really, I wish you all the best."

"Jealous?"

"Oh yeah. Completely." Cate looked at Zaide Romanza again. "Are we done? Or are you planning to invite me to your bachelorette party?"

"Do you want him to know you are here?"

"No," Cate answered. "Don't tell him."

That encounter would be too awkward for words. Especially when they reached the part where Revelin would want to know who had mutilated his brother.

"As you wish," Zaide Romanza said. "I will keep him out of your path, but do take care not to place yourself in his."

"Considering I've done nothing but sit alone in a room, or sit alone in the woods, I don't think that will be a problem."

"We need to discuss that as well."

"Am I screwing up your hostile-takeover timetable?"

"If that means what I believe it does, then yes, you are," Zaide Romanza said. "You can't sit here forever."

"I think I probably can. We could find out, but when forever gets here, one of us is going to look really stupid."

"Yes, I suppose so," Zaide Romanza said. "Dine with me this night, and we shall discuss it."

"Oh, I wish I could, but I don't want to," Cate said. "Thanks for thinking of me, though. It means a lot."

"If you do not come willingly, I shall send guards to drag you there."

"I'll throw them off the balcony."

"I'll send more."

"I'll throw them, too. I'll throw everyone you send until there's a pile so high it blocks the sun," Cate said. "Oh, the fun we'll have."

"Then I'll gather innocents from the castle, the city surrounding it, the villages, or wherever else I can find them, and kill them one by one," Zaide Romanza countered. "The longer you make me wait, the more I'll kill."

Cate studied the queen of Feond. She still wasn't getting anything off the other woman, but there was no need to ask if she was serious. If Cate was morally ambiguous, Zaide Romanza was a black hole where morals went to die.

"Rhona has a family," Zaide Romanza continued casually. "Were you aware of that? Two little whelps—girls, I think, but their sex does not matter. Deny me, and I'll start with them."

Cate stood to confront the queen. "If you kill them—if you touch them— *any* of them—you'll never get anything from me but pain," she said. "Your pain, if that wasn't clear. I will make you feel pain, but that's the only thing I'll ever do for you."

"Well, when tonight gets here, one of us is going to look really stupid," Zaide Romanza said. She gestured inside. "But for now, Rhona is waiting."

And thus ended another session of idle and active threats. Cate glanced at the healer waiting bedside. "Did you send her to spy on me?"

"I sent her to care for you."

"And spy on me in the process?"

"My word, Mireille, how paranoid you are."

This coming from the woman who had just threatened to kill an unspecific number of innocents if Cate didn't have dinner with her.

"It's not paranoia if it's true," Cate said.

"I have, at my disposal, a great number of spies, each far more effective than a blind healer. If I did want to spy on you, do you truly believe I would use her instead of them?"

"Yes."

"You're incredibly tiresome."

"You're not the first to think so."

Cate returned inside and joined Rhona. As the healer murmured a greeting, Zaide Romanza breezed through the room on her way to the exit.

"Enjoy your day, Mireille," the queen said. "I look forward to tonight."

"What will happen tonight?" Rhona asked once the doors had closed.

"She wants me to have dinner with her."

"Will you?"

"Haven't decided yet. Do you have any children, Rhona?"

"Two daughters, my lady. They work in the kitchens mostly, but on occasion they deliver and fetch items on my behalf," Rhona said. "Have you any children?"

Cate laughed. "Thankfully, no. That would be a disaster on the order of the Hindenburg and Titanic combined."

Rhona nodded, choosing not to comment on Cate's gibberish. "Well then, lay down and let me do my work."

There were no words to properly describe how much Cate hated this part, but she pulled her shirt over her head and did as Rhona requested.

"It's an unusual pattern, these wounds," the healer said as she removed the bandages.

What was unusual about a psychopath carving his fucking name into your skin? Cate squeezed her eyes shut and buried her face in a pillow. She wasn't there anymore, and he couldn't hurt her again.

No one could.

"Could we maybe not talk about that?" she asked.

"As you wish, my lady."

"You could tell me about your daughters, though. If you wanted."

Her voice betrayed how close she was to crying. Rhona heard it, too, registering it in the same calm manner in which she seemed to do everything, and launched into a description of her children. Cate hated the pity, but hearing a normal person talk about normal things was neutralizing, and the tension gave way little by little—replaced with a glaring truth.

She couldn't repay Rhona's kindness by putting her kids in danger. Looked like Cate would be dining with the queen that night. Yay.

"Your back is healing nicely," Rhona said when she had finished.

Yeah, right. Cate retrieved a new shirt and vest combo from the clothing trunk and put them on. "If you say so."

"It is the truth," Rhona said. "I would not lie about that."

"What would you lie about?"

"I beg your pardon?"

Cate slid on her boots. "Nothing. Never mind."

Though Rhona was quiet as she packed away her things, Cate heard her concern and suspicion. She concentrated entirely on Rhona's mouth, so she wouldn't miss the question when it was asked.

"What is troubling you, my lady?"

"It's nothing. I'm fine."

Rhona did not believe her and required a moment to process her disappointment. "Well," she said then, "if you have no further need of me, I must take my leave."

"Where are you going?"

"Back to my surgery. I have some poultices and tinctures to prepare for her majesty's court."

"Could I...Can I go with you?"

"To my surgery?"

"Yes."

"To do what?"

Hide. Cate shrugged. "Watch you make poultices and tinctures?"

Befuddled, Rhona nodded. "If it pleases you, my lady."

What pleased her was how quiet Rhona's mind was. Composed. No big emotions, no all-encompassing thoughts to devour her whole. Being in the healer's presence was soothing, and that was something Cate sorely craved. They walked together through the halls, Rhona giving directions and Cate making nervous chatter until they arrived at the surgery.

It was much darker than Cate's room. There were no glass doors to allow in the maximum amount of natural light, just several smaller and much less effective rectangular windows. Multiple tables held the tools of Rhona's trade: a variety of bottles, bags, bowls, mortar and pestles, knives, spoons. It looked like chaos, but Rhona would surely be able to find anything a person needed without trouble.

As Rhona set to work, Cate drifted to the nearest window, over which hung a line of drying plants and herbs.

"I'm sorry if it seems like I'm stalking you," she said, examining the plants. She didn't recognize any of them. "And I'm sorry that I can't stop talking. It's a pretty shitty coping mechanism, I know."

"Perhaps you might tell me why it is you wanted to accompany me this morning."

"I've been considering a career as a healer."

"Have you?"

Cate turned from the window. "Sure. Why not? You all seem to be super feisty. I could be feisty."

Rhona concealed a smile. "What is the real reason?"

"I'm not doing anything," Cate confessed. "I'm sitting around, lying around, not doing anything. Again! I'm doing it again, and that's not what...That's not what I want. It's what I always seem to do, but it's never what I want."

Rhona reached for a bowl. "What do you want to be doing?"

Wasn't that just the $64,000 question. Cate leaned on a table. "I used to want to go home."

"What changed that?"

Everything. Once upon a time, home had been a townhouse in Boston, a cabin in Maine, but how could she live there, knowing the truth about Laura? That life had been nothing but lies, lies, and more lies. No, she couldn't go there.

She couldn't very well return to the rebellion, either. That bridge had been burned. Except 'burned' wasn't the right word, was it? No, what had happened in Enimode had been more like the bridge on the River Kwai. Smithereens. That's what her bridge was.

That left Mairéad, she supposed, where there was an estate with her name on it. Not *her* name, exactly, but it didn't matter because she had the right face. She could go there, take her place as lady of the manor, and close the gates. Keep everything and everyone out. Idwal Kai would kill himself to make sure she stayed hidden, if that was what she ordered him to do.

Cate sighed. "I don't know where that is anymore."

"Perhaps home is not a place," Rhona said. "Perhaps home could be a person or persons."

That didn't seem likely. At least not in Cate's case. Who'd make that list? Laura hadn't been real, Daniel and Fiona likely accomplices. Friends had been few and far between following Laura's faked death, and if anyone—*anyone*—had honestly cared about her on this side of the portal, she would have destroyed that alongside James's cottage.

"I don't know who that is, either." Cate stopped leaning and tilted her head to examine Rhona. "Are you a plant?"

Rhona's face crinkled with confusion. "Am I what?"

"Did Zaide Romanza send you to spy on me? Was your mission to ingratiate yourself to me, and—"

"My mission was to tend your wounds," Rhona said. "My mission was to restore you to health, my lady. That is all the queen has ever said to me where you were concerned."

Sounded like the truth. *Felt* like the truth. Still, an operative would be trained to sell lies. Perhaps she should pose a harder question.

"How many people did I kill?" Cate asked.

Rhona stopped working. "I don't know that you were to blame."

"I was. How many died?"

Rhona sighed but didn't answer the question. She maintained her tight grip on her emotions, keeping Cate in the dark.

"Zaide Romanza didn't want to tell me, either," she said.

"I do not hesitate because the queen has ordered me to," Rhona said. "I do so because I am afraid—"

"Of me?"

"Should I be?"

Yes. "You're full of impossible questions today, aren't you?"

"Is that truly such a mystery?"

Yes. "Depends on who you are, I guess," Cate said.

Rhona moved around the table, patting the surface until coming across a cloth-covered jar. She felt the leaves inside of it, then set it down, and reached for another. This time, she nodded, apparently satisfied, and held out its contents.

"Here," she said. "Fetch me some of this from the forest."

"You want me to leave the castle?"

"I was merely making a suggestion. You're the one wanting something to do."

"What if I don't come back?"

"You did yesterday."

"What if I leave the castle today and decide to run away?"

Rhona shrugged. "I'll send someone else to fetch me what I need."

"While armed guards are sent after me?"

"Are you under the impression that you're a prisoner, my lady?" Rhona asked. "I can assure you that you're not. Prisoners are not given rooms in the castle. Prisoners are chained in the dungeon."

"I've been a prisoner ever since I showed up in this universe," Cate said. "Though an extremely compelling argument could be made that I've been a prisoner from the moment I was born."

"Do you plan to spend much time feeling sorry for yourself?"

Cate folded her arms across her chest. "Maybe."

"Well, while you're at it, bring me some of these leaves from the forest."

Rhona shook the plant, and Cate took it from her hands. "Do you want the entire plant, or just the leaves?"

"The entire plant, if you please," Rhona said, now holding out a leather bag. "Roots and all."

Cate claimed the bag. "Fine."

Rhona smiled and went back to her work. "You'll find it near water. Streams, rivers, lakes—"

"I know what water is."

"Then why are you still here?"

Cate laughed as she walked out of the room. After saddling the same silver mare as the day before, she rode away from the castle and returned to the woods.

The plant grew near water, but Rhona hadn't said where that water could be found. There was a lake somewhere—Cate had seen it from the balcony—but where that lake was in relation to her current location, she didn't know. Should she try to find it, or should she look for another source?

But how did one go about finding water in a forest? Cate had no idea. The goddess had never put her adoptive daughter through any sort of survival training—they'd never even gone camping. That fact was much odder now that her fake mother had been revealed to be some kind of earth goddess. One would have expected an earth goddess to make sure her fake daughter was one with the earth. But Cate had always settled for being one *on* the earth.

What, then? She couldn't look for something green. Everything was green, so she'd have to look for mud. Or animal tracks, maybe. Those could lead to water, or from water. Everything needed water to survive, right?

Against all odds, and after what seemed like hours of pointless wandering, Cate discovered water in the form of a small stream. She dismounted and searched for Rhona's plant on either side of the bank.

"Don't wander too far, Silver," Cate said as they grew farther apart.

The brook widened as she made her way upstream, the current quickening, until it was a swiftly moving river. That was wrong—it didn't work like that. It wasn't the natural order of things. Streams became rivers, not the other way around. Why was this one different?

Hastening her pace, she traveled along the bank as though her life depended upon it. She couldn't explain it, her need to keep going, going, going, but it was as large as life itself.

As the grass and mud gave way to white rock, the river became a waterfall-fed pool. Cate crept as close to its base as she could, the spray saturating her from head to toe. Her focus switched from the water to the rock beneath her—smooth and white, accented by various shades of gray. She knelt to touch it, fingers first grazing the cool stone, then trailing into the unnaturally warm water.

"Mireille."

Her head snapped up at the wraithlike whisper. What was that? Who?

"Mireille."

Was it coming from the waterfall? Lifting her hand, Cate leaned to the right. There was something back there. A cave? She stayed in her crouch as she studied it.

"Come, Mireille."

Going any farther would be a mistake—even if there wasn't some creepy ghost voice calling her name. She had no way of knowing who or what was in that cave. Something scary could have decided to make its home there. Something with claws and teeth.

"Don't be afraid, Mireille."

Of course, she was pretty goddamn scary herself.

She eased behind the waterfall and into the cave. The water on the other side was calm and blue—a Caribbean blue that illuminated the darkness. It was even warmer than it had been on the other side, giving the space a sauna-like quality. The faint scent of sulfur hung in the air—something of which she should have been more wary—but she pushed on, a narrow path of smooth white stone guiding her.

How far down would the cave go? How far would she walk? How far *could* she walk? The path was tapering. Common sense would suggest it would end eventually or become so narrow that it would be impossible to continue on. She should stop, turn back. There was no telling what she would find—if anything—and she had left her ride roaming at will. If the mare became lost, it would be an awfully long walk back to the castle, and the survival of Rhona's daughters—and others—depended upon her return.

She stopped short, skidding on the wet stone. Nothing in that cave would be worth their lives.

"Mireille," the voice whispered. "Don't go, Mireille. I can help you. I can give you what you want."

That was doubtful. She didn't even know what she wanted. Not really.

"Sorry, Casper," she said. "I've got plans."

Carefully, she turned but slipped and fell. Her arms flailed as they searched for something to stop her descent, and her left arm came down hard, palm slicing open on a rock's sharp edge. A cry drowned as she plunged into the water. She stayed there, eyes open and marveling at how clear the water was. When her lungs began to burn, she pushed up and broke the water's surface, gasping for breath. Her palm throbbing and bleeding, she swam to the waterfall, then slithered onto the rocks and out of the cave.

Once again on dry land, Cate flopped onto her back to catch her breath and examine the gash running diagonally across her hand. Returning to the water, she washed out the wound, using her thumb to flush out any dirt. When it was as clean as it would get, she tore a strip from the bottom of her shirt and wrapped it around the injury, using her teeth to tie it off.

She looked at the sky. What had happened to all the daylight? How late was it? It had been fairly early in the day when she had left the palace; the sun hadn't even reached its peak yet. Granted, she was far from an expert in telling time without a clock of some kind, but the sun now appeared to be long past noon. Had she really spent that much time looking for water?

She glanced at the cave. Maybe it hadn't been the water. What the hell was that place?

That mystery would have to be unraveled later. If evening was nigh—which it certainly seemed to be—she didn't have time to waste. She had to find Silver and hightail it back to the castle.

There was no sign of the mare in the immediate area. Cate whistled to no avail, then set herself to trudging along the riverbank. Oh yes, letting her wander had been such a great idea.

Cate found the mare contently cropping grass near where she had left her. The mare lifted her head at her rider's approach but didn't bolt—a small favor for which Cate was grateful. Taking the reins in hand, she pulled herself into the saddle and steered them toward the palace.

She had a dinner to attend.

chapter 41

Without the aid of magic, moving the camp was a far more elaborate process. A location had been selected to offer the most natural protection, a source of water, and an easy route to Labhras. They couldn't lose their lifeline. Given their current status, the rebellion's relationship with Lord Emrys was more important than ever.

Slowly, carefully, they moved, doing so over the course of days to avoid the risk of attracting attention. James doubled and tripled the number of guards, but no sign of either of the queen's sisters or the king's men revealed itself.

There had been a lull like this before, where the fighting had stopped, and the rebellion had received an unexpected reprieve. It hadn't made sense to him then, and it made even less sense now. They were more vulnerable than ever—for what were their enemies waiting?

When the camp was once again settled, James was left with nothing to do but fall back into its routine. He resumed taking the morning watch, using a horse as his mount, as Bearach was unable to carry him. Gair accompanied him most mornings and rode with him one day to Eluned when their watch had ended.

They rode through the city gates amidst a group of travelers seeking entrance and broke off to make their way to Orla's. When the horses were settled in her stable, they left and walked toward the palace.

The last time James had stood before the wall, it had hummed, vibrating with potency. It made no noise now, but when he dragged his fingers along it, the pain was the same. Dropping his hand, he flexed his fingers and retreated to stand with Gair in the shelter of a shadowed alley. He leaned against a building and contemplated the walls he could see, as well as the one he couldn't.

One unsolvable problem after another. That's what his life had become.

"Cate threw you through one wall," he said. "Perhaps she could throw you through this one, too."

"We'd have to find her first."

James smiled. "Aye, that is the problem with that plan."

Why had he bothered coming here? What had he hoped would happen? A door would magically appear because Cate was no longer inside?

"Captain," Gair said, pointing toward the palace.

A smallish lad dressed in Aelhaeran colors darted through the gates, a wax-sealed piece of folded parchment clutched in his hand. James straightened as the lad disappeared from view. When the lad finally reappeared, he slipped unseen around the crowds and passed through the palace gates.

"Let's go," James said.

Back at camp, Iestyn was training with Ilya. Each held a dagger, and she taught him how to strike and block. They moved slowly through the exercise, stopping only when Ilya noticed their audience.

"You boys want a lesson, too?" she asked.

"I need to speak with Iestyn," James replied.

Dagger in hand, Ilya said, "Go on, then."

She was suspicious of his motives and was right to be. He was about to ask a boy to put himself in danger on the rebellion's behalf.

"Iestyn, do you know where the soldiers' barracks are on the palace grounds?" James asked.

"Aye."

"If I took you to Eluned, would you be able to find a soldier in the palace and give him a message from me?"

Ilya's arms fell to her sides, the hand holding the dagger readying the weapon as though she were considering using it on him. As an actual strike was unlikely, James focused on the boy, leaving Gair to watch Ilya.

Iestyn's fear was gradual. "Captain...the king."

"He won't realize you're there. You'll only go to the barracks for as long as it takes to find my friend"—James grimaced inwardly at having described Willem as such—"and give him my message. The king won't be anywhere near there, I promise you."

When the boy's fear was replaced with uncertainty, James added, "You don't have to do this, Iestyn. I can find another to carry my message."

Ilya nodded. "I think that would be—"

"I'll do it," Iestyn announced. "If Mam says I can."

"Aye," James said, "we'll talk to her."

"I'll go now," Iestyn said.

He handed his dagger to Ilya and scampered away.

"Are you going to talk to that lad's mother?" she demanded.

James sighed. "Ilya."

"What do you mean to say to her?" she continued. "Llian, I know you lost your husband at the king's soldiers' hands, but would you mind terribly if I sent your son into a nest of them?"

"Well, perhaps not that exactly," James said. "We need to get word to the queen's guard, and this is how we get it done. Iestyn can do this; he's the only one suited for it. He'll be all right. No one will notice him."

Ilya shook her head. "You don't know that. You can't guarantee he'll go unnoticed. You can't promise he'll be all right."

"Neither can you guarantee he'll be all right if he stays here," James argued. "We're in trouble, Ilya—all of us. We're vulnerable, exposed, and they could come for us any day now. They already should have, and you know it. We can't sit around and do nothing because the threat to one boy is too great."

"You'll get him killed."

"Aye, maybe."

"Llian will never agree."

"Make her agree," James said. "We're doing this, Ilya. We're taking this chance. Whether or not you approve."

"James—"

"No," he said. "If you want her permission to use her son, you had better get it because I won't wait."

Ilya nodded. "I'll talk to Llian. You convince the queen."

"I won't have to convince her of anything."

"When you tell her you're planning to sacrifice a child, you will."

"I'm not planning to do it," he returned. "Just willing."

"Well, that's much better, then, isn't it?" Ilya sighed and stepped closer to him. "Don't do what Dana did. Don't lose your way because of the girl."

"This has nothing to do with the bloody queen."

"I'm not talking about the queen," Ilya said. "We need you, James. Don't be reckless; don't get lost."

"Talk to Llian," James said, walking away.

Gair followed him to the queen's tent. Eion stood guard outside of it, and James pointed to him. Gair stopped at Eion's side, and James entered alone. The queen sat at the table, chatting with his grandmother. Apparently, they finally had acquired that second chair.

"What is it?" the queen asked.

"I must speak with you," he said. "Alone."

The queen nodded and touched Sarai's hand. "Will you please excuse us?"

Sarai rose, patting his arm as she passed. "Be nice."

"Your grandmother has been exceptionally kind to me," the queen said as Sarai departed.

"That's how you know you're not family."

The queen smiled. "I am certain that is not accurate," she said, gesturing to the empty chair. "Would you care to sit?"

At a table with her? He wouldn't.

"I understand I am not your preferred company," the queen said, "and I will not be insulted should you remain standing, but please, sit if you'd like. Depending on how long this discussion may take, sitting may be more comfortable."

"You care about my comfort?"

"Yes."

"Why?"

"Because you fight against my husband. Because you saved my life more than once. Because you brought my sister back. Because—"

"I lost her again."

"You did not lose her. Her departure was her choice, and I am certain she has had scant few of those extended to her. She left on her own. She'll return the same way."

James studied her, searching for Cate and not finding her. Odd that two people with the same face could look so different.

He sat. "Your lover doesn't want her to come back."

"Dana is no longer my lover. As you well know."

"Why do you want him to stay?"

"I understand that he has fallen from grace, that he has lost the favor of those he once led," the queen said. "I see it all around me here, in every face—yours included."

"He should stay because we are miserable?"

"He did lead once and did it well, I think. He rallied so many to his banner—the bold, the afraid, the reluctant. You, me," the queen said. "He brought us all together and kept us together."

"Abandoned us together?"

"We could stand on our own then, and we have," the queen said. "I saw him that night you came to my chambers. I saw the wounds he carried. He should have died."

"That has been said about him more than once."

"Yes, indeed, it was said just days ago in Enimode, was it not?"

"Aye, and days before that in Tanuba," James said. "What of it?"

"Have you ever considered that he was not here because he was never meant to be? Dana should have been dead more than a month ago. If he had died as he should have, we would have been forced to stand on our own anyway. Are we punishing him for that which he could not control?"

"That's bloody ridiculous. He didn't die. He walked away. He *chose* to walk away."

"Destiny and fate are oftentimes cruel mistresses."

"I don't believe in destiny or fate."

"Sometimes, I believe, that does not matter."

James shook his head. "You want to pardon him. You want *us* to pardon him."

"Does he not deserve the chance to redeem himself? Do we all not deserve that?"

"I don't know."

"What about Mireille—Cate?" the queen asked. "Is she worthy of such consideration?"

Was she? James shook his head again, agitated. "It's not the same, him and her. It's different, what they did; it's—"

"It's not what you came here to talk about."

"No," he said, unable to properly disguise his relief, "it isn't."

"What did you wish to discuss?"

James looked at the table and reached out to flatten the curling edge of a map. "We need eyes in the palace, someone who can tell us what the bloody hell is happening behind those walls," he said, and the queen nearly bolted from her seat. He sighed. "Oh, sit down—I don't mean you. You wouldn't do any good. From what I understand, you can't pass through your sister's defenses anyway."

"Can you?"

"No."

"Then what do you propose?"

"I thought we might ask your guard."

"Willem?"

"Aye."

"I asked him to protect my sons."

"He's still aware of what's happening in the palace. Perhaps he can tell us about this invisible, roaming band of soldiers razing villages and leaving messages."

"We already know who is responsible for that."

"Aye, and now we need to find out where she might send them next."

"He will not be willing to help you."

"That's why you'll ask him."

The queen nodded. "How?"

"We'll bring you to a safe place within the city walls, and send word to Willem to meet us there."

"Will he come if you ask him?"

"I believe he will, if I mention you," James said. "He's already tracked us down once to inquire after you. He'll come a second time."

"They announced that I was dead. He would have heard that."

James shrugged. "We'll tell him the truth. If he thinks there's a possibility that you're alive, he'll come."

"He will not think that I am...her?"

"No. Willem can tell the difference."

"How will you get word to him?"

"There's a lad in camp familiar with the palace grounds," James said. "He should be able to get inside, find Willem, and deliver our message. The rest will be in Willem's hands."

"A lad? A child, you mean."

"Aye."

"You'll put him in danger."

"There's some risk, aye," James conceded, "but if we had another way to do this, we would have done it already."

The queen looked away, unhappy and unwilling to say so. Finally, she nodded. "When?"

"A day or two," James answered. "I need to...There are things to be done first."

"Very well."

Hanah entered the tent then, and they looked at her as she bowed her head in greeting. James stood to leave. Hanah made a disapproving noise in her throat and stopped him.

"Don't you ever bow before your queen?" she demanded.

"She doesn't want my bow." James looked at the queen. "Do you?"

The queen shook her head. "I would not expect it, nor would I ask for it. Indeed, I consider it a great victory that you have stopping referring to me as a whore."

"Have I?" James backed away. "My mistake."

Before turning around, he thought there might have been the hint of a smile on the queen's face. Perhaps there was something of her sister in her yet.

———⟊⟊⟊———

It was dark by the time Cate returned to the palace. For the sake of Rhona and her daughters, she hoped Zaide Romanza was a fan of eating late. Cate slid from the saddle and trapped an escaping groom to give him possession of the mare.

She went next to Rhona's surgery, holding her breath until she found the healer alive and at work, crushing something with a mortar and pestle. Two young girls worked at her side. The daughters, she assumed. They were all accounted for, then. Good.

"I decided not to run away after all," she announced. "At least not tonight."

The girls stared, but their mother didn't even raise her head.

"The guards will be delighted," Rhona said.

Cate crossed the room, clothes squishing as she walked. Frowning, Rhona felt her way toward Cate, who caught Rhona's searching hands and set them on her waist.

Rhona patted Cate's clothing. "Did you go swimming?"

"Not intentionally." Cate placed Rhona's hand on her injured palm. "Have any spare bandages?"

"What did you do?"

"Fell."

"Girls, go help in the kitchens," Rhona ordered, and they obeyed without hesitation. To Cate, she said, "Did you clean it out?"

"I stuck it in a river. Does that count?"

Rhona didn't respond as she took Cate's uninjured hand and led her back to the table at which she had been working. Cate sat on a stool at its side and watched the healer unwrap her makeshift bandage and prod the gash.

"I'm sorry if I'm hurting you," Rhona said.

"You're not hurting me. Don't worry about that."

Rhona released Cate's hand. "There's a bottle of wine on the table. Fetch it for me, please."

Cate looked the table over, locating the wine at the other end. Holding out her good hand, she waved it toward herself. Magic carried the bottle straight to her, and she placed it into Rhona's waiting fingers.

"How did you..." The healer's voice faded. Realization took its place. "You have magic."

"You didn't know?"

Fear pushed realization out of the way. "I suspected, but..."

"You don't have to be afraid of me, Rhona. I won't hurt you."

"I am not afraid of you, my lady. Just afraid *for* you."

"You don't have to worry about that, either," Cate said. Her irritation was stoked when Rhona's fear morphed into sadness and pity. She sighed. "Can we move this along? I have somewhere I need to be."

"Yes, my lady." Rhona removed the cork from the bottle. "This will hurt."

No, it wouldn't. Twisting to avoid the scent, Cate was silent as Rhona poured the deep red liquid over her palm. Her mind registered the minor discomfort—but that's all it was. There was no hurt to be found.

"Did you bring me my plants?" Rhona asked as she continued to work.

"Got sidetracked, and then wet, so no," Cate said. "But I'll go again tomorrow."

Rhona wrapped a linen strip around the wound. "There's no need. I can easily ask another."

Cate looked at her. "And take away my quest? You've given me purpose—I've got to see it through."

"Well, if you must." Rhona finished with the bandage. "Remove your shirt now. Those dressings on your back will have to be replaced."

"I'll let you take them off, but I don't have time for anything else right now," Cate said, looking over her shoulder. Had the girls even made it to the kitchens? Why had she allowed them to leave? "Zaide Romanza's waiting. If I don't show up soon, a massive fit will be forthcoming. Trust me when I tell you that you do not want that. Not tonight."

Rhona considered this and nodded again. "The air will be good for the wounds. If needed, I'll replace the bandages in the morning."

"Yeah, great," Cate said, pulling off her shirt. "Sounds like a plan."

Rhona worked efficiently, and soon Cate was off and running back to her bedroom to change into dry clothing. Afterward, servants directed her to the great hall, and Cate walked in to find Zaide Romanza sitting upon her throne, eating from a tray set at her side. A man stood to the queen's left, his hands behind his back. Together, they watched Cate approach.

"Sit, won't you?" Zaide Romanza gestured to the chair on her right. The tray of food—meats, cheeses, and fruits—sat between them.

"I think I'll stand," Cate said.

Zaide Romanza shrugged and waved to the man. "This is Torin. He'll fetch you anything you like."

Cate looked at Torin, gradually becoming aware of the lust he bore for Zaide Romanza. She closed her eyes as it worked its way through her. Boy, this was a fun power.

"Something wrong?" Zaide Romanza asked.

Cate shook her head and opened her eyes. "Is there anything other than wine?"

"Of course. Ale, whiskey—"

"Whiskey works."

Drinking herself to death hadn't worked in Tanuba, but she was much more desperate now. Maybe she'd be able to commit fully this time.

She sat and watched Torin fetch her drink. "Have you been screwing him long?"

"Screwing?"

"Having sex with."

Zaide Romanza looked at Torin as he returned, and Cate felt another rush of desire—this time Zaide Romanza's. Cate gripped the arms of the chair, hoping that it would pass before Torin reached her. Though her body was currently aching to lick every inch of his naked flesh, she didn't actually want to do that.

"Oh," Zaide Romanza said. "How did you know?"

Admitting the truth seemed like a dumb idea. If Zaide Romanza hadn't already figured it out, surely Cate wasn't meant to spell it out for her. It hadn't proven true yet, but a secret kept could possibly turn into a weapon later, right?

Cate shrugged. "Lucky guess."

Torin handed Cate a cup. "My lady."

She managed not to grope him as she took the cup, and he returned to his position at his playmate's side. Slowly, the fervor drained out, and Cate's body settled. Sampling the whiskey, she felt herself mellow further.

"What happened to your hand?" Zaide Romanza said, her fingers brushing the bandage.

"Cut it."

"Did Rhona tend it?"

"Are you going to kill her daughters?"

Zaide Romanza leaned back. "Not tonight. You are here, after all, and I am a woman of my word."

Yeah, right. Cate sipped more whiskey, and a warmth that was not lust spread through her. "Yes, Rhona tended my hand."

"Good. Now tell me what happened in the forest today."

"How did you know—?"

"I do have sentries, and those sentries have eyes," Zaide Romanza said. "They watched you ride into the forest and watched you ride out again. What did you do there?"

"Went sightseeing."

"What did you see?"

What was Zaide Romanza hoping—or expecting—to hear? Had Cate triggered something in the cave? Some sort of magical silent alarm? If so, what was in that cave that interested the queen of Feond?

"Trees, more trees, some ferns, and then some trees," Cate said. "I wasn't really there to see the sights. I just wandered around aimlessly, thinking."

"About what?"

Should she answer? Zaide Romanza had been the most instructive when it came to magic. She sincerely wanted Cate to unlock the secrets behind her potential, so while her views on the harmful nature of magic were skewed in a different direction than Cate's, the basic information could be worthwhile.

"Mostly I'm trying to understand what I can do. I want to be able to control it—out of necessity, more than anything else, but I want control. It's just..." Cate sighed. "Everything's emotion-based, right? It seems that the stronger the emotion, the stronger the magic. In my case, it's been the strongest when my life's on the line. Anger or fear is behind the power, so what am I supposed to do? Be angry and afraid all the time?"

"Aren't you already?"

Pretty much, yeah. Cate shrugged. "Sometimes, I'm just sad," she said. "But it's different—the big things, I mean. Yes, I'm angry and afraid all the time, but what I did to Zoltano, to Laorans...It was different. *I* was different."

"You are different," Zaide Romanza said. "You are clinging to this notion that you are human, that you are as ordinary as every other soul in this castle, but you're not. This has been said many times before, but you are not ordinary. You are not human. When you stop warring with yourself over this simple truth—that you are different and are meant to be so—I believe you will find yourself no longer angry nor afraid. You will find yourself at peace."

Cate drank more whiskey. She wasn't human. That thought wasn't new; like Zaide Romanza had said, this was not the first time that theory had been suggested. But if she wasn't human, what was she?

The doors to the great hall opened then, slamming loudly against the walls. Startled by the sudden noise, Cate dropped her cup. Liquid sloshed and spilled over her breeches, and she rocketed out of the chair, shaking whiskey from her fingertips.

"Your majesty!"

Cate froze as she recognized the deep male voice. Revelin. Fuck, it was Revelin. What the hell was he doing here?

"Revelin," Zaide Romanza said, depositing her goblet onto the tray. "I wasn't expecting you so soon. Good trip?"

Revelin stalked across the room. "I have come to announce my arrival. That is what you..."

As his voice trailed off, Cate lifted her head to meet his eyes. Shock and confusion flooded her veins. Shit, she hated this power.

Zaide Romanza stood. "Revelin, may I present Mireille Coileáin, Darian Coileáin's lost daughter."

"What are you doing here?" Revelin asked.

A plethora of snarky responses invaded her brain, but Cate uttered none of them.

"Oh, I forgot," Zaide Romanza said. "You two are already acquainted, aren't you? How foolish of me to forget."

She hadn't forgotten; she had orchestrated this entire encounter. Revelin knew it, too, and he had no more powers than a clown making balloon animals. Zaide Romanza leaned over the tray, examining her choices. She selected a grape and popped it into her mouth, chewing lazily.

"I sense there's some tension between you," she said after swallowing. "Shall I give you a moment alone?"

"Yes," Revelin said.

"No." Cate broke off the staring contest with Revelin to look at Zaide Romanza. "A woman of your word, huh?"

Before Zaide Romanza could respond, Cate froze them both where they stood. Torin stumbled back, gaping at his mistress in wide-eyed shock. She had forgotten about him.

Torin glanced at her quickly, reluctantly, and flattened himself against the wall when he saw her watching. Cate grinned, stepped off the dais, and walked out of the room. Let him spread the tales of what she had done. The more people who were afraid of her, the better.

Leaving the palace, she used magic to prevent anyone from seeing her enter the stable. The same magic got her past the two grooms working the night shift, and she let it lapse as she eased into Silver's stall. The mare checked over the new arrival before turning back to her hay. Cate sat in the corner that would offer the most protection from anyone looking in on the mare and let her head drop back against the wall.

Would Zaide Romanza have freed herself yet? What about Revelin? What would happen to him? Fionnbar had been released when she had touched him. If she hadn't, would he ever have stopped living the still life, or would it have just worn off eventually? Maybe Revelin would be stuck like that until she went back for him. If that were the case, he'd be waiting for the next *forever* because she wasn't going back there for anything.

Which did beg the question of where she was going to go. As glamorous as hiding out in a stall was, it was a stop gap at best—and a shitty one at that.

Running away was damn appealing, but the problem with that plan—besides the part where she was planning to run away yet again—was that her list of safe harbors was dwindling fast. She'd have to find somewhere new.

Not that it mattered where she went. Zaide Romanza would know where she had gone, or would at least have the capability of finding out. She wouldn't leave Cate alone. Neither would Omur. Neither would anyone else. None of them would ever leave her alone. She'd told James that—or something like that—back in Gweneria, and it was still true. It would never end because they would never leave her alone.

Not unless she made them.

That's what it always came back to, wasn't it? She could pretend all she wanted, hide all she wanted, but there was no other way for it to end. If this was going to stop—if she wanted to get clear of it—she would have to make it happen. Burn them all to the goddamn ground.

Starting with the queen of Feond herself. Zaide Romanza was already there—shouldn't Cate take advantage of that?

She should. No use in making a second trip. She'd kill Zaide Romanza, then move on to Omur, Maddox, and even the Black Wolf, if she happened to cross paths with him. She'd cleanse the whole damn world of assholes. And when that was done, she would...Well, she'd do whatever the hell she wanted, wouldn't she?

It was probably too soon to be sure, but she suspected copious and reckless self-medication was in her future. *Was* her future.

Yes, she had killed before—Zoltano, the guard, the untold number here in Feond—but none of that had been planned, premeditated. What she did now would be. There wouldn't be a shield of any kind to hide behind. It would be murder, plain and simple. Who did that? What kind of sick lunatic did something like that?

Besides her.

She laughed silently and slid onto her side. Her body shook with noiseless tears. They had won, hadn't they? Goddammit, they had won. This was what they had wanted the entire time. An indiscriminate killing machine—that's what they wanted her to be, and that's what they were getting because here she was—lying on a bed of straw, making plans to go on a murder spree.

Fuck.

"Mireille?"

She jumped, unaware that anyone had entered, and looked at Revelin standing in front of her. How long had he been there? As she scrambled to sit up, his emotions slammed into her like a freight train, shoving her back against the wall.

"What are you doing here?" he asked.

She didn't answer—couldn't answer—as his onslaught of turmoil was too busy clogging up every part of her. Pushing it back out again took effort, leaving her exhausted to the point where sleep would be inevitable. There always was a silver lining.

"Have you nothing to say?" Revelin pressed. "What are you doing in Feond?"

She gritted her teeth and slapped on her game face. "Hiding mostly. What are you doing here? Well, I guess I know what you're doing here, and who—congratulations on that, by the way. It's not every day you agree to get hitched to someone whose very existence you despise."

"I had no choice."

Cate stood. "Sure you did."

"Had I not agreed to marry Zaide Romanza, it would have fallen to Eamonn to do. I had to spare him."

"Still a choice."

She walked out of the stall, brushing hay from her clothing. A pair of grooms gawked, and she snarled at them to get out. They bolted into the daylight, and Cate stopped short. Daylight. Sunlight. That meant...Had she lost time again? Terrific. At least she had survived another night. Kudos to her.

"I thought you were dead," Revelin said.

She nodded. "I get that a lot."

Grabbing her shoulder, he spun her around. "What happened to you?"

She laughed. "You're kidding, right?"

"Did my brother take you?"

"Yes."

"Against your will?"

Cate looked at him in disdain. "Yeah."

"Why?"

"He was a sick bastard."

"Who never laid hands upon you, nor ever showed interest in doing so."

"On Haleine, maybe. But not me. He laid hands on me."

"What did he do?"

Time to go. She turned, but Revelin blocked her path. Her hands became fists that she hid behind her back. He didn't know what she could do, and despite his current line of questioning, he didn't deserve to find out. Not like this.

"Did he hurt you?" Revelin asked.

Cate stepped forward, hands falling to her sides. "Of course he hurt me. That's what he does—did. He hurt me, and he probably hurt an untold number of women before me. He was an absolute horror of a human being, and you and everyone else let it happen," she said, body shaking and power churning. She forced it down, determined to maintain some semblance of control. "That, in my humble opinion, doesn't make you much better than him. Might even make you worse.

"Yet, you seem to think you're entitled to know what happened—that you're allowed to *ask*—and you're not," she said. "I have zero interest in helping you play out whatever emotions you think you're required to show."

"I do not—"

"You'll say you're sorry; you'll say if you had only known. You'll say that if you had known, you would have done something. You would have stopped him. If you had known, you would have killed him for it," she said. "But the problem is that you did know. You knew all along what he was like, what he was capable of doing, and you did nothing. You don't get to ask what happened. You don't get to ask what he did to me.

"But what the hell—I'm feeling generous, so let's play Show and Tell." Her fists became hands again, fingers working to remove her vest. "Where would you like me to begin? Should I tell you how he intended to rape me and then rape me again? About how he would have done just that if he had been able to get it up that first night? About how, even with everything he did do, I somehow have to be *grateful* that he didn't do worse? Or maybe you'd like to hear how he amused himself instead. Is that what you want? Do you want to hear about the beatings? The cutting? Burning? Flaying? Should I tell you how he suspended me from the ceiling and—"

"Stop."

"No."

Dropping the vest on the floor, she pulled off her shirt and let it fall. Nothing to hide behind now, for either of them. Revelin stared, mind mercifully blank with sheer shock as his eyes roamed over her exposed torso.

When his gaze turned to the floor, she snapped, "No, look at me, dammit. Look. You wanted to know, so look." She spun around to show him her back. "Take a good, hard look at what your brother's hands did."

His shock turned to revulsion, twisting her stomach. Resisting a sudden need to vomit, she turned around.

"Perhaps, your highness, you would rather discuss choice," she said. "My choice was to surrender to the torture and the pain—let him rape me, let him kill me—or fight back. So that's what I did: I fought back, and I killed him. You've probably been blaming Dana all this time, but it was me. I killed him. I *murdered* your brother with my own two hands, and I couldn't have enjoyed it more."

Revelin stared. She couldn't get a proper read on him; his emotions were a cannonball in his gut.

"Why would you tell such a lie?" he choked out.

"Why would you think it was a lie?"

"I saw his body. I saw what was done to him, and—"

"And what? You think he deserved better?"

"How could *you* have done *that*?"

Cate held up her hands and wiggled her fingers. "With these. Slid right through his skin like butter. Soft butter—the kind that's been left out for a while. It wasn't hard."

"Stop," Revelin begged. "Please, stop."

"And warm, too. It was—*he* was warm. Not that I'm surprised—98.6 and all—but that man, who was so hard and cold, turned out to be quite the opposite on the inside. Warm and soft and...fragile." Cate looked at Revelin. "You've never had your hands inside anyone before, have you? Too bad—it's a real rush."

Revelin continued to stare, now horrified with her actions. "How did you...How *could* you?"

"I assume you're asking how it was physically possible for me to do that, and not why I would do such a horrendous thing, because if it is the latter, I can show you my back again. You didn't vomit the first time, but maybe the second viewing will be the charm. I could explain in excruciating detail how excruciating it is to have a psychopath strip pieces of your skin right off your body. Would that help?"

Revelin nearly vomited then. He needed a moment to compose himself. Cate took advantage of the lull to find her shirt.

"Yes," he said when he was able. "How?"

Cate smiled. "Sorry, tough guy. Share time's over."

He had to go. He wouldn't want to; he'd want to stick around and ask a million more questions, but she wouldn't be able to hold on through it all. Her façade was fading fast. It wouldn't be long before she imploded—perhaps literally—and that was something no one should witness.

"That was your cue to leave," she announced. "In case you were curious."

"Mireille, I—"

"Have nothing more to say," she finished. "Which works out because neither do I. You know where the door is. Use it."

He didn't move, just looked at her with eyes so sad, it made her hurt. She shook her head.

"I guess I'll use it." She walked past him, and this time he let her go.

"I am sorry," he said.

She faced him and threw her arms out to her sides. "Well, hallelujah!" she exclaimed, affecting the accent of a Southern Baptist preacher. "I'm healed! Praise the Lord!"

Dropping her arms, Cate stalked out of the stable. No longer caring who saw her, or who was in the way, she stormed across the courtyard and through the palace, returning to the solitude of her borrowed chamber. She almost made it to the bed before dissolving into tears.

She huddled on the floor, leaning against the bed for support, and cried, cursing herself with each sob. She was so damn sick of crying. What the hell was wrong with her body that she couldn't control that? The earth's elements were her bitch, and people's minds were her personal playground, but she couldn't command her own tear ducts. Why?

She vomited, falling forward to void the contents of her stomach. The second and third times she retched, it was only bile because there hadn't been much in her stomach since she'd boarded the damn ship to Tanuba.

How long had it been? How many days had passed? How many more goddamn days would she have to do this, live like this? How much longer would she have to *live*?

No. Focus. She had to focus on the here and now. Revelin was coming. Revelin would come. The man had no idea how to read social cues, even when they were loud and shouted in his face. Even if it was the last thing she wanted, he would come anyway. Once he finished processing the horror-scape that was her body—once he finished throwing up because of it—he'd be at her doors, asking if she was all right when she was so obviously not. Zaide Romanza would probably accompany him, too, eager to watch firsthand as Cate unraveled beyond repair.

She couldn't be there when they came.

But where would she go?

Not having an immediate answer only increased her misery, and she pressed her face into the bedding to muffle the sound. She couldn't do this—just sit there and cry. It was weak and pathetic, and they were coming. She had to go. Where didn't matter. It just had to be *away*. From here, from them, from everyone. She could take Silver and ride off into the forest and just keep going, going, going until she found a place. The edge of the goddamn world, maybe, or somewhere even farther. If there were two worlds, there could be more. One of them was bound to be safe. One of them had to be—

A snarl splintered her thoughts, and she swallowed her sobs upon hearing it. What was that? Who was—?

Oh no. Déjà vu washing over her, Cate pulled back and looked at the bed, her clothing, and the tapestries on the wall. Oh *no*. Touching her tear-stained cheeks, she turned toward the balcony and the two hell hounds waiting there.

"Shit," she breathed.

She barely had enough time to cover her head with her arms before the creatures burst through the glass. As soon as the shards stopped flying, she stood and looked at the doors. Running away wasn't an option. Not now. If the devil dogs followed her through the palace, all sorts of people would die—and not the ones who deserved it. It never worked out that way. She'd have to stay. Keep their focus on her. Shouldn't be hard—she was the one they wanted.

Two hell beasts against one. The odds weren't great, but they could have been worse.

"All right, boys," she said, moving away from the bed, "if you want me, come and get me."

Almost as if they had been waiting for that invitation, they charged, snarling, snapping, and salivating.

She threw out both hands. "Stop!"

They didn't. She glanced at her palms, shook them out, and tried a second time with no better results. The neruals tackled her, and she shrieked.

She went down hard, bones snapping beneath their weight. Their mouths roamed her skin, but only one sharp tooth punctured her flesh, running the length of her left arm. She groaned. What were they doing? Why weren't they ripping her to shreds? Why were they *sniffing* her? That hadn't been in the vision.

Fine. Whatever. Let them sniff her all they wanted. If they were busy doing that, they weren't killing her, or anyone else, and that gave her time to do something.

She gathered power deep in her stomach, a bright, white ball growing in size and intensity. As it reached its boiling point, she curled in—that one tooth now working its way across her thigh—and set it free.

The release hurled the devil dogs to opposite ends of the room, while Cate flew straight up, leaving her body behind. She hung oddly in the air for a few seconds—a ghost once again—before landing back in her own skin. She struggled to sit up, to stand, and by the time she managed it, the neruals were approaching again. The beast closest to her snarled.

She bared her teeth. "Bring it, Cujo."

He came at her, while the second lagged behind. Tag-teaming it. How thoughtful. Cate held out her hand toward the fire, smiling when it formed in the center of her palm. She stood her ground, waiting to see the whites of his yellow eyes before throwing the flames at them.

When contact was made, he yelped the way a man would, the way a canine would, and dropped to the floor, howling and covering his burning face. His hand-paw hybrid clawed at his eyes.

Cate stepped closer, fascinated by his pain. It had been so easy to cause. All that fear—and for what?

The second neural hit her then, its teeth sinking into her shoulder. She screamed as they slammed into the floor. Her head struck stone, and the world went black but came rushing back when Cujo sunk his claws into her stomach and his teeth into her leg. Her cry was strangled by pain and became a giddy laugh as her body twitched and bled.

So *that's* what the fear was for.

Her right hand flopped on the floor, stretching and searching for any kind of weapon. They had shattered the doors; there was glass everywhere. Could she use that? Or maybe a chunk of the frame, if one were jagged enough. Would there be a piece large enough to make a difference? Did she even have any other freaking options?

A slice of pain down her palm told her she had found what she needed. Dragging the glass shard to her, Cate maneuvered it into a useable position, embracing the hurt it caused. It was all right. That pain would set her free.

Or so she hoped.

She brought the shard up and stabbed wildly at the nerual closest to her. With a sharp, ear-piercing howl, it pulled away. She'd struck something valuable. Encouraged, Cate pushed up and lashed out at the other beast, slashing the glass across his singed muzzle. That did nothing, so she stabbed at what was left of his eyes until he had backed off as well.

Guzzling air, she stayed on the floor but dragged herself back until she came against a wall. The neruals huddled together in front of the balcony. They communicated with yips and growls, but it was no language she could understand. She watched them with heavy eyes growing heavier.

What a horrible time to fall asleep.

The glass dagger slipped from her fingers, and she looked at the floor to find it, but could only see blood pooling there. So much blood. Had it all come from her? Why couldn't she feel it? Shouldn't she feel it? Shouldn't it *hurt*?

The neruals stalked toward her. They didn't rush this time—why bother?—one on two legs, the one she had blinded on four. How could she end this? Could it even be done, or was her only way out to let them finish what they had started? Not that it would take long. Not when her blood was abandoning ship at such a rapid rate.

What would happen when she ran out?

Haleine had told her once that blood didn't matter, that an oceanful could be spilt, and she would only wake up, alive and whole.

Would that apply to Cate, too?

She'd find out soon enough. That black void was roaring back and showed no signs of abating. The last time she had seen it was before she had turned the tables on Zoltano. But he had been a man—just a man—and Cujo and his friend were about as far away from that as a creature could get. She didn't know how to stop them, plain and simple.

One more push. She could do one more push, couldn't she? As long as there was a single drop of blood in her veins, she'd have power—wasn't that what Omur had said? There had to be at least one drop still in there somewhere.

Using every last ounce of strength she could muster, Cate shoved against the air, carrying the motion as far as her ruined body would stretch. The neruals, caught in the riptide, were swept away. Pulled from the room and over the balcony's edge, they disappeared from view. Cate slid to the floor, rolled onto her stomach, and didn't move again.

How long would it take to die?

Her eyes closed, incapable of doing anything else, as her heart and brain slowed to a crawl. Not long, then. That was good. No reason to drag it out.

She continued to float away, an errant feather in a lazy breeze. There was no white light, not for her, but it was all right. She was more comfortable in the dark anyway.

Hands flipped her body over, the sudden infusion of pain pulling her back down. Voices—frantic and freaked—filled the air, and Cate opened her eyes to see him hovering over her. The man. Zaide Romanza's pet. What was his name?

He squatted at her side, his disgust at her condition making her ill. Twisting around, he yelled at some unseen person to fetch the queen. He shouldn't have bothered. Zaide Romanza would have known that the neruals were in her castle. She would have known that Cate was facing off against them. If Zaide Romanza wasn't already there, it was because she didn't want to be.

"Torin," Cate said when his name came to her.

He looked at her, and her arm snaked out, her hand catching him by the throat.

"Hope you don't mind," she said, coaxing the life out of him and into her, "but I need to take this."

CHAPTER 42

Haleine woke up screaming.

She doubled over, pain infusing every inch of her body, and the cot on which she had been sleeping tipped over, spilling her onto the ground. Brighid rushed into the tent and knelt at her side. Haleine lay paralyzed as blood seeped from her body.

"Your majesty?" Brighid said.

"I-I am dying," Haleine gasped. "The blood—it is everywhere."

Brighid pulled away, shouting for Hanah. Haleine lost sight of her, but the tent was soon aglow with soft light. Brighid returned, lantern in hand. Setting it at her side, she ran her hands quickly over Haleine's limbs.

"There's no blood, your majesty," the girl said. "There's nothing."

That wasn't right. Haleine could feel it, the hole where her stomach used to be. She pressed her hand against it, finding her body solid and her fingers free of blood.

Hanah burst in. "What is it? What's happened?"

"I am fine," Haleine said, sitting up. "They should not have disturbed you. It was naught but a dream. It was..." She swallowed as she realized what she had seen. "It was Mireille."

No one in the tent reacted to the name. They knew her as Cate, Haleine supposed.

She looked at Hanah. "I need to talk to James."

Hanah turned to Brighid. "Find him, please."

As Brighid darted from the tent, Hanah dropped to her knees to perform her own examination. Haleine found it futile to argue with the healer and submitted to the inspection.

"There isn't a mark on you," Hanah said. "Not one scratch."

Haleine placed her hand on her stomach and rubbed gently. The pain was abating, but she would not easily forget its grip. Her twin had been terribly injured; her pain wouldn't fade so quickly.

"It felt so real," Haleine said. "I thought I was dying."

"You're not," Hanah soothed. "You're fine."

"Yes, I am," Haleine said. "I fear Cate is not."

Hanah sat back, unsure of how to respond. Uncertain that Mireille was worthy of her concern.

"I had a dream, Hanah, a terrible dream," Haleine said. "My sister may be dying—she may be dead—and I do not know—"

"Like you said, your majesty, it was naught but a dream."

Haleine shook her head. "It wasn't. Not for her."

Anger ushered James inside the tent, Dana sliding in after him. Neither man was armed, and both were dressed in trousers and linen shirts. They must have been sleeping when the summons came. Dana stepped into the corner opposite from her, while James stood before her, his irritation plain. He did not like having been sent for by her. Haleine rose, Hanah offering aid.

"I know where Mireille is," Haleine said.

His agitation took on a new focus. "How?"

"I saw it, the same way I knew what happened in Tanuba."

James nodded. "Where?"

"Feond. In Eacha Donn," Haleine said. "The palace, I believe. There were...dragon tapestries on the walls—that's her crest. Zaide Romanza's."

"She's with Zaide Romanza?" Dana asked.

Haleine looked at James as she answered, "Yes."

"Hardly worth sending for me in the dead of night," James said.

"She's hurt," Haleine offered. "She's been gravely wounded."

"How?" Dana asked.

Haleine looked at him. "There were...creatures of some kind, and Mireille was torn apart by them. I felt it all." She turned to James. "You know that happens. You know what one of us experiences, the other feels."

James said nothing.

"We should—we should go there. To Feond," Haleine continued. "We should...rescue her, save her."

"You don't know that she needs saving," Dana said.

"She's in Feond, Dana. No one goes there deliberately," Haleine argued.

"Omur and Maddox did," he replied.

"She did," James said.

"We don't know that," Haleine insisted. "We don't."

"You said yourself that leaving was her choice," James said. "Whatever's happening, she's on her own. We have other things with which to concern ourselves. Cate can't be one of them. Not anymore."

"You can't mean it," Haleine said.

James shrugged. "It doesn't matter what we do. It would take too long to travel to Feond," he said. "If she's hurt as badly as you claim—"

"She is." Haleine put her hand over her stomach.

"Then we'd never get there in time to make a difference. Even if Faolan would be willing to help us get there as quickly as possible—which he wouldn't—it wouldn't matter," James concluded. "We'd have no way to get into the palace. There would only be more walls we couldn't hope to breach."

"We'll have to try," Haleine said. "She needs—"

"She doesn't need anything from us—certainly not our help," James said. "She has never needed our help, nor wanted it, for that matter."

Haleine's shoulders sagged. "You don't know—"

"I don't know what? Tell me," he demanded, stepping toward her. "Tell me what it is about that girl that I don't already know."

Dana came out of the corner, and Hanah slid closer to her. James ignored them, his focus fixed on Haleine.

"You call her your sister, but you don't know the first bloody thing about her," James said. "You've barely spoken to her. You haven't argued with her, you haven't fought with her, or at her side. You haven't sat up all night with her, night after night, watching her cry and knowing there's not one damn thing you can do to help her. You haven't done any of that, but I have. I've done all of it, and still you mean to tell me there's something I don't know?"

"James, we must do something," Haleine pleaded. "If we don't help her—"

"She can take care of herself!" James shouted.

He advanced, fuming and reckless. Dana placed himself in front of Haleine and shoved James back.

"None of this is the queen's fault," Dana said, his voice barely more than a growl. "Act like it."

James stared. The air thickened with the possibility of a physical altercation, and Hanah eased around Haleine. James caught the movement and retreated to the back of the tent, his hands forming fists at his sides. No one spoke, nor moved, as they waited to see what he would do next. After some time, his hands opened and his shoulders slumped. Dana nodded then and returned to the corner.

When James turned around, his eyes on the ground, Haleine said, "We need to do something."

"No, we don't," he responded. "Not for her."

Though his words were quite convincing to the others—she could feel Dana's overwhelming support—Haleine could tell there was a lack of conviction behind them. James was only saying what he thought he should. Mireille had wronged his family, his people, his cause; she had done so much damage, surely he was supposed to hate her. But he didn't. He wanted to—it would be easier—and part of him did, but the whole of him did not.

He had already gone to great lengths for Mireille once, and every conversation they had had since only reinforced Haleine's belief. Indeed, he knew her sister well—he had come to care for her so deeply—and he hated himself for it.

"I will agree to this. I will consent to ignore what I have seen and will allow my sister to fend for herself, but you should know something, James ap Seoras," she said. "I shall not always be inclined to indulge your tantrums where she is involved."

He offered her a hostile smile. "Why should I concern myself with what you're inclined to do?"

"Because not only am I your queen, but you also happen to be in love with my sister," Haleine said, irritated by his continued lapse of common courtesy. "You will be best served if you at least attempt to be civil toward me."

"In love with your sister?" James said, incredulous. "The hell I am."

"The hell you aren't," Haleine replied calmly. "Please stop embarrassing yourself. You are fooling no one."

"I don't know what you're talking about."

"Then you are the only one."

A noise sounding much like laughter came from Dana's corner. When both she and James looked at him, he coughed and pounded his chest.

"Sorry," he said. "Didn't mean to interrupt."

Neither Haleine nor James were amused. Together, they glared at him, united in that, if nothing else. James broke first and looked at her.

"We're going to Eluned in the morning to talk to your guard," he said as he walked out.

Haleine nodded. "I will be ready."

———◦◦◦———

Dana followed James out of the tent, giving Haleine one last glance to assure himself that she was nothing more than annoyed. James disappeared into the darkness, but Dana did not go after him. He imagined that, for the moment at least, neither of them had anything to say to the other.

Locating a lantern, he went in search of Faolan. There were questions that only the pegasus could answer, and Dana dare not delay any longer in seeking them. Faolan wouldn't want to speak with him; they had barely spoken since that day in Enimode when Dana had been banished. Even now, the rift continued. Faolan was not alone in his disdain, either.

It all led to one hard truth: Dana was not welcomed in the rebel camp.

He kept his head bowed as he made his way through it, but he remained aware of the stares coming at him from every direction. It was night, and most people slept, but there were still enough awake to stare. And whisper. Some he could hear clearly, others not, but they were all the same. He didn't belong there; he wasn't wanted.

There had been a time when the opposite was true—a time when he couldn't walk through the camp without being waylaid by something requiring his attention. But it would seem that time had ended.

James had told him this would happen—that it had happened. Dana had walked out on them when he should have been at their head.

They'll not follow you anymore, James had said. *Don't you understand that?*

He did understand. He did not know how to change it, nor if he could. But perhaps saving the life of their new leader would be a start.

Faolan stood with Lorcan and Luisiúil at the edge of camp. All three witnessed his arrival, suggesting they had anticipated his appearance.

"We need to talk about Cate," he said.

"What about her?" Faolan asked.

"She'll destroy them both—Haleine and James," Dana said, "and I won't allow her to have either one."

"That's ambitious of you."

"Faolan!"

"What would you like me to do?"

"Tell me what happened in Tanuba. What happened in Enimode?" Dana said. "What is James not telling us?"

"What makes you think there's something he's not telling you?"

"I know him, and I bloody well know you, too," Dana said. "There's something you're not telling us."

"Oh, there's a lot I'm not telling you."

"Then tell me!" Dana exclaimed. "I'm fighting your goddamn war here—the least you could do is be forthcoming about what you know."

"Do you really want to talk about doing the least you could do?"

"I want to talk about Cate," Dana said. "What happened to her? One moment she's helping us, and the next she's tearing us apart, limb by limb. What happened to her? What *is* happening to her?"

Faolan looked away.

"I only want to keep them alive—as do you," Dana said. "If you know something that could help me do that, please...just tell me."

Faolan and Luisiúil looked at one another. What were they saying? Would Luisiúil side with Dana or the pegasus?

"What is it?" Dana asked.

"Faolan," Lorcan said, "you should not—"

Luisiúil's piercing whinny interrupted the warning. Dana stepped back as the mare pawed the ground and bolted away.

"Tell him," Lorcan said, following Luisiúil into the darkness.

"Tell me what?" Dana asked.

Faolan looked at him. "I think the magic is too much for Cate. I think it may be controlling her more than she is controlling it."

"Can she control it?"

"She can. She has, but not consistently so," Faolan said. "If she doesn't learn how to master it completely, she'll be lost."

"Dead?"

"So to speak," Faolan said. "She wouldn't be Cate anymore. She'd be that...thing who destroyed the cottage. Who nearly destroyed Laorans. Dangerous, soulless—"

"Soulless?"

"Yes."

"What do we do? What can we do?" Dana asked. "Can she be saved, or is it too late?"

"I don't know. Controlling the magic has to be her choice, and if she chooses not..." Faolan looked away again. "If she chooses not, our deaths would only be a matter of time."

"Could you force the choice?"

"That," Faolan said, looking back, "is what landed us in this particular predicament to begin with. Two sides, forcing her to choose."

Dana nodded. "All right, then, what if she didn't have to learn to control it? What if we took the choice away?"

"How would you—?"

"Can't you...suppress her magic somehow? Bind it, strip it, or...I don't know what it would be called, but can't you? You, Luisiúil"—Dana waved in the direction the mare had gone—"Laorans—all of you together—can't you do something?"

"It may be possible, but again, I don't know. We've never had to do anything like this before."

"Then you have to find out," Dana said. "You have to find out because we can't be unprotected. We can't leave Haleine unprotected, and I'm not saying that because I love her."

"I know."

"Then do it," Dana said. "Find a way to bind Cate's powers before it's too late."

"In order to do this, I'll have to leave camp and, very possibly, this world," Faolan said. "And it could still all be for naught."

"It won't be. It can't be."

"It may be," Faolan insisted. "There's a reason why this war is happening now—why the dark gods waited centuries for them. Cate and Haleine—this world has never seen anything like them before. A way to suppress her magic may not exist."

That would leave them with only one option, then. Dana looked at the ground. "If it is too late, will Laorans help us stop her?"

"Of course she will."

"No, Faolan. Will Laorans help us kill her?"

The pegasus hesitated. "You want to kill Cate."

"If we have to. *Only* if we have to." Dana shrugged. "If we can."

"She can be killed."

"I ran Omur through with a sword," Dana said. "Haleine put a dagger in her heart, yet they didn't die."

"It won't be easy, but it can be done," Faolan said. "No one is immortal."

"Omur has lived for—how many did you say? Seven hundred years?"

"Longer."

"Longer," Dana echoed. "Yet, you claim no one is immortal?"

"No one is," Faolan said. "Omur could be killed if the right weapon was used."

"What is the right weapon?" Dana asked, but Faolan offered no answer. "Something else we need to know, then."

"Yes."

"Haleine also said…" Dana swallowed. "She said that what one of them experiences, the other feels."

"Yes," Faolan said. "I've witnessed it from each of them. I watched Haleine bleed from a cut Cate received, and Cate carries a scar over her heart from—"

"Aye," Dana interrupted. He didn't need to hear more. "We have to sever the bond between the sisters. I don't want Haleine to feel us killing her twin."

"Dana—"

"We may have to kill her, Faolan. You know I'm right."

"Bond or no bond, Haleine will feel her sister's death."

"But she doesn't have to suffer needlessly. Aye, she will feel Cate's death, but she doesn't need to feel my sword running through her sister's body. I can spare her that. I owe her that. *We* owe her that."

"If you kill Cate, Haleine will never forgive you."

Dana nodded. He was far too aware of that already. "If I have to kill Cate, I will. If it will save this miserable world, I will do it, even though *my* world will be destroyed," he said. "Find me the weapon, Faolan, and I'll use it."

"I can try. That's all I can promise you," Faolan said. "I don't know how long it might take, or how long I might be gone."

"We'll manage until you return."

"Keep Haleine safe."

Dana turned back to camp. "Always."

—⟪⟫—

When dawn came, Lucius insisted upon accompanying Haleine to Eluned. His concern for her safety had increased greatly, leading her to conclude that Hanah must have told him what had transpired the night before. He meant to protect her from any danger—including that which might have come from his own leader. James understood the reasons behind Lucius's presence as well but merely shook his head and said, "As you will."

Unicorns carried them to Eluned, Haleine riding double with Lucius, while the boy they would send into the belly of the beast sat with James. Dana rode alone at the rear, silent and sullen.

They left the unicorns in the trees near the hidden passage. James and Dana made for the wall as Lucius held back both Haleine and the boy. Once the door had been opened, and Dana indicated that it was safe, they proceeded. Haleine led the way, determined not to allow Sighle's jibes and whispers to affect her.

"Lucius, you have the queen. Iestyn, you're with me," James said upon reaching the end of the passage. "Meet at the tavern. Dana, make sure we can get in."

James put his hand on the boy's shoulder and guided him into the city, walking toward the palace. Dana nodded at Lucius before raising his hood and leaving them as well. Haleine lifted the hood of her own cloak and walked with Lucius out of their protected alley.

She only knew when they had reached the tavern when she saw Dana leaning against a wall. He didn't move except to open a door, and Lucius ushered her inside a lantern-lit stable. James and the boy had not yet arrived.

"There is a stool, your majesty, if you would care to sit," Lucius said.

She glanced at it. "What did Hanah tell you about last night?"

"Your majesty?"

"It is not a secret," she said. "I seek only to understand your intentions."

"My intention is to keep you safe."

"From whom?" Haleine asked. "What did Hanah tell you?"

"She told me you accused James of being in love with Cate," he said after a moment's hesitation.

"It was not an accusation," Haleine replied. "Just a rather accurate observation and a gentle warning."

"A warning?"

His voice betrayed his concern, and Haleine sighed. "You don't have to protect me from James, Lucius," she said. "He is not a threat. Not to me."

"Your majesty, I—"

"Yes, he is angry, and he bears me no love, but he won't harm me. As much as he would like to deny it, James ap Seoras is a good man, and that will win out in the end." Haleine sat upon the stool and laid her hands in her lap. "But you should not tell him I believe so. He would only take it for a challenge."

Lucius smiled. "Aye, your majesty."

The door opened again, and James stalked in with the boy at his side and Dana on his heels. He looked around. "Are we all here?"

"We are," Lucius said.

James turned to the boy. "Iestyn? Are you ready?"

The boy nodded. "Aye, Captain."

"Tell me again what you're meant to say."

The boy stumbled through his memorized message, and James pressed him to do it again. *Go to the barracks, and find the queen's guard. Tell him the queen awaits him at the tavern.* Over and over, the boy recited it.

"Good," James said when he was satisfied. "You'll remember the way?"

"Aye, Captain."

James led the boy outside, returning alone.

"Should the message not have been written down?" Haleine asked. "Something written in my hand, something tangible, that Willem could see with his own eyes?"

"No," James said, not looking at her. "If anyone stops Iestyn for any reason, there's nothing to find. If he's caught with a letter, he's guilty for sure."

"What if he forgets?"

"He won't forget."

"What if they torture him?"

"They won't torture him."

Haleine nodded. She hoped he was right. "Iestyn's quite young. How did he come to join the rebellion?"

James leaned against a stall door and looked at her. "His father died, attempting to protect your twin from a band of soldiers hunting for you. He thought she was you, and the soldiers killed him because of it. We took in the rest of his family—Iestyn, his mother and brother. They've been with us ever since."

"It was good of you to take them in," Haleine said.

"What else would we have done?"

She nodded. "What else indeed."

They fell into silence. There was no telling for how long the boy would be gone. There was no guarantee he would ever come back. James believed that no harm could come to Iestyn, but Haleine could clearly recall the day her husband had murdered a boy right in front of her. She saw his face, his fear. Oh, how he had looked at her, his terrified eyes pleading for help, and she had not saved him. Maddox had put a blade through his heart, and Haleine had watched him die.

Now she had allowed another boy to cross the king's path. If Maddox found him, if Maddox discovered whom the boy served, Iestyn would not come back.

Tears formed behind her eyes, but she did not want to let them out. James would see; he would point to them, mock them and her, and claim she was not fit to serve, that she was too weak for any purpose. She did not wish to argue with him, not again. Not when she could offer no evidence to the contrary. Carefully, she raised her hand to wipe the tears away.

"Your majesty?" Lucius murmured. "Are you all right?"

Of course he had seen. Haleine quickly cleared her eyes and stole a glance at James to see if he had taken notice.

"I'm fine, Lucius," she said. "Thank you for your concern."

"If you require—"

"I require nothing. Thank you."

More silence followed. It was not broken until a woman entered from an inside door. She walked toward them; the three men glanced at her but did nothing. She was someone they knew, then.

She greeted Lucius by name and gave Haleine nothing more than a passing glance on her way to speak with James. Dana joined their conversation, but Haleine could not hear what was said.

"Who is she?" she asked.

"Her name is Orla," Lucius answered. "She is the alewife here and a friend to the rebellion."

"She knows them well," Haleine said as Orla kissed Dana's cheek.

Lucius nodded. "They were acquainted before the war began. As I understand it, her history with Dana is particularly long."

Haleine watched Dana interact with the alewife. She had never seen him be anything to anyone else before. He had only ever been her lover. Even when they had first met, even within the confines of his rebellion, he had never been anything else. How had he viewed her?

When Orla departed, Dana and James took turns standing outside, while Haleine and Lucius did not move at all. How long would they stay here? It had been early in the day when they had arrived, but there was no telling whether Willem would be in the soldiers' barracks, or when he might return. He had been tasked with guarding her sons, and he would not shirk that responsibility.

Finally, the door opened again, and the boy came through. Her relief was swift but was quickly curbed by Willem's subsequent entrance. She stood. The motion caught his attention, and he looked at her. His eyes remained hard and cold as he examined her from afar.

"It's your bloody queen," James said, passing him.

"Willem," she said.

Eyes softening, he crossed the space between them, dropped to his knees in front of her, and bowed his head. "Your majesty."

His voice was raw, the mark of a man trying too hard to avoid showing emotion. She waved Lucius away and reached beneath Willem's chin to raise his head.

"Thank you for coming here today," she said.

"I needed to know, your majesty, whether the boy had spoken true."

She nodded. "My sons, are they…"

Willem's eyes darted in Dana's direction. "They are well. I've not failed you this."

"You've never failed me."

"I beg your pardon, your majesty, but it is believed that you are a dead traitor," Willem said. "I failed you."

"Not while my sons live. Any failure belongs to me," Haleine said.

She looked at James, once again leaning against a stall door. His arms were folded across his chest, and his fingers tapped erratically against his ribs, suggesting he was not nearly as patient as he would appear. When he saw her glance, he gestured that she should move along.

"We have brought you here today to ask for your aid," she said to Willem.

"Anything, your majesty."

"There is a detachment of my husband's army roaming the country and destroying villages, but none have ever seen them," Haleine said. "The rebellion seeks to stop them, but we cannot track them, nor do we know where they intend to strike next. Do you know anything about them that could help us?"

Willem stood and looked at the three men his king considered enemies. "The man who rides at their head is called Garbhan. The king named him captain before his departure for Tanuba. Garbhan is hungry for prestige and seeks to gain it by destroying you."

"Have you ever known where they were going?" James asked.

Willem shook his head. "I only hear what they have done."

"If they were to plan another attack, could you find out?"

"Normally, I have a trusted man in every regiment that leaves the palace walls," Willem said, "and Garbhan knows this. He has never included any of mine amongst his soldiers. It is well known that my allegiance is tied to the queen, and—"

"You know nothing," James finished, "and you will continue to know nothing."

"In this matter, yes, that is likely," Willem said. "Garbhan is very careful, much more so than our previous captain. He does not wish for me to be aware of anything he does."

James pushed off the stall and stalked to the end of the stable where Dana and Iestyn stood. He said something to Dana, too softly to be heard, but the frustration was evident. Willem watched them carefully.

"The man you set to protect Sighle," Haleine said, recalling her guard's attention. "Is he still with her?"

"Yes, your majesty. Bronagh serves her as well."

"Bronagh," Haleine said. "What does she believe? About me?"

"She believes you are dead. Your...twin told us that lie."

Haleine nodded. "It will be best that she continue to do so. For a time at least."

"I will tell her nothing, your majesty," Willem said. "Why do you ask about the man who guards your sister?"

"I want to know that she is watched; I want to know what she does," Haleine said. "Has she ever left the palace?"

"No, your majesty," Willem said. "She barely leaves her chambers, except to..."

"What?" Haleine prompted.

"Lady Sighle visits your sons nearly every day."

His tone caused Haleine to sink back onto the stool. "Has she done anything to harm them?"

"No, your majesty, she never so much as touches them, but there is something that I..."

"You don't trust her," Haleine supplied, and Willem nodded. "You are right not to. Is there no way to prevent her visits?"

"Not without your command, I think," Willem said.

And perhaps not even then. Haleine nodded. "Thank you for coming, Willem. We won't keep you any longer."

Willem looked at Dana and James before kneeling in front of her. "Do you wish me to leave you here?" he whispered. "With them?"

She put her hand on his cheek. "I wish for you to keep my sons alive. Please, Willem, will you do this?"

He covered her hand with his own. "Until my dying breath, your majesty."

He pulled away and stood. He bowed to her and walked out of the stable without looking at any of the rest.

"What do we do now?" Lucius asked. "If we can't find out where the soldiers are going—"

"We stop it from within; it's the only way," Haleine said. "We get into the palace, and we stop my sister."

"And her wall? How do we defeat that?"

Haleine looked at Lucius. "You promised me an army. I think that will do."

CHAPTER 43

Falling
 Falling
 Falling
Nothing to see, nothing to do but
Wait and fall
Fall and wait
For it to end
To hit bottom
Concrete, bed of spikes, shark-infested waters—it wouldn't matter what was there.

The fall would kill you.

Not her, though. Never her. Nothing could kill her. This would be just another link in an endless chain of disappointment. Razor-sharp rocks replaced with a trampoline to force her up, up, up again.

Back into a broken body. Back into a broken life.

When she finally hit, she bolted upright, swallowing a scream and panting heavily, as she took in her surroundings. A bed—her bed. In her chambers. In Zaide Romanza's palace.

Had it been a dream? Cate hauled up her shirt to expose her stomach. No big, gaping hole. Arms and legs were intact, too.

Another damn dream, then.

How much had been a dream? If the hell hound encounter hadn't been real, perhaps the same was true for other things. Revelin, for example. Maybe she hadn't actually confronted him in the stables and performed half of a miserable striptease for him. Maybe he hadn't put in an appearance at dinner, either. Maybe he wasn't even in Feond. It was probably just her stupid brain, taking her fear of those scenarios and turning them into one mega-nightmare for her to experience over and over again.

Her brain was such an asshole.

She rubbed the heels of her palms into her eyes. No more seeing for her. Not that night—not *any* night, if she could manage it. Perhaps she could go back to the woods and stumble across the same storm that had robbed Rhona of her sight. Or find a spike or a dagger, or some other sharp, pointy object, and jam it right into her brain. That would be a surefire way not only to make sure she'd never see anything ever again, but also that she'd finally get some goddamn sleep.

"Miles to go before I sleep," someone drawled. "Remind me—who wrote that?"

Unaware that she hadn't been alone, Cate dropped her hands and turned to see herself sitting in a chair in the corner. Haleine? No, not Haleine. She sounded like Haleine—and was dressed to the nines the way a queen should have been—but whoever it was, it couldn't have been her twin. Haleine never would have been able to quote Robert Frost.

"What, are we, like, triplets now?" Cate said.

Her newest doppelganger smiled. "No, not triplets."

Cate slid off the bed. "Who are you supposed to be, then? My spirit guide? Ghost of Christmas past?"

"You."

"Me. Well, that's interesting," Cate said. "So, what is this?"

The doppelganger rose. "The beginning."

"Of what?"

"You seem tense. Having a rough day, pet?"

"Pet?"

The doppelganger walked toward her. "A term of endearment."

"I'm not your pet."

"Aren't you? Is a pet not something with which one plays and perhaps feels a modicum of affection for?"

"That's a toy."

The doppelganger grinned as though Cate had given her a winning lottery ticket. "Then my toy you shall be."

"Oh, fuck off."

"That is needlessly rude, but I understand the reason for your pain. This is what happens when you allow yourself attachments. The emotion is what hangs you in the end."

It had been ages since Cate had last heard that sentence. Yellow-eyed Iestyn had said it in a dream. Hearing it now was a shock, a bucket of cold water dumped on her head.

"I don't have attachments," she spat.

"Of course you do. If it hadn't been for your brown-eyed boy, my task would have been completed long ago."

"My what?"

"Your...What did you call him? Oh yes, your human security blanket. Your...goddamn body pillow."

James? She was talking about *James*? "He's nothing," Cate said.

"The lady doth protest too much, me thinks," the doppelganger said. "He's everything. You know it; I know it. Don't be ashamed. If you live amongst them long enough, it's bound to happen. We are not immune to human weakness when exposed to it for as long as you have been."

"Possibly because I *am* human."

"You don't believe that. You can't."

Guess she couldn't lie to herself. "I have to believe it," Cate said.

"Why?"

"It's better than the alternative."

"The alternative," her doppelganger echoed. "Do you mean me?"

Cate nodded. "I think maybe I do."

"Zaide Romanza told you true. If you give up your ridiculous sense of humanity, you'll not hurt anymore."

"Being you will hurt a lot."

"Just not us," the doppelganger said. "Isn't that what matters most?"

"I'm not sure even I'm that selfish."

"Oh, don't sell yourself short, pet. Your capacity for selfishness is limitless."

That was more on the true side than not. Cate dropped her head into her hands. "What the hell is happening here?"

"Allow me to enlighten you," the doppelganger said. "I feel no pain; I only inflict it. I am strong, and you are not. I am untainted by the mortal coil, while you are infested with it. But I can end that for you. I can take away your pain, your misery. You would never hurt again, and all you would have to do is stop running from and fighting against your destiny."

Cate backed away. "Can't run from something that doesn't exist. Well, I suppose you could, but why waste the energy?"

"Why waste the energy fighting a battle you can never win?"

"You don't know that I won't win."

"Don't I?" the doppelganger said. "You want to kill every last one that has done you wrong. You can't do it alone."

"Yes, I can."

"No, *I* can. *You* can't."

"Maybe I'll get help."

"Who would help you?"

That would be a short list—a *very* short list—but somewhere in Lira was a group of people with a similar list of enemies. They wouldn't like combining forces with her, but would they do it to end a few reigns of terror?

"I'll think of someone," Cate said.

"Your brown-eyed boy? There's not a day goes by that he doesn't curse your name."

"Only my name?" Cate shook her head. "You can stop now. This—whatever this is—it won't work. I won't let you in."

"You already have. Zoltano would have killed us had you not. You had given up."

"I fought back."

"*I* fought back. You surrendered. You welcomed death, so I stopped it."

"Where were you, then, when I was ripping out that bastard's entrails?"

The doppelganger pressed her hands together as though she meant to pray. Cate assumed she didn't.

"In your hands, your arms, your skin." The doppelganger laced her fingers. "In that moment, I was you, you were me. In that moment, we were one and the same."

"Well, that's not excessively complicated."

"Permit me to simplify things for you. I came from the womb of a woman long since dead. She called me Mireille, and the goddess stole me from her and gave birth to you," the doppelganger said. "The goddess truly is your mother. She gave you life and name. If she had never come for me, you never would have been born."

"That's not true," Cate said, though it felt very much like the opposite.

The doppelganger gave her a look. "You're making a fool of yourself now. Stop it."

A flare of anger surged through Cate. "What happened to you, then? If you're so strong and high and mighty, what happened to you? How did I ever have control? How did you ever let me exist?"

"Oh, do calm down. I was an infant at the time. I was trapped, caged inside of you, useless and forgotten, until your brown-eyed boy brought you here." Her doppelganger indulged in a secret smile. "I've always thought it rather maudlin that you loved the one person who made it possible for you to die."

"I'm not dead yet."

"You're drowning," the doppelganger said. "But it's all right, love. Fight, if you want. Flail your little arms, and keep your head above water for as long as you want—for as long as you can. This is what was meant to happen. You've fulfilled your purpose, Catherine Cole. You carried me through these long years, shielding me from the harm the world inflicts upon a soul. Mayhap I should call you my mother, as indeed you have acted as one to me."

"Maybe you shouldn't."

The doppelganger extended her arms toward Cate. "My protector, my savior, my life-giver, who kept me safe from human weakness—the very cancer that now eats away her soul. Are these not things a mother does for her child?"

"How the hell would I know?"

The doppelganger dropped her arms. "So bitter you are, but you needn't fear, Catherine Cole. I won't cry for you when you're gone."

"I'm not going anywhere."

"You are, and so much sooner than you realize."

"How do you figure that?"

The doppelganger moved forward again. "You weren't made for this life, this world. You don't know how to find your way and are content to run and hide. I stay; I fight, and ever since you came here, you have called upon me to do what is hard, what is necessary to survive."

Cate hit the wall, and the doppelganger was on top of her impossibly fast.

"Every time you do," the doppelganger continued, "I grow stronger while you grow weaker. It won't be long before I take you, whether you want it or not. When that happens, I will crush you completely. I will cut you out of me like the tumor you are. I will—"

"Oh, let me do this one," Cate interrupted. "You'll tear the flesh from my bones and play my ribs like a xylophone?"

Her doppelganger smiled. "Your retorts will not save you. This is destiny," she said. "You remember your mythology, don't you? Even Zeus could not question destiny."

"Because he's so relevant to this discussion?"

"To break with destiny, to question it, is to introduce chaos into the world."

"I know we like to talk big, but chaos was here long before me. Pretty sure it'll be here long after me, too."

"You'll take it to the grave with you."

"I'm not planning on dying."

The doppelganger stepped back. "How do you do that? How do you lie to yourself like that? You believe you're human; you believe you'll live. Tell me how you do this."

"I will get out of this alive," Cate said. "I know my way out, and it's not through you."

"Such sweet lies. It doesn't change what he feels. Or you."

"When I'm done, it won't matter what anyone feels."

Her doppelganger smirked. "Keep telling yourself that, precious. I enjoy a good laugh."

Her evil twin disappeared, and Cate woke with a start in another bed in another room. She lifted her head to check it out. Small and dark, lit only by a pair of lanterns on either side of the door. No windows. No natural light. The antithesis of her most recent accommodations. Had she finally made it to the dungeon?

She sighed and let her head drop back on the pillow. Well, this sucked. Into which dream world had she been pulled now? The one with ravenous devil dogs, or the one with her very own evil twin?

More evil twin.

As her body ached from head to toe, this probably wasn't a dream at all, just the return of reality—the world where she was an out-of-control, telekinetic empath with massive injuries all over her person. To be expected, she supposed, following a death match with a pair of hell hounds. The pain was strangely refreshing. It had been a while since something had hurt more than her back.

"You killed him."

Zaide Romanza's voice was taut, livid, and sliced through Cate's inner monologue like a knife. Interesting. She hadn't been aware that anything could upset the queen of Feond.

Checking her stomach for a big, gaping hole that didn't seem to be there, Cate found Zaide Romanza sitting in a chair on her right. "Yeah, you'll have to be more specific. I've killed a fair few, remember?"

"Torin," Zaide Romanza said. "You killed him."

Yes, she had done that. Sucked the life right out of him as though he'd been a jelly donut. Who knew she could do such a thing? Who would have thought that she ever would?

Besides Mireille. Omur. Zaide Romanza. Faolan. Dana, probably. Gair and Rhydwyn. James…

"So? You'll find another pool boy soon enough, I'm sure." Cate felt her arms and shoulders. The only marks on them had come from Zoltano. "Why do you care who I killed? I thought that's what you wanted me to do."

"Not him."

"Oh. Well, perhaps you should have been more specific before encouraging my gratuitous killing spree tendencies." Cate closed her eyes again. Shit, her head hurt. "How did the devil dogs find me?"

"Devil dogs?"

Her head hurt more as she struggled to recall their proper name. "Neruals. Did you send them?"

"I imagine you summoned them."

"I think I would have remembered doing that."

Zaide Romanza stood and took Cate's left hand, pressing three fingers into the bandage-covered gash on her palm. Cate's eyes flew open as she yanked her hand free.

"What are you doing?" she exclaimed, propping herself up.

"Causing you pain," Zaide Romanza responded. "You told me you cut yourself in the forest. Where in the forest? Tell the truth."

"I followed a stream that became a river that opened into a pool fed by a waterfall. Behind the waterfall was a—"

"A cave."

"Very good."

"Did you cut your hand inside the cave?"

"On a rock, yes."

Zaide Romanza returned to her chair. "Do you know what would happen if some mere mortal stumbled across that pond and that waterfall?"

"Obviously not."

"Nothing would happen. Even if they were to spend their entire lives in that spot, searching for that cave, they would never find it. It exists only for those of us blessed to be more."

Cate laughed. "Yeah, this has been a real blessing."

"How many times would you be dead by now were you not blessed with this magic?"

"That's beside the point," Cate said, sitting up. "If I hadn't been *blessed* with this magic, the neruals never would have come for me when I was an infant. If I hadn't been *blessed* with this magic, I would have been Mireille Coileáin—I would have known my mother, my father, my sisters. I would have been some average, boring girl who grew up to marry whatever creep her father had made a deal for. If I hadn't been *blessed* with—"

"You never would have been average, nor boring."

"Maybe not, but I wouldn't have blood on my hands, and I definitely wouldn't have lines and lines of people—and some non-people—all waiting for their shot at killing me," Cate said. "You'll have to shut up and deal with it if I don't find what I can do to be a blessing."

"Do you think Mireille Coileáin would whine as incessantly as you do?"

"If she had to deal with you, absolutely."

Cate swung her legs over the side of the bed. Her head swimming, she gripped the edge of the thin mattress and looked at her lap. What the hell was she wearing? She lifted a hand and plucked at the unfamiliar sleeveless shirt and woolen leggings. New clothes weren't completely unexpected—the devil dogs would have torn her last outfit to shreds—but she hated the idea that she had once again been naked and unconscious in front of an untold number. Who had dressed her this time?

"Something wrong?" Zaide Romanza asked.

How many people had seen? Given how pissed off the queen of Feond seemed to be, she had probably invited the entire population of the palace—if not the city surrounding it—to participate. Cate was better off not knowing.

She shook her head and stood. "Just tell me what bleeding in a cave had to do with the neruals trying to eat me alive."

"By bleeding in that cave, you allowed them to catch your scent. By bleeding all the way back to my castle, you left them a trail straight to you. How pleased they must have been, after spending your entire life hunting for you, to have found you at last."

A black leather bodice was draped over the end of the bed, and Cate slipped it on, lacing it tightly. The more layers she had, the better. Finding her boots on the floor, she stuck her feet inside and walked away. It didn't take long to reach the other end of the chamber.

"You really didn't send them," she said.

"I did not," Zaide Romanza replied. "What good would that serve? Sending the Black Wolf didn't prove worth the cost; why would those brainless beasts be different?"

Cate looked at Zaide Romanza over her shoulder. "What did you say?"

Zaide Romanza sighed. "That I was not responsible for—"

"Not that." Cate turned around. Her head didn't hurt anymore. "The other thing."

"I said nothing else."

A slow smile spread across Cate's face. "No, you didn't. You thought it."

Uncertainty pushed Zaide Romanza out of the chair. "What are you doing?"

"Reading your mind. Feeling your emotions," Cate said. "I couldn't do it before, but it's loud and clear now. Your boy must have given me a real boost. Thanks for putting him in my path."

"What you claim—it is impossible."

"It really isn't," Cate said. "Tell me why the Black Wolf wasn't worth the cost. What did you hire him to do?"

Zaide Romanza's face remained impassive, but inside she was bordering on panic. Guilt and fear swirled like the beginnings of a tornado.

"Go on, then," Cate commanded. "Tell the truth. Say it out loud."

"I engaged the Black Wolf to kidnap you and compelled Zoltano to see to your torture," Zaide Romanza said. Her eyes were wide with disbelief at her tongue's betrayal. "We needed the monster, not the girl. Your physical pain was the only proven way to get what we wanted."

"Why hire the mercenary? Why involve Zoltano? Why not do it yourself?"

"To protect myself from your wrath. You would seek to kill those responsible, and I had no desire to be your target."

"You told the Black Wolf to make sure I blamed Omur for it," Cate said, taking a step forward. "Because you wanted me to rip off his head instead of yours."

"I did."

"How much? How much did my kidnapping and torture cost? How much was I worth?"

"You are priceless," Zaide Romanza said. "In comparison, the Black Wolf worked for mere trifles."

Cate took another step. "How much?"

"Everything Zoltano had," Zaide Romanza said. "Including a lordship."

Lord Weylyn Lann. Cate had to admit it had a nice ring to it. "Well, I'm glad you got a bargain on ruining my life."

"Life? What life?" Zaide Romanza's eyes flashed as she fought Cate's coercion. "You should thank me for what I've done. Because of me, you will have the life you were meant to live."

Cate smiled. "Yeah. Thanking you isn't exactly what I had in mind."

Zaide Romanza shrank back. "Have you decided to kill me, then?"

"A while ago, actually."

"To kill me is to go against the dark gods."

"Killing you and going against them are two different things. They still have hope. You don't."

"The dark gods do not deal in hope."

"Well, then, I guess you're all screwed."

Zaide Romanza flattened herself against the wall. "Guards!"

"Really?" Cate laughed as the door slammed open, and the sound of armed men filled the space. "Don't move," she said to Zaide Romanza, then turned to the new arrivals. "Take a nap, boys."

The guards dropped to the floor, armor and weapons clattering. The man closest to her had a dagger in his belt, and she held out her hand for it. As soon as it settled on her palm, Cate spun and threw the blade into Zaide Romanza's stomach. The queen of Feond screamed and sank along the wall until she sat on the floor, bloodied hands holding the handle.

"Sorry about that," Cate said as Zaide Romanza pulled out the blade. "Not the stabbing, just the placement. I was aiming for your heart, but I guess I haven't quite mastered the art of throwing knives. It's all right, though. This is better. Now we can chat."

The dagger fell from Zaide Romanza's hands. "I-I won't beg."

"Don't recall asking you to beg." Cate crouched in front of her. Picking up the dagger, she tucked it inside her bodice. "Where would I find the Black Wolf?"

"I don't know."

"Sure you do. Where is he?"

"In the wind. He doesn't want to be found by you."

"Smart lad," Cate said. "Where might that wind take him?"

Zaide Romanza's eyes closed, her shoulders slumping as her head lolled to the left. Cate sighed and slapped her across the face.

"We're not done yet," Cate said when Zaide Romanza looked at her. "Where do I find the Black Wolf?"

"Can't you let me die in peace?" Zaide Romanza groaned.

"Not until you tell me what I want to know."

Zaide Romanza smiled, a trickle of blood appearing at the corner of her mouth. "G-go to hell. That's where you'll find him."

Cate nodded. "See you there."

She stood and took one last look at the queen of Feond. Turning around, she ran her eyes over the collection of sleeping soldiers before lifting her head to see Revelin standing in the doorway and gawking in utter terror. Guess it hadn't been a dream after all.

"Hey," she said. "Back for a second show?"

He staggered inside. "What are you doing?"

She shrugged. "Getting you out of your wedding."

"What—what is...Did you kill all these people?"

Cate jerked her thumb toward Zaide Romanza. "Just that one, and technically, she's not dead yet. The others will wake up soon. Soon-ish."

Revelin laughed, a brief appalled sound, as he worked his way toward her. His head was filled with nothing but white noise. He looked at the soldiers, then leaned to his right to glance behind her, registering the sight of his dying bride-to-be with an indifference that made Cate smile.

"Dare I ask why you did this?" he said, straightening. "Or am I not allowed to pose such a question?"

"You can ask. I just won't answer." Cate met him in the center of the room and placed her hand on his chest. "No matter what she tells you, let her suffer. No fair making it quick, okay?"

Revelin gaped at her. "I do not—I do not understand."

"You will," she said, hands dropping down to unbuckle his sword belt. "Now, as fun as this has been, I have to be moving on. Places to go, people to kill—that sort of thing, you know?"

As she removed his belt, Revelin searched her face, looking for, and not finding, the girl he had left behind in that Tanubian courtyard. "Mireille—"

"It's Cate." She patted his cheek and walked away. "See you around, lover."

———

Revelin watched Mireille disappear from the room. She was always doing that—one moment, standing before him, and the next...vanishing without warning. Without a trace.

He should have stopped her, called for other guards to apprehend her. He should have done *something*. The murder of a royal was a grave offense—the murder of two even more so. He could not allow her to walk away.

However, he said nothing as he looked at the now-empty doorway. She may have been gone, but he could still see her and all that his brother had done—the cuts, burns, bruises, and the still-healing signature carved across her back. He might never be able to see anything else.

A fitting penance, he thought, for a sin of inaction. She had spoken true that morning in the stables—he had known of what Zoltano was capable, but never had he acted upon it. Never had he stopped it.

Eamonn had charged him with a similar crime. Revelin was not a man of action, and so many had suffered because of it.

"Revelin," Zaide Romanza said.

He turned. She sat on the floor, hand covering a stomach wound gushing blood. The blood surprised him; he had expected to see only lies pouring out.

"Please," she said, shoulders twitching. "R-Revelin, please."

Was she begging him? For what did she ask? Surely she did not think him capable of saving her. She was not stupid; she had to understand she was beyond help now.

It was odd, his lack of emotion. So long had he hated this woman, he would have thought he would feel *something*—relief, pleasure, anything—upon witnessing her demise. But it had been the same with Zoltano's death. Revelin had had only apathy to offer his brother's corpse but could not even summon that much for the queen of Feond.

Where do I find the Black Wolf, Mireille had asked.

Ties to Tanuba found here. Why?

Revelin crouched before Zaide Romanza. "Why did she ask you where to find the Black Wolf?"

As a smile crossed her lips, Zaide Romanza gasped for breath. "H-heard that, did you?"

"Did you hire him?" Revelin asked. "Did you order him to poison my mother?"

The smile widened. "I did that...m-myself."

Robbed of breath, Revelin went to his knees, hands braced on his thighs. "Why?"

She laughed. "Y-you're so s-stupid."

"Why would you do that? My mother loved you," he said. "What did you stand to gain?"

"O-only that which y-you could never understand."

His chest ached with a sudden desire to hurt her. Mireille had disarmed him, but he still had hands. That would be more satisfying—wrapping his fingers around her throat, throttling answers from her—than any weapon, but try as he might, he could not seem to lift them.

Let her suffer, Mireille had told him. *No fair making it quick.*

Had she done something to him?

"W-what's the m-matter, Revelin?" Zaide Romanza wheezed. "N-nothing to say?"

"You surprise me," he said, choking down his hatred. "I did not believe you capable—"

"Of k-killing your mother?"

"Speaking the truth."

"I l-lied far less t-than you t-thought."

Her eyes closed. She was fading. It wouldn't be long before she was gone.

He sighed. "Who is your heir? You have no children, no siblings, no family at all, of which I am aware. You must name someone."

There was movement behind him. The guards awakening, perhaps, or the arrival of others. They did not speak, and he did not look at them, keeping his eyes fixed on Zaide Romanza.

"Who do you name?" he urged.

Her eyes opened. "I have...brother. H-half brother."

"A half brother?" Revelin said. "Then your father..."

"F-fucked...a maid, yes." Her eyes slid shut again. "H-he...doesn't...k-know. O-only me...and n-now you."

Her body slumped to the right, and Revelin caught her, easing her onto her back. He placed his hand over the hole in her gut and pressed down. She came awake with a groan, the sound soon turning into a feeble laugh.

"So cruel, R-Revelin," she gasped. "I...k-knew you...h-had it in y-you."

"Tell me his name. Tell me where to find him. I will see him located and crowned."

Another laugh, this one weaker still. "I w-would have liked...to h-have s-seen t-that."

"Who is he? Tell me."

Her bloodied hand came up, fingers twisting in his shirt. She pulled him down as she lifted herself up and uttered the name in his ear. Releasing him, she sank to the floor.

"Run and give him my crown," the queen of Feond said with her dying breath. "I dare you."

Revelin stayed on his knees and stared.

CHAPTER 44

The morning after Haleine's reunion with Willem, she sat with Lucius, Ilya, and Dana in her tent and discussed an attack on the palace. Neither Lucius nor Ilya were pleased by Dana's presence, but they allowed him to stay. He stood behind Haleine at the back of the tent as the siblings quarreled.

"An army?" Ilya said to her brother. "You promised the queen an army? Where were you planning to get an army?"

"We could raise the men," Lucius said. "Lord Emrys could—"

"Raising an army to storm the palace goes beyond what Lord Emrys would be willing to do for us," Ilya said. She pointed to Dana. "He would tell you the same if he weren't too afraid to speak."

Haleine glanced at Dana to see a smile briefly cross his face. He did not, however, offer a differing opinion.

"Even if we could raise an army to rival the king's," Ilya continued, "there remains the problem of gaining access to the palace itself. We'd need to lay siege to it, and that would never—"

"Why don't we?" Haleine asked. "If a siege is our best chance—our only chance—of breaching the wall, and the palace itself, then we must do it."

Ilya shook her head. "It will take too long; it'll be too conspicuous. We couldn't possibly plan a siege of the palace in the middle of the city that would go unnoticed by anyone. Your sister would know, your majesty, if no one else, and I doubt very much that she would be passive as we dismantle her wall on our way to dismantle her."

"Dismantle," Haleine echoed.

"Stop," Ilya amended. "We need to stop your sister—and Omur and Maddox and potentially Cate—however it needs to be done."

It was safe to mention her twin's name. James had ridden out that morning to take a turn guarding the borders. No one bothered to dissuade him. Haleine had declared that plans would be made in his absence, and only then would he be informed. No one had argued that decision, either.

"Yes," Haleine said, "we do need to—"

She stopped when a crack like lightning drowned out all other sounds. It faded, replaced by screaming. Lucius and Ilya bolted from the tent. Dana followed but soon returned, his hand on his sword.

Haleine stood. "What is it?"

"Stay behind me."

"Oh, I'll do no such thing," she said, but when she tried to leave, Dana blocked the way. "What are you doing? Stop this!"

"Haleine, please," he begged, "just stay behind me."

"What is out there that has you so terrified?"

"That would be me."

As Dana whirled around, Haleine looked past him to see Mireille. Wild and otherworldly. Haleine stepped back, and Dana drew his sword. Mireille's cloudy-blue eyes flickered toward it, and a smile crossed her lips.

"What are you doing here?" Dana asked.

Mireille looked at him. "You seem far less dead than when I saw you last. Good for you."

"What do you want?" Haleine asked.

Mireille's eyes found her. "I want to talk to you, which means your boy toy can put the sword away. He won't be needing it."

Dana neither moved nor sheathed his weapon.

Mireille shrugged. "Or don't. It's not like it would do you any good anyway. If I had come here with nefarious intentions, you'd already be dea—"

"Why would you wish to speak with me?" Haleine interrupted. "What do we have to talk about?"

Mireille laughed. "You're kidding, right? What *don't* we have to talk about?"

"How did you find us?" Dana asked. "We go to great lengths to keep enemies from crossing our borders."

"James. He's this giant beacon of misery. Made it real easy to find you."

"He is angry," Haleine said.

Mireille nodded. "I know. What about you? Are you angry?"

"Should I not be?" Haleine asked. "You destroyed much when you left Enimode the way you did."

"Yeah, well, in my defense, if you hadn't interfered, the only thing with holes in it would have been Laorans."

Her smug tone was galling. "That is neither amusing nor accurate," Haleine snapped. "Did you or did you not put a dagger in a man's leg?"

"Leg, not heart," Mireille said.

"You slashed his chest open."

"Flesh wound." Mireille's eyes darted around the tent, not focusing on anything. "I didn't want to kill him, only stop him from getting in the way."

"But you did want to kill the goddess."

Mireille's face lost some of its detached poise. "I don't know. Maybe."

"You don't know," Haleine said, unable to disguise her disgust.

Mireille caught the tone, the crack in her confidence repairing itself as quickly as it had appeared. "Yeah, that's right. I don't know," she mocked. "You'll have to forgive me, but I don't have the solid grasp on my emotions that you do. Tell me, Haleine—attempted suicide lately?"

The cool sting of shame trickled through Haleine's body. "What did you want to talk about?"

"The possibility of making a deal."

"What sort of deal?" Dana asked.

"The sort where both sides get something they want." Mireille looked at Dana. "You know, Ken Doll, I'm not actually talking to you. You can leave."

"I'm not going anywhere."

Mireille smiled viciously. "Not a deadbeat rebel leader anymore, huh? How nice. Your lemmings must be thrilled."

"Mireille," Haleine said wearily, "please state what you want."

"I want your number one fan here to go elsewhere."

"Dana," Haleine said, "will you please oblige my sister?"

Dana hesitated, and Mireille added, "I won't hurt your girl. I need her alive."

That did nothing to reassure him—Haleine could see it, feel it—and she touched his arm. "Please, Dana."

He nodded and walked out of the tent.

Haleine sat and looked at Mireille. "He'll not go far, you realize, and he'll hear every word we say."

"No, he won't," her twin replied. "Not if I don't want him to."

Magic, then. Haleine took a closer look at her sister. "How do you do it?"

"What?"

"The magic. You have control over what is inside of us. How did you do it?"

"I didn't come here to talk about this."

"Do it anyway."

"You're not my queen. You can't order me around."

Haleine watched her calmly, waiting for her to relent. Finally, Mireille sighed.

"I don't know how, okay? Not really. Just…something happened in my brain. It was like the ultimate cheat codes had been entered in—not that you know what that means, but it was like that. Type in a code, and all of a sudden, I can just do all these things I couldn't do before." Mireille shook her head. "I didn't learn it; I didn't earn it. I just…A switch—not that you would know what that is, either—but a switch that hadn't been flipped on before suddenly was, and...presto change-o. Scary, cosmic powers."

"How? What spurred it?"

"Ah, well, let's see...there was the time when Omur sent a man to run me through with his sword, followed by that time Zaide Romanza had a man hold my hand in a fire. Those were pretty motivating," Mireille said. "Then, of course, there was the road trip from hell with Satan's spawn. It's amazing what a person's willing to do when..."

Haleine looked away. She was well aware of what her sister had endured. She would never forget the sight of Mireille lying on that wooden floor.

"You saw that?" Mireille asked, her voice tight. "What do you mean you *saw* that? How did you—?"

"I don't know how. Not really," Haleine echoed. How had Mireille known her thoughts? "I see things sometimes, and others, I will feel them. But all that I can do—have done—has been passive. With few exceptions, I have never done anything like that which you have achieved."

"Yeah, it's a real achievement."

Mireille's voice was steady, but Haleine could feel the despair beneath it. Mireille shook her head as though such emotion were a flighty, worthless thing.

"Did you feel it, too?" Mireille asked. "Did you feel everything they...I felt it when you put a damn dagger in your chest, so you must have—"

"I felt it."

Mireille laughed, short and nervous. "And the scars? You have those, too?"

Scars? What scars? Haleine's horror was naked on her face as she shook her head. "I had only bruises. They faded."

"Lucky you." Mireille folded her arms across her chest. "Can we talk about the deal now?"

"Yes," Haleine said, looking at her twin in a new light. What was she hiding underneath her clothing? "What do you want?"

"I want to be not here anymore. I want off of this fucked-up planet, and I want you to help me get there."

"How?"

"Maybe you don't know, but we have the ability to open doors between places. Not like, one room to the next or anything normal like that—not that we can't do that, but I'm talking about doors between countries or, I sincerely hope, worlds."

"Worlds?"

"Yes, worlds," Mireille said. "Maybe nobody told you this, either, but the goddess of which you are so very fond took me from our family when I was an infant and transported me through the veil of time and space to an entirely different world where magic is in short supply, but overpriced coffee is available on every street corner."

"You believe I can help you return there?"

"It's a working theory. I can open portals between countries all on my own, but I can't manage worlds," Mireille said. "I thought maybe if we activated our Wonder Twin powers that it'll be enough to help me—"

"Run away?"

"Do you want me here?"

Haleine did not know. That one simple thought was enough to put a crooked smile on Mireille's face.

"This is my proposal," she said. "I help you fight Omur and Maddox. I help you reclaim your castle. In exchange, you help me open a portal out of this hellhole. Do we have a deal?"

"You have me at a disadvantage."

"Life's unfair like that. Do we have a deal, or do I walk?"

"What will you do if we are unsuccessful in opening your portal, and you cannot get back to your other world?"

"Go as far away from here as I can get. I'm guessing there are entire continents on this earth of which you're not even aware. You probably think the damn thing's flat. I'll go to one of those and be far, far away from you and yours, and everyone else."

"You'll be alone."

"That's kind of the point."

"That is what you want? To be alone? To live a solitary existence?"

"It doesn't matter what I want," Mireille said. "Do we have a deal or not?"

Haleine nodded. What else could she do? "I will agree to this arrangement under one further condition."

"You want to know more about us," Mireille said. "What we are. What we can do."

"Yes."

"You'd also like to know how I knew that's what you were going to say."

"Very much so."

"As best I can figure, we're some kind of telekinetic, pyro-prone empaths," Mireille said. "Who can occasionally see the future. And control people's minds."

"Control people's minds?"

Mireille shrugged and scratched the side of her neck. "Yeah. You might have done it and not realized it. That's how it started with me."

Had she? How horrible. Feeling ill, Haleine asked, "But...what does it mean? What is a telekinetic, pyro-prone empath?"

"Telekinetic means that you're able to move objects with your mind." Mireille glanced around the tent and waved her hand at the baskets along the back wall. They rose and hovered in the air, falling only when she dropped her hand. "Pryo-prone is—"

"How did you do that?" Haleine stared at the baskets and their spilled wares.

"Magic. It's magic. Remember the magic? The super fun bullshit that's ruined our lives?" Mireille said. "Hasn't anyone ever told you *anything*?"

"Since your arrival, Faolan has been—"

Mireille made an odd noise in her throat. "Don't say his name. I'm not interested in dealing with that Machiavellian jackass with wings right now, or ever, really—which will make his imminent appearance all the more perfect for me."

"His appearance will not likely be imminent. He's not currently in camp."

"Where did he go?"

Haleine registered her twin's suspicion and shook her head. "I don't know. He declined to tell anyone his destination or purpose."

Mireille focused on the tent wall. "I don't think that's true."

"Why?" Haleine asked, but Mireille offered nothing else. She nodded. Later, then. "What of the rest of it? The...pyro-prone part?"

Mireille smiled. "That's not an accurate name for it, but..."

She looked at the lantern on the table and held out her hand. Haleine glanced between the lantern and her twin, unsure as to Mireille's intent, until the source of light moved. The lantern was now empty, its flame resting in the center of her twin's palm.

Haleine stood, mouth open in shock. How could Mireille do that? Hold fire and not even cry out? She gingerly touched Mireille's outstretched arm. "Does it not burn?"

"Not anymore," Mireille answered.

She closed her hand, and the flame reappeared in the lantern. Haleine pried open Mireille's fingers to see her palm. The fire had not damaged it at all.

"It's not just fire," Mireille said, shaking her hand free. "We can manipulate other elements, too—earth, maybe wind and water. I haven't done all of that, but—"

"Who told you about this, about the magic?" Haleine asked. "Who taught you?"

"Omur and Zaide Romanza got me started. I did the rest on my own."

"How?"

"Trial and error," Mireille responded as her hand became a fist again. "The murder of a few innocent bystanders. Using a goddess as target practice. That kind of thing."

Legs suddenly weak, Haleine sank back into her chair. The murder of innocents. The assault of a goddess. How could Mireille be so cavalier about such things?

"Oh, sorry. Was that too callous for you? Let me try again," Mireille said. "I...closed my eyes real tight, wished upon a star, and believed in myself. It was a true life-affirming experience."

Irritation replaced Haleine's repulsion. She shoved it down and said, "Tell me the rest of it."

"I think you're already familiar with the rest of it," Mireille said. "You told me you experience things—things like what your stalker feels?"

"Stalker?"

"Dana."

"Yes, I am always aware of his emotions."

"What about those with whom you haven't been intimate? Are you aware of their feelings, too?"

"When they are strong, yes, I seem to be. James included," Haleine added, making note of the change in her sister's smug expression. "Though one would not need to be an empath to understand his turmoil."

"I'm not sure why you think I would care about his turmoil."

"Neither did he," Haleine said. "You broke his heart, you know."

The corner of Mireille's mouth twitched. "Cost of doing business."

"Is that what you will tell him?"

"He doesn't need me to tell him anything."

"I think you may be wrong about that." Haleine looked Mireille over and sighed. "Is that all? Is that everything? All we can do?"

Mireille laughed. "We can do pretty much anything we want. Isn't that enough for you?"

"You misunderstand," Haleine said. "I ask because I saved a woman. She was dying, and I stopped her from doing so. Later, I brought Dana back very much the same way. I *healed* them."

"Good for you, Florence Nightingale."

"No, I fear you still do not understand," Haleine said. "I healed them with my hands and naught else. It was as though their wounds had never existed."

"Nifty."

"Have you worked any magic similar to that?"

"Well, when I was dying, I sucked the life right out of the nearest passer-by in order to keep myself alive. It worked, obviously, because I'm here, and he's very, very dead." Mireille shrugged yet again. "Maybe we're not so identical after all."

Haleine stared. "How many have you killed?"

"I don't know the exact number. There are four that I do know about, plus an unspecified number in Feond," Mireille said. "It was probably a lot, though, because no one wanted to tell me."

"You don't care, do you? You don't care how many there were."

"I can't care. If I start caring..." Mireille shook her head. "If I start caring, it'll be worse."

"What will?"

"Maybe someday, if you get over that pesky humanity of yours, I'll tell you," Mireille said. "Is that it? Are you done now? Can we finally discuss what to do about your husband and his puppet master?"

"They're not the only threat, you know."

"If you mean Zaide Romanza, you don't have to worry about her anymore."

"Does that mean Feond's queen is one of your four?"

"So what if she is? You gonna shed a lot of tears over her loss?"

"Not her loss, no," Haleine said.

"What, then? The loss of my innocence? Of me?" Mireille said. "You don't have to worry about me. I'm fine."

"You seem it."

Mireille's mouth quirked. "Good effort, Haleine, but in the future, maybe you should leave the sarcasm to the professionals."

Haleine sighed. "I do not care about Zaide Romanza. Whatever fate she was dealt, I am certain she earned it. But she was not to whom I was referring."

"Who was?"

"Sighle."

"*Sighle?*"

"Yes, Sighle. Do you know about her? Have you met our sister?"

"Yeah." Mireille laughed. "I met our sister. I met our sister *and* the man she decided to screw."

"Screw?"

"Fuck."

Haleine flinched and looked at the ground. "Who?"

"I'll give you a hint," Mireille said. "It's someone you were already planning to kill."

Haleine's head snapped up. "Please tell me Maddox hasn't—"

"No, she's fucking Omur. She was, anyway. I did request they stop, but I'm guessing they didn't listen," Mireille said. "I don't know if you think that's any better; the scene I happened to witness was rather nauseating, but at least it wasn't…" She shrugged. "It could have been worse, I guess."

"She's a child."

"Yet, thirty seconds ago, you claimed she was a danger. Why? What has she done?"

Murder. Gleeful murder, all done without a single care. Loreton, Rushwick, and Hythe. So many had died. How many more would follow? How many more lads would have their guts made into inkwells, all in the name of a game whose rules Haleine did not understand?

"Are those villages?" Mireille asked. "Loreton? Rushwick? Hythe?"

"That's rather unnerving, you know," Haleine said.

"Wait until it starts happening to you," Mireille responded. "So, Sighle attacked villages?"

"My husband's men were the ones to do it. Sighle was not there, yet she was…"

"Controlling them?"

"I believe so, yes," Haleine said. "I went to Loreton, and I…I touched a boy, and I saw it—his death. Sighle may not have been there, but she was the one to wield the knife."

Mireille nodded. "What was that inkwell thing?"

"That boy…She used his blood to write a message on a wall, demanding that I be given over to her," Haleine said. "She has done the same in every village so far. A man writes the words, but does so in her hand."

"And she wants you?"

"Yes."

"What are you still doing here, then?" Mireille asked. "You don't seem the type to sit back and let others die in the name of saving your own ass."

Haleine looked at Mireille. "I tried to surrender. I went to Eluned to do as she wanted, but I was unable to get into the palace. There was a wall, a barrier of magic, and I—I could not pass."

"She wouldn't let you in?"

Haleine shook her head. "She taunted me, challenged me, but I do not understand what it is she wants."

Mireille laughed again, the sound chilling. "I told Bronagh there was something wrong with that kid. I just knew. I didn't know what it was, and I didn't realize she was *this* screwed-up, but I knew there was something off with her." She released another huff of amusement. "Shit. She hides it well."

Yes, she had done that. "I've seen the things she's done, yet I hardly believe it," Haleine said. "She's only a child."

"No, she isn't."

"She is. You weren't there. You weren't there when she was born; you did not witness her first steps, her first words. You do not recognize her hand because you did not teach her to write. You did not—"

"You're right—I didn't. I wasn't there," Mireille said. "Which is maybe why I can accept her for what she is, and you can't."

"What is she, then?"

"Someone who, by your own admission, orchestrated a lot of deaths. Someone who used a boy's gut as an inkwell. Someone who sure as hell isn't a child—no matter how much she may look like one."

"It was Omur. It had to be. He did this to her. I left her alone, and he corrupted her, made her—"

"Maybe."

"Maybe?"

"There's an awful lot of prophecy that suggests we were born this way. If that's true, it makes sense that she could have been, too," Mireille said. "We had the same parents, after all. Well, I assume we had the same parents. It's not like I know—"

"We did," Haleine said. "Do not insult our mother's memory."

"You mean the mother I have no memory of?" Mireille asked. "Is that the mother whose memory I shouldn't insult?"

Tears pricked at Haleine's eyes, and she had to look away again. They hadn't talked like this—about this—before. There was so much they didn't know about the other. How would they ever say all that needed to be said?

"We don't," Mireille said.

Haleine looked up. "Mireille—"

"No, Haleine, we don't. We *can't*," her twin said. "There's big, bad evil on the horizon, and you want to stroll down nineteen years' worth of memory lane? Do you know what that would be like? You're probably imagining some cute, little jaunt through a picturesque forest filled with nothing but giggles and good times, but it'll be more like Mad Max on the Fury Road. I know you don't know what that is, but it's not good, and it sure as hell isn't something we do when the shootout at the O.K. Corral is imminent."

Once again, Haleine stared. She had understood very little of Mireille's outburst, but the sentiment behind it was plain enough.

"The deal—the deal that you accepted—is Maddox and Omur six feet under in exchange for my ticket out of here. Nothing else. I answered your questions about the goddamn magic, but you get nothing else," Mireille stated flatly. "We're not going to bond. We're not going to braid each other's hair, or invent some secret twin language. We're not sisters. We're nothing but identical strangers who had the misfortune of running into one another. Do you understand me? You get nothing else."

Haleine broke her stare and nodded. "Omur will not be easy to defeat. Dana ran him through with a sword, and he did not die. He has powers."

"We have some powers of our own," Mireille said. "And judging by his obsession with our powers, I'm guessing they're better than his."

Haleine shook her head. "I don't want them."

"I don't think we get a choice in that."

"We can choose whether we use them, and I choose not. I will not surrender my humanity."

Mireille scoffed. "What does humanity have to do with anything?"

"Before, when I did...what I did—"

"Attempted suicide?"

"Magic. When I worked that magic—or however it was called—I was so desolate, so lost, and to do that again, to *be* that again, would be truly terrible. It is not a human thing, what we can do."

"Being human is overrated."

"Do you believe that?"

"I don't believe anything. Safer that way," Mireille said.

"Listen to you. Look at what this magic has done to you!" Haleine exclaimed. "Look at what it has made our sister! How can you—?"

"I didn't want to die," Mireille blurted. "All right? I didn't want to die, so it was either that, or this, and I chose this because I didn't want to die. Do you understand that? Can you? Can a person so obsessed with killing herself even comprehend someone else's need to survive?"

"I comprehend it very well, I assure you."

"I didn't want to die," Mireille repeated, softer, sadder. "I thought maybe I...I wanted to live, so I did what I had to do to keep on living. Sometimes I think I chose right, but..." She shook her head. "But that's it. That's all. I didn't want to die."

They were quiet then, as Mireille again looked off at something Haleine could not see, her hands rubbing her upper arms. Haleine brushed tears from her face, certain Mireille would not care to see them.

"Mireille," Haleine said, "I—"

"Maddox and Omur," Mireille interrupted. "We should each take on one, at the same time—divide and conquer, you know? If Omur's distracted, then he can't do whatever it is he does to Maddox. Maybe that'll be easier; I don't know, but since you choose not to risk your humanity, I should take Omur. Unless you're feeling suicidal again. Then I'll take Maddox, and you can—"

"No," Haleine said. "Maddox is mine to kill."

"Great. You kill him, and I'll deal with Omur." Mireille rubbed her arms harder. "Could we work out the specifics of this plan later? Tomorrow, maybe?"

Haleine nodded. "Do take care of yourself, Mireille," she said as her twin walked away. "Sister or no, I would be quite distraught if something were to happen to you."

"That's only because you don't know me." Mireille stopped and turned around. "Our deal only extends to Maddox and Omur. You know that, right? You'll have to deal with Sighle. You, by yourself. I won't get involved in that."

"Sighle is not to be dealt with. Not by you, not by anyone. She is to be stopped—she must be stopped—but..." Haleine sighed and looked at the ground. "They want to kill her, and I cannot allow that to happen. I will not allow that to happen. I will find a way to save her."

"I'm guessing destiny will tell you that you can't."

Haleine lifted her head. "Fuck destiny."

Mireille grinned. "Now that sounds like a plan."

James had left Gair behind when he rode out that morning. He was in no mind to tolerate the company of anyone—even that of a long-steadfast companion—and bade the man to stay behind.

Lorcan had assured them that the camp's magical protections were back in place, but James had taken Bearach and set out to ride the entire perimeter of camp to see for himself that they were safe—or as safe as could be.

They had not quite completed their circuit when the unicorn stopped short, nearly throwing his rider.

"We need to return," Bearach said.

The unicorn offered no other information, and they pounded the earth as they made their way back. The last time Bearach had done this, James had returned to camp to discover that Enimode had been attacked. What had happened this time? Had the king's men finally found them?

Gair waited outside of the camp, holding the reins of a lovely silver-gray mare James had never seen. The threat could not be imminent, then.

"What's happened?" James asked, sliding from Bearach's back. "Where did that mare come from?"

"She's here," Gair answered.

She. There was no need to ask to whom Gair referred. There could only be one.

"Where?"

"With the queen."

Heart pounding and blood boiling, James charged to the tent. Why had she returned? What did she want? The camp atmosphere was muted—had she done something? Reappeared in the same manner in which she had departed? Had more people been hurt?

Brighid and Eion stood guard outside of the queen's tent, but neither attempted to stop him as he pushed inside.

Cate was gone. The queen sat at the table, her fingers covering her mouth. She either had not seen him or was ignoring him, but Dana, crouched in the corner, took notice. He stood but didn't speak.

"Where is she?" James asked. "Why has she come?"

The queen looked at him. Her hand slid down, fingers coming to rest against the base of her neck. "You didn't tell me about the scars. You should have."

He shook his head. "I don't know what you're talking about."

"You are a bloody poor liar, James ap Seoras," the queen said.

"So I am," he replied. "Where is she?"

The queen looked away. "Here. She's here in camp."

"Where in camp?"

"I don't know."

"You don't know?" James looked at Dana. "Tell me you at least put a guard on her."

"There is no need for that," the queen said. "She won't hurt anyone."

"Tell that to Rhydwyn," James spat, spinning around to leave.

"Rhydwyn is fine, James," the queen declared. "It is you with which we must concern ourselves."

The force behind her words made him stop. "Me?"

"You have wondered why she is here, why we have allowed her to run around unescorted," the queen continued, "but have you spared a thought as to *how* she is here? She never should have been able to find us, yet here she is. She passed right through every protection set in place. Do you know how she managed it, James? How she found us?"

Judging by the queen's harsh tone, he was somehow at fault. He faced her and waited. The queen stood, Dana at her side. He watched James with troubled eyes, hands flexing as though preparing to intercede. Why did he do that? Was Dana expecting him to attack the queen? What was she about to say?

"How?" he asked, looking from Dana to the queen.

"Your anger. Your misery," the queen said. "It served as map and key for her. It led her straight to us."

"Did she…Why did she come?" James asked.

"She offered her help in defeating Maddox and Omur."

"In exchange for what?"

"For my help in sending her away."

Away. "Where?"

The queen shook her head. "Wherever she was before you brought her here, I suppose. She did not say."

James nodded. "If she's still here, it must mean you agreed to her terms."

"I did, yes."

"You decided to trust her."

"I did, yes."

James looked at the ground. How had she done it? How had she found that ability within herself?

"How many of us will die because you did?" Dana said.

James glanced at him. His distrust of Cate wasn't new, but his dissension from the queen's opinion was.

"I do not think she wishes to harm anyone," the queen said.

"She may do it anyway," Dana argued. "Faolan believes she can't control it."

The queen turned to Dana. "You spoke to Faolan about her?"

"I did, aye."

"When did you do this? Why did you—?"

"Because she'll break the pair of you and leave you devastated—if not dead—if we don't find a way to contain her," Dana said, anger rising. "Neither of you should be lost to her or because of her. It would be a waste."

"What did you do?" the queen demanded, her voice low.

"I asked Faolan to help me keep you alive. I asked him to help me stop her."

"To kill her," the queen accused. "That's what you mean, isn't it? You asked him to help you kill her."

"Only if it becomes necessary," Dana said. "Which it very well may."

"That was not your decision to make," the queen said.

"I should stand aside and watch you kill yourself?"

"You did before," the queen said. "Why should it be different now?"

"Haleine," Dana said, "I only—"

"No. You're done. You may go."

Dana did not fight to stay. He stalked out of the tent, leaving James alone with the queen. She required a moment to compose herself before she could look at him. When she resumed speaking, her tone was less severe.

"I know what I accused you of, and I understand the conflict you now feel. You love her, you hate her, and they're so tightly intertwined you do not know where one ends and the other begins. Please believe me when I tell you that I understand this," she said. "What I am about to ask you to do is unforgivable, but she is attuned to you, James." The queen hesitated before adding, "Be sure to use it to our advantage."

James walked out. Gair fell in step with him. He asked no questions, which suggested that he had heard what the queen had said. No reason why he shouldn't have. Tent walls could only conceal so much.

"Do you know where she is?" James asked.

"No, Captain."

That was all right. Wherever she was, she wouldn't remain unnoticed for long. Word would get back to him. He would find her wherever she hid, then he would—what? What would he do? What *could* he do? The queen claimed Cate was attuned to him, that it could somehow be made into an advantage, but the validity of that was doubtful.

If they were somehow linked, she never would have left.

"Find Ilya," James said, looking at Gair as he entered his tent. "Nothing in this camp—"

"Hey."

Cate. Her voice cut through him—the sharpest blade he ever had encountered—and he drew his sword before he realized what he was doing. Almost as quickly, it was ripped from his hand and sailed across the tent. She caught it and lowered it to her side, then met his stare.

They were her eyes. Clear, blue. Hers.

She looked away when Gair drew his own sword. "Just don't," she said.

James put his arm out to stop Gair, to protect him should Cate decide to retaliate. Her face contorted in irritation.

"Oh, I'm not going to retaliate," she said. "Give me a break."

"How did you—?"

"Know what you were thinking?" Cate shrugged. "Magic, mostly. But I also have the ability to read your very obvious body language."

Magic. He blinked. If she had the ability to read his mind, she would only be more dangerous.

Cate nodded. "True. But only if I'm not on your side."

James dropped his arm and glanced at Gair. "Leave us."

"Captain," Gair protested.

"Go," James ordered. "Now."

Gair backed out of the tent. He did not stay, rushing off, likely to tell Ilya, or perhaps Dana, of Cate's whereabouts. James looked at her.

"Are you?" he forced himself to ask. "Are you on our side?"

Cate looked at the weapon she held. She released the handle, but the sword remained upright. Her hand hovered over it, her damn magic keeping the blade from falling. She sighed, twisting her wrist, and the sword flew back to him.

"No," she answered as he caught it. "But before you retaliate, you should know that I'm not on anyone else's side, either."

He maneuvered the sword so he could use it if need be. "What does that mean?"

"It means I'm on my own side. The side of Cate," she said. "Turns out, there is a lot less physical trauma on the side of Cate. At least for me. Might be kind of selfish, but thus is the side of Cate."

He had been a part of that physical trauma. Not only that, but he had been the cause of it. The start of it. The sword fell to his side. "Why did you come here?"

Cate looked as though someone had hit her. "James, you didn't..." She shook her head. "I, uh, I'm here to—I made a deal with Haleine. I help her— *you*, all of you—deal with Maddox and—"

"Not that. Why did you come *here*?"

"I didn't know where else to go."

"So you came here."

She shrugged. "I didn't think you'd want me mingling with the general population."

"Are you a threat to them?"

"I don't want to be, but who would trust that?"

"The queen."

Cate conceded that with a nod. "I guess all those suicide attempts damaged her brain." When he didn't respond, she looked at the ground. "I made a deal with Haleine, so while I need to be in this camp, I don't have to be in this tent, nor anywhere near you. If you'd prefer me to go elsewhere, I'll happily go. I just thought that whatever was going to happen between you and me should be private and not in front of a studio audience.

"I imagine you want to yell; you seem like you want to yell, and there's no one anywhere who would argue that I don't deserve that and worse," Cate went on. "I wouldn't even argue with it, if that's what you wanted to do, and you know how much I love to argue. But I wouldn't this time. I mean, I did some pretty unforgivable things—"

"I know what you did."

Cate nodded. "Right. You were there; you saw the whole thing. You saw everything I did, and—"

"I know what you did," James repeated. He was somehow calm. Where had his anger gone? "I know everything you did. I don't need you to remind me of that."

"Then what do you need?"

"Where did you go? What did you do there?"

"It doesn't matter where I went."

"The queen claims you were in Feond."

"She's right."

"She also claimed you were gravely injured."

"She's right about that, too."

"You don't appear injured."

"I got better."

"Your recovery is remarkable—even by your standards."

"You have no idea."

"What does that mean?"

"That you have no idea," she said. "And I refuse to explain it to you for that reason."

"I don't think you get to do that."

"I think I get to do whatever the hell I want to do," Cate countered. "You need me a lot more than I need you."

"Then leave," he said. "You don't have to be here, and no one wants you to be."

She nodded. "Dana and I should start a club."

"Why did you go to Feond?" he asked. "Why did you go to Zaide Romanza?"

"I don't know. I'm not trying to be difficult; I honestly don't know. I remember leaving Enimode, and I remember waking up in Feond. I don't know what happened in between."

"What did you do there?"

"Got in touch with my inner...sorceress? Witch? Person with magical abilities not normally found in people?" She sighed. "I don't know what the proper term for it is, or even if there is one, but I learned some of what I can do."

"Only some?"

"I wasn't there very long."

"Why did you leave?"

"I killed the queen. Thought sticking around after that wouldn't be the best idea."

"Coming here was?"

"It's only for a little while. Then I'm gone."

"Who will you kill on your way out?"

"None of yours," Cate said. "If things go according to plan."

"Will they?"

"Depends on the plan," she said. "You only have, like, three questions left. Make them good ones."

Cate watched him without looking directly at him. Did she know what he was thinking now? Was there a way to stop her from doing so?

"Not so far," she said. "Well, unless I'm distracted by something else, I suppose."

"I didn't say that out loud."

"I know."

"That's an unfair power you have."

"No shit," Cate said. "Especially in a world where aspirin doesn't exist."

"Why did you kill Feond's queen?"

"Long story."

"Tell me."

"She hired the Black Wolf. She's the reason I...She's the reason."

"Why did she—?"

"To make me what I am today."

If only he knew what that was. He nodded but didn't say anything else.

Cate gestured toward the entrance. "If you're done, I'll just go find—"

"I'm sorry," he said.

Her face showed her confusion. "You're what?"

"Sorry. I'm sorry."

"You know, out of the two of us, I didn't expect you to be the one apologizing."

"I let them lie to you. I shouldn't have."

"Did you know the truth about Laorans before I forced it out of her?"

"No."

"Then you didn't let them lie to me."

"I knew Faolan had been dishonest."

"That's what he does. It's hardly your fault."

James looked away. Was nothing his fault?

"I'm sure lots of things are your fault. But this isn't," Cate said. After a pause, she added, "Sorry."

She was attuned to him. That's what the queen had told him. He sighed. "As long as you are here," he said, "you will stay with me, and we will stay away from everyone else."

"All right."

"You will not use any magic."

"Sure. That sounds like a reasonable request."

James bristled at her tone. "If you cannot agree to that, you cannot stay here."

Cate looked at the ground. "I'll agree to whatever you want."

"This is what I want."

"Great. Anything else?"

"I'll let you know."

"You do that."

He stared at her, searching for truth and not caring if she knew he did it. She kept her eyes adverted. If she was aware of his thoughts, she had decided not to comment upon them.

"Do you know how to win this war?" he asked.

"Not yet," she said. "But I know where to start."

—◈—

Mireille was coming. Mireille wasn't hiding any longer.

No, there was no place for her to hide, not when she had murdered Zaide Romanza and left Feond burning in her wake. The act had been a shrill scream that even Omur could hear.

He was energized—agitated by the death of his conspirator, pleased that it hadn't been him—and bolted from her bed, hastily dressing and departing without a word to the girl he left behind. Sighle knew where he was going, and what he would do there, but she lingered as the rest of what Mireille had done settled in her mind.

Mireille had returned to her brown-eyed boy and his rebellion to strike a bargain with her twin. Together, Sighle suspected, their powers would only grow until they were impossible to defeat. Neither she nor the gods she served were interested in testing that theory.

Mireille had to be stopped.

Only one thing now tied her to this world. One shred of a soul kept under careful guard.

There was only one thing to be done about that. The risk would have to be taken.

When Sighle entered the library, Omur and Garbhan were already hard at work, a map spread on the table before them. They had made their plans every day, and every day Sighle had turned them aside. *Wait, wait, wait*, she had commanded. Wait to see what Mireille would choose to do.

Now Mireille had chosen, and Sighle would do the same.

"The rebels were here before," Garbhan said, tapping the Aerona Forest with his finger. "We will start there and work our way out."

"No." Sighle placed her hand on top of his and guided it across the map—east, then south—until they arrived at the Donasien Woods. "Here. You will start here."

"Here." Garbhan tapped the name. "We will start here."

She stood on the tips of her toes to whisper her next request in his ear.

"Do be sure to kill the brown-eyed boy."

CHAPTER 45

The isolation tent was small and cramped, offering barely enough room for the two people meant to sleep there. The only furnishings were two threadbare bedrolls lying side by side, and a low stool upon which a lantern sat. As the holes in the tent itself would provide enough light when there was light to provide, Cate didn't think the lantern was strictly necessary. All it contributed were more shadows for her demons' frolicking pleasure.

She wasn't the only one with demons. James was struggling with a few of his own. He hadn't mentioned them out loud—he hadn't said *anything* out loud since he had deposited her there and demanded that she not leave. Much to her surprise, he left her then and went off to deal with other camp business—namely, making sure everyone knew she was back, that they were prepared for the worst.

It sucked to hear it, to feel it, and to understand that it was a completely rational decision. He was only looking out for his people, his cause. She had proven to be a risk to both. No going back from that.

When he returned, she lay on her side, her back to him, and pretended to be asleep. He unbuckled his sword belt and collapsed on the empty bedroll. His exhaustion leeched into her, but his thoughts kept them both awake.

He didn't know what to do, neither with her nor about her. The options ranged from nothing, absolutely nothing, to strangling her in her sleep, to simply asking if she was all right.

It was the last that broke her heart. Somehow, even after everything she had done to him, his family, his rebellion, he still had some sliver of himself—however small—that gave a shit about her well-being. How did he do it?

Mostly, though, he hated her. That was good; she was more comfortable with that. She knew what to do with that. It made sense, too. There was no real reason why he shouldn't despise her, just as there was no real reason why she shouldn't feel the same way about him. Maybe that made them even. Maybe that was how he was able to bring himself to worry about Dana and Faolan—and their plan to kill her.

A plan, a plot, a scheme—maybe it wasn't any of those yet. They had the desire to do it and had formed an exploratory committee to figure out how to fulfill that desire.

Dana had given himself away. He had stood at Haleine's side and telegraphed his intentions without realizing he was doing it. James and Haleine hadn't found out until later, while Cate was waiting in James's tent, but she had felt their reactions, too—a combination of horror and disapproval.

Another surprise. Who would have thought that James would have a problem with someone plotting to kill her. Certainly not her, but there it was. He didn't want them to pursue it further. Cate, personally, only wished them luck. It wouldn't be an easy task.

James eventually succumbed to fatigue, and as he softly snored, Cate rolled onto her back. It was raining now. Fat water drops worked their way through the tent's ventilation system and landed near her feet. She curled up and counted down the minutes until Faolan returned.

He'd show his little face before long. Wherever he had gone, he would have sensed her presence in camp and would come rushing back, desperate to protect his investment. It was honestly amazing that he hadn't shown up already. He must really have wanted her dead.

Her right hand began to burn then, and Cate sat up to examine it. The lantern's feeble light revealed a perfect, little scorch mark forming in the center of her palm. It hurt, but not much, and she looked at it, smiling when she realized from where it had come.

Haleine was playing with fire.

That was true in more than one sense, but Cate focused on the literal and blew on the burn. It was curious that she should feel this when Haleine had been spared the brunt of Cate's trauma. Not that she was complaining—she wouldn't wish that experience upon anyone—but somehow Haleine had only suffered bruises, and those had faded. What had protected her from the rest?

Pressing her hand into the grass, Cate drew life from it to heal the minor wound. Did Haleine know she could do the same? She'd healed others with magic—would she use it on her own behalf?

Cate hoped not. That was a slippery slope down which she was still falling.

Faolan returned with the sun. She felt his arrival but nothing else. Perhaps that was to be expected. He was an animal, after all, and it was possible her magic didn't extend that far. It was also possible that he knew how to shield himself, how to keep her out of his mind and emotions—provided he had those—and everything else except the rebel camp.

He wouldn't be happy with her presence, but he would see reason. Recognize her particular brand of help, as well as the rebellion's need to accept it. She wouldn't be around for long; he'd understand that, too. That wasn't her style anymore. Get in, do the damage, get out. That was her motto now.

She told that to a kid once, imparted that bit of wisdom while teaching him the broad strokes of fencing. Was he still alive, or had he gotten himself killed because she had made him think he could fight? She looked at James. If she asked, would he tell her?

He woke the same way he had fallen asleep—gradually and reluctantly. He studied the tent's apex before looking at her.

"Morning, sunshine," she said. "Sleep well?"

He grumbled as he stood. He picked up his sword and buckled the belt around his waist.

"Don't you want to inquire as to how well I slept?" she said, sitting up. When in doubt: be a jerk. Perpetuate the hate. "All things considered, it wasn't the worst, but it probably would have been better if I had a cot."

James grunted.

"How come Haleine gets one and I don't?" she asked.

"She hasn't attempted to kill anyone lately."

"Neither have I."

James looked at her, his eyebrow raised. "Really?"

"I successfully killed everyone I set out to," she said. "And a few I didn't."

"Not the goddess."

Interesting response. Cate shrugged. "True, that didn't go so well. I'll have to try harder the next time."

James stared at her, unimpressed, and reconsidered his stance on Dana's quest. He didn't even let up when Gair entered the tiny tent, the saddlebags she had brought from Feond draped over his shoulder. In all the turmoil, she had forgotten about them.

She stood. "Oh good. I was hoping the airline hadn't lost my luggage."

Gair dropped the saddlebags at her feet and stared. He was mad. Beyond mad. Probably because she had launched him into orbit shortly after slicing open his brother, but she supposed there was no way to know for sure.

"How's my mare?" she asked. "Did she get settled in all right? I would have taken care of her myself, but I've been under tent arrest."

"Mare?" James looked at Gair. "What mare?"

Gair gestured to Cate. "Her mare. The silver."

James looked at her. "Where did you get a horse?"

"Stole her from Zaide Romanza's stables," Cate said.

"Before or after the murder?"

"After." She looked at Gair. "Is she all right?"

"Aye," Gair said.

"Good," Cate said. "Thank you."

Gair did not care for her gratitude. His eyes hardened as his hands formed fists. Some people were just determined to hold a grudge.

"Was there something more, Gair?" James asked.

"The queen has summoned you—both of you."

James swore under his breath, and Cate had to bite the inside of her cheek to keep from smiling.

"Aye, fine," he said. "We'll be along."

As Gair departed, Cate crouched to sort through her bags. If she was about to face down Judge Haleine and a jury of the angry, she should make an effort to look less like a homicidal wildling.

"You stole a horse," James said.

"And a wardrobe. It seemed a shame to leave them behind. Waste not, want not, you know?"

"Aye," he said. "Hurry and dress. I don't want to keep the queen waiting."

"I would've thought that you'd balk at being summoned by her, that you would make her wait, just for the sake of making her wait."

"Not this time," he said. "We get this over with as soon as possible."

Cate watched him walk out. "I'll second that."

When they arrived at Haleine's tent, the queen of Lira was holding court. She sat in the center of the space, her hands resting primly in her lap. Her right hand was wrapped with a linen bandage, and Cate clenched her own hand upon seeing it.

Faolan stood on the table to Haleine's right, watching every movement Cate made, however slight. She still couldn't get a read on him. Dana, Ilya, and Lucius all stood behind their queen, but it was Dana on which Cate focused.

He was on Haleine's left, close enough to intervene should it become necessary. The fingers of his right hand were extended and flexing, closing the distance to his sword. If she did anything he didn't like, he would be ready.

His determination to protect Haleine was almost adorable. Too bad it would get him killed.

Haleine gestured to the empty chair across from her, and Cate sat, careful not to mirror her twin's posture. As James hovered behind her, she didn't need to look to know that his stance echoed Dana's.

If any of them managed to walk out of that meeting alive, it would be a damn miracle.

"For those of you who may not already be aware," Haleine began, "my twin and I have struck a bargain. Mireille has agreed to help us battle Omur and end Maddox's rule. Afterward, I will help her leave this world."

Faolan, Ilya, and Lucius were the only ones who hadn't already known about the deal. Faolan looked at her, and Cate felt the first inklings of emotion from him. He was intrigued. Lucius took the announcement in stride, but Ilya did not. She had a tight grip on her emotions, so Cate was blind to her intentions until the warrior woman said, "Maddox and Omur? What about Sighle?"

Ilya didn't notice the agony on her queen's face. Cate could see it, though. *They want to kill her*, Haleine had said.

Cate looked at Ilya. "The deal only extends to Maddox and Omur. The deal does not include Sighle. I have no qualms with her; therefore, she is not my problem. She is your problem, to be dealt with by you at your convenience. Or inconvenience. I don't care which."

"You wouldn't be saying that if you knew what she had done," Ilya said.

"Burning villages, murdering people, using them as a source of ink?" Cate said. "I know what she's done. I just don't care."

Haleine looked sharply at her. "Mireille—"

"No." Cate stood to better confront Ilya. Dana stepped forward, hand wrapped around his sword. She pointed at him before James could react in kind. "Knock it off, Ken Doll. No one's in danger."

"Dana, stand down," Haleine ordered, and he reluctantly obeyed.

Cate looked at Ilya. "You're not here to challenge or tweak the deal. The deal is an entity that exists outside of you. It cannot be altered by you or them" —she gestured to Dana and Lucius—"or anyone else in this tent, this camp, or this *universe* who is not either your queen or me.

"As such, your only purpose here is to aid in the development of a plan to take out Maddox and Omur. Sighle is not up for discussion. If you're not on board with any of this, keep it to yourself. I'm not interested in your feelings. In fact, I insist you bottle that shit up and seal it tight.

"If you can't follow these guidelines as I have laid them out, find an exit."

She sat down again and glared at each of them in turn. Dana glared back. Ilya, however, was looking rather superior.

"Tell me, then," she said. "How do you plan to defeat Sighle's wall?"

"I don't know yet," Cate admitted.

Ilya smirked. "Well, I feel my confidence rising already."

"Give me a break, all right?" Cate said. "I only found out about the damn thing yesterday."

"Why weren't you aware of it before?" Dana asked. "You were in the palace with Sighle, weren't you?"

Cate shrugged. "I didn't get a lot of yard time during my incarceration. I was mostly kept behind locked doors."

"Those work on you?" Dana scoffed.

The former rebel leader really wasn't a fan. He sent nothing but metaphorical daggers in her direction. He hated what she had done to Haleine, and what he thought she would do to James. The second part seemed unfair, but he was probably right.

"They did then," Cate answered. "So, before we do anything else, I suppose I should check out this mysterious wall."

"What then?" Dana challenged.

Cate looked at him. "I find a way through it. I'm here to kill Omur, and if he's on the other side of that wall, then that's where I'll go."

"You mean to kill Omur," James said. "That's your plan?"

She twisted around. "He won't step aside because we ask him nicely."

"You mean to kill Omur," James repeated. "You, by yourself."

He was sliding back into protection mode. Goddammit. What exactly would she have to do to break him of that need to keep her safe?

"Yeah, me by myself," she said. "It's the only way."

"She's right," Faolan said.

James looked at the pegasus. "You wouldn't let the queen do this."

"You're right. I wouldn't want Haleine to face Omur, but it doesn't matter. Cate has to be the one to do this. She's the only one who can face him and hope to survive."

Cate snorted. "The only one you wouldn't care about if she died, you mean."

Faolan hesitated. "That, too."

"Bloody hell," James said. "This is insane."

"No, it's not." Cate stood and turned, gripping the back of the chair as she leaned toward him. "This is how it has to be. I'm the one who's strong enough to kill him. Me. No one else."

Not even James could argue with that. He held her stare a moment longer, then nodded. "I'll take you to Eluned today."

"Thank you," she mouthed, and he gave her another nod that was nothing more than a miniscule jerk of his head.

"No," Dana said.

James glanced up, hand moving to his sword. Cate placed her hand over his and shook her head when he looked at her. She turned to Dana.

"You can't do this, Haleine. You can't involve her in this," he continued. "I know my opinion means nothing; I know I have no right to even offer it, but you cannot do this."

"Dana," Haleine said.

"No. Banish me if you want, Haleine, but don't do this. Whatever help you think she may provide is not worth the risk. She can't control it. I've told you that. Faolan will tell you that, too, and I believe she would as well." Dana looked at Cate. "None of us know which side she serves, but neither does she."

All eyes were on her again, but Cate didn't argue. The man did have a point. She couldn't control the magic—at least not consistently. There were times when she hadn't been in control, and other times when she had been precisely that. Neither had worked out too well for the poor souls in the blast radius.

"If I wanted to destroy you, I would have done that already," she said. "And it would have been easy, too, because not a single one of the precautions you have taken would do a damn thing to slow me down. Reconcile yourselves with the fact that you're not worth the effort. None of you are."

The tent filled with a heavy silence as its occupants stared at her, their brains wrapping around her words. Would they view it as a threat and an insult, or see it for what it really was?

James walked away. "We're leaving, Cate."

She followed. "Good talk," she said to the others. "Let's do it again sometime."

"Don't you dare make him die for you," Dana spat, venom in his voice.

Cate turned without breaking stride and saluted him.

—⚘—

When they departed for Eluned, James requested that Faolan accompany them. The pegasus agreed readily, leading James to conclude that he was eager to watch Cate, hoping to prove Dana correct, or perhaps fulfill their deadly mission. James glanced at Cate, unwilling to think more on the task itself, but she looked back at him and smiled, suggesting that she already knew.

As none of the unicorns would agree to carry Cate anywhere, they took her stolen silver mare and walked out of camp. James led the horse, Cate at his side and Faolan hovering behind them.

"I'm no expert," Cate said, "but we might make better time if we get *on* the horse."

"We will. Just not yet," James said. He looked at Faolan. "Open a portal to somewhere near the city, but not so close that it can be detected by those within it. Cinna, perhaps, or Nechtan."

Faolan glanced at Cate. "Not Nechtan. It's too populated."

"Cinna, then," James said. "Will you do it?"

"I can do it," Cate offered.

"No, you can't," he said. "No bloody magic, remember?"

She shrugged. "Whatever you say, Captain."

"Don't call me that," James said. "Faolan?"

Faolan opened the portal, and Cate coaxed the mare through. They emerged onto Cinna's main road, in the center of a village that had never been rebuilt following the soldiers' attack.

"You can wait for us here," James said to Faolan.

The pegasus kept his eyes on Cate. "No. I'll come with you."

The forest was silent and the ground damp from the night's rain, so they made little noise as they galloped down the road. Cate rode in front, James behind her with his sword on his back and his hands as lightly on her sides as he could manage without falling off. When they neared Eluned, James claimed the reins and directed the mare to the hidden passage.

"Let me tether the horse," James said, dismounting. "Then we'll go."

"No need," Cate replied, stroking the mare's neck. "She won't go anywhere. Will you, Silver?"

"You need to tether her. She'll wander off."

Cate slid to the ground. "No, she won't."

James looked at the mare. "Magic?"

"Nope. Just really well trained," she said, heading for the passage.

"Get back here!" he hissed. "I need to make sure it's clear first."

"It's clear," she called back.

James glanced at Faolan.

"It's clear," the pegasus said.

James sighed. "Stay here. Make sure the mare doesn't wander off."

"That mare's not going anywhere," Faolan said. "I'm staying with you."

James and Faolan followed Cate inside the city walls. By the time James had secured the door behind them, Cate's head was tilted up, and her hands patted the air.

"Magic?" he asked.

"No, just practicing my mime routine," she responded. "All I'm lacking is the beret. Striped shirt, grease paint, red kerchief. You know."

He didn't know. The sarcasm was distracted, and he stayed quiet to allow her examination. Faolan perched on his shoulder.

Cate dropped her hands. "Huh. She is evil, isn't she?"

"Can you breach it?" Faolan asked.

Cate looked up again. "Don't know yet. Let's go see the rest of it."

"Put your hood up first," James said.

Cate turned, an amused grin on her face. "Sighle probably already knows we're here. I don't think a hood will do much good."

"She's not the only one looking," James said. "Put your hood up."

Cate rolled her eyes but did as he asked. "What about our flying fashion accessory? I'd say he's the most recognizable of us all. It's not like this place is crawling with tiny, flying horses."

"I'm not a horse," Faolan said.

"You're the queen's bloody twin," James said, raising his own hood. "You don't think you're recognizable?"

"Well, not anymore," she said. "I'm wearing my hood."

James shrugged the pegasus off his shoulder. "Faolan knows how to stay out of sight. He can monitor our movements from afar. Cate, if your sister already knows we're here, we're running on borrowed time. We need to focus on the wall now."

"Aye, aye, Captain," Cate said as she stepped out of the alley.

James nodded to Faolan, then went after her. Cate walked, hand out. If she touched the wall, it did not appear to hurt her.

"You promised you would never call me that," he said.

"I lied. I'm evil, remember?"

"You're not evil."

She laughed. "Once more with feeling, maybe."

"What?"

"Nothing," she said. "Can you tell the wall's there? Can you see it or anything like that?"

"I thought I heard it once—humming, aye?—but I can't see it. Walked right into it the first bloody time. I didn't realize it was there."

"What happened when you did?"

"Pain. It's the same every time."

Cate looked at him. "Every time? How many times have there been? God, James, if it hurt, why didn't you stop?"

"I had to keep trying. I had to get you back," he said. "What else should I have done?"

She looked away. "Does that still happen? The pain? I mean, if you were to touch it."

He cautiously reached out, gritting his teeth when his hand made contact with the wall. "Aye."

She shoved against his chest, knocking him off balance. "What is wrong with you? Don't do that."

James shook out his arm. "You're the one who asked."

"Well, I didn't mean for you to actually put your hand on the magical wall of pain."

"You don't have to worry about my bloody hand," he said. "Just tell me if you can breach the wall."

"Maybe. It's hard to be sure," she said. "What's Haleine's plan to get inside? Does she have one?"

"Gair tells me she wants to lay siege to it."

Cate shook her head. "Won't work. It'll take too long."

"I believe Ilya told her the same thing."

"You believe? Gair told you?" She looked at him. "You weren't there?"

"They've taken to discussing strategy in my absence."

"Why would they do that? Aren't you the leader?"

"The queen fancies herself to be in charge."

"Imagine that," Cate said, grinning. "You sent Gair to spy on them?"

"They were talking in a tent."

"Is he listening today?"

James shrugged. "I want to know what they say."

"About me."

"Among other things."

Her smile disappeared. "Come on. I need to see more."

They walked along the wall, drifting in and out of crowds to avoid passing patrols of soldiers. Cate touched the wall when near enough, and James watched the palace. Was Omur aware of their presence? Was Sighle? Cate seemed to think so. Should he be relieved or concerned that the youngest Coileáin had not acted?

"Relieved," Cate said absently.

"I didn't say that out loud."

"Sorry," she said, eyes traveling to the palace. "I didn't..."

"Cate? What's—?"

"Shut up," she ordered.

James fell silent. He glanced at the palace and the crowds surrounding them, then searched the sky and rooftops for Faolan. He could see nothing amiss.

"Oh. *Oh.*" Cate laughed. "Well, that's kind of genius."

"What's genius?" he asked, but she wasn't listening. She stared intently at the palace, or the wall, or something else he couldn't see, her expression darkening every moment. "Cate? Is something wrong?"

"We have to go," she said. "Now. We have to go now."

Snaring his cloak, she dragged him back the way they had come.

"What is it?" he asked, prying her hand loose. "What's wrong?"

"Where's the nearest exit? Is it where we came in, or is there another one that's closer? It's okay if there are a few guards keeping watch or whatever— I can get us by them—we just have to...We have to get out of here."

"Aye, the passage is closest," James said. "What's the matter? What has you so panicked?"

"She wants Haleine; Sighle wants Haleine, right?" Cate said. "But she wants a certain version of Haleine."

"What does that mean?"

"Your queen is reluctant to embrace magic. She thinks it's destroyed her sisters, so she chooses not to use it, lest she be destroyed herself," Cate said. "But Sighle has decided to force the issue. If Haleine wants in—if any of you want in—she has to be the one to bring the walls a-tumblin' down."

"With magic?"

"With magic," Cate confirmed. "Haleine's the key."

"You're certain?"

"I can feel it. I can..." She looked around. "I can hear it. Her."

"Sighle?"

Cate nodded. "Yeah, her. I can hear her, or the magic, maybe—I don't know which; there might not be a difference—but I can hear it. It's calling to Haleine."

"All right, good—that's good," James said. "But why are we running away?"

Cate looked over her shoulder. "She knows I know it."

There was something else, something she was too afraid to utter; he could see it in her face.

"I am not afraid," she said.

"Stop reading my mind!"

"Stop making it so easy!" she exclaimed. "And stop thinking that I'm afraid. I'm not afraid."

"Then what aren't you telling me?"

"Nothing. There's nothing, okay?" she said. "Sighle doesn't want me running back to Haleine and spoiling her game, which means the doors are slamming shut, and if we don't get out of here soon, we'll be..." Slowing down, she sighed and pointed. "Too late."

James looked on ahead. Soldiers. More than a few. More than he could handle on his own. He stepped in front of Cate, his hand going to his sword.

"We need another way out," he said.

Cate snorted. "Astute observation, Captain Lira."

"Is everyone in your world always so bloody sarcastic?"

"Only the most fortunate," she answered. "Okay, what if I—"

"Run," James said as the guards came straight at them. He grabbed Cate's hand and pulled her along with him. A glance back showed the guards were keeping pace.

"James," Cate said, "I can—"

"Shut up," he commanded, wildly looking around.

Where could they go? Orla's? No. The men were too close; he couldn't risk leading them to her door. Where, then? It didn't matter, did it? Unless they could lose the soldiers, they wouldn't be able to escape anywhere. How could he gain some distance on them?

"I could—" Cate called.

"No, you can't!" he shouted.

"Here!" Faolan said, swooping into view. "Turn here. To the left."

James obeyed and immediately swore. Faolan had directed them to a dead end. James hit the wall with his fists as the soldiers blocked their only exit. He whirled around, shoved Cate behind him, and drew his sword.

"James," she said, putting her hand on his arm, "I can—"

"No." He knew what she could do; he couldn't let her slip again. "Stay behind me."

He pushed her back. She crashed into something, but he didn't look. There was no time. The soldiers were advancing, weapons out and ready.

Twenty men. He could...He could never defeat twenty men. Not here. Not on his own. Cate could—no. He couldn't involve her in this. Twenty men. He would have to find a way.

Cate approached again, and he put his free arm out to keep her from coming closer.

"I can help," she said. "Let me help."

"No bloody magic," he said, preparing to lash out at the first man. "You promised."

The soldiers stopped then, all of them. James put both hands on the sword, but the men merely turned around and walked away.

James maintained his defensive position. "What just happened?"

Cate laughed. "We weren't the droids they were looking for."

He lowered his sword and looked at her. "What did you do to them?"

"It wasn't me." She gestured to Faolan with her thumb. "The Great Gazoo here worked some kind of Jedi magic mind mojo on the black hats."

James gawked. "He...what?"

Cate looked at Faolan. "I don't know what you might call it, but you entered their minds and suggested they go elsewhere, didn't you?"

"You could tell?" Faolan asked.

She nodded. "I could tell."

James looked between the two of them, an inkling of understanding washing over him. "You can do that, Faolan? You can—"

"Mind control," Cate interjected. "That's essentially what it is, regardless of what fancy name he might have for it. He invades a person's thoughts and takes away their free will."

"Please stop explaining things," Faolan said.

James focused on the pegasus. "Is that true? Is that what you do?"

Faolan sighed. "On occasion, yes, I have done that. When I had to."

James glanced at the other end of the alley. The guards hadn't reappeared. He looked at Cate then. Unable to make sense of the expression on her face, he returned to Faolan.

"Have you ever done that to any of us?" he asked.

"Tell the truth," Cate said quietly.

Faolan looked at her. "Yes."

James shook his head. He couldn't have heard that correctly. "Who? Dana?"

"Yes," Faolan said.

"Me?" James asked. The pegasus didn't respond, which was more than enough answer for him. "You did that to me."

"You were going to say no," Faolan replied. "I needed you to say yes."

James blinked. "You...you needed me to say yes," he echoed, disbelief and realization combining to turn him numb. "And you..."

"Uh-oh," Cate said in a singsong tone. "Somebody's in trouble."

His disorientation only increased as he looked at Cate, then back at the now-silent pegasus.

I needed you to say yes.

"Find your own way out," James said, throwing the sword on the ground. "I'm done."

chapter 46

As James disappeared, Cate retrieved the fallen sword. It was, perhaps, not wise to let him go, but they both might benefit if he was given some alone time. Finding him later wouldn't be difficult. His emotions were shouting at her through a megaphone and showed no signs of abating. She'd be able to find him in the dark. With her eyes closed.

"Did you have to do that?" Faolan asked, his voice dripping with annoyance.

"What? Tell him the truth?" she asked. "It didn't seem like you were going to, so I took a stab at it. I'd apologize for messing up your slave labor, but we both know that would be a lie."

"Take a stab at it?" Faolan said. "Interesting phrase."

"I know lots of interesting phrases. Want to hear another one?" Cate didn't wait for a response. "'Not Nechtan.'"

"If you heard that, then you heard what came after," Faolan said. "Nechtan is too large a town. There was too much risk of being seen."

"You know how to stay out of sight, don't you? Isn't that what James told me? You know how to stay out of sight, so you would have known how to avoid every last soul in that town," she said. "What's in Nechtan that you didn't want me to see?"

"There's nothing in Nechtan. I'll bring you there right now, if you'd like."

Cate smiled. "You're only making that offer because you know I'm going after your boy."

"James is not my boy."

"No, he isn't." She laughed. "Definitely not anymore. You really screwed up that one."

Faolan's head tilted, but he didn't ask about her word choice. "He was better off not knowing."

"Like I was with Laorans?" she asked. "You won't be able to reason or lie your way out of this. You stole away a man's free will—you took away his choice—and now he knows it. Nothing to do now but deal with the fallout."

"Fallout?"

"Consequences," Cate said. "Or is that another word with which you're unfamiliar?"

I'm coming for your brown-eyed boy, your lovely brown-eyed boy, Sighle sang, obscuring Faolan's answer.

Not again. James had been right when he thought something else had spooked her. Amidst all the taunts for her twin were whispers targeted directly at Cate. Threats—*promises*—that James would come to harm. Just seemed prudent to get him as far away from that danger as she could.

"Something wrong?" Faolan asked.

She looked at him. He hadn't heard that? No, why would he? It wasn't meant for him.

I'll make him scream and cry and bleed, that lovely, brown-eyed boy.

"Gotta go," Cate said. "Have fun with your lies."

She left the alley, concealing the sword under her cloak before hitting the street. The soldiers had vanished entirely, gone wherever Faolan had sent them. Feeling like a bloodhound trained to sniff out torment, she discovered James's trail and followed it.

He'll be so brave, yet die anyway, that lovely brown-eyed boy.

Cate slowed. Those lyrics were new.

And you'll be left to dig a grave for your lovely brown-eyed boy.

She turned. The song seemed to have ended, but Sighle's smile still hung in the air. Cate could *hear* it. That little shit was so pleased with herself. Cate marched toward the palace with laser focus, her determination driving others out of her path. She stopped in front of Sighle's wall.

"Listen up," she said, attracting the attention of everyone within earshot. "If you lay one finger on him—if you even *look* at him—you and I are gonna have a confrontation."

Oh, I know, came the response. *I am counting on it.*

The arrogance set Cate's teeth on edge. Stepping back, she drove her fist forward, sending reverberations rippling along the wall. Yes, she could breach it. Quite easily, as it turned out. Sighle's screams filled Cate's head, and she staggered back, hands pressed over her ears. Stares were contagious, the number of people focused on the hooded figure picking a fight with an unseen enemy only growing. Too many people. It would be dangerous to stay much longer.

"Maybe you shouldn't," Cate said as she walked away. "There's a reason they want me."

Getting out of the city was easy after that, and Cate followed James's trail to the clearing where they had left Silver. She found him there, sitting on the ground, his back against a tree. He frowned as she approached.

"You suck at running away," she said. "I would have been in a different country by now."

"Not all of us have your talent." James tipped his head back to look at her. "Your bloody mare wouldn't go anywhere."

Cate smiled and glanced at Silver. "The very best anti-theft system around," she said before offering James the sword. "You forgot this."

His eyes ran up both her and the sword. Though it wasn't audible, he sighed and reached for the weapon. He laid it on his right, and she sat on his left.

"Are you all right?" she asked.

A half-smile formed on his face. "That truly is an awful question, isn't it?"

"Only when one is as damned as we are."

"Is that what we are?" James said. "Damned?"

"You disagree?"

"I don't know."

"Well, that makes you a much better person than I am, although that probably goes without saying." She prodded him with her elbow. "What's your plan?"

"I don't know that, either."

"While it's nice to have company in that regard, you shouldn't just sit here. It's not like this is an overly populated corner of the world—I mean, you guys keep going in and out without anyone noticing, but..." She shrugged. "It's better to keep moving, right?"

"Aye."

Cate stood and held out her hand. "Okay, then. Come on."

"Where?"

"Back."

He laughed silently, shoulders shaking, and took her hand. She pulled him to his feet, and he slung his sword across his back. He mounted first, then reached for Cate. She used his boot as a stirrup, just as she had done in the same spot once before. He was remembering the same event, but she chose not to comment on it.

Once she was settled, James leaned forward and took the reins, steering Silver away from the city. Cate relaxed against his chest and let him take command. It was good for him to have something else to focus on, even if it was only the ride back to camp.

But they didn't go to camp. Instead, they left the woods and galloped in the opposite direction along a wide, well-traveled dirt road. Where were they going? Whatever destination he had in mind was kept close to the vest, protected by endless layers of anger, keeping Cate blind to his intentions until they arrived in Enimode.

She straightened upon recognizing it. Was it too late to jump off and run the other way?

They rode through the center of town on their way to the farm. Or what was left of it. Her stomach performed an impressive, if nauseating, array of gymnastics as they returned to the scene of her crime. She sure had done a number on the place, hadn't she? As James dismounted and walked away, she stayed on Silver's back and gaped at the cottage's remains.

They hadn't closed the door when they left. What was the point in closing the door when the back wall had been blown out? Cate could see clear through to the woods behind the cottage. She had done that—picked up a full-grown man and threw him through a goddamn wall—and then finished off with a display of magic so destructive, they had been forced to abandon their home completely.

Fuck.

Why had he brought her here?

She looked at a still-retreating James and sighed. The answer had absolutely nothing to do with her.

The barn was intact, as was the corral at its side, so she turned Silver loose inside the fence before searching for James.

He was crouched in front of his parents' graves, sword on the ground at his side. He didn't seem to be thinking or feeling much. Shock, maybe. Resignation? Or perhaps just calm, quiet control over himself and his emotions—because that was possible when she wasn't involved. He picked up a handful of dirt and held it for a moment before letting it slip through his fingers. When he repeated the action, she stopped. Whatever this was, she shouldn't get in the middle of it.

But before she could make an escape, James glanced over his shoulder.

"Sorry. I didn't mean to interrupt," she said. "I'll just…I'll go wait with Silver. Take your time."

"If Faolan hadn't…If I had said no"—James looked at the graves—"they might still be alive."

She moved closer. "Or you might be dead, too. You, and them, Aaron, Sarai—all of you." Cate shrugged. "Maybe not Sarai. She's pretty scary—Death might not dare come for her."

James looked at her, confusion mixed with some incredulity all over his face.

"Sorry," she said again. "But it's true—the first part, anyway. Maybe they would be alive, but there's every chance that you wouldn't be. You were a farmer, James. Swordplay wasn't a part of your daily routine. If you hadn't learned how to fight, the soldiers might have killed you the first time around."

"Aaron learned."

"He learned because you got suckered into the rebellion," she said. "I don't condone what Faolan did, or how he did it, but it's possible that by doing so, he saved your life. Aaron's life, too, by extension."

"Sounds like condoning to me."

"Yeah, well, what would you know about it?" Cate said. "You can't play the 'what if' game, James. Take it from someone who knows—there's nothing down that road but madness and futility. Until a way exists to open a portal to the past, what's happened can't be changed. We can only move forward."

"Familiar with moving forward, are you?"

"I read a lot."

James stood. "It'll be getting dark soon. We should go."

"If you need more time—want more time—we don't have to leave. We could crash in the barn and set out again tomorrow. If you want."

He shook his head. "We should keep moving."

But he went down again, his rush of anguish shoving her back. Unconsciously, he reached for another handful of dirt. As it slipped through his fingers, rain started to fall, and Cate looked at the overcast and darkening sky. They weren't going anywhere until morning.

Returning to the corral, she rounded up Silver and moved her into a stall in the barn. Though it had been abandoned, the scent of farm animals was heavy in the air. Where had all the livestock gone? There had been cows and sheep and horses before, but none of them were there now. What had happened to them? Lost? Stolen? Wherever they were, she had to assume their absence was her fault. How considerate of her to so thoroughly destroy James's livelihood.

By the time she finished caring for Silver, the rain was on the verge of a downpour, and James hadn't yet appeared. She ventured out to fetch him, finding him in the same spot. Putting her hand beneath his elbow, she gently lifted and was surprised when he rose without a fight. Grabbing his sword, he accompanied her back to the barn.

Once inside, he stripped off his sodden cloak, draping it over a stall door, and abandoned the sword in a corner. He checked on the mare and was either satisfied with Cate's work or too disinterested to care. He said nothing as he climbed to the loft. Cate waited a moment before following.

He sat against the wall at the other end, elbows resting on bent knees and his head angled toward the dimming light coming from the opened loft doors.

"Do you mean to shadow me everywhere I go?" he asked.

"Depends on where you go."

"We should go back."

"It's raining."

"Afraid to get wet?"

"Yes," she said. "Just like any wicked witch would be."

James nodded as though he had understood what she had said. He really wasn't in any shape to go anywhere that night.

"The camp will still be there in the morning," she said.

James started to nod, but it turned into a shake of his head. "I don't want to be there, I don't want to be here. I don't know what to do."

"Don't do anything. Tonight, at least. It's not a very good long-term plan, but it's all right for a night."

"It's a waste of time."

"That's one of its biggest perks."

James said nothing after that. Cate lingered near the ladder, unsure as to whether she should stay or go.

"What do I do?" he asked. "What do I do about Faolan? How do I remain in that camp when all I want to do is throttle that miserable little beast?"

"Don't stay." She slinked forward, sticking to the edges to give him as much space as possible. "You don't have to be there. You could leave. You could walk out, walk away, and never be heard from again."

James shook his head. "I can't do that. If I did, I would be no better than—"

"Me?"

"Dana."

"He and I are a lot alike, you know," Cate said. "Yet, you're only angry at him."

"I've been angry at you, too. I *am* angry at you."

"As you should be."

"Don't do that. Don't tell me what I should be. What you think I should be."

"Sorry."

"I'm angry at both of you."

"But not in the same way," she said. "You think about forgiving me. You don't think about that with him."

James laughed, but it lacked any humor. "I hate that bloody power."

"You're not alone in that."

"It's different, you and him."

"You're right. It is," she said. "When I walked out, I destroyed your home and put your family in mortal peril. Not to mention the entire rebellion. When Dana walked out, he hurt your feelings."

James made a dismissive gesture. "It doesn't matter anyway. I can't leave the rebellion. My family's there, all the people there...You're there—or you will be. You're not leaving."

At least he hadn't included her as part of his family. There was hope for him yet.

"I made a deal," she said. "I'm here until it's done."

"I didn't make a deal. I didn't do anything. I was going to say no—you heard Faolan. I was going to say no, and he *made* me agree." James looked at her, and she froze. "What do I do?"

"If you can't leave, you stay," she said. "You stay, and you deal with the thing that made you want to go in the first place."

"How do I deal with that?"

She shrugged again. "How the hell should I know? Dealing has never been one of my strong suits. But, seriously, though, fuck the pegasus."

"Fuck the pegasus?"

"Well, don't actually fuck the pegasus," she said. "Unless it's consensual, and you're into that kind of thing, but..." She sighed. "You're not going back for Faolan. He doesn't have anything to do with it. You're going back because the fight's not finished. You're going back because it's the right thing to do."

"That must be why it feels so miserable."

She laughed as she sat across from him. "That's for damn sure."

"You came back," he said.

"That's just selfishness. I only did it because I need Haleine's help. If I could leave this world on my own, I'd already be gone."

"Faolan would send you away, if you asked. He would do it tomorrow without you having to do anything in return."

Cate nodded. The pegasus would. He had never wanted her there in the first place, and now she was nothing but a threat to everything and everyone he was interested in protecting. He would send her away without hesitation.

"I don't want his help," she said. "I'm sure you can relate to that."

"Aye." James looked at her. "If you're so selfish, why did you come after me?"

"Was I supposed to stay with Faolan?"

"You did make a deal with the queen."

"With Haleine, yeah," Cate said, emphasizing her twin's name. "Not her pet."

"Where she goes, he follows."

"Unless he's off, trying to work out how to kill me."

James's jaw clenched. "Who told you?"

"No one directly, but I got it off Dana, Faolan, and Haleine. It was stronger in them than her."

"The queen doesn't...She was angry with them for plotting against you."

Was James actually *defending* Haleine? Cate understood that some sort of shift had occurred—the meeting that morning demonstrated that he maybe didn't harbor the same blind hatred toward her twin anymore—but she hadn't realized that he would ever consider shielding the woman to whom he would only refer by a title.

"But she didn't stop it, either," Cate said. "It's all right, though. She shouldn't stop it. Neither should you. As far as back-up plans go, it's not a bad one, and you should have a back-up plan. Just in case."

"In case of what?"

"In case they're right," she said. "I know you brought me here to take Haleine's place, but it won't work. We're not interchangeable. We're opposites. She's good, and I'm...not good. I'm bad. Very bad. Everything I touch turns to evil, and I'm incapable of doing anything else."

"That's not true."

"We're crashing in the barn right now because I threw a temper tantrum. It's true."

"It's not. You've done good, Cate. You've done right by the rebellion."

"By trying to kill their goddess?"

"By recruiting Emrys."

She looked at him. "Chuckles came through?"

"Aye. Because of you."

"Dana, you mean."

James shook his head. "You."

"Even if that were the truth, it doesn't change anything," Cate said. "I still can't be here. It's not safe."

"What happened before, Cate, I won't—"

"Not that. I'm not talking about that," she said. "*I'm* the danger. It's safer for you—for everyone—if I'm on the other side of the portal. If I stay here, you'll lose."

"Cate—"

"I don't know who I am anymore, James. *What* I am," she blurted. "I mean, look at my hands. I have the same hands—they're exactly the same—and to look at them you wouldn't think that they were capable of...They're the same, and I have the same brain, the same *everything*, but I'm not the same. I'm not that girl from Boston anymore—she's gone; that girl you found is gone—and I don't know..." She sighed. "I'm not always in control of it. And even when I am, it's still too...You should have a contingency plan. You should know how to kill me. You have to know how to kill me."

"Cate."

"You have to be willing to kill me."

James shook his head. "I won't do it. I won't."

Which was why she couldn't stay. Another stretch of silence followed, and Cate looked at the ladder. Maybe she should go hang out with Silver.

"Well," she said, standing. "I'll leave you to your brooding."

"Tell me about the girl from Boston," James said.

"Why?"

"Why not?"

"I told you—she's in the past, and the past doesn't matter."

"The past always matters," James said. "Tell me about her. Tell me what your life was like before I ruined it. Or tell me anything else; I don't care. I just need..."

To be distracted. She did know a thing or two about that. Cate nodded and sank back to the floor. "I was a student. I was studying literature—books, stories, you know?"

"Studying books?"

His tone suggested that such a thing was just as big a waste of time as doing nothing. She shrugged. "It was something to do. It was never a passion."

"Is that what people in your world do? Pursue their passion?"

"The lucky ones do."

"And the unlucky?"

"They go through the motions. They do what they can to survive. Sometimes only that."

"Does that mean you were unlucky?"

"No." Cate looked out the loft doors. "I was very lucky. The goddess set up a nice life for me to live."

"What would you be doing if I hadn't...interfered?"

"Studying more books," she said. "Shakespeare, maybe, or the Romantics."

"Romantics?"

"Poets. Do you have poetry here?"

James smiled. "Aye, we have poetry."

"That's good. That shows there's...I don't know, beauty or whatever. Humanity, maybe. What separates us from the animals is our need to create, right?"

James laughed, the sound much friendlier than before. "I don't know. I don't know what you're saying."

"Yeah, me neither."

"I never know what you're saying."

"Yeah, me neither." Cate sighed. "I didn't want to be like this, you know. Evil, out of control—I didn't...It wasn't what I thought would happen. Omur and Zaide Romanza going on and on about all this bullshit, and I thought...I thought that's all it was. I thought I'd be stronger, more stubborn—"

"You're plenty stubborn."

"Not stubborn enough, though, because they were right," she said. "About what I would do, how I would feel—they were right about everything. I guess you really can't escape destiny."

"Destiny is a goddamn lie," James said. "Destiny, fate, prophecy—all of it. It's nothing but a game you can't win."

"Well, we're clearly not winning."

The wind picked up then, driving the rain inside. James stood and walked to the other end of the loft, returning with a quilt.

"Where did this come from?" she asked when he dropped it in her lap.

"It was kept up here for Dana," James replied, fiddling with something she couldn't see. "If he returned to the farm late at night, he would sleep in the loft. My mother left that and a lantern for his use."

The soft glow of lantern light filled the space. It didn't give off any heat, but Cate still felt warmed.

"You two go back a long way, huh?" she said.

James hung the lantern from a hook in the ceiling. His lips moved—offering a response, maybe—but she didn't hear it. She didn't hear anything but a familiar banshee wail as she looked at the gently swaying lantern and the hook upon which it hung.

Suddenly, the barn was gone, and Cate was the one dangling from a hook. Head pounding, leg bleeding, door opening, and there was malice, malice everywhere and not a drop to drink.

"Cate?" James said. "Are you all right?"

It stopped then, a needle scratching a record. She squeezed her eyes shut. If he was here, she wasn't there. She wasn't there. She wasn't, she wasn't, she wasn't.

"Cate?"

When she opened her eyes, the room above a tavern was gone, replaced by the loft and James gazing at her in concern. Her stomach felt heavy, and her heart thumped against her rib cage. Could he hear it?

"Are you all right?" he repeated.

She swallowed hard. "I'm fine. Just tired, I guess."

"You should get some rest."

Like that would happen. "You first."

He closed and latched the loft doors, then sat next to her. "Thank you for this."

She set the blanket between them. "I didn't do anything."

"Aye, you did. Not so selfish after all, are you?"

That, and more. He'd figure it out one day. She shrugged. "Just repaying a debt. You did it for me. You would do it for me. You hate me—rightfully so, by the way—but you'd still do it for me."

"I don't hate you."

She grinned. "Against your better judgment?"

His resulting laugh was mordant. "Aye."

She looked at him. "I really am sorry. I know I didn't say it—wouldn't say it—but I am. I didn't want to hurt you or Rhydwyn or Gair or anyone else. I only wanted to hurt her. I'm sorry you were caught in the crossfire."

James stared straight ahead, and Cate couldn't help but see what he was remembering—her, destroying his family's life. She relived it along with him, finding it intolerable to watch herself from his eyes, and twisted away to erase fresh tears.

"It wasn't you."

At first she thought she had misheard him, or that it had been a stray notion he hadn't meant to think. Wiping the tears from her cheeks, she turned to see him looking at her.

"It wasn't you," he repeated.

She watched the words leave his mouth, unable to deny that he had stated this concept deliberately.

"It wasn't anyone else," she said.

"It wasn't you."

Three times now. He didn't honestly believe that, did he? He couldn't. She studied him, waiting for a hint of disbelief, uncertainty—*anything* that would prove he didn't legitimately think someone else was responsible for the events that had transpired there.

"It wasn't you," he stated for the fourth time. An attempt to convince himself? To convince her? "Your eyes, your voice, Cate, your manner—none of them belonged to you. It wasn't you."

Five times. Damn. He really did believe it, didn't he? He may not have been sure what it meant, or even if it absolved her of anything, but he believed it just the same. She pitied him.

"That's a nice theory, James. There's only one thing wrong with it."

"Aye? What's that?"

"It's not true," she said. "Why would you say it? Why would you think it? Why would you want to?"

He didn't say anything, but he didn't have to. His resolve weakened, and the memory pulled her in before she could stop it. The rebel camp at night, a shouting match with Haleine—why couldn't she hear what they were saying?—soon replaced by another encounter—this one softer, sadder. No more anger, just sorrow and regret. As Haleine spoke, Cate strained to hear the words, but James's protections snapped back into place, and she was quickly returned to reality.

"What did Haleine say?" Cate asked, rubbing her temples to ease the dull aching in her head. Apparently, being expelled from a person's memories came with side effects. "That night in the tent, or the other time, what did she tell you?"

James turned away. "How many times do I have to tell you to stay out of my bloody head?"

"At least once more, it would seem," Cate said. "What did she tell you?"

He shook his head. "She didn't tell me anything. Or, if she did, I wasn't listening. I'm not in the habit of doing that, you know."

What was he hiding? If he had admitted to the assassination plot against her, just how bad was this secret? She dropped her hands.

"You listened to this," she said. "What was it?"

Try as she might, she couldn't get anything off him, either. How was he shielding himself? Everything else had come so easily; how was she meeting resistance now? Superior self-control? Willful determination? Divine intervention? Cate glared at the roof briefly, in the event that it was the last.

"Haleine doesn't know anything about me—you know she doesn't," Cate said. "Whatever she told you, there's every chance that she was wrong."

She turned her back and settled on her side. James didn't do anything but stare at her, his eyes boring holes in the back of her head.

"She wasn't wrong," he responded.

Cate didn't know if he had said it or thought it, but she curled inward as the truth of his statement and the meaning behind it infused her.

Shit.

Faolan had followed James and Cate out of the city and along the road to Enimode, maintaining as much distance as possible to keep his presence undetected. The precautions hadn't appeared to matter, as Cate was so fixated on James, she was blind to everything else.

James was the key. To keeping Cate grounded, in check. He was the only one with any semblance of control—of influence—over her. She would help them save the world only because James was in it.

Faolan had to ensure it stayed that way.

It could have been the only way to protect the world *from* her. He had told Dana that he would find a means of killing her, should it become necessary, and he had tried to do so. But he had suspected that his search would be for naught. Apart from a single prophecy, nothing was known about the twins, so there was nowhere to look, no one to ask for answers. There was nothing for Faolan to find, no help to be had.

Making James more valuable than ever.

Their enemies likely knew the same. Faolan couldn't leave James vulnerable to them. If something were to happen to him...If Cate would save the world because James was in it, what would she do if he were gone?

He couldn't allow James from his sight.

He would have to do so, however. There was the remainder of the rebellion to consider. When James failed to reappear, panic would break out—

especially with Cate's involvement—and Faolan couldn't allow that to happen, either.

After Cate led James into the barn, Faolan returned to the rebel camp. The atmosphere was calm, oblivious—their departure not yet lengthy enough to attract suspicion. It changed only as he grew nearer to Haleine's tent.

James's shadows—Rhydwyn and Gair—prowled outside of it, restless in the absence of their leader. Did they understand why James had left them behind? Rhydwyn noticed him first, nudging his brother into awareness, and together they stared at him until he entered the tent and the overt panic within.

The worst of it radiated from Ilya and Lucius as they argued over a course of action. Ilya was in motion, pacing from one end of the tent to the other, while Lucius stood behind Haleine, his clenched fists the only outward sign of his concern. Dana stood in the far corner, arms folded across his chest. Only those who knew him best would recognize the worry in his stance. Haleine was calm as she watched Faolan fly across the tent and land on the table at her side. Did she already know what news he carried?

"James should have been back by now," Ilya said. "Something must have happened. Captured, killed—we'll have to send people to the city."

"We won't be able to get into the palace," Lucius said tiredly, a sign that they had discussed this before.

"Then we'll get word to the queen's bloody guard," Ilya said. "We'll ask him to—"

"Or," Haleine interrupted, "we could simply ask Faolan."

"Faolan?" Ilya looked at Haleine, then saw him. "Where is James? Isn't he with you?"

"No," Faolan said.

Ilya stiffened. "Where is he?"

"He's unharmed," Faolan said. "They both are."

"What happened?" Ilya demanded. "Where is he?"

"He left me in Eluned," Faolan said. "He didn't mention where he was going."

Ilya's eyes narrowed. "Why did he leave you behind?"

Faolan hesitated. "He said he was done. With the rebellion."

Lucius and Ilya's disbelief and outrage was immediate. Dana looked at him in suspicion, but Haleine remained serene. She had heard the lie buried in the truth.

"He wouldn't do that," Lucius said.

"No, he would not," Ilya agreed, staring down at Faolan. "What happened? Was it...her? Did she do something?"

Her. Cate. Faolan looked at Haleine, still staring, and Ilya nodded as though he had answered her question. She turned to Lucius.

"I told him," she seethed. "I told him—*begged* him—not to get lost. How could he—?"

"We don't know that he's lost," Haleine said. She glanced at the others. "Leave us, please. I need to speak with Faolan."

Lucius obeyed immediately. Ilya was fraught with suspicion but departed. Dana lingered until Haleine turned to him.

"You as well," she said. "Contain any rumors about James to those within this tent—and his two men skulking outside of it."

Dana nodded. "Aye, your majesty."

As he walked out, Haleine looked at Faolan. "Where are they?"

"I imagine he went home," Faolan said. "I imagine she went with him."

"You imagine, or you know?"

He sighed. "They were in Enimode when I left them. I assume they haven't gone elsewhere."

"Will they come back?"

"I don't know."

Haleine nodded. "You're allowing them to think Mireille is responsible for this."

"Perhaps she is responsible."

"Is she?"

Certain Haleine already knew the answer, Faolan didn't respond.

"I know this is what you want," she continued. "I know what Dana asked you to do, and I know that when you leave here, you are searching for a way to murder my twin. Why should it matter if they believe her guilty of this? The more they hate her—"

"I don't want to murder your twin."

"Yet, you seek to learn how to kill her."

"What should I do, Haleine?" Faolan said. "There is a prophecy that claims she will destroy everything, and I need to prevent that any way possible."

"Not this way," she said. "I told Dana this, and now I shall tell you the same. You are not to pursue this further."

"I will always pursue whatever I must to safeguard the goddess and this earth," Faolan said. "You should know that better than anyone."

"Perhaps not as well as Mireille," Haleine said. "What did you do to her? What drove her to attack the goddess?"

Faolan didn't answer that, either, but Haleine didn't seem to notice.

"I thought it was the torture—that she was in so much pain, she didn't know what she was doing. But each time I asked, James told me that my questions would be better directed to you," Haleine said. "Tell me what you did to make her turn on us. Tell the truth, Faolan."

There it was. Cate had made the same demand of him, and her power had compelled him to obey. Had she taught Haleine to do the same? Haleine's command lacked her twin's strength—he felt the sway, but not the same urge to comply. Still, he decided to answer. The secret didn't matter anymore.

"What did Mireille tell you about Laorans?" he asked.

"She said the goddess took her as an infant and brought her to another world."

"Nothing about her mother?"

"She never knew her mother. Our mother."

"Not Rhoswen," Faolan said. "The woman who raised her. Did Mireille tell you anything about her?"

Haleine shook her head. "Who was she?"

"When the neruals came for your sister, Laorans and I stopped them—I've told you that," Faolan said. "We had to keep Mireille protected, you understand. We didn't know why they wanted her, but even if we had, we still would have taken her. It was the only way to keep her safe."

"What does this have to do with her adoptive mother?" Haleine asked. "Who was she?"

"Taking her away wasn't enough," Faolan said. "Another world without any further protections could still leave her vulnerable. We couldn't chance that."

"What did you do?"

"Laorans took on human form to care for Mireille," Faolan said. "She acted as Mireille's mother—*was* Mireille's mother—because it was the only way to keep her safe."

"And Mireille didn't know the truth," Haleine said. "About her mother, about herself, about anything."

"No."

Haleine looked away, shaking her head. "That wouldn't be enough. Not on its own," she said. "What else is there?"

"As the conflict here worsened, maintaining a human persona became more and more difficult," Faolan said. "Laorans was weakened tremendously and continued to deteriorate until she was left with very little choice."

"What did she do?"

"She had to let go of her human guise. She had to let Mireille's mother die."

Haleine's calm disappeared, replaced by revulsion. "Without telling Mireille the truth?"

"We couldn't—"

"Of course you could! Don't you dare try to claim otherwise," Haleine spat. "How could you do that to her? How could Laorans? How could you allow her to believe her mother was dead?"

"Her mother was dead."

"She wasn't! She isn't!" Haleine exclaimed. "Yet, you've allowed Mireille to grieve that loss. I know that is a pain you cannot comprehend, but—"

"I watched you mourn Rhoswen," Faolan said. "I comprehend it well enough."

"Then you have no excuse."

"We didn't want her to suffer. We didn't plan for that to happen."

"When have any of your plans ever worked?"

Haleine pushed out of her chair and walked away. Faolan stayed quiet as she hovered near the entrance, hands on her hips. Would she stay, or would she walk out on him again?

"It's slipping away from you," she said.

"What is?"

She turned around. "Control."

That it was. He couldn't deny that.

"You have woven a tangled web of lies and half-truths, designed to keep your pawns where you wanted them," Haleine said, stepping toward him. "But it's tearing now, and all your captives are finding their way free. Did you believe you could hold us in thrall forever?"

"Forever was never the intention," Faolan said. "Winning the war was."

"I hope you find your sacrifices are worth the cost."

"They will be. And if they're not...Well, that will hardly matter, will it?"

"It matters, Faolan. What we do, how it's done—that may be the only thing that does matter," Haleine said. "You cannot save the world at the expense of those souls within it. The war may be won, but there will be nothing left."

"I'm doing what needs to be done—whether or not you agree with it," Faolan said. "If I didn't—if I hadn't—hope would have been lost long ago. *All* hope."

Haleine returned to her chair and sat. "You don't have to kill Mireille."

"Maybe not yet, but that could change—and probably will," Faolan said. "I have to know how to do it."

He braced himself for another argument, but Haleine merely looked at him with sad eyes growing sadder. What was she thinking? He used to be able to read her so easily, but that was gone now. A wall had been built between them—fueled by her magic and his lies—and he had no confidence in his ability to tear it down.

"Find out what you need to know," she said. "But the decision to use it rests with me—and only me."

"And when it becomes necessary?"

"If."

"*If* it becomes necessary?"

"Then I will say so. Until such time, however, she has pledged her aid to this rebellion, and I intend to hold her to her word. James will help her keep it."

"I hope you're right."

"Do you believe I'm wrong?"

"I believe that James is all that's keeping Mireille on our side, but the truth remains that he failed to keep her in check before."

"That failure was yours."

"I didn't mean..." Faolan sighed. "Yes, my lies—Laorans's lies—were the cause, but James couldn't keep her from turning. Why would it be different now?"

"Because now Mireille knows what she can do, and she hates herself for it." Haleine looked toward the tent's entrance and called, "Lucius, do stop lurking and come in."

Lucius stepped inside, dressed for traveling. He bowed to Haleine. "I apologize, your majesty. I didn't wish to interrupt."

"You're not interrupting," she said. "Do you need something?"

"Just to tell you that I'm riding to Eluned to search for James, or for news of him," Lucius said. "Rhydwyn and Gair mean to accompany me. We will find his trail, your majesty."

"There is no need to do that. It will only put you at risk," Haleine said, looking at Faolan. "James is unharmed, and regardless of what Faolan has claimed, he will return before the next day is done. You will remain here. All of you."

Faolan held Haleine's gaze but felt Lucius's glance slide back and forth between them.

"Yes, your majesty," Lucius said and backed away.

"A vision?" Faolan asked once the man had gone.

Haleine shook her head. "Hope."

CHAPTER 47

As soon as James had fallen asleep, Cate covered him with the quilt and moved away.

He loved her.

He *loved* her.

He loved *her*.

How? Why? What, he couldn't find a wolverine or a honey badger to love instead? It had to be *her*? Goddamn masochist.

She'd have to stop it. He couldn't love her. It was too stupid, too dangerous. He knew it, too; he'd been thinking about it the whole damn time, either forgetting or not caring that she could hear every last syllable.

But what would it take? His feelings had been dented by what she had done to him, his family, his cause, but remained largely intact. Those transgressions should have been deemed unforgivable—ask the entire goddamn rebellion—but he continued to defend her to anyone who had the audacity to point that out. Including herself.

How could she make him change his mind? No—not his mind. His *heart*. His mind wasn't the problem. His mind was already well aware of the reality and was shouting that truth from the rooftops, but his heart...his heart was a different story.

She looked at James, illuminated by the flickering light. Yes, the heart was the problem.

As he started to dream, she went below and paced from one end of the barn to the other while silently reciting multiplication tables. When the rain stopped, she went outside and gulped fresh air.

Maybe she should leave him there. Let him wake up in the morning to discover her gone. Would that be cruel or kind? Maybe it would be both. How would he view it? A relief, or a violation of the agreement they had made upon her return?

If it were the second...would that be enough to make him hate her?

She didn't want to find out. Not there. Not ever, truth be told. Maybe she could take her own advice and do nothing. Just for a night. The problem would still be there in the morning. She'd figure something out then.

Or she could just tell herself the exact same lie the next night, too.

Leaving the barn door open, she returned inside to sit with Silver. The mare was lying down, and Cate wedged herself in between her warm body and the wall. Closing her eyes, she used the stall as support and waited for dawn.

James woke with the arrival of the sun, making enough noise to rouse the mare. Silver lurched to her feet, but Cate stayed still and waited.

"Cate?" he called out, voice tinged with panic. "Cate?"

She opened her eyes. He moved across the loft and climbed down the ladder, his anger twisting her stomach. The night away had done nothing to improve his temper.

"Here," she said when his boots had settled on the ground. "I'm here. With Silver."

He peered at her over the top of the stall. "What are you doing?"

"Sitting."

"Why?"

She shrugged as she stood. "I couldn't sleep, and I didn't want to wake you, so I came down here."

"For how long?"

"Not long," she lied, easing out of the stall.

"I thought you were gone," James said, fetching his sword and buckling the belt back in place.

Thought, or hoped? Cate couldn't tell. Now that he was closer, his emotions were strangling her. Her arms formed an ineffectual shield across her chest.

"You asked me to stay with you," she said. "Well, demanded it, really, but I told you I would."

He nodded. "Aye," he said and glanced out the opened door. "Why couldn't you sleep? Nightmare?"

Of sorts. "Just restless," she said.

He looked at her, debating the validity of her statement, and she lowered her eyes to the ground. They both knew she was lying. Would he call her out or allow it to slide?

He let it pass. She didn't blame him; it was the easier choice.

"There isn't any food here," he said, "but if you're hungry, I can—"

"I'm fine."

"You don't sleep or eat anymore?"

She sighed. "You don't have to do this."

"Do what?"

"Worry about me. Care," she said. "I really am fine."

"Aye, you're always bloody fine, aren't you," he returned. A shake of his head followed. "Do what you want. I'll tend to the mare, and we'll go back to camp."

She nodded, skittering out of the way when he approached the stall. Tendrils of love and hate tightened around her heart, and she grimaced. Somehow, it had hurt less when Haleine had stabbed herself. But that made sense. That pain had belonged to Haleine. This pain was all hers. And his.

James spoke to the mare in soft, calming tones as he brought her out of the stall and headed for the door.

"I don't have to go with you," Cate said when his back was turned. "Not if you don't want me to."

He stopped to look at her. "What about your deal?"

"I'll work around it. I don't have to go back to the camp, if that's what you want."

He looked away. "As if what I want matters."

She watched him lead the mare outside. "You have no idea how much," she murmured.

Sitting on the ground, she softly banged her head against the wall. She had to get out of this goddamn world just as soon as she could. It would be better when she was gone. *He* would be better. Not to mention safer.

With a groan, she buried her head beneath her arms and stayed like that until James called her name again. She looked at him, standing in the doorway.

"Are you planning to sit there all day?" he asked. "Or are you coming?"

Was there a third option? "Yeah," she said. "I'll be right there."

As he disappeared again, Cate pulled herself to her feet. The barn seemed to have doubled in length, and when she finally made it outside, Silver pranced in the paddock while James leaned on the fence, waiting.

"Last chance to blow off the rebellion," she said.

He pushed off the fence. "Let's go."

They walked out of the village with nothing but a lit lantern and the mare. James led them into the woods and pressed his hand against a large tree. A door opened in its trunk, and Cate's jaw dropped.

"What the hell is *this*?" she asked.

"The road back," James said, leading Silver inside.

Cate chased after him. "Has this been here the whole time? What even is this thing?"

"A tunnel."

"Okay, I know it's a tunnel. That's not what I'm asking."

"What are you asking?"

"Well, for starters, how long is it? Where does it go? Is it just the one tunnel? Does it only run from Enimode to the camp, or are there others? If there are others, how do you know where to go? Are there signs? Is it here all the time, or does it only exist if one enters it? What's powering it?" She stepped close to the wall and carefully stroked it. "Faolan, right? Faolan and his merry band of unicorns? They must be so pissed that I'm in here right now."

"Pissed?"

"Oh, angry—not drunk or peeing. Though I suppose they could be doing all three," Cate said, catching up to James. "Hey, do you ever worry about it falling down on you? What if you were in here and the magic collapsed? You'd be squished under all this rock or dirt, or whatever's here when there isn't a magic tunnel running through it. But that's not right, is it? You'd be...Hell, I don't know what you'd be. Dead, for sure, but as to the manner of that death—that I don't know. It probably doesn't matter what it's called. It's still a shitty way to go. Unless it doesn't hurt. Do you think it would hurt? It might not. It could be, like, one minute you're there, and the next you're not. What do you think?"

James looked at her but didn't say anything.

"Sorry. I know I'm talking too much," she said. "I'm surprised, I guess. It's weird because after everything I've seen and...well, done, I didn't expect to be surprised by anything ever again, but here I am, flabbergasted by an underground tunnel made of magic. I just can't wrap my brain around it. How did you do it?"

"Do what?"

"Reconcile this. The magic, all of the freaking weird shit," Cate said. "How are you all right with it?"

"Who said I was?"

"You seem like you are, and I have a pretty good handle on your emotions."

"That's unfair."

She shrugged. "Such is life."

"I'm not all right with it. It's bloody unnatural what you do. What you've done," James said. "You can hold fire in your hand and conjure a door out of nothing to transport yourself and others across an ocean in a single step. You threw me across a room and Gair through a wall. Lightning came out of your hands in a near-successful attempt to murder a *goddess* just before you disappeared in a ring of fire that should have killed you, but here you are—alive and well, and with a pretty good handle on my emotions—whatever that means. You know what I'm thinking before I even think it, and—"

"Not before. It's more instantaneous. Maybe a one-second delay, but not before."

"Still unnatural."

"Quite," Cate agreed. "Which brings us back to my question. Why so calm in the face of such unnatural acts?"

"What other choice is there?"

"Freaking out."

"Freaking out." James repeated the phrase slowly, as though determining how the words felt on his tongue. "What does freaking out entail?"

"Depends on the one doing the freaking out. You could scream, cry, tear your hair out, or scream and cry while tearing your hair out, or—"

"How will any of those resolve the situation?"

"Oh, they don't."

"Then why bother?"

"Everyone needs an outlet, my friend," Cate said.

"Outlet?"

"Release."

James looked at her again, then nodded. "That they do."

The conversation lapsed, Cate unable to sustain it, and they walked the rest of the way in silence. There were no signs, and no other alternate paths appeared, but when he led them back above ground, Cate was instantly aware of the rebel camp's proximity. Thought-based, then? The travelers need only think about their destination, and that's where the tunnel would take them? Cate had to admit that was pretty damn impressive.

Both Rhydwyn and Gair met them outside of camp. Had they known James was returning, or had they just been waiting there since he had left them behind the day before? The faithful dogs, lost without their master. Neither appeared happy.

Rhydwyn was particularly pissed off. Not that anyone normal could tell from his complete lack of expression. She hadn't had a face-to-face with him yet, and looking at him now proved that she might be better off avoiding such a meeting. But as she had recently attempted to butterfly him like a shrimp, she probably owed him an awkward encounter. Or maybe the chance to do the same to her. Did they believe in 'eye for an eye' here?

"The pegasus returned last night," Gair said in greeting. "He wouldn't say what had become of you."

"He didn't know," James said. "Is he in camp now?"

Gair shook his head. "Disappeared at dawn."

"Good," James said, leading Silver away.

Rhydwyn blocked Cate's path before she could follow. She looked him over and smiled. "Down, boy. You're not equipped for this fight."

Leaving Lenny and Squiggy behind, she entered the camp and rejoined James as he transferred Silver into another camp dweller's care. Their conversation went beyond the horse, but Cate wasn't paying attention. News of their return was spreading like wildfire, soon capturing Dana's interest. He made a beeline for them, Cate waiting to see him before nudging James.

She pointed to Dana. "Incoming. Twelve o'clock."

"What?" James looked in the direction she had indicated and swore softly. "Go on, then," he said to the man holding Silver. "See the mare settled."

"What happened to you?" Dana demanded upon reaching them. "Where have you been?"

"Enimode," James answered.

That gave Dana pause. He glanced at Cate. "Faolan told us you walked away, that you were done."

James looked at Cate, too. "He was wrong."

"Why did he think that at all? What happened?" Dana asked.

James shook his head. "It doesn't matter. I'm back now."

"James—"

"It wasn't her fault, Dana."

James took off, this time disappearing into their isolation tent. Cate hesitated. Following him didn't seem to be getting either of them anywhere. Perhaps she should go find Haleine.

"What happened?" Dana asked. "What did you do?"

"I didn't do anything." She shrugged. "I didn't stop anything, either, but I didn't start it."

"Then who—?"

"Faolan. It's always Faolan, isn't it?" she said. "When he told you what happened, I'm sure he didn't mention his role in it, so if you want to throw around some accusations, you should begin with him."

"But you did something."

"Pointed out a hard truth," she said. "That's all."

It was her turn to make a dramatic exit, and she did, only to be stopped by Dana's hand on her arm. She turned to look at his fingers wrapped around her.

With a flash of fear, Dana released her and stepped back. "I meant what I said before. I don't want him to die for you."

"Actually, you said, 'Don't you dare make him die for you.'"

"I mean it, either way," Dana said. "Don't let him die for you. Don't let that happen. He deserves better."

Cate smiled. "Bold words coming from a man who made his lover want to kill herself."

Dana's face reflected the gut punch, and he nodded. "Perhaps, then, that's how I know," he said. "As angry as he may be, James cares for you; he cares what happens to you, and we both know that..."

That she would meet a bad end. He was right—they both did know that. Why was he reluctant to say it?

Dana sighed. "Protect him from that. Please. Don't let him die for you. If you care about him at all…" He shook his head. "Make him stop caring. Please—do that for him. To save him."

He wasn't asking for anything that she hadn't already decided to do, but Cate looked at Dana for a long time. She couldn't make herself stop. To his credit, he didn't flinch beneath her extended scrutiny.

Finally, she nodded. "I'll see what I can do."

Inside their tent, James had stripped himself of his cloak, but the agitation remained firmly wrapped around him. She'd have to use that against him. He'd hate her for it.

But that was the point.

"Were you talking to Dana?" he asked.

"You could call it that, I suppose."

"What were you talking about?"

She took off her own cloak and laid it over his. "He wanted to know what I did to you."

"I told him you didn't do anything."

"I guess he didn't believe you."

James nodded and looked at her. "I don't think—" He swore. "Are you bleeding?"

Was she? Cate examined herself, finding the injury on her left arm. "I guess so. Look at that."

James ripped her shirt sleeve. Holding her arm at an awkward angle, he examined the wound. "How did this happen?"

Hell, she didn't even know *when* it had happened. "I must have caught it on something when we were running away yesterday," she said. "A nail, maybe."

He released her. "I'll take care of it."

Cate shrugged out of her vest and dropped it on her bedroll. "There's nothing to take care of. It's not even bleeding anymore. It'll be fine on its own."

"Like your back was?" James accused, and she froze. "You're bleeding through your shirt."

She carefully worked her hand under her shirt to touch her back, drawing away damp and reddened fingers. Yep. Her back was bleeding again. Would it ever heal?

James sighed. "I'll find Hanah or my grandmother."

"No."

"No?"

"Don't bother. It's fine. I'm fine."

James made a noise of disgust. "Stop being a bloody martyr."

It would be hard to find a better opening than that. Cate closed her eyes and breathed deep. Now or never. Putting it off would only make it harder.

Opening her eyes, she laughed. "I'm not a martyr. A martyr is someone who would rather die than give up his or her religious beliefs, and my only religious belief is that I have none. I'm just someone who would rather die of infection than apologize. That doesn't make me a martyr. That doesn't make me much of anything."

James pulled back, immediately wary. "What are you doing?"

"How many things would you be willing to die for?" she asked. "Tens? Hundreds? Thousands? More? How many people are in this camp? How many people are in this country? Would you be willing to die for all of them?"

"Cate, what are you—?"

"I wouldn't die for anything or anyone. Somehow, you've been seeing nobility where there's only narcissism. I'm not a martyr; I'm not a savior. I don't have a noble bone in my entire body. Two hundred and six bones to be found, and not one of them gives a shit what happens to this place, or the people in it, because I'm only looking to save myself," Cate said. "Haleine, Laorans, you—all of you—you could die tomorrow—you could die today— and I wouldn't care."

"You're lying," James stated, flat and seething at the same time. "I don't know what you're trying to do, Cate, but you're lying."

She nodded. "You're right. I am lying. If you all died, I would care. I would celebrate; I'd do a goddamn jig on your graves because that would mean there were fewer people around to try to make me care about shit I don't care about."

James backed away, eyes narrowed in suspicion. "What's happened, Cate? What are you doing?"

"Just trying to be truthful. You know how big I am on the truth. Truth and trust—that's my ballad, isn't it? Yours is honor and duty, and I have given you nothing but grief for it," she said. "It's insufferable, isn't it, how much of a hypocrite I am. Don't you want to throttle me for my high-mindedness? For my holier-than-thou attitude?"

"Stop it, Cate. Stop it now."

"Come on, James! You're fighting for your life here. You're fighting for everyone's life. You're fighting for the goddamn preservation of goddess and country, and what do I do? I come in here and make everything worse," she said. "You've spent all this time beating your brains out, trying to please me, trying to convince me to help you. You've fought battles for me, shed blood for me and because of me—you *died* because of me—but have I ever done anything except make your life that much harder?"

"You have, Cate. You—"

"I haven't," she said. Calm, cool, collected. The exact opposite of how they both were feeling. Shoving down the truth, she carried on. "The reality is, James, that you were willing to die for me, and that kills you because you brought me here to save the world, but now you know I'm the thing that will destroy it."

He shook his head. "That's not true."

"You can't lie to me, James. You were never very good at it, even before I could read your mind, so let's stop pretending. Let's not pretend you're all right with me being here because you're not. Let's not pretend you're conflicted about your feelings because you're not. Let's not pretend you don't know what you want to do because you know exactly what you want to do.

"Every single second since I showed up here, you've stood there, looking at me and wishing you could run me through with your sword," Cate said. "And it has nothing to do with Laorans or this ridiculous war. It's because of me. I could have blown a hole right through the goddess. I could have split the world in two, and you would still hate me because I took your trust and threw it in your face."

He was desperate, angry, as he paced in a tight circle while his hands clenched and unclenched. Once he had done that because of what Zoltano had done to her. Now, however, he did it because of what she was doing to him. His hand went to his sword once, twice, three times, and he came at her, stopping only when he was right in her face.

"You know nothing," he snarled, his voice low and dangerous.

She didn't flinch. "Enlighten me, then. What did I get wrong?"

"I would *never* die for you," he spat and stalked out of the tent.

The truth to his words was a knife twisting in her gut.

Cate closed her eyes. "I wouldn't want you to."

———◈———

The morning had passed without a sighting of James nor Mireille, and Haleine had worried that perhaps her hope had been misplaced. She did not eat the breakfast Hanah brought and dismissed Lucius when he arrived for her daily lesson, choosing to sit at the table with her knees drawn to her chest, her eyes closed and head bowed, as she strained to discover any sign of her twin.

It wasn't until the sun had reached its apex that Haleine was successful. She became conscious of Mireille first—wary and weary—and then James. The depth of his fury made her short of breath, and it was a pit only growing deeper.

What had happened?

"Your majesty?" Dana said. "Haleine?"

She opened her eyes and looked at him as she straightened, already knowing what news he brought.

"They're back," he said.

She nodded. "Are they hurt?"

"They don't appear to be."

That did not mean they were unharmed. Indeed, Haleine thought quite a lot of damage had been done. "Did you speak to them?"

She suspected not. Neither James nor Mireille would consider Dana a viable confidant. James would not deign to talk to her, either—not without proper goading—but would Mireille?

Dana shrugged. "They didn't say much. Both claimed it was not her fault."

His tone more than suggested he believed that to be a lie.

"It is possible that they are telling the truth," she said.

"It's also possible that she has bewitched him into believing so."

"She wouldn't do that to him," Haleine said. "What did they tell you?"

"James said nothing else. Your twin claims the fault lies with Faolan."

That was likely true. Had the blame belonged to Mireille or Sighle, Faolan would have said so, but he had told her so little about the situation that there was no other conclusion for Haleine to reach.

She nodded. "I believe Mireille may be right. When Faolan returns, I will..."

Her twin's heavyhearted melancholy swept into her without warning, and she braced herself against the table.

"Haleine?" Dana said. "Are you—?"

"What did you do?"

"Do? I don't—"

"What did you do to Mireille?" Haleine looked at Dana. "You either said something, or did something, because she is...What was it? What did you do?"

"She's what?" Dana said. "Are we in danger?"

Haleine slumped as the agony slowly dissipated—her twin attempting to regain control. "I rather think you are," she said. "What did you do to Mireille?"

"I did nothing to her."

"Then you said something. What was it?"

Dana threw his hands in the air. "I told her not to let James die for her. I asked that she protect him from that. From herself."

Haleine closed her eyes. Yes, there it was. She could feel James now. The pair of them screamed at her, misery and ire swirling like a storm. Unlike Mireille, he made no effort to calm himself.

"He cares for her, and he'll suffer for it," Dana continued. "I requested that she—"

"Make him stop caring?"

"Aye."

"You found a way to kill her after all. Faolan shall be so pleased."

"Oh, I've hardly killed her," Dana said. "Nothing, apparently, can do that."

Haleine opened her eyes. "You will have to leave."

"Leave?"

"Yes," she said, rising. "I argued for you, for your presence in this camp. Not one single soul wanted you here—*wants* you here—yet, I fought to keep you. However, I see that I was wrong. You cannot stay—not if this is your agenda."

"Haleine."

"You have decided not to trust Mireille, to hate her, and I do not care about that," Haleine said. "But you seek to undermine her, and in doing so, you undermine our cause."

"I'm *protecting* our cause."

"Yourself. You protect yourself, Dana. Once again, you are acting as the man, not the leader."

"I'm not the leader!" he exclaimed. "I'm not. That's been made perfectly clear."

"You're going against the leader."

"I'm protecting him," Dana said. "She is poison, and she will kill him."

"Did you listen to James when he told you the same about me?" Haleine asked. "Your feelings do not matter, Dana. We need her. *I* need her. I cannot do this alone."

"You're not alone, Haleine."

"I have never been more so, and that has never been more evident," she said. "Do you remember when you promised me answers? Together, you claimed, we would discover the truth of what I was—what I am—but it was an ill-fated oath you swore that day. Neither you, nor Faolan, nor anyone other than Mireille could have done such a thing.

"For days now, we have quarreled about armies, and we can rally as many as we desire, but it won't matter how many men we have if I can't put an end to the source of this strife. Men did not start this, and neither will men finish it. That shall fall to me to do, and whether my sisters are with me or against me is not your decision. Mireille is with me now; she is here, she is able to help me, and I badly need her to do so. If you are neither willing nor capable of understanding her importance, then you must leave."

He walked to the other end of the tent, keeping his back to her. After a moment, he sighed heavily and turned. "We always fight. Why can't we stop?"

"Dana, you cannot—"

"I don't want to fight with you anymore. Please, Haleine. Let's not fight."

"Then surrender."

He laughed. As he looked at her, she was acutely aware of everything he was feeling. What a strange, horrible power this was. Mireille had it quite right.

"Haleine, I…" He shook his head. "I don't believe James ever called you poison."

"That was a missed opportunity," she said. "He should be ashamed of himself."

Dana smiled, but his amusement faded quickly. "He'll always put her first, won't he? No matter what she does—no matter how much he might hate her—he'll still put her first."

"Yes."

"How do we stop it?"

"Why must it be stopped?"

"You know why. You must."

"And you must know why it can't," Haleine replied. "Mireille has done as you requested, and now their broken hearts are bleeding freely. You think it will protect him, but it will only serve to ruin them both. However it happened—regardless of whether it should have happened at all—they need one another, Dana, and they need you to understand that. I need you to understand that as well."

"If we don't stop it, it will ruin them anyway."

"And so it may, but that decision does not rest with either you or me," Haleine said. "They have given so much to this fight; they have sacrificed and lost, yet found something in each other. Be it love, comfort, understanding, respect—its name does not matter. It does not belong to you, and you were wrong to interfere."

Dana looked at the ground. "You're wrong not to."

"Am I? There was a time, not long ago, when you put me first, despite the cost. Then came the time when you stopped," Haleine said, meeting Dana's eyes as he raised his head. "Look where that led. Mayhap they will fare better."

As Dana stared, her head grew light, her thoughts hazy. His emotions fighting for position with the others, she thought, until the tent tilted and the world began to turn. This was something different. A vision.

"Haleine?" Dana said. "What's wrong? Is it Cate?"

She looked at the ground, but it only made the world spin faster. "No. It's—"

Her knees gave out as the vision overtook her. Dana caught her, and she lay awkwardly in his arms until it had passed. Once it had, he picked her up and carried her to the cot. He laid her upon it, then knelt and smoothed the hair out of her face.

"Vision?" he said.

She nodded, unable to speak, and brushed his hand away. He stayed at her side, his hand near hers.

"Should I fetch Hanah?" he asked. "Sarai? Anyone?"

She shook her head. "No. Y-you have to..."

"What did you see?"

"Soldiers."

"Coming here?" he asked, and she nodded. "When?"

"I-I don't know. I didn't—"

"It's all right. We'll find out." Dana glanced over his shoulder. "I need to tell James and Ilya. Are you—?"

"Go," she bade, then grasped his fingers to prevent him from leaving. "There were so many of them. I fear we shall be outnumbered."

Intertwining their fingers, Dana brought her hand to his lips and kissed it. "We always are," he said against her skin before releasing her.

"Dana," she called as he walked away. When he looked at her, she said, "We don't always fight."

He smiled sadly. "Aye, your majesty."

chapter 48

Bert and Ernie had been left to guard her, or perhaps they had taken it upon themselves. Cate didn't know which. What was certain was that they sought to protect others from her. They stood outside the tent, on high alert, swords out and ready.

Kind of a waste, considering she had no real desire to go anywhere or do anything, but if it made them feel better to stand there, she would tolerate it without comment. She definitely wouldn't tell anyone that Rhydwyn and Gair—as well-intentioned as they were—wouldn't be able to do anything to stop her, should she decide she did want to do something. They'd only be a minor obstacle in the way of what she wanted.

Probably good that she didn't want anything.

She should be tracking down Haleine, explaining Sighle's catch-22, and forcing her twin to do things she didn't want to do. She should be rallying the troops, storming the palace, killing despots, and booking her one-way ticket out of this hellhole. Every minute wasted was another minute spent in this goddamn place, but Cate could do nothing but lay on her side and cry into her sleeve as quietly as she could.

Following the escape of one loud sob, Rhydwyn came into the tent to check on her. Cate held her breath to stop her shaking and closed her eyes to give off the illusion of sleep. He stared at her briefly but left once satisfied that she wasn't up to any magical mischief.

She lay on her back then, treading water in the lake of worry into which the camp was still sinking. The more people who knew what she had done, the larger and deeper the lake grew. The majority of them hadn't been in Enimode for her swan song, so seeing how the gossip must have spread was interesting in an utterly demoralizing kind of way. No one much wanted her within their borders, and she couldn't blame them for that. She didn't want to be there, either.

Definitely not now.

It would only be for a short time. It would. Just days, maybe. Or even hours, if she ever worked up the will to leave the tent and talk to Haleine. The first step was always a doozy. The rest would be easier. Defeat Sighle's defenses, take out the black hats. Both doable.

Then, maybe, she could finally get the hell out of Dodge.

Leaving this goddamn world was looking better and better with every breath. She didn't need to go back to Boston. She could become someone else altogether—carve out a brand-new life that had no ties to anyone or anything. Boston could just be a way station on her journey to elsewhere.

Mexico was supposed to be nice. White sand beaches and tequila—what could be bad about that? She had a trust fund big enough to make a career out of being a drunken beach bum.

Was it far enough away, though? Maybe it wasn't isolated enough. Too easily accessible. Too many frat boys. Perhaps Bora Bora would be better.

James's return forced her to stop brainstorming remote places in which to become a hermit. As he stopped to ask the boys if she had done anything, she rolled over to face the opposite wall. Gair answered that she was asleep, and James dismissed them before coming inside.

A full minute passed where he did nothing but stare at her back. She scrambled to think of a song to sing, but nothing came to mind, so she quickly resorted to silently reciting multiplication tables to keep from hearing or feeling anything happening in his head. A gale of tangled emotions ranging from anger to despair slammed into her anyway. It was too much; she couldn't take it and squeezed her eyes shut until the storm had lost some of its potency.

Eventually, the staring stopped, but the anger didn't. He funneled it into sharpening blades, each stroke sending out waves of hate aimed at her.

She lay awake, thinking and feeling while wanting to do neither. What the hell was she doing? Why didn't she just get up and leave? He wouldn't stop her—*couldn't* stop her—and she had shit to do. Places to go, people to kill. None of which could be accomplished from a damn tent.

She pushed off the bedroll, determined, but the vision forced her back down and kept her there. Curling into a ball, she gritted her teeth against the assailment and watched as a pair of neruals—one missing an eye—tore through the rebel camp's population. People and unicorns screamed and died, all of them cut down by those razor teeth and claws, and she couldn't stop it.

"James," she croaked, once the vision had ended. She flopped onto her back, feeling as though she had been flattened by a steamroller. "James."

He ignored her. She called his name a third time, and when he didn't acknowledge her, she slipped off one of her boots and threw it at him. It bounced off his shoulder, and he whirled around, dagger in hand.

"James," she repeated.

He looked at her but didn't lower his weapon. "What's wrong with you?"

"We've got trouble."

"Trouble?"

"Right here in River City."

"What?"

"Nothing. Look, something's coming, all right?" she said, forcing herself up. "My spidey sense is tingling in a big, ole danger-is-heading-right-for-us kind of way."

He lowered the dagger. "Your what is doing what?"

"Okay, I don't know if you'll remember this, but I have visions of things. Did Faolan ever explain that to you? Haleine has them, too, so they're not necessarily evil, but I see things—pictures in my head. Most are events that have already happened, but there was that one forward-thinking vision that came true to the tune of neruals launching themselves through big glass windows in a damn near-successful attempt to tear me into bloody ribbons."

"What did you see this time?"

"I saw the neruals in this camp, killing everyone," she said. "They're coming after us, and I think they're coming now."

"Someone's sending them here?" James asked, putting the dagger back in its sheath.

"I haven't been bleeding in any caves lately, so probably."

"Bleeding? What does bleeding have to do with it?"

"It's how they found me the last time. I cut my hand in a cave, and they followed the trail back—"

James grabbed her arm and thrust up her torn sleeve to expose the skin. "You bled in Eluned. You bled in Enimode. Between this and your back, you bled all the way here."

Cate looked at the newest cut on her arm. "Okay, maybe I inadvertently sent for them, but the who or the how doesn't matter at the moment. What does matter is that it's happening, and we have to prepare."

"We?"

"You, all right? You have to prepare."

"Faolan and the unicorns are protecting the camp. We'll be safe here."

"Maybe, maybe not—probably not, as I was able to walk right through those defenses without breaking the smallest of sweats—but this isn't the kind of thing you risk. This is the kind of thing you run away from as fast as your little legs will carry you."

"You want to run," James said. "What a surprise."

"Yeah, see, here's the thing about fighting neruals: you can't," Cate said. "I know because I tried. I have been there, done that, and got the T-shirt. I used it to keep my internal organs from becoming external organs, so if it's all the same to you, I think I'll sit this one out. But if you want to try taking them on, best of luck to you. I'm sure you'll do great."

He looked away, contemplating doing just that.

"Oh, come on! You cannot do that!" she exclaimed. "You cannot fight these things. You have to get these people out, James. You have to raise the alarm and get everyone somewhere safe. Yourself included."

"You want us to leave the protection of the camp."

"It'll be a whole lot less protected shortly."

"You want us to flee," James said. "Why? What's out there, Cate? What trap has been set?"

"Trap? What are you..." She looked at him, mouth gaping, as she realized his implication. She always did have the shittiest timing ever. "I'm not trying to set you up for an ambush or anything like that. I'm not in cahoots with Sighle or Omur or anyone else. I'm not setting you up to die," she said. "I may have said and done some things—some quite recently—that could possibly lead you to such a conclusion, but it's not true. I'm only telling you what I saw and what I think needs to happen next. If you want to deal with it differently, go right ahead, but deal with it. Just don't waste any more time. You're running out of it fast."

He didn't move. Damned and determined until the end. Cate nodded and sighed.

"Consult with Haleine. Maybe she had the same vision. Maybe she's trying to convince Dana of the danger right now—though I'm guessing she wouldn't need to work too hard to do that. Consult with Faolan. He's a liar, too, but at least you know he'll do whatever's necessary to keep this thing going," she said. "I don't care what you do, James, but please, do something. Everyone here will die if you don't."

James picked up his sword and pushed out of the tent. Cate recovered her boot and went after him. The camp was in motion, lending credence to her suggestion that Haleine had experienced a similar vision. James wove his way through the commotion, head bent as he conversed with Rhydwyn and Gair. Cate trailed behind them, her eyes on Dana.

Dana spotted James first and headed toward him but hesitated when he saw her. His eyebrow raised in question, and she nodded brusquely. His subsequent relief pissed her off, and she envisioned herself kicking him in the shins. A rush of satisfaction ran through her when Dana stumbled, then bent to rub his leg.

"Has anyone seen them?" James asked Dana.

Dana straightened. "How did you know about them?"

"Cate had a vision."

Dana looked at her. "You had a vision of the soldiers?"

"Soldiers?" James said before Cate could ask the same question. "What bloody soldiers?"

"Haleine had a vision of the king's men heading right for us. Our sentries just confirmed it," Dana said. "But if not the soldiers, what are you talking about?"

"Neruals," James said. "Where's Faolan?"

"Neruals?" Dana echoed. "What are—?"

"Giant, evil man-dogs who want to eat your face," Cate interrupted. "Where's the pegasus?"

"I-I don't know," Dana said. "I'm sorry—giant, evil man-dogs?"

"Who want to eat your face," she repeated. "When they get here, don't let them cut you, or do that face-eating thing. If you do, you'll die."

Dana ran his hand through his hair. "Bloody hell."

"Yes," she said, "that's exactly what will happen here if we don't get everyone to a safe place soon."

"The magic will keep them out," Dana said.

"I bet you said that about me, too, didn't you?" Cate glanced at James. "Tell him."

James muttered, "Cate believes the magic will not keep out the neruals. It did not, after all, keep her out."

"It might work on the soldiers," she said, removing another metaphorical dagger from her heart, "but after the devil dogs punch a hole in that magic, it won't keep anything out."

Rhydwyn and Gair watched their captain, waiting for a command, but both Dana and James surveyed the camp. None of them wanted these people to die.

"The bright side," Cate continued, "is that the neruals will probably take care of the soldiers for us."

James's eyes shot in her direction, objecting to her word choice. Rhydwyn and Gair hadn't cared for it, either. She should not have included herself as one of them.

"For you. The neruals will take care of them for you," she corrected. "Of course, that will mean everyone here will already be dead. I could be wrong, though. Maybe no one will die. Maybe no one or no thing intending to do harm will get through the wall—because magic's infallible like that—and all this worry will have been for nothing. Or...I'm not wrong. That's a possibility, too."

James looked at Dana. "Ask Ilya if she has a count on our enemy yet. If not, she's to get one. Then find Faolan and tell him—"

"I don't think Faolan's in camp," Dana said.

"Talk to the bloody unicorns, then," James said. "We need to know if Cate's right, if there are other threats out there."

"Oh, Cate's right," she interjected. "But don't take my word for it."

"I won't." James turned to Rhydwyn and Gair. "Make sure everyone who can fight is armed and—"

"You're going to stay here," Cate said. "You're actually going to do that?"

"What else do you want us to do?" James demanded. "We have no place to go."

"Labhras. What about Labhras?" she asked. "I know you've moved since I was here last, but are you close to Labhras? Would Chuckles help?"

"Chuckles?" Dana said.

"Emrys," James translated. He looked at Cate. "Aye, he could help, but would he? There's a great difference between feeding us and allowing the whole of the rebellion inside his gates."

"He could be persuaded," she said. "You have both the queen and his bestest buddy, Dana, at your disposal."

James shook his head. "He met you, not the queen."

"While I was pretending to be the queen. As Haleine is actually the queen, I'm guessing she could—"

"You guess? You want to risk all these lives on a guess?"

She nodded and glanced at the other three men in the circle. "Don't stab me, okay?"

Before any could question the request, she put her hands on either side of James's head and forced the vision into him. His hands covering hers, he screamed until the vision ran its course and she released him.

He staggered back, staring at her as he struggled to breathe properly. When he collapsed to his knees to vomit, Cate held out her arm behind her to keep the now-terrified trio back.

"He's all right. I didn't hurt him," she said. "Calm down and give him a minute."

"Calm down?" Dana demanded as James purged a second time. "What did you do to him?"

"I showed him what's coming. That's all. If you wait a minute—a moment—he'll tell you himself."

James lurched to his feet. "Order the evacuation. Everyone goes, unicorns included. Now—do it now," he gasped. "Get the queen to Labhras to beg on our behalf."

"James?" Dana said. "Are you—?"

"Do it now," he said. "We haven't time to waste."

Dana glared at Cate but said nothing as he ran off. James looked at Rhydwyn and Gair.

"We'll need fighters, but not too many. There have to be enough to protect our people on the move," he said. "Weapons, too. We'll need lots of weapons."

"You're going to fight them?" Cate asked.

But of course he was. He would take his guilt and anger and his goddamn white hat and charge head-on into the fray. She could see him doing it, standing on the front line, acting as a one-man shield wall between his family and the evil that wanted to devour it.

James narrowed his eyes. "How did you—?"

"I know what you're thinking. I know what all of you are thinking." Cate pointed to Gair. "He's trying to work out where best to slip a dagger between my ribs. It's about here." Looking at him, she jabbed three fingers into her left side. "Thrust up for maximum damage." She pointed to Rhydwyn next. "He's planning to put one in my heart." She looked at him. "By the way, there's some debate going on as to whether I actually have a heart, so you might want to consider sticking that dagger somewhere else. Eyes, for example. Eyes are always good; if you shove it in there far enough, you're bound to hit the brain." She turned to James. "And you, my good sir, are not only wishing that you had never met me, but also that I had never been born. Just so you know, that wish never works out as well as the wisher hopes it will. Do what you want with that; I just thought you should be informed of the risks." She took a step back and looked at the three of them in turn. "Well? Did I get anything wrong?"

She hadn't. She already knew that she hadn't.

James looked at Rhydwyn and Gair. "Go."

"If you do what you're planning to do, you will die. You and them"—she pointed to Rhydwyn and Gair as they determinedly marched in the opposite direction—"and all those other fighters you collect. You will die."

"We all have to sometime," James said.

"Yeah, and as true and deep as that statement is," she said, "you don't have to sacrifice yourself and others in such a monumentally absurd, waste of a way. You don't have to do this, not this time. Not like this."

"You tell me demons are about to fall on us, and the king's men are close enough that our sentries have laid eyes on them," James said. "You tell me that we must run, that we must flee—and we do—but we need time. *They* need time, and they need someone to provide it. Every moment I can delay our enemies—every moment I can hold them back—is another chance for these people—*my* people, *my* family—to survive another night."

"I get that, I do, James. I want that time to be bought and paid for, but not if this is the price. If you go out there, you will die," Cate said. "It won't matter how many people you take with you or how many weapons you have—seriously, unless you have a rocket launcher lying around this camp somewhere, you are outmatched. Hell, even if you do have a rocket launcher lying around the camp somewhere, you'll be outmatched. These things kill with a scratch, and you won't be able to hurt them."

"I don't need to hurt them, just slow them down."

Cate shook her head. "You can't. You'll fail."

"Then I'll fail. But I have to do this—there's no other way. Don't you see that?"

She could make him change his mind. Make him run away with everyone else. It wouldn't be hard, and it would save his life. He'd find out afterward, and he'd hate her more than he already did—if such a level could even exist—but did it matter if he hated her more? If the goal was to make sure he didn't die here and now, did it matter? If he hated her, it meant he was alive to do so.

She could make him change his mind. One sentence. Ten words. A goddamn haiku—that's all it would take, and she could make him change his mind. Save his life.

She swallowed. "There's one other way."

"Aye? What's that?"

One sentence, and she could save his life.

"I'll do it," she said instead.

James laughed and walked away. She growled under her breath and ran to catch him.

"I'm serious," she said.

"You were serious about running away not long ago. Didn't you say you wanted to sit this one out?" he asked. "Well, go! Do it! Go...*sit*! Go do whatever you want to do—just do it somewhere else far away from here."

Cate stopped her pursuit. He now hated her more than Dana. Mission accomplished.

"I am going to do this, and you can't stop me!" she screamed. "I will save your sorry ass, and I won't even let you thank me for it afterward!"

Never breaking stride, James extended his arm out behind him and flipped her off. Despite everything, she smiled.

"That's my boy," she murmured.

She turned and stalked through camp, hunting for Dana. The bedlam had heightened, fueled by the threat of an unknown danger and the sudden rush to escape. Ilya stood in the center of it, shouting instructions, and Cate caught a brief glimpse of Aaron and Sarai joining the line of those prepared to flee. Dana stood in the back of a wagon, catching bundles tossed to him by people Cate didn't recognize.

"I need armor," she said, looking at him. "Where would I find it?"

"An armory," he answered. "Where's James?"

"Preparing for battle."

Dana dropped the bundle in his hands and searched the chaos. "Battle? But we're leaving. Doesn't he remember that? It was his order. Everyone goes. We're going to Labhras so we can avoid battle."

"He's not. He's planning to face the demons and ghouls in order to buy the rest of you time to get away."

"He'll be killed."

Cate climbed into the wagon to dig through the rebellion's possessions. "That's what I told him."

"Leave off a moment," Dana shouted to the others, then looked at her. "You have to stop him."

She jumped up. "I can't stop him. I *can't*. I destroyed whatever bond there was between us today because you asked me to, and now he won't listen to me. I told him he would die. I told him everyone he dragged into this would die, and he didn't care. I can't stop him. All I can do is try to save him." As Dana stared, Cate resumed her search. "I assume you won't mind if I die for him."

Dana worked his way to the front of the wagon. He opened one bundle, then another, and threw something to her. "Try this. And these."

The first item was a brown leather breastplate, smaller and narrower in size, with buckles on the left-hand side. She held it to her chest. Seemed like it would work. The second piece was a pair of leather, fingerless gloves that would cover her arms almost to the elbow. She slipped them on, Dana lacing them for her. After he helped her fit and secure the breastplate, she jumped out of the wagon.

"Good enough," she said. "Now get the hell out of here."

"We're going." Dana climbed out of the wagon. "Will you need weapons?"

"I am a weapon."

"Powerful enough to save James?"

That was the wrong question to ask. Yes, she was powerful enough to save James. But consistency...that was another story. She looked at him. "What do you have?"

There were no rocket launchers, but Dana supplied her with a matching pair of short swords and a leather harness to hold the swords on her back. There were knives, too—one for each boot and one for her belt.

"Thank you for the assist, but you really do need to leave," Cate said. "And whatever you do, don't tell Haleine what's happening here until it's over. You have to keep her alive."

"She's already gone to Labhras; she'll be safe there," Dana said. "With all the confusion, she shouldn't notice your absence until..."

"Until it's too late," Cate finished.

"Aye."

"Good. Make sure it stays that way."

"Keep him alive," Dana said. "If you can."

Cate nodded and walked away.

James and nine other men waited at the edge of the emptying camp. Their armor was mismatched and incomplete, primarily limited to ill-fitting breastplates. All carried swords, and most had bows and quivers of arrows. The rest carried a variety of other weapons—maces, pikes, and axes—but it wouldn't be enough to make even a bit of difference against what was coming.

James stood apart from the rest, leaning against a tree, and staring straight ahead. She had seen him fight but hadn't seen him like this—a man on the edge, a man preparing to fight. He was eerily calm for someone who knew he was about to die. She would have admired it, if it hadn't been for the fact that it would kill him.

"Come to watch me die?" he asked when she stopped alongside him.

"Had to make sure I got that front row seat," she said and rapped his tarnished silver breastplate. "Nice armor."

"It's borrowed."

"From whom?"

"A man I killed."

"So it's useful armor." She sighed. "There are ten of you."

"You can count. Good for you."

"What do you think you'll be able to do with ten of you?"

"Kill ten of theirs."

"There's more than ten men coming here."

"Doesn't matter."

She suppressed another sigh. "Do you know where they are?"

"The soldiers are nearly here," James said. "No one knows about your wolves but you."

She nodded. "Is your plan to wait for the soldiers?"

"The goal is to delay them, to keep them from following the others. So long as they do that, there's no need to engage before we have to."

"That's good. Smart," Cate said. "You know, except for the part where you're going to die."

"I'm so glad you approve." He finally looked at her and pushed off the tree. "What are you doing?"

"Saving your sorry ass. Remember?"

"Do you even know how to use those weapons?"

"Do you care?"

"No."

He didn't, either. The truth was poison hitting her bloodstream.

"There's still time to run, James," she said. "Run like hell, and save ten more lives today."

"I already told you I wouldn't do that. I already told you why."

She stepped closer to him, her arm grazing his. "I will do this. I will get you the time you need. I can do this, and I will do this. Trust me, please, and go."

He shook his head and walked away. "Why would I trust you?"

"I lied before," she called, following him. "In the tent, when I said all of those things about wanting you to die, and wanting everyone else to die, and...everything else, I didn't mean it. I lied, I lied, I lied."

He rounded back on her. "You think I don't already know that? How bloody ignorant do you think I am?" he shouted. "Of course you lied! I don't know why you bloody did it, but I know you did."

"James," she pleaded.

He shook his head. "No. Tell me why—tell me the truth here and now—or walk away and never speak another word to me again. Don't you dare do anything else."

She did neither. If she confessed, he might forgive her. He *would* forgive her; he was that special kind of stupid. If he hated her now—for any reason—it would be better. Her death was crashing through the forest, growing closer with each breath. If he hated her, he wouldn't care.

But the soldiers would kill him. Cate felt them, too. Twenty heartbeats belonging to twenty men intent on slaughtering anyone in their way. Then there were twenty more, and twenty after that. More followed, too many to count. The exact number didn't matter because James had Rhydwyn, Gair, and seven other men. Ten dead men walking.

"They're coming!" someone screamed.

"Enjoy your jig," James spat.

He abandoned her without a second thought and ran toward the voice. Cate watched him go, then looked over her shoulder. The neruals were pounding the earth in their haste to kill her. If she followed James, if she tried to help fight the soldiers, there was no telling who the devil dogs might encounter first. She had to meet them. She had to leave James to his own fate and go meet her own.

"See you on the other side," she said to his disappearing form.

She ran, heading straight at the neruals, and skidded to a halt in a small clearing. This was it—a good place for a fight and not a bad place to die. She removed the blade from her belt and dragged it across her upper arm, flicking the blood on the ground.

"Come and find me," she said, returning the dagger to its sheath. "I dare you."

She stayed in plain view, wanting them to see her. No time for games. This battle wouldn't be won with guerilla tactics. It would be messy, physical, and ugly. There was no way around it.

James couldn't avoid it, either. Her entire body convulsed when the first arrow went through his left shoulder. She hadn't expected it, and the force threw her to her knees. Pressing her hand against her shoulder, she pulled it away, expecting to see blood, but finding none. Guess she wasn't quite as connected to James as she was Haleine.

She could still see him, though, as he stumbled and dropped to one knee to work through the pain. Quickly—he had to do it quickly. The danger was still there, looming, threatening. He'd have more than an arrow in his shoulder if he didn't recover soon.

"Get up, get up, get up," she chanted. "Fight, goddammit, fight!"

The neruals burst into the clearing, snarling and snapping their jaws. Cate got to her feet. Her hands were shaking as she reached for her swords.

"We'll have to make this quick," she announced, drawing the blades. "I have somewhere I need to be."

They snarled in response before dropping onto four legs. She braced for their attack, but they stayed on their bellies like two well-trained dogs awaiting a command.

Cate stepped back. "What are you doing? Why aren't we fighting? What's your game here?"

"There is no game," a new voice answered. "They are not here to fight. At least not against you."

Cate took her eyes off the devil dogs to give the clearing a quick glance. No one. Just a voice—male and sinister—she didn't recognize.

"I don't have time for this," she said. "Show yourself, or I'm gone."

She waited only a fraction of a second before turning her back on the devil dogs and walking away.

"Don't go," the voice implored, directly behind her. "Stay."

Cate spun on her heel, swinging a sword in a high, wide arc. The blade sliced through the neck of a translucent man with brilliant blue eyes. Upon impact, the man turned into blue-and-white smoke, then reformed into his human shape.

"Nice entrance," she said. "Who the hell are you?"

"At this moment, your only friend."

"I don't need a friend."

"No, you need an army."

"You have one for me?"

The ghost gestured to the neruals. "Indeed I do."

Cate laughed. "Well, that sure is tempting, but I'm not all that interested in being ripped to shreds again."

"They are not your enemy."

"Oh, they ripped out my stomach because we're friends? I feel so much better about that experience now."

"You fought them. Did you expect them not to fight back?"

"What did *you* expect? I knew what they had in mind, and I—"

"How did you know? You saw it? Your vision told you what was to come?" the ghost said. "What you do not understand about visions, my dear, is that they only—"

"I'm not your dear."

"You are most dear to me."

"Who are you? Do you have a name?"

"I have several. On this earth, I am known as Yelsneh. I do not know if that name is one you have heard, but both Omur and Zaide Romanza will have told you about me."

That would make him one of the evil overlords. Cate sighed. "I definitely do not have time for this."

"You have all the time in the world. However, the same cannot be said for your boy. If you do not leave now, you'll never save him," Yelsneh said. "You do wish to save your boy, don't you?"

"He's not my boy."

Yelsneh smiled. "You claim time is short, yes? Let us not waste it with lies."

"Then tell me what this is."

"Only what I have said. You wish to save your boy, and I wish to help you do it."

"Why?"

"If I help you, perhaps you will help me."

"Help you kill a goddess, you mean."

"Yes, of course. For all the mistakes they made, I don't believe either of my servants were ever unclear about that," Yelsneh said. "Accept my offer. You will not save him any other way."

"His life in exchange for mine?" she said. "Guess we know who's getting the better end of that deal."

"It's not your life I want. It's hers."

Killing the goddess would kill James anyway. He was willing to die for the cause; she couldn't very well save him at the sacrifice of it. No, if she wanted to save him, she had to get back there and do it herself.

Shaking her head, she opened her mouth to tell Yelsneh off when James sustained a blow to the head, followed by another hit to the chest. His useful armor was failing him again, and as Cate choked back a sob, the ghost of a god smiled.

"How do I know they won't kill everyone anyway?" she asked.

She couldn't stand there and live his death. Couldn't and wouldn't. She wasn't strong enough for that. It was completely selfish, but she didn't care. She'd figure a way out later.

"You will have their control, and they shall kill only those you want dead. You have merely to think it, and it shall be done. When your battle is over, dismiss them, and they shall return to my side."

"There's at least a hundred soldiers," she said.

"Fewer now. Your lad and his men are not completely helpless," Yelsneh said. "But there could be twice the number, and it would not matter. They will prevail. You will prevail."

Pain shot up her right arm, and Cate didn't bother to conceal her scream as she dropped both swords. Her arm felt broken. Did that mean James's arm was broken? That was his sword arm—if it were broken, he wouldn't be able to fight. If he couldn't fight, he would die. Whatever she was going to do, she had to do it now.

She looked Yelsneh right in his ghostly blue eyes. "If you screw me on this, if anything you've said proves to be a lie, Laorans won't be the one I'll destroy."

Yelsneh extended his arm. "Likewise."

She put her hand in his before she could change her mind. His fingers slid along her skin, wrapping around her arm just below the elbow. She gasped as the cold burned its way through her, the arm guards failing to do their job. Ice spread through her body, leaving her feeling different. Strong, capable.

Lethal.

She released the god and looked at the neruals. "Shall we?"

Magic carried her and her temporary allies back to the rebel camp. She reappeared in a ring of fire that spread to the men closest to her. They yelled and screamed, and terror spread from one man to the next.

King's men only, she thought, and a moment later, the soldiers screamed for other reasons as the neruals began their bloody work.

She searched the melee for any sign of James or the other nine. Soldiers rushed her, and she brushed them away, leaving their deaths to the devil dogs. Were any of the rebels still alive, or had she delayed too long?

She stopped, closing her eyes and bowing her head. She had to be able to sense him. Feeling all his goddamn pain had to come with some benefits, right? If she focused hard enough, channeled her inner homing pigeon, she could find him. Would find him.

Pain suddenly gushed from her right shoulder, the force pitching her forward, and she opened her eyes. He had been shot. Again. Another arrow. Head whipping from side to side, she scanned the field for him, finding nothing but an arrow sitting in her own shoulder.

Oh. *She* had been shot.

Twisting to examine it, she saw the man responsible readying another arrow. She waited until it was flying before whirling around to catch the shaft in midair. The archer's eyes widened, and he froze, disbelief holding him in place as she advanced upon him.

"I think you dropped this," she said when they were face to face.

Grabbing the breastplate's collar, she jammed the arrow in his neck. Watching the life leave his eyes was tempting, but she still had to track down James and the others. This man would have to die without an audience.

She dropped him and resumed her quest, checking each body she came across. When she found a blank-eyed Gair, his throat cut, she stopped and stared.

There was no reason why she should be shocked. Hadn't she told James this would happen? Ten men versus one hundred—weren't too many ways for that to end. And yet...

Kneeling at his side, she gripped Gair's cold, bloodied hand and slid her fingers over his eyes to close them.

"I'm so sorry," she whispered. "Rest in—"

"Well," a man's voice interrupted, "if it isn't her majesty, the queen."

She looked at the speaker. Tall, obviously strong. A gash over his left eye bled, and more blood trickled from his nose. A red-stained sword rested in his left hand. She could smell Sighle all over him. Another meat puppet.

She looked from him to the rest of the field. The neruals had done well. The number of men still standing could be counted on two hands. The devil dogs appeared behind her, preparing for another bout, but Cate shook her head.

"I'll take it from here," she said, getting to her feet. "Run along home, little doggies."

She didn't watch their departure, but neither did the meat puppet. They stared at one another until the air settled.

"We've been looking for you," the meat puppet said.

She stepped over Gair's body. "Now you found me."

"The king will be so pleased."

She continued toward him, glancing around to count the remaining men. Five were still breathing and walking, and they formed a line behind the meat puppet.

"The king can kiss my ass," Cate said, focusing on Sighle's toy. "As can you."

She came across another body then, the silver catching her eye, and she knew who it was before she looked. James. His face was bloodied, his nose broken. Two arrows had pierced his armor. One was the left shoulder hit she had felt earlier. The other was lower, in his gut below the breastplate. A third arrow rested in his left leg. His right arm appeared to have been mangled, still attached to the rest of him by habit alone.

Was she too late? Had Yelsneh lied to her?

"He went down hard, that one," the meat puppet said. "Must have had something to live for."

"Something worth dying for," she corrected.

"You?"

His tone was cheerful, as though they were two strangers on a train making polite chitchat to pass the time and not enemies standing on a blood-soaked battlefield. In that moment, she decided she would kill him.

"No, not me." Cate walked around James and stopped in front of her sister's puppet. Would Sighle feel what she was about to do? "Hey, do you want to see a trick?"

He was forming a question when she put her hand through his armor and his chest and pulled out his heart. He looked at it, the query on his lips falling away. A fresh line of blood oozed from the corner of his mouth.

"Neat, huh?" she said as he crumpled to the ground.

The remaining five men gaped in open horror, not one taking a single step toward her. She smiled and crushed the heart in her hand.

"Die," she commanded.

They obliged nicely—one by one, clutching at their chests and falling to the ground, dead, like their leader and all the rest.

Dropping the heart's remains onto the meat puppet's corpse, she returned to James and collapsed at his side. She picked up his right wrist. No pulse, but that didn't mean anything; his arm was broken, the circulation screwed up, or whatever. It didn't mean anything. She reached for his left hand and breathed a massive sigh of relief when a pulse was located. It was faint, hardly worth speaking of, but it existed. He was alive, but just barely. That was all right—she could work with just barely.

She snapped off the arrows in his chest, leaving the heads inside him, and worked the breastplate buckles on his sides. Fingers shaking, she carefully removed the front piece, tossing it away. It clattered as it landed, and his eyes fluttered open, immediately finding and focusing on her.

"Hi," she said.

"Ca—" He coughed, blood sputtering from his lips.

Afraid he would choke, she lifted him onto his side and caught a glimpse of the bloodied back of his head. Because he needed a goddamn head injury on top of everything else. Shit.

When the fit passed, she eased him onto his back and wiped the blood from his mouth. Dragging his upper body into her lap, she wrapped her left arm around him to support his head.

"Is...is it b-bad?" he gasped.

She nodded. "I've never seen anything worse."

"Good. Don't—don't w-want...to b-be b-boring."

Laughter burst out of her, jostling James, and he groaned.

"Sorry, sorry," she said, pushing the hair out of his face. "I'm sorry. I didn't—"

"I-is it...o-over?"

"Yeah, it's done. You did it; you saved them."

"Proved...you w-wrong."

"You did that, too," she said. "You should—you should stop talking. Save your strength."

James smiled. "W-what for? W-won't...need it...n-now. Y-you—"

He swallowed, then gasped and choked, his body convulsing. Cate gripped him tighter and waited for it to end. He'd be okay. She made a deal. This, too, would pass. It had to pass. She made a deal. For him. She made a deal for him, and he would be okay. He had to be.

Afterward, his body went limp, eyes closing as his head lolled away from her. She stared at the exposed side of his neck, at the spot where it met the jaw, and waited, waited, waited to see it beat.

It would beat. It would. She made a deal. He would be okay.

The pulse stayed hidden, but drops of water appeared on his skin. Was it raining? She looked to the sky, but it was blue and cloudless, a gorgeous day for a massacre. Looking back at his neck, her vision blurred with tears. *Tears.* Crying—she was crying.

She laughed, then apologized for shaking him again, but there was no response. No pain-soaked moan, no plea that she stop finding amusement in situations that were anything but funny.

"James?"

She nudged his head in her direction, shoving down her rising panic and grief. His eyes were still closed, their lids pale and bruised. He looked small in her arms. He looked...

Gone. He looked gone.

Panic came in hard and fast, unchecked, and swallowed her whole. "James? James? James! Come back. Come back, come back. Please, come back. Come back to me, okay? Come on, James, please, you have to come back," she urged, her dwindling composure dissolving faster and faster. "You have to come back. You have to stay, James. Don't go. You can't go. Stay, please, stay. You have—you have to stay. With me. You have to stay with me. Please, James. Don't go. Please, James, please—"

His eyes opened once more. "Y-you've got me."

She nodded. Unable to contain her relief, she cried harder, tears dripping off her nose and chin. They splashed against his forehead and cheek, joining those she had left on his neck.

Cate leaned in and pressed her forehead to his, nothing but her tears between them. "I've got you."

CHAPTER 49

Before sending Haleine to beg Emrys on the rebellion's behalf, Dana had told her one thing: be brash, be bold. Cate had held a dagger to the man's throat; Haleine would have to be prepared to do the same.

Haleine had acknowledged his words with a brisk, distracted nod before riding off with her trio of guards. Dana had stayed behind to aid in the camp's evacuation, awaiting word that she had been successful. When it came, he escorted the last group out of camp and rode as hard as he could to Labhras, trying not to think of what he had left behind.

As he rode through the keep's gates, Haleine was hard at work, helping to settle the new arrivals. Emrys stood apart, overseeing everything without involving himself in it. They locked eyes, and Emrys nodded. A summons. Dana dismounted from his horse—a silver mare with which Cate had reportedly arrived—and left her in a groom's care.

"Do you know what it is that I have done this day?" Emrys asked when Dana had joined him.

"I do, aye."

"The king will come for me when he hears of this."

"We will stop him before he can, Jaspaer."

Emrys laughed. "Don't lie to me, lad."

Dana shook his head. "I wouldn't lie to you."

"Remember that." Emrys pointed to Haleine. "That is not the same girl to whom I spoke before. Who is she, and who is the other one?"

Dana contemplated his response, but not for long. Emrys had made a great sacrifice that day. He had earned the truth.

"That is the queen of Lira," he answered, watching Haleine. "The woman who came to you before was her sister—her twin. I am sorry they deceived you, but it meant our survival."

"What of the sister now? Is she the one the king declared dead?"

"To the best of our knowledge, aye."

"Is she dead?"

Haleine fainted, and Dana leapt from the platform, Emrys trailing after him. Lucius reached her first and knelt at her side.

Dana remained standing. "What happened?"

Lucius shook his head. "She just went down. I don't know why."

A vision. It had to have been a vision. What might she have seen? Cate? What would she make of it?

"It doesn't matter what happened," Emrys said. "Bring her within."

Lucius looked at Dana, eyebrow raised, and Dana nodded. Lifting Haleine, Lucius followed Dana and Emrys into the keep. The lord of Labhras led them to his own chambers, and Lucius laid Haleine upon the bed. Dana stayed near the door, watching as she slowly woke.

"Dana," she said. "Is he here?"

"I'm here." Stepping around Lucius, Dana sat on the edge of the bed.

She grabbed his tunic and pulled herself up. "Where are they? What's happened to them?"

Dana didn't answer. He couldn't; he had promised Cate that he would say nothing for as long as he could, and it had been a vow worth making. Given all they still faced, keeping Haleine out of harm's way was, perhaps, more important than ever.

"Dana, tell me right now what—" Haleine gasped, covering her ears with her hands. She closed her eyes and screamed.

"What's happening to her?" Emrys asked. "Should I summon the physician?"

Dana shook his head, unwilling to look away from Haleine. "No, it's fine. She's all right," he said. "Don't ask me to explain this yet, Jaspaer. I'll do it later, but not now. Please. Just wait."

When the second vision had run its course, her hands fell to her sides, and Haleine looked at him with tears in her eyes. "What did you let her do?" she asked. "I told you, Dana, I told you that you couldn't—"

"James stayed behind to fight, to buy us time to escape, and she stayed with him," Dana said. "She wanted to save him, and I didn't stop her. I didn't want to."

Haleine's face softened. "Dana."

"She asked me not to tell you until it was over. She wanted to make sure you stayed away. That you were safe."

"It's over now," she said. "We must go back."

"We'll go back, then," Dana said. "But you must stay here."

"No."

"Yes. Please," he said. "Just until we know it's safe."

"As if anything is ever that," she said. "I will return, Dana. I will not stay behind."

"I know. I still had to try," he said, then turned to Emrys. "Could we trouble you for some horses?"

They returned to the camp with Lucius, Brighid, Eion, and a handful of others, leaving the bulk of the rebellion to protect the rest behind Labhras's walls. Emrys offered to send men with them, but Dana declined. They needed to see for themselves what had happened before others were involved.

The camp was trampled now, no longer a home, but rather a graveyard littered with the blood and bodies of men and horses. Their own mounts bucked and shied, unwilling to proceed any farther, and were tethered to trees a safe distance away. Lucius muttered something about the perimeter, but Haleine paid him no mind as she pressed on, her concern for Cate and what she had seen overriding anything else.

Dana drew his sword and followed her. "Search for survivors," he called to those behind him. "If they're ours, get them back to Labhras. If they belong to the king, finish them off."

Their search would not last long. The carnage was shocking, even to his war-hardened eyes. No one would have survived this. No one *could* have.

Haleine walked amidst it all, hands covering her nose and mouth, guarding against the sights and smells of a brutal slaughter. One mangled corpse was indiscernible from the next, severed limbs and spilled guts entwining. Others had burned to death, their charred remains still smoldering. Odder yet was the line of five men who had died seemingly untouched and the lone man with a hole in his chest where a heart should have been.

What had done this? It couldn't have been human. Dana lifted his head in search of Haleine but finally found James and Cate. He stopped to stare.

Cate, an arrow in her shoulder and arm dangling uselessly at her side, sat on the ground, supporting James's head and shoulders. The broken shafts of two arrows protruded from his chest, while a third, untouched arrow sat in his leg. There was blood—too much blood—and Dana's limbs grew heavy and numb with realization, the sword falling from his hand.

No one could have survived. Not even James ap Seoras.

"Haleine," Dana said, his voice breaking under an assault of grief. "Here. Over here."

He staggered toward the horrible scene before him. It wasn't supposed to end like this. Not with James lying in a pool of his own blood.

"Cate?" Dana said.

Her head snapped up, revealing a face streaked with grime, blood, and tears.

Haleine swept past him and knelt before James. She put her hands on his cheeks, peering at his face. "Is he alive?"

Why did she ask? Couldn't she see it? Neither Dana nor Cate answered, but Haleine was already running her hands over James, fingers beneath his jaw, around his wrists.

She looked at Dana. "He's alive."

What? How? Dana looked at Cate. How had she done it?

"He's not lost, not yet," Haleine said to her twin. "I can save him. I *will* save him, Mireille—I promise you."

Cate remained silent, looking as though she didn't recognize the woman sitting in front of her.

"We must lay him down," Haleine said. "Help me lay him down, Mireille, and I will save him. You know I can do it."

Cate neither moved nor spoke.

Haleine looked at Dana. "Help me."

He nodded and forced himself to move, dropping to the ground at Cate's side. He kept his eyes on her face as he reached for James.

"You can let him go, Cate," he said. "We've got him; you can let him go."

She didn't acknowledge him, either. Slowly, he maneuvered his hands beneath James's body, taking whatever space Cate ceded to him. When she pulled away completely, Dana eased James onto the ground.

"His arm is broken," Dana said. "His nose, too."

"The arrows first," Haleine said. "They need to come out."

Dana used his dagger to slice through James's padding and shirt. Tossing them aside, he pushed James up to examine his back.

"The heads are in him," Dana said. "They didn't go all the way through."

Haleine nodded as she moved her fingers along James's broken arm. "Cut them out."

"Cut them out?" he echoed. "Haleine, you can't—"

Cate pushed back in, knocking Dana askew, and reached into James's chest, through the skin. Easing one head out, she threw it to the ground. Dana bolted to his feet, and both he and Haleine stared as Cate repeated the act. When she had finished, James's chest showed no additional sign of injury.

Cate removed the arrow in James's leg and stood. "What are you waiting for?"

Dana couldn't speak for Haleine but thought that, like him, she was waiting to recover from her shock. She looked from James to Cate and back again, her jaw dropped.

"Do it, Haleine," Cate snapped. "Otherwise, I'll use Ken Doll here, and do it myself."

Haleine looked at Cate, then Dana, and nodded. "Back away, both of you," she ordered. "Dana, do what you can for Mireille's shoulder."

Dana looked at Cate and the arrow in her shoulder. He gently tugged on her uninjured arm.

She whirled around, fury in her eyes. "Try it, and you'll lose that arm."

He released her, unwilling to chance it. "At least allow me to remove the arrow."

She looked at the arrow, then contorted her body to put a hand on its shaft and yanked it out without uttering a single sound. She dropped it and glared at him. "It's out. Happy?"

That wasn't the word he would use. "Cate, please, let me tend your shoulder. Haleine will take care of James. He'll be all right, I promise."

"Like your promises are worth anything."

"Let me take you out of here."

She shook her head, still staring at James. "I know my way out. You can't get me there."

She turned on her heel and left. Dana glanced at Haleine, still working on James, then followed.

"Cate, please! Wait," he called.

He nearly faltered when her progress came to a halt, but it wasn't until he reached her side that he realized she had stopped because of Faolan, hovering before her.

"Dana, Cate," the pegasus said. "What happened?"

"I could crush your throat," she said. "I could reach out and crush it before you knew what was happening. It wouldn't even be a challenge."

Faolan backed away. "Cate, I—"

"Did you ever think that maybe you did just what they wanted?" she asked.

"Every day," the pegasus answered.

The response meant nothing to Dana, but Cate smiled.

"I guess you do know how to tell the truth," she said. She glanced back toward the field. "When Haleine's done, when he's…Tell her to open the door. It has to be her. Sighle made it that way, to force Haleine into it. The magic. She has to—it has to be Haleine. You won't get in any other way. So tell her that. Tell her to open the door."

"Open the door," Dana echoed. "What does it mean?"

"Haleine will know."

"If she doesn't?"

"She will. Tell her not to take forever. A dead man's a dead man, no matter how much you might fuss," Cate said, then reached out and snagged Dana's tunic, pulling him close. Her next words were for him alone. "This fight belongs to Haleine. Don't take it away from her."

"What fight?" he asked.

She offered no reply as she released him and walked away. Dana repeated his question, but she ignored him.

"What fight?" he shouted, chasing after her yet again. "Dammit, Cate, tell me!"

She stopped, but instead of answering him, her entire body swayed, and he reached her in time to hear her say, "Oh shit," before falling to the ground with a thud.

———

One hundred men had been sent from the palace. One hundred men against his ten. A fool's errand—*suicide, you mean,* he heard Cate say.

Sacrifice—that's what it had been. He would sacrifice himself so that others might live.

Killing yourself for no good reason, she interjected. *Suicide.*

Suicide—aye, it had been that.

But it had to be done.

No, it didn't.

Starting with bows, they had used the cover of trees and brush to ambush their attackers. Aim, fire, run. Aim, fire, run. They were good shots, all of them, but their efforts were laughable. Arrows hit knees and sank into throats, bringing down mounts and men, but no matter how many fell, too many remained.

Men encroached farther into the abandoned camp. Cover was lost, and bows were exchanged for swords. Swarmed by the enemy, they were struck down easily but got up only to be knocked down again.

Again and again they did this, and James would keep doing it, too. They wouldn't win; they couldn't win, but neither did they have to. Delay the enemy, give their people the chance to get to safety—that's all they sought to do, and James would find a way to push through whatever the soldiers threw at him.

And he did. Until they killed him.

He had fought their leader, and he had lost. Pain in his chest, his head, more pain in his legs, his arm. His body had been replaced by pain. He had fought; he had lost. He hadn't gotten up again.

But now he had to...had to what? He couldn't remember. His head hurt so badly, he couldn't remember. There was the fight, the dark, and the pain. And Cate.

Cate.

His heart beat faster. He wanted to put his hands on his chest, to quiet the sound, but he couldn't feel them, couldn't find them.

What about Cate? Was she in danger? No, she was the danger. But that wasn't right, either.

Why couldn't he remember?

Why did it have to be her?

He remembered fighting the captain. The captain was winning; the captain would win. James had no weapons left, apart from his wits, and he had long ago exhausted those. Even if he hadn't, they'd be useless against the captain's skill and sword.

He remembered the strike. As soon as it had started, James knew it would end his life. He watched it coming as though the captain were moving deliberately slow to teach a pupil a correct stance. He had died at the hands of a talented swordsman, fighting for what mattered. Noblemen would say there was honor in that—that it was a good death—but that couldn't be right because he wasn't dead.

Was he?

No, Cate said. *You're unconscious and bleeding from the damn head. Among other things.*

He recalled the strike. But there was something else, too. The sword. The grip. Aye, that was it. The captain's grip had changed before contact had been made. That was a thing to be admired. The agility and skill involved in such a feat was breathtaking, as odd as it sounded, and James had appreciated it in the moments before his death.

But he wasn't dead.

Nope.

What was he, then? He couldn't see, he couldn't move. Mayhap he was a prisoner, blinded and incapacitated at the captain's hand. Perhaps he wasn't dead, but he was dying.

Still a drama queen, I see. If you're dying, what am I doing here?

Cate.

Whatever supported him gave out then, and James fell as though dropped from a great height. The landing robbed him of breath, but there was no pain. He could feel his arms and legs once more, but there was nothing to see but darkness. He sat up, checking his body for injuries and finding none. How was that possible?

"Cate?" he called, getting to his feet.

"Yeah. No need to shout."

"Where are you?"

"Around. Fighting tooth and nail to get out of this mind meld—unlike someone I know," she said. "Are you planning to set up permanent residence here, coma boy?"

Around. Around. What did that…Aye, she was there. He could *feel* her. She was not solid—a spirit, perhaps—but she was there. He could feel her surrounding him. How odd that he should be able to do such a thing.

"Where are we?" he asked. "What is this?"

"This is a damn inconvenience," she said. "I'm busy. I have places to go, people to kill—that sort of thing, you know."

Places to go, people to kill. He nodded. "You mean to go to Eluned."

"That I do. Just as soon as I get the hell out of here."

"You mean to go on your own."

"It was always going to be like that," she said. "Me, on my own."

He shook his head. "Don't go. Not like this. We can find another way."

"Not one that won't get you killed."

What did that bloody matter? "Omur will kill you."

"Then again, he might not. I'm not exactly defenseless."

"Sighle, then. What if she tries to stop you?"

"She won't."

"What if she does?" James pushed. "What if her powers are greater than yours?"

"They're not."

"How do you know?"

"Why do you care?" she asked. "One way or another, it'll be over. One way or another, I'll be gone."

"You know why I care. I know you do," he said. "Please don't pretend otherwise."

"James—"

"Don't go, don't do this, Cate, please. We'll find another way. You don't have to do this. Not this way. Not alone."

A deafening hush followed. Had she found her way free? Was she gone?

"Cate?" he said, his voice straining to stay composed.

"It's not up to you to save me."

"If not me, then who?"

"It doesn't work that way."

"Damn you, you don't know that. You don't know everything."

"Maybe that's true," she said, pulling away. "But I do know this."

If he remained silent, she would disappear. She'd leave him in the darkness and go to her death without another thought.

"I don't want you to sacrifice yourself for this," he blurted.

Another pause.

"You'd feel differently if you knew what I've done," she said.

"I don't care, Cate. Bloody hell, I don't care what you've done."

"You would if you knew," she said, her tone fierce. "If I told you—"

"Then don't tell me," he spat, just as viciously. "Don't say one bloody thing more, except to say that you won't do this. That you'll let us find another way."

"No. This is what you brought me here to do, and I am finally ready to do it," she said. "Please, just let me do it."

She was slipping away, sand through his fingers, and he exclaimed, "Wait! Cate, wait! Just tell me..."

She hesitated, the sensation—how could he *feel* it?—momentarily robbing him of breath. He asked; she waited. If only for a moment, she waited because he had asked.

"Tell you what?" she said. "The clock's ticking, cowboy."

"Have you any advantage over them?"

If there was something, one small thing she had that Omur didn't—that Sighle didn't—maybe he could let her go. If she wasn't just running off to her death, then maybe—just maybe—he could live with it.

"There is one thing," she said. "One thing I have that they don't."

"What? What is it?"

A soft sigh followed, and a shower of shimmering embers appeared in the darkness. Lifting his head, James watched them float and drift around him, holding out his hand to catch one in his palm.

But the ember fell away as her hand settled on his chest, over his heart. His fingers followed the line of her arm—there; she was there, solid, real, and standing before him. He searched her face for any sign of injury. Her eyes looked bright. A trick of the light, or was she crying? His question was answered when one tear, then another, rolled down her cheek.

"Cate?" he said, brushing away her tears. "Are you all right? Are you hurt?"

She shook her head. "Don't. Just..."

Taking his face in her hands, she pulled him down until their foreheads touched. As his hands skimmed down her sides to her waist, James closed his eyes, absorbing the nearness of her, and though he couldn't see it, he knew she did the same.

"You were supposed to hate me," she said.

"I do," he said, his voice soaked in exhaustion. "God, I do."

She laughed quietly and pressed her lips to his. The kiss was tentative, almost teasing, to start, then deepened. For an instant, there was no war, no lies, no magic in all the world. Here, he was healed; here, he was whole, and he gripped her tightly, unwilling to leave this place.

But the moment was fleeting and ended all too soon. She stayed close, her fingers lacing together behind his neck. He opened his eyes but didn't move, afraid of driving her away, terrified of losing her.

"I'm sorry," she breathed. "I am so sorry."

"Cate?"

She kissed the corner of his mouth, his cheek, and then his ear.

"A death wish," she whispered into it.

With that, she pulled away, turning to ash before his eyes, leaving him immediately and impossibly empty. The pain of withdrawal only increased as what she had said—and what it meant—registered with him.

A death wish.

"Cate!" he shouted. "Cate, no! You can't!"

But she could. She did. She was gone, irretrievably gone, and James was more lost and wounded than ever.

A death wish. A goddamned *death* wish! She would march to Eluned and put herself in their path, and she wouldn't care if it killed her.

"Damn you, Cate!" he screamed. "Do you hear me? Damn you!"

An explosion of blinding white light knocked him off his feet. He hit the ground hard, but there was no pain. In the center of the light stood the woman he had seen in Enimode. Laorans. Uncertain as to what he should do, he got to his feet, only knowing what he would not do.

"I'll not bow before you," he said.

The goddess smiled. "I would not expect it."

"Where am I? What is this?"

"You are safely within the walls of Labhras, in the lord's keep, recovering from your injuries."

"No, that's not the truth. It can't be."

"Why not?"

"Because...Because I-I died. I was dying. Am dying. Cate—"

"She kept you alive."

"She didn't say."

"She didn't want you to know."

You'd feel differently if you knew what I've done.

James shook his head. "No, that isn't right. It's—if I'm not dead, how am I *here*? And Cate, she was here as well. It has to be that—"

"You are not dead, James ap Seoras. It is your mind that wanders, searching for that which you feel you have forgotten and lost."

He hadn't forgotten Cate; he'd never be able to do that. But losing her...

"Did she mean what she said?"

"It may well be so."

Fury propelled James forward. "You will let her die? What kind of being are you that you would let a girl—*that* girl—sacrifice herself for something as meaningless as your own existence? She was your daughter; you were her mother!"

"Yes, that is true."

"Why don't you care? Why won't you stop her? Your presence is not known on this earth, apart from stories told to children. You give nothing and bring nothing but pain. Why will that girl's death for your sake make it better?"

"She is not a girl."

"Woman, then!" he shouted. "Why does she have to die for you?"

"Tell me, James ap Seoras," the goddess said, "were she to die and this battle continue, would you lose yourself in grief? Would you surrender?"

What were these questions? Cate grew farther away with each heartbeat, and he was faced with this? He shook his head, not quite looking at the goddess. "I haven't yet. I never will."

"That is why you were chosen, my dear one."

"Chosen?"

"Dana never did tell you," Laorans said. "He knew the answer right enough, but he never did say it."

James shook his head again. "Why are you telling me this? I don't care what Dana—"

"I think perhaps you do," the goddess said. "You were swept into this strife not out of love for country, not out of love for self, and certainly not out of love for me. You were pulled into this out of love for your adopted brother, and while it is true that he has fallen upon this path, you have always been there, willing to carry his banner because it was his.

"You did not need another reason. You did not need to believe in me. It is this simple fact—this simple truth—which led me to choose you for this task. My most reluctant soldier," the goddess said, laying her hand on his cheek, "you have become a most valuable savior for us all."

"I am no one's savior," James said. "Hers, least of all. I didn't protect her. I failed."

"You have not failed, neither her nor your cause. Out of all that you have lost, you have found for yourself a name and a strength that cannot be denied. You stood in Dana's stead and became the followed, not the follower. It is what you were meant to do."

"Destiny?"

She shook her head. "Standing on your own is never destiny."

"What of her destiny? Does it decree that she must die?"

"For all that is written, there remains a great deal that is unwritten. You are not a puppet, James ap Seoras, and neither is she. You must have faith that all shall work itself out as it was meant to be."

He smiled. "Faith in you?"

She laid her hand over his heart. "Faith in yourself, dear one. Faith in her. She has made her choice and started on that path. Now you must continue along yours. Do not fear it, for she does not fear hers, and fear shall only

761

hinder you from what you seek. Be strong, James ap Seoras," the goddess said. "For her, for them, for you."

The goddess faded, replaced by the same glaring light that had ushered her in. It dissipated, leaving darkness and pain in its wake. James had been returned to Labhras, and the dream—or whatever it had been—was over.

His eyes flew open. "Ca—" he shouted, but the throbbing of his head forced him to cut the cry short.

"James."

Turning his head, he breathed a heavy sigh of relief. "You're here," he said, grabbing her hands. "Oh God, you're here. I thought—"

Her eyes widened, and as she shook her head, James realized his mistake and let her go.

"James," the damned queen of Lira said, "I am so sorry."

Cate had said that, too. *I am so sorry.*

He struggled to sit up. "Where is she?"

"James, please lie down," the queen said, pushing against his shoulders. "You mustn't do this. Nor is there any need. Mireille is here. She is fine; I promise you that."

"Oh, and I should trust you?"

"Yes. Yes, you should," the queen said, exasperation apparent. "Stop fighting me, James."

"Never," he said, but as Dana entered the room, worry written all over his face, James fell back upon his elbows. "She's gone, isn't she?"

Dana nodded. "I don't know where she went."

"I do." James lurched off the bed. This time, neither Dana nor the queen hindered him. "We have to get to Eluned."

⸻ ∿ ⸻

Cate sat on the ground in the woods, her back against a tree. Fingers digging into the ground, she fought a losing battle to regain some semblance of control. Her body shook with the force of her sobs, and she couldn't stop it.

He asked her to wait, and she had.

She had woken up on a narrow bed, alone in an unfamiliar room, with only one thought: getting the hell out. Getting away without talking to anyone, without seeing anyone. The sooner the better, the faster the better. There was nothing for her amongst the rebellion, and staying would only make them bleed more.

She had made them bleed enough already. She didn't want to do it anymore.

Besides, she had places to go and things to do there—people to kill, a destiny to avoid. Couldn't do any of that in Labhras.

Her armor and weapons were gone, along with her boots and shirt. Someone had tended her wounds, the bandages wrapping around her shoulder and chest. Cate used her nails as daggers to shred the linen and found her shirt draped over the end of the bed. Pulling it on, she left the room.

She wandered barefoot through empty hallways until she found an exit. The bailey had been full of bodies—too many bodies—and emotion—thickening fear, anger, and devastation. The onslaught choked her, threatening to take her down, take her out, but she pushed it away, shoved it down, and kept moving.

They couldn't see her if she didn't want them to. They couldn't touch her if she didn't let them. He asked her to wait, and she had, but it wouldn't happen again. He wouldn't get near her again. She wouldn't let him. She could do that for him, if nothing else.

She had made it into the woods before surrendering to her weakness and the *feelings*—hers, his, theirs—setting up residence in her heart. Her hands clutched her stomach through her bloodstained shirt—his blood, spilled for her, because of her, because she couldn't save him.

He asked her to wait, and she had.

Shit, shit, shit—she had to stop this. She had to shove it down, out, and away, into the ground where it belonged, into the air, into the ether—anywhere other than in her. Places to go, people to kill—she couldn't do it like this.

She had to do it, then. Had to. Let go of the humanity, turn it off. Embrace the not-human side of her. It was the only way she could do this, stop it, survive it.

She did want to survive, didn't she?

Hugging her knees to her chest, she squeezed her eyes shut and envisioned the humanity draining into the ground. Muscles relaxed; pain, heartbreak, and the rest of the spectrum disappeared until nothing remained. When she opened her eyes again, she was free.

"Mireille."

The voice belonged to the deity she had once considered a mother. Cate laughed as she uncurled and punched the ground, sending radiating tremors through the earth.

"Are you leaning-impaired?" she asked. "What the hell are you doing here? Don't you know what I did? The deal I made?"

"Yes."

"Then get away from me!"

Staggering to her feet, Cate hunted for Laorans, finding her on the other side of the tree. Apart from her long, flowing dress, she looked very much like

Laura. Laura's wardrobe had been more fitted. Boston business woman on the go.

"I'll do it, you know," Cate said. "I'll do it right now. I don't care."

"You do care," Laorans said. "You care a great deal."

Cate walked away. "Past tense."

"You can't do this. It is not a switch you can turn on and off, Mireille."

"It is if I want it to be."

"And this is what you want?"

Cate turned around. "That was your opportunity to go, to leave, to get as far away from me as you can because I will end you. I traded your life for his, and it was the easiest decision I have ever made. You threw me to the goddamn wolves, and he pulled me out again. He's the only one on this side of anything that matters."

"Yet, you strive to sacrifice everything for which he has fought."

Fire formed in her hand, and Cate stepped toward the goddess. "Stop using him. You and everybody else just love to use him, to evoke his name like it's some talisman that'll protect you from me," Cate said. She threw the fire away, and a nearby tree burst into flames. "It won't. Nothing will protect you from me."

Laorans looked at the burning tree and put an end to the flames with a wave of her pale hand. "Let's not burn down the forest."

Cate laughed. "I'm threatening to destroy both you and this earth, but you're worried about a forest fire?"

"Threatening, yes, you have done this."

"You don't believe I'm serious."

"I believe you're hurt, so hurt," Laorans said, pressing on when Cate let out a loud, rude guffaw. "I believe your heart has been broken, your trust betrayed, and all hope you once held seems irretrievably lost. The fault is mine—I wronged you greatly, and nothing I could ever say could repair the damage I have done, but I do not believe—and I never shall believe—that you, my beloved daughter, wish to do this."

More fire appeared in Cate's hand. She held it low, at her hip, but did not release it. "You're wrong."

"Why, then, did you burn the tree, and not me?"

This time, Cate landed a direct hit in the center of Laorans's chest. The goddess shrieked and disappeared, leaving the fire to drop onto the soft dirt of the forest floor. Waving her hand to extinguish the flames, Cate searched for a sign of the goddess. She found none.

"What do you believe now?" she said to the empty air.

She opened a portal with a single, simple gesture.

"Ready or not," she said, stepping inside the black hole. "Here I come."

Her next step put her in a library. Omur was at the other end, sitting behind a massive desk and issuing orders to three white-haired men standing in front of him. As her arrival had gone unnoticed, she leaned against a bookshelf and watched them act as though what they did had meaning. She expected it from the mortals, but it surprised her coming from Omur.

Emotion is what hangs you in the end. Cate almost smiled.

"So, this is where a power-hungry, bottom-feeding lunatic hangs out," she said loudly. "What's wrong? The throne room occupied?"

The meeting stopped, its participants turning to look at her. She focused solely on Omur. He was the only one who mattered.

"Hi honey," she said. "I'm home."

Omur pursed his lips. "You. Why are you here?"

"I thought I might take my chances with destiny after all," she said. "If it's good enough for Zeus, it's good enough for me."

"Zeus? Who is this Zeus?"

"Focus, Twinkie. Zeus isn't what's important here. Zeus is mythology," Cate said. "Much like this world will be when I'm through with it."

Omur looked at his minions. "Leave us."

The three men bowed and turned to go, but Cate moved in front of the doors.

"Sorry, but you'll have to stay," she told them. "I can't have you running around telling everyone Haleine's back."

"They should not hear what we have to discuss," Omur said.

"I agree. Still, they're staying."

Omur sighed irritably. "What game do you suppose you're playing?"

"No game."

"Then what do you want?"

Cate set the minions on fire. They screamed, they screeched, they burned. Omur gasped and gaped.

"I want to destroy the world," she said. "Thought maybe you could help."

CHAPTER 50

As James cut an unsteady path out of the room, Haleine did not stop him. He would go regardless of what she said or did, and what happened next would be easier in his absence.

Dana stood in the doorway, watching James. "We need to go. He'll leave without us."

She nodded. "Let him. Tell Faolan to close the tunnels so that his travels might be delayed. If we slow his progress, it will be over by the time he reaches the city."

"What will be over?"

In her mind's eye, Haleine watched Mireille approach Omur. *I want to destroy the world*, her twin said. *Thought maybe you could help.*

"Mireille is in the palace." Haleine looked at Dana. "That is where you and I must go as well."

"What about the wall?"

"I will get through the wall. I have to," Haleine said. "We made a deal, and I have to be there to do my part. I can't let her do this alone, so I will get through the wall. I will tear it down, and—"

"I don't think you have to tear it down," Dana said, shaking his head. "Cate told me...She said for you to open a door."

"Open a door? What does that mean?"

"She said you would know. She said that it has to be you. That Sighle made it that way."

"To force me into it," Haleine said. "The magic."

"Aye."

"Open a door."

"Aye. She said you would know."

Why would Mireille think that? Open a door? What could that...*We have the ability to open doors between places.*

She had to open a portal.

Faolan flew into the room and landed on a table. "Why is James leaving, and why is he doing it in such a manner that would suggest the whole of the king's army is chasing him?"

"He's going after Cate," Dana said, "who apparently has gone to the palace."

"Why would she go there?" Faolan asked.

I want to destroy the world. Thought maybe you could help.

"Because we struck a bargain," Haleine answered. "Faolan, I require you to render your tunnels unusable. James can't get to Eluned before this is done."

"Before what is done?" Faolan asked.

"I also need you to help me open a portal."

"A portal?" Dana said.

"To where?" the pegasus asked.

"The palace. My chambers there. They'll be empty, so no one will—"

"That will never work," Faolan interrupted. "It's already been tried, and—"

"Not by me," Haleine said. "I can do this, Faolan, and with your help, I will do this. It will work. Mireille said so."

"How are you certain that she's told you the truth?"

"James didn't die," Haleine said. "Please, Faolan, I dare not waste more time."

"What do you intend to do once you're inside the palace?" Faolan asked.

"Follow through with our plan. She will kill Omur, and I will kill my husband."

Faolan seemed to shrink in size. "You shouldn't...you shouldn't do this alone."

"Dana will accompany me, and he shall perform the task should I fail, but I will do this on my own."

"You can't take this fight away from her, Faolan," Dana muttered. "Help her."

Faolan lowered his head. "I'll help you."

"Thank you," Haleine said.

"Recall every detail you can about your chambers," Faolan said. "Everything you remember, envision it now. Hold on to it—don't lose focus."

She closed her eyes to do as he instructed. When she had it in her mind, and could feel the magic churning inside, she said, "Now what?"

"Open the door. Any way you can."

She nodded. Her success would depend entirely upon her belief. If she needed a door to open, she would have to make one.

Dana swore, and Haleine opened her eyes. A black hole hung in the air, and she marveled at the sight until her lapse of concentration caused it to shrink. She shoved aside the awe and focused on growing the portal.

As soon as it was large enough for a man to fit through, Faolan ordered them to go. Dana grabbed her hand and dragged her through the hole with him.

The next step brought them into her chambers, and the portal closed as soon as they were free of it. Dana continued to hold her hand and reached for the other, watching her closely. As her equilibrium was lost in a surge of magic, Haleine was grateful for his assistance.

"Your majesty? Is it you?" Bronagh asked.

Haleine found her standing near the fire, jaw dropped and eyes watering. "Yes. I have returned."

The maid was as still as a statue, but inside, turmoil and disbelief were shouting. Haleine's own eyes filled with tears.

"There are questions to be asked and answered on both sides, Bronagh, but it must wait a while longer," she said. "I need to find my husband now. Do you know where he is?"

Bronagh was crumbling—Haleine could feel it—but she said, "The great hall, your majesty. Look for him there."

Haleine nodded and looked to Dana. He helped her to the doors, but once they were through, she walked on her own.

As she made her way through the palace, she did not hide her presence nor her identity, leaving an endless number of gawking servants in her wake. Dana stayed on her heels, his sword loosed from its sheath and held low at his side, but there was no need. There were no guards to oppose them.

Nor were there any guards in the great hall where the king was holding court. Together, Haleine and Dana stood outside the doors.

"No guards," he murmured.

"They're not afraid of us," she said. "A mistake for which they'll now pay."

As she moved forward, Dana seized her elbow and held her back.

"You have no weapon," he said, holding out a dagger. "Take this. Just in case."

It was *his* dagger, the one he had given her months before. The one she had used to...*Just in case*. It was what Faolan had said to her. Dana had wanted her to have it to protect herself from Maddox. Just in case. Now he offered it to her again.

"Dana," she breathed.

"I want you to live," he implored. "Take it, please."

Haleine nodded and tucked the blade into her belt behind her back. "You're not to interfere, and you're only to kill him if he first kills me. Watch the doors, and do not allow anyone to enter," she said and walked into the hall.

Dana followed her in, closed the doors, and stood in front of them. The court parted ways as she continued onward. Whispers filled the room, finally catching the attention of the man sitting upon the throne. In his lap sat one of Haleine's ladies-in-waiting. The woman gasped when she saw her queen and scrambled out of Maddox's lap.

"Your majesty!" the woman exclaimed. "I—"

"Leave this place," Haleine commanded.

Her attendant did not waste any time. She rushed down the dais steps and past Haleine, who turned to watch her flee. Others departed as well, and when the exodus had reached its end, Dana once again closed the doors. Haleine surveyed those who remained—a mixture of nobles and servants. Good. She would require witnesses for this.

"Now, which one are you?" her husband asked as he came down the steps. "You're here with him"—Maddox gestured to Dana—"so I think perhaps you're the woman I married, but how can I be sure? After all, both of you should already be dead."

"One of your many mistakes," Haleine said. "You trust to others what you should do yourself."

"Shall we remedy that now?"

"Yes. Let's."

"And your pet?" Maddox pointed to Dana again. "Will he be joining us?"

Haleine shook her head. "This is not his fight."

"I'll kill him afterward, then."

"There won't be an afterward," Haleine said. "Not for you."

"Come to kill me, have you?"

"I have."

Maddox circled her. "Your twin once threatened to kill me. Do you know what happened to her?"

Haleine smiled. "Do you? Because I think you'd be surprised by the answer."

"Nothing surprises me anymore."

"Let's change that, shall we?"

"When did you become so bold?"

"The proper question to ask would be why I ever stopped."

"Oh, I already know the answer to that, my fickle love."

"I was never your love," Haleine said. "Fickle or otherwise."

He stopped in front of her, a cruel smile twisting her lips. "You truly mean to fight me."

"I do."

"With what? You have no weapons."

"You're wrong."

As she looked into her husband's harsh face, her daring diminished. How would she possibly do this? She had fought him before and had failed every time. What if she failed again? What would happen to all who depended upon what she did now?

A sparkle in his eye told her that Maddox had noticed the waning. It was all the warning she received before he lunged at her. She jumped back, instinctively, before she could stop herself. Maddox ceased his pursuit and laughed.

"Is that your weapon? Running away?" he asked. "Won't it be rather difficult to kill me when you're too frightened to even"—he leapt the distance between them, grabbed her arms, and pressed his forehead against hers—"be near me?"

Tears formed in her eyes. "I am not afraid of you."

"Liar." He laughed again and kissed her forehead before pushing off. Turning his back and spreading his arms, he played to his audience. "What will it take, Haleine? What will I have to do to get a proper fight out of you? Kill your bastard lover? I recall you fought me the night you thought him dead; if you see it happen, will you fight me then? Or—no." He grinned at her. "Someone fetch me a stable boy—the one with the biggest, saddest eyes. Bring him here so that I might slaughter him. A present for my wife."

"If you want to slaughter someone," she said, "slaughter me."

He spun and brought the back of his hand across her face. "Gladly."

She hit the floor. As she pushed herself up, he kicked her stomach, and she fell again. She didn't move this time, and Maddox continued to rain down blows and insults.

"Haleine," Dana said.

His tone was soft; she thought no one else would have heard, but she could. His voice cut through everything, and she turned her head toward him. He had not left the doors, though the glean of sweat on his brow suggested he had attempted and failed many times over. His face was crushed by anguish, and when she heard his voice again, his lips did not move.

Come on, Haleine. Get up. Fight him. Haleine, please, you have to fight him.

She looked at her husband. How many times had he done this? How many times had he left her bruised and battered? How many bones had he broken? This was not new, his abuse and torture. She had endured it all before. What could he do to her that he hadn't already done? What could he do that she hadn't already survived?

But she had to do more than survive now. She had to fight him. She had to—

No, she didn't have to fight him.

She only had to kill him.

All voices, all noise, faded, and Haleine breathed as though it were her very first breath. A moment of peace and clarity followed, one that was soon broken by Maddox's shrill scream.

"I'm going to kill your whore, Dana!" Maddox brought his cruelty to a sudden halt. "Will you stop me? Do you care? Or shall you thank me for ridding you of such a pathetic creature?"

Haleine stood, slowly, unsteadily. "I am no one's whore."

Maddox's head snapped in her direction, his wolf's grin bright, and she threw herself at him.

She didn't have to fight him. She only had to kill him. Scratching, clawing, kicking, she attacked him. He laughed at her attempts, as he always had, batting her away, toying with her, until he shoved her back.

She stumbled, breathing heavily. "Why haven't you killed me? God knows you've had the opportunity. Chance after chance, you've had to do it, to kill me, to kill him"—Haleine pointed to Dana—"and you've failed to do it every time. Why? Why can't you kill me? Are you truly that inept? Are you afraid?" She laughed. "You are, aren't you? You're terrified! Won't it be rather difficult to slaughter me when you're too fright—?"

Maddox grabbed her by the throat and slammed her into a wall. Her arms smacked against the stone, her right hand inching behind her back as her left slapped ineffectually at him.

"Mayhap one day the minstrels will sing songs of your greatness. Mayhap they'll weave beautiful tales of your valiant effort to save your people and of the love you bore for your mongrel," Maddox said. "But mostly I think they'll sing of your tragic death at the hands of the king too powerful to be defeated."

Haleine neither looked away nor blinked as she pulled the dagger from behind her back and thrust the blade upward beneath his sternum. His eyes widened, and his mouth dropped open as he fought to breathe. She twisted the blade, and Maddox released her. As she fell to the floor, Maddox stumbled away. His jerking hand latched onto the dagger and pulled it out. Balance lost, he fell, landing hard on his back. Haleine struggled to stand, then walked to where he lay and watched his once-harsh eyes fill with tears.

"Perhaps they'll have something else to sing about now," she said.

The room was completely quiet as Haleine stared at the man who had been her husband. When the last of his life had left him, she swept past his corpse and climbed the dais steps. She sat on the king's throne and looked out at his court. Slowly, they sank to their knees and bowed their heads.

Only Dana remained standing. His face had split into a brilliant, wide grin, the love he bore for her shining brighter than any sun ever could.

"Long live the queen," he said.

—◦⁓◦—

The burning of three bodies took considerably longer than Cate had expected. They had screamed at first—of course they had—as their skin fried and flaked, limbs flailing independent of the bodies to which they were attached. Eventually, the cries stopped. Soon only bones would remain. Those would take longer to turn to ash, but it was all right. She had time. Omur hadn't moved yet.

He stared at the human barbeque pit. Cate let him. It was important that he process all that she had said and done. Though, if he was having trouble grasping things now, she didn't have much hope for the rest of their encounter.

"You want to destroy the world?" he said finally.

As she hadn't stuttered or suddenly switched languages, she didn't respond. She walked the outer edge of the room, running her hand along the cold stone wall and the warm leather spines of books. Stopping at a tapestry bearing the Liran crest, she studied the unicorn before focusing on the sword and shield hanging beneath it.

"I trust you will forgive my reservations," Omur said. "But for far too long, you have been Laorans's daughter."

"Sugar and spice and everything nice," Cate agreed. She ran her hand along the blade. It, too, was cold. Fitting for an instrument of death. "What can I tell you? I was going through a phase."

"And?"

He was annoyed with her. He'd been fond of his trio of yes men, so he hadn't enjoyed her entrance very much. But he wanted to tread carefully. She was the chosen one, after all, and she had just fried three innocents. Somewhere, she imagined, the dark gods were wetting themselves with excitement.

"And what? I'm over it now. You saw to that." Cate removed the sword from its holder. "Would you like to hear how this will work?"

"How what will work?"

"The end of the world, you moron." She sighed. "You know, I have spent a lot of time with Team Good, mostly marveling at their stupidity and wondering how it is they ever managed to survive for so long, but now? Now that I'm here in the inner sanctum with the evil point man himself, it doesn't seem like such a mystery anymore. Or an accomplishment, really."

Omur flushed with anger. "If you think you can enter this chamber and insult me so—"

She dropped the sword and faced him, miming zipping her lips shut. Omur fell silent and pawed at his closed mouth.

"I think I can enter this chamber and insult you in any manner of my choosing. I think I can do anything and everything I damn well please because I have been from one end of this island to the other and had the crap kicked out of me at each and every stop," she said. "As you were responsible for each and every one of these incidents, and I have now come here to save your sorry ass, the least you could do is let me finish, you stupid fuck. Do you understand me, or shall I just kill you?"

He stopped fighting and nodded. She released him, and Omur slumped against the chair.

"This is how it will work," she said, trying to ignore how damn good his physical pain had felt. "I start the apocalypse. Your bosses swallow the world in darkness, chaos, and misery while I retire to Mexico and find out how many margaritas this not-quite-human body of mine can tolerate. Or maybe it'll be Bora Bora and whatever cocktails they happen to drink there. Wherever, whatever—it doesn't really matter.

"What does matter is that—wherever I am—I never hear from anyone or anything in this dimension ever again, thus leaving me free to work toward the alcohol-induced coma of which I have so recently dreamed. How does that sound to you?" she asked, picking up the sword. "Before you answer, keep in mind that your other option is me beating you down and crushing you like the tiny, insignificant flea that you are."

Omur ran his fingers over his lips. After a moment, he laughed. "Destroyer her name shall be, and she shall come for thee."

"Cute couplet," she said. "Did you think of that all on your own?"

"That prophecy came from Sighle. She is, as it turns out, touched with the Sight."

"She's touched all right. I can't argue with that," Cate said. "It's curious, though, how you came by such a prophecy when you were given explicit instructions to stay the hell away from her."

Cate rested the sword against her shoulder and took her first steps toward Omur. He still wasn't afraid of her. Well, she'd change that soon enough.

"Are you threatening me again?" Omur asked. "And with what? A weapon you don't know how to use?"

This time, she laughed. "First of all, I do know how to use this, you silly, sad, little troll. Second of all, do you think I even need this? Didn't you hear what I did in Gweneria? In Enimode? In Feond? I didn't need a sword then, and I don't need one now. I just like the way it feels in my hands. You must know what that's like."

"I dare say Sighle does."

Cate tilted her head to the right, and Omur was propelled out of the chair. When she swept her arm out to the side, the desk slid to the opposite wall. Omur lay on the floor, staring at her.

"You should seriously consider not talking to me that way anymore," she advised, advancing upon him. "There's a new moon rising and a new sheriff in town, and things will go badly for you if you don't. Of course, they might go badly for you anyway. I am destroying the world after all."

Omur opened his palm and hurled two bright orbs at her. She dropped the sword and held out her hand. The orbs stopped in midair until she flicked her wrist and sent them careening into the wall.

"Is that the best you've got?" she asked as the wall exploded in a shower of stone, leather, parchment, and splintered wood. "Because, if it is, you are so screwed."

"You cannot destroy the world," Omur said.

Cate retrieved her sword. "Destroyer her name shall be, and she shall come for thee. Nope, my job description's clear."

"Our lords do not wish for the destruction of the earth."

"Your lords. And, sure they do. Metaphorical destruction, maybe, but destruction just the same. This earth doesn't do them any good. This earth with its humanity is useless to them," she said. "Like Cate, this earth needs to be cleansed. Like Cate, this earth needs to be broken. Worn out, worn down until it's unrecognizable to itself or anyone who cares to save it. And like Cate, this earth is ready to fall. The heroes of the piece don't know what it is they're fighting for anymore, and you can't ask for anything better than that.

"What the dark gods need now is death. Horrible, widespread death followed by a cleansing fire to char the land and every soul in it. From the ashes will be reborn their Utopia. They will mold it to their liking, and on the seventh day, they'll rest," Cate said. "Well, I am making up that last part, but I imagine there will be a celebration of some kind. Where do you think you'll be when that happens? At their side? The faithful servant evermore? I don't. Would you like to know why?"

She held out her hand, palm up, and a fireball appeared, feeling oddly cool. Like the stone, like the sword. Strange, but it fit, too. Her eyes were on the fire, but she saw Omur's mind as the first kernel of undeniable fear rooted there. It almost made her swoon.

"Because I can do this," she said, "and you can't."

She pivoted on her heel and threw the fireball at the unicorn tapestry. Lira's crest disintegrated to ash. The symbolism was almost too much. She turned back to Omur, nearly cowering on the floor.

"You see, when I'm done, your lords will throw a parade in my honor, or do whatever you all do around here to celebrate a hero," she said. "I won't be around to see it but, then again, neither will you. I guess you can hope they turn your ashes into something pretty. Or—considering the rather large tool you were in life—something functional."

He stood. Inside, he was mustering courage. It was a nice effort, but it wouldn't be enough. It wouldn't come close. He'd already let her in. Some part of him feared her now, and that was a door he wouldn't ever be able to close. He could and would fight like hell, but he'd lose in the end.

And she would win. Or whatever passed for it these days.

"You are wrong," he said.

"You still think you're part of the in-crowd, huh? Okay, let's test that theory," she said. "I'll start the murder and mayhem portion of our evening—beginning with you—and just as soon as Yelsneh or one of his fine friends shows up to tell me to stop, I will. But here's my theory"—she dragged the sword tip across the floor as she approached him—"they won't interfere because you were never meant to deliver the world. You were only meant to deliver me. And now you have. Job well done."

She stopped in front of him. His mind raced, trying to figure out the precise moment when he had lost control. She smiled and stood on her toes to look him directly in the eye.

"What makes you think you were ever in control?" she whispered.

He hit her across the face, and she fell to the floor. The sword spun out of her physical reach. Sitting up, she wiped the blood from the corner of her mouth. His confidence soared. It would take longer now.

"I can't believe I didn't see that coming," she said. It made sense, though. He had acted on impulse, and she remained blind to that.

"I have always been in control," Omur hissed. "I have been devoted to this purpose long before you were born."

"Hate to nitpick, but there wasn't a purpose before I was born."

"There was prophecy."

Cate punched the air, sending Omur sprawling back against the wall. As she got to her feet, he retaliated and hit her shoulder with another of the energy balls she had dispatched earlier. Spinning around, she hit the floor again. She pressed her hand against her shoulder and pulled it away to see it covered with blood.

"Oh, bad move, Twinkie," she said. "You're not incurring any favor with the new regime here."

"That is no concern of mine. I will never bow to you."

She closed her hand into a fist and stood. "Of course you will. It's what you've been waiting for your entire life. Everything up until this point was a waiting game. Screwing with Haleine, screwing with the rebels, screwing with Cate? It was you biding your time, waiting for me and this day and this moment." She smiled. "It's funny, you know? Laorans, Faolan—all of them—believe disaster was averted the day she rescued me from the neruals. They don't realize how much was planned. They think they've been doing well—thwarting the enemy at every turn and holding evil at bay—but they don't realize how perfectly it was done, or how perfectly everyone played their assigned part. It'll make for an interesting third act, I'm sure, but the funny part—the real punch line of it all—is that you don't know it, either."

His courage and confidence diminished as uncertainty set in. Doubt, she found, wasn't quite as good as fear or pain, but they were just around the corner. If she pushed him a little more, a little bit harder, they'd be there.

"How are you so sure you are apart from it?" he asked.

"Because I was never a part of this world. Not like you or Zaide Romanza. I had another life, you see, in a galaxy far, far away, in the land of hot, running water. Your lords wanted it that way, and they went to a lot of trouble to make sure that happened because it was the only way to ensure they would have exactly what they wanted," Cate said. "A vessel with the power and desire to destroy every square inch of this universe.

"You probably think that description applies to you, but it doesn't. While you may not care about a great deal of the world, you care about enough that it taints you. Sighle infected you like Revelin ruined Zaide Romanza, and that makes you just as weak as the rest of them," she said. "Emotion is what hangs you in the end, and I don't have that problem. Not anymore."

He attacked again. Two more orbs hurled in her direction, but she waved them away as though they were nothing because they were nothing.

"If you do that again," she warned, "I will rip out your throat."

"You won't get close enough."

She slapped the air, leaving Omur covering his stinging cheek.

"Won't have to," she said. "Haven't you been paying attention? This isn't a matter of best man wins. This is destiny, written in blood and carved in stone. You can't change it, you can't fight it, you can't deny it. Destiny is what destiny does, and she will take what she wants!"

Cate shouted the last of it at him, and for the first time, he looked and felt like a man beaten. The sensation was powerful, so strong that when it hit, she rocked back on her heels and laughed.

"Shit," she said.

She sounded out of breath, exhilarated, punch drunk—and she was. She put her hands on either side of her head, afraid that if she didn't hold it together, it would come apart. It would explode and cover the floor and the walls and the goddamn books with his misery and her joy.

Who knew it would feel this good? She hadn't felt this way in so long—just so damn *good* that she wanted to throw her head back and laugh full and loud—and not because something was ironic or tragically comic, but because she was *happy*.

No more pain, no more torment. Just like the brochure promised.

"Not to change the subject," she said, walking away, "but this power is fan-freaking-tastic. Seriously, I can't even begin to describe the awesomeness that is this feeling. I should have been clearer with myself instead of trying to be all clever or mysterious because this is amazing.

"But it's unfair, really. I came here with all these noble intentions—well, maybe not *noble*. I did come here intending to screw with you and exploit your belief in destiny until I tore you down so much that you were like—I don't know—like a smurf or something, but I did start off wanting to do good, wanting to do what's right," she said. "I didn't realize that euphoria was a part of the evil benefits package when I made that plan, though. And now I'm conflicted because if feeling this good is wrong, what the hell's the point of being right?"

Letting her hands fall, her head remained intact, and she smiled. How far could she go?

"Sorry about that," she said, turning back to Omur. "I didn't mean to keep you wait—"

Omur's fist made contact with her face. She dropped to her knees and laughed until she felt the cool metal tip of her sword pressed under her chin. She adjusted her head slightly in order to see him.

"Nice sucker punch," she said. "Really, very sneaky."

"Should you move," he said, "should you even blink, I shall cut you from ear to ear."

She grabbed the blade and shoved the pommel into Omur's stomach. While he groaned and stumbled, she ripped the sword from his hand and threw it behind her. He lunged for her, and she propelled him across the room. When he hit the wall, he attempted to stand, but she swept her arm from one side to the other and brought him down again. She stood and walked toward him.

"Shouldn't have bothered with the warning," she said. "You should have just killed me because, good or evil, I'm going to bleed you dry. The only real thing in question at this point is how much I'll enjoy it.

"It's odd, though. You'd think one with your sense of self-preservation would've known that, but you never learn, do you? It's amazing. It's dumbfounding that after all our time together—after all the violence and all the empty threats—that you haven't figured it out. Move, and I'll kill you. Breathe, and I'll kill you. Blink, and I'll kill you. Yet, here I am, still blinking, still breathing, still moving," she said, closing in on him. "Here's a little fortune cookie wisdom to take with you into the afterlife: man—or whatever you are—cannot threaten death when he fears his own."

"I fear nothing," Omur said. This time when he attempted to stand, she let him.

"That's true in its own way. Death isn't something to be feared. I know it; you don't. I've accepted that which you have not. It's why I'm here and you're there, standing only because I have allowed it. But now I'm bored, so here endth the lesson, as I impart to you the knowledge which has escaped you all my life." She paused for dramatic effect. "Death isn't the evil. I am."

She held her hands as though something sat between them, and Omur was paralyzed from the neck down. He knew what she was about to do. He knew he was beaten. She smiled and snapped his neck without laying so much as a finger on him. The power in her swelled like a tsunami, and she lowered her arms as she was swept away by it. Omur's body landed with a thud on the floor. He didn't move, nor did she suspect he ever would again. She waited a few minutes, but he stayed dead.

"Well," she said, "that was anticlimactic."

As there was nothing more to be gained by hanging out in a crumbling library with a collection of corpses, she headed for the door. Before she could escape, a bright light flooded the room. She glanced over her shoulder to locate its source, then turned around to stare.

Omur's body hovered in the air, encircled by a white sphere. It rotated, steadily accelerating, as the light increased its brilliance. Somewhere in the distance, a voice suggested that she run, but Cate stayed rooted to the floor, fascinated by the grotesque display. The corpse spun faster, gaining such speed that it became impossible to tell what it was.

Without warning, the sphere ruptured, sending waves of energy and light racing throughout the room. Cate braced for the impact, but it threw her into a wall of books. Landing on her stomach, she covered her head with her arms to protect it from a cascade of the written word. After the last volume had fallen, she rolled onto her back, repressing some major whimpering. Had she broken every bone in her body, or did it just feel like she had? She honestly couldn't tell. What the hell?

Sighle's face appeared in her view. "I did tell you to run. You should have listened."

—◊◊◊—

Sighle watched her sister's eyes slowly fade back to blue, then studied her many wounds. "You're hurt."

"No shit." Groaning with the effort, Mireille sat up. "What the hell was that?"

"The dark gods, reclaiming their servant."

Mireille gingerly prodded her injured shoulder. "Well, the dark gods sure do have a flair for the dramatic."

"As do you, I think." Sighle offered her sister her hand. "Death isn't the evil? I am?"

Grinning, Mireille allowed Sighle to pull her to her feet. "I couldn't resist," she said. "And you're one to talk, Little Miss Destroyer-Her-Name-Shall-Be."

"Was he pleased?"

"Right up until the moment I snapped his neck," Mireille responded, limping away.

Sighle looked at the spot where Omur's body had been. Other than scorch marks on the floor, no sign of him remained.

"It always is anticlimactic," she said. "The mothers who raised us would have us believe that to kill a man—or even one masquerading as such—is a much grander affair than it is to either you or me. They would have us believe that such an act will shred the soul, but we remain intact. It washes off us, as though it never touched us. We inherited that from our father. I know you have no recollection of him, and that is a terrible tragedy, for Darian Coileáin was a man well worth remembering."

Mireille laughed. "Seriously—what made you like this?"

"I made me."

"No, come on, tell me—what happened to you? Something must have."

"Why must something have happened?"

Mireille stopped at the scattered remains of the men she had burned. Carefully, she picked her way amongst them, hand rising toward her mouth, as an emotion Sighle couldn't name invaded her body. Did Mireille grieve their loss? Three men whose names she did not know, three men whose names she would never learn? Why did she care about them?

Swallowing hard, Mireille said, "No one is as fucked up as you are without a reason."

"You desire a reason?"

"Me? No, I'm just curious. Haleine, on the other hand..."

"She wants more than a reason," Sighle said. "She wants an excuse."

"Pretty much." Mireille sighed and looked at her. "You know, we're probably about thirty seconds away from being swarmed here. If you don't want your secret identity revealed, you should be running along."

"No need to be concerned about that. We won't be interrupted."

"This castle is crawling with a cast of thousands, and I just blew a hole in the wall and burned a bunch of people alive," Mireille said. "Someone would have noticed that, poppet. Someone's coming."

"Indeed, you did blow a hole in the wall and burn a few men where they stood. Omur exploded right before your eyes. You two really did make quite the ruckus," Sighle said. "Every brave soul within this palace should already be at those doors, and yet, I hear no one and see no one other than you and me."

"What did you do?"

Sighle shrugged. "Ensured our privacy. No one will come near this room. Not until I am far away from here."

"And where might you be—" Mireille shook her head. "Nope. Don't tell me. I don't care."

"Oh, that's not true. If I were to kill your brown-eyed boy, you'd care very much."

Mireille's head snapped in her direction, eyes darkening rapidly. "Then you best not kill the brown-eyed boy."

Sighle smiled at the growl in her sister's voice. "Then you best not make me."

"I don't know if this is part of some game, or if you legitimately believe it's a good idea to go up against me, but either way, stop it." Mireille stalked toward her, no longer mindful of where her feet fell. "If you push me, you'll lose—and I don't think that's something you want."

Sighle backed against the wall, allowing her sister to trap her there. "You know nothing of what I want."

"I know you want to live, and I know that in this entire damn universe, there's only one other person who wants that, too," Mireille said. "I know you believe you're the smartest, most infallible being to ever walk the earth, but guess what?" She gestured to the scorch marks where Omur's corpse had laid. "So did that guy, and now he's dust in the wind."

Sighle leaned forward. "I am better than him. I won't make the same mistakes."

"No, you'll make other ones. That's how it works," Mireille said. "You'll fuck up, your enemies will close in on you, and the only thing standing between you and becoming your own exploding ball of light will be the sister whose life you've made endlessly miserable." She patted Sighle's cheek. "How do you think that will work out for you?"

Sighle did not answer as the vision tore through her. Closing her eyes, she slid to the floor and watched Mireille kill her. Though no less brutal, the act had changed since she had seen it last. The river of fire was gone, replaced by Mireille herself. Her hands ripped into Sighle's chest, extracting from it a heart still beating. Sighle screamed—both the girl dying and the one bearing witness to it—and the vision ended, leaving her breathless for more reason than one.

It changed. The vision had changed, yet she still died. Mireille still killed her. Sighle had not expected that. Did it mean she had failed? Or would every road—regardless of what she did—lead to death?

Perhaps she would die in the service of her lords after all.

Sighle opened her eyes and looked at Mireille, almost surprised to see no heart in her hand.

Mireille stepped back. "I hope whatever you saw just now scared the shit out of you."

Rubbing her chest to ease away the lingering ache, Sighle asked, "You didn't see?"

"No, but judging by that scream a minute ago and the look on your face now, I'd guess it was a nice preview of your death at Haleine's hands."

Sighle smiled. "She won't be the one to kill me."

"Maybe not, but if you push her past her breaking point, she won't stop the one who does," Mireille said. "People are getting tired of fighting. They're getting desperate, which means they'll be less discerning about what they're willing to do—or who they're willing to kill—to end that fight. And that includes Haleine."

Sighle laughed. "I don't fear Haleine. Our sister will never act."

"There's a dead king in the throne room who might have something to say about that." Mireille shrugged. "But believe what you want. Do what you want. So long as you leave James out of it, I don't care."

"Then why bother with a warning?"

Mireille glanced around. "Maybe it doesn't roll off me quite as easily as it does you."

"It will someday," Sighle said, getting to her feet. "You are the destroyer."

Mireille's jaw clenched but quickly relaxed. "Don't call me that. It's not who I am."

"There are quite a few corpses in quite a few countries who might have something to say about that," Sighle said. "I may have played a game or two with Omur, but they were based in truth. You are the destroyer. It was spoken, written—"

"Yeah, well, I don't care if there's an interpretive dance. It's not me."

"No, because you're Cate, and Mireille is some separate entity trapped inside you," Sighle mocked. "You think it will absolve you from all the terrible things you've done because it wasn't you. It was her."

Mireille's eyes filled with tears. "I don't believe that. There won't be any absolution for me."

"Especially not after the deal you made with our god."

"Your god, maybe."

"Your benefactor, then," Sighle said, and Mireille shrugged. At last they had come to it—the one question that mattered, the one answer that would define their future. "Will you do it? Will you do as you promised?"

Mireille looked at her left arm, where the imprint of a hand had been burned into the skin below the elbow. Sighle circled her, watching and waiting for her response. Would they be allies or foes? She might be willing to die for an ally.

"No," Mireille said. "I won't."

"Your life will be forfeit, if you do not."

Mireille smiled crookedly and walked toward the doors. "Try not to lose too much sleep over it."

Sighle pursued her. "The goddess will live and you will die because a mortal man wishes it?"

Mireille whirled around. "Because I'm not a slave. Not to destiny, not to any fucking gods, not to you—not to anything."

"Only your heart."

"Better than being whatever the hell you are."

"It's a waste."

"It's *my* waste. It's *my* life," Mireille said, pounding her chest. "And neither you nor your puppet masters get a say in that."

"I am no puppet."

Mireille looked at her in disgust. "Oh, of course you are, Lamb Chop. You've got nothing but strings on you, and a big ole hand shoved right up your ass," she said. "As smart as you are, I'm sure you'll figure that out someday. When you do, drop me a line, okay? I still won't care, but—"

"You made a bargain, Mireille Coileáin," Sighle interrupted, closing the distance between them. "You should do as you promised."

Mireille spread her arms. "And yet, here I am, not doing that."

Another Coileáin woman lost to love. How disappointing that Mireille had proved to be just as weak as her twin. Sighle stepped close to her sister. "I thought you would be different."

"Did you?"

"I thought you would be stronger, better."

Mireille shook her head. "I'm just me."

"Yes, I see that now," Sighle said. "I should kill you where you stand."

"Well, you could try. It might not help."

"I think it might help a great deal, but they wouldn't want that, our gods. They want you."

"They can't have me."

"No, they can't. Not as you are now, anyway," Sighle agreed. "But I can't allow you to go free."

"Is that so?"

"Yes. You leave me with no choice."

Mireille scoffed. "There's always a—"

Stretching, Sighle slipped her fingers inside Mireille's skull, paralyzing her sister. Mireille stood slack-jawed and pliant as Sighle culled her memories.

When she had found what she wanted, she removed her hands, and Mireille collapsed, landing on her side, head resting on her outstretched arm.

"I'll have to do it myself," Sighle said. Humming softly, she settled on her knees to trace the scars adorning her sister's arm and wrist, then grasped her hand. "So ill-used. Perhaps you will thank me for this."

Their magic combined, the portal opened easily, and Sighle could not help but be awed by it. It was a lovely thing, dark and terrible. What lay on the other side? What would it be like there? The taste of the air and the sharpness of sound—dull and quiet, or brash and bold? How simple it would be to find out. One step, two, and she would know. One step, two, and she'd be gone.

But as she fed her sister's body to the shadows, Sighle stayed behind. Her work was not yet done, and there was somewhere else she needed to go.

Haleine could have Eluned. Sighle never had intended to stay.

Once the portal had closed, she took a cloak and nothing else, bid farewell to Nonna, and fetched a horse from the stables. As the palace wailed beneath the weight of magic and death, she galloped out of the city and into the forest.

When the brown-eyed boy passed her on the road, he didn't look at her. Sighle let him go and turned her horse toward the sea.

It was time to go home.

About the Author

Armed with an assortment of purple pens and medieval weaponry, M.J. Fifield is prepared for a very specific apocalypse. When she isn't writing, she's reading on the beach or bravely fleeing from the lizards living in her mailbox. M.J. lives with her family in Florida. Visit her online at mjfifield.com.

www.ingramcontent.com/pod-product-compliance
Lightning Source LLC
Chambersburg PA
CBHW050116030726
47505CB00007B/1902